DREDD

An Abaddon Books™ Publication
www.abaddonbooks.com
abaddon@rebellion.co.uk

This omnibus published in 2012 by Abaddon Books™,
Rebellion Intellectual Property Limited,
Riverside House, Osney Mead, Oxford, OX2 0ES, UK.

10 9 8 7 6 5 4 3 2 1

Editor-in Chief: Jonathan Oliver
Desk Editor: David Moore
Design: Parr & Preece
Marketing and PR: Michael Molcher
Creative Director and CEO: Jason Kingsley
Chief Technical Officer: Chris Kingsley

Judge Dredd, Judge Giant and Galen de Marco
created by John Wagner and Carlos Ezquerra.
Psi-Judge Anderson, Chief Judge Hershey and the Four Dark
Judges created by John Wagner and Brian Bolland.
Dredd vs Death based on the PC/PS2/Xbox game
Judge Dredd: Dredd Vs Death,
script by Tim Jones, Kevin Floyer-Lea and Paul Mackman.

ISBN: 978-1-78108-077-1

Printed in the US

DREDD

COLLECTING

DREDD VS DEATH BY **GORDON RENNIE**
KINGDOM OF THE BLIND BY **DAVID BISHOP**
THE FINAL CUT BY **MATTHEW SMITH**

ABADDON BOOKS

W W W . A B A D D O N B O O K S . C O M

DREDD
VS
DEATH

GORDON RENNIE

IT WAS THE smell from the rotting corpses of his wife and daughter which finally forced Vernon out of the apartment he had shared with them for the last five years.

He wasn't sure how long he had been in there with them. Time seemed to have altered its flow in the days since the whole of Mega-City One had fallen into this place which must surely be something close to Hell. The perpetual gloom that cloaked the city and enveloped the tops of the highest city blocks made it difficult to tell day from night, but by his reckoning it could only have been a few days since reality, as the citizens of Mega-City One had known it, had simply ceased to exist.

Just a few days. Not long enough to account for the rapidity with which the city had fallen apart. Not long enough to account for the overwhelming stench of weeks-long decay emanating from behind the closed door leading to the small apartment's bedrooms. But more than long enough to account for the growing sensation of gnawing hunger in his stomach.

The city's power supply was intermittent now, but even that couldn't account for the speed at which the food in the icebox had rotted away. There was something in the air which seemed to seep into absolutely everything, bringing festering decay in its wake. Even the contents of the packets of synthi-stuff in the kitchen cupboards had become mouldy and rotten, and Vernon hadn't been able to keep down more than a few mouthfuls of the raw synthi-noodle flakes he had tried to eat.

All he could do was sit there in the semi-darkness of the apartment, shivering against the unnatural cold that seemed to creep right into his very bones, listening to the terrible sounds that echoed through the deserted street-canyons outside – and wonder when it would be his turn to meet the awful, shapeless source of those sounds.

The stench got worse every day. It touched something deep inside Vernon, something dark and growing. Finally, he found the courage to flee the apartment and venture into the terrible, frightening world outside before his sanity finally gave way, before the terrible, groaning hunger within him caused him to look at that closed door and think of the bodies festering away behind it with something other than revulsion and a distant, mournful despair.

He stepped out into the corridor, closing the apartment door silently behind him, leaving behind forever the life he had lived there. The flickering corridor lights illuminated a scene of derelict decay. Slime dripped down cracked walls onto mildewed floors. Strange patterns of mould and moss crawled across walls and ceilings, finding nourishment from ultra-synthetic surfaces which should have provided none.

Just a few days, Vernon reminded himself. All this has happened in just a few days.

Most of the apartment doors which lined the corridor were closed. From behind some, he heard a few faint sounds of life: sobbing or weeping, or disjointed, mumbling words which may have been snatches of some half-remembered prayer. From behind one – 78/34, the Kirschmayers, he remembered, and Mr Kirschmayer was a deputy lieutenant in the block's Cit-Def unit – he heard a broken, maniacal cackle. From another, a few doors along – 78/42, Mr and Mrs Voogel, who had been friendly with him and his wife – he heard eager, hungry, scratching sounds.

One door at the end of the corridor stood open, with the welcome, reassuring sound of a voice on a Tri-D coming from within. Vernon found himself running eagerly towards it. Tri-D at least meant some kind of normality, a reminder of what had until recently been a huge part of everyday life in Mega-City One, when the city's thousands of media outlets poured out a brain-numbing torrent of game shows, vidverts, chat shows, info-blips, newscasts and shock jock tirades into the over-saturated minds of the citizens. Someone talking on a Tri-D meant that maybe someone was explaining to them the cause of the madness that had engulfed the city – and that maybe, just maybe, someone somewhere was doing something about bringing an end to it all.

"Good morning, citizens," hissed the eerie, sibilant voice on the Tri-D. "Once again, a sinister black pall has settled over the entire city, blocking out all light and hope, while the temperature will be somewhere round about zero, meaning that you can leave the corpses of your friends and loved ones to fester for a while longer yet. If you are foolish or brave enough to venture outside, remember that the curfew is still in force and that you will be shot on sight... which would be a real pity, since we have provided so many other more interesting and painful ways for you to die."

Vernon was at the door now, staring in at the figure suspended from the ceiling, hanging from the synthi-leather belt wrapped round its neck, the other end attached to the lighting fixture in the ceiling, and at the figures – a woman and two children – all dead from single gunshots, lying sprawled on the floor beneath its dangling feet. But it was the ghoulish, cackling apparition on the apartment's Tri-D screen that monopolised his attention.

"Although, really, we should be grateful to you all," it continued to hiss in its monstrous voice. 'Many of you have already given up hope and lost the will to live. Some have already begun to starve, and disease is spreading rapidly throughout all parts of the city. Faced with this, many of you have already chosen to take your own lives rather than await your fate at the hands of my brothers and their servants.'

The creature broke off, laughing shrilly to reveal an animal-like mouth crammed with sharp-fanged incisors. With a start, Vernon realised that the thing on the Tri-D screen was actually female.

"All this pleases us very much," the monstrosity continued. "Your help in achieving our great work is very much appreciated. Even now, our brothers work tirelessly to bring justice to you all, but they are few, and you are so many. Be patient, remain in your homes and they will get to you in time."

The creature's voice was rising, moving swiftly towards a shrieking crescendo: "It is a momentous task we have set ourselves. To purge this city, to cleanse all of you, its teeming millions. To grant you eternal absolution from the greatest crime of all... life itself!"

Vernon started to run, fleeing from that voice and from the terrible, awful things it was telling him. Even as he fled down a stairwell choked with corpses, climbing over the bodies of neighbours and strangers, he could still hear the final words of the inhuman, mocking creature on the Tri-D pursuing after him.

"With your help, we will turn this city into a monument to justice, a home fit only for the innocent. Where the only sound will be the blessed silence of the grave, and where the only sign of life will be the flies crawling amongst the vast mounds of your rot-bloated corpses. With your help, all this will soon come to pass... TOGETHER, SINNERS, WE WILL BUILD OUR GLORIOUS NECROPOLIS!"

HE NEVER COULD remember how long he had wandered the city for, or how he had managed to survive. He imagined he must have found food from somewhere, scavenged from the many derelict city blocks or shopping precincts, for the hunger pangs were not such a problem anymore. Deep down, he knew he had probably gone mad. But what did it matter, he reasoned to himself, when the whole city had also gone mad?

He glimpsed other wanderers like himself, other survivors and scavengers, but warily stayed clear of them. Several times, he saw larger groups of survivors, on one occasion several hundred strong, but always he hid until they had passed by. One of these groups spotted him and called out to him, urging him to come back and join them, but he kept on running. They were doomed, he knew. They had the invisible mark of death upon them – he had seen it clearly in the faces of the nearest of them – and he had no wish to join their fate.

On another occasion, a Judge patrol spotted him. Vernon didn't know why, but he knew that the Judges were part of what was going on in the city. He had taken off running as soon as he saw them. The Judges had chased after him, firing at him with their Lawgivers, but Vernon had managed to lose them somewhere in the darkness of the Hel Shapiro Underway. Bored with the chase, the Judges had given up and gone into the nearest building, looking for easier targets. Even from several kilometres away, Vernon had heard the gunfire from their weapons as they roamed at whim from apartment to apartment and level to level within the massive city block.

ON THAT OCCASION, he had been fleeing from gunfire, but it would be the same kind of sound which ultimately led him to the moment of glorious rebirth, when he was to discover where his own new destiny lay.

He heard them from afar: rippling bursts of gunfire, tight and coordinated. There were always plenty of gunfire sounds in the city, but something about these seemed different in a way he could not explain. Carefully, going against every new instinct he had developed surviving on his own on the city's devastated streets, he crept towards the sound, drawn in by something invisible yet undeniable.

He found his destiny in Whitman Plaza. The surface of the square had been violently ripped up, transformed into a series of giant craters which were now being used as mass graves. There were Judges everywhere, herding in groups of citizens in their hundreds, barking harsh orders at them, lining them up in neat rows at the lips of the craters and then sending their lifeless corpses tumbling down into the burial pits amidst crashing volleys of Lawgiver fire. Some of the people in the mass graves were still alive, and an occasional laughing Judge would fire into the pits with rippling bursts, making the corpses piled down there dance and jerk as the high-velocity Lawgiver bullets tore through them. Those they missed were left to die, suffocating beneath the weight of the new layers of corpses that soon fell down to join them.

Vernon picked a path across these burial pits, drawn inexorably towards something in the centre of the square. Judges were all around him, but none saw him. Death was everywhere around him too – in the dismal, tainted air he breathed, in the lifeless, bloodied mass of flesh he crept across – but something or someone had decided that he was to be spared from it all. Taking up a position at the edge of one of the craters, crouching down to stifle the dying moans of one of the bodies he was standing on, he looked upon the figures that had drawn him on to this place.

They were standing in the centre of the square, surrounded by their Judge servants. Hover vehicles known as H-wagons, restless and lethal, circled overhead, standing guard over the new masters of Mega-City One.

There were four of them, and Vernon knew instantly who – what – they were, as soon as he saw them.

Death. Fear. Fire. Mortis.

The four Dark Judges. Creatures from another dimension, the news-vid reporters had said, with a thrill of fear in their voices. Twisted, evil entities who had decided that all crime was committed by the living, and that, hence, the greatest crime of all was life itself. They had wiped out all life on their own world and had then discovered a means to cross the dimensions to find Mega-City One. Twice before, the city had come under attack from them, with thousands of citizens losing their lives, but each time the human Judges of the Justice Department had fought back and defeated them, seemingly destroying them for ever.

But, like some creature from an old horror-vid, the Dark Judges refused to die and would return again, each time seemingly more deadly than ever. Now they were back once more, and this time killing not thousands but millions. The entire city was theirs, and they would not rest until they had killed every living thing in it.

Judges, seemingly under some kind of twisted mind control, were moving amongst the columns of captured citizens, randomly pulling people aside and herding them forward to be personally judged by the four creatures. Terrified citizens were herded in groups of a hundred or more into a smouldering crater, where Judge Fire immolated them en masse with blasts of lethal, supernatural fire from his burning trident.

His three brothers stood waiting as their Judge servants brought their unwilling subjects forward to them. The creatures had been busy, Vernon could see. Pairs of Judges carried off the lifeless remains of those who had been selected to be personally judged by the Dark Judges, and the pits set aside for each of the Dark Judges' victims were all nearly full.

Pleading and sobbing, each citizen was brought forward in turn to meet their fate at the hands of one of the Dark Judges. The Judges attending Mortis wore their helmet respirators down, Vernon noticed, to fend off the decayed stench from the rot-corrupted flesh of his victims, while even from this distance he could clearly see the frozen looks of sheer terror on the unnaturally twisted features of the victims of Judge Fear.

But it was Judge Death above all who captured Vernon's attention.

He stood like some regal overlord, his Judge servants making his victims kneel on their knees before him as they were brought forward to be judged.

"Rejoice, sinners! Soon you will be free from the crime of life, and the burden of your terrible guilt will be gone!" he hissed as each was made to kneel before him, before reaching down almost as if to bestow a blessing upon them. His claw-like hands melted seamlessly through flesh and bone, passing mysteriously through organs and innards until they unerringly found the heart, before those same long, inhuman fingers closed around the vital organ and squeezed all life from it.

The victims fell dead at his feet, the same look of horror and fear stamped into all their faces. Instantly, each corpse was picked up and tossed into the nearby pit, before the next victim was dragged forward to meet the same fate.

Vernon was awestruck by what he saw. Here was something far more than a supernatural bogeyman, the extra-dimensional fiend of the old news-vid reports. Here was a creature beyond life and death, an unholy, blasphemous god; terrible in his glory, undying, immortal, a taker of lives and guardian of the secrets of what lay beyond death. Had Vernon been one of those the Judges were bringing before Death, he would have fallen to his knees willingly and without being forced, in voluntary submission to this most glorious and terrible of creatures.

Death paused in his work, looking up as though suddenly sensing something amiss. From behind the iron grille of his helmet, undead eyes gazed out in search of what it might be. He gave a low hiss of irritable displeasure as his gaze picked over the thousands of corpses in the craters surrounding him. He did not like to be disturbed in his work, not when there were still so many sinners waiting to be judged.

Vernon cringed in terror, pressing himself into the tangle of cold, lifeless flesh beneath him as he felt Death's eyes searching him out, inexorably finding the spark of treacherous life amidst the otherwise pleasing landscape of death. The icy grip of fear took hold of Vernon's body as Death's gaze fell upon him and, horribly, he felt the creature's long, cold fingers picking through his mind, almost as if he were physically kneeling before him to receive the Dark Judge's lethal blessing.

His body convulsed and the beating of his heart slowed... and stopped. For a moment, he knew what it was to stand on the very edge of the abyss of death, and then the fingers withdrew, and the gaze of Death was lifted from him. Whatever Death had found in the mind of one helpless and terrified human had pleased him.

Death withdrew his deadly tendrils from Vernon's soul with a long, low hiss of satisfaction and turned his attention back to the business at hand. "The crime is life... the sentence is death," he ritually intoned and, seconds later, another corpse joined the thousands of others in the burial pits.

Vernon crept away, still only dimly aware of the significance of what had just happened. Death had found him, had judged him – and had found him worthy of something other than extinction.

There was something more though, something the Dark Judge had left within him. If he closed his eyes and concentrated, Vernon imagined he could just see it, a slick, hard, black pearl planted amongst the living tissue of his brain.

He had been marked by the Dark Judge. Marked not for death, but for life. For a purpose that was yet unknown to him, but which he already knew he would faithfully and devoutly carry out when the time came, for he knew that if he did Death's bidding, then he would be suitably rewarded.

"I don't want to die," he intoned to himself as he crept away again. "I don't want to die. Not now, not ever. I don't want to die."

One

"ANYTHING HAPPEN WHILE I've been away?" Burchill asked, helping himself to a few generous gulps from Meyer's cup of now lukewarm synthi-caf.

Meyer sighed in unhappy resignation. Being a Judge-Warden wasn't exactly the most exciting duty in the Justice Department, and keeping watch over the things they kept down here in the Tomb wasn't exactly the choicest duty posting in the Division, but it was having to work with jerks like Burchill that was the worst thing about this job. Worse even than the mind-numbing boredom and the extra creep-out factor of the nature of the... things encased within the crystalline cube-prisons only a few steps from where Meyer sat at the duty-console.

"Nothing much," she told the smug Psi-Judge. "You're welcome to watch the vid-logs, if you want. We've got the whole of the last eighteen months since you were last here still on file. Not much to see, I'll grant you, but I think maybe Sparky might have done something like blink or change the flicker pattern of his flames a month or two ago."

Burchill snorted into the cup of synthi-caf. "Sparky! It was me that christened him that, you know that? Sparky, Spooky, Creepy and Bony, that's what I called 'em one night, a year or two ago. Glad to see it's caught on while I've been away."

Meyer bristled in irritation again. Psi-Judges were notoriously highly strung, and other Judges were expected to cut them a little extra slack, but Burchill was just an annoying creep. Duty regs said that there must always be a Psi-Judge on duty in the Tomb, to protect against any dangerous psychic activity from the things imprisoned down here, but the Psi-Judges selected for the job were rotated every three months since there were concerns about the effects on a Psi's mind of long-term exposure to the creepy vibes generated by the four detainees held in the Tomb. It had been a year and a half since Burchill had been on Tomb duty – or "spook-sitting", as he called it – and Meyer didn't think that was nearly long enough.

"Yeah, ain't you just the Department comedian?" she commented, the sarcasm bare in her voice. "And, hey, by the way, feel free to finish the rest of my synthi-caf, why don't you?"

"Thanks. Don't mind if I do," laughed Burchill, draining the last of the contents of the plasti-cup.

"No! Don't you d–" began Meyer, way too late, as the Psi-Judge casually flipped the empty cup over his shoulder, throwing it towards the thick red warning line painted on the floor behind him, which divided the underground room into two distinct halves.

On one side of the line were the duty-consoles for the two Judges – one experienced Judge-Warden and one Psi-Judge – which Tomb regs required to be at all times on duty here, as well as the elevator entrance back up to the surface. On the other side of the no-go line were the four entities imprisoned within the Tomb.

Even before the plasti-cup had crossed the line, hidden sensor devices buried within the walls of the chamber had detected the movement and were tracking the object's progress. As soon as it entered the no-go area marked by the line, multiple sentry guns placed at various points around the chamber opened fire, using precise telemetry data fed to them by the room's remote sensors.

The cup was instantly vaporised, struck by several laser beams simultaneously. All that remained of it was a fine residue of ash, which drifted slowly down to settle on the ground on the forbidden side of the red line.

Meyer cursed, and punched a button to open up her duty log. "Thanks a lot. Now I'm going to have to make a report on that."

Burchill laughed, and settled down into his seat in his duty-post across from her. "Hey, look at it this way: at least I've given you something to do now, which makes a change down here."

FROM BEHIND THE substance of the crystalline barrier, from behind the walls which had imprisoned him and his brethren for too long, Death watched his captors. The failure of their great work, the collapse of their grand vision of the Necropolis, had been a galling experience. And defeat at the hands of their old enemies, Dredd and Anderson, had been even more so. The destruction of their physical bodies, the entrapment of their ethereal spirits within these crystal prisons, where they were almost completely cut off from each other and unable to plan the continuation of their holy work, all this was bad enough, but worst of all was seeing sinners so close by – sinners guilty of the worst crime of all, the crime of life – and being unable to bring due punishment upon them.

Although Death could not actively commune with his brothers, he knew that they felt as he did. Within his prison, Fire blazed with angry, vengeful rage. Next to him, Fear writhed in agitation, his spirit twisting in on itself. On his other side, Mortis's restless spirit-shape formed and reformed itself, prowling round the borders of its prison, endlessly testing the strength of the walls and psychic wards which had been put in place to contain him.

Of them all, only Death was at relative peace. While the others raged and turned their anger on themselves and the seemingly unbreakable walls of their prisons, he watched. And waited.

And now, perhaps, his patience was being rewarded.

Death recognised their new gaoler, the Psi-Judge. He had been here before, and Death, probing subtly and tentatively at the edges of the man's mind, had sensed the interesting possibilities within. There was weakness within this one, Death understood, weakness that could be exploited to his advantage. The man had gone away again, as they always did, but Death had waited patiently for his return, silently laying his plans.

In the city beyond were the special ones, the ones who knew the Dark Judges for what they truly were – liberators, come to free all from the sinful burden of life – and who were eager to help Death and his brethren in their glorious task. Death had encountered several such special ones, and had put his mark upon them, knowing that one day he might have need of them. That day was soon, he knew now, and his call had already gone out to them.

Secret acolytes in the city beyond this place, and now a weakness here amongst their guardians. Yes, now he had everything he needed.

Patience, brothers, he whispered silently to the occupants of the other three cells. Soon we will be able to begin our great work anew. Soon, Necropolis will be ours once more.

Eyes, RED AND hungry, blazed at her from out of the darkness. She tried to move, to draw her Lawgiver, but the darkness around her was a living, sentient thing. It wrapped itself around her, snagging her limbs, dragging her down.

She felt herself falling, down into the dark. From above her came the angry, cheated snarl of whatever had been pursuing her.

She hit the ground with a clattering impact. She felt dust on her face, smelt withered, ancient decay and felt something dry and brittle beneath her fingers. Opening her eyes, she saw she was lying on a carpet of bones. Raising her head, she saw the litter of bones – human remains, she noticed, seeing identifiable skulls and bone shapes amongst the graveyard detritus – stretching out as far as she could see. The vague tombstone shape of vast buildings, cracked and ruined, loomed up out of the surrounding gloom. There was something horribly familiar about the whole scene.

Deadworld, she wondered to herself, remembering her past experiences in the nightmare world which had given birth to the Dark Judges?

Or Necropolis maybe, she asked herself, noticing with growing disquiet how much the surrounding buildings resembled the familiar outlines of Mega-City One?

No, none of these things, something whispered inside her. Not something from the past. Something from the future, something dreadful that had yet to happen...

Pulling herself to her feet, she heard a chorus of menacing growls from the nearest of the buildings. Backing off, she heard more of the same sounds from the buildings behind her. And from those to her left, and then her right.

Surrounded on all sides, she checked the ammo counter on her Lawgiver and waited for whatever was out there to come to her.

She didn't have to wait long. From out of the buildings they came, a black wave of shadow figures, snarling and hissing at her in hungry anticipation. She opened fire with her Lawgiver, firing off quick controlled bursts as per Academy of Law standard training. The bullets tore into the ranks of the shadow things, giving rise to an outraged chorus of howls of pain and anger. A dozen or more of the things tumbled to the bone-littered ground, to be fallen upon mercilessly and ripped apart by the others swarming close behind.

Despite the carnage, the others came right on at her, swift and relentless. As they closed in on the Judge, heedless of the Lawgiver bullets tearing through unnatural flesh, they merged into one great shadow-shape, a black and red collage of maddened, hunger-filled eyes and crimson-dripping fangs.

They bore down on her, dragging her to the ground, and the last conscious thing she remembered before the red veil descended was the sensation of talon-like fingers raking into her and sharp, needle-like teeth worrying at her flesh.

After that, there was only the darkness, and the overpowering smell of freshly spilled blood.

MY BLOOD, SHE thought, awakening with a shuddering start. The thin synthi-satin sheets of the bed were soaked with perspiration; the short vest she wore – definitely not Department-approved, which was probably why she wore it – clung to her sweat-soaked skin.

Coming out of the nightmare, it took her a moment to remember where she was: the small and predictably spartan temporary quarters assigned to her within the dorm-wing of Psi-Division Headquarters. Closing her eyes, she received a few brief but gruesome mental after-images of the nightmare she had just experienced.

"Grud on a greenie, that was a doozie," she murmured to herself as she leaned forward to flick-activate the intercom control on the panel set into the wall beside the bed. Instead, she hit the wrong switch, and made the room's small Tri-D screen activate into sudden and noisy life.

"...it's Fluffy, darling... he's dead!" bellowed the voice on the Tri-D, making Anderson look up with an involuntary start. She saw a husband-and-wife pair of citizens, both of them straight out of the usual dumb vidvert Central Casting, by the looks of things, crying and cradling the white-furred corpse of something she assumed was supposed to be a dead rabbit. At that moment, the vid-generated background of an ordinary city block apartment wiped away, and a tall, rather intense-looking man in a spotless white lab coat stepped into shot, smiling in a supposedly disarming but actually rather scary manner at the camera.

"Dr Dick Icarus, chief scientist from EverPet! What are you doing here?" exclaimed the wife character in a way that probably made the vidvert director wish he'd gone for digitally generated actors after all.

"I'm here... for Fluffy!" declared the freaky mad scientist type, brandishing a syringe filled with an alarming-looking, glowing green liquid, and quickly injecting the noxious stuff into the dead pet. Almost instantaneously – because vidvert airtime didn't come cheap, naturally – the animal sprang back to life and went hopping off out of shot.

"He's alive! But HOW???" shrieked the wife-actor in amazement, no doubt seeing a dazzling career ahead of her in walk-on roles in middle-of-the-night graveyard slot soap-vids.

"It's all thanks to this," boasted the wacko in the lab coat, holding the syringe and its contents up to camera. "EverPet's revolutionary new Pet Regen Formula. That's right! Now there's no need for death to part you from your most beloved animal companions. For only a small monthly fee, and regular injections of Pet Regen, EverPet can bring your furry little family members back to life. So dial 555-REGEN and resurrect your pet tod–"

"Bringing dead pets back to life... only in the Big Meg," Anderson muttered, hurriedly switching off the Tri-D before what was shaping up to be a predictably dumb and irritatingly catchy musical jingle started playing. Second time lucky, she activated the intercom.

"Psi-Control – Anderson. Just picked up something. Could be a pre-cog flash, maybe a big one."

The answering voice on the radio-link was politely sceptical. "You sure about that, Anderson? We've got more than thirty other Psi-Judges asleep in the dorms, not to mention the full-time pre-cogs down in the Temple, and none of them are interrupting my duty shift to report on picking up anything. You sure it wasn't just some REM sleep phantom bogey stuff?"

Anderson fought to keep her temper under control. "You know my rep, Control. You're not talking to some rookie Psi straight out of the Academy. I know the difference between a nightmare and a genuine pre-cog flash."

"Okay," sighed the voice of Control. "You want me to log this as a possible pick-up. We both know the routine. Tell me what you thought you picked up, starting with surface impressions first."

Anderson closed her eyes, bringing her psi-powers to focus on the images still burning in her brain. A moment's concentration, a careful sectioning off of the various areas of her mind to prevent random and subconscious psi-spill from polluting the memory of the images she had picked up, and then she was ready to replay the nightmare she had just experienced.

"I see blood, Control. Lots of blood."

"I MEAN, JUST what the drokk is it with these so-called 'Church of Death' freakoids, anyway? The Big Meg is what I like to call a broad church, with room for all kindsa wackos, freaks, gomers, spazheads and nutjobs, sure, but there's still gotta be some limits, ain't there? Now, all you regular listeners out there know that good ol' Drivetime Sam ain't no bigot – except when it comes to muties, Alientown freaks, Juggernaut fans, stuck-up Brit-citters, assorted Euro-cit trash, those big-mouthed domeheads from Texas City, Luna-cit weirdos and especially those dirty Sov-Blokers – but usually I say 'live and let live'. Except in the case of these Death cult creeps.

"You know the freaks I'm talking about, right? Loons that paint their faces like skulls, dress up like it's Halloween and worship – yeah, you heard me right, I said WORSHIP – Judge Death and his three fellow extra-dimensional freakshow buddies? That sound SANE? That sound LEGAL? That sound like the kind of thing we should encourage our innocent young people to get into, when they could be out there getting into juve gang rumbles, taking illegal narco-tabs, setting fire to winos or doing any of the other traditional things the juves of today get up to?

"'Of course not, Sam,' I hear you say, 'that's why the Judges are rounding these freaks up as soon as they appear.' Which is fine by ol' Drivetime Sam, but I say we should all be doing our part too. You know any of these wackos, you think some of your neighbours might be perverted sickos who have a shrine to the Dark Judges hidden in their apartment, then there's only one thing to do. Let the Judges know about it. Dial 1-800-KOOKCUBE, and tell 'em Drivetime Sam told ya to do it.

"Okay, so that's the Rant of the Hour slot and our statutory public information obligations taken care of for the time being, so now it's back to our usual mix of travel-time news, made-up stuff about the private lives of vid-celebs and phone-in chat with you, the dumb, feeble-minded and pathetically attention-seeking ordinary cits of Mega-City One. First on the line is Chuck Cheedlewidge, who we understand is some dweeb who wants to tell us that the weird growth on his neck has started channelling the spirit of the late Chief Judge Goodman. Ooowww boy, now where did I put that kook cube num–"

Galen DeMarco switched off the radio with a curse that would surely have earned her a verbal reprimand from any of her old Sector House shift commanders. Like millions of other citizens, she couldn't stand arrogant, opinionated shock jock creeps like Drivetime Sam. Then again, like millions of other citizens, she also couldn't help tuning in to hear what he was going to say next.

"So much for all those dull citizenship classes they made me take," she said to herself. "If I really wanted to blend in with the rest of the population, all I had to do was listen to the meatheads on talk radio."

She looked out the series of wide bay windows that lined one entire wall of her apartment, relishing the spectacular view it gave her across the central core sectors of MegEast. In the distance, behind the towering bulks of Sax Rohmer Block and the DaneTech Building, one could just catch a glimpse of the Statue of Judgement standing guard near Black Atlantic Customs and Immigration, while off to the east the afternoon sun reflected brightly off the gilt-metalled giant eagle facade of the Grand Hall of Justice. Clustered for tens of kilometres around it were a host of other Justice Department ancillary facilities, including the Academy of Law, Psi-Division HQ and the Tech 21 labs, as well as City Hall, the glittering stratoscraper headquarters of nearly every giant mega-corp company worthy of the name, and several of the most elite and exclusive luxy-blocks and con-apt buildings in the entire city. When foreigners thought of Mega-City One, this was the sector they thought of: the soaring, gigantic-beyond-belief buildings, the colourful, teeming millions of citizens and the seemingly never-ending number of fads and crazes which these citizens invented to occupy their time, and the dominating and ever vigilant presence of the Justice Department. Right outside her window was a snapshot of all the allure, glamour and splendour of the biggest, craziest and most powerful Mega-City on the face of twenty-second century Earth.

The reality, DeMarco knew, was nowhere near so exciting and exotic. Over on the West Wall, on the city's border with the Cursed Earth, the Department fought what was practically a non-stop war against the hordes of muties who tried every night to get into the city. There were areas of the city, most notably parts of City Bottom or some slum sectors such as the notorious Pit, where the Judges had all but ceded control to perp gangs that were more like small standing armies than criminal groups – not that anyone in the Department would ever officially acknowledge this. Eighty-seven per cent of the population was unemployed, and too many of them chose some form of lawbreaking as an alternative pastime. The cits invented new crimes faster than the Judges could pass laws to deal with them. The city's iso-cubes were full to bursting, the kook cubes even more so.

Statistics said that sixty per cent of citizens were likely to suffer some form of serious mental breakdown some time in their lives, mostly due to the pressure of twenty-second century life as it was lived in Mega-City One. They even had a term for it – Future Shock Syndrome – and the kook cubes were full of the plentiful evidence of its virulence and widespread adoption.

Statistics said that fifty-three per cent of citizens were afraid of being murdered by their neighbours. Maybe with good reason, though, since another survey also suggested that seventy-seven per cent of citizens – including, simple arithmetic suggested, many of the respondents from the other survey – actually had given serious thought at least once to the idea of murdering whoever was living next door to them.

It was the Big Meg, the craziest and most violent city on Earth, home to four hundred million citizens, every one of them a potentially violent criminal, and Grud help her, she loved every over-populated, crime-ridden, polluted and blood-stained square metre of it.

Looking down from the penthouse level of the two hundred storey apartment block, she could see the stacked snarl of megways, skeds, overzooms, underzooms, pedways and shoppo-plazas that passed for the Mega-City One street system. It was times like this that she missed those streets the most, missed being a Street Judge and being out there on patrol, dealing with all the madness and mayhem the city had to throw at you.

Boredom was the biggest problem for her now. More than twenty years with the Department, and every minute of that time she had always been busy doing something. She had money, of course – the fortune she inherited from her father more than ensured that, unlike the rest of the ordinary cits, she'd never have to worry about where her next cred was coming from – but like a lot of other cits she had had to deal with the boredom.

Setting herself up as a Private Investigator after she had left the Justice Department hadn't been her idea, but she had to admit that it was a gruddamned good one. Her connections within the Department gave her more leeway than that afforded to others in her profession, and, while it would never beat the buzz of having to quell a full-scale block war after pulling an energy sapping, sixteen-hour double shift of street patrol, it was better than sitting in your luxury apartment all day painting your nails and watching the Tri-D, which is what she figured most of her neighbours seemed to do.

Since she didn't have to work for the money, she tried to pick and choose her cases, sifting through the run-of-the-mill surveillance, insurance fraud and employee-vetting jobs that came walking in through her office door. She passed a lot of these kind of jobs on to some of her competitors, only keeping on the cases that interested her. The ones that involved the stuff that slipped through the cracks of the Justice Department's attention, the ones that made her feel she was still doing some good for someone. She had an office downtown, close to City Hall, but a lot of the time she preferred to work out of her apartment.

Which was what she was supposed to be doing now, she reminded herself guiltily as she called up a number on her phone. It rang, and was immediately answered by an auto-message program. DeMarco gave a silent prayer of thanks. As a Judge, the security of the badge and uniform had always allowed her to erect a professional barrier between her and the cits she dealt with. As a cit herself, she was still learning about how to deal with people in emotional distress.

"Hello? Mrs Caskey? It's Galen DeMarco. As I promised a few days ago, I'm calling to give your progress report on what I've found so far. I've talked to some of Joanna's friends at her college, and, according to them, she had got involved in some college fringe society that calls itself the 'Friends of Thanos'. I did a little digging on these creeps, and found that..."

She checked herself here, trying to work out an easy, sympathetic way to tell a mother that her daughter had probably run off to join a cult of death-worshipping loons.

Damn it, she thought to herself. Why did the Academy learning program have more than fifty compulsory courses on combat techniques and only one brief one on Cit Relations?

"Well, uhhh... I have reason to believe that they're maybe connected in some way to a group you might have heard about on the vid-news recently, a group called the Church of Death. I'm not sure, but it's possible she might be with them... It's possible some boy she met might have persuaded her to join. I'm looking into it now, and I've already got a few leads I want to follow up about this cult, maybe even be able to track them down. Don't worry, Mrs Caskey, whatever you've heard on the Tri-D about these people, it's probably just the usual exaggerated vid-news stuff. I'll contact you in a few days, by which time I'm fairly sure I'll have some good news about your daughter."

She hung up, thinking that maybe the Academy of Law training wasn't so bad after all, since at least it taught you how to lie with conviction to the cits. She had some leads on this Death cult alright, but her gut feeling was that these Church of Death creeps were a cut above your usual Mega-City One lunatic fringe/apocalypse cult bunch of wackos.

She had a lot to do now, she knew, but she couldn't help looking out the window at the city again and wonder, for what was maybe just the twentieth time that day, where Dredd was, and what he was doing right now.

TWO

JUDGE DREDD'S FIST smashed into the perp's face, spreading most of his nose across his face and making a trip to the iso-block med-unit for some dental reconstruction surgery a likely event in this creep's immediate future.

One of the perp's buddies used the moment for his advantage, slipping around Dredd and trying to blindside him. The Judge turned and pivoted as the perp came at him with a pig-sticker blade. Dredd swung his daystick twice, swiftly. One sharp crack of reinforced plasteel on bone broke the wrist of the creep's weapon-hand and sent the knife skittering across the rough rockcrete surface of the alleyway. The second caught him neatly on the top of the skull and booked him a place in an iso-block med-unit alongside Creep Number One.

Creeps Number Three, Four, Five and Six looked slightly disconcerted about this. They hung back for a moment, weighing up the odds. Creep Number Four, with slightly fewer disfiguring facial tattoos than the rest of the gang, was maybe the brains of this particular outfit, and the others seemed happy for him to do all their collective, half-witted thinking for them.

"Don't matter what the name on that badge says!" he shouted, weighing up the odds, doing all the necessary mental arithmetic and still coming up with very definitely the wrong answer. "There's one of him and four of us, and he can't take us all. Get him!"

They rushed at him together. Dredd's Lawgiver was in its boot holster, within easy reach, but he made no move to draw it. None of these punks were packing guns, and so far there didn't seem to be any just cause for the use of deadly force against them.

Besides, he thought to himself, it had been a slow day so far, and he could probably do with a workout.

Creep Number Five hit the ground first, taking a plasteel-reinforced Judge's boot to the groin and a daystick blow to the temple. Creep Number Three followed swiftly, courtesy of a knock-out punch to the jaw. Creep Number Four drew back, looking like he was having second thoughts about the whole thing. Dredd gave him something else to think about instead: a daystick jab to the solar plexus which sent him reeling to the ground, winded, the follow-up kick from a boot swiftly reintroducing the perp to the violently regurgitated remains of his synthi-fries and Grot Pot lunch of only a few hours ago.

If Creep Number Four was the brains of the outfit, then Creep Number Six must have fancied himself as the brawn, throwing himself at Dredd with a savage roar. Dredd bent slightly, caught him in the ribs with the hard edge of his eagle-shaped shoulder pad and used the creep's own momentum against him, judo-throwing him over his shoulder and sending the perp face-first into the surface of the wall behind him. The pattern of the rough brickwork, now stamped deep into the skin of the unconscious thug's face, made an interesting new addition to the mosaic of ugly tattoo markings already there.

With the six perps lying unconscious or groaning on the ground around him, Dredd finally relented and lifted his foot from the back of the original perp – Creep Number

Zero, he supposed he should call him – who had been lying there helpless, hands cuffed behind his back and pinned to the ground by Dredd's foot, during the entire fight.

"Control – Dredd. Seven for catcH-wagon pick-up, Mohammed Alley, just off Spinks and Foreman."

"Wilco, Dredd," came the crackling reply over his helmet radio. "What are the charges?"

Dredd looked at the seven subdued figures around him. "Six of them on Attempted Judge Assault – five years." Dredd paused, looking at the six groaning, bleeding perps lying around him. "Tell the catcH-wagon crew there'll be no problem figuring out which ones they are. The other one…"

Dredd looked round at the colour-splashed and still-wet graffiti wall decor behind him.

"Scrawling – one year's cubetime."

Scrawling was a common enough Mega-City crime, Dredd knew, and Sector House Chiefs were required to order regular crackdowns on it in some of the worst-hit areas. Dredd had made thousands of arrests for scrawling in his years on the streets, and this one had at first seemed no different from the rest when he had come across an illegal scrawler – Creep Zero – still at work on his latest graffiti masterpiece at the mouth of the alley.

What had been unusual, though, was when Creeps One to Six turned up to dispute Dredd's arrest of their buddy. Scrawl wars were common amongst the city's street gangs, with gangs leaving provocative scrawl-tags on their rivals' turf and then protecting their own gang territory – often with lethal force – from reprisal scrawl attacks in return. Gang members protecting their gang's scrawl artists wasn't that uncommon, but what was very much out of the ordinary was a gang willing to do the same thing if it meant attacking a Judge.

Especially if that Judge happened to be Judge Joe Dredd.

Dredd looked again at the scrawl design the scrawler had still been working on when he arrested him. He saw a cartoon depiction of a familiar-looking ghastly figure, a figure which Dredd knew all too well, but which the scrawler would only have seen in brief and heavily Justice Department-censored news-vid images. The figure, a grinning ghoul wearing a crudely imagined parody of a Judge's uniform, was surrounded by a chemically treated fluorescent paint halo of glowing black energy. Written beside it, in large and still unfinished letters, was a single stark message: "DEATH LIVES!"

Despite the cartoon crudeness of the thing, despite the mundane setting of a typically grubby and garbage-strewn Mega-City One alleyway, there was something strangely unsettling about the image, almost as if the scrawler had subconsciously tapped into some greater hidden reservoir of fear and dread.

Sensing he was onto something, Dredd bent over the nearest prone body, ignoring the injured perp's groans of pain as he quickly searched him. Like all the other gang members, the perp's clothes were uniformly black, but, beneath the fresh dye marks, Dredd could still see the evidence of the ganger's original and quite different gang colours. Likewise, while his arms bore traditional juve gang tattoos – Dredd recognised them as belonging to the Sid Sheldon Block Big Spenders Crew – the ones on his face were most recent, and different from the gang tattoos. Flaming skulls, vampire bats, clawed hands coming out of graves and similar cartoon-gothic imagery seemed to be the predominant style here.

Standing back up, he reactivated his helmet radio link.

"Control – Dredd. Extra to that last call: possible evidence tying my perps into these Church of Death creeps."

"That's a check. We've been seeing more and more of this amongst the sector juve gangs. Could just be the latest passing street gang fad."

"Or it could be something else, Control," growled Dredd. "Fads don't make gangers attack Judges the way these punks tried to attack me. Slap a mandatory extra five years onto all their sentences for membership of an illegal organisation, and have them all run through the interrogation cubes to find out what they know. It's time we came down hard on these Death cult freaks."

"Wilco, Dredd..." responded the voice of Control, before suddenly assuming a more urgent tone. "Just got something coming in. Armed assault at the Bathory Street med-supply warehouse. Judge Giant on the scene and requesting assist from any nearby units!"

Dredd looked at the seven subdued perps around him. Bathory Street was only five blocks from here, just off Ingrid Pitt Plaza, and it would take him less than a minute to secure his perps for catcH-wagon pick-up. Cuffed together, and with most of them already beaten unconscious, he didn't figure it likely they would be going anywhere before the catcH-wagon crew arrived.

"Wilco, Control. On my way."

JUDGE GIANT DIDN'T believe in vampires.

Which was not to say he'd not witnessed some freaky stuff in his time as a Judge, of course. Even as a cadet, during the darkest days of Necropolis he'd faced off against no less a creep than Judge Mortis. And then there had been the whole Judgement Day thing, with the dead – yeah, the freakin' dead – rising from the grave and forming into one big zombie army to try and destroy everything and everyone. Since then, he had seen or heard about all kinds of weird stuff – tribes of werewolves in the Undercity, alien monsters with acid for blood attacking the Grand Hall of Justice – but he still didn't believe in vampires.

Which was perhaps a pity, since "vampires" seemed to be exactly what he was faced with right now.

He'd already pumped six Lawgiver rounds into one of the freakers, but now here it was again, popping up from behind the cover of those crates of med-supplies to take another shot at him. It didn't look much like what Giant thought of when he thought about vampires – no fancy burial suit, no black cape lined with red synthi-satin, and so far it hadn't turned into a bat or a plague of rats, or anything really freaky like that – but the fangs, the pale, dead-white skin pallor, the superhuman strength and the blood-crazed hunger all seemed to be present and correct.

And guns? Vampires weren't supposed to fire guns at you, thought Giant, ducking back round the corner as the hail of bullets from the thing's spit pistol popped holes into the surface of the doorway beside him.

A security guard's corpse, throat brutally ripped out, lay in the corridor behind him. The perps' means of entry into the building had been anything but subtle. The building was closed to the general public and its doors and windows were impressively secure, considering the amount of proscribed drugs kept in the place for use by the city med-units they would have to be, but the perps – Giant knew there were an even half-dozen of them – had simply ripped through the front door to get in.

Yeah, with their bare hands, Giant reminded himself, remembering seeing what had looked unpleasantly like claw marks gouged into the metal of the door.

After that, they had gone on the rampage through the building, brutally killing everyone they found in the place before breaking into the large central room they were in now, where the repository's main med-supplies were kept.

Arriving minutes after the break-in had been reported, and moving through the building in the perps' murderous wake, Giant had automatically assumed that they must be stimmed-up hypeheads, breaking into the place in a desperate need to feed their narco-addiction. Professional perps would have been long gone so many minutes after the alarms were first tripped. These creeps might be vicious – Giant had counted seven corpses on his way in here – but they were also amateurs, and now he had them trapped in the main storeroom.

Like juves in a synthi-candy store, he had thought to himself. Probably too busy getting stimmed-up to even remember that the Judges were coming to throw their punk-ass butts into a Detox Cube if they didn't get out of here fast.

He'd pretty much abandoned the hypehead theory, though, when he came across two of the things feeding on the dead security guard. The creeps were hunched over the corpse, lapping eagerly at the blood pouring out of its ruined throat, too busy in their meal to register the Judge's approach at first.

They'd looked up at him in fury at having their meal interrupted as he aimed his Lawgiver at them and called out a warning. They'd hissed at him in raw anger, baring their teeth and showing him their fangs – and then reached for their own weapons.

He'd shot both of them, quickly and expertly, putting them down with a piece of clinical precision marksmanship worthy even of Dredd himself. Then they had got back up, run into the cover of the main storage area and started firing back at him.

Giant took stock of the situation, trying to evaluate what he'd seen with what he still thought was impossible. A glance down at the dead security guard – throat savagely laid open, eyes wide in disbelief at the circumstances of his death, killed by vampires right here in the biggest city of the twenty-second century – told him that the impossible was what he was dealing with right now.

Well, if it looks like a vampire, acts like a vampire and tries to rip your throat out just like you'd expect a vampire to, then… thought Giant, deciding it was time he took the fight back to these things.

He darted out from the corner where he had been sheltering, heading for deeper cover inside the storage room. The move instantly provoked a hail of bullets from the two perps, but luckily any kind of marksmanship ability with automatic weapons didn't seem to be such a high agenda item with the undead.

The warehouse space was divided into a maze of wide aisles separated by pallets of med-stuff, and row upon row of storage shelving which stretched all the way up to the building's high ceiling. Giant ducked into the first aisle he came to, which seemed to be solely devoted to the storage of artificial cybernetic limbs. There were thousands of the things there, bionic arms and legs stacked floor to ceiling, everything from the cheap and basic models that any cit could get on the City Mega-Care program to the high-performance, top-of-the-range bionic-enhancement deluxe jobs favoured by the top professional athletes and sports celebs. Giant wondered for a second if someone knew something he didn't, and was stocking up in advance of some forthcoming rerun of the Apocalypse War, before returning his attention to the problem at hand.

He heard fast, eager footsteps behind him, and turned to see one of the perps following him in, charging down the aisle towards him. No sign of a weapon, but from the way it bared its fangs at him and flexed its talon-fingers in keen anticipation, he figured it had other ideas about how it was going to kill him. He fired instinctively, pumping three Lawgiver rounds into its chest. Three heart shots, each one a perfect ten score. The vampire staggered a little, and the change in pitch of its snarling seemed to suggest that this had hurt it some, but it was still on its feet and coming at him.

Department regs didn't allow Judges to carry religious ornamentation, so the idea of waving a crucifix at it was a complete non-starter, and only Psi-Division had access to the exotic stuff like silver-bladed boot knives and holy bullet Lawgiver rounds – so just how the hell was he supposed to kill the drokking thing?

Giant remembered Judgement Day, and Dredd's sanguine advice when they had been the first to encounter the zombie menace while on a Hotdog Run out in the Cursed Earth: "Pick your targets and shoot for their heads."

It had worked for zombies – and so had Hi-Ex and Incendiary too, though the latter only worked if you had the luxury of enough time to wait for the things to burn to death – so just how much difference was there between vampires and zombies?

Giant got his answer soon enough, firing off another burst of shots as the thing leapt at him. Its head exploded in a bloody pulp, and he hurriedly stepped aside to avoid its flailing corpse as it flew past him to land on the floor behind him, where it continued to twitch spasmodically.

Giant was just beginning to congratulate himself on his newly-achieved status of vampire-slayer, when the next one stepped out at the opposite end of the aisle from the other one. And this sucker was a lot closer and a lot angrier-looking.

"Hold it right there, freak! You're under arrest!" Giant barked, aiming his Lawgiver right at it, wondering as he did so if the undead were entitled to the same Justice Department regulation warning as living perps.

It leapt at him, faster and more agile than the first creature. Giant, following years of drilled-in Academy of Law training, put three textbook shots into its chest before amending his aim in light of what he'd just learned, and snapping off another three at its head.

It twisted out of the way, tucking its head down protectively, although one of the shots drilled through its cheek and blew away its lower jaw. This only seemed to make it even madder, Giant noticed.

The monstrosity crashed into him, slashing at him with its claw-like nails, tearing rents in the bullet-resistant material of his uniform. Giant fell, taking the vampire with him. He dropped his gun, unable to bring it to bear on the squirming thing clinging tightly to him, and used both hands to try and tear the thing off him.

Its strength was incredible, even more so when Giant realised that his attacker was a young girl, probably no more than about twenty years old. Her shrieks of rage were shrill and hellish and she seemed possessed by a frenzied, almost superhuman strength and tenacity. Her head darted down towards his exposed throat, elongated fangs eager to bury themselves in the soft flesh there. Giant desperately blocked the attack with his arm, and she sank her teeth into the tough material of his kevlar-lined Judge gauntlets, chewing into it to get at the meat beneath. If she could bite through the stuff his gloves were made of, Giant didn't even want to think of what kind of quick work she would make of his jugular vein, and his efforts to get away from the thing became all the more frantic.

His heart sank as he heard more footsteps running along the corridor behind him. If it was another one of these things, he knew he was doomed.

"Out of the way, Giant. Give me a clear shot."

The voice, authoritative and unmistakable. Suddenly, Giant was pretty sure he wasn't going to die anymore.

"Dredd!" he called out. "I know it sounds crazy, but they're vampires. You need to…"

There was a sound of a Lawgiver shot, and the thing on top of him was snatched away, the top of its head blown clean off.

"Shoot them in the head," finished Dredd with typical steely calmness as he stood over Giant, offering a hand to help him to his feet. "Figured that was the best way to go, soon as I saw it."

Dredd looked down at Giant, at his torn uniform, unsure whether the copious amounts of blood splattered across it belonged to Giant or to his attacker. "You injured?"

Giant climbed to his feet and recovered his Lawgiver, for the first time getting a good look at the thing which had almost just killed him. Scratch twenty. That thing had been no more than seventeen, tops.

"Only if you count my pride, I guess."

"How many more of the creeps are in here?"

It had been Dredd who had rescued Giant as a juve, keeping him on the straight and narrow and enrolling him in the Academy of Law, making sure that his life would have some real purpose. Dredd had been a permanent fixture in Giant's life for almost as long as the younger

Judge could remember, and was the nearest thing to a father he would ever have, even if neither him or Old Stony Face would ever admit it.

Still, no matter how long he had known Dredd, Giant would never fail to be impressed by the way Dredd dealt in the same stoic and matter-of-fact way with absolutely every freaky and weird thing the city had to throw at him. Whether it was vampires, zombie armies, extra-dimensional superfiends or apparently indestructible Cursed Earth headbutting cyborg maniacs, it was all just another day on the streets for Joe Dredd.

"Security cams picked up six of them when they broke in, so I figure that means four of them left. Watch your back – some of them are armed with more than fangs and bad breath."

"So am I," said Dredd, bringing his Lawgiver up to bear. "Let's go find them."

It wasn't too hard. The creatures had left a trail of destruction through the interior of the warehouse, randomly smashing everything and anything along the way as their frustrated search continued for whatever it was they had come here to get. That search had apparently ended at one of the refrigerated storage rooms off the main warehouse space. The thick metal door had been ripped off its hinges. Hungry snarls and chill, refrigerated air drifted out of the room beyond. Dredd silently motioned with the barrel of his Lawgiver towards the sign beside the entrance to the room: Synthi-Plasma Storage.

"Figures, when you think about it," said Giant. "What else would a bunch of vampire perps pull a heist job for?"

Both Judges tensed, automatically bringing their Lawgivers round to bear as another one of the vampire creatures shambled out of the freezer room, its face dripping with bright-red synthi-plasma, its arms laden down with packet after packet of the stuff. Gorged on the blood substitute, almost drunk on the taste of it, it stared in stupefied surprise at the two Judges. Finally, something within its brain clicked, and it made to unsling the stump gun it wore over one shoulder.

"Picnic's over, freak. Hi-Ex!" barked Dredd, giving the command to his Lawgiver's voice-activated shell selector, aiming his gun at the target's central body mass.

Both Judges ducked as the area in front of the entrance to the freezer room was suddenly painted bright crimson as the vampire and the twenty-eight one-litre plasti-packs of concentrated synthi-plasma blood it was carrying exploded under the impact of the Hi-Ex bullet.

Giant recoiled back, splattered with the stuff. Some of it had got into his mouth, and he spat it out in disgust, revolted by its taste. If he ever turned vamp, he figured he'd probably end up starving to death, if that was the only kind of chow he was expected to go for. His vision was a red smear, and he was still wiping clear his helmet's face visor when he heard Dredd's Lawgiver firing again.

The remaining three vamps were holed up in the freezer room, probably armed and ready to blow away anyone who tried to storm in there after them. Which Dredd wasn't about to do – not when his Lawgiver had everything he needed to encourage them to come out to where he was instead.

"Ricochet," he ordered, firing off a brace of shots through the freezer doorway. He hadn't bothered taking aim, and couldn't even see the targets he was firing at. With Ricochet rounds, though, he didn't need to.

The rubber-tipped titanium bullets weaved a deadly pattern in the close confines of the freezer room as they bounced off metal walls, bursting the racked packets of synthi-blood by the dozen and biting into vampire flesh. In seconds, the floor of the room was centimetres deep in blood spilling out from the bullet-exploded storage packs.

Possibly more enraged by the destruction of their food supply than any damage caused to them by the bullets, the vampires charged out wildly to face their attackers. Lawgivers at the ready, Dredd and Giant were more than prepared for them.

Dredd shot the first one with an Incendiary shell. Howling in agony as its body exploded into flame, the creature threw itself back into the freezer room, rolling and splashing about on the blood-covered floor in a vain attempt to put out the volatile and hungry phosphor fire which ate relentlessly into its undead flesh.

Taking a cue from Dredd, Giant picked off the next one with a Hi-Ex shot, splattering its shredded remains against the nearest wall. This was going to be a messy one for the clean-up crews, Giant guessed, and he hoped the Tek-Judge forensics squad that was soon going to be crawling all over this place were packing spatulas and scraping tools with their tech-kit, to gather up all the evidence now sliding down the walls.

Dredd coolly took care of the third creep as it leapt at him with apparent lightning speed, claws and fangs ready to tear him open. It was fast, but not fast enough. For a moment, it seemed to almost defy the laws of physics, hanging suspended in mid-air as Dredd's rapid-fire spray of bullets struck against it. Then it was moving again, hurled backwards by the relentless force of the shells still being fired into it. A final burst decapitated it as it struck the far wall. Head and body fell to the ground several metres apart.

Yes sir, a very messy one for the poor slobs in the clean-up crews, thought Giant.

Dredd took in the aftermath of the brief but spectacularly gruesome fight, casually prodding the remains of the nearest vamp with the toe of his Judge boot.

"Creeps don't seem in too much of a hurry to turn into dust when they're dead either, or whatever it is they're supposed to do in the horror stories."

Giant bent down to study the scraps of the one he had tagged with the Hi-Ex shot. It had been wearing what looked like ordinary citizen's clothes. No fancy evening suits. No red synthi-satin lined opera cloaks. "You think we're looking at something normal here, not necessarily supernatural?"

"Bloodsucking freaks that shrug off standard Execution rounds aren't exactly what you'd call normal, even for this city, but I'd rather look for some rational answers before we call in the Psi-Div spook chasers," Dredd said.

He shifted impatiently, re-holstering his Lawgiver. Giant sighed inwardly. He knew what was coming next.

"Meat-wagons and clean-up units are on their way," said Dredd, already moving to leave. "Stay here and supervise, Giant. I want full forensics back-up on this one. Let me know what they find. Anyone wants me, I'll be finishing the rest of my patrol shift."

Giant watched him go. No, Old Stony Face never changed. Vamps, freaks, muties and weirdoes Dredd took in his stride, but every chance he got, he always pulled rank and left someone else to deal with the paperwork.

Three

It was the paperwork Hershey hated the most.

Well, she also hated the meetings, the drafting of minutes, "resolutions" and "mission statements", the inane photo-op PR events, the occasional obligatory chat show appearance to show the citizens the allegedly friendly face of the Justice Department, the mind-numbing meet-and-greets with foreign dignitaries and ambassadors, the endless briefings from her policy advisors on a thousand different and tediously uninteresting but vitally important subjects.

But, most of all, she decided, she hated the paperwork. It was only now, two years after being elected Chief Judge of the most powerful city in the world, that she fully appreciated why Joe Dredd had turned down the post on several occasions in the past, when it would otherwise easily have been his for the asking.

"My place is on the streets," Dredd had always said.

"Yes, Joe," and those within the Justice Department who, like Hershey, knew him best, could always have silently added, "because that's where you're the furthest away from the drokking paperwork."

Not that she blamed him, really. Sitting here in the Council of Five chamber within the Grand Hall of Justice, listening to Judge Cranston of Accounts Division making his quarterly budgetary report to the Council, she wished with all her heart she was out there with him, putting down a block war or two, or even re-fighting the Apocalypse War all over again.

Grud, even the time she had been kidnapped, completely paralysed and almost tortured to death by Fink Angel had almost been preferable to this.

"Furthermore, looking at our overseas balance of trade figures for this current fiscal quarter, and taking into account our projections for the next fiscal quarter, as well as the standing moratorium on non-essential trade with the former Sov-Blok cities and the ongoing renegotiation with Sino-City as regards their Most Favoured Nation trade tariff status, we can predict with some modest confidence that, as far as the budget deficit for both this quarter and the next two is concerned–"

"Thank you, Judge Cranston," Hershey interrupted with what she hoped was the correct amount of tact. "Unfortunately, I have several other pressing appointments following this meeting, so thank you, but we'll read and review your budgetary report and recommendations later, and let you know our decision before the end of the week."

She kept on going before the flustered-looking elderly Accounts Division Senior Judge could protest. "Moving on to the next item on the agenda: the rise in incidents involving members of the so-called 'Church of Death'. Hollister?"

Judge Hollister, the Council's only member who wasn't already a Justice Department Divisional head, had been assigned to brief the rest of the Council members on the problem. Hershey was amused to see that, for once, Hollister had actually turned up for a Council meeting in proper Judge uniform. As a senior member of the Wally Squad, she had occasionally attended meetings in various kinds of civilian attire, some of them downright scandalous. Hershey wondered what Silver, one of her predecessors as Chief Judge and a notoriously prudish stickler for the rules, would have had to say if one of his most senior Judges had turned up for a Council of Five meeting wearing the fishnet tights and low-cut halter top outfit of a common slabwalker, as Hollister had once so memorably done.

"Most Sector Chiefs are reporting a rise in crimes associated with the cult. Up until now, it's been relatively small-time stuff; pro-Death scrawl-graffiti, juve gangs swapping their gang tags for cult symbols, the occasional case of pet animal sacrifice."

"And now?" said Hershey.

"Now we're seeing a sudden spike in these crimes, not just in number, but also in terms of their seriousness," replied Hollister. "Juve gangs claiming an association with the cult are banding together to start violent rumbles with the other gangs. Street preachers claiming to be pronouncing the 'Gospel of Death' have started appearing – we're picking them up as soon as they appear, of course – and some of them have even taken to the airwaves on illegal pirate radio stations to spread the word even further.

"My anti-pirate monitoring units have already tracked down a number of these illegal broadcast stations, and identified and arrested those responsible," interjected Tek Chief McTighe testily, keen to counter any suggestion that his Tek-Judges weren't already on top of the situation."

"Granted," agreed Hollister, "but what we're dealing with here is something more than a few pirate broadcasters. We're looking at Death cult-related crimes all across the board. More worryingly, we're seeing a noticeable rise in missing persons cases. We believe the cult may be tied into a lot of these."

"You think they've maybe graduated from pet sacrifice to something more serious?" asked Judge Niles, head of the Public Surveillance Unit and, in Hershey's opinion, probably the most astute mind in the room.

"Human sacrifice? The cult grabbing victims off the streets?" answered Hollister. "It's possible, but we think it's more likely that a lot of these are simple runaways. Juves or dropouts running off to join the cult."

"So they're actively recruiting now?" noted Buell, the gruff and no-nonsense head of the Special Judicial Squad, the division of the Justice Department charged with rooting out corruption within the force itself. "If they're recruiting, they must be organised. Do we have any idea of the kind of numbers they might have, or how they're organising or funding themselves?"

Hershey nodded in silent agreement. Typical Arthur Buell, his question cutting right to the heart of the issue.

"Nothing so far," admitted Hollister. "Grud knows we've rounded up enough of these loons, but the ones we're seeing so far are strictly small fry, lone kooks picking up on the Death cult vibes on the streets at the moment, or loosely associated local groups like street gangs or the odd kook collective. If there's a central leadership or organisation to the thing, we've yet to see any real hard evidence of it."

Ramos, the head of Street Division, shifted impatiently in his seat. "We've seen this kind of crap before, surely?" he said, with typical Street Judge bluntness. "Last month it was half the juves in the city painting red stars on their foreheads, calling themselves stuff like the 'Sons of Orlok', pledging their undying allegiance to East-Meg One and swearing to avenge its destruction. This month it's worshipping the Dark Judges, and next month it'll be something else. Sick as it is, it's probably just another fad. Maintain control of it, round up a few of its most visible proponents and make examples of them, and it'll soon blow over, just like that whole 'Kool Kommunista' thing did."

Several heads round the table nodded in quiet agreement. Hershey looked towards the man sitting on the far side of the room, seated beside Cranston and amongst the other non-Council member divisional heads. Even though the accountant and these others had no right to a vote when it came to making Council of Five decisions, Hershey still welcomed the opinions of her divisional chiefs, especially when it came to matters relating specifically to their own division's field of expertise.

Like now, for example. When it came to anything to do with the Dark Judges, Hershey didn't believe in leaving any possibility unconsidered.

"Psi-Chief Shenker, Death and the rest of his super-creep buddies are supposed to be your bailiwick. What does Psi-Division have to add to everything we've heard so far?"

"Nothing much, Chief Judge," came the Psi-Chief's answer. "Whatever this supposed cult's activities involve, it doesn't seem to have generated any significant psi-presence to be picked up over the psychic white noise thrown out by a city of over four hundred million human minds."

"Nothing at all, then?" asked Hershey, aware of the thinly veiled sharpness in her voice. Psi-Division's success in predicting city-threatening disasters had been less than stellar, most notably in the case of the so-called "Doomsday Scenario" event of the previous year, when organised crime group the Frendz almost seized control of the entire city. Like many others within the Justice Department, Hershey's faith in Psi-Division's effectiveness had been severely tested by such events, which went a long way to explaining why Shenker had swiftly lost Psi-Division's long-held seat on the Council after Hershey's election to the position of Chief Judge.

The Psi-Chief, a quiet, slightly fussy man, paused, looking vaguely uncomfortable, before venturing an answer. "We have had one unsubstantiated pre-cog warning in the last few days, relating to a possible supernatural threat against the city, Chief Judge, although as far as we can tell, there's nothing in it yet to suggest any connection to the Dark Judges or this Death cult phenomenon."

"Just one?" queried Hershey, puzzled and slightly irritated. Whenever possible, Psi-Division policy was to cross-check possible pre-cog warnings from any of its operatives with any secondary visions picked up from other Psi-Judges, especially those amongst the Division's supposed powerful and specially trained pre-cogs. Usually, it took verification from several other Psi-Judges before the alarm bells would start ringing loud enough to be heard here within the Grand Hall of Justice.

"Who did the pre-cog warning come from?" asked Hershey, suspecting she already knew the answer.

"Well... Anderson," said Shenker reluctantly.

There was a series of muted sighs from several Judges in the room. Although no one questioned Anderson's psi-abilities – she was without doubt Psi-Division's top operative – her reputation could only be described as... troublesome, at best. She could be irreverent, highly strung, insubordinate, even downright mutinous at times, and was becoming increasingly questioning of Justice Department methods and policy. That was Anderson all over, and Hershey knew that she wouldn't be the first Chief Judge to have problems with Psi-Judge Cassandra Anderson.

Nevertheless...

It had been Anderson who had dealt with Judge Death the first time he had ever appeared in Mega-City One, trapping his spirit within her own mind at a cost to herself which few here within the Council of Five chamber could ever possibly imagine.

When the other three Dark Judges had struck, freeing Death and slaughtering the inhabitants of an entire city block, it had also been Anderson who, along with Dredd, had stopped them. The pair had followed them back to the ghastly netherworld where the fiends had originally come from, and apparently destroyed them for good.

They had returned again once more, though, tricking Anderson into unwittingly bringing them back to life, but she had redeemed herself for that terrible mistake, devising a way of trapping them forever in extra-dimensional limbo. Or so it had seemed at the time.

And then, in the nightmare that had been Necropolis, it had been Anderson who had enabled Dredd to deliver the killing blow, destroying the power of the twisted beings known as the Sisters of Death and allowing the Judges to take control of the Mega-City back from Death and his foul kin.

Every time the Dark Judges had struck, Anderson had been instrumental in stopping them. There was no denying that Anderson had a special link with Death, almost certainly down to having the creep taking up joint residence in her brain for over a year, so Hershey wasn't about to ignore any chance, no matter how slight, that there was any threat to the city involving Death and the other Dark Judges.

"There's a cult dedicated to the worship of Death on the rise in the city, and Psi-Division's top telepath has a vision about a possible supernatural threat. Coincidence?" asked Buell, making Hershey wonder if her SJS Chief didn't have a few mind-reading powers of his own.

"Let's assume not, at least for the time being," replied Hershey, looking to Shenker. "Have Anderson brought in. I want a full face-to-face briefing from her on what it was she thought she picked up."

"And the Church of Death?"

"As you suggested," she told Ramos. "We come down hard on them, right across the board. Brief all the Sector Chiefs to round up any and all Death cult agitators in their sectors. Any of them who look like they might know anything get a full tour of the interrogation cubes. Until we know anything better, we assume there might be more to these muncheads than just another passing fad. Agreed?"

There was a brief show of hands round the table. Unanimous agreement.

"Very well," Hershey began. "Next item on the agenda, the increase in illegal alien smuggling at the spaceports. Judge Blunkett of Immigration Division will give us his report..."

* * *

COWED AND FEARFUL, cringing and repentant, the vampires bowed in submission before the angry figure on the altar's vid-screen.

"With so much at stake, at this late hour, and you fools couldn't contain your blood thirst for a day or two longer?"

Hissing in fear and contrition, the vampires grovelled even closer to the stone floor, afraid to even glance up at the figure on the vid-screen before them.

"Your children grow hungry and impatient," said the priest, shuffling forward in his dark green and amber cult robes to address the hidden speaker on the vid-screen. "Impatient at having to remain in hiding for so long, impatient for the glorious moment when the Dark Brethren are at last released from their imprisonment and we, their children and faithful servants can come out from the shadows and finally claim this city as our own."

There was a keening of agreement and anticipation from amongst the congregation of vampires, some baring their fangs in murderous and barely restrained blood hunger at the thought of the slaughter to come.

Many kilometres away, secure in his own hidden sanctum, the figure on the vid-screen sighed in thinly veiled irritation. They had their uses, these things, but ultimately they were at best a mistake on his part, yet another failed experiment on the route to his ultimate goal. Like these Death cultist fanatics whom he had found and with whom he shared at least some beliefs, he would use them to his own ends. And then, when they were of no use to him any further...

He broke off from that distracting, if not entirely unpleasant, train of thought, reminding himself that there were still important matters to be attended to first, and that these creatures he had created and these ignorant fools he had gathered to him were still the only tools he had at hand to carry out those matters.

"Believe me," he told the coven, the more conciliatory and understanding tone in his voice evident even over the static interference of the heavily code-scrambled vid-link, "I understand your impatience, and there is no one more eager to see our Dark Lord and his Holy Brethren returned to us, but there is still work to be done first, and we cannot afford any more mistakes now. If the Judges discover our plans, everything we've worked for up until this moment will have been pointless. You understand me? The Dark Ones will remain held prisoner by the unbelievers, and you will have failed them in the holy duty they have asked of us."

"I... I understand," the Death cult priest said, bowing his head in fearful contrition.

Fear and religious awe, the figure on the vid-screen marvelled to himself. That's how to make these fools do as you want. Keep them properly subdued, remind them who it is that they believe speaks through you and dress up everything you say in the right amount of portentous-sounding quasi-religious gobbledygook, and you can get them to do just about anything.

Even die for you, he thought with a smile. As would be amply demonstrated soon enough.

"Excellent," he said aloud. "Contain your hunger and impatience just a little longer, my children. I know the serum I provide you with is not enough to satisfy you, but I promise blood enough to feed the hunger of all of you, just as soon as the psi-witch is no longer a danger to us."

"Andersssssson..." Her name was a collective hiss of pure hatred from the members of the coven.

"Yes, Anderson," affirmed the figure on the vid-screen, further stoking the fires of the vampire coven's hatred. "The witch who has defied our masters time and time again, the one who has always been there to lead the Judges against them. The one who has even foolishly believed that she had actually succeeded in destroying that which cannot be killed!"

The coven snarled and hissed in rage at these reminders of past transgressions against their holy masters. The figure on the vid-screen waited a few moments for the sounds of their anger to abate.

"You still have her under surveillance?" he asked the priest, who nodded eagerly. "Then do our masters' bidding – and kill her!" commanded the figure on the vid-screen. "This time, when the Dark Judges are set loose to continue their holy work, Judge Anderson will not be there to stop them!"

Sitting there secure in his hidden sanctum, he leaned forward, hitting the switch to kill the vid-link, cutting off in mid-snarl the coven's predictable sounds of enthusiastic and bloodthirsty approval.

He tapped his fingers lightly on the console keyboard, calling up the floor plans which it had cost him much effort and money to secure from the supposedly impregnable Justice Department computer files.

He looked over the precious schematics for perhaps the thousandth time, mentally tracing out the pre-planned entry points, his eyes automatically seeking out those vital places which a hundred or more detailed computer simulation assaults had shown to be the most tactically vital or weakly defended. There would be casualties during the attack, of course, but that wasn't really going to be too much of a problem, was it? Not when he had a small army of death-obsessed fanatics and bullet-resistant vampire servants at his disposal?

Allowing himself a small smile of satisfaction, he closed his eyes and thought of the glorious transformation that would soon be his.

He was so close now, so close, and, the blundering incident at the med-supply repository aside, everything was going perfectly to plan.

"SO MUCH FOR that plan," muttered DeMarco to herself, drawing herself further into the shadows of the doorway from where she had been keeping hidden watch for most of the last few hours.

Another vehicle drew up, depositing a further group of figures outside the seemingly derelict dockside warehouse which she now knew to be the headquarters of the Church of Death.

In truth, the place wasn't much to look at, just another run-down old pre-Atomic Wars building in a street full of similar abandoned heaps in a neighbourhood almost now completely derelict due to the pollution overspill from the lethally toxic waters of the nearby Black Atlantic shore. But then again, DeMarco reminded herself, if she was setting up a secret and highly illegal cult dedicated to the worship of a mass-murdering, extra-dimensional super-freak, wouldn't this be exactly the kind of generally forgotten place she'd choose to hide out in too?

Her original plan had been to sneak into the place and reconnoitre it, to discover if it really was the cult's headquarters and see if she could find any clue about the whereabouts of the Caskey girl.

The constant flow of people in and out of the building – she had counted over fifty people arriving or departing in the last hour alone – had swiftly put paid to that idea.

"Grud, this place is almost as busy as Remembrance Square on Apocalypse Day," she muttered to herself again, as the warehouse's loading doors screeched up noisily and a medium-sized hov-truck slid forward into the street outside. Its rear panel doors were still open, and DeMarco saw a small platoon of figures in the now-familiar garb of the Death cult scrambling aboard. One of them suddenly looked round, straight toward where she was hiding, and DeMarco hurriedly pressed herself deeper into the shadows of the doorway.

Still, the brief moment she had seen the cultist's face was enough time for her Street Judge-trained instincts to get a glimpse of the creep, and she registered a shockingly pale and gaunt face with fierce, red-rimmed eyes and...

"Fangs?" she breathed to herself, wondering just what she had gotten herself into here. She was also pretty sure that almost all of them had been armed with a mixture of firearms: stump guns and automatic spit guns, the weapons of choice amongst most of Mega-City One's criminal fraternity.

She supposed that this was the point when she should do what any good cit was required to do, and call in a crime report to the Justice Department. Leave it to the Judges, that's what ordinary citizens were supposed to do. There was just one problem with that theory: Galen DeMarco didn't consider herself to be just another ordinary cit. She was an ex-Judge – she had been a Sector Chief before she left the Department, for Grud's sake, in command of a force of hundreds of Street Judges and responsible for the safety of the millions of inhabitants of an entire city sector – and she still had an experienced Judge's training and instinct, so no way was she just going to turn and walk away, leave it for someone else to deal with like a good little cit was supposed to.

Besides, she reminded herself, she was a Private Investigator, and she had a job to do and a responsibility to her client. And to her client's daughter, the still-missing Joanna Caskey.

DeMarco had gone to town on one of these "Friends of Thanos" creeps at Joanna's college, and, after searching his apartment (illegal entry: minimum five-year sentence, the Judge part of her mind dutifully reminded her) and finding a large stash of highly illegal narc-stims there (failure to report a crime: automatic minimum five-year sentence) she was fairly sure that the girl was here, and probably being held against her will. Apparently, her unwilling informant had told her, there was something special about the Caskey girl's aura, and she had been chosen for some unspecified "special purpose".

None of which DeMarco much liked the sound of at all. She told herself that even if she called it in now, the Judges might still not arrive in time to stop whatever was going on in there.

No, she decided, she had to get in there herself, find the girl and discover what exactly these creeps were up to. Then, she promised herself, she'd put in a call to the Judges, once she had done her duty to her client and got the Caskey girl safely out of there.

There was a guard left at the still-open loading doors. He was wearing robes with identifiable Church of Death markings (membership of an illegal organisation: five years), was openly carrying a well-worn pump-action stump gun (possession of an illegal weapon: two years) and, even as DeMarco watched, paused to light up a cigarette (illegal smoking in a public place: one to three years mandatory).

"Creep sure is racking up the crime count," DeMarco murmured to herself. "At this rate, he'll probably be catching up with me soon."

The guard was standing with his back to her now, looking along the street while taking a long draw on his cigarette, although DeMarco wondered why he even bothered smoking the thing down here. If he wanted to dramatically cut his lifespan and pollute his body with lethally toxic substances, then a few good big lungfuls of the stuff that passed for air down here would do the job just as easy.

Reaching into her pocket to make sure that her pistol with its add-on stun beamer (unregistered modification of a licensed firearm: six months to a year, that little Judge voice reminded her) was still there, she slipped quietly from her hiding place and began sneaking across the street towards the guard's unprotected back.

The first plan had been a bust, she told herself, so let's see how this one worked out.

Four

ANDERSON WAS REVVING up her Lawmaster, before pulling out onto Tinto Brass Memorial Expressway for a long, looping, random patrol circuit of the inner sectors of MegEast, when her bike radio crackled into life.

"Anderson – Control. Chief Judge Hershey wants to see you. Report your position; we're sending an H-wagon to pick you up and take you to the Grand Hall of Justice."

"Not necessary, Control. I'm a big girl now, I can get there on my own."

She broke off communications before she received Control's no doubt exasperated repeat of the instructions they had already just given her. Even though she was a telepath, she didn't have to be a mind-reader to know what was probably going through the mind of an anonymous Comms Judge back at the local Sector House Control.

That Anderson. Always making trouble, always thinking that normal regs don't apply to her. Grud knows why she's still even a Judge.

To be honest, Anderson asked herself the same thing a dozen or so times a day at least. She thought she'd left the Justice Department and even Mega-City for good before – "Cassandra's little hiatus away from us" was how Psi-

Chief Shenker referred to that period, with a wry smile – but, despite herself, she had eventually returned, called back by something inside her.

She loved Mega-City One, but she hated it too. She had hated being a Judge too, had hated and fought against the monolithic authoritarian weight of the Justice Department and much of what it stood for as well, but still she had come back, realising that this was all she knew and was where she was needed most.

Like now, for instance. The last time she had come back it was because, even from halfway across the galaxy, she had sensed a premonition that the Dark Judges were going to strike once more, and she had arrived back on Earth just in time to stop Death and his three super-creep amigos from escaping again.

And this time? What was the source of that vision she had, and that growing, creepy feeling at the back of her mind? Was it linked to the Dark Judges in some way?

Anderson didn't know, but she intended to find out and, while the immediate prospect of an audience with the Chief Judge didn't exactly thrill her, she hoped that it would go some way to putting her mind at rest. Death and the other Dark Judges might be contained under the highest security in the Tomb level beneath Nixon Penitentiary, but, as the Justice Department had discovered to its cost too many times before, imprisonment or even their apparent destruction hadn't been enough in the past to reduce the deadly threat they represented to every living soul in Mega-City One.

Checking the non-stop flow of Traffic Division info-updates scrolling across the screen of her bike computer, Anderson saw that Tinto Brass was severely congested at a point a few kilometres ahead, with serious delays at the Brucie Campbell Interchange caused by fans travelling to the smashball game at the nearby Juggernauts stadium and the aftermath of yesterday's brief block war spat between the Kylie and Dannii Minogue twin con-apts.

"Grand Hall of Justice – best alternative route from present location," she barked to her bike computer in the approved Justice Department tone of voice.

"Wilco. Please stand by," responded the onboard computer in a voice Anderson had long come to call Justice Department Techno-Soulless. She'd heard that some of the younger Judges coming out of the Academy these days liked to have bike computers with a selection of changeable audio circuits. Apparently some bright spark at Tek-Division had even made it possible to have your bike speaking to you in a synthesised version of Dredd's own unmistakably terse and no-nonsense tones. Anderson grinned at the thought – Grud only knew what Dredd thought of that. Then she smiled to herself again at the realisation that, to many of the younger Judges hitting the streets these days, she must seem almost as much a piece of Justice Department legend – "relic" would be the more unkind term they used amongst themselves in the Sector House locker rooms – as Old Stony Face himself.

A moment later, the screen on the compact instrumentation panel in front of her displayed the requested map route, with secondary and even tertiary alternatives suggested as optional extras. Anderson selected the main route and guided her Lawmaster away from the expressway and onto an off-sked ramp, keeping one eye on the scrolling flow of traffic data as she did so. Like any good Judge, she knew the city's main roadway map by heart, but the day-to-day traffic situation was so chaotic, affected by everything from freak Weather Control mishaps to major block wars, and not forgetting the seemingly random basis on which the planners down at City Hall decided to carry out roadwork repairs and construction projects, that any seemingly simple trip from A to B could end up taking in unplanned detours to C, D, E and F along the way.

She hit the off-sked ramp at an easy 150 kph, turning onto it in a casual manoeuvre that would not have met with approval from any Bike Skills tutor at the Academy of Law – and which would have quickly drawn angry beeps and honks of protest from the vehicles behind her, had she been anyone other than a Judge.

Three lanes back, unnoticed by Anderson, the hov-truck which had been following her jumped lanes to match her manoeuvre, drawing a chorus of complaint from the motorists around it. Anderson, speeding off and accelerating up to 200 kph now, didn't notice as the vehicle slid onto the sked ramp behind her, bringing its own speed up to catch her.

She was on Joey Ramone Undersked, travelling east towards Sector 44. From there, she would cut off at Linneker Junction, catching the Tushingham Expressway for half a sector until she hit Slab 12 with its For Justice Department Use Only express lanes, which would allow her to open up the throttle and cruise all the way to the Grand Hall at a cool 350 kph. In less than fifteen minutes, she figured, she'd be pulling into the Grand Hall's motor pool levels.

When it came to beating the big city traffic, Anderson mused to herself, there were times when being an agent of a rigidly authoritarian law enforcement regime definitely had its advantages.

A juve skysurfer swooped in low above her, buzzing the speeding traffic below him and briefly mooning a party of outraged-looking elderly Brit-cit tourists sitting on the top deck of a strato-bus. He laughed at their reaction and briefly posed theatrically for the cameras of the delighted party of Hondo-cit tourists sitting behind the more uptight Brit-citters, and then hit the uplift throttle on his board, zooming back upwards and making the complex task of juggling high-speed aerodynamics with balancing the requirements of the skyboard's notoriously delicate and unreliable anti-grav field look as easy as riding an escalator.

Anderson supposed she should call the incident in to Control and have an aerial unit pick him up. Grud knew a stickler like Dredd would already have done it as soon as he spotted him, probably with good justification. Pulling illegal low-level flying stunts like that, the juve was a danger to himself and others, and maybe a few months in the Juve Cubes would cool his heels a little and do him some good.

On the other hand, she thought, watching the skysurfer accelerate away, dodging with masterful skill through two lanes of aerial traffic and then gliding gracefully up across the strong thermal updrafts from the stacked rooftops of the giant city blocks below, Anderson couldn't help but marvel at the momentary illusion of complete freedom the juve seemed to represent.

"Enjoy it while it lasts, kid," she murmured to herself. "Trust me, the rest of life in this city is all downhill from where you are now."

Distracted by her thoughts and the skysurfer's antics, she didn't even notice the hov-van pull almost level with her in the lane opposite. It was the psi-flash, screaming through her brain with nerve-shredding intensity, that warned her scant moments before the panel door at the side of the van nearest her slid open and a hail of automatic weapons fire was blasted out at her at near point-blank range.

Anderson swerved.

And braked. Hard.

She ducked too, leaning forward fast and hugging the chassis of her Lawmaster as a hot stream of bullets passed through the space where her head had been a brief moment ago.

The gunfire raked down the side of the bike. Anderson's violent swerve manoeuvre took her away from most of it, but she still heard shots ricocheting off the bike's armoured bodywork or shattering its sidelights. Something punched into the calf of her leg, while another red-hot shell tore painfully into the tough, bullet-resistant material of her Judge boot.

No biggie, she thought to herself. I'm a Judge. I've been shot plenty of times before.

She veered away from the van, into the next lane and the path of traffic flowing in the other direction, forcing her to violently swerve again to avoid smashing into oncoming vehicles. A bright red Foord Strato screamed by, passing close enough for Anderson's Lawmaster to leave scrape lines along the length of its gleaming paintwork. Anderson caught a lighting-speed glimpse of the horrified expressions of the car's occupants – mother, father and their population regs-permitted two juves – and then they were gone before they could realise just how close they came to having Psi-Division's top telepath smeared all over the front of their family car.

She was behind the van now, wondering how long it would be before back-up might arrive, wondering if she could stay alive long enough for it to matter. By now, some of the cits in the passing cars might be making emergency calls to the Justice Department. Roving spy-in-the-sky anti-crime surveillance cams might already have picked the incident up, beaming the images of it back to the local Sector House Control, while the Traffic Division cameras would surely have picked up something of it, although, unless a human supervisor was present, it might take the autobot programs that each monitored the images from thousands of such cameras some time to realise what was happening.

A personal heads-up call from her probably wouldn't do any harm at this point either, she thought.

"Control – Anderson. Am under attack, Joey Ramone U-sked, between Fred Fellini and Pete Bogdanovich Interchanges. Perps are driving a black, late-model Kryton-Skesky hov-truck. Am in pursuit and still under fire."

Right on cue, she was reaching for her Lawgiver even as the rear doors of the van burst open. She saw her attackers clearly this time. Four of them, wearing familiar-looking green and amber robes, and aiming their weapons at her.

Death cultists, she realised with a chill. In her book, at least, the Church of Death had just become something much more than another passing craze amidst Mega-City One's usual quota of harmless loons and jaded thrill-seekers.

She swerved again as they opened fire. What they lacked in accuracy, they more than made up for in sheer ferocity of firepower. Spit shells smacked into the rockcrete surface of the sked, gouging huge chunks out of it, or smashed into the front of her Lawmaster, shattering against its array of powerful headlights or ricocheting off its densely armoured eagle badge facade. One lucky shot drilled through the armoured casing of her bike computer and the thing died with a noisy electronic squawk, cutting off any reply that she might have been expecting to hear back from Control.

Stray shots flew everywhere, causing mayhem amongst the traffic behind her. She veered off again to a position directly behind the hov-truck, drawing her attackers' fire directly back upon herself and away from the other vehicles on the road. She wasn't in a hurry to get killed today, but she didn't want innocent cits to get hit by any bullets meant for her.

In doing so, she caught an unexpected break. Her attackers had completely emptied their magazines and were now struggling as fast as they could to reload their guns.

I'm being attacked by a hit-squad of amateurs, she thought to herself. If these creeps kill me now, I'll probably never live it down.

She could see them clearly. The hood of one of them slipped back, and she saw a shockingly pale face, a pair of red eyes staring at her in hatred, a mouth snarling open to reveal...

Fangs, she wondered to herself, remembering the things from her psi-flash nightmare?

The cultist raised his reloaded spit gun to fire at her again.

"Not going to happen, freak," Anderson said, beating him to the punch, as she raised and fired her Lawgiver at him.

As was normal with Psi-Judges, she wasn't the greatest shot the Justice Department had ever seen. The extra-intensive psi-training at the Academy of Law came at the expense of some of the other regular skills taught to all Judge cadets, and she was never going to be able to beat someone like Dredd on a Sector House firing range – but, nine times out of ten, her Lawgiver shots went exactly where she wanted them to. This time was no exception.

The two shots punched into the white-faced freak's chest, knocking him backwards. A second later, though, he was back on his feet, reaching for his dropped weapon and snarling in even greater hatred.

Body armour, thought Anderson. That's what he must be wearing under those robes. There's a couple of light and flexible armour types – stuff like the new shokk-hard jackets favoured by Mega-Mob blitzers – that can stop anything up to a Lawgiver AP round.

Then Anderson saw the freak's face again, felt for a moment the burning hatred in those unnatural red eyes and sensed the awful hunger behind that hatred, and suddenly knew that, no, there was no armour hidden underneath those robes. She had just put two shots straight into this freak's chest cavity, and it hadn't even phased him.

The other three were getting ready to fire again too. One of them was fumbling with an object in his hand, and Anderson got another psi-flash as, in her mind's eye, she saw the object leave the cultist's hand; saw it explode against the front of her bike; saw both her and the Lawmaster burning furiously, wreathed in unquenchable flames. Saw herself falling screaming from the saddle as she burned alive in agony, her body smashing into the surface of the road and then lying there lifeless and yet still burning. By the time the nearest back-up unit arrived a few minutes later, there would be hardly anything left of her to scrape up and deliver to Resyk.

Phosphor bomb! her mind screamed to her in warning at the weapon in the cultist's hand.

Her own hand stabbed the handlebar-mounted fire control switch for her Lawmaster's main armament, sending out a long, roaring stream of shells from the twin-linked cannons on the bike's front. Large-calibre shells raked the rear and interior of the hov-van, ripping through metal bodywork and human flesh with equal ease. The phosphor grenade, blown out of its owner's hand, exploded inside the van with devastating effect, and Anderson had to manoeuvre hard to avoid the ferocious fireball which suddenly burst out of the vehicle's open rear doors.

Its whole interior ablaze, including its driving compartment, the vehicle swerved violently across the lanes of the sked. A flailing figure covered head to toe in flame fell out of the still-open side door and hit the surface of the road with a sickening crunch. Anderson followed the vehicle on its careering course, hitting her bike sirens to alert all oncoming traffic of the danger, although the sight of the fiercely burning and out-of-control vehicle was surely enough to make the driver of any oncoming vehicle sit up and take notice.

Suddenly, without warning, something detached itself from the flame-filled furnace that was now the van's rear compartment. It was a human figure, covered in fire. It leapt – flew, almost – from the rear of the van, covering the nearly ten-metre gap between the burning van and Anderson's position in an astounding feat of strength, landing on the bullet-scarred front of the Lawmaster with a bone-jarring impact.

Anderson recoiled back in her saddle in disbelief, finding herself staring into the inhuman eyes of the thing as it launched itself upon her. Most of its clothes were burnt away by the fire which crawled over almost all of its body, and Anderson could clearly see the gaping holes on its torso from the wounds inflicted by the bike cannon shells and her two Lawgiver shots. It was the same freak she had already shot twice in the chest.

It leapt across the front of the bike at her, forcing her to relinquish control of the bike's handlebars as she brought an arm up to block a lunging bite from that fang-filled mouth.

With her onboard computer knocked out by a lucky bullet hit, the Lawmaster was now effectively out of control.

The monstrosity locked its hands round her throat, pressing forward eagerly toward her. Her nostrils were filled with the stench of burning meat, and she could feel the heat from the flames starting to blister those portions of her skin that weren't protected by the fire-resistant material of her uniform.

The thing's face – Anderson no longer thought of her attacker as now being anything remotely human – loomed up in front of her, only centimetres away from her own. Its red eyes bored into her with a terrible intensity. For a moment, Anderson involuntarily brushed minds with the thing, tasting the hunger and hatred which consumed it. There was something else there, something hidden at the back of its mind…

She focused her psi-talent, pushing violently through the repellent barrier of the creature's hunger-thoughts and into the remnants of the ravaged mind beyond. In that briefest of moments, she plundered what she could from the creature's own memories. She saw the gleaming antiseptic surfaces of a high-tech laboratory… a dingy warehouse front, possibly somewhere down at the Black Atlantic docks, judging by the pollution haze hanging in the air…

She pushed in still further.

Some kind of religious ceremony, heads bowed in fear and awe before some kind of altar… A figure speaking on a vid-screen, its face hidden from view, its voice sending a thrill of fearful obedience through the mind of the thing…

Further. Still further. Not memories now, images of events still to happen.

Doors opened to reveal huge caches of weapons, eager hands reaching in to snatch up what they can… Dozens of creatures identical to the thing Anderson was now fighting crammed into the compartments of hov-transporters, a sense of almost unbearable hunger and eagerness running through them as they neared their destination… A set of schematics marked with a 'Justice Department: Highly Classified' security notification... Guard tower points, security bypass procedures, level after identical level of corridors lined with small cube-like rooms... Cells... An iso-block?

With a sickening realisation, Anderson knew in an instant what these freaks were up to. She broke off the psi-contact, snapping back to the reality of what was still happening to her right this moment. The sucker's hands were still around her throat, burning into the material of her uniform, strangling her. She felt herself start to black out. From somewhere far away, but somehow coming swiftly closer, she heard an urgent roaring sound...

She threw herself backwards off the saddle, taking her attacker with her, hurling themselves both off the Lawmaster a split second before it crashed into the front of the huge jugger-transporter, the sound of the impact as the Lawmaster was smashed apart momentarily drowning out the blaring roar of the giant vehicle's batteries of warning horns.

Falling backwards at a 100 kph or more, it was times like this Anderson wished she had paid more attention to the Department regs about the compulsory wearing of helmets. She desperately twisted in mid-air, putting her attacker's body between her and the road surface now rushing up towards them, figuring she might as well let him hit it first.

It worked, mostly.

They hit the ground and rolled for fifty metres or so, the rough surface of the sked making them pay for every bone-breaking, skin-shredding metre. The creature took the worst of it, as Anderson had hoped, but at least it didn't have to worry about being on fire anymore. Not when most of its burning skin had been scraped off along the way.

Anderson fared better, her uniform and protective pads saving her from the very worst of the variety of injuries on offer.

She came to rest on the edge of the sked's hard shoulder, still conscious, and started counting the damage. A couple of ribs were gone, and she suspected one of them might have punctured a lung, judging from the white-hot spears of agony she felt every time she took a breath. Her left leg was bent back at a decidedly unpleasant angle, and she didn't need to try to pick up any pre-cog visions to see some serious time spent hooked up to a speedheal machine in her immediate future.

The pain was bad, real bad. She knew some psi-tricks to block a lot of it out, but they would have to wait. The most important thing now was to let everyone else know what it was she had seen inside the mind of that creature.

She was just reaching down for the communicator stored in her utility belt when the hand, charred and almost fleshless, reached out to grab her.

The creature, incredibly, was still alive. Its body was smashed, its skin was burnt away from it in huge, terrible patches, yet it still wouldn't accept the inevitable and just roll over and die. It was crawling up the length of her body, making a horrible, hissing, gurgling sound from its ruined throat.

Pinned to the ground, weak from pain, Anderson was helpless to stop it. Her Lawgiver was long gone, knocked from her hand as they fell from the back of the bike, and probably now crushed beneath the wheels of the jugger-transporter. Which only left her with...

Ignoring the screaming pain from her broken leg, she reached down for the boot knife secreted there. Her hand found it just as the creature pressed itself down at her throat. Its mouth hung slackly open, revealing the jutting fangs there. Anderson's hand flashed up, stabbing the knife's blade right between the thing's open fangs.

Psi-Judges were equipped with silver-bladed boot knives as standard these days. Anderson didn't know what this fiend was or where it came from, but she was pretty hopeful that this might finally be enough to kill it. Silver blade or no silver blade, ramming the point of a boot knife right through the roof of its mouth and straight up into its brain was sure to have some kind of effect.

It did. The creature gave a choking cry and fell forwards across her, its fangs closing around the hilt of the knife still gruesomely jutting out from between its clenched jaws.

Using almost the last of her rapidly failing strength, Anderson painfully pushed the thing off her and reached in desperation towards the communicator lying on the ground nearby.

A black, nauseous wave of unconsciousness rushed up towards her. She struggled to hold it off for a few more precious moments. She had to radio in what she knew... Had to let the rest of Justice Department know what was about to happen...

Had... to...

She heard sirens in the distance, coming closer. Her fingers brushed against the hard casing of the communicator. Her vision swam. And dimmed.

THE BACK-UP SQUAD found her less than two minutes later. She was unconscious, lying in a spreading pool of her own blood. The first Judge on the scene gingerly knelt over her, feeling for a pulse and relieved to find one, weak though it was.

"Control – Varrick. Med unit urgently required down here on Joey Ramone. Alert anyone who needs to know – Psi-Judge Anderson's down and in a bad way."

"Wilco, Varrick. Med assist on its way."

"Hold on, Anderson. Help's coming," Varrick said gently to the near-comatose Psi-Judge. Two years ago that had been him, lying bleeding into the ground of a block plaza after being caught in the crossfire of a juve gang rumble, and he knew from experience how much it meant to hear a friendly voice or just to know somehow that someone's there with you, watching out for you, while you're lying there helpless and injured.

He reached down to take her hand, noticing as he did so that she had her back-up communicator held in it. Her finger was on the call switch, although she'd passed out before she could activate it.

Five

"HEY, WHAT WAS that?"

Burchill looked up in irritation from the book he was reading, his concentration broken by the sudden sound of Meyer's voice. Dull as it was, Dredd's *Comportment* was supposed to be required reading for any Street Judge.

Despite the mood of breezy nonchalance Burchill affected whenever he was on duty down here, he hated this posting, and seriously resented having to come back to the Tomb for another three months of sitting here doing nothing.

Which was why he had put in a request for permanent reassignment to something a little more interesting than guard duty in the Tomb, once this latest three-month stint was up. Something like open patrol assignment, say, maintaining a visible Psi-Division presence on the city streets and giving psi-specialist back-up to the ordinary Judge on patrol.

Which meant he'd have to undergo a series of re-evaluation tests at Psi-Div HQ, to see if he was suitable for more responsible duties.

Which meant having to brush up on his knowledge of Street Division and the way the Street Judges operated.

Which he couldn't do, if Meyer kept on drokking interrupting him.

"What?" he said testily.

Meyer indicated the instrument panel in front of her. "The needle on Containment One. Did you just see it move?"

Sighing in undisguised irritation, Burchill laid down the book and looked at the matching instrumentation on his own duty station. There were huge and expensive batteries of delicately calibrated electronic sensor devices trained on the four containment capsules on the other side of the no-go line. Much of it was designed to measure or detect any kind of psi-activity on the part of the four beings imprisoned in those capsules. If Spooky, Creepy, Sparky and Bony were up to anything, it was supposed to register on these instrumentation panels.

Which it never did, because nothing – absolutely nothing at all – of any interest ever happened down here in the Tomb.

"Nothing here," he answered. "You sure you didn't just imagine it?"

Meyer didn't look amused. "Check the log record," she ordered. "You know how the regs work."

Burchill punched up the sensor readings for the last few minutes, giving an unimpressed grunt in response to what he saw. "Okay, so there was a tiny micro-spike on One, forty-three seconds ago, but nothing to get your panties wound up about. Less than point-three of a psi-joule. Despite what the Tek-heads say, you know how random some of this junk is. One of the perps in the cells a hundred levels above has himself a real hot erotic dream one night, and sometimes the instruments down here pick it up. Satisfied?"

"Not yet. You still know what regs say. I need you to do a psi-check."

Now Burchill was getting really irritated. Despite the flippant names he gave them, the four things in those containment cells seriously creeped him out sometimes, and he really hated having to do what he was now required to do.

He sat back in his chair, closed his eyes, doing his best to empty his mind of the usual mental clutter as he brought his psi-abilities into focus. He reached out, overcoming the instinctive mental recoil from the sheer evil power of the things on the other side of the no-go line and, for the briefest possible moment, scanned the psi-activity within the chamber, looking for anything out of the ordinary. He hated doing this. What made it even more unnerving was knowing that Meyer, sitting across from him, had her hand on the grip of her Lawgiver, ready to draw it and put a Standard Execution round through his brainpan at the first sign that he had become possessed or psychically controlled by any of the occupants of the containment units.

After a few moments, he opened his eyes again, seeing Meyer looking at him intently.

"Anything?" she asked, the tension clear in her voice.

"Not a thing," he replied. She stared at him hard for a few moments more – like maybe she's expecting me to start sprouting tentacles or levitate into the air with my head spinning round in circles on my shoulders, he asked himself, incredulously? – and then visibly relaxed, bringing her hand up from under the desk where her Lawgiver was secured.

"With these creeps, it's always best to be sure," she said, perhaps in way of partial apology.

"Whatever," grumbled Burchill, going back to his book again.

"*A Judge's first weapon is not his Lawgiver or his boot knife or his daystick,*" he read. "*It is his Judge badge, and the natural authority it gives him...*"

Oh brother, Burchill thought to himself. Old Stony Face might still be Mega-City One's greatest lawman bar none, but when it came to writing, he'd all the slick prose style of the late, great Mayor Dave the orang-utan.

WITHIN HIS PRISON, the spirit of Judge Death hissed to itself in silent pleasure. Yes, this one was pleasingly weak, not even aware of Death's growing control over his deep-buried subconscious. He saw only what Death wanted him to see and nothing more.

Death was pleased. Equally pleasurable had been the event he'd just detected from afar. Since the time he had first come to judge the sinners of this place, his fate and that of the psi-witch Anderson had always been intertwined. He still rankled at the memory of his imprisonment within her, trapped by the frightening power of her mind, unable to escape her comatose body, the two of them put on display together in a museum, of all places.

The memory of that first defeat, that first humiliation, still fuelled his hatred against this city and the sinful life that teemed within it. It was this connection between them that had allowed Anderson to defeat him and his brothers several times since, but that connection worked both ways. Just as Anderson could sense him, so too was he sometimes psychically aware of her, even while he was imprisoned down here, weakened and disembodied.

Her aura was like a distant glimmer of light in the darkness of his thoughts, torturing him with the knowledge that she still existed, despite all his attempts over the years to extinguish that light forever.

Now, though, the light was faint. Barely perceptible and unusually dim. She was not dead, he sensed, or at least not yet, but her life force had been seriously diminished. Perhaps for good, he hoped.

His servants in the city beyond this place had done well. Anderson was no longer a threat to he and his brethren, which meant that those same servants were now ready to take the final step.

The spirits of his foul companions writhed in psychic restlessness, demanding to know when they would be free.

Soon, brothers, he whispered to them in a voice that only those who had passed beyond life and death could ever know. *Very soon now. I promise.*

HERSHEY RESISTED THE urge to yawn. They had almost reached the end of the Council session, which was traditionally Kook Time, when the Council discussed what Hershey secretly called AOOC.

Any Other Outstanding Crap.

Last on the Kook Time agenda was a concern about some new bio-product that had come onto the marketplace a few months ago. Med-Division had given it a clean bill of health and approved the patent, but there had been a number of complaints about it from the citizens. For reasons that Hershey still wasn't quite sure about, no one at Justice Central had been able, or perhaps cared enough, to make a decision about what to do, and so the case had gradually risen up through the hierarchy of the Department until the Council of Five, which regularly debated issues vital to the security and existence of a city of over four hundred million people, found itself now arguing about a novelty medical treatment for raising pet animals from the dead.

Only in the Big Meg, thought Hershey, using a Street Judge's customary dismissive opinion on all the weirdness and craziness that passed for daily life in Mega-City One.

"After the events of Judgement Day, we're aware of many citizens' objections to the idea of a product which brings dead flesh back to life," Hershey said, gesturing towards the computer file compilation of the several tens of thousands of complaints they'd received from the citizens about the EverPet adverts that had been running for weeks on the Tri-D networks, "but we have Med-Division's most stringent assurances that the treatment only works on the simpler nervous systems of animals like common household pets, and definitely not on human beings."

"Quite so," nodded the representative from Med-Division. "We went down to Resyk and pulled dozens of corpses off the conveyor belts there and dosed them with increasingly huge quantities of the Pet Regen formula. We got nothing so much as a twitch from any of them. And besides," he added a hint of a smile, "a chemically reanimated cat, budgerigar or goldfish isn't quite in the same league as an army of millions of flesh-eating zombies knocking on the gates of the West Wall."

"My thoughts too," agreed Hershey, glad that the issue looked like it was going to be quickly resolved. "Any other comments?"

"Well, there are the fiscal benefits to consider too," volunteered Accounts Judge Cranston, pouring over the tables of carefully prepared statistics he'd brought with him. "Besides the standard twenty-five per cent sales tax charged on the product, there's also the extra income we'll derive from the necessary re-issuing of new pet licences."

"Meaning what, exactly?" Ramos asked, showing the same kind of impatience as Hershey.

Cranston shuffled through his beloved piles of paperwork. "Well, the cost of a general pet licence is one hundred credits, with some of the more dangerous or alien pet types also requiring an annual additional inspection fee on top of that. In all cases, however, a pet licence becomes legally null and void when the animal dies. If a pet owner then wants to use this product to bring their beloved creature back to life…"

"Then they'll have to buy a new licence," Niles smiled, instantly seeing where Cranston was going. "And the Department in effect will receive double the licence money for the same animal."

"Indeed!" beamed Cranston, making quick-fire calculations on his desktop analyser. "So, with fifteen million, three hundred thousand and twenty-seven pet licences currently issued, and assuming that at least ten to fifteen per cent of pet owners might take advantage of this product, we can probably expect to accrue additional revenues somewhere in the region of…"

Hershey, however, had already heard all she needed or wanted to. "Enough to settle the issue, I imagine. Unless anyone has any other points, we'll assume the Pet Regen product is allowed to remain on sale – for the time being?" She looked around the room, seeing only nods of agreement, and gratefully brought the Council meeting to an end for another week.

"Very well, then. If there's no other business to be discussed..."

"Just one item," interrupted a new voice from the other end of the room. All heads turned to see Dredd standing in the council chamber doorway. The Council of Five meetings were supposed to take place in closed session, with no one permitted to enter without the Chief Judge's permission. A guard of armed Judges was posted in the corridor outside, to make sure of this. Dredd, however, was always a special case. There seemed to be an unofficial and unspoken understanding, established many administrations ago, that Dredd had automatic and unrestricted access to the Chief Judge whenever he required it.

When Dredd spoke, Hershey knew from long experience, it paid for Chief Judges to pay attention to what he had to say. She sat back in her chair, signalling for her old street patrol partner to continue.

"What's the official Department policy on vampires?" he asked.

Six

ANDERSON STRUGGLED AND fought against the darkness that surrounded her. She was back in the nightmare world she had seen in her earlier pre-cog vision – only this time it was much, much worse.

She was running through the empty streets of the city again, her feet crunching gruesomely on the carpet of bones which littered the ground. From all around her, she heard the growling and snarling of the vampire creatures. At first she thought they were hunting her, but then she realised they had no interest in her.

There were thousands of them, maybe even tens of thousands. The vampires were flooding through the city streets like a living tide of darkness, converging on one central point. In the distance, Anderson could see their destination: a vast prison tower, forbidding and impenetrable. The teeming creatures threw themselves at its walls, tearing at the seamless stonework with their claw-like hands, gnawing madly at it with their bare fangs. Teeth shattered against dense, unyielding stone. Taloned fingers were shredded down to the bone, but still the creatures persisted in their crazed task.

Their toil and mindless sacrifice finally paid off. A crack appeared in the blood-smeared surface of the wall, then a second. The creatures redoubled their efforts, tearing eagerly at the weakened stonework with a renewed fervour. The cracks widened, vast blocks of masonry tumbled out of place…

There was a scream of hellish triumph from within the breached prison tower, echoed a moment later from the snarling throats of the thousands of creatures gathered around its base. A wave of darkness poured out through the breach, accompanied by the overpowering stench of pent-up decay and corruption.

There were presences within that darkness, the fetid feel of their psychic auras so sickeningly familiar to Anderson. Four voices, so terribly familiar also, hissed in unison: "At lassssst. Now the great work continuessss. Thisss time, there will be no esssscape for thosssse guilty of the ultimate crime – the crime of life!"

THE BRIEF BUT urgent series of beeps from the devices monitoring Anderson's vital signs was enough to bring the med-bay orderly over in a hurry to where the unconscious patient lay on the bed of the speedheal machine. Anderson was out of danger now, but her body still needed time and rest to allow the speedheal procedure to go to work on her injuries, and so she was still under sedation.

The orderly leant in close to study the readings on the monitor beside the bed. She frowned, seeing a sudden momentary spike in the patient's brain activity. That shouldn't be happening, not with the sedatives that had been administered, and under the technology the speedheal machine used to accelerate the body's own healing processes. Still, she thought to herself, Anderson was a Psi-Judge, wasn't she, and who knew what went on in the minds of those frea–

She jumped back suddenly, dropping the tray of instruments she had been carrying, as Anderson's hand snatched out and grabbed her by the wrist.

Anderson's eyes fluttered open, which should have been nearly impossible, considering how much sedation she was under. She locked eyes with the Med-Div auxiliary, her grip tightening on the frightened woman's wrist. Using strength she shouldn't by any rights have at the moment, she pulled the orderly closer, her lips forming half-mumbled, slurred words, every one of them taking a supreme effort of will to get out as she struggled against the black walls of near-unconsciousness which still pressed in on her from every side.

"Nixon Penitentiary... D-Dark Judges... Tell Dredd, warn the Chief Judge... before it's too late..."

"VAMPIRES?" ASKED HERSHEY doubtfully, looking at the naked corpse of the thing lying on the autopsy slab in front of her.

They were in a forensics lab deep within the Grand Hall of Justice. This was where Dredd had had the remains of the perps from the Bathory Street med-repository attack brought for examination, and whatever the Forensics Teks had found had been enough for him to bring the Chief Judge down here in person.

The corpses of the perps killed by Dredd and Giant were spread out on various autopsy slabs around the large room, with various combined teams of Tek- and Med-Judges working over them. Hershey had received Dredd's verbal report of what happened down there on Bathory, and had heard all about how hard it had been to truly kill any of the perps. Hi-Ex, Incendiary and rapid-fire had been the order of the day, it seemed. The corpse on the slab in front of her, the top half of its skull clinically removed by a Standard Execution round from Dredd's Lawgiver, was definitely one of the more presentable pieces of evidence that Dredd had given the lab technicians to work with.

"Yes, most assuredly. Not that they seem to be the kind of things that sleep in coffins and have any kind of unlikely aversion to sunlight, garlic or random religious symbols – but they're definitely vampiric in nature," Tek-Judge Helsing beamed, using a forensics tool to proudly show off the most interesting details of the specimen on the slab in front of them. Helsing was a typical forensics Tek, probably more at ease poking through the innards of some horribly mutilated corpse than talking to real, live people. His complexion was only a ghost of a shade darker than that of the bloodless thing on the autopsy slab, and he looked like he probably spent his every waking moment under the thin, antiseptic light of the windowless forensics labs.

"Look here," he indicated, drawing back the corpse's lips to reveal its unnaturally long and sharp fang teeth. "And here too," he added, lifting up one of the corpse's hands and displaying the long, cruel talons that passed for the fingers there.

"Plenty of Bite Fighters get fancy dental work jobs like that, to give them an advantage in the ring," noted Hershey, "and we've seen the combatants in underground bash'n'slash fights coming back from the Hong Tong chop shops with surgically altered hand weaponry just like that."

"These aren't surgical alterations," said Helsing. "They're the result of some kind of massively accelerated bio-evolutionary change."

"Mutants, then?"

"Of a sort, but these things didn't evolve naturally. They were deliberately created. Probably as recently as a few short months ago, they were still ordinary human beings."

"And now?"

"Bio-engineered vampiric creatures, their body chemistry altered to an extreme degree by massive infusions of a gene-reprogramming retrovirus. Their systems are saturated with the stuff, although unfortunately we haven't been quite able to identify it yet."

"What are its effects?" Hershey asked, staring in mild disgust at the thing on the slab. In twenty years on the streets, she had seen countless thousands of dead bodies, had attended Grud-knows-how-many forensics examinations like this, but there was something uniquely disquieting about the corpse in front of her.

"Unnaturally high levels of strength, almost superhuman resistance to physical injury–"

"Giant and I can vouch for that," grunted Dredd.

"So that the only way to put them down for sure is to inflict massive physical trauma to their central nervous system," Helsing concluded.

"Blow them up, set them on fire or just shoot 'em through the brain," commented Dredd. "It worked during Judgement Day and it works with these creeps too."

"So far I'm only wondering why we aren't pumping our personnel full of the same stuff," quipped Hershey. "I assume there's some drawback to it."

"Alterations in brain chemistry probably cause violent psychosis and, in the long term, true death or complete derangement, but the main immediate and adverse side-effect is this–"

Helsing deftly slit open the arteries of the creature's wrist, and pressed down with his fingers. Hershey wrinkled her nose in distaste as a milky and pale pink liquid wept out of the wound.

"The retrovirus consumes the haemoglobin in the body's blood supply at a quite astonishing rate. Combined with the psychotic effects, anyone infected with the retrovirus will be consumed by an overpowering need to find fresh supplies of haemoglobin to keep the virus's long-term side-effects in check."

"Blood thirst," noted Dredd dryly. "Now we know why these creeps were raiding a blood bank."

"You said a *retrovirus*," said Hershey, picking up on the unpleasant implications of what she was hearing. "These creatures can kill by biting their victims, and traditionally the victims of vampires are supposed to rise from the dead and become vampires themselves. What are the chances the victims of these things might become infected by the virus too, and turn into yet more vampires?"

"We've already thought of that," Helsing smiled cadaverously. "The bodies of the victims from the Bathory

Street massacre are being transferred over from Resyk. We'll give them full tests for any signs that they might be infected with the retrovirus."

Hershey nodded in approval. After Judgement Day, another outbreak of the dead coming to life and attacking the living was the last thing the city needed.

Or almost the last thing, she thought to herself, remembering the news that had come in about Anderson shortly after the Council of Five meeting had broken up. The implications of that weren't too thrilling either, not with her best Psi-Judge unconscious in a med-bay when trouble relating to the Dark Judges was maybe on the agenda again.

"And we're sure that these were the same things that attacked Anderson?" she asked Helsing.

"The report from the clean-up crew at the attack scene indicates they might be," answered the forensics specialist, "but the ones in the truck are too badly burned to do anything with. There's one specimen on its way here. I'll get to work on it as soon as it arrives."

"The clean-up crew say the thing they scraped up had fangs and had taken enough damage to kill maybe a dozen Kleggs," pointed out Dredd, with his customary impatience. He gestured to the half-dozen charred and exploded corpses in the room around them. "Sound familiar? We know now why the creeps Giant and I met were robbing a blood blank. Big question now is: why were they so keen to see Anderson dead?"

The question was a troubling one, the possible answers to it even more so, thought Hershey. "Something she knew? You think this is all connected to that pre-cog vision she had?"

"Too much of a coincidence to be anything else," said Dredd with trademark certainty. "Anderson gets a psi-flash of a possible supernatural threat to the city. Next thing we know, she's been jumped by a bunch of wannabe freaks from an old cheapo-horror vid-slug."

He gestured at the thing on the slab. "These things didn't fly over the West Wall on bat wings. Someone created them. So: who, and why?" He looked at Helsing. "We got an ID on any of them?"

"Not yet," conceded the Tek-Judge unhappily. "The massive genetic changes caused by the retrovirus has so far made identification by DNA match impossible, and the physical changes to their facial features and hands is making slow work of any attempt to identify them by normal fingerprinting or photofit ID methods. If they're on the citizens register, we'll find out who they are eventually, but it'll take time."

Hershey considered what they had so far, and wasn't pleased with the answer she came up with. "What we really need is more information, and fast. As soon as Anderson's conscious, I want–"

As if on cue, Dredd's helmet radio crackled into life.

"Dredd – Med-Judge Caley, head of Med-Div operations, Sector House 42. Got a message for you from Psi-Judge Anderson. She says you've got to get down to Nixon Penitentiary fast. She says the Church of Death and some bunch of vampire creeps are about to try and bust out the Dark Judges!"

Dredd and Hershey looked at each other in alarm. It was Hershey who replied to the voice on the radio: "Anderson's conscious? How does she know this? Why isn't she reporting this to us herself?"

Over in the Sector House 42 med-unit, Caley blanched as he recognised the voice now interrogating him over the radio link. Talking to Dredd made him nervous enough, but now he had the Chief Judge on his back too.

Unhappily, he glanced over at the now-empty bed of the speedheal machine.

"That's just it, Chief Judge. Anderson's gone. None of us could stop her. She just got up and took out of here running, just a few minutes ago!"

* * *

ANDERSON EXITED THE turbo-lift, still jogging. Her barely healed leg, the one that had been badly broken only a few hours ago, hurt like hell. So did her ribs. But only every time she took a breath, she reminded herself with a smile.

In fact, most of her still hurt like hell. She stuck a few more stim-tabs into her mouth from the bottle she'd grabbed on her way out the med-bay. They took the edge off the pain, and allowed her to overcome the effects of the sedatives that had been pumped into her, but mostly she was running on pure psi-fuelled adrenaline. A properly trained Psi-Judge could turn their psi-ability in on themselves, using it to push their body often well beyond normal human endurance limits. It wasn't recommended, though. The comedown, when their reserves of psi-power finally ran dry, could be brutal, sometimes even lethal.

Anderson figured that was a problem she was just going to have to deal with when it came. Of course, considering what it was she was just about to do, and who she was just about to go up against, she might be dead long before then.

That's it, Cass, she reminded herself. Just keep looking on the bright side of everything.

She arrived at the Sector House's motor pool level, sprinting across a maintenance bay towards a line of parked Lawmasters. The instrumentation panels of several of them showed a green light on their status panels. All systems running, and engines refuelled and ready to go. Better still, they all had scatter guns locked into place too, which was a relief, since she had lost her Lawgiver back there on Joey Ramone and hadn't had any time after her escape from the med-level to stop by the Sector House armoury and pick up – you mean "steal", Cass, she reminded herself ruefully – a replacement for it.

She jumped onto the nearest of the bikes, slipping her Department-issue ID card into the slot and punching in her personal recognition code. The bike computer screen blinked into life in acknowledgement.

"Hey! You can't just take one of those," shouted a Tek-Judge, running towards her from the motor pool admin office. "I need to see something from the Watch Commander before I can let you ride that outta here!"

"Anderson, Psi-Division!" she told him, waving her badge at him. "Sorry, friend, but the paperwork's going to have to wait for another time."

What the hell, she thought to herself. I've only broken about half a dozen Department regs in the last few minutes. Stealing a Lawmaster is just adding one more to the list.

The Tek-Judge's protests were drowned out in the powerful roar of the Lawmaster engine as Anderson gunned the thing into life and headed at speed out of the motor pool.

A few seconds later, she was out of the Sector House and lost amongst the seemingly never-ending flow of the city's traffic. She looked around her, getting her bearings. She was on Megway 126, heading east towards the core sectors of MegEast. If she stayed on this route, it would eventually take her to Sector 57, where Nixon Penitentiary was located.

On the other hand, the turn-off for the McFly Spiral was just coming up, which would take her to the Black Atlantic dockside sectors.

Much closer, she thought to herself. 57 was way too far away, and she'd never get there in time. Dredd would have to deal with whatever was about to happen at Nixon Pen without her. In the meantime, she had urgent business down at the docks.

She hit the accelerator controls, abruptly changing lanes and taking the turn-off for McFly. She realised then that she still had her uniform tunic and utility belt gripped in her hand. She would just have to finish getting dressed on her way to the docks, and at least it would give the citizens some unexpected entertainment.

After all, it probably wasn't every day they saw a half-undressed Psi-Judge struggling to put on the rest of her uniform while riding a Lawmaster at high speed along the megway.

Seven

BEING AN ISO-CUBE guard sure could be boring, Judge-Warden Kiernan grumbled to himself. Nixon Penitentiary was a maximum-security facility, maybe the most impregnable iso-block in the entire city. Some of the most dangerous perps on the Justice Department's files were kept under lock and key here, and that wasn't even counting the four… things they had locked away down in the basement, he reminded himself. But it still didn't make guard duty here nearly as interesting or exciting as it maybe sounded.

Mostly, his duties involved patrolling the prison building's eighty levels of iso-cubes, or closely monitoring the prisoners' activities during the few hours a day they were actually allowed out of their iso-cube cells. Over fifteen thousand perps were held here, with several hundred arriving or being released every day, and Kiernan reckoned he'd seen just about every kind of perp there was, everything from the ordinary cit doing a six-month stretch for Jaywalking, Littering or Slow Driving, to the hardened lifers who were never going to see the outside world again: the Mega-Mob blitzers, responsible for dozens of gangland hits and carrying sentences totalling hundreds of years; the Judge killers, whose crime carried an automatic life sentence in a justice system where life imprisonment meant exactly what it sounded like; the juve gang thrillkillers, who would spend most of the rest of their young lives in here in payment for those few hours of murder-spree fun.

You name it, thought Kiernan, if there's a law against it, then there was someone in Nixon Pen who had been locked up for doing it.

And then there were the four monsters in the basement, but no one really liked to talk or even think about them. As dull as iso-block guard duty sometimes was, Kiernan would much rather be dealing with all the freaks, psychos and stone-cold killers in the main population levels than the creepshow inhabitants of the Tomb.

Kiernan shivered involuntarily. Sometimes he swore he could sense the vibes from that place, feel it creeping up from deep underground below the prison, subtly affecting the minds of everyone inside it. Psi-Div said that was impossible, that the prisoners in the Tomb were under full containment and that there was no possible chance of any psi-radiation leakage, but Kiernan and the rest of the Judge-Wardens in the Pen weren't so convinced. Vividly macabre nightmares were a frequent complaint amongst both guards and inmates and even for a max-security facility holding so many dangerous perps the Pen had much more than its fair share of fights and violent disturbances amongst the prisoners.

Everyone's on edge round here, thought Kiernan. It's this place, and it's not just the creeps in the cubes who want to get out of here.

His radio buzzed. "Thinking about that transfer to a West Wall guard duty assignment again?" laughed the voice of Sprange, his partner on this duty shift. "Mutie raids, rad-storms blowing in from the Cursed Earth, dodging the falling crap from low-flying dog-vultures? You don't seriously think any of that is better than this?"

Kiernan laughed in return, and looked over to where his opposite number was stationed. The two of them were on the prison's H-wagon rooftop landing pad, manning the two gun turrets positioned there to defend the facility from aerial attack. The airspace around Nixon Pen was restricted, strictly forbidden to civilian traffic, and the only flyers which came near the place were Justice Department H-wagon transports, delivering high-risk category prisoners who were too dangerous to be conveyed by ordinary catcH-wagon road vehicles.

As guard duties went, this was one of the dullest, but at least it got you outside.

"Hey, at least on the West Wall, your job's to stop creeps breaking in. All we do here is–" began Kiernan, only to be cut off by Sprange's alert-sounding tone.

"Hold it, Solly. You picking this up?"

Kiernan glanced at the scanner screen in his turret console, and looked up into the darkening evening sky for confirmation of what the scanner showed him.

"Check. A hov-transporter, a big one judging by the scanner readings, inbound our way. We expecting any more perp deliveries tonight?"

"Not according to what I know. Hold on, I'll check with Control. Those muncheads in Perp Transfer are always doing this to us. You ask me, they're the ones who should be finding out what it's like to go on West Wall duty, not chumps like you..."

Kiernan waited, watching the hov-transporter coming towards them. It was in restricted air-space now, and this was just about the point when it should be hitting its retro-jets to slow down to land while signalling in to them with the correct recog-code.

It was doing none of these things. Instead, if anything, it seemed to be increasing its speed. And so were the two identical craft coming in right behind it, on the same approach course.

"They're not Justice Department flyers, and they're not responding to hails!" warned Sprange, bringing his turret round to bear.

Kiernan fumbled to do likewise, losing precious seconds as he got the unlock code wrong on his weapon's auto-targeter. By the time he had got his weapon activated it was too late. He looked up in horror as the first hov-transporter came straight at him. Whoever was in the cockpit must be some kind of madman, Kiernan realised, because the pilot wasn't even trying to bring it in on retro-jets; instead, he was simply going to crash-land the transporter on the roof. Kiernan's last act was to press the firing controls on his turret weapon, sending a long line of explosive shells into the nose of the lumbering hov-transporter, raking the cockpit and blowing apart anyone seated there.

It didn't matter, just as Kiernan had already sickly realised. Gravity and the vehicle's own momentum would finish what the pilot had started.

The transporter hit the roof of the prison in a shower of sparks and screeching metal, belly-flopping right across the wide area of the landing pad and smashing into Kiernan's turret, ripping it right off its mountings and hurling it over the far edge of the roof.

Sprange, in the other turret, fared better, at least for a while. He concentrated his fire on the second flyer coming in, riddling its cargo compartment with armour-piercing shells and destroying a power-feed to the underbelly grav-lifters. Stricken, the transporter dropped out of the sky on a downwards trajectory that ended with it pile-driving itself into the body of the iso-block some thirty levels below. Amazingly, many of the creatures inside the transporter would survive the impact. Unfortunately, the more human occupants of the hundreds of iso-cubes on those levels would not, and many were crushed or burned to death as the transporter's engines drove it deep into the structure of the building.

Alarms were going off all over the building. Up on the roof level, the third transporter was coming in to make the same kind of makeshift landing as the first. Sprange concentrated his fire on it, aiming for the engines and trying to cripple or destroy it before it could land. He was still firing when he noticed the dark figures streaming out of the wreck of the first craft down. He didn't know who these freaks were or why they were attacking a heavily defended maximum-security iso-block, but he was just about to show them what a dumb proposition that was.

He spun the gun turret round towards them, bringing his targeting scope to bear and switching the fire selector on both guns to rapid-fire wide dispersal. These babies could cut up armoured steel like it was synthi-cheese, and Sprange couldn't wait to show these chumps what they could do to a packed mass of human bodies.

Before he could fire, however, the door behind him was wrenched off its hinges and dozens of clawed hands reached in to violently pull him out of the gun turret. He was borne aloft into the midst of the baying pack of creatures there, screaming as he realised what was about to happen to him.

The monstrosities descended on him eagerly, claws and teeth hungrily tearing into his flesh. They had been waiting a long time for this. The serum the master provided staved off the worst of the blood thirst that consumed them, but it was nothing in comparison to a taste of the real thing.

"ROCKING JOVUS, WHAT was that?!"

Meyer and Burchill had felt the impact of the transporter crashing into the iso-block, although this deep underground it had registered as little more than a faint rumbling tremor. Even that, however, had been more than enough to break the eerie, perpetual calm of the Tomb.

Seconds later, alarm lights started flashing on their consoles. Meyer flicked switches on her comms board, trying to raise someone in the prison levels above to find out what was going on, but no one seemed in too much of a hurry to answer. She flicked through channels, getting back only static in answer to her calls. Finally, she found an open frequency – someone's helmet radio was broadcasting, even if they themselves weren't talking – and she could pick out identifiable sounds. What she heard didn't exactly thrill her.

It was gunfire, and the frantic sounds of human panic.

She drew her Lawgiver. "Stay alert," she told Burchill. "I think there's some sort of prison riot going on above."

She locked her gaze on the thickly armoured slab of the sealed elevator door, the only way in or out of the Tomb. You needed about ten different security codes to even begin to think about getting into that thing up there on the surface, never mind starting it up and using it to come down here. As added security back-up, every metre of the elevator shaft was monitored, and anyone trying to climb down it surreptitiously would trip a dozen or more alarms and run into a seriously nasty surprise at a point about halfway down, where the hidden robot sentry guns were located.

"Stay alert," she repeated again to Burchill. "Until we know what's happening up there, we assume anything coming out that elevator is going to be bad news."

Burchill barely heard her. The Psi-Judge's attention was fixed on the four containment cubes on the other side of the line, and he stared at them in unnatural concentration... as he listened to the voices whispering inside his head.

THE RECENTLY DECEASED Judge-Warden Kiernan would have been very unhappy if he could see the events unfolding throughout Nixon Penitentiary at the moment. However else you might want to describe it – chaotic, gruesome, a murderous bloodbath – you certainly couldn't describe it as being boring.

Senior Judge-Warden Scholker and his riot squad, en route to the rooftop H-wagon landing pad, would be the first to agree with that. As far as Scholker was concerned, all hell seemed to be breaking loose inside his beloved Nixon Penitentiary. Some kind of large flying vehicle had crashed into the iso-block, causing several fires and major casualties on levels 54 to 57. The impact and subsequent fires had also damaged the security systems in the prison, and Scholker was getting confusing reports about armed perps being loose on some of those floors, although where these perps came from, no one could yet figure out, since they didn't seem to be inmates. He had been on his way to the section affected by the crash, with the firm intention of busting heads and restoring order, when he got the call to head to the roof level instead. The turret crews there had reported engaging incoming aerial targets, but nothing had been heard from the Judge-Wardens on duty up there since.

Scholker fumed in impatience and tightened his grip on the stock of his scatter gun as he watched the level numbers tick past on the elevator control panel display. No creep was going to get away with mounting a mass break-out attempt – if that was really what they were dealing with here – on Nixon Pen. Especially not on his shift.

"Get ready," he growled to his squad. "Whoever's up there, we'll give 'em–"

That was all he said, before the doors rumbled open and the tide of vampire creatures which had been waiting for the elevator's arrival swept in at them with a howl of ecstatic glee. Scholker's finger couldn't even close on the trigger of the scatter gun before a vampire ripped his throat out with one sweep of its claws.

WITH SCHOLKER AND his squad obligingly bringing the large transport elevator up to where they were lying in wait, the vampires now had a means of entry down into the rest of the iso-block. They swept into the place, more than two hundred of them, shrugging off Lawgiver bullets and scatter gun shots, killing everything in their path. Some, overcome by blood-thirst and the temptation of having so much prey trapped helplessly all around them, broke into cube after cube, feeding on the defenceless and terrified inmates they found inside. Most of them, though, retained sufficient self-control and presence of mind to follow out their master's instructions.

Guard points were overwhelmed, control rooms seized, security systems destroyed or sabotaged. As they were slaughtering their way down through the levels of the prison, those vampires which had been aboard the second hov-transporter and had survived its crashing impact into the building were doing likewise.

In a way, Sprange had done the Church of Death a big favour. Starting from the levels where the transporter had hit the building, they were able to reach the iso-block's main control centre on level 45 far quicker than had been anticipated. After breaking into the place and killing the command staff there, they were able to bypass the security codes and open every iso-cube door in the prison at a point far earlier than had been expected, way back when this crippling attack had first been planned.

SHERMAN "SHARKEY" McCANN didn't like being locked up. In truth, he didn't like most things, but most of all he didn't like Judges, which was why he had kept killing them. He'd killed six of them – although a couple of them had been those wannabe Judges who drove the catcH-wagons and did all the cleaning up after the real Judges had finished doing their Law stuff, so Sharkey wasn't too sure if they really counted – before the drokkers caught up with him.

Sharkey hadn't liked getting caught, and had liked being shot even less. He'd taken three Lawgiver shots, one in the arm and two through the chest, and the Med-Judges had fitted him out with a crappy paper lung after one of those shots in his chest had royally messed up one of the perfectly good human lungs he'd had all his life. Still, Sharkey took quiet pleasure in the fact that the Judges hadn't been able to kill him, not even with three Lawgiver slugs. Better still, it had been Dredd himself that had pulled the trigger on those shots. Sharkey knew that the rest of the Judges were secretly afraid of him, 'cause otherwise why would they have had to call in their top lawdog to bring him in?

Yeah, he took three shots from Dredd, and he still wouldn't lie down and die for them.

Not that Sharkey liked Dredd much either. Dredd had shot him. It was because of Dredd that he was in here, with this crappy paper lung that didn't work properly, that gave Sharkey a pain in his chest every time he took a breath, never mind what the Med-Judges said about the pain all being in his head. Sharkey knew the pain was real, and every time he took a breath and felt it cutting into him, it made him think of Dredd.

Oh man, but there was one lawdog Sharkey would like to add to his score. He fragged Dredd, and he knew he wouldn't ever hear any more sniggering behind his back from the other cons about how he wasn't really such a big, bad Judge-killer 'cause some of the badges he scragged weren't real Judges.

This was what Sharkey was thinking, and wasn't really that much different from what Sharkey was normally thinking, when the hov-transporter had hit the iso-block about ten levels above where his cell was. Sharkey's cube didn't have a window – like everyone knew, only narks or rich creeps who could bribe the Judge-Wardens got cubes with windows – so he didn't see the rain of burning wreckage from the crash tumbling down the outside of the building. But he sure felt the impact and he sure heard every gruddamned alarm in the place going off right afterwards.

After that there had been a lot of screaming and shouting, and then a heap of gunshots, and then just a whole lot more screaming. Looking out the tiny aperture in his cube door, Sharkey hadn't been able to see or figure out much of what was supposed to be going on, even if he did fleetingly see some freak in a Halloween monster mask run down the corridor outside. Which just didn't make much sense at all to Sharkey.

It was a little while after then that there was a familiar-sounding clunking noise, and Sharkey's cube door swung open. Sharkey stepped forward and peered cautiously out into the corridor. It turned out that Sharkey's wasn't the only cube door to have been opened, 'cause there was everyone else in the corridor standing there and peering out just like Sharkey was.

Best of all, the only guard in sight was the dead one slumped against the wall at the end of the corridor. Sharkey moved fast, getting to the Judge stiff before anyone else and helping himself to whatever he had.

Sharkey knew enough to leave the stiff's Lawgiver in its holster – try pulling the trigger on that sweet little package and you can kiss your flipper goodbye – but he was happy to help himself to the scatter gun.

Satisfying himself that the weapon was in working order – Grud, but it felt good to have a gun in his hand again after all these years – Sharkey looked up, seeing the faces of his crew looking expectantly at him. Some of the other cons, the ordinary Joe cits doing the kind of joke cube-time that you counted in months instead of years or even decades, stayed in their cubes, too afraid of what was happening, but Sharkey's crew knew what the score was.

"Find some more weapons," he told them. "We're gonna bust our way outta here and maybe have some fun while we're doing it."

"THERE'S SERIOUS TROUBLE at Nixon Pen. Let's roll!"

The message crackled through the helmet radios of more than eighty Judges, all of them mounted on Lawmasters and heading at speed out of Sector House 57. The call had come in only a few minutes ago. Nixon Penitentiary was under attack, and every Street Judge in the Sector House had been scrambled in response. Off-duty Judges were rudely roused out of dorms or sleep machines, Judges who had just come in from an eight-hour duty shift immediately got ready to hit the streets again. Emergency response units were being pulled in from other sectors, and more units from their own Sector House – pat wagon crews, riot squad teams, even Sector House admin and auxiliary staff to plug the holes in the ranks of the Street Judges – would follow them up soon enough, but these would be the first Judges to arrive at the scene and bring the situation at Nixon Pen back under control.

They were travelling along Minnie Driver Megway towards the prison, bike sirens blaring en masse, when the ambush happened.

A juggernaut-transporter jackknifed itself on the road ahead of them, overturning and completely blocking the road, crushing half a dozen other vehicles and their occupants in the process. At the same time, ten or more roadsters travelling along behind the Judge convoy suddenly skidded to a halt, blocking off the road behind the Judges and cutting off their escape. Hidden snipers on the block plazas and pedways on either side of the road opened fire at the Judges below. Seconds later, their comrades at the roadblocks in front of and behind the Judges joined in too.

Corralled in, the Judges took cover behind their Lawmasters, returning fire at targets whenever they presented themselves. It didn't take them long to identify their attackers; their coloured robes and the way in which they fought with almost suicidal abandon soon gave the game away.

"Death cultists!" shouted a senior Judge, picking off a black-cloaked, skull-tattooed sniper perched on top of a Sump Industries advertising billboard overlooking the roadway. "And if it's death these freaks are looking for, then today's their lucky day!"

"IT'S HAPPENING EVERYWHERE, Dredd. We're getting reports of attacks and violent disturbances involving Church of Death cultists all across the board!"

Dredd studied the tactical display on the H-wagon's control console. A pattern quickly appeared to him.

"They're centred around Sector 57, and Nixon Pen. Every incident is either designed to cut off one of the main routes to Nixon or tie up units that would otherwise be sent to deal with the trouble there."

"That's a roj," said the voice of Hershey over the radio link. "These Death cult kooks are coming out of the woodwork everywhere. They're doing everything they can to keep us away from Nixon Pen. There's thousands of them, but at the rate we're mopping them up, they'll all be either in the cubes or on their way to Resyk by the end of the night."

"If we don't get more units into Nixon fast, the whole city might be following those creeps along the Resyk conveyor belts," Dredd said grimly.

He'd commandeered the fastest H-wagon available at the Grand Hall of Justice as soon as Anderson's warning had reached him, but it had barely even taken off before the news of the attack on the prison had come through. Anderson's warning had been passed on too late, and the Death cultists had already made their move. It was minutes after that, as the H-wagon sped across the sky, that the first reports started coming in about the other Death cult attacks.

Like Hershey said, the Church was coming out of the woodwork, throwing everything they had into slowing the Judges down. Small groups of heavily armed Death cultist commandoes were on the loose in several sectors adjacent to 57. A human wave of unarmed, chanting cult members had blocked off Bachman-Turner Oversked, cutting off yet another approach to Nixon Pen. Lone cultists were going on killing sprees in crowded plazas and ped-precincts, and a report had just come in that a Death cult suicide bomber had detonated herself in the lobby of Sector House 58. Several block wars had suddenly flared up – the ever-feuding Minogue twin con-apts had been the first, eagerly renewing simmering hostilities once more

– and it seemed too much of a coincidence for the Death cult's involvement not to be suspected.

Dredd had intended to rendezvous at Nixon Pen with the local Judge units already at the scene there and then take command of the operation to restore order in the prison. At the moment, with roads blocked off and most of the available reinforcements tied up in dealing with the Death cult attacks, he was going to be the first unit to reach the place. He needed more Judges, and he needed them now. He activated his helmet radio.

"Giant – Dredd. Where are you?"

"About twenty minutes behind you," came the reply, "with four H-wagons' worth of riot squad units and a couple of heavy weapons teams. There's another ten wagons of the same taking off now, about another ten minutes behind me. We'll rendezvous with you at Nixon Pen, and–"

"No time," growled Dredd. "These Death cult creeps are trying to bust out the Dark Judges. The whole city's at risk now."

Dredd could see Nixon Pen through the H-wagon's cockpit window; a dark, forbidding-looking tower standing starkly against the illuminated backdrop of the city's spectacular skyline. Part of the building was burning, and even from this distance Dredd felt a sense of the chaos that had suddenly enveloped the place. Grud only knew how bad it was inside.

He signalled for the H-wagon pilot to begin his approach. "I'm going in on my own right now," he told Giant. "I'll meet you inside."

TWO MINUTES LATER, the H-wagon touched down briefly on an emergency landing platform on the side of the prison building, then at Dredd's signal took off almost immediately afterwards. There were probably hundreds, if not thousands, of escaped and dangerous perps on the loose inside the prison, and Dredd had no intention of leaving an H-wagon sitting there on the landing pad for any of them to try to seize and make their aerial escape in.

Dredd was left standing alone on the landing pad, with the door into the main prison levels in front of him. He deactivated its coded locking mechanism with his override card, drew his Lawgiver and stepped into hell.

Eight

THE HI-EX SHOT caught the vampire in the midsection, blowing it and the one next to it apart in the same single, bloody blast. The third creature leapt over their smoking remains, fangs bared in anger.

"Hungry, creep?" Dredd asked it. "So chew on this!"

He fed his kevlar-reinforced fist into the creature's mouth, feeling its fangs break against the armoured material of his Judge glove. Two Lawgiver shots into its chest gave it something more to howl about. Dredd knew the shots wouldn't kill it, but they would keep it distracted for a few more seconds – and a few more seconds was all he needed.

Grabbing it by the shoulders, he hurled it backwards, smashing its head into the cell door opposite and then, before the creature could recover, he propelled it in the other direction across the narrow corridor, throwing it through the broken doors there and into the elevator shaft that dropped through fifty levels of this section of the iso-block building.

The vampire fell, uselessly flailing its limbs and howling in equally useless fury. Dredd didn't know if the fall would kill it – as he had been finding out ever since the battle at the Bathory med-repository, these creeps took a lot of killing – but he was fairly sure he wouldn't be seeing that particular example again in a hurry.

He continued on, following the route down to the next level. Power to the elevators and grav-tubes was gone, possibly as a built-in security measure when the alarms had first gone off, possibly as a result of damage done to the building's power supply either by the impact of the crash or sabotage by the rioting prisoners. Either way, the only way down through the building was on foot.

Dredd was heading for level 10, where the elevator entrance to the Tomb level was located. So far, he'd managed to fight his way down through twenty-six, with another twelve still to go. His combat responses had fallen into a pattern on the way down through those twenty-six levels.

Vampires got Standard Execution rounds to the head, or Hi-Ex or Incendiary shot special deliveries. Any armed perps he came across – and there were thousands of them loose within the prison – and who were dumb enough to get in his way got the Standard Execution treatment, no more questions asked. Everyone else got a single warning and, if that didn't work, they got a brief but efficient first-hand demonstration of Dredd's unarmed combat ability and renowned daystick head-busting skills.

It was a crude but effective system, designed to get him to where he wanted to go with the minimum of delay and using the minimum of ammunition. Even so, in the twenty-six levels he'd covered so far, he'd still managed to go through four whole Lawgiver magazines, and his supply of Hi-Ex and Incendiary shells was now at a premium.

At the moment, nothing else mattered other than getting to that express elevator to the Tomb, and Dredd was forced to press on, going against his every instinct by ignoring all the other law-breaking going on in the prison around him. If the Dark Judges escaped, the chaos happening now in Nixon Pen would be as naught compared to what could result across the entirety of Mega-City One.

Giant would be touching down with his riot squad reinforcements soon enough. Dredd had been in constant radio communication with him, giving him updates on his progress so far. Thanks to Dredd, when Giant and his squads stormed into the place, they would already know where the worst trouble spots were, and where to apply the most force to swiftly bring order back to the prison.

He found the stairs from the level below and was down them in seconds, applying his daystick to the two shiv-armed escaped perps who stepped out of the shadows halfway down, demanding that he first pay the "entrance toll" to the next level. Dredd left them where they fell, unconscious and bleeding.

"Giant – Dredd. Two more for you, level 22, bottom of Stair B. Attempted Assault on a Judge: five years apiece onto their sentences, on top of the general counts for Rioting and Attempted Iso-Cube Escape."

Level 22. Twelve more levels to go.

LEVEL 19.

Turning a corner, he ran into a mob of fifty or more escaped perps, all of them armed with a variety of makeshift weapons, all of them doing their best to slaughter each other. Freed from their cubes, and with no sign of any living Judge-Wardens, the prisoners had so far been at liberty to pursue their own violent agendas. Many of them, like the fifty creeps here, were using the opportunity to reignite some ancient gang feuds.

Dredd didn't have time to deal with a distraction like this. A precious Hi-Ex shot into the ceiling stopped the fighting and grabbed their attention. Two more Standard Execution rounds into the heart of a perp – probably one of the gang leaders – who tried to fire a stolen scatter gun at him grabbed their attention even further.

Fifty pairs of hostile eyes regarded him with sullen hatred, fifty hands grasped the handles of makeshift clubs or shivs, fifty minds imagined how good it would feel to bring those clubs down hard on that helmet or bury those shivs hilt-deep into that chest. Dredd coolly stared down every one of them, daring any of them to make their move. Not one did.

"Lay down your weapons and return to your cubes," Dredd commanded, bringing his full, natural authority to bear in what could almost have been a textbook moment straight out of his own *Comportment*. "Wait there – and don't even think about leaving them again. Judges will be here soon enough to deal with all of you."

"Drokk that!" shouted some big creep who had stripped off to the waist, his filed teeth and scar-crossed skin marking him out as a former bite-fighter. It was time for the classic equation. "There's one of him, and–"

He never got to finish it. Dredd's Lawgiver sounded once and the perp hit the floor, a Standard Execution round drilled through the centre of his forehead.

The other creeps took the hint. By the time Dredd reached the end of the corridor, there wasn't one of them left in sight.

LEVEL 16.

"Giant – Dredd. Make sure someone picks up the four creeps in the Level 16 med-bay. Life sentences all round – murder of a Med-Judge. Any problems finding them, just look for the four perps with my Lawgiver slugs in each of their kneecaps."

LEVEL 15. HE was getting close now, and running into more vampires along the way. Some of them were sluggish and bloated from feeding on the plentiful supply of unwilling blood donors they had found in the iso-cubes around them. Some of them weren't, but sluggish or still hungry, they all went the same way.

By the time he found the way down to the next level, he had taken care of another eight vampires, at the cost of most of another Lawgiver mag and an extra minute's delay. It was time Dredd knew he didn't have to spare.

"GRUDDAMNIT, WHAT'S KEEPING them up there?" cursed Meyer, frustrated at her attempts to raise anyone on her console radio. "Why isn't there anyone there to tell us what's happening?"

"Yessss. Do it now."

The sound came from behind her. It was Burchill's voice, but at the same time it wasn't. Meyer spun round, seeing Burchill standing right in front of the no-go line and staring in what she could only describe as mesmerised adoration at the things imprisoned on the other side of it.

Being chosen for Tomb duty meant that she was no shrinking violet, and was more than capable of taking the kind of swift and cold-blooded decisions necessary for keeping the four most dangerous beings in Mega-City One safely under lock and key. She didn't hesitate, snatching for the Lawgiver stored in the specially built holster under her console desk. She had seen Burchill's combat scores, and knew that she was both quicker on the draw and a better shot.

She shot him four times, just as he drew his own Lawgiver, hitting him three times in the stomach and once in the chest. Each time she hit him, his body jerked weirdly, as if it was suspended on strings.

Also like a puppet on strings, it refused to fall down, no matter how hard it was struck.

Burchill continued moving as the bullets pummelled into him, drawing his own Lawgiver with a horrible, awkward slowness, a gruesome rictus grin fixed on his face which only seemed to grow wider as each bullet tore through him.

Finally he raised it to face her and returned fire, even as Meyer's fifth shot hit him in the throat in what should have been an instantly lethal wound. His own shot took her through a lung. She dropped to the floor, coughing blood.

She heard his weird, shuffling footsteps coming towards her across the room, heard the blood from the four or five fatal wounds she had inflicted on him pumping out of him and splashing onto the ground. She stretched out to reach for her Lawgiver, almost managing it before his boot came down hard on her fingers, breaking them all.

She sobbed in pain as he reached down to grab her under the arms, dragging her roughly across the room. She tried to struggle, but could not. She tried to call out, maybe hoping desperately to be able to reason with whatever remnant of Burchill remained in the thing which had hold of her now, but all that emerged was a choked and bloody cough.

She groaned again as he took even firmer hold of her, lifting her bodily up with a strength which he simply shouldn't have had. She saw where they were now, right at the edge of the no-go line, saw the four things in the crystalline containment cubes looking at her as their possessed servant displayed her to them, almost as some kind of offering. She felt herself being lifted up higher, suspended high above Burchill's head – and suddenly she knew what was about to happen to her.

He threw her. She suddenly found her voice again and screamed, although the sound was abruptly cut off a moment later amidst the hissing chatter of the sentry lasers as her hurled body sailed across the no-go line and was instantly cut apart in the bright tangle of laser fire.

The alarms had started going off as soon as the hidden sensors in the room had registered the sound of Lawgiver shots. A whole chorus of further, more strident ones went off now, as Burchill's body jerked round to open fire at the two control consoles, riddling them with rapid-fire Standard Execution rounds. Hi-Ex rounds unerringly found both the sentry gun sensors and then the hidden guns themselves.

Now that it was safe to do so, Burchill stepped forward to stand before his masters and do the final things necessary to release them. The alarms kept ringing, both in the Tomb and in the prison above, but Burchill knew that there was no one left up there to hear them.

LEVEL 12. ALMOST there now.

The bloodsuckers had been through this level like an impossibly virulent plague, and many of the corridors were choked with the corpses of their victims. Dredd heard screams from an open iso-cube door ahead. Approaching it at a run, he glimpsed in and saw a prisoner being attacked by one of the vampire creatures, the vampire pinning down its victim and biting bloody chunks out of his neck and shoulders.

Dredd raised his Lawgiver and shot the creature through the back of the skull as he ran past, never even breaking stride. The victim was still, weakened by shock and blood loss, and looked in a bad way. Dredd didn't know who he was or what his crimes were, but even as an iso-block inmate he was due the same cold, dispassionate mercy accorded to every citizen of Mega-City One.

"Giant – Dredd. Vamp victim in urgent need of med-treatment, Cube 47, Level 12. If he's still alive when you get to him, put him into med-unit quarantine until we find out what effects there might be from a bite from these things. Same goes with any other vamp victims you find."

SHARKEY COULDN'T DROKKIN' believe it! Him and his crew were down on Level 10 somewhere, heading downwards all the time. They'd lost a couple of guys along the way – Long Louie had got shivved in the riot they'd had to blast their way through up in Level 33 and good ol' Marv had been jumped by one of those bloodsucker freaks somewhere in the 20s, and, boy, was Sharkey not in a hurry to run into any more of those freaks – but they were still in pretty good shape and on course to reach one of the lower level exits outta the Pen.

They had just shot their way through a security point down here – two Judge-Wardens had tried to stop them, but Sharkey and a few scatter gun blasts had nixed that idea – when Sharkey caught sight of him on one of the vid-monitor screens.

Dredd! Right here in the Pen, running along a corridor somewhere.

Sharkey glanced at the monitor reading. Level 11, Subsection 4A, it said. Sharkey grinned. That was only one level above them, and, better still and judging by the direction he was heading towards the level exit drop-tube, Dredd was heading straight this way.

Sharkey wasn't big on all that Holy Church of Grud prayer-mumbling stuff, but he decided there and then that someone up there must like him. First of all they get him sprung from his cube, and now they obligingly drop Dredd right into his lap, and if that wasn't just too sweet, then Sharkey didn't know what was.

Of course, he'd added to his Judge-fragger score a couple more times today, but all the ones he'd killed had been Judge-Wardens, and Sharkey didn't really think they rated that much higher than those other kinds of phoney Judges who drove the med-wagons and handed out the parking tickets.

But Dredd... Well, he was the biggest, baddest Judge of them all, wasn't he? So fragging him would make Sharkey the biggest, baddest Judge-killer of them all, wouldn't it, and then there wouldn't be anyone laughing behind his back at him no more, would there?

Besides, Sharkey reminded himself sourly, thinking of that paper lung in his chest and the pain it caused him every time he breathed, him and Dredd had some history together, and he still owed the lawman some payback, didn't he?

He picked up his scatter gun and checked its load. Plenty of shells left, more than enough to take care of business, even with a tricky drokker like Dredd.

"Gonna be a change of plan, boys," he told his crew. "Got some unfinished business to settle up before I get us out of here."

BURCHILL'S HANDS MOVED over the small control console, their movements stiff and awkward. The four shadowy beings in the crystalline containment cubes focused their powers more heavily upon him, redoubling their efforts to remain in control of his mind and body. The material their prisons were composed of blocked virtually all their powers, and the vassal's body had sustained too much damage to allow them to keep it alive for very much longer. Time was running short, but they were too close now to even think of the possibility of failure.

"Release us!" hissed the voices in Burchill's head, forcing his body to carry out the Dark Judges' bidding.

He hit the final command key and a robot arm unfolded from its cradle in the chamber roof, smoothly snaking down towards the four crystals held in their heavy mechanical restraints. The restraining grips holding the crystal cubes in place were built into the deepest foundations of the iso-block building, and were designed to survive even a major earthquake. Nothing had been left to chance that might allow the creatures held here to be accidentally released, but it had always been hoped that sometime in the future a means might be found to destroy the Dark Judges' disembodied spirits once and for all. With that in mind, there had to be a way of opening up the virtually indestructible crystals to get to the things contained inside them, since the crystals protected the Dark Judges from harm just as much as they protected the city from their escape. The holding chamber's designers had no doubt imagined the deliberately engineered release of the creatures taking place under carefully controlled conditions, with a large number of Psi-Judges on hand to keep them under psychic control. What was happening now was probably beyond their worst nightmares.

A lance of stellar-hot laser energy shot out from the las-drill attachment on the end of the robot arm, cutting into the ultra-dense material of the nearest crystal's surface with a piercing sonic shriek. In just over a minute, its work was done and it was already moving on to the next crystal in line as a thin stream of what looked like greasy smoke poured out of the tiny, centimetre-wide hole that had been las-drilled through the wall of the crystal.

As the other three Dark Judge spirits writhed in impatience, the smoke from the first crystal coalesced in mid-air, slowly reforming itself into the familiar visage of the greatest enemy Mega-City One had ever faced.

"Freeeeeeedommmmm!" Judge Death hissed in triumph, over the shriek of the las-drill and the continuing chorus of warning alarms.

KOOM!

Dredd rolled for cover as the scatter gun spoke loudly again. The desk he had been sheltering behind just a moment ago exploded, throwing shredded paperwork and a spray of cold synthi-caf into the air around him.

"Remember me now, Dredd? Thought you'd seen the last of Sharkey McCann, didn't you?" called the voice from up the corridor. "You made a big mistake last time we met, lawman. Shoulda made a better job of your aim last time you pulled a trigger on me. You only get one chance with a guy like Sharkey!"

Sharkey McCann? Who the drokk was Sharkey McCann, Dredd wondered? He'd put tens – Grud, maybe even hundreds – of thousands of perps into the cubes in his time. His ability to recognise perps from memory alone was legendary within the Justice Department, but even he couldn't be expected to remember every two-cred punk and small-time jerk who had crossed his path during his forty years on the streets.

Still, at least all this dumb creep's jawing had allowed Dredd to get a good fix on his position.

"Ricochet!" he commanded, firing a single shot up the corridor. It hit the far wall of the foyer area at the end and rebounded back at an angle. He heard a choked-off scream of pain and surprise, followed by the sound of something hitting the floor.

"Sharkey!" The call came from one of the other armed perps, who came popping up from behind the overturned desk he had been sheltering behind. Dredd wasn't about to pass up the gift of a free target, and sent him sprawling back behind the desk again with a single shot.

Another creep broke cover from behind a doorway off the foyer, firing two shots with his scatter gun. The weapon was set on wide spray. Dredd ducked as he felt the sizzling flurry of hot lead rip through the air around him. He tracked the target, manually adjusting his shell selector setting as the creep ducked behind the open, heavily armoured door of a high-security interrogation cube. The creep might have thought he was safe from harm there, but the Armour Piercing shell that Dredd put through the thick metal slab of the door said otherwise. A second later, there was the sound of another body hitting the floor.

Dredd strode forward out of the abandoned Judge-Warden duty station area where the perps had thought they'd had him bottled up. He hadn't killed them all, but experience told him he'd more than made his point. The three remaining, terrified-looking perps standing there waiting for him with their hands in the air and their guns dropped at their feet obviously agreed.

Dredd glanced down at the corpse of what he assumed was Sharkey McCann on the ground at his feet, noting the surprised look on the creep's face and the bullet hole dead centre in his back which had gone through to find the creep's heart.

"How's my aim this time, creep?" he asked the corpse as he tossed three set of handcuffs to the three surrendered perps.

"Cuff yourselves to the wall over there," he commanded, gesturing towards the holding bars on the side of the room. "Judges are on their way. If you're not here when they arrive, I guarantee I'll come looking for you."

Dredd ran on down the corridor. He was halfway down it when his memory put the name and face together. *Sherman "Sharkey" McCann: sentenced to life back in 2016, for the murder of a Judge.*

A Judge-killer, then. So no big loss there.

Still, the incident had been yet another troubling distraction along the way. A delay which might yet cost the city dear.

THE SCREAM OF the las-drill died away as soon as its job was done, and the robot arm glided smoothly on to the last of the crystal containment cubes. The same stream of foul smoke poured out of the hole to coalesce into shape beside the other disembodied Dark Judges.

The spirit form of Judge Fear took his place alongside Death and Fire, as the drill went to work on the final crystal containing the spirit of Judge Mortis.

Now that it was now longer needed, the lifeless body of Psi-Judge Burchill lay discarded on the ground nearby, like a puppet with its strings most definitely cut.

THE LATE JUDGE-WARDEN Meyer had been right in thinking that anyone wanting to access the Tomb level from the main prison building would have needed ten different security clearances even to make it to the elevator entrance. Sometimes, though, there were exceptions.

"Dredd, alpha red priority!"

The double set of thickly armoured blast doors obediently rumbled open before him and he ran through them without breaking stride. The sentry guns lining the corridor beyond submissively swivelled away as he approached and then swivelled back after he had passed, guarding his back. The Tomb and its entrance level within Nixon Pen had their own independent power source, and so were unaffected by the damage inflicted on the iso-block's security and power systems. The computer controlling them was now responding to the order, the combination of Dredd's name and voice recognition pattern, together with the command code he had given it, these all combining to override all other considerations.

"Activate elevator!" he barked while still a good ten paces away, making it through the heavy blast doors just before they rumbled shut, saving himself a few more precious seconds.

The ride down was a speedy one, considering how far below ground the Tomb level had been buried. For Dredd, with the safety of every citizen in Mega-City One at stake, it still seemed to take forever.

He squeezed himself through the doors as soon as they began to open again, his Lawgiver held at the ready. He took the situation in at a glance, seeing the two dead Judges, the bullet-riddled control consoles and the disabled security systems. The las-drill he destroyed with a single Hi-Ex shot, but it was too late, because its work was already done, and the stream of spirit matter was already flowing out through the fissure that had been cut into material of the crystal.

The spirit of Judge Mortis coalesced alongside those of its brethren, the four Dark Judges hissing together in shared triumph.

"Free at last," they exalted. "Free to continue our great work."

The atmosphere inside the Tomb was charged with dark psychic power. Even Dredd, who was double-zero rated for psi-sensitivity and thus mostly immune to any kind of psi-attack from the Dark Judges' spirit forms, could feel it, like a pressure between his temples. There was a foulness there too, a creeping sickness, the sense of something tainted hanging invisible in the air of the place. The Dark Judges were toxic, completely poisonous to everything around them. Even in spirit form, their deadly, corrupting power could still be felt.

They began to flow through the air of the chamber, heading towards the metal grille openings of the chamber's air-conditioning system. Dredd instinctively opened fire at them, spraying a dozen or more Lawgiver rounds into them, knowing just how futile the gesture was even as the bullets passed harmlessly through the creatures' insubstantial forms to strike the walls of the chamber.

They flowed with ease through the grilles and into the narrow conduits beyond. Dredd knew that the air-conditioning was supposed to be secure, with dozens of fail-safes built into it to prevent anything – even something gaseous – making it in or out of the Tomb, just as he had no doubt at all that the Dark Judges would find a way to elude all such safeguards. They were too cunning, too dangerous, to allow anything as mundane as air filters or vacuum-sealed plasteel slam-barriers to stop them now.

The others were gone, but the Death spirit lingered for a moment, floating tauntingly in the air before him. Dredd stared dispassionately at the leering visage of what was probably his oldest and greatest enemy.

"Patience, sinner," it grinned at him. "Your time to be judged will come soon enough."

Dredd raised his Lawgiver to give Death his reply, but the spirit-thing was already gone, flowing into the grille after the others, leaving behind only the mocking echo of its chilling laughter. Dredd activated his helmet radio to deliver the bad news to the rest of the Justice Department.

"Alert the Chief Judge. Tell her we were too late. The Dark Judges have escaped and are loose in the city."

Nine

JUST AS NIGHT fell, disembodied, invisible, the spirit-forms of the four Dark Judges passed across the face of the vast, teeming future city which had once come so tantalisingly close to being theirs forever. The city bustled with life as day turned to evening. The bars, clubs, restaurants, hottie houses, shuggy halls, vid palaces, juve joints, poseur parlours and all-nite shopperamas were starting to fill up with the night's customers, and the zoom trains were running at double frequency in the busiest central sectors, bringing in millions more citizens to the bright lights of the city's main attractions. It was Sunday night. Which meant that the familiar phenomenon known to the Justice Department as Sunday Night Fever was just beginning to bite, as countless millions of citizens went out to drown their sorrows or vent their anger and frustration against the fact that the following morning would bring nothing but the prospect of another long week of unemployment, boredom and poverty.

This was also the time when the tour party flyers took to the city skies in droves, each one packed full of foreign tourists who gawped down in stupefied amazement at the ocean of light that was the Big Meg by night. For these visitors, no matter how large they had previously thought their own mega-cities to be, there was no sight like it.

Light and life stretched out everywhere below them; giant city blocks clustered together to form bright, glittering constellations, vehicle-filled megways threading between them and looking from this height like living rivers of light; the spaceports and strat-bat ports were blazing galaxies of light, throwing out the comet-like engine trails of craft blasting off for somewhere new every few minutes. Few ordinary flyer vehicles were capable of ascending to the height necessary to see the city in its entirety, where it stretched from the shores of the Black Atlantic in the east to the sullen, ominous darkness of the Cursed Earth rad-wastes to the West, so for those looking down on it from the tour flyers, it seemed as if Mega-City One was all there was to the whole world.

For these sightseers, the sight was simply amazing. For the spirits of the Dark Judges, moving invisibly amongst the drifting flyers, it was simply hateful and frustrating. So much despised life teeming beneath them, so many sinners waiting to be judged.

They were travelling at great speed, riding the invisible currents of psychic power that flowed across the face of the city, drawn inexorably towards a point somewhere just over the horizon. They were being called, they knew, and allowed the call to carry them to their ultimate destination.

A summoning spell, they realised. Their followers were calling the Dark Judges to them, to a place that had already been prepared, where Death and his brethren would be garbed in flesh again so that they could continue their great work of eradicating the crime of life from this world.

Passing unseen amongst the tourist flyers, Death amused himself for a moment by plucking thoughts from the minds of those sinners within the craft. He had always known that there were other cities in this world, other clusters of pestilent life waiting to be judged, but the number and variety of them which he found within the minds of those sinners surprised even the Dark Judge.

Brit-Cit... Simba City... Banana City... Hong Tong...

Hondo City... Oz... Ciudad Espana... Cal-Hab... Puerto Nova... East-Meg Two... Sino-City Two. So many different places. So much disgusting life. So many guilty souls awaiting judgement.

"Patience, sinners. Your times will all come," gloated Death to himself, deliberately echoing what he had told Dredd earlier, thinking now of all the glories that still awaited even after Mega-City itself had fallen to him and his brothers.

There was still much to be done here first, of course. Their old enemy Dredd had arrived just too late to stop their escape, and he and the rest of his troublesome kind were still a danger to Death and his brethren at this early stage of their escape. Clearly something must be done to distract Dredd and those like him, while the Dark Judges and their servants prepared for the next stage of the great work.

Death could sense the one who had set all this in motion. He was one of those few sinners whom Death had allowed to live long ago, choosing him for some greater task and setting his invisible mark upon him. That mark was there still, like a hard black stone planted within the mortal's mind, and the chosen one had passed it on to the things he had created, the Hungry Ones. And they, in turn...

Death hissed in pleasure to himself, seeing a sudden opportunity to keep Dredd and the others from interfering in their plans for a little longer.

"Concentrate, brothers," he told the others. "Focus your energies. Let us put one more obstacle in the path of those who would try to stop us completing our work."

"FOR GRUD'S SAKE, will someone go and see what that banging sound is?"

Unlike their colleagues in Street Division or on general Sector House assignment, the specialist staff of the central Tek-labs didn't work in shifts, and many of them were off-duty now, leaving the labs mostly empty for the night.

Which suited Helsing just fine. He didn't like noise and he didn't like company, at least while he was working, and the few other Judges and auxiliary staff still on duty in the labs knew to keep their distance and give the Forensics Chief some space.

Helsing picked up the las-scalpel again and bent down over the corpse to take another tissue sample from its inner organs. The results of the last few sample tests had been inconclusive, but he felt sure that he was getting close to what he was looking for. Despite its startling gene-altering properties, there was something tantalisingly familiar about the chemical composition of the as-yet-unidentified retrovirus. The Justice Department computers still hadn't found a match for it yet anywhere in their mind-bogglingly huge file repositories, but Helsing trusted his own instincts more than any computer, and felt sure he had seen a protein chain profile much like it before – and recently too. If only he could get a better idea of the way it reacted and replicated, then perhaps–

The sound occurred again, breaking his concentration. A dull booming noise coming from somewhere to the back of the labs, near the refrigerated mortuary rooms where specimens and evidence still awaiting analysis were stored. The corpses of the victims from the Bathory Street massacre had arrived just after Hershey and Dredd had left the lab, and–

The sound came once more, louder and more insistent. A hammering, drumming sound, like fists pounding on metal.

Laying down his las-scalpel with an exaggerated sigh, Helsing went to investigate. The lab was deserted and he seemed to be the only one here. Acting on a vaguely disquieting afterthought, Helsing went to his desk and retrieved his Lawgiver from one of the drawers. As a Tek-Division lab specialist, he had never fired the weapon in anger – the closest he ever usually got to actual perps was when they turned up as evidence on his autopsy slab – but Justice Department regs required him to attend marksmanship courses at least once a year at the Grand Hall of Justice's firing range.

He walked towards the source of the sound, which was definitely coming from one of the locked mortuary rooms. Even as he watched, he could see the metal door shaking on its hinges, as something or someone relentlessly hammered on it from the other side. By the looks of things, the lock on it would only last a few moments more, and then there was the matter of the angry, animal-sounding, growling and moaning noises coming from whatever was on the other side of the door.

Calmly and methodically, Helsing reached down for his belt radio handset. "Control – Helsing. Unidentified intruders in the Forensics lab. I need some back-up down here as soon as possible."

He had barely finished speaking before the door lock gave way with a scream of snapping metal. The occupants of the mortuary chamber beyond tumbled out, snarling and hungry as they quickly spotted Helsing and started shambling eagerly towards him.

Helsing had lived through Judgement Day and knew what zombies looked like. How these zombies had come into being, whether the corpses of the vampires' victims had been reanimated by scientific or psychic means, these were questions the forensic scientist in him would have to wonder about later, assuming he was going to live through this. Right now, the only part of him that mattered was the Judge part, and his reactions were textbook perfect.

He brought his Lawgiver up to bear, drawing a bead on his first target, and fired. The zombie's head exploded and it tumbled soundlessly to the ground, where the others trampled over it in their mindless, stumbling rush to get to Helsing.

Helsing took aim at the next nearest one, wondering if his first shot was a fluke, since to be frank his marksmanship scores on those annual firing range courses were barely above the Department required minimum.

One way or another, he figured he was soon going to find out. The zombies were almost upon him, and there was still no sign of that back-up.

"SAY THAT AGAIN, Giant?"

"It's happening all over the prison, Dredd. Corpses are coming back to life again. Anyone who was killed by the vampires' bite is getting back up again as a zombie."

Grud almighty, that's all we need, Dredd cursed to himself. Vampires, Death-worshipping freaks, the Dark Judges and now the walking dead. This case was turning into a real late-night vidshow horrorfest.

"You able to handle things at your end?"

There was a pause on the radio link. Dredd could hear screams and Lawgiver fire in the background. Giant's riot squads had touched down a few minutes ago, and were methodically working their way down through the iso-block from its uppermost levels, rounding up escaped perps and gunning down any of the vampire things still on the loose. More H-wagons full of reinforcements were on their way, and it was confidently expected that Nixon Penitentiary would be back under full Justice Department control before dawn the next day.

Of course, that was before they had found out about the zombies, Dredd grimly reminded himself, listening to the dead air over the radio link with Giant.

"Giant?"

He heard a chorus of snarling sounds over the radio link, coming from somewhere close to Giant, followed by a series of rapid-fire Lawgiver shots. A moment later, the Judge came back on the radio.

"Sorry, Dredd. For a moment, a couple of the things got closer than they were supposed to. Yeah, no problems here. Zombies I can handle. I was there with you for Judgement Day, remember? It's Death and those other three creeps I'm worried about."

"Same here," answered Dredd. "Everything else they're throwing at us is just a distraction to keep us busy while they make their next move."

He was in the elevator now, travelling up from the Tomb to rejoin the effort to take back the prison. Might as well make himself useful, he thought, until they got a fix on the Dark Judges' position. To do that, of course, they really needed...

"What about Anderson?" he asked, knowing that Giant would easily pick up on the note of anger in his voice.

"Your guess as good as mine, Dredd. No one's been able to track her down since she broke out of med-bay and boosted that Lawmaster."

"Wilco, Giant. I'm coming out the elevator now. I'll do what I can down here, until your squads can make it down to meet up with me. You hear anything about Anderson, let me know. Dredd out."

He exited the elevator and marched along the corridor, the security doors obediently rumbling open in front of him. Sharkey McCann's three accomplice perps were exactly where he had left them and had cuffed themselves to the wall as ordered. They quaked visibly when they saw Dredd coming back towards them again.

"That's the idea, creeps," he warned them as he strode past. "Just make sure you keep it like that."

Out in the stairwell, he could hear the snarling and moaning sounds echoing from the levels above. He recognised it from Judgement Day. Zombies, lots of them. And on the move, coming down the building towards where he was. He could hold this stairwell by himself, he knew, as long as his Lawgiver ammo lasted, but how many of the things were there, and how many other ways down that were now standing unguarded?

Dealing with these creatures would take time, time he didn't have. Not with the Dark Judges on the loose somewhere out there in his city.

So where the drokk was Anderson?

*   *   *

JUDGE ANDERSON WAS almost in a trance as she piloted the Lawmaster at speed through the dark and mostly deserted streets of the city's dockside areas. She had switched her radio off some time ago, finding the angry calls from Control demanding that she report her position immediately too much of a distraction while she concentrated her psychic abilities on finding the Church of Death's headquarters.

She was getting close now, she knew, homing in on the place she had seen in the mind of the vampire thing. She could sense how close she was – just as she could sense that something had gone terribly wrong at Nixon Pen, and that the Dark Judges were free once more.

She could feel them too, floating somewhere in the psychic ether over the city, sense their hunger and eagerness to begin their sick work again as they looked down at all the life spread out below them. Something was calling them, she could sense that too, a summoning spell of some kind, and she was now using her psi-powers to focus in on it, following it back to its source, just as the Dark Judges themselves were now doing.

She sped on, entering the maze of warehouse-lined streets clustered around the old dockside district. Dredd hadn't been able to prevent the Dark Judges escaping from their prison. Now it was up to her to stop them taking on physical form again.

INSIDE NIXON PEN, the walking dead were on the move. Something was calling them too. Obeying some invisible summons, they left the places where they had died at the fangs of the vampires and flocked out into the corridors and cell-wing landings, crowding the stairwells, some even tumbling down the powerless grav-tubes, in search of a way out into the city beyond. Some were trapped and picked off by Giant and his men as they pushed down through the prison building, retaking it level by level. Others ran into the immovable obstacle of Dredd who had taken up station in one of the lower level stairwells, and was mowing them down by the dozen just as fast as he could reload his Lawgiver. But even he was just one man with just so many bullets, and, just as Dredd had already grimly surmised, there were other stairwells and other exits.

The zombies flooded out of the prison building in their hundreds, breaking through locked doors and barriers by sheer weight of numbers, passing unhindered through guard posts and security checkpoints left unmanned as more and more Judge-Wardens had been called away from their posts to deal with the rapidly spreading disaster that had enveloped the prison.

Most of them were still not even cold yet, raised from the dead before the heat could leave their bodies. Most wore the bright yellow uniforms of the iso-cube inmates, marked with prominent target symbols on their front and back, but there were the uniforms of Judge-Wardens amongst them too. Perp or guard, the vampires hadn't discriminated when it came to satisfying their blood-thirst.

All of them were splattered with gore and bore the marks of the circumstances of their own deaths: clawed-open throats, teeth-ripped jugulars, some even eviscerated or with their rib cages brutally pulled open and chest plates smashed through to expose the empty hole where blood-gorged hearts had hungrily been ripped out. The retrovirus was in their polluted bloodstreams, infecting their nervous systems and replicating within it, bringing them back to life again as these shambling, ravenously hungry creatures, connecting them to the vampire-things which had killed them and infected them with their bite, connecting them further to the figure who had created the vampires, and connecting them finally to the Dark Judge whom the vampire creator ultimately served.

The zombies poured out of the prison, heading towards the lights of the city beyond, eager to feast on human flesh and spread that infection even further.

JUDGE ASHMAN HAD graduated from the Academy to make full Street Judge status in 2018. She had still been a cadet when the zombie war known as Judgement Day had happened, and had missed the whole thing. Her class had been amongst those put on alert to join the battle on the West Wall perimeter, bringing desperately needed reinforcements to plug the gaps in the Justice Department defences as they struggled to fight off the massive zombie army encroaching in on the city from the Cursed Earth. In the event, the zombie war had been over before they could go into action, won not on the bloody battle lines along the West Wall borders or in the similar, desperate battles taking place at every other Mega-City on the planet, but in the tunnels beneath the mystic Radlands of Ji, where Dredd and a small, elite band of Judges from all across the world had destroyed the power of Sabbat the Necromancer and broken his psychic control over his deathless hordes.

Ashman had always wondered what it would have been like to be there on the West Wall in the darkest hours of Judgement Day, fighting off an enemy coming at you in countless numbers; an enemy that shrugged off wounds that would have killed any living human; an enemy which came on mindlessly and relentlessly, never tiring or despairing, its only motivation being the most basic animal impulse to kill and eat its prey.

Now she was about to find out. She and her partner Farrer were the first Judges to make it through the Death cultists' ambushes and roadblocks, and they were just pulling up on their Lawmasters in front of Nixon Pen when the horde of zombies started flooding through the iso-block's broken gates. Their Sector House Control was in radio communication with Giant and his squads within the prison, and so the two Judges had been warned what to expect when they arrived.

On the other hand, being confronted by a shambling, howling, flesh-hungry mob of the walking dead was a career first for both young Judges, and it took them some vital moments to adjust to the situation.

"Holy Jovus!" shouted Farrer, only a few months as a Street Judge after being promoted and transferred over from more sedate duties in the Justice Department's Traffic Division. "There must be hundreds of them! What do we do?"

"This," answered Ashman, dropping to one knee, taking aim with her Lawgiver and opening fire with calm, accurate precision at the first ranks of the approaching zombie horde. Farrer hesitated a moment, then followed suit.

Zombie after zombie fell to the ground, bullet holes drilled through their skulls. As each one fell, though, others instantly came forward to take its place, all of them pushing eagerly forward toward the two Judges.

"Code 99 Red!" Ashman shouted into her helmet mic, giving the Justice Department emergency code that signalled a Judge in trouble, designed to bring the nearest back-up units scrambling to their assistance. "They're out in the open here at Nixon Pen. We need help down here now!"

She looked over at Farrer, relieved to see that he didn't seem to be showing any more signs of panic. "How you doing?" she shouted over to him, raising her voice to be heard over the sound of Lawgiver fire and the hungry moans of the zombies.

"Sure beats being back at Traffic and giving out parking tickets and speeding fines!" he shouted back, blowing the top of the head off a zombie dressed in the shredded remains of a Judge-Warden uniform.

"Reloading!" he called over to her again, as his Lawgiver gave a warning beep to signal that its magazine was now empty.

"Covering you," confirmed Ashman, picking off a zombie from her side of the firing line and then rapidly switching her aim over to those on Farrer's front, shredding three of them with a single Hi-Ex shot. A few moments and six more destroyed zombies later, her own Lawgiver gave the same warning alert.

"Reloading!" she shouted, reaching down to her belt pouch for a fresh magazine. "Covered!" confirmed Farrer, bringing his aim round to return the favour. This time, however, the arrangement didn't quite go according to plan.

A zombie stumbled forward towards Ashman, taking advantage of the lull in fire from her position. Farrer saw it and nailed it with one shot, but his aim was slightly awry and he only blew off the lower half of its face. His second, hastily fired shot only winged it in the shoulder, while his next two shots, fired in growing panic, both missed it completely.

The dead thing came on at Ashman, growling hungrily, a mess of blood and juices dripping from the ruined remains of its face. She dropped her Lawgiver with a curse, snatched her daystick from the loop where it hung from her belt and swung it with every bit of strength she could muster. There was a sickening crunch as the blow struck the zombie and it fell lifeless to the ground, its brains dribbling out of its smashed-in skull. Ashman ducked down, trying to scoop her Lawgiver up from the ground, but the flailing hands of several more zombies reached out, trying to grab hers, and she snatched them back quickly, shocked by how close these others had got now. She retreated back, abandoning the precious weapon to the advancing things.

Things were bad, but a glance over at Farrer's position told her they were about to get a lot worse.

In trying to cover her, Farrer had been forced to take his fire off the zombies advancing on him, and now they were upon him. He must have switched to Incendiaries as they closed in on him, because several of them were ablaze, something that didn't seem to trouble the mindless things too much as they clustered in on him, hungrily falling upon him.

"Farrer!" she shouted in anguish, hearing his screams as the zombies started to tear into him with their teeth. The flames covering the bodies of those struck by Farrer's Incendiary shots quickly spread to the others packed in close around them, and soon the whole pile of them would be ablaze. Not that this would be enough to deter them from eating Farrer alive as they all burned away to nothing together.

Farrer's Lawgiver lay teasingly nearby, knocked aside by a hungry zombie but, like any other Lawgiver, it was coded solely to its owner's palm-print, and Ashman knew it would be as dangerous to her as it would be to any other perp who foolishly tried to pick it up and fire it.

The zombies were closing in on her too. She turned and ran back towards her Lawmaster, popping a stumm gas grenade as she did so and throwing it behind her back into the midst of the pursuing zombies. Designed to incapacitate and render unconscious rioting citizens, the non-lethal gas would do nothing to walking, reanimated corpses which no longer even had the need to breathe, but Ashman hoped that the thick cloud of white gas that spewed out of the grenade would at least succeed in blinding or confusing them for a few vital moments.

Her bike! She had to get to her bike. Its twin-linked cannons would make short work of these things, and there was the scatter gun in the bike's saddle holster for more close-up action too.

She made it onto the bike, was starting up its engine with one hand and pulling the scatter gun from its holster with the other, when the lead zombie grabbed her. She smashed an armoured elbow pad into its decaying face, knocking it away, but plenty more were already closing in. They grabbed for her, their fingers clawing at her body and the pieces of her uniform, the creatures mindlessly unable to distinguish one from the other as they tried to pull her apart. She was dragged off the bike, giving an involuntary wail of despair as she felt herself being pulled down, felt the first teeth bites starting to worry at her flesh. The scatter gun was still in her hand but it was useless, the arm holding it pinned to the ground by the weight of a zombie body.

She looked and saw the barrel of the gun pointing towards the underside of her bike's fuel tank. A Lawmaster's fuel tank was heavily armoured, but at this extreme close range, and firing into one of its more vulnerable and lesser armoured sections...

She felt something nuzzling roughly at her throat, and then felt the sharp pain of something biting excitedly into the flesh of her neck. After that, what came next was easy. A defiant curse on her lips, she pulled the trigger of her scatter gun.

THE EXPLOSION IMMOLATED everything in a five-metre radius around the bike, killing Ashman and more than twenty zombies. The other remaining creatures took little interest in the charred and scattered remains of what only moments ago had been living prey.

Confused by the explosion and the sudden, disappointing lack of living flesh to consume, the zombie mob began to break up, individuals or groups of the creatures shambling off to begin their own search for more tasty prey. They would spread out into the sector around the prison with alarming speed, and the retrovirus-infected and partially consumed corpses of their victims would rise a few hours after death to join them. For days afterwards, the citizens of Sector 57 would hide behind their doors as the Judges and eager citizen squads of volunteer zombie-killers hunted the creatures down and destroyed them. After that, disappointed by the lack of further targets, some of the more over-enthusiastic volunteer groups of zombie-hunters would ignore the Justice Department's order to disband, preferring to instead turn their guns on any unfortunate citizen who in their opinion looked too suspiciously zombie-like. The last of these renegade zombie-hunter groups would be rounded up by the Judges after the notorious Oliver Street Soup Kitchen Massacre, when the vigilantes would learn that the line "Well, they kinda looked like zombies to us" was not a legitimate excuse for the murders of thirty-seven homeless street bums.

All this, however, was still to come. Right now, the only thing that mattered was the zombies and their growing hunger.

In life, Mikey "Swifthands" Liebling had been an expert pickpocket and thief. Known as a "dunk" in Mega-City criminal underworld slang, his favourite hunting grounds had been the city's many large and busy shopperamas and mega-malls. Cube-time was an occupational hazard of his chosen profession, and he had been about halfway through a five-year sentence when the attack on Nixon Penitentiary had happened and to his eternal surprise a vampire had torn through the door of his iso-cube and ripped his throat out. Now, in death, only the vaguest and most fragmentary memories of the circumstances of his life remained in the mind of the zombie-thing which he had now become.

The thing that had been Mikey Liebling dimly remembered a place near the prison, a place where it had gone before, a place where it had found in plentiful abundance the things he had gone there looking for. As Mikey "Swifthands" Liebling, what it had been looking for back then were crowds of people and plenty of inattentive shoppers who wouldn't even notice that their wallets or cred-cards were gone until minutes after Mikey had struck. The needs of the thing that used to be Mikey Liebling were far different, but something told it that it would still find what it was looking for now in that selfsame place.

Slowly, acting on the most dimly held trail of memory, he stumbled off on his own, not even noticing as first one and then another zombie mindlessly followed him. Many others wandered off in other directions, following their own random and unknowable impulses, but, by chance or instinct, the greater part of the horde shambled off after Mikey as he mindlessly led them to their night's feast.

DREDD EXITED THE prison a few minutes later, taking in the situation at a glance. The pattern and number of zombie corpses and the remains of the two dead Judges told him the story of almost everything that had happened out here. Grimly, he bent down over the remains of one of the Judges, picking up the heat-fused badge lying there. The name on it was still barely legible: Ashman.

He had never known Judge Ashman, but she and her partner had both died bravely, fighting by themselves against overwhelming odds. Too many Judges had died already today as a result of the events at Nixon Pen. As a senior Judge, Dredd would see to it that these two, at least, would receive posthumous commendations for their courageous actions here.

Going over to the Lawmaster that still remained intact, Dredd used his autokey to open its stowage pod, rummaging through it in search of the spare Lawgiver magazines that every Judge carried with their bike supplies. The battle in the iso-block had left him seriously short of ammunition, and he needed every spare mag he could find. It had been a busy night, and Dredd didn't have to be a Psi-Judge to realise there was probably a lot more to happen yet.

He clambered onto the Lawmaster, activating his helmet radio as he did so.

"Giant – Dredd. What's the situation?"

"Not good, but getting better, Dredd. We've retaken the top thirty levels, and we've probably already seen the worst of the opposition we're going to encounter. Besides, given a choice between us and those vampire creeps, most of the perps in here would prefer us any day. They know we're the only thing that's going to protect them from the vamps and they're surrendering to us whole levels at a time."

"Back-up?"

"On its way, thank Grud. They'll be here any minute to secure the lower levels and prevent any more of these creeps getting out."

"You'll have to manage with a couple of units less when they get here," Dredd told Giant. "I need them to deal with these zombie things."

"Understood, Dredd. Any idea where they went?"

"Working on it now. Dredd out."

Dredd rode off at a slow pace along the prison's approach road. He flicked on the bike's front-mounted powerful UV beamer, flooding the area in front of the bike with ultraviolet light. Since they were dead, the zombies would generate nothing in the way of body heat as their bodies eventually cooled to room temperature, but it had been less than an hour since most of them had died, and there were hundreds of them grouped together en masse, so Dredd figured they had to have left some kind of heat trace behind him.

He was right. The UV beam revealed the faint but discernable marks of hundreds of pairs of feet on the ground in front of him. They were heading in a disorganised pattern away from the prison and towards the more populated areas of the city, but at a point a hundred or so metres on, there was an abrupt break in the pattern. Some continued on towards the pinnacles of the city blocks in the distance, but the greater part of the zombie tracks broke away from the main skedway, taking a side-road instead. Dredd followed those ones, accelerating off in pursuit. Even before he saw the bright, gaudily coloured sign pointing the way ahead to the large and equally gaudily coloured building in the near distance, he already knew where the zombies were heading.

"Control – Dredd. Be advised: large group of zombies, estimated several hundred strong, on their way to the Winnie Ryder Mega-Mall. Am in pursuit."

Ten

JUDGE ANDERSON TURNED her stolen bike onto the dark, warehouse-lined street, recognising it immediately as being the same as the one she had seen in the mind of the vampire. The psychic summoning call which she had been following up to this point was overpoweringly strong this close to its source, and it was with a real mental effort that she finally managed to wrench her mind separate from it. She didn't need any psi-powers now, just plain old Judge's instincts, and her first act was to switch on her bike radio to report in.

As soon as she did, the urgent-sounding voice of Control came flooding through to her. "...repeat, Control to Anderson, call in your location and situation immediately. This is a direct order from the Chief Judge. You must respond immediately, Anderson!"

Oh Grud, she thought to herself. Well, I knew I was going to get into trouble when I started out on this thing.

"Control – Anderson," she started, cutting off Control's immediate angry response. "Have located the Church of Death HQ. They're on Jack Kevorkian Street, down in the old Black Atlantic dockside district. Get everything you've got rolling and on its way here fast. My hunch is the Dark Judges are going to be putting in a surprise guest appearance down here any minute now."

"Understood, Anderson. Maintain position and wait until back-up units are–"

"Jovus, didn't you here me, Control? I'm talking about the Dark Judges! They're going to be here any moment. This is the place where they'll get new bodies again, and if that happens then Grud help us all. No time to wait for back-up – I'm going in now!"

She broke off radio contact again, cutting off Control's expected objections in mid-sentence.

Roaring along the street, she saw two figures on the road ahead of her. They were both wearing robes marking themselves as members of the Church of Death, and both were armed. Guards, posted to keep a lookout on the street outside.

"Well, so much for trying to sneak in the quiet way, Cass," she told herself as she saw them pointing in alarm towards her and unslinging their spit guns.

She didn't have her Lawgiver, and the scatter gun was too unreliable firing at this range from a moving Lawmaster.

"Bike cannons it is then," she decided, hitting the weapons' firing switch.

Thirty-millimetre armour-piercing cannon shells chewed up the road surface, cutting a line directly towards one of the guards. The line reached him and suddenly he wasn't there any more, disappearing in a spray of blood and bullet-shredded clothing.

The other guard was running for her, opening fire with his gun. Anderson crouched low on her bike, as bullets whistled over her head. She'd been shot already today, and had no intention of having it happen to her again. Still, there was another problem to deal with. The street ended in a dead-end, which Anderson was now rapidly approaching on a speeding Lawmaster.

Time to kill two birds with one stone, she thought, wrenching the handlebars, hitting the brakes and throwing the big bike into a controlled braking skid. The Lawmaster hurtled sideways in a wide skid manoeuvre, slamming at speed into the gunman. He flew through the air, slamming into the wall at the end of the street some twenty metres away. By the time what was left of him had messily slid down the surface of the wall to land on the ground, Anderson had already dismounted from the now stationary bike and was sprinting towards the warehouse building that housed the cult's headquarters.

Another cultist emerged from the doorway, raising his gun to fire at her. Anderson didn't even bother with the scatter gun in her hands, and let fly at the creep with a powerful psi-blast right into the centre of his cerebral cortex. The gunman hit the ground as if he'd been pole-axed, lying there drooling, with a glazed and stunned expression on his face. In direct breach of Psi-Div regulations, Anderson hadn't even tried to regulate the strength of the blast she'd hit him with, and the after-effects of the attack would be unpredictable. The creep could wake up in a couple of hours with a raging migraine, he could wake up in a couple of days with the mental age of a small child or he could lapse into a persistent vegetative state and never wake up again at all. With so much at stake, with the Dark Judges on the loose again, Anderson frankly didn't care which way it went for the Death-worshipping freak.

Scatter gun at the ready, Anderson charged into the lair of the Church of Death. And her psi-senses screamed at her in warning, telling her the Dark Judges had already arrived ahead of her.

DeMarco was still waiting for the right moment to make her move. A sick feeling of growing dread inside her kept on telling her that she'd probably already missed her chance.

Maybe she should have done the good cit thing after all, and just called the Judges much earlier on, before she'd slugged that guard and dragged his unconscious body into a nearby alleyway, stripping and cuffing him before putting on his Death cultist robes and just walking into the place wearing them, mingling unnoticed among the other Death worshipper freaks.

Or maybe she should have done something when the ceremony started and they'd brought out Joanna Caskey.

The ceremony was taking place in the central warehouse area. The windows of the large room had all been blacked out and the walls covered with black and red drapes, embellished in gold and silver with what DeMarco assumed were supposed to be arcane, magical symbols. The only real source of illumination in the place came from the numerous tall, black candles around the room, and most of these were clustered in what was obviously supposed to be an altar area on the elevated stage at the front of the room. So far, so run-of-the-mill hokey occult mumbo-jumbo, DeMarco decided; half the sectors in the city probably had hidden set-ups like this, bored cits looking for some kinky, illicit thrills by dressing up in these mad monk outfits and mumbling some cod-Latin gibberish before stripping off and getting down to the real point of the exercise.

However, it was when they dragged the girl out that things started to turn deadly serious.

They had drugged her with something, that much was plain to see, and she had lain down all too placidly on something that was clearly and gruesomely supposed to be a sacrificial altar. There were four other similar slabs there too, two of them on each side of the sacrificial altar, and with a stone column with more occult markings upon it standing at the head of the altar. There were four other shroud-covered figures lying upon the slabs beside the altar. From where she was standing amongst the Death worshippers at the rear of the congregation, DeMarco couldn't make out anything of the bodies under those shrouds, although she couldn't help but notice the reverence with which any cult members up there on the altar platform treated the four figures lying there whenever they came near them.

If DeMarco was having any thoughts about slipping quietly away and alerting the Justice Department to what was going on now, these were swiftly ended when the doors to the place were sealed and two long lines of cloaked and hooded figures were marshalled into place on either side of the main congregation. DeMarco didn't much care for the sound of snarling and growling coming from beneath those hoods, and she liked it even less when the hoods came off and she saw the shockingly feral faces of the fanged, white-skinned things beneath them.

The vampires – DeMarco couldn't really think of any other term to describe them – hemmed the congregation in, leading them in the droning chant begun by the priest figure on the altar platform. The priest stood over the altar, a gleaming black, horned skull in one hand – the remains of some kind of Cursed Earth mutie specimen, DeMarco imagined – and a curved-bladed dagger in the other. DeMarco didn't like the look of that at all, and realised that she was going to have to do something about this.

She had been edging slowly forward for a while now, taking advantage of the darkness and the semi-trance state into which many of the congregation members seemed to have entered to slip forward surreptitiously, row by row, creeping towards the front. There were over a hundred of them and only one of her, and all she had was her pistol held inside her robes and her training as a Judge, but she had a job to do, and she wasn't going to stand by and watch these sick freaks kill an innocent girl.

Up until now, DeMarco still wasn't completely worried. If worse comes to worst, she told herself, she was going to use her first shot to save the girl from whatever they had planned for her, and then use the rest of the clip to kill as many of these creeps as she could. It was only when the four spirit-shapes started materialising in a greasy cloud of dripping, dark-coloured vapour in the air above the altar platform that she finally realised just how far out of her depth she was here.

"Yes!" the four voices hissed in unison. "Complete the ceremony. Give us flesh once more!"

The air was charged with psychic power. The congregation's chanting was nearing its frenzied climax. The vampire things prowling round the sides of the room were filled with a terrifying anticipation and excitement. Unable to control itself any longer, one of them leapt upon a member of the congregation, hungrily tearing out his throat. Several more of the creatures rushed to join the feast, and their eager snarling and the scent of freshly spilled blood only added to the highly charged atmosphere inside the place.

The priest stepped forward, raising his dagger. DeMarco slipped her pistol out from her robes, mentally drawing a bead on him as she raised the weapon to fire. Two in the chest, one in the head, she decided, and then everything else for the creeps around her. The dagger in the priest's hand began to descend. DeMarco's finger began to tighten on the trigger.

There was a loud gunshot explosion from behind her – a scatter gun shot, DeMarco's Judge training instantly told her – and the doors there crashed open. Two more scatter gun blasts sent the cultist guards there flying through the air.

"Justice Department! Party's over, freaks!" shouted a commanding female voice.

"Andersssson!" the four things hovering in the air above the altar hissed as one, their voices full of hatred. And something else too, DeMarco detected. There was fear there too.

"Kill her!" they ordered their followers. "Finish the ceremony. Give us flesh!"

The priest raised the dagger once more, getting ready to strike. DeMarco beat him to it, putting two slugs into his chest, as promised. The one intended for his head instead found its way into the big creep in front of her, who had turned and tried to grab her as she began firing.

There were more scatter gun blasts from behind her, together with the screams and howls of dying cultists and vampires. Whatever Anderson was doing back there, she was going about it the right way. DeMarco pushed forward through the throng of panicked cultists, trying to get to the figures on the altar platform. She pistol-whipped one cultist who tried to block her way and delivered a swift kick into the crotch of the next creep who came running at her with the same idea. The rest of the time she simply cleared a path through with her pistol, firing blindly into the bodies of any robed figures that stood before her.

Somewhere in the distance, above the sounds of the melee, she thought she could hear the sounds of Judge sirens. Lots of Judge sirens, in fact. Help was on its way and closing fast. DeMarco just hoped she could stay alive long enough for it to matter.

Incredibly, the priest creep was on his feet again, still holding the knife and staggering determinedly towards the girl on the altar. Ignoring for a few vital seconds everything else going on around her, DeMarco took careful aim again and put two more slugs into his back. Her gun clicked on empty the third time she pulled the trigger.

The creep was still staggering forward, but he had lost the knife now.

"Yes, serve us," the spirit-shapes commanded him. "Be our sacrifice. With your own life's blood, make us flesh again."

The priest pitched forward with the last of his strength, throwing himself forward against the stone column. As he touched it, smearing the blood from the bullet wounds in his chest across its surface, the spirits of the four Dark Judges gave a hellish shriek of triumph. The stone suddenly seemed to suck the life out of the figure clinging to it. Sorcerous energy crackled forth from it, touching first the disembodied spirits of the Dark Judges and then moving down into the four forms beneath the shroud covers. The spirits of Death and the others flowed with the energy stream, allowing them to take possession of the corpses their devoted followers had so carefully prepared in advance for them.

It all happened with surprising speed. One moment, Death and his super-creep pals were floating about in the air in spirit-form, and the next the four corpses on the slabs were rising up with preternatural speed and an awful, unnatural stillness. The shrouds of Death and Fear fell to the ground at their feet. The one covering Fire fell away in burning fragments. That covering Mortis simply rotted away into stinking, mildewed pieces in seconds.

There they stood, reborn again: Death, Fear, Fire and Mortis. The four Dark Judges, who had expunged all life on their own world and had come to this one to do the same here.

One of the Death cultists clambered eagerly up onto the platform, throwing himself down to kneel, hands clasped in supplication, at the feet of Death. "Master!" he begged. "Grant me eternal existence. Let me join you there in the glorious realm beyond life and death!"

"With pleasure, sinner," cackled Death, sinking his hands seamlessly through the shell of the man's skull and squeezing its contents with his clawed fingers. The cultist fell dead at the monster's feet, the frozen expression of pain and horror on his face suggesting that the experience had been somewhat different from what he had hoped.

"Don't be shy, sinners. Who's next?" Death asked with an inviting leer, looking round, his cold, inhuman gaze finally settling on DeMarco. She wanted to reach for the spare ammo clip she had on her, load it into her pistol and empty it into the thing in front of her, but found she couldn't.

She couldn't do anything, in fact: move, scream, call for help or turn her gaze away. All she could do was stare back into that ghoulish caricature of the face of a Judge, as Death loomed up towards her.

"NO!"

It was Anderson's voice, and there was real power in it, enough to break whatever psychic spell Death could cast over his would-be victims. With a shock, DeMarco realised that it hadn't been Death that had been moving, it had been herself, shuffling unwillingly and unconsciously towards him to receive his twisted sentence of judgement.

Death looked up, all interest in DeMarco forgotten as he saw his old nemesis come running towards him. There were other Judges arriving on the scene too, crowding in through the door behind her, and DeMarco could hear the distinct heavy engine thrumming of at least one large H-wagon circling above the building. But the Dark Judges had sightless eyes for only one person here.

"Anderssson," hissed Death. At his gestured command, one of the vampires hurled itself at her. She blew its head off in mid-air with a scatter gun blast and kept on moving.

"Anderssson," gloated Fear, throwing one of his vicious mantrap weapons into her path. Another scatter gun blast sent it flying out of harm's way, and still she kept on moving.

"Anderssson," blazed Fire in hatred and raised his burning trident weapon, sending out a blast of supernatural flame. Anderson twisted out of the way and the blast struck behind her, consuming several panicked Death cultists and reducing them to charred scarecrows in seconds.

Anderson strode forward, firing the scatter gun, and the weapon's high velocity shot load tore into the Dark Judges' bodies. Their Church of Death servants had done their work well, and each of the creatures was dressed in an exact replica of their familiar uniform, which themselves were grotesque, twisted parodies of the uniforms worn by Mega-City One Judges. DeMarco watched as Death slid one long, bony hand down to his version of a Judge's utility belt, reaching for the object attached there, reaching for what looked like a–

"Teleporter!" shouted Anderson in angry warning to the other Judges following in behind her. "For Grud's sake, shoot them. Stop them before they can teleport away!"

She opened fire again with the scatter gun, the roaring sound of the weapon joined seconds later by the crash of massed Lawgiver fire. A hail of Lawgiver fire, including Hi-Ex and Incendiary shells, struck out at the Dark

Judges, but it was already too late. A dancing nimbus of energy surrounded the four figures on the altar platform, and the volley of gunfire passed harmlessly through their dematerialising forms as the activated devices teleported them away out of the Judges' reach.

"There is much work to be done, but we will meet again soon, Anderson," hissed Death as he shimmered into nothingness, his gloating gaze fixed on Anderson. A moment later, he was gone, his final words left echoing psychically in the minds of those left behind. "This time, we will not be stopped so easily…"

Not wasting any more time, DeMarco scrambled forward up onto the altar platform, standing on the spot where the Dark Judges had been only moments ago. She heard the ominous clatter of a scatter gun being cocked directly behind her.

"Don't shoot! Family man!" she shouted, realising that in these robes she looked like any other Death cultist, and giving the traditional code phrase used by undercover Judges to identify themselves to other members of the Justice Department.

"Turn round. Slowly."

DeMarco did as ordered, seeing Anderson there, a hostile, suspicious look in her eyes, the scatter gun levelled straight at DeMarco's body. The look in the Psi-Judge's eyes intensified for a moment, and DeMarco felt cold psychic fingers picking through her mind, searching for the truth about her identity.

The fingers withdrew, the odd look left Anderson's eyes and the gun barrel was lowered.

"You're DeMarco?" asked Anderson, surprise evident in her voice. "The one that used to be Sector Chief in 303? The one that…"

Anderson's voice drifted off, but DeMarco knew what she had been about to say.

The one that's supposed to have tried to get Dredd into the sack with her? Yeah, that's me, ma'am. Guilty as charged.

"I guess that means I can lower my hands now without worrying that you're going to shoot me?" DeMarco said, continuing what she had been doing and going over to the prone figure of the girl on the altar slab.

"What are you doing here?" asked Anderson.

DeMarco laid a finger on the girl's neck, feeling for a pulse – and finding one. It was weak, but it was still there, thank Grud.

"Closing a case and saving a girl's life," she replied. "I guess you've got some important calls to make. Make sure one of them is for this girl. Grud knows what kind of drugs these freaks pumped into her. We need to get her into a med-unit fast."

Anderson nodded in understanding, and reached for her belt pouch radio.

"Control – Anderson. Things didn't go so well down here at Jack Kevorkian. Thanks to these cult creeps, the Dark Judges now have bodies and teleporters. They've escaped and are still on the loose. Wherever Dredd is, and whatever he's doing, tell him to drop it now. I need him to help track them down again before they start trying to wipe out the entire city."

Eleven

FERGUS MUNCLIE LIKED being a living mannequin. Sure, it wasn't the greatest job in the world, but it was still a job – and that was a damn site more than most people in this city could ever say. He was the only guy on Level 271 of Jack Yeovil Block who even had a job, and the only other person in his extended family who had one was that dumb jerk of a brother-in-law of his, who had somehow managed to land a gig down at Resyk as a Part-Time Assistant Trainee Blockage Cleaner. Fergus had been down there once to see him, and hadn't been too impressed by what he saw. His brother-in-law worked in the sub-basement maintenance area directly below the main fat-rendering vats. The acidic fumes down there were pretty nasty, especially when the Resyk conveyor belts were running at full capacity, which was pretty much most of the time, and as far as Fergus could figure out, his brother-in-law's job mostly involved crawling about inside pipes and run-off troughs with the partially dissolved remains of recycled human organic matter dripping down on top of him.

No, Fergus was much happier where he was. Sure, he had to cross two sectors to get there, taking three zoom train interchanges and a hover-bus journey to do it, but any job was better than no job, he figured.

He had been employed as a living mannequin at the Ryder Mega-Mall for the past three years. Some people couldn't handle the job, having to stand still for eight hours a day, minus lunch-breaks, but Fergus adored it. It got him out and about amongst people, and he enjoyed being the centre of attention, as passing shoppers stopped to check out what he was wearing, and gangs of juves pulled faces and made gestures at him through the glass, trying to make him move or react. He was good at it too, able to come up with some truly novel and dynamic poses and hold them for hours at a time, able to look good in whatever they required him to model each day, and skilled at really selling the product, tailoring the intensity and excitement of his pose to whatever it was he was supposed to be modelling.

The mall management moved him around a lot, but most of the time he spent his work days in the window displays of shops like Kneepad-U-Like, Mosgrove & Thung and Ugly Kid Joe's; solid, respectable, middle-of-the-marketplace chains found in every mall and shopperama all over the city.

Of course, what he really dreamed of was a move up to the top tier: the prestige gigs working in the window displays of high-class retail outfits like Sump Couture, Khaki-a-Go-Go and Military Junta. All the mall's mannequins took home the same pay cheque amount at the end of the week, but the mannequins in those particular stores were still rated a cut above the rest. They got to put on the most daring, imaginative and outrageous poses – poses that the traditionalist management of family orientated stores like Mosgrove & Thung would never approve of – and in the staff canteen they always sat at a table of their own, never mixing with the other mannequins. All the other mannequins hated them, of course; all the others wanted to be where they were.

Fergus was pretty sure he was getting close to that dream now. His posing work a few weeks ago in the "Give Me Victory, or Give Me Death" window display of

Harv's Sports Gear & Armoury had been the talk of every mannequin in the place. Better still, while he had been standing there in the display, dressed in a Juggernaut strip and holding a copy of the Inter-Meg Smashball trophy aloft in one hand and the blood-dripping, severed head of one of his shop dummy opponents in the other, he had seen none other than the assistant display arranger from Sump Couture sidle past the outside of the shop, clearly sent to check out his work on the sly.

Yeah, Fergus was pretty sure that he was on his way up, and that soon enough it would be him there in the window display of those places, modelling all the latest in high-Meg fashions.

Assuming, that was, that he didn't get eaten by rampaging hordes of zombies in the meantime.

They were everywhere in the mall. Where they came from, Fergus had no idea. What they wanted, though, was clear enough. Trapped there in the Cursed Earth safari-wear display outside Ronnie Radback's, he had watched as at least half a dozen people were eaten alive right there in front of him. He was wearing the latest in anti-rad fashion and had a machete in one hand, swinging it in frozen motion at the head of the giant fibreglass ant coming out of the ground in front of him, but the weapon was useless, as fake as the cardboard rad-counter in his other hand, so all he had to depend on to keep himself alive were his wits and his Grud-given abilities as a living mannequin.

On the plus side, he knew he could remain in this pose for hours yet. The zombies were everywhere, milling all around him, one or two of them even brushing against him, but as far as he could tell, they were simply too dumb to realise that he was flesh and blood, and not the inanimate object he appeared to be.

On the minus side, his display partner today was the new kid, the girl who had just started last week. Fergus hadn't been happy with being paired with her. Her stance ability was all wrong, she had no idea about dynamic posing, her muscle control was sadly lacking – and now, to top it all, she was probably going to get him killed and eaten.

She was playing his wife in this display, cringing in fear before the giant ant model while showing a very customer-pleasing amount of leg and cleavage, as Fergus, the intrepid Cursed Earth explorer, strode forward to defend her. She didn't have to fake that frozen look of terror on her face anymore, but she was visibly trembling in barely contained panic, and her skin glistened with a clammy fear-sweat. She couldn't take much more of this, and when she screamed, tried to run or even just moved, the zombies were going to realise she and he were there amongst them.

They could hear screams from all around, echoing through the cavernous space of the multi-level mall, along with all the snarls and moans of the zombies as they fell upon the terrified shoppers within the place or fought amongst each other for some of the choicest scraps of meat. There were security droids hovering around the place, spraying the zombies with knock-out gas or zapping them with stunner shots, although as far as Fergus could see these attacks were as much use against the things as the stern cease-and-desist warnings issued by the droid units. The droids were designed to take legal, non-lethal action against shoplifters, pickpockets, juve troublemakers, loiterers, buskers and mimes, but apparently their programming didn't cover eventualities like zombies invading the place to eat the shoppers.

Incongruously, in amongst all the carnage, the mall's auto-ads kept on running, broadcasting out their hard-sell messages to terrified shoppers and the roaming packs of zombies that were hunting those same shoppers.

"Important new Mega-Mall research by top scientists has proved that buying things may actually boost your immune system, clear your complexion, improve your eyesight and sex drive, and even significantly reduce cholesterol, so get those creds out, shoppers, and spend, spend, spend! Your continued health and well-being may depend on it!" boomed a tannoy announcement, as a gang of juves in the ground level vid-arcade pulled out their illegal las-blades, preparing to go down fighting against the zombies now crowding into the place.

"Grot Pot! When a snack's this cheap, delicious and easy to prepare, who gives a drokk about nutritional value?" suggested the Grot Pot dispenser machine at the entrance to the level one drop-tubes, unaware that most of its customers were being attacked and eaten by ravenous zombies.

"Take two bottles into the shower?" squealed a holo-ad projection of a near-naked female model in the main foyer, looking down blindly on a pack of zombies tearing apart a screaming family of Fatties. "Not me! With Otto Sump's new Sham-Poo, I just stink and go!"

"Tired? Stressed? Bored of a lifetime of endless unemployment and poor-quality leisure time?" asked a wandering hov-unit, trying to sell its ads to the corpses strewn along the main concourse. "Why not take a vacation in our new Cursed Earth holiday work-camps? We promise back-breaking hard labour, brutal overseers and the best protection from the surrounding hostile mutie tribes that money can buy!"

"Brit-Cit! Where outdated tradition, and useless pomp and ceremony still reign triumphant! And all of it just a quick trip away through the Black Atlantic tunnel!" boasted another hov-unit in a typically snooty Brit-cit accent, as it followed its rival in the holiday ad business along the same concourse.

The hov-units weren't going to be doing much business amongst the shoppers tonight, but they seemed to have attracted the attention of the zombies, and a group of the things were shambling along the concourse behind them, drawn in by the sound and movement generated by the devices. Which meant, Fergus knew from long days watching them go round and round, that they were coming straight towards him and the girl.

The girl gave a whimper of fear and shifted slightly.

"Don't move! Just let them pass us by!" Fergus hissed urgently through gritted teeth, knowing it was probably not going to do any good. She was too far gone, and probably going to start panicking any second.

The hov-units were past them now, still blaring out their ad messages. The zombies were only a few metres behind them. The girl moved again, and gave a stifled scream. The slight sound or movement was enough to catch the attention of at least one of the creatures. It looked round towards the display, studying the two immobile figures there with its dead, blank gaze. It took a step towards them, and then another one–

There was a loud, shocking report of a gunshot. The zombie fell one way, most of the contents of its skull went the other way, propelled out in a gory spray by the bullet that had just passed clean through its head.

More gunshots rang out, felling more of the creatures. Some of the shots lacked the fatal headshot accuracy of the first and instead hit the zombies' bodies, making the creatures dance and stagger under the impact of multiple hits. Fergus heard the pounding of heavy booted feet coming towards them along the concourse. Like any other citizen of Mega-City One, he recognised the sound immediately. Unlike many of those citizens, though, he thought it was the happiest sound he'd heard in his life.

Thank Grud, the Judges had got here at last.

Six of them came pounding along the concourse, gunning down zombies as they went. The bullet-riddled shape of one of the creatures picked itself back up off the ground and threw itself snarling at the lead Judge. Without breaking stride, and while gunning down another undead freak at the same time, the big Judge simply grabbed the zombie as it attacked him and hurled it over the side of the concourse, sending it crashing down onto the roof of the luxury Foord Falcon grav-speedster on the Mega-Mall prize giveaway promotional stand on the ground-floor concourse, three floors below.

The big Judge turned round, and Fergus recognised him from his voice even before he saw the name on the badge on the Judge's chest.

"Spread out," Dredd commanded the other Judges. "Two-man teams. Secure the exits on this level and check for any cits that might be hiding around the place. Remember, if it's moving but it hasn't got a pulse, shoot it in the head."

Dredd paused, glancing round at the two immobile mannequin figures. "And you two can quit playing possum. Danger's over now. Clear the area, citizens. That's an order."

WITH THE MALL'S entrance and exits secured, and with the bulk of the surviving staff and shoppers who had been in the place when the zombies attacked now safely evacuated, the clean-up op could begin. No zombies could get out of the mall, and the only thing that was going to be coming in through its doors were more and more Judges, so Dredd didn't think there was much more of a problem here, and gladly relinquished command of the situation to a Tac Watch Commander from Sector House 57.

That the situation at the Ryder Mega-Mall was now more or less under control didn't exactly please Dredd. It had been nothing more than an annoying distraction from his main duty, and it wasn't even over yet. Reports were coming in of more zombie attacks in the area around the iso-block as the creatures spread further out into the sector, although it seemed as if the main concentration of the things had been trapped here at the Ryder Mall. Now all that was left to do was a tedious but necessary mopping-up operation throughout the rest of the sector to prevent the zombie contagion spreading any further.

Judges were flooding in from all the adjoining sectors now, adding to the available manpower. By all accounts, there were almost as many Judges as surviving perps inside Nixon Penitentiary now, and Giant reported that the situation there was well under control. The remainder of the vampires and any zombies that had remained in the building were now confined to just three levels in the prison's lower sections, and Justice Department heavy weapons teams armed with flamer units were already on their way to remove their polluting presence for good from the prison.

Two problems down, but what was by far the biggest issue was still unresolved. The Dark Judges were still out there somewhere and every minute they remained free, the danger to every living person in Mega-City One increased accordingly.

"Control – Dredd. Any update on the Dark Judges?"

"Negative, Dredd. We've got Anderson and half of Psi-Div scanning for them, and so far they've come up with zip. No reports of any sightings coming in either, and every slab jock in the Department is out there looking for them. If Death and his pals are out there, they're managing to keep a real low profile."

"Give 'em time, Control. Maybe they're planning something, but they'll turn up sooner or later. When that happens, all we can do is follow the trail of dead cits."

"Wilco, Dredd. Chief Judge says she wants you and Anderson together on this one. We're sending an H-wagon to pick you up."

Dredd considered the situation for a moment. He was no longer needed here, and he and Anderson together had proven themselves in the past to be the best weapon Mega-City had against the Dark Judges, but too many unanswered questions still remained.

Someone had created the retrovirus that had given birth to the vampire and zombie creatures.

Someone, possibly that same someone, had carefully planned the attack on Nixon Pen that had allowed the Dark Judges to escape.

The members of the Church of Death were no different from the fanatical kooks who filled the ranks of at least a dozen other similar illegal crank-cults, but someone had organised and funded those creeps, turned them into a weapon to be used against the Justice Department at the crucial moment of the Dark Judges' escape.

Someone was behind everything that had happened so far, and Dredd and the rest of the Justice Department didn't have a clue yet who that someone could be.

First things first, decided Dredd angrily. First we deal with Death and the others, then we find out who was responsible for this whole mess.

"Understood, Control. Awaiting H-wagon pick-up. Dredd out."

He was at the outside of the mall, supervising as meat-wagons and med-wagons arrived to take away the dead and injured, and pat-wagons delivered more Judges to deal with the situation inside the mall. As he watched, a group of injured cits were brought out of the place. Six of them were stretcher cases, and the walking wounded were splattered with gore and nursed blood-soaked bandages showing where they had been clawed or bitten in zombie attacks. A Med-Judge accompanied them, saw Dredd and came running over to him.

"The wounded are starting to stack up now, Dredd. We've got over two hundred injured cits, all the victims of zombie bites. What little we've got to go on with these things all suggests that they were reanimated by a retrovirus passed on to them by bites from the things that attacked Nixon Pen. What do we do if the retrovirus affects living victims the same way?"

"Quarantine?" asked Dredd.

"That's what I'm thinking," nodded the Med-Judge, grimly. "If I've got a couple of hundred injured cits here who are maybe going to turn into vamps or flesh-hungry zombies in an hour or two, then we need to do something to either cure them or contain them."

"Good point," agreed Dredd, activating his helmet radio again.

*   *   *

"IT'S AN INTERESTING question, Dredd," said Helsing, bending over the zombie specimen on the autopsy slab in front of him. Even with most of its cranium missing, destroyed by one of Helsing's own Lawgiver shots, they weren't taking any chances with the thing. It was secured to the table by metal restraints, and there were armed Judges standing by in the room to make sure that the zombie and the rest of its equally dead friends weren't going to pull any more surprise resurrection stunts. Helsing was glad of the guards' presence, and was fairly sure that if they had arrived a few moments later when he had first raised the alarm then he would probably be lying stretched out on one of his own autopsy slabs along with the rest of the dead meat on display here.

"As far as I can tell," he continued, talking via radio link to Dredd while he neatly sliced into the zombie's body with his trusty las-scalpel, "the virus changes structure when it jumps from the vampires and into the bloodstreams and nervous systems of their victims. It degenerates, becoming less effective, so that when the dead tissue is reanimated, virtually all the higher brain functions are lost, and all that remains are the most basic and animalistic urges such as hunger and aggression."

"But is it contagious?" asked Dredd, a clear note of impatience in his tone.

"To anyone non-fatally bitten by these things? I'm not sure, I'm afraid. I'll have to do tests on blood samples for the bite victims, but it's my hope that the more degenerative form of the virus only affects dead tissue. In fact, it was only when I saw it in its degenerated form that I realised where I had seen it before–"

"You've seen this virus before? Where?" The note of impatience in Dredd's voice had suddenly been replaced by one of alert interest.

"In molecular form, it's strikingly similar to the chemical formula recently patented by the EverPet Corporation."

"Pet Regen? The stuff that brings cits' dead pets back to life?" The disbelief in Dredd's voice was clear.

"Basically, yes," answered Helsing calmly. "It's very possibly an early test-form of the final product."

There was a pause on the radio link before Dredd answered: "Good work, Helsing. Keep me informed if you find anything else. Dredd out."

Helsing bent down over the corpse again, wincing from the pain in his arm. He'd had the wound dressed and had allowed a Med-Judge to administer him some minor pain-killer tabs, but nothing that would interfere with his thought processes or cloud his judgement, and he had absolutely refused the Med-Judges' suggestions that he go into med-bay for observation.

One of the zombies had got a little too close for comfort, and had taken a bite out of Helsing's left arm before the Judge had managed to jam his las-scalpel deep into its brainpan. Despite the worrying certainty that he, too, now had the retrovirus coursing through his bloodstream, Helsing tried to look on the bright side, telling himself that having a personal stake in this case would give his work an extra added impetus.

After all, now he was in the same boat as the other injured citizens who had been bitten so far, and if the retrovirus was contagious in this fashion then it really rather was in his interest, just as much as theirs, that he find a cure as soon as possible.

Humming quietly to himself, he applied the las-scalpel to another part of the zombie's exposed innards, calmly continuing his work.

SOMEONE HAD DELIBERATELY engineered the virus that had created the vampire and zombie creatures. Someone had organised and funded the Church of Death and had mounted a successful operation to free the Dark Judges from their prison – but now Dredd had a good idea just who that someone might be.

"Control – Dredd. Been a change of plan. I still need that

H-wagon, but the rendezvous with Anderson will have to wait. If she needs back-up, recommend Judge Giant for the job. Tell my pilot to pick me up and then plot a course at double-speed for the EverPet Corporation's HQ, and give me everything you've got from Central Records on the company."

AFTER SO LONG shut away in the darkness, disembodied and under constant guard, it was good to be free to kill once more. Their servants had done well – the teleporters were a good copy of the devices the Dark Judges had used on their own world – and now those devices had brought them to this fine place where there were so many sinners to be judged, and no interlopers with their guns to interrupt Death and his brethren in their sacred work.

Fire lashed out with his burning trident. More of the crude dwellings burst into flame. Screaming figures stumbled amidst the inferno, burning from head to foot. The others fled from where they had been cowering, flushed out from hiding by the flames, herded by further blasts from Fire's trident straight into the deadly embrace of the other three Dark Judges.

Death pushed a hand into the chest of one sinner, his fingers twisting amongst the arteries of his heart. With his other hand, he thrust into the back of another fleeing figure, withdrawing it again almost as quickly, leaving Death clutching his gory, dripping prize in triumph. The man kept on running for a few steps more, and then collapsed to the ground, an expression of utter and horrified disbelief fixed on his face. Death threw the still-beating heart into the spreading flames and then moved on to judge more of the sinners.

Mortis looked down at the begging, whimpering figure kneeling before him. There was decay in this one already, he could sense. Disease festered within him, his insides eaten away by the bottles of low-grade meths-brew he had been consuming for years. All it would take to bring it out to full bloom in the sinner's body was the merest touch from the Dark Judge.

Mortis's fingers stroked the man's face, leaving deep, pus-filled boils where they brushed the skin. Almost instantly, the man fell writhing to the ground, maggots boiling out of his rotting flesh as it sloughed away wholesale from his bones. Mortis hissed in pleasure, and strode on to bestow his gifts to the next sinner in turn. Where he walked across the uneven, broken ground, where his feet made contact with the polluted soil there, maggots and other carrion insects sprang out of the earth in the wake of his passing.

Fear flowed out of the shadows of a heap of crumbling war ruins, seemingly appearing from nowhere to the rabble of sinners who had been fleeing the wall of flame behind them. The barred gate of his helmet visor gaped open, and the first few sinners in line caught a glimpse of what lay behind that visor, and fell lifeless to the ground, their hearts frozen solid like blocks of ice, fireworks exploding amongst the darkness of their dimming vision as their brains were wracked by a series of instantly fatal embolisms.

The others turned and fled, seeking escape amongst the ruins. Fear spread his cloak wide, revealing the living darkness that lay beneath the garment. Shadow-shapes, moving too swiftly to be properly seen, flew out of that darkness and flitted after the escaping sinners. As each shadow-shape found its target a sinner fell to the ground screaming and writhing, their minds filled with images of the things they had previously glimpsed only on the furthest fringes of their worst nightmares. Fear stalked forward to find his prey and finish them off, his mystic senses guided by the screams in the darkness and by the delicious taste of the victims' terror.

Death stood upon a small mound of the corpses of his victims and exulted in being free once more. The place they had found – the place destiny and their teleporters had brought them to – was one of those places where the lost and dispossessed drank to blot out the worst details of their existences. Of all the inhabitants of this city, these were amongst the most wretched and miserable, with little or nothing left to live for, but still they had tried to run when the Dark Judges had appeared amongst them. As all foolish mortals did, they had tried to survive rather than surrender to the inevitable.

What was it about these sinners, Death wondered, that they wanted to compound their crimes by hanging onto the sin of life for as long as they could? With more co-operation, with more understanding of what it was he and his brethren were trying to achieve, their great work would be done all the sooner, and then first this city and then the rest of this world would know peace at last.

The giant towers of the city loomed up around this area of waste ground where the lost ones had made their home on the ruins of one of the city's past wars. So many wars these sinners fought amongst themselves, and still they had not succeeded in wiping themselves out. So disappointing. That was why their great work was so necessary, Death knew. If the sinners did not have the courage to end their own existences, then it was the task of the Dark Judges to do it for them.

The sound of H-wagon engines interrupted Death's contemplation. He saw the running lights and search-beams of the aerial vehicles coming closer across the darkness of the ruins, and realised that time was short.

He called his brothers to him. Some of the sinners still lived, fleeing in terror into the darkness and towards the city lights beyond, but it did not matter. Their escape was only temporary and they, like the rest of this doomed city, would be judged soon enough.

"They have found us," said Fire. "We must leave this place and continue our work elsewhere."

"There are only four of us, and many of them. They will be determined to stop us, just as they have stopped us before," said the dead, cold voice of Mortis.

"We are still weak from our long captivity," noted Fear, his whispering voice like a cold shiver running down the spine. "Perhaps we should return to Deadworld to gather our strength. We have more power there than we have here."

"Or perhaps Deadworld should come to us."

It was Death who spoke. The other three Dark Judges looked at their leader. With all their minds psychically linked, it took only a moment for them to realise the intent of his words. His plan was instantly met with a low chorus of approving hisses.

"I will gather the sacrifices and go to the Under-Place to prepare the way," whispered Fear. This too met with an approving chorus of hisses.

It was Death that spoke next. "They seek four of us together. If we are apart, they will be confused. Their forces will be spread thinly as they attempt to find us. The carnage we other three bring will distract them. They will not realise what it is we plan to do until it is too late to stop us."

Death looked at the other three Dark Judges. "Judge well, brothers. When next we meet, in the Under-Place, this city will finally be ours."

THE H-WAGON REACHED the spot less than thirty seconds later. Powerful search-beams played over the place, and Tek-Judges aboard the vehicle scrutinised monitor screens that displayed the entire area on spectrums far beyond the power of the naked eye, but there was nothing to find.

The Dark Judges were gone.

ICARUS SAT IN the darkness of his laboratory, quietly satisfied with the way events were proceeding. The Dark Judges had been freed, and so soon his own elevation to a higher state beyond life or death would begin. Of course, the Church of Death which he had secretly set up and then funded had been virtually wiped out by the night's events, but that didn't really matter, not in the grand scheme of things. Those fanatics had died happy in the knowledge that they had helped set free their precious masters and, more importantly, their role in Icarus's plans was over now anyway. After that, he really didn't care what happened to them. The only thing that mattered was what was going to happen to him tonight.

Rebirth.

Transcendence to a new and greater level of existence. That was why he had freed the Dark Judges, so that they could elevate him to the same status of everlasting life that they had achieved. The Dark Judges existed at a state beyond life and death, and so soon would Icarus.

"You cannot kill that which does not live," he murmured to himself, picking up the large syringe of fluid that lay on the desk before him. It contained the Regen retrovirus in its final, perfected state, and was far removed from the debased stuff which he had tested on the Death cult members to create his vampire creatures, or the even further adulterated muck which he had marketed as the EverPet product in order to fund his work.

No, the contents of that syringe represented his life's work. Everything he had striven for since the scales had been lifted from his eyes during the time of Necropolis was held within the dark, swirling liquid inside the syringe.

He picked it up, pushed the needle into his skin and pressed the injection switch. The liquid flooded into him, mixing with his bloodstream, the retrovirus molecules instantly attaching themselves to his blood cells, beginning the rapid process of reprogramming his DNA in preparation for what was to come.

The final stage would be death itself, the virus spreading to infect every cell in his body, going to work on his necrotised flesh. Icarus had a range of chemical substances that would bring on his own death quickly and painlessly. Many of them were the same Justice Department-approved compounds used in the city's chains of euthanasia clinics.

Still, none of them seemed quite appropriate, Icarus felt. For his death, for rebirth and transcendence to the state of eternal undeath, something more dramatic than mixes of toxic chemicals was called for, surely?

As if on cue, the radio intercom on his desk buzzed.

"A Justice Department H-wagon landing outside. There's a Judge getting out of it."

"Just one?" asked Icarus, puzzled.

"Just one," answered the Death cultist in charge of security at the facility. "It looks like it might be Dredd."

Dredd! Icarus's mind thrilled at the news. How appropriate, he thought. Fate was obviously at work here. Dredd was death incarnate. The biggest mass murderer on the planet, the man who had pressed the button on East-Meg One and consigned hundreds of millions of people to nuclear oblivion, the man who had given the brutally necessary order that would condemn billions more people to death during Judgement Day.

Yes, how appropriate, Icarus decided. This was destiny, this was fate. This was clearly how things were meant to happen.

"Stop him," Icarus ordered over the radio, knowing that there was no way the defenders he had left would ever be able to stop Dredd, even if he was on his own. "Make sure he doesn't get to the lab."

Yes, Dredd would come here, and Icarus would allow Dredd to kill him and elevate him to his destiny.

And then, after that?

Icarus was distracted for a moment by another barrage of angry fists pounding on the thick vault doors behind him. He smiled, thinking of the creatures contained behind those doors. Vampires, newly created and still filled with the worst after-affects of the virus flowing now through their veins.

So let Dredd come, Icarus smiled. After he had fulfilled his purpose and sent Icarus on the path to his destiny, he would find his supposed victory to be very short-lived indeed.

Twelve

DREDD EXITED THE H-wagon at a sprint. He'd been on duty now for over twenty hours, which wasn't completely unusual for him, but in that time he'd fought a couple of dozen vampires, battled his way through the middle of a prison riot, missed preventing the escape of the Dark Judges by the skin of his teeth, single-handedly taken on a couple of hundred zombies and commanded the clean-up op at the Ryder Mall which had saved the lives of hundreds of cits.

Even by his standards, it had been an eventful day – and it wasn't over yet.

Now, though, he could feel the exhaustion starting to build up in his body. He'd been a Judge for over forty years, and had pushed himself to the very limits of human endurance just about every day of every one of those years. His body was a machine, crafted from fifteen years of the toughest training on Earth at the Academy of Law, honed to near-perfection from four decades patrolling the streets of the biggest, most dangerous and crime-ridden city on the planet.

But even the best machines start to wear out after a while, Dredd knew. The Justice Department knew it too, and they'd already lined up his replacements, clones from the same precious bloodline as himself. The first of them was already on the streets. How long did Dredd have left, people secretly wondered within the Department? How long could he keep on pushing himself at the same rate that he had sustained for so many years?

For as long as necessary, Dredd told himself. For as long as his city still needed him.

He'd downed some standard-issue pep tabs in the H-wagon to fight off the worst of it, and from long experience he knew they'd keep him alert and on his feet for another six hours or so.

Long enough to stop the Dark Judges and save his city? Grud only knew, but Dredd hoped it would be enough.

Through the speakers in his helmet, Control fed information through to him straight from the files held in the giant MAC computer system at the Grand Hall of Justice.

"Icarus, Dick. Real name: Martins, Vernon. Born 2078, Betty Boothroyd Maternity Med. Graduated Meg U, class of 2101, first class honours in Biochemistry. Employed as biochemist at DaneTech Industries, 2102-2115. Specialist field of research: Longevity and age retardation."

Dredd was at the doors to the lab facility, using his override card to open the doors as the calm voice of the Justice Department's anti-crime super-computer continued to feed him information.

"Left to establish own company, 2015. EverPet Corporation. No criminal record. Admitted for psycho-cube observation, 2112-13, following death of wife and daughter in citywide Necropolis disaster of 2112."

A spell in the kook cubes. That caught Dredd's attention. Not that Martins, or Icarus, or whatever he wanted to call himself, was unique in that respect. Necropolis was like an open wound in the city's psyche; sixty million citizens had died, and tens of millions more had suffered severe mental trauma, filling the city's psycho-blocks to maximum capacity for years afterwards. Some had recovered sooner than others. Clearly, the psycho-cube docs had thought Martins/Icarus was one of them, but now Dredd knew different.

Using MAC's resources, he'd uncovered a lot on the H-wagon ride out here. All the information had been there all along, for anyone who wanted to go digging for it. Dredd knew that, with over four hundred million citizens to watch over, the Justice Department couldn't keep a close eye on all of them, but there were enough anomalies in the records to have maybe raised at least a few questions in someone's mind.

EverPet's financial records were a revelation. The Pet Regen product was a commercial success, but the company was still trading at an enormous loss. Their public accounts records showed huge large amounts of money being ploughed into unspecified "research projects". Using MAC's high-powered analytical abilities, Dredd had quickly found out what that really meant.

Money had been transferred to overseas accounts and then shifted back into the city in the guise of charitable donations to various minor religious organisations, all of which, Dredd suspected, would quickly be revealed as mere fronts for the Church of Death. Other funds had been siphoned off to set up the facility Dredd was about to enter now, even though there was no official record of the place in the list of the company's property holdings.

A secret lab, hidden away from the prying eyes of the Justice Department. A biochemist with a history of mental disorder, connections to the Church of Death and whose research speciality was the reanimation of dead tissue.

Didn't need forty years on the streets to put this one together, Dredd figured.

Icarus, for whatever reasons of his own, had funded the Church of Death, created its vampire shock-troopers, freed the Dark Judges and caused the deaths of a lot of cits and Justice Department personnel. The mood he was in now, Dredd would be happy now to just put a few Standard Execution rounds into the murdering creep at the first provocation, and let some of the big brains down at Justice Central figure out all the hows and whys of whatever it was Icarus was hoping to achieve from all this mayhem.

"Help you, sir? I'm afraid this facility is closed to the general public, but if you want a tour of the main EverPet labs, then our Citizens Relations office will be happy to arrange it. Their office hours are 0900 to 1700, and you can contact them on–"

Dredd silenced the security droid in the foyer with a single Armour Piercing shot, instantly transforming it into just so much expensive junk. Another shot silenced the alarm that had started shrieking as soon as his first gunshot rang out. His override card took care of the second and more serious set of security doors, and then he was through and into the lab complex proper.

The H-wagon Dredd had ridden in on was a command model, with a fully equipped mobile armoury of Justice Department standard-issue weaponry. Dredd hadn't been shy about helping himself to whatever he thought he was going to need. When he exited the H-wagon, he had been carrying enough weaponry to fight a small block war all on his own.

Beyond the doors, a group of Death cultists were waiting for him. High on hate and eager for death, they charged down the corridor towards him, firing off indiscriminate volleys of bullets at him. Dredd raised his Lawgiver and introduced them to the gun's rapid fire setting, giving them an object lesson in what tight, accurate bursts of fire were all about.

Four of them hit the ground in as many seconds, Resyk-bound. Dredd popped a stumm grenade and let the rest of the survivors share its contents out amongst themselves. Respirator down, Dredd strode on through the midst of them. Choking and retching, completely incapacitated by the effects of the gas, Dredd knew none of these creeps were going anywhere in a hurry. One of them still managed to rise staggering to his feet. Dredd slammed him hard in the face with the butt of his Lawgiver. The creep ate floor, fast and sudden. Next stop for him would be a med-unit to fix his broken nose, busted teeth and severe concussion, before the Judge-Wardens threw his deranged butt into an iso-cube for the next twenty years or so.

Dredd strode on. A chorus of snarls and growls warned him what was waiting for him round the next corner. Dredd figured that Icarus's retrovirus didn't do much for IQ and common sense when it came lying patiently in ambush. He also figured that, since they had been voluntarily infected with the virus, Icarus's vampire-things were, to all intents and purposes, legally dead. That being the case, they weren't entitled to the same legal rights as any ordinary, decent citizen that still had a pulse, and hence Dredd's next actions weren't governed by the regulations that normally applied in matters relating to the correct use of the proper and legal amount of force to be applied in carrying out his judicial duties.

And besides, he reminded himself... both the retrovirus and the Dark Judges were clear and present dangers to the lives of everyone in Mega-City One, meaning that any extra-judicial force he chose to employ was officially permitted under the terms of the Security of the City Act. Short version: no arrest, no warning shot, no shooting to wound. These creeps were going straight to Resyk.

Dredd reached for the first of the surprises he'd taken from the H-wagon armoury, popping the safety caps and timer fuses on them and throwing them almost casually round the corner. The explosions came just a second later, but Dredd had already moved into the cover of the near wall to avoid the dual waves of flame and shrapnel that came roaring round the corner.

A vampire, completely bathed head to foot in fire, came staggering round the corner. The phosphor chemicals from one of Dredd's grenades had already burned away its eyes and face, but somehow it could still sense his presence. It turned and came charging towards him, screaming in rage and pain. A moment later, anything that was left of it was decorating the walls, floor and roof of the corridor, liberally distributed there by the Hi-Ex shot Dredd had calmly snapped off.

Round the corner waited more evidence of the aftermath of the phosphor and fragmentation grenades that Dredd had just used. The shredded and burning remains of several more – Dredd estimated at least four – vampires littered the place. One of them, its lower body torn away by shrapnel, its remaining upper half charred and burning, still managed to summon up the strength to start crawling towards him, making a hideous mewling sound as it scrabbled at his Judge boots with its burning claws. Dredd put two Standard Execution rounds through the top of its head and carried on.

It was at the next corridor junction that he started to run into trouble. He was just finishing mopping up the combined group of vampires and cultists who had foolishly imagined they could lure him into some kind of crossfire ambush there. He'd picked off the first few of them with shots from his Lawgiver, demolishing one of the barricades they'd been sheltering behind with a double-blast of Hi-Ex. Heatseeker hotshots had flushed the remaining cultists out of hiding. The vamps, whose inhumanly low body temperature barely registered with the Heatseeker warheads' targeting systems, Dredd took care of with one of the other weapons he was carrying, hosing them down with a spread of rapid-fire explosive shell fire from the Colt M2000 Widowmaker.

The M2000, a replacement for the old Lawrod weapon in providing Judges with some additional heavier firepower for on-the-street use, had first come into widespread service during Judgement Day. It had proved highly effective then against zombies, so Dredd didn't see why vampire targets would prove any more resistant to its devastating effects.

He wasn't wrong. The vampires disintegrated bodily under the impact of the volleys of high-calibre shotgun shells. One of them, which had come at Dredd with an industrial las-burner, was blown clear across the corridor by the impact of the shells into its body, hitting the far wall with a sick, wet splat.

It was only after the roar of the weapon's fearsomely loud gunfire reports started to die away that Dredd heard the other sound coming from the corridor behind him: the loud, pounding tread of metallic feet, too heavy to be anything human, too regular and steady to be anything other than a droid. And not just any kind of droid.

War droids were supposed to be illegal in Mega-City One. Even before the Second Robot War, when crimelord Nero Narcos had used an army of war droids to try and overthrow the entire Judge system and install himself as the city's new ruler, the manufacture and ownership of any kind of combat-orientated robot unit was highly illegal. The Justice Department had its own war droid reserve resources, of course, although a scheme under the late Chief Judge McGruder's administration to make up the growing shortfall of patrol Judges by putting robot Judges onto the city streets had not met with success, Nevertheless, the private ownership of such droids was forbidden.

Such devices were still available elsewhere, of course. Asiatic mega-cities such as Hondo Cit, Sino Cit and Nu-Taiwan did a roaring trade in war droid manufacture, and even in Mega-City One there was always a thriving underground black market in war droid units still left over from previous conflicts, stretching all the way back to events as long ago as the early twenty-first century Volgan Wars. In fact, the ABC Warrior unit, dating from the mid-period Volgan Wars, was still highly prized for its combat abilities, even now more than a hundred years after its original construction, and there were those collectors and aficionados of such things who considered the ABC unit so durable and easily adaptable that they claimed they could still be in active service even thousands of years from now.

Dredd dived, rolling for cover, as the metal brute stomped up the corridor towards him, opening fire with its own inbuilt weaponry. Bullets ricocheted off walls and careened off the stone floor as the droid's weapons systems tracked Dredd, his speed and reflexes managing to keep him just that vital hairsbreadth ahead of its targeting sensors.

He dropped the M2000, knowing its high-calibre shotgun capabilities, although devastating against unarmoured human opponents, would be useless against a heavily armoured droid. The droid kept on coming, its thunderous footsteps cracking the stone of the floor. It was too big and heavy to be one of the sleek new Hondo-cit jobs that had been coming onto the market in the last few years, and superior targeting programs on the Nu-Taiwan models would most likely have found him and vaporised him by now, so Dredd's best guess was that it was probably an old Sov-Blok unit, probably even pre-Apocalypse War. The details didn't worry him; if they wanted to, the Tek-Judges could try and identify it from whatever scrap metal was left when he had finished taking care of it.

He came out of the roll, Lawgiver in hand, firing as he went. Armour Piercing shells ricocheted off the droid's armoured carapace, barely even denting the thick armour there to protect its CPU core. A Hi-Ex shell took care of the heavy spit-blaster mounted on one of its shoulders. Dredd was just about to fire a second shot to destroy the mini missile launcher on the droid's other shoulder, when it hit him with the auxiliary electro-gens built into its chest unit. Crackling lightning bolts of electricity filled the corridor in front of it, leaping from metal wall to metal wall, striking Dredd multiple times. The heavily insulated material of his uniform's bodysuit saved him from the worst of it, but the blasts still threw him several metres back, slamming him painfully against the corridor wall. His Lawgiver flew from his nerveless grasp, landing far away from where he fell.

He slumped to the ground, hearing the stone-cracking impacts of the droid's footsteps as it stamped forward to finish him off, its servo-motors growling in what sounded almost like eager anticipation.

Muscles cramped with pain from the effects of the electricity blast refused to respond. Dredd's vision swam, the heavy, deadening weight of imminent oblivion pressing in on the edges of his consciousness.

Get up, old man, he told himself. You're not out for the count yet, not while your city's still in danger.

The reminder was like a shock to the system. He was moving even as the droid's giant metal fist jack-hammered down towards him, pile-driving into the area of the floor where only moments ago Dredd's head had been resting. He scrambled away from it, reaching out for the nearest weapon which instinct and more than forty years of combat experience told him should still be lying right where its previous owner had dropped it.

The las-burner wasn't designed for combat use, and wasn't a particularly easy thing to operate, usually requiring a physically strong operator or even work-droid to wield properly. Its main purpose was to cut up dense materials like metal or reinforced plasteel. Perps had quickly found its uses when it came to slicing through inconvenient obstacles like vault doors and walls. It probably didn't say anything about it in the manufacturer's manual, but disabling maniac war-droids seemed to be another one of the multi-faceted tool's many useful applications.

In an impressive feat of strength, Dredd swung the heavy device one-handed, activating its power supply with a flick of his finger. The tool's las-beam instantly hissed into life, projecting several feet from its end, burning with a cold, clear light that made Dredd's eyes hurt, even through the polarised visor guard of his helmet.

The las-burner sheared through the armoured metal of the droid's right arm as if it was nothing more substantial than raw munce. The metal monster's hand fell to the ground with a loud clunk, twitching in distressed reflex, sparks and oily black hydraulic fluid spraying out from its severed end. The droid made a dull roaring sound that was either a mechanical expression of pain and anger or merely a change in the pitch of its servo-motor system as it shut down the flow of power and fluid to the damaged limb.

Dredd was moving again, rolling between the thick metal tree trunks of its legs as it swivelled round in search of him, trying to bring its remaining weaponry to bear on this one unexpectedly troublesome human target. Designed mainly for frontal assault, the droid was more vulnerable to attack in its more weakly armoured rear sections. Hefting the las-burner, Dredd quickly got to work on the backs of its legs, slashing into the joint-pistons and power cables there.

Hamstrung, with both legs disabled, and bellowing in impotent mechanical distress, the three and a half metre tall droid pitched forward onto its face, with a crash that reminded Dredd of the sound of a con-apt building or small-sized city block being demolished.

It lay there, emitting strange mechanical growls as its servo-motors whined in protest, flailing its one still-functioning limb about the place in futile protest. A few more brief seconds' work with the las-burner put paid to even this much activity from it. Dredd walked away, leaving the now-deactivated weapon buried deep into the fused slag that had been the droid's CPU unit.

ICARUS HAD BEEN surprised how easy it had been to track Dredd's progress through the complex by the sound of the gunshots alone.

First had come the loud and intense sounds of several different guns firing at once, as Dredd encountered and dealt with the main groups of Icarus's security detail at the main entrance points to the lab. After that, the gunfire had become more sporadic as it crept closer to where Icarus was and Dredd penetrated further into the complex, encountering the occasional wandering vampire or small pocket of Death cultist resistance. Amidst these had come the odd explosion, the sounds of those also coming progressively closer as Dredd methodically destroyed lab after lab, wiping out years of Icarus's research into longevity and various possibilities for sustaining life after death. It didn't matter, Icarus knew. He already had everything he wanted from his research, and it was coursing through his veins now, changing his mind and body in ways that puny, mortal intellects like Dredd's could never imagine.

The last explosion had come about half a minute ago, no doubt caused by Dredd laying waste to the lab just down the corridor, where the vampires' blood serum food supply was produced. If that was the case, then by Icarus's calculations he should be entering the...

Right on cue, the lab doors obediently opened in response to the Justice Department override device's command. Dredd walked in, his Lawgiver aimed at Icarus. Apart from the two of them, there wasn't another living soul in the lab.

"Dick Icarus? Fun-time's over, creep. You're under arrest."

"Really? On what charges?" Icarus's tone was casual and breezy, his voice deliberately raised to distract Dredd's attention away from the faint pounding sounds on the incubator vault door on the wall to the side of them.

"Don't get cute, punk. So far tonight, you've been responsible for the deaths of thousands. Grud knows how many more are going to die before we take care of the things you've unleashed on this city."

"Aren't you even going to ask me why?" asked Icarus, glancing down at the weapon he'd left on the desk top beside him. It was only an arm's reach away. All he had to do was–

"No need. You'll tell us everything we need to know soon enough, as soon as we get you into an interrogation cube," promised Dredd. "Why you did it, what you know of the Dark Judges' plans, any more little surprises you had planned for us. You won't hold anything back for too long. We've got interrogation techniques that'll make you tell us things you didn't even know you knew, and that's even before we bring in the Psi-Judges to go creeping around inside your mind."

"I did it because I want to live forever, and because the Dark Judges have the power to grant me that wish." Icarus was almost shouting, as much to drown out the sounds from behind the vault door as from the sense of rising excitement he felt within him. The moment was so close now, so close...

Dredd wasn't impressed. "So thousands have to die to feed your sick fantasy that the Dark Judges will give you eternal life? Grud alone knows how you managed to convince anyone to let you out the kook cubes, Icarus. The only wish the Dark Judges are ever going to grant is a death wish. You'd have to be completely insane to ever think you could make a bargain with those things."

Dredd was walking across the room towards him now, reaching into a belt pouch for the handcuffs to secure his prisoner. The noise from the vault door finally drew his attention. He paused, glancing suspiciously over at the door.

"What you got in there? More bloodsuckers?"

Icarus knew it was now or never. "Why don't you see for yourself," he screeched, making a grab for the weapon on the counter.

It was a good choice of weapon, he thought. A Flesh Disintegrator, instantly recognisable to someone like Dredd, and instantly lethal to anyone on the receiving end of its organic matter-destroying field. Icarus had had cause to use it several times before, in dealing with difficult-to-control lab specimens infected with some of the early versions of the retrovirus, and he could happily attest to its deadly capabilities.

He knew he wouldn't be able to grab the weapon, pick it up and fire it before Dredd could fire his own weapon. But then, as Icarus reminded himself, that was something he didn't have to worry about.

His hand was barely on the weapon's grip before the first Lawgiver shot punched into him, followed by two more in the space of a heartbeat, all three closely hitting in a tight cluster over his ribs. Icarus felt his heart explode, torn apart by the bullets' paths through his body. He had wondered many times what this moment would be like. His knowledge as a medical research scientist and his experiences from studying death in all its many forms over the last eight years suggested to him that it would all be quick and refreshingly pain-free. His knowledge and practical experiences had lied to him, he now knew; being shot dead hurt, and seemed to take much longer than you would reasonably expect.

A tremor passed through him. The formula coursing through his bloodstream seemed somehow to realise the fact of his imminent death, and was reacting accordingly. Icarus felt it release some of its strength into him, and he began to rise again to his feet, still clutching the disintegrator weapon, still bringing it up to bear at its target.

Dredd, caught by surprise by the fact of the nondescript-looking scientist's unexpected resilience, almost hesitated for a moment.

Almost.

Three more shots ripped into Icarus, hurling him backwards, knocking the gun from his hand. The scientist sank to his knees, blood pouring out of him. In spite of the pain from his torn-apart innards, he still managed to look up at Dredd and smile.

"Me, I know I'm coming back. For you, though, this is the end of the line."

He fell dead to the ground, Dredd at the same time spotting the small remote device held in Icarus's other hand. Icarus's hand had squeezed around it at the moment of death, activating it, and now the vault door on the far wall was sliding open. An alarm blared in warning, and over it Dredd could clearly hear the excited snarls and ravenous growls of the things behind that door.

They poured out of the vault: vampires, maybe a hundred or more of them, naked and newborn, hungry for blood, keen to start killing and spread their retrovirus further.

When they had joined the Church of Death and volunteered to undergo Icarus's retrovirus transformation process – a "rebirth into a glorious state beyond life and death", he had promised them – they had imagined that they would become natural-born predators, with nothing to fear and none strong or brave enough to stand against them. They were wrong.

Dredd's Lawgiver and M2000 roared together, their combined firepower blasting into the first few rows of vampires, picking them up and hurling their bullet-shredded bodies back into the ranks of those following on closely behind.

Dredd's marksmanship was almost as good with his left hand as it was with his right, and he kept up the punishing hail of fire with both weapons. The M2000 was difficult to control one-handed, but at this range, and with the weapon's devastating area of effect, all he really had to do was keep it trained on the general area of the open vault door, forcing anything that tried to come through that doorway to pass through the barrier of gunfire. His Lawgiver was in his left hand, picking off any vampires that managed to make it relatively unscathed through the curtain of Widowmaker fire. Vampire after vampire was knocked back, screaming and hissing, by the combined fire of both weapons, but there were still many more vampires in the vault than Dredd's guns had bullets for, and he was fast using up the magazines in both of them.

The M2000 was the first to run dry. With its final shot, it hit an enraged vampire that it had already hit at least once before, flaying its flesh even further and hurling it once more back into the vault with the others. Dredd dropped the weapon, knowing he didn't have the time to reload it.

He emptied his Lawgiver of its remaining Incendiary shells, firing them into the mass of bodies in the vault's doorway, buying himself a few more seconds as the vampires retreated back, hissing and snarling, from the wall of flame that was now between him and them.

He reached for the weapons pack holding the last of the ordnance he had brought with him from the H-wagon. He activated it with a flick of a switch and threw it into the vault, throwing himself at the heavy vault door as he did so, slamming into it hard and using every bit of his strength and body weight to push it shut. Slowly, painfully, it swung shut. For one terrible moment, a mere hand's breadth before it sealed shut again, Dredd felt the weight of the vampires hurl against the other side of the door, threatening to push it back wide open again in seconds, but a moment later the device he'd thrown into the vault went off, and all that remained after that was the terrible roaring sound from beyond the doors.

A second after that, Dredd pushed the door fully shut, the door's seals engaged and the vampires were trapped amidst the inferno now raging inside.

Dredd had grabbed the thermal bomb as soon as he had seen it in the H-wagon armoury, intending to use it as a weapon of last resort in case Death and the other three super-creeps showed up at Icarus's labs. They hadn't dropped by to pay their respects to their liberator, but, as it turned out, the thermal bomb had still come in handy after all.

Detonating inside the thick-walled vault, it had immediately raised the temperature inside the place to well over three thousand degrees. The air beyond the reinforced doors would have ignited instantly, and everything combustible in there would be reduced to ash long before the oxygen supply had been burned up. Dredd could feel the heat radiating through the thick metal of the door, and knew that the clean-up crews would probably need to use las-burners to cut through into the vault afterwards, since the heat inside it now would almost certainly have melted and fused the door workings.

He didn't care. The Teks and Meds could come and take what evidence they needed from the wreckage of the labs, but, as far as Dredd was concerned, Icarus and his vampires were now one less problem to deal with tonight.

Satisfied the vampires were destroyed, he stepped away from the door, speaking into his helmet radio.

"Control – Dredd. Clean-up crews required at the Icarus labs. Tell Chief Judge Hershey the vampire outbreak has been cut off at source now."

"Roger, Dredd. And Icarus?"

Dredd glanced at the corpse lying on the floor nearby. Was it his imagination, or had the corpse somehow changed in the last few minutes? It looked different somehow, larger and strangely swollen. Despite that, he was still clearly dead. Something else for the Teks and Meds to look into, Dredd supposed.

"As dead as Judge Cal," Dredd replied. "Make sure the clean-up crew get him properly bagged and tagged. I want him delivered to Helsing at Justice Central Forensics for a full autopsy. Any word on Death and the other three creeps yet?"

"Plenty. They've hit random points across the city four times now, but every time we got there they teleported away. They seem to have split up after the first attack and are operating solo, which is a new strategy, but the death count is already reaching block war level. We've got a confirmed sighting of Mortis at Clooney Memorial – Giant's on his way there now – and Anderson's picked up a psi-flash hunch that something might be about to happen at the Churchill Smokatorium. She's heading there herself."

"And the other two? Death and Fear?"

"Nothing yet, Dredd. We've got every spare badge we've got out on the streets, and a citywide alert's been given. If they turn up anywhere, you'll know about it as soon as we do."

*   *   *

IT WAS THE overpowering psychic stink of pure evil that alerted every Psi-Judge in the Academy of Law to Fear's presence in the building as soon as he teleported in. And it was the sound of the cadets' frantic screaming, mere seconds later, that alerted everyone else.

Tutor Judges came running in response as word spread throughout the building that something terrible was happening in one of the dorms reserved for Psi-Judge cadets. They hammered uselessly on the door of the dorm, unable to break it down. Fear had sealed it using one of his mantrap weapons, and it would need more than brute strength to overcome the device's mysterious psychic properties.

Meanwhile, for several long and terrible minutes, the Dark Judge was able to run amok in the dorm, with thirty young and helpless Psi-Judge cadets trapped in there with him.

The sealed door finally succumbed to a fusillade of Lawgiver fire and the combined psychic efforts of three Psi-Judge Tutors. What they found when they charged in, Lawgivers at the ready, was something from their worst nightmares. Fear was gone, teleporting away again, but leaving behind him the slaughtered remnants of an entire class of Psi-cadets.

However, it would be several minutes later, after Judge Tutors had finished the grim task of compiling a roll call of the dead, that the most terrible thing of all would be discovered. Four of the cadets were missing. A search of the entire Academy was ordered, but it was already clear to all what had happened to them.

Fear, for whatever twisted reasons of his own, had taken them. The four cadets were in the clutches of the Dark Judges.

Thirteen

ANDERSON HAD ALMOST to be restrained from jumping
out the hatch of the H-wagon while it was still in mid-
air above the Smokatorium. Anxious and impatient, she
forced herself to wait as it came into land, her feet hitting
the ground only seconds after the tarmac there had been
heat-scorched by the after-blast from the H-wagon's
underside thrusters.

There were Judges everywhere, cordoning off the
Smokatorium building from the rest of the city.

"Rosen?" she asked the nearest officer. He pointed
to a harassed-looking female Judge nearby, who was
issuing orders on the radio from the back of a pat-wagon.
Anderson strode over to her.

"I'm Anderson," she told her. "What's the situation?"

Rosen looked at her for a moment. Anderson didn't
need to use her telepath abilities to know what she was
thinking. Anderson's reputation – as a troublemaker, as
a maverick, as the best Psi-Judge the Justice Department
had, as the woman who had saved the city from the Dark
Judges several times before – preceded her everywhere she
went within the Department.

"He's inside," Rosen said. "Somewhere in the main

Smokatorium hall levels. He ported in while we were still evacuating the place."

"Casualties?" Anderson asked.

Rosen grimly nodded her head. "Too Gruddamn many, cits and Judges. It would have been a lot worse, though, if your warning hadn't reached us. There's still some cits trapped in there, we think, but we got everyone else out." She paused, looking at Anderson. "We were ordered to wait for your arrival. You're here, so what do we do now?"

She's scared, thought Anderson. She probably hasn't been on the streets more than five years. She must be good to have made it to Tac Watch Commander this early in her career, but she's too young to have been with the Department during Necropolis. She's never met the Dark Judges before, all she knows about them are the bogey man stories she's probably heard about them at the Academy – and now she's scared about facing the reality behind those stories.

"Just secure the area while I go in and get him," Anderson told her.

"On your own?" Rosen asked, doubtfully.

Anderson knew exactly what Rosen was thinking. There were now several dozen Judges on the scene. Leaving aside those needed for crowd control duty, that still left more than enough to provide Anderson with all the back-up she would ever need.

"If you give him the space to use that flame weapon of his, Fire's the most lethal of all the Dark Judges," Anderson told her. "He can kill fifty of us just as easily as one with that thing. No point losing any more people than we have to. Besides, I've handled all four of these creeps before. One of them on his own shouldn't be too much trouble."

The last comment was said with half a smile. Anderson looked around. "Now all I need to do is find a gun to use."

At Rosen's signal, a Tek-Judge handed her a Lawgiver. "Straight from Tek-Div central armoury, already programmed to your palm-print. It arrived just before you did."

Anderson smiled and took the weapon, testing its feel and weight. It gave a series of coded bleeps, its built-in micro-computer acknowledging her palm-print signature and signalling that it was now in the hands of its rightful owner. She checked the ammo counter, seeing that it was already fully loaded. She had a feeling she was going to need every one of those shots, and all the other ones in the spare magazines she was now cramming into her belt pouches.

"You heard about what happened at the Academy of Law?" asked Rosen.

Anderson nodded. The news had reached her while she was still en route aboard the H-wagon. Four Dark Judges individually on the loose, and now four Psi-cadets taken, not to mention the massacre of the rest of their class. The problems just kept multiplying.

The snatching of the four cadets was a new and worrying tactic. The Dark Judges didn't take prisoners or hostages, not before now; the only thing they were interested in was spreading death to every living thing that came into contact with them. So what did they need the cadets for, and why specifically Psi-cadets?

With a heavy feeling of foreboding, Anderson guessed she would probably find out the answer soon enough. Assuming she survived the coming encounter with Fire.

She hefted her Lawgiver and looked at Rosen. "Okay, I'm ready."

PEOPLE WERE ALWAYS jealous that he had a real, honest-to-grud, genuine job, Ernesto Kopinski knew. He wasn't so sure, though. Of course, it was a real job, not some airy-fairy pretend kind of job like that dumb jerk of a brother-in-law of his had.

Standing around all day pretending to be a shop dummy, what kind of a job was that for a grown man? Ernesto's job was different. It required skill, application, dedication, not to mention several tedious days of introductory training. It served a useful purpose, to the city and his fellow citizens, and, most importantly of all, it couldn't be done just as well by an inanimate object, unlike the so-called job that dumb jerk of a brother-in-law of his had.

Which still didn't mean that it didn't suck.

He crawled forward through the low-roofed tubeway, his thick armoured boots splashing through the bubbling acidic gruel that swirled around his ankles. More of the same kind of gruesome organic gunge dripped from the leaking pipes overhead, splattering on the acid-proof material of his protective hood and overalls. The pressure tanks on his back hissed and gurgled, and he adjusted the pressure gauge on the barrel of his sprayer gun accordingly. His task was to crawl around down here all day, clearing blockages in the run-off pipes and sluiceways leading out from the main fat-rendering tanks overhead. Strictly speaking, it was really a job best performed by maintenance droids, but the dripping acids and metal-corroding fumes made that an expensive proposition and so, bearing in mind Mega-City unemployment was still running at over eight-seven per cent, it was far cheaper and easier to use human workers.

The business of Resyk was death. Or, more specifically, the breaking down and recycling of human organic material as the corpses of dead cits were delivered to Resyk from all over the city. Once here, they were reduced to their most useful base constituents for later use in a bewilderingly large array of commercial products and substances. Resyk ran day and night, and only the very richest citizens who could afford interment in a private cemetery – or, for the truly rich and dying, a place in cryo-facilities such as Forever Towers – could avoid that final trip along the Resyk corpse disassembly conveyor belts. "We use everything except the soul!" was the proud boast of Resyk management, and there was a steady belief amongst Mega-citizens that the scientists in Resyk R&D were working on ways to remedy even that little oversight.

None of this, however, was at the forefront of Ernesto Kopinski's thoughts right at this moment. All he wanted to do was clear this new blockage, finish his shift and get the drokk out of here with the minimum of acid burns or inhaling of too many of the toxic fumes.

"Ray? Billy?" he called out, thinking he could see two forms in the drainage chamber ahead of him. Ray and Billy were supposed to be working this area on this shift, and the blockage they had been sent to clear was still there, causing an overflow that was now threatening to back up all the way to the bile pumps.

Gruddamnit, if he found out that they had been slacking off again, sneaking off down to the illegal card games run by one of the conveyor belt's assistant foremen in the maintenance sub-bay next to the bone-grinders, then there was gonna be trouble...

He stepped into the drainage chamber, seeing the two figures lying there in the swirling, acidic chem-fluids. Working at Resyk, you got used to the sight of corpses real fast, and Ernesto had no hesitation in deciding that both Ray and Billy were as dead as you could get. They could only have been dead for a short while, though, otherwise they would already have started dissolving into the bubbling tox-brew they were lying in. Ernesto had seen a lot of corpses, but he had never seen two like these, especially with what he could only describe as frozen looks of horror on their faces.

He was just reaching for his radio headset to report on what he had just found, when he heard splashing sounds from the sluice-duct to his right and looked round to see the silhouette figure of a Judge coming towards him. Sure, it was a real thin-looking kind of Judge, wearing some kind of extra funky looking uniform, but Ernesto knew there were all kinds of Judges with all kinds of different uniforms, and so he didn't see anything to get worried about – not until the thing he had thought was a Judge stepped out into the dim light of the chamber and reached out towards him with something that was more like a ghoul-claw than a human hand.

"Greetingsss, sssinner," it hissed. "Rejoiccce. Judgement is here."

DREDD WAS STILL in the air, aboard his H-wagon, when the news broke.

"Dredd – Control. Got a query for you from the clean-up crew at the Icarus lab location. You sure about call on the Icarus stiff? The meat-wagon crews say there's no sign of the body."

"That's impossible, Control," Dredd snarled into the radio mic. "I put six Lawgiver slugs into him, every one a kill shot. The only place that creep was going was Resyk. Tell them to check again and–"

"Hold it, Dredd," the voice of Control abruptly cut in. "Something coming in over the radio net now. Reports coming in about a possible Death sighting... Wait, that's confirmed! We've got a positive lock on Death's position."

"Where?" Dredd's voice, instantly commanding.

"Only half a sector away from your current position, Dredd. He's at Resyk, and he's killing every living thing in the place."

The H-wagon pilot must have been monitoring the conversation, because the vehicle was already swerving round in an abrupt change of course, accelerating off towards Resyk.

"Wilco, Control. I'm on my way. Dredd out."

BEING DEAD WASN'T nearly as dramatic as one might have imagined, Icarus had decided. For a start, he still had consciousness, although he wasn't sure how much that was to do with the retrovirus which was now steadily transforming his recently dead body. The seat of his consciousness was still tied to that body, and he was aware of his surroundings and what was happening around him, but the sights and sounds were oddly dimmed, almost as if he were experiencing them all in a strangely detached, fugue-like state. He knew he was still within his body, but he had no sense of physical existence, and any kind of sensation of pain or bodily awareness was completely absent. Which was probably just as well, he decided, considering the six Lawgiver bullets which had torn his insides apart.

As far as he could tell, he was somewhere in the Undercity, carried there by the last few vampires which had remained in hiding in his lab during the confrontation with Dredd. He had no idea where they were taking him, or why. To be honest, he wished he could communicate with them in some way. On the other hand, even if he had been able to, he wasn't sure they would take any notice of his commands any longer. The way they were moving, the way they seemed to work together in perfect accord without speaking, he got the distinct impression they were acting under the direction of some outside force.

His creations were no longer his to command. For the first time since he had taken his first steps on the long road to this point, Icarus began to feel a vague uneasiness about his presumed pact with the things he had set free from Nixon Pen.

Meanwhile, while he dwelled on what Dredd had told him about the wisdom of making deals with the Dark Judges, his former servants continued on their mysterious journey, carrying him deeper and deeper down into the darkness of the Undercity beneath Mega-City One.

GIANT STILL WOKE up sometimes at night in his dorm cubicle at the Grand Hall of Justice, sweaty and panicked from nightmares about his first encounter with Judge Mortis. The experience had been a defining one for him. And almost a fatal one too, he grimly remembered. Mortis had kept right on coming at them, as he and the others had pumped round after round of Lawgiver fire into the Dark Judge's rotted, ossified body. Even after a decapitating Hi-Ex round, the

Dark Judge had simply picked itself up again and reattached its head to its body before continuing the pursuit.

Mortis's touch was literally death, and Giant could still remember the putrefying stench that had filled the air as he watched the flesh rot away in mere seconds from the body of one of Mortis's victims. The memory, together with the fear of those hands ever bestowing the same deadly touch on his own flesh, had stayed with Giant a long time. He had been a cadet back then, of course, not one of the rising stars of the Justice Department and Dredd's chosen right-hand man, but some things you don't forget. Especially in your nightmares.

And now here he was, ten years later and about to confront the source of those nightmares again.

He was leading a squad of Judges down the corridors of Clooney Memorial Hospital. So far, it hadn't been difficult to work out which direction Mortis had taken. Like Dredd said, all you had to do with the Dark Judges was follow the trail of corpses.

Mortis hadn't been here long – it was less than twenty minutes since the alert had gone out and Giant had jumped aboard an H-wagon and maybe broken the Department's aerial speed record to get here – but, by Grud, Mortis had been busy in that short time. He had been going from one ward to another, slaughtering every living soul he found, and the rooms and corridors of the place were choked with corpses and filled with that same awful and familiar reek of decay. Not even the droids had been spared, because Mortis's touch affected more than just flesh. Giant had already passed the rusted and corrosion-pitted remains of several robo-docs.

They were in the isolation ward now, and there were screams coming from further up the corridor. Mortis had been busy here too, going from room to room dispensing his version of justice, the occasional locked or sealed door proving no barrier to his material-corrupting touch.

Grubb's Disease. Rad-sickness. Creeping Buboes. 2T(FRU)T. The oddities of twenty-second century life threw up a bewildering variety of new and dangerous diseases, and this was where the sufferers of such contagious ailments were treated. Of all the deadly contagions that had been loose in here, though, Mortis was by far the most lethal.

The corpse of a fattie wearing a hospital smock was blocking the corridor. This one was fresh, the flesh on it still in the process of accelerated rotting, its body looking like a deflating tent as the decaying bulk of its mountainous belly melted away, leaving bare the bones of its massively expanded rib-cage. Giant vaulted over it, homing in on the continued sounds of screams from just up ahead. They were close now.

"No, please! I-I'm sick!" came a voice from up ahead. "I got Super-Duper Creeping Buboes, or something real bad like that. You... you don't wanna touch me or you'll catch it too, I guarantee!"

"Life itself is a sickness, sinner," snickered the unearthly voice of the Dark Judge. "Death is the only sure cure."

Giant rounded the corner, seeing a terrified cit in a patient's smock in Mortis's grip. The cit was screaming, Mortis's horrific decay touch already going to work on him. Too late to save this poor creep, thought Giant, bringing his Lawgiver up to bear.

"Rapid fire," he ordered his squad. "Blow that bony freak to pieces."

Mortis looked towards them, hissing in irritation, the screaming cit still caught in his lethal grasp. In one movement he turned and hurled the cit at them, using him as a human shield, throwing him into the full fury of the Judges' weapons fire.

If the cit wasn't dead already from the effects of Mortis's touch, then he surely was now, as the hail of Lawgiver bullets struck him, tearing apart his decay softened, putrefying body and spraying Giant and his squad with the leftovers.

If Giant had somehow ever forgotten how deceptively fast the Dark Judges could move when they wanted to, he got a sudden reminder now. Mortis was in amongst them in the blink of an eye, cackling in malignant glee as he went about the business of bringing judgement to the Judges.

Furio, a ten-year veteran who had been Giant's second-in-command, was the first to die, collapsing in a rotted heap as one of Mortis's claws punched right through him. Willot, whom Giant had first met when he had been briefly posted to Sector House 301 to help Dredd in his mission to clean up the city's most crime-ridden sector, was next to go. Screaming in agony as tumours and lesions spread in seconds through his body, Willot tumbled backwards, thrashing and writhing, knocking Giant to the floor.

In the time it took Giant to kick Willot's disease-bloated corpse away from him and realise that he had lost his Lawgiver in the fall, Mortis had already killed Judges Powers, Hiassen and Goldman. That left only Giant to be judged.

Mortis loomed over him, reaching down towards him. Giant stared into the empty sockets of Mortis's skull head, feeling the tug of the powerful psychic spell the Dark Judges were capable of casting over their victims.

"Come, sinner, why try to resist? Fighting me is useless. You cannot escape your fate."

Mortis's hand descended towards Giant's face. The Judge's own hand snatched down, finding and drawing his boot knife in one smooth motion.

"Heard it before, freak. It might have had more effect ten years ago, when I was still a frightened kid – but not now."

Giant's hand came up to meet Mortis's, the knife he was holding stabbing hilt-deep through the centre of Mortis's outstretched palm, stopping the Dark Judge's taloned fingers just centimetres away from Giant's face.

Mortis hissed in anger. His powers of decay were already going to work on the blade piercing his unnatural flesh, and the metal of the knife blade was quickly starting to crack and erode away in rusted flakes. Giant had only delayed Mortis for a few seconds, but those few seconds were all the defiant Judge needed.

Giant brought his feet back and lashed out with both legs, catching Mortis square in the chest with two Judge boots, propelling him backwards. Mortis crashed into the wall opposite with a dry, bony rattling sound, but recovered almost immediately and pulled himself up again. Giant rolled, grabbing his fallen Lawgiver and aiming it at the Dark Judge as Mortis advanced upon him again.

"We've met before, freak," he reminded him. "Remember this?"

The Hi-Ex shell tore Mortis's head off. Whatever he was made of, however light and frail his leathery, mummified skin and wasted, brittle bones appeared to be, the Dark Judge was a lot tougher than he looked. Anything else would have been blown to shreds by the same shot.

As it was, it was still enough to stop him in his tracks as he bent to pick up the skull and reattach it to the snapped-off, bony stump of his neck. Giant had seen this trick before. What was new, though, was that he found out Mortis could still speak even with his head separated from his body.

"Foolish mortal," rasped the voice from the bodiless skull. "When will you learn? You cannot kill that which does not live…"

"Tell it to someone who gives a drokk," replied Giant, firing a brace of Incendiaries into the body of Mortis.

Even as the hungry flames took hold of him, Mortis still took the time to wait for his head to reattach itself. Meanwhile, up until now, Giant had been acting on instinct, just trying to survive the encounter moment to moment. Now, seeing the open doorway to the place directly behind where Mortis was standing, he suddenly saw a way to bring this whole thing to an end.

He charged forward towards Mortis, even as the Dark Judge staggered forward towards him. The fiend was wreathed in flames, a fact which would soon force him to abandon his current body, but not before he took one last sinner with him, it seemed. Even after his body had been destroyed by the flames, Mortis's spirit would still survive, roaming the city until it found another host form to occupy and possess. If that happened, Mortis would rise again, free to continue the same kind of carnage that had occurred here and elsewhere.

Giant wasn't about to let that come to pass.

He shoulder-charged straight into Mortis, turning his face aside and holding his breath to avoid scorching his lungs with super-heated air from the flames that were now all over Mortis. It was like charging into a pillar of solid granite. A pillar of solid granite that had been set blazing alight. A lancing shot of agony told Giant he had probably just dislocated his shoulder and maybe cracked his collar bone into the bargain. Numerous points of growing pain told him he was on fire down most of that same side. Giant could already hear the sirens of the med-wagon that would probably soon be rushing him to the nearest Sector House med-bay.

Even so, what he had intended to do still worked. Mortis reeled backwards and through the open doorway behind him. Giant slammed a fist into the door-seal switch, not stopping to beat out the flames that were eating into the material of his armour and bodysuit until he was sure the door had slid securely shut.

He stared through the transparent material of the door, watching Mortis burn. Most of the Dark Judge's clothing and unnatural flesh had burned away now, leaving little more than a skeleton covered in flame. Still, he wasn't ready to die yet and staggered forward, pressing one burning, skeletal hand against the transparent wall of the room he was in. His rattling hiss of fury increased sharply in volume as the material of the wall stubbornly refused to yield to his decaying touch.

"Reinforced glasteel, freak. Supposed to be able to last for centuries, maybe even longer. Maybe if you tried long enough you could rot through it, but I don't think you've got the time to do that, have you?"

Mortis's body was already starting to collapse, too much of it eaten away by the flames to allow him to sustain it any longer. He abandoned it with a final, whistling shriek, his spirit flowing out of it as it crumpled to the ground to form a small pyre of burning bones.

Mortis's spirit-form prowled round the borders of the room, restlessly seeking a way out, hurling itself against various portions of the floor, ceiling and thick glasteel walls. Giant laughed at its growing fury.

"Oh yeah, and it's airtight too, didn't I tell you that? You're in a quarantine cube. They use them to keep suspected contagious disease cases in isolation until they know what they're dealing with. That's what you are, freak: a disease. And now I've got you where you belong, in quarantine."

Watching the furious contortions the thing behind the glasteel walls was now going through as it relentlessly and futilely sought an escape from its new prison, Giant reached for his radio.

"Control – Giant. I need a Psi-Judge squad to Clooney Memorial. I've got Mortis trapped here in spook form. Tell them there's no rush, I don't think he's going anywhere else in a hurry right now."

One down, three to go, thought Giant. He wondered how Dredd and Anderson were doing with their own super-creep Dark Judge freaks.

As ANOTHER BLAST of supernatural fire blazed out towards her, Anderson dived for cover. She hoped Dredd and Giant were doing better than her.

She rolled past the shrunken and flame-blackened corpses of another row of smokers and popped up out of cover to snap off another few Lawgiver shots at Fire. Not that it would do any good, she reminded herself.

Every time she encountered the Dark Judges, they always brought something new to deal with, some new, never-revealed-before ability or power they could use to counter the Judges' best efforts to track them down and destroy them. In the past, it had been teleporters, psychic possession, mind control, the ability to body-hop when their own bodies were destroyed and then to rise up again in the flesh of the next nearest corpse. This time, though, Fire had found a brand new trick of his own and, by Grud, was it a doozie.

He could use the unnatural heat of the supernatural flames which permanently surrounded him to vaporise bullets before they could strike him. Incendiaries were useless against this particular Dark Judge, of course. Falling back on what had worked against him before, Anderson had fired off several rounds of Hi-Ex shells as soon as she caught sight of him within the main Smokatorium hall – only to see them vaporised as they struck the shimmering heat barrier around him. Every Standard Execution round she had fired since had gone the same way, either vaporised instantly or ineffectually striking Fire in the form of little more than a thin spray of molten droplets. Now, as the Dark Judge hunted her through the smog-filled, corpse-strewn interior of the Smokatorium, Anderson began to suspect she was in serious trouble.

She had borrowed a helmet from one of the Judges outside. Its respirator and visor provided some protection from the poisonous, choking fumes of nicotine and tar that surrounded her, but her eyes still stung from the effects of the thick cigarette smoke that hung heavy in the air of the place. Anderson always knew she would probably die in the line of duty one day, most likely at the hands of a major-league perp like one of the Dark Judges. Except she had figured it would probably be Death that would do the honours, not Fire. And she had always imagined her death as taking place somewhere a lot more glamorous than a city Smokatorium.

There were several Smokatoriums in the city, being the only places in Mega-City One where citizens were legally allowed to smoke. Anderson could never see the attraction in the filthy habit; there were enough unpleasant and hazardous things that could happen to you in this city without deliberately poisoning your body with the after-effects of inhaling burning tobacco. The circumstances in a Smokatorium, where smokers sat in rows wearing protective suits and smoking tobacco products through filter mouthpieces fitted into the air-sealed helmets they wore, made the whole thing look even less attractive than it already was, but the Smokatoriums were still very popular. Dedicated and die-hard smokers still flocked to them to smoke everything from the finest, hand-rolled cigars from the Cuban Wastes to the cheapest brands of Brit-Cit cigarettes. Only in a Smokatorium was smoking legal, and the money generated in the hefty smoking taxes imposed on everyone using them was always a welcome addition to the city's financial coffers.

Now the lifeless smokers sat in rows where they had died. With visibility poor due to the thick, choking cigarette smoke that filled the place, and with all sound muffled by the head-enclosing helmets worn by all smokers, many of them had probably never even known what had hit them as Fire stalked from room to room, incinerating everyone he found in all of them with fiery blasts from his trident weapon.

Justice Department med-programs and health education vidverts always stressed that smoking killed. Now the proof of that was here in abundance in the Churchill.

"Good to see you again, Anderson," cackled Fire. "Looking for a light?"

Anderson dodged again, narrowly avoiding another fire blast that struck the wall behind her, setting it instantly ablaze.

There were now numerous blazes burning throughout the building, some of them spreading rapidly, all of them started by the Dark Judge's deadly trail of destruction through the place. Idly, Anderson wondered if that meant she was still going to burn to death even if she managed to defeat Fire, and then decided that she would probably still be long dead by the time there was any danger of the building burning to the ground.

Even more idly, she wondered why the building's fire control systems hadn't kicked in by now. After all, Smokatoriums were just one big fire hazard, so surely there must be...

Fwooosh!

She barely moved in time, as the hungry tongues of supernatural fire licked out towards her. She rolled away from them, feeling the flames caressing her back and legs, imagining her skin starting to blister even under the heat-retardant material of her uniform.

She sprang back up and ran, snapping off several Heatseekers at the Dark Judge, knowing that they would have no difficulty in locking on to him, just as she knew that they would probably be almost completely useless against him.

Fire laughed as the tiny, buzzing heat-seeking bullet missiles vaporised harmlessly in the heat-shimmering air in front of his flaming skull face. His laughter was dry and crackling, like the sound of hungry licks of flames.

"Anderson, always so fast and so fortunate. But how long can you stay that way? You have to remain fortunate all the time. I only have to get fortunate once."

He stalked forwards across the wide space towards her, swishing his trident impatiently in front of him, tracing patterns of fire in the air.

He's been toying with me, Anderson realised, but now the game was coming to an end and Fire was clearly intent on closing in for the kill. Anderson instinctively backed off away from him, realising with a sick feeling that she was being herded into a corner with no other means of escape.

Desperately, she looked around her, looking for a way up. All the exits were behind Fire, as was a window looking into a small control room. No way out that way, since the only way out of the control room was a locked door leading back into the Smokatorium hall.

And yet... there was something about that small room that drew Anderson's attention back to it again.

A control room, but a control room for what?

Something – a hunch or intuition – told her to glimpse upwards towards the roof of the high-ceilinged chamber. As soon as she did, she knew she had found a way to defeat Fire, and she was moving even before she had consciously started to formulate the plan that was about to save her life and put paid to at least one of the Dark Judges.

Fire brandished his trident and a column of flame leapt from it, chasing after Anderson as she ran. Heat splashed against the wall behind her, melting the surface of the wall's material, leaving a burning map of the direction of Anderson's sprint as it chased after her along the wall, always lagging a few precious moments behind her.

Anderson fired off a series of shots. Fire laughed in malign satisfaction at what he thought was a sign of growing panic in the mind of the Psi-Judge, since none of the shots came anywhere near him. In fact, Anderson had hit absolutely everything she had been aiming at.

The first few shots shattered the viewing window of the control room, making things a lot easier for Anderson for the moment when she would hurl herself through it a few seconds later. The last shot – a Rubber Ricochet – hit the tiny panel set into the wall on the far side of the chamber, shattering the glass panel over it and hitting the large red emergency switch beneath the glass.

Not bad shooting, Cass, Anderson congratulated herself as she leapt through the smashed control room window and tumbled across the console inside, hearing the Smokatorium's sprinkler mechanism finally kick in in response to her activation of the building's fire control systems.

Water gushed down, smothering the fires here and elsewhere throughout the building. Judge Fire walked through the downpour, giving off a cloud of hissing steam as the falling droplets of water noisily vaporised as soon as they came into contact with the flames of his body. The flames he produced did seem noticeably diminished by the effects of the sprinkler downpour, but they were supernatural in origin, and Anderson doubted that anything could completely douse them as long as Fire's spirit remained in possession of its host body.

Fire laughed as he stalked closer. "Foolish Anderson, did you really think this would have any effect at all?"

Anderson waited before replying, carefully measuring Fire's progress towards her. She was trapped inside the control room, with nowhere inside it to take cover. One blast from Fire's trident weapon would obliterate everything inside the small room. If Anderson had misjudged anything at all, she knew she probably only had a few seconds to live.

"No, creep," she answered, grabbing hold of the big lever handle on the control console in front of her. "I did it so you wouldn't guess that I was really planning to do this."

She hauled on the lever, her action instantly rewarded by the ominous sound from the chamber roof of something large and heavy powering up. Fire hesitated and then looked up. Anderson didn't know if Dark Judges could actually visibly express panic and alarm, but she supposed that this must be what she was seeing now, as Fire saw what was happening up there in the chamber roof.

Each day after it closed, the Smokatorium underwent a rigorous cleaning process, a giant rotary fan in the ceiling of the main chamber sucking the nicotine-choked air out of the entire building and into a series of rooftop filters where it was cleansed and purified of all traces of tobacco taint before being safely expelled out into the general atmosphere of the city. That was what the huge fan-blades now spinning with increasing speed up there in the chamber roof were usually used for. Now Anderson had them in mind for a completely different purpose entirely.

As far as she could see, as the air began to swirl round the chamber in a rapidly growing vortex, Fire was going to immediately do either one of two things. One of them still meant almost immediate certain death for Anderson.

Instead, he did the other, reaching down to the teleporter device on his belt instead of aiming his trident and blasting Anderson to oblivion. His burning fingers reached out to activate the device, but Anderson was already firing her Lawgiver. She had flicked the shell selector to Armour Piercing, hoping that the solid, diamond-hard titanium bullet would have more chance of making it through the slightly diminished hazard of Fire's heat aura. It was a gamble, but a calculated one.

The bullet hit and shattered the teleporter device before the Dark Judge could activate it. His screaming hiss of anger was lost amidst the growing hurricane roar of the effects of the giant fan mechanism overhead. Fire vengefully raised his trident to send a scouring, fiery blast into the control room, but it was already too late. The weapon was pulled from his hand by the force of the wind vortex that now filled the chamber and went flying upwards towards the spinning blades. A second or two later, Fire followed it, sucked up into the fan's hungry mouth along with all the other loose material in the chamber. Corpses, charred fragments of corpses, the litter of ash and hundreds of cigarette ends: all of it went tumbling upwards into the blades. The last Anderson heard of Judge Fire was his unholy shriek of rage as his body passed through the fan rotors and was dashed to pieces by the spinning blades.

Wedging herself beneath the console to prevent herself suffering a similar fate, she shouted into her helmet radio, praying that the Justice Department units waiting outside could hear her voice over the roar of the vortex blasting around the chamber.

"It's Anderson. I've destroyed Fire's body, but his spirit is still going to escape. It's going to be coming out the air vents on the Smokatorium roof any second. If there's any H-wagons in the vicinity, get them there pronto. Tell the pilots to use their underside airlocks. Evacuate the air from the airlock then hover over the vents and pop the airlock hatch as soon as Fire comes out. The sudden vacuum should suck him right in. It worked before, during Necropolis. Let's see if it works again."

She crawled out from under the console, anchoring herself securely to it as she disengaged the fan rotor control. The tornado force wind died away almost instantly. A few seconds later, Anderson gratefully received the message she had been waiting for over her helmet radio.

"That's a roj, Anderson. Manta-tank Four reports it's got Fire in the bag. Word's just come through that Giant has got Mortis under containment too, over at Clooney Memorial."

Two down, two to go. Anderson found herself almost giving a silent prayer of thanks. Cruel and capricious, contrary and whimsical though they may be, the gods of Mega-City One were being relatively charitable today. As bad as the carnage had been so far, it could still have been a lot worse if all four Dark Judges remained on the loose.

"Any word yet on the other two?"

"Death's turned up at Resyk. Dredd's there now."

Resyk was five sectors away. Anderson knew that, even if she left now on a fast-travelling H-wagon, she would still get there too late to be of any help there. Dredd would have to handle Death without her, but if anyone could deal with the most dangerous and unpredictable of the Dark Judges, it would be Joe Dredd.

"Copy. Any sign of Creep Number Four?"

"Judge Fear? Nothing so far, not since he hit the Academy of Law. Looks like he's gone completely to ground."

INDEED HE HAD, quite literally.

Fear was down there in the darkness beneath the city, preparing the way for what was to come next. Through the psychic links that connected all four Dark Judges, he already knew of the defeat of at least two of his brethren, but it was only a temporary setback, at worst. Soon his work here would be complete. Then the power of the Dark Judges would be multiplied many times over, and they would at last be able to bring justice to this city and then the sinful, life-filled world beyond.

He had gathered others down here in the darkness to aid him. Some were their would-be servants from the city above, the humans and the transformed Hungry Ones, who all foolishly believed that they would be joining Fear and his brethren in the dark new world they would soon be creating. Others were the simple, debased things that lived down here in the Under-Place already. Fear had found their primitive minds surprisingly and pleasingly easy to control. Seized by terror, possessed by a mind-numbing dread of the Dark Judge, they made useful enough slaves for the moment, but, like all of the Dark Judges' other erstwhile servants, they would be judged along with all the others when the time came.

Fear watched as his servants and slaves hauled the final plinth into position, bringing it into carefully judged alignment with the others. Nearby, the Hungry Ones held the moaning, terrified figures of the four kidnapped Psi-cadets. The vampires growled softly to themselves in irritation, their blood thirst held in check only by the all-powerful command of the Dark Judge.

There was the other prize too, although Fear barely recognised it as being the same human who had served them so faithfully in engineering their escape from their prison. Fear almost cackled aloud to himself at the idea that this wretched thing had thought itself worthy of being elevated to the same status as he and his brethren. The foolish mortal's desire for life-beyond-death was motivated purely by a terror of dying. Yet how could dying be something to be avoided, when death was the natural state to which all living things should be despatched as quickly as possible?

Still, thought Fear, there were interesting possibilities in this new form their servant had created for himself. These human forms he and his brethren inhabited, even when strengthened by the power of the Dark Judges' psychic possession, had too often proven to be too fallible for the great work at hand.

Perhaps, he mused, they would find a use for the corpse when the portal was opened and the business of judging this world began in true earnest.

Fourteen

IF THE BUSINESS of Resyk was death, as the facility's slogan proudly proclaimed, then it was certainly a claim that Judge Death had taken seriously. By Dredd's estimation, by the time he and the other Judges arrived there, the undead creep had already slaughtered his way through most of the staff of the entire day shift, as well as the crews of several meat-wagons making deliveries to the place, and also four separate and well-attended funeral parties there to see their loved ones off on their final journey along the Resyk conveyor belt.

Dredd and the others had burst in on the fourth of these funeral parties, a mass event for sixteen victims of the recent Minogue Sisters conflict, just as Death was consoling one grieving window in his own unique way.

"No need to thank me, sinner," he hissed, laughing as he thrust one skeletal hand into her chest and squeezed her heart dry. "You'll be with him again soon enough."

Dredd caught his old foe's attention with three Lawgiver rounds through the head and chest. His fourth shot shattered the teleporter device hanging from Death's belt, destroying it with just the same intent as Anderson's earlier ploy.

"Now you're going nowhere, creep, except back to the place you escaped from," Dredd told him.

Death hissed angrily, discarding the lifeless corpse still held firm in his grip. Anderson had already found out that the Dark Judges were again exhibiting some unnerving new abilities this time around. Now Death was about to prove that Anderson's experience with Fire was no fluke. At a single gesture from Death, the lids flew off the row of coffins against the far wall where the corpses would be loaded down onto the conveyor belt below, and the bullet-riddled bodies of the sixteen block war combatants climbed out to attack the nearest living things around them.

"Just a taste of what is in store soon enough for you all, sinners!" Death hissed as the reanimated corpses hungrily charged at the terrified mourners.

Dredd didn't know how far Death's newfound zombie-making abilities extended, but the tactic had already achieved its immediate purpose. While the attention of Dredd and the other Judges was on the zombies, Death had already made his escape from the room.

"Teague and Goddard – with me!" Dredd shouted to the two Judges nearest him. "The rest of you – take care of the situation here!"

Dredd was already running through the door, pursuing Death along the catwalk that ran along the length of the huge processing hall, following the conveyor belt below and the corpses stacked up on it on their progress towards the Resyk grinders. Teague and Goddard came running along behind Dredd, both of them good back-up men whom Dredd knew he could depend on against a perp as dangerous as Death. All three Judges snapped off shots at Death. Lawgiver rounds punched into the Dark Judge's lifeless body, doing little to no real damage but keeping the pressure up on the fleeing figure.

Suddenly and without any warning, Death turned and went on the offensive. He reached out and, with one skeletal hand, snapped off a two-metre length of steel tubing from the guard rail of the walkway. The amount of force needed to do this was impressive, showing the supernatural strength hidden within the Dark Judge's deceptively emaciated and cadaverous frame. What Death did next was even more impressive.

He hurled the steel pole like a javelin, sending it hurtling towards his pursuers. Dredd ducked, barely avoiding the missile as it flew past him at near bullet-like speed. Judge Teague, following in close behind, wasn't so fortunate or agile. The pole struck him full in the chest, impaling itself through him, and he collapsed to the ground with almost a metre of blood-slicked metal jutting out of his back.

His partner Goddard grabbed at him before his body could slip under the guard rail and fall onto the conveyor belt below.

"Call for med-assistance and stay here with him until it arrives," Dredd ordered grimly, knowing that Death had just further successfully whittled down the odds against him, promising himself that Teague was going to be the very last of Death's victims today.

Time to bring this chase to an end, decided Dredd, firing off a brace of Hi-Ex shells at the fleeing figure in front of him. Death eluded all of them, as Dredd suspected he would, but the Dark Judge hadn't been his primary intended target.

The shells exploded into the grillwork of the walkway in front of Death, blowing it apart. Suddenly there was nothing supporting that end of this section of the walkway, and so, with a loud groan of rending metal, it collapsed from beneath Death's feet.

The Dark Judge plummeted, spilling onto the Resyk conveyor belt. A second or two later, Dredd landed on the same belt, about twenty metres behind him, having jumped from the walkway to continue the chase.

Death rose to his feet, snarling: "Fool! You still think you can defeat me?"

"Willing to give it my best shot, creep," countered Dredd, raising his Lawgiver.

Before he could fire, through, he felt something scrabbling against the material of his Judge boot. Looking down, he saw one of the corpses there hungrily trying to gnaw its way through the toe of his boot. A Standard Execution round through the crown of the corpse's skull put paid to that idea, but now more reanimated cadavers were rising up all around Dredd on the conveyor belt.

More proof of Death's newfound zombie-making ability. They came at Dredd, snarling and clawing, all of them hissing at him in an eerily familiar voice.

"Fool! You cannot stop me now!" gloated one of them, just before Dredd blew its head off with a burst of Lawgiver fire.

"Give up, you have already lost!" mocked another, as a kick from Dredd sent it flying off the conveyor belt and into the giant metal rollers that kept the whole mechanism churning along.

"Why struggle when the end is inevitable?" suggested another, shrugging off the blows that Dredd pounded into its dead face. "Soon Mega-City One will be judged. Equal justice for all, that is what we will bring."

The corpse collapsed, lifeless, back to the ground as Dredd delivered a blow powerful enough to drive its nose bone back into the decayed mush of its brain. For every zombie that fell, though, at least another one rose up to take its place. They threw themselves at Dredd remorselessly, clawing and biting at him, tearing away shreds of both his uniform and the skin underneath as they tried to drag the Judge down by sheer weight of numbers.

Dredd shot, punched and bludgeoned his way through all of them, showing the same indomitable, die-hard determination that had kept both him and his city alive so many times before.

Suddenly, there were no more zombies in front of him. Only Death himself awaited, and Dredd barely had time to react as the leader of the Dark Judges lunged at him. Dredd knocked aside the clawed hand that might otherwise have squeezed the life out of his heart. The important thing, he knew, was to keep Death's hands away from him, and for this he brought his daystick into play, weaving it in the air between him and his old foe, using its weighted tip to parry away any of Death's sudden, darting attacks.

Equally important, Dredd knew, was to keep Death distracted, so that he didn't realise what was happening behind him, and just how close they were getting to the end of the conveyor belt.

Dredd had rarely been this close to his ancient enemy, and the stench from Death's lifeless, decaying flesh was almost overpowering. The most dangerous of all the Dark Judges literally reeked of evil and death, souring the air around him, tainting everything that came into contact with him.

Death lunged forward again. Dredd hit him a daystick blow to the side of neck that would have killed anything living, but this time Death's attack was in deadly earnest, and he didn't retreat back again. His long, thin fingers darted out, sinking through the armour of Dredd's shoulder pad to penetrate through into the flesh beneath. To Dredd, it felt like being stabbed by five burning icicles of frozen venom. His whole right arm blazed with pain and then went completely numb. His Lawgiver dropped from fingers suddenly rendered senseless and he fell to the ground, the numbness creeping slowly into the rest of his body.

Death bore down on him, his other hand poised to push into Dredd's chest to find and close on his heart.

"Hurts, doesn't it?" cackled the Dark Judge, flexing his fingers inside the meat of Dredd's shoulder, exploring the contours of the bones and muscles in there. If he was expecting any cries of pain from Dredd, he was to be disappointed. "Don't worry, though. Your pain and sin will soon be at an end."

Death's other hand hovered over Dredd's heart. He leered down at his old enemy, their faces only centimetres apart. "Any famous last words?"

"Yeah, creep – eat helmet!"

Dredd's head shot up, the armoured crown of his Judge's helmet smashing into Death's grinning visage. Bone shattered, teeth went flying. As viciously brutal head-butts went, it was a move worthy of Mean Machine Angel himself.

Death reeled back, spitting teeth and curses. If his claws hurt as they went into Dredd's flesh, it was little compared to how much they hurt as they were ripped back out again. The entire shoulder and arm and a good part of Dredd's chest were shot through with white-hot needles of pain. The lawman hauled himself to his feet, fighting off the wave of nausea that welled up inside him. He couldn't allow himself to succumb to it, not when Death was still a threat. His gun-hand was useless, so he scooped up his Lawgiver with his left hand instead.

Death came lurching straight back at him. Dredd's Hi-Ex shot caught him square in the chest, blowing him backwards and knocking him to the floor of the conveyor belt.

They were only a few metres from the end of the belt now. After that, there was nothing but the drop into the corpse-grinding machinery. Death was starting to draw himself up again, his chest blown open but the rest of his body otherwise intact. Dredd ran at him, not giving him a chance to decide how to react.

Dredd leapt upwards, grabbing the bottom rung of the overhanging maintenance ladder with his one good arm, swinging both legs out as he did so to catch Death full in the face with the soles of both Judge boots.

"How about it? Any famous last words for me?" asked Dredd, as Death flew backwards over the end of the conveyor belt. Any answer he might have come back with was lost in the whirring thunder of the machinery below, machinery which was designed to render the human form – even one possessed by the spirit of a Dark Judge – down into its most basic constituent elements.

Dredd hauled himself painfully up the ladder, not sure he was going to have the strength to make it to the top. From long experience, he knew he was going to be spending a lot of recuperation time in a speedheal machine after this.

"Dredd!"

Goddard's voice. Dredd gratefully grabbed the hand wearing a Judge glove reaching down towards him. A few seconds later, he was being pulled back up to the safety of the overhead catwalk.

"Teague?" he asked.

"The Meds have got him. They say he should pull through. Where's Death?"

Dredd glanced down into the churning machinery below. "He got recycled."

He activated his helmet radio. "Anderson – Dredd. Scratch Death off the list, at least for the moment."

"Copy that, Dredd. I got a sudden psi-flash when he hit the grinders. Trust me, you really don't want to know what his last words actually were, but you can be sure they were about you."

Two Med-Judges came running up, concern written all over their faces. Dredd waved them away in annoyance. In forty years on the streets, he'd been shot, stabbed, beaten, blown up and burned to within a centimetre of his life almost more times than he could remember. Whatever his injuries were this time, they could wait.

"He's out there in spirit form again. Any idea where he's heading now?" Dredd asked Anderson.

"The Undercity," came the reply. "That's all I could pick up from him before I lost contact again. I think Fear's down there too, with the missing Psi-cadets. I'm picking up a trace of their psi-presence. I'm on my way now to the Gate 38 Undercity entrance. How soon can you meet me there?"

Dredd thought of his injuries. Sensation was gradually returning to the shoulder where Death's fingers had penetrated his flesh. As sensations went, the lancing bolts of pain he was now experiencing there weren't exactly what you would call comforting. Clearly, the smart thing to do would be to get his injuries fully checked out in a Sector House med-bay before he did anything else.

"Meet you there in twenty," he told Anderson.

Fifteen

THE UNDERCITY. THE ruins of Old New York, abandoned and forgotten. A festering blight which Mega-City One's original architects had dealt with by simply building over the top of it, burying the decaying streets in a vast rockcrete shell which served as part of the foundations of the shining future city they erected above it.

The Undercity may have been abandoned, but that did not mean it was uninhabited. Criminals often sought refuge in its sheltering darkness from the prying eyes of the Justice Department. As refuges go, though, the Undercity was one fraught with dangers all of its own, for its derelict buildings and eternally dark alleys were home to mutants, outlawed cults, tribes of troglodyte cannibals and sinister outcasts from the city above.

When Judges could no longer serve on the streets, many chose to take the Long Walk, bringing Law to the lawless regions that bordered Mega-City One. It was often a matter of locker-room debate amongst Street Judges about whether the wild, mutie-inhabited rad-deserts of the Cursed Earth were any more dangerous and challenging as a Long Walk choice of destination than that dismal, sunless place directly beneath the streets they patrolled every day.

Dredd and Anderson had both been in the Undercity before, and its eerie ghost town streets and crumbling, derelict twentieth century buildings and remains of skyscrapers held little that they hadn't encountered before.

"More troggies in front of us," commented Anderson casually, registering the dim shapes moving in the gloom ahead of them, just beyond the furthest fringes of their flashlight beams.

"I see 'em," answered Dredd. "Nothing to get worried about. Light's usually enough to scare them off. If that doesn't work, the sight of a Lawgiver or a Judge badge will do the trick. They know better to mess with us."

Anderson ducked sharply, barely avoiding the axe weapon that was hurled at her from out of the shadows in front of them.

"You were saying?" she asked, bringing her Lawgiver up to bear as the troggies rushed at the two Judges.

They were in the area known as Central Park, having followed what had once been Park Avenue north from where they had entered the Undercity at Gate 38. Anderson didn't know what Central Park had been like back in the days of Old New York, but now it was an overgrown, tangled maze of petrified, leafless trees and weird thorny vegetation that still somehow managed to thrive down here in the absence of natural light. It wasn't the kind of place you chose to enter unless it was strictly necessary. Anderson was tracking Death's trail, following his psychic spoor. The Dark Judge's disembodied spirit had passed this way, and recently too. Which meant Dredd and Anderson had to follow him in there too.

Dredd levelled his M2000 Widowmaker. He was just about to fire – at this range, the gun would wreak carnage amongst the charging troggies – when Anderson suddenly knocked his gun barrel aside.

"Wait, there's another way!" she shouted, changing the shell selector switch on her Lawgiver and firing the gun up into the air.

The flare shell exploded in the darkness overhead, bathing the whole scene in eerie, brilliant luminescence. The troggies, the spectrum of their vision atrophied through generations of life in the lightless depths of the Undercity, screamed as one and turned and fled, their hands shielding their sensitive, light-damaged eyes.

Dredd lowered his gun and looked at Anderson. "Didn't know you had a soft spot for troggies, Anderson. My way would still have been better. At least then they wouldn't have had a chance to regroup and come back for another shot."

"It wasn't their fault, Dredd," explained Anderson. "They're just simple, scared creatures. You were right when you said that normally they would be too afraid of us to attack, but something made them. I sensed it just as they attacked, and it was almost as if they were possessed by their own terror. Their minds were filled with nothing but–"

"Fear?" said Dredd. "With a capital F?"

Anderson nodded gravely. "Looks like Death and Fire weren't the only ones to pick up a few new tricks this time around."

THE TROGGIES TACTIC hadn't worked, so next time the Dark Judges used their other remaining servants. A few minutes further on, as Dredd and Anderson cleared a thicket of petrified trees, they were attacked by what must surely have been the last of the vampires and Church of Death fanatics.

This time around, Anderson wasn't so concerned about preventing a bloodbath.

Volleys of Heatseekers from her and Dredd unerringly sought out and found the warmer human bodies of the cultists amongst the lines of vampires. After that, with the cultists taken care of, the two Judges could both go to town on the remaining undead.

Anderson switched Lawgiver mags, loading one filled with nothing but Hi-Ex and Incendiary shells. Lawgiver special rounds might be expensive, but Anderson didn't think that Accounts Division would be querying the cost of any excessive use of them in this particular firefight.

In the space of a few seconds, three vampires exploded apart under the impact of multiple Hi-Ex rounds, while the same number were transformed into stumbling, screaming mannequins of flame by Incendiary hits. Over on his side of the battle, Dredd was doing plenty to keep up his share of the kill tally. The M2000 kept up a steady rate of fire, obliterating anything that came within five metres of Dredd's position.

Despite the carnage that was being inflicted upon them, however, the bloodsucking freaks just kept throwing themselves forward. They were probably psychically controlled too, Anderson realised, but why were Fear and Death throwing their remaining followers at her and Dredd in such a reckless, suicidal fashion?

A glance at the torch-lit area beyond the scene of the battle quickly told her the answer. She didn't immediately recognise the standing stone structure erected there, but she recognised its purpose, and she could clearly sense the strong psychic vibrations emanating from the shimmering patch of darkness between the pillars of the central stone arch. Even as she watched, she saw a group of figures hurrying towards it. The disembodied spirit of Death was with them, her psi-senses told her, and so were four other distinctive psi-presences.

"Dredd!" she shouted in warning. "They've opened up a gateway to Deadworld! That's where they're taking the Psi-cadets!"

"Cover me!" Dredd shouted, running forward, blowing apart the first vampire trying to stop him. Anderson dropped to one knee, gripped her Lawgiver in two hands and began picking off targets, Hi-Ex blasting anything that looked likely to get close to her fellow Judge.

Dredd, still running, drew his Lawgiver. The M2000 was good enough for the kind of work it was designed for, but he was a Street Judge, and a Lawgiver was his stock in trade. Bullets spat out at him from amongst the standing stones; armed cultists left behind to guard the gateway. Dredd picked them off with ease; all the suicidal determination and crazed religious fanaticism in the world was no substitute for Academy of Law training, where a cadet's marksmanship training began at age five.

The last cultist fell to the ground, and Dredd was in amongst the stones now. He was approaching the gateway when a shape amongst the surrounding darkness detached itself from the shadows and flowed towards him.

Alerted by her senses a scant split-second earlier, Anderson managed to shout out a warning. The shape hissed in anger and hurled something at her. Anderson cried out in pain, and fell to the ground as she felt the mantrap device's jagged metal teeth bite into her leg, penetrating right through to the bone. Dredd spun round, instinctively firing several shots into the shadow shape's central body mass, and then the most mysterious of the Dark Judges was upon him. And, for the second time in his life, Dredd found himself gazing into the face of Fear.

The first time had been almost twenty years ago. He had been a younger man then, of course, completely sure of himself and his abilities, afraid of nothing, free of any of the doubts and fears that came with age.

And now? What was he afraid of now, when he had once taken the Long Walk into the Cursed Earth after losing faith in the justice system he'd served all his life? When he knew that he was no longer irreplaceable, when he knew that the Justice Department had a whole new series of clones sharing the same bloodline as him coming through the Academy?

Death? No. Everyone died, and death had been an ever-constant factor through his life, for as long as he could remember. He did not fear death, he knew.

Failure. That was what Dredd was secretly afraid of now, and that was what he saw there in the terrible black void within Fear's open helm.

He saw his city defeated and destroyed in a thousand different ways. He saw its walls crumble, and the teeming millions of howling, vengeful muties pour through into the city beyond. He saw a city ruled by a hundred different versions of lawlessness, but in all these visions the end result was the same: its citizens, free to do what they wanted, falling upon each other in a murderous display of the very worst aspects of unfettered human nature. He saw times when the place where Mega-City One stood was nothing more than a vast smoking crater or a dead landscape of nuked-out ruins. He saw the city empty and abandoned, its giant towers slowly crumbling to dust, with no clue as to what happened to its vanished inhabitants. He saw his city under occupation by its enemies, its citizens brutalised and enslaved.

He saw all this, and in every vision he knew what he saw had happened because he hadn't been there to stop it. One day, death, old age or bad luck would catch up with him, and then Mega-City would fall.

Fear hissed in satisfied pleasure as he sensed Dredd's worst nightmares bubbling to the surface. At last, he had found something that this most stubborn of sinners was afraid of. It was all Fear needed to push the door open further into Dredd's mind and flood it with sensations of pure, unadulterated terror. In moments, the sinner would be lying dead at Fear's feet, his eyes stretched wide in final horror at the things the Dark Judge had unleashed into his mind, and then Fear's triumph would be complete.

"Yes," the cold, ghostly voice of Fear whispered. "Look deeper. Gaze into the face of Fear and know what true nightmare looks like."

Dredd looked, and for a moment stood on the edge of the precipice. Then he remembered three things, and the shadowy terrors waiting for him down there in that abyss retreated back into the shadows, snarling in cheated anger.

He was Joe Dredd, a Judge of Mega-City One, and he wasn't going to lie down and die as long as his city still needed him.

"Told you once before," growled Dredd, reaching down to his belt pouch. "Maybe you don't remember, so here's a quick reminder...

"Gaze into the fist of Dredd!"

Dredd's fist smashed into the empty helm that was Fear's head. The Dark Judge reeled back, hissing in outrage. A moment later, though, Fear was rising up again, damaged but still intact.

"The years have made you weak, sinner. Now you no longer have the strength to defeat me!"

"Don't bet on it, creep," Dredd told him. "Check your headspace. I left something for you in there."

Dredd hurled himself aside as the frag grenade he had left inside Fear's open helm exploded. The blasted remains of Fear crumbled to the ground, trails of black vapour already starting to seep out of it as Fear's spirit abandoned its destroyed host body.

Dredd didn't waste any time. The suction trap device was in his hand even before the Dark Judge's spirit had finished seeping out of its former body. He threw it, its small anti-grav generator and gyro-stabilisers activating immediately. It hovered above Fear's abandoned body, powerful motors kicking in to draw in everything in the air around it, including the gaseous stuff of Fear's escaping spirit. Fear gave one last hissing scream as his spirit-form was drawn inexorably into the device, and then the trap sealed itself shut again. It fell to the ground, its power used up, giving little hint of the malign monstrosity now safely held inside it.

Dredd picked it up, and looked over to where Anderson was limping towards him. The mantrap, its jaws prised open, lay behind her, as did the corpses of the last few vampires who had foolishly thought she was trapped there helpless.

He tossed the suction trap over to her. "Souvenir of your trip to the Undercity, courtesy of the Psi-Div Teks."

She caught it, wincing it pain from her injury. Fear's mantrap had done a real number on her leg, Dredd saw.

"Three down—"

"And one to go," Anderson said, looking at the swirling darkness of the dimensional gateway. "Death's escaped back to Deadworld, and he's taken the Psi-cadets with him. Grud knows what he's planning to do with them."

"Nothing good," decided Dredd, reloading his Lawgiver before moving off towards the gateway entrance.

"Wait, Dredd! You can't go through that thing on your own! You need me there too!" Anderson started limping forward after the other Judge, but her injured leg suddenly gave way beneath her. Giving an involuntary cry of pain, she fell forward. Dredd caught her and lowered her gently to the ground.

"You'll be more of a liability than a help in Deadworld, with that leg," he told her. "Wait here for back-up. Anything except me tries to come back through that gateway, use Hi-Ex to demolish the whole thing. Check your chronometer – I'll be back within an hour."

"And what if you're not?"

Dredd was already walking away towards the mouth of the portal.

"Then Hi-Ex it anyway. If I don't make it, then at least we haven't left the door open for Death to come back. Whatever he's planning, I'm going to make sure it ends on Deadworld."

And then he was gone, swallowed up by the swirling darkness of the gateway.

DREDD'S BOOTS CRUNCHED noisily on the carpet of bones at his feet. The bleached litter of human remains stretched out in all directions, for as far as the eye could see in the perpetual twilight gloom of Deadworld. How many were there, Dredd wondered. Hundreds of millions? Billions? However many, it could never be enough for the Dark Judges. They had exterminated all life on their own world, and now they wanted to export this same nightmare to Dredd's world.

Dredd had been on Deadworld before. The carpet of bones, the twisted buildings with giant, screaming faces emerging out of them, the eerie, eternal silence that hung in the air, the sinister gloom that cast a lifeless pall over everything – all of it was familiar to him, like the memory of a particularly bad dream.

This is what my city will look like one day, he reminded himself, if we ever fail to stop Death and the others.

They were just ahead of him, he could see, mounting the bone-scattered steps of what had probably been this world's version of the Grand Hall of Justice. There weren't many of them left now, Dredd saw. Four vampires or cultists, each one carrying one of the Psi-cadets, and another group carrying something large and shroud-covered on a makeshift stretcher. Dredd couldn't see the disembodied spirit of Death, but he knew it would be here somewhere, hissing commands and sinister exhortations to its servants.

The bloodsucking freaks disappeared inside the vast, fortress-like building. Dredd picked up his pace, hoping to catch them before they could begin whatever it was they were planning. He got halfway to the entrance of the building before, with a dry rattle like someone expiring on a slab, the inhabitants of Deadworld began to come to life again.

Skeletal fingers reached up to claw against the soles of his Judge boots, trying to pull him down into the writhing bone carpet at his feet. Empty skulls shouted out hate-filled insults or defiant threats, all of them speaking in Death's own hissing, mocking tones. Dredd kept on going, in places actually wading through the layers of human remains as they rose up around him.

They came up in massed groups, the tangled mess of bones creating strange skeletal hybrids as the fragments of different bodies were freely used to form brand new composite forms. Roaring blasts from Dredd's M2000 blew them back into the bone-dust from whence they came. He kept on firing, destroying group after group just as fast as they rose up to face him. Those few that survived the furious barrage succumbed easily enough to punches or blows from his weapon butt, collapsing back into the ground whenever they were struck with enough force. It was grim, tiring work, but Dredd was in little real danger from the waves of skeletal figures that threw themselves at him. The real point, he knew, was to keep him busy and delay him from reaching Death's lair.

He broke through at last, reaching the entrance to the fortress in a few paces and discarding the now empty Widowmaker as he sprinted up the steps towards the open doorway ahead. The skeletal things pursuing him collapsed as one, the bones of the closest ones tumbling rattling down the steps behind him.

After that, Dredd was through the doorway, which took the form of a giant screaming mouth, and into the lair of the Dark Judges.

IT WASN'T DIFFICULT to work out which way to go. The rising sound of the chanting echoed through the dead, empty corridors and chambers of the place. All Dredd had to do was follow the sound back to its source.

The Judge found Death and the others in a vast, high-ceilinged chamber deep inside the fortress complex.

The four Psi-cadets were tied down on the top of crystal slabs, grouped around a structure that was like a more elaborate version of the gateway portal in the Undercity. Crackling bolts of psi-energy leapt from the cadets to the dark, stone-like material of the new portal that dominated one wall of the place. As each bolt struck, flickering power runes became visible, carved into the surfaces around the edge of the portal, and the glowing, swirling haze at the centre of the gateway seemed to grow slightly larger and more ominous every time.

Dredd strode forward, sheer instinct warning him of the waiting ambush vital moments before it came. The vampire that leapt at him got a Standard Execution round through its head for its troubles. At the same time, however, a cultist hurled a dagger at him from his other side. Unable to dodge the weapon in time, Dredd simply chose the most expedient course and used his free hand to block the blade which would otherwise have found his heart. A brief grunt of pain was his only reaction as the spinning knife sank through the material of his Judge gauntlet, impaling him through his left hand.

Dredd had better things to do than react to the injury. The knife-throwing creep got two shots through the heart back in return, and so did his pal while he was still fumbling to aim his spit pistol. Half of what he had left in his Lawgiver's magazine took care of the rest of the Dark Judges' remaining servants. A few seconds later, the last of the gunshots faded away, the last of the cultists slid to the floor, and Dredd declared the Church of Death officially out of business.

He ran forward towards the nearest of the Psi-cadets, intending to free them. As far as he could see, he and the four cadets were the only things left alive in the chamber...

And as soon as he'd formed the thought, the... the thing appeared out of the shadows on the far side of the chamber.

"Hello, Joe," it cackled in a voice that was both horribly familiar, but still somehow different. "Surprised to see me back so soon?"

"Icarus!"

Dredd knew this wasn't really the deceased Dr Dick Icarus, aka Vernon Martins, that he faced now, even as the surprised exclamation of the name escaped from his lips. For one thing, Icarus was dead. For another, the last time Dredd had seen him, he hadn't been three metres tall and covered in thick bony plates of armour that rose out of his mutated, virus-warped flesh.

"Not quite," growl-hissed the thing in a voice that was half Death's, and half something even stronger and yet more monstrous. "Our servant's spirit has left this flesh, but his sinful attempts to attain eternal life would seem to have had their uses. His serum flows in this body's veins, transforming its dead flesh. Now it is truly indestructible, a fitting new form to contain my spirit and a vessel with which to continue our great work."

As the thing spoke, Dredd could see Death's own ghastly visage emerging at moments from the pulsing mass of flesh that was its face. It was still changing, still transforming before Dredd's eyes.

"Indestructible?" sneered Dredd. "Fine in theory. Let's see how it works in practice."

His Hi-Ex shots caught the Death-thing square in the chest, blowing it backwards off its feet. It landed heavily and twitched for a moment, lying in a spreading pool of its own fluids and exploded flesh. It lay there for a moment, but then began to climb to its feet again.

Dredd watched, seeing its flesh knitting back together, layers of hard bone-shell pushing up through the surface of the skin to provide additional natural armour. In what seemed like seconds, the thing's body had regenerated itself. If anything, in fact, it actually looked slightly larger, more powerful and menacing than it had before he had shot it.

The Death-thing growled in pleasure, pleased at this test of its new body's abilities. Dredd didn't give up. Standard Execution rounds struck against its bony armour, to little effect. A Hi-Ex round to the face wiped the gloating smile from its face, but only for a moment. After that, the smile just grew back again, along with the rest of its face. Several Incendiary rounds burst against it, setting it ablaze. The phosphor-fed flames caught for a moment but died away again, unable to affect the stuff of the thing's unnatural body. What little flesh had been burned flaked away in blackened scales, to be instantly replaced by newly regenerated tissue.

Death was shambling towards him all this time, forcing Dredd to circle away from him, keeping the altars with the Psi-cadets on them between the Dark Judge and his prey. A moan escaped from the lips of the cadet nearest Dredd, as another current of rippling psi-energy leapt out from her towards the portal. Death gloated at the sound, as if it was the sweetest music.

"Yes, with the energy from these little ones, I can open the dimensional gateways to their full extent. The Sisters of Death will be found and returned to us. Deadworld and your own corrupt dimension will merge together as one. I will cross over again to free my brothers. In this body, with our two worlds merged into one, I will be invincible, and all will finally be judged!"

"Right. And what makes you think we're going to stand here and let that happen?"

It was Anderson's voice. Dredd turned to see the Psi-Judge standing at the entrance to the chamber. She looked seriously haggard, worn out by everything she'd been through in the last twenty-four hours. Then Dredd remembered his own experiences in the same period, and realised he probably looked just as bad.

"Anderson! Thought I told you to–"

"Stay and guard the gateway in the Undercity? Yeah, well, you know me, Dredd. I never was much good at following orders. So how do you want to handle this?"

"Free the cadets. I'll keep gruesome here busy while you do it," Dredd ordered, snapping off another series of shots at the foul thing containing Death.

The brute charged forward, knowing that it was now under serious threat. Dredd hit it with everything he had, and then some more, just for good measure. The Death-thing staggered under the crippling impact of multiple Hi-Ex shells. Rapid-fire bursts tore into it. Incendiaries set it ablaze. Armour Piercing shells drilled through the bony plates of its chest, futilely seeking out vital organs to puncture and burst.

The Death-thing absorbed it all, and just kept on coming. Dredd stood his ground, knowing that every bullet impact still delayed it for one crucial moment more, giving Anderson more time to free the cadets. He risked a glance back, seeing that she had now freed the first of them. He had only looked away for the barest of moments – but when he looked back the Death-thing was right on top of him.

It lashed out at him with its claws. Dredd felt razor-sharp talons shred apart the armour of his eagle shoulder pad and then he was flying through the air. The bone-jarring collision with the wall only added to the damage Dredd had just suffered, but even as he fell to the floor, he was reloading his Lawgiver and taking aim at Death's monstrous new form as it bore down on him once more.

Three Hi-Ex rounds staggered it in its tracks. A raking blast of Standard Execution rounds blew out both of its eyes.

Two cadets freed now. Weak and confused though they were, they still ran to help Anderson free their remaining companions.

An Armour Piercing shot erupted though the back of the beast's head, unleashing a torrent of black, slimy matter from inside the Death-thing's skull. Double blasts of rapid-fire took away its knees. It stumbled for a few seconds as its body regenerated the damage, and then kept on coming.

Three cadets free now. They huddled together in fear as Anderson hurried to free the last of them.

Dredd protected them, standing there pumping round after round into the Death-thing's body as it remorselessly came on at him. With a hellish shriek, it lashed out with one hand, knocking the weapon from Dredd's grip, grasping him by his now empty gun-hand as it hauled him up off his feet, dangling him in the air in front of its grinning face.

Death squeezed, enjoying the spreading grimace of pain on the face of his old enemy as every bone in Dredd's hand was crushed, the broken bones grinding together under the relentless pressure of Death's grip.

Dredd blacked out for a few moments. The Death-thing dropped him with a disappointed shrug, and then prodded at the groaning figure lying at its feet. "Wake up, sinner," it hissed. "Judgement time is here at last!"

"Got that right at least, freak," Anderson challenged, standing with the four Psi-cadets clustered around her.

"You wanted to use these kids' abilities for your own sick reasons. Let's see how you like getting some of it back at you in return."

She and the cadets linked hands, linking minds at the same moment.

Psi-blasting was only taught to Psi-cadets in their last two years at the Academy of Law, and the cadets had just begun their training in it. Anderson had, however, had more than a few years' practice. She focused their power through her own mind, amplifying and focusing it, adding her own considerable psychic strength to theirs.

What hit Death was the psychic equivalent of a close-range blast from a sawn-off scatter gun. His bestial form reeled back, screeching in psychic and physical pain. Injuries he had thought safely regenerated spontaneously opened up again. Wounds blossomed across his body, overwhelming this new form's ability to deal with them. Death screeched hideously again, feeling his control slipping over his host body, feeling its strange, unnatural flesh begin to rebel against him.

"Now, Dredd!" shrieked Anderson, bringing her own Lawgiver up to bear. Dredd rolled and grabbed his own fallen gun. His gun-hand was useless, and his other hand was still injured, but as long as he could hold a gun, Dredd was still to be considered completely lethal.

The two of them opened fire simultaneously, and Death's new body was destroyed utterly in a few furious seconds of combined Lawgiver fire. Death's spirit was already abandoning the thing, even before the burning, shattered fragments of it hit the ground.

"Uh-uh," warned Anderson, focusing her psi-powers again. "Your non-corporeal butt's going nowhere, except back with us."

With her mind still linked to those of the Psi-cadets, she reeled Death's screaming, struggling spirit-form in with relative ease. At the last moment, she broke off all psychic contact with the others – cadets that young and inexperienced weren't up to having a super-creep like Judge

Death crawling around inside their minds, Anderson wisely decided.

Death's spirit flowed unwillingly into her, held fast in the iron grip of her psi-power. It was inside her now, and she felt the old, sickeningly familiar lurch of repugnance as everything he was reached out to taint her mind and soul. With a final, wrenching mental effort, she seized hold of him and pushed him down into the dark, buried place in her mind which she had prepared for him. His screams of psychic rage filled her mind as he was forced in there and she slammed shut the mental barriers that would hold him there until she was ready to undergo the long and stressful process, assisted by a carefully chosen group of other experienced Psi-Judges, that would be necessary to extract the Dark Judge's spirit again and force it into another, more permanent prison.

Her strength gave way as soon as she knew she had Death under control. She stumbled and fell forwards, only to be caught by Dredd, who by any rights should barely have been able to stand himself.

"I'm… I'm alright," she assured him, weakly. She could still feel Death inside her mind, squirming frantically against the barriers of his psychic prison. "But I can't hold him forever…"

She gestured towards the now-deactivated portal, which showed only blank stone where minutes ago there had been the swirling darkness of the extra-dimensional void. "Whatever you've got left, use it to destroy that. Even if they ever get out again, this is one option that's not going to be available to them again. And then, after that…"

She looked at the four still-traumatised cadets. One of them was quietly sobbing to herself. Under normal conditions, had this been a Hotdog Run or any other kind of live training mission, that would have earned a cadet a reprimand, or perhaps even have been grounds for failure and instant dismissal from the Academy. Under the circumstances, though, even Dredd wasn't going to comment.

"After that, we go home," Anderson promised.

Sixteen

"AND THE GATEWAY in the Undercity?" asked Chief Judge Hershey.

"Destroyed also," Psi-Chief Shenker assured her.

Hershey sat back in her chair, digesting everything she had heard in the last few hours as the Council of Five had convened in special session to discuss the aftermath of the recent carnage caused by the Dark Judges' escape.

It could have been a lot worse, she reminded herself, looking at the death toll figures that scrolled across the screen of the small desk monitor in front of her. It still made for grim reading but yes, she told herself, it could have been a lot worse.

The Church of Death was officially no more, its members either dead or locked up for life in the cubes. EverPet had been shut down, and Icarus's secret research work seized by the Justice Department before anyone else could try to replicate it. Even before Justice Department Med-scientists had started going through it in detail, Judge Helsing had been able to successfully replicate a cure for the effects of Icarus's retrovirus. There would be no more outbreaks of any plagues of undead in Mega-City One for the foreseeable future.

Harsh lessons had also been learned. A new prison to hold the Dark Judges had already been built. Death and his three brethren would be its only inmates, and the facility's location was a closely guarded secret, even within the ranks of the Justice Department. Security procedures at the facility would be ultra-rigorous, with several systems of fail-safes in place. There could hopefully never be a repeat of the events that happened at Nixon Pen.

"We've heard all the reports now," Hershey announced to her assembled Division heads. "Does anyone else have anything to add?"

Ramos cleared his throat noisily and shifted in his seat. Hershey looked expectantly towards her head of Street Division. She could already half-guess what he was going to say.

Ramos pointed to the thick stack of files on the table in front of him. "With respect, Chief Judge, we've had full reports on all the facets of this incident, from all the senior Judges involved. Giant. Helsing. Grud, even Anderson managed to file something…"

Hershey interrupted him. "If you're wondering about Dredd, I remind you that his preliminary report is there in front of you, along with all the others."

"Yes, his preliminary report," emphasised Ramos, who was infamous in the Justice Department for his strict belief in the importance of proper paperwork. "But when can we expect to see his complete report?"

Despite the gravity of the events they had been discussing here at the Council meeting today, Hershey still had to fight to suppress a slight smile as she answered Ramos's query.

"The Meds tell me Dredd is still undergoing speedheal treatment. I'm sure, however, he'll be looking forward to catching up on his paperwork and submitting a full written report to the Council when he returns to active duty in a few days' time."

*   *   *

"But, Dredd, you can't leave the med-bay yet! You've got to give the speedheal time to take full effect, and the Chief Judge's office said that they were to be informed before–"

Dredd's only response was a trademark menacing glower as he hit the activate switch and the elevator doors slid shut in the face of the panicking young Med-Judge.

Riding the elevator down to the Sector House motor pool level, Dredd activated his helmet radio. He was immediately immersed in the non-stop flow of comms data that was the strangely comforting background buzz to the daily life of every Street Judge in the city.

"Item: suspected mob blitz reported, Tony Soprano Skedway…"

"Item: riot by Human League anti-droid agitators in progress, Robot of the Year Show. Riot squad in attendance, Judge Giant commanding…"

"Item: multiple vehicle pile-up, Mo Mowlam Megway. Extra meat- and med-wagons required urgently. Sounds like a real mess down there on Mowlam…"

"Item: Justice Central reminds all units that there's a full moon tonight. Expect an increase in futsie crimes and general psycho activity. Additional kook cube space has been allocated for tonight's quota of loon-related arrests…"

Dredd flexed the muscles of his gun-hand as he listened to the litany of item reports. The speedheal treatment had been a perfect success, reknitting the broken bones in the hand in almost record time, and the Meds had assured him there was no nerve damage, but the hand still felt slightly stiff and unresponsive to Dredd's own hyper-critical sense of self-judgement. What might seem more than good enough to anyone else was more often than not completely insufficient for the exacting standards Dredd set for himself.

What he needed, he decided, was something to give him a chance to test his combat responses and Lawgiver-handling skills under real combat conditions.

"Item: block war flaring up at the Minogue Con-apts. Looks like Kylie and Dannii are renewing hostilities again. Units already at the scene requesting Senior Judge assistance."

The elevator doors opened, and Dredd walked out to where the vehicle pool Tek-chief had a fully fuelled and ammo-loaded Lawmaster already waiting for him.

"Control – Dredd. I'll take command at the Minogues. I'm on my way."

HIS BRETHREN AT times fought and raged against the even more restrictive confines of their new place of imprisonment, but Death remained still and silent, content for the time being to merely observe the conditions of the barriers and wards that held them in check, and study the minds of their human jailors.

Slowly, imperceptibly, the thinnest, most invisible tendrils of his psychic aura crept out to explore the limits of this new place and of the living minds that inhabited it. He was patient, never rash or greedy, and his slowly expanding knowledge of all that was happening around him passed beneath the psychic perceptions of the batteries of Psi-Judges who were there day and night to keep watch over him and his brothers.

There were possibilities even here, Death sensed. Dim and remote they may be right now, but Death was patient in a way in which his still-living jailers were not, and after all he had all eternity to wait and plan, if need be.

"Patience, brothers," he consoled the others, whispering to them in a voice so quiet that it existed at a level never even suspected by the living. "One day we will be free again, I promise, and then our great work will begin again."

ON THE OTHER side of the dimensional void, in the empty silence of Deadworld, something stirred amongst the jumbled litter of ancient bones that was all that remained of the original victims of the Dark Judges.

Death had been wrong when he had thought he had seized control of an empty vessel when his spirit had flowed in to take possession of Icarus's retrovirus-mutated corpse. Some vestige of the body's original owner had lingered, remaining trapped and helpless within the prison of its own dead flesh, powerless to intervene as the Dark Judge had claimed that same flesh for himself.

That same remote vestige had survived the destruction of its body, but in being freed from that dead flesh, it found it had merely exchanged one prison for another, larger one. It wandered the far reaches of its new prison, receiving no response to its increasingly frantic entreaties for help.

Dr Dick Icarus, aka Vernon Martins, had achieved his wish at last. Here in the empty, still spaces of Deadworld, he would live forever, lingering bodiless and alone for all eternity, with nothing but the dead bones to hear his whispered, begging pleas to be granted the oblivion he now so desperately craved.

THE END

THE
KINGDOM
OF THE
BLIND

DAVID BISHOP

For Steve MacManus,
the unsung hero of 2000 AD.

Prologue

IN A METROPOLIS not short of oddly shaped buildings, the Mega-City One Museum of the Twentieth Century still succeeded in bewildering most who saw it. Designed by architectural genius Foster St Normandy, the museum had been conceived as a fifty-storey replica of a handheld vacuum cleaner. Few people recognised the resemblance because even fewer still owned such a device, once eponymously known as a Dustbuster. In the year 2126 such objects were museum pieces, antiques from a bygone age before the advent of cheap domestic robots.

To Foster St Normandy, this was the point of his award-winning and controversial design. The building was to be filled with relics from the twentieth century, so why not have the building itself resemble one of those relics? To the citizens' committee that approved his design without ever seeing it, the end result was a fifty-storey embarrassment. The committee became a laughing stock and the building, inevitably, became known as the Dustbuster.

None of that mattered to Judge Dredd as he waited in the shadows of McGraw Alley opposite the museum. He had been inside the building once before, pursuing a perp through the displays of tea-towels, digital watches and real paper books. Now the lawman was planning to take another look – if Jesus Bludd ever arrived. The Judge activated his motorcycle helmet radio.

"Dredd to Control, am in position. Where's our target?"

"Control to Dredd, he's en route to you now. ETA – three minutes."

"That's a roj." Dredd cut short the transmission before turning to the nervous juve behind him. "Get ready. He's nearly here."

Blake Ryan nodded, teeth biting into his bottom lip. Seven days ago he had been just another twelfth year cadet, one of more than a hundred approaching the end of their training at the Academy of Law. Anyone wanting to become a Judge in Mega-City One was required to undergo thirteen years of intensive study and tuition, passing many stringent tests and checks before being empowered to dispense instant justice. Once they graduated, each new law enforcer would have the authority to act as judge, jury and – when necessary – executioner. For this responsibility they forswore love and sex, devoting almost every waking moment to upholding the Law. They could be killed at any moment by a perp and had to be willing to kill just as quickly.

RYAN HAD BEEN unsure what to expect when called to the Academy administration office a week earlier. His marks had been good, his report from the last Hotdog Run excellent, and nobody could fault his attention to duty or detail. But one doubt had niggled at him. A few hours before receiving the summons, Ryan had been among a group of cadets subjected to a random psi-scan. Such incidents were commonplace, designed to detect any mental aberrations that might indicate a cadet was unsuitable for the badge. Could he have failed without even realising it after twelve years of study?

The red-haired cadet had reported promptly to the administrator's office to find a senior Street Judge waiting for him. But it was not just *any* Judge – it was Dredd! The man was a living legend, someone all the cadets aspired to emulate. He had saved the Big Meg on countless occasions over the years from threats like the alien superfiend Judge Death or agent provocateur Orlok the Assassin. Dredd had risked his life time and again for the city and its four hundred million residents, without asking for, or expecting any thanks. Even his books on judicial comportment were set texts at the Academy.

Meeting this mythic figure for the first time, Ryan was surprised by the Judge's appearance. Rather than being mighty or muscular, Dredd was trim and lean, his body all sinew and coiled energy. He might be pushing sixty but his back was still ramrod straight, posture upright and imposing.

From what Ryan could see beneath the helmet, Dredd's face was grizzled and gaunt, a line for every year on the streets etched into the impassive features. And that voice – a rasping growl of rockcrete and iron, heavy with authority and gravitas.

Ryan had begun stammering something but Dredd quickly interrupted, cutting straight to the point. "I had all the cadets from your year scanned earlier today. Out of them, you scored highest in the criteria sought," he growled. "Your thoughts are almost impenetrable to direct psi-probing."

Ryan had nodded. This unusual capacity had been noted years before. It was a useful gift but would be of limited application on the streets.

"Do you recognise the name Jesus Bludd?"

The seventeen-year-old cadet did and said so. Part of his training included a study of the major figures in Mega-City One's criminal underworld. There had been a power vacuum following the demise of gang boss Nero Narcos five years earlier. Bludd was among those who emerged from the shadows to claim some of the territory Narcos involuntarily vacated. But unlike the others, Bludd kept his face out of the news media. Rather than trying to foster a cult of personality, he worked hard at remaining invisible, always staying one step removed from those who enforced his will. Bludd had never served time for any crime; he was untouchable. But the stain of his influence had been spreading.

Ryan related all of this before Dredd spoke again. "We have been trying to get an undercover operative close to Bludd for years. But he surrounds himself with psykers, powerful mindreaders able to detect any Wally Squad Judge trying to infiltrate Bludd's inner circle. No one sent in undercover has ever returned alive." Dredd uncrossed his arms and leaned forward to watch Ryan's face. "We have received word that Bludd is making a rare excursion from his penthouse to visit the Dustbuster. He has tickets to see the Evil Empire exhibit that's just opened in the 1980s section. We want you to make contact with him there. With luck, you might succeed where others have failed."

"And if I don't?"

"Then you will receive a funeral with full judicial honours. Well?"

"How will I make contact?"

ONE WEEK ON and he was primed for meeting one of the Big Meg's most dangerous crime bosses. Tutors from Psi-Division had worked round the clock to enhance his mental defences, implanting the roots of his cover story deep into Ryan's psyche. Academy records were forged and the cadet summarily expelled for gross insubordination and violent misconduct. The best dunks in the cubes had been training Ryan in the art of picking pockets. Now all that remained was a close encounter with Jesus Bludd.

Dredd rested a hand on the cadet's shoulder. "There's still time to change your mind. Nobody will think any less of you. This assignment is voluntary. No demerits will be placed on your file if you back out, even now."

Ryan did not hesitate. He was proud to be chosen and ready to risk his life. Every day on the streets as a

Judge would be dangerous, he told himself, so there was no point shying away from the life that came with the badge. If he completed this mission and returned alive, it would mean an instant upgrade to full eagle status and a commendation on his record. "I'm ready," he told Dredd.

"Good," the Judge replied. "You better get inside."

JESUS BLUDD SIGHED as his hoverpod flung itself through the sky above Mega-City One. It was too long since he had been out of the penthouse. Life atop Emil Jannings Block was luxurious, but Bludd was a child of the streets. He had grown up fighting for his life on City Bottom and still felt a wistful nostalgia for those days. It was nonsense, of course. Nobody wanted to scratch out such a meagre existence. But he could not deny the thrill that living on his wits had offered.

"Are they still watching us?"

"Yes," the woman beside him replied. She studied a holographic patchwork of tiny screens, her hands pulling different images forward to be studied before being cast aside. "PSU cameras have not let this vehicle out of their sight since we left Emil Jannings."

Bludd nodded, light gleaming off his coarse black hair, the locks slicked-back close to the scalp. His was an unremarkable face but for the implacable, intelligent eyes and cruel mouth. Bludd's tongue frequently darted out, like a serpent's, to moisten his lips. His neck was almost as broad as his head, leading down into powerful, muscular shoulders. He had a heavyset body but the bulk was born of muscle, not fat. He dressed in a dark blue tunic and trousers, unadorned by the usual kneepads or accessories most ordinary citizens wore. "Such attention is only to be expected. We don't give them many chances to observe our movements so closely, do we, my dear?"

Kara smiled, switching off the holo-screens. Like Bludd she was in her early thirties, her face unlined by age or injury. Her body was trim and taut, every sinew detailed by the skin-tight garment of black silk that clung to her. She was wearing a blonde wig cut into an asymmetrical bob, the fringe sloping from left to right across her forehead. Stark black and white make-up heightened the angularity of her features, a tear of mascara drawn on to one cheek. "No, we don't. Shall we go down now?"

Her lover smiled. "I was wondering when you would ask."

SEVERAL MINUTES LATER the hoverpod shuddered to a halt outside the museum, its robot chauffeur emerging to hold open the passenger door. Kara stepped out first, slyly wiping a trickle of moisture from the corner of her mouth. Bludd followed, his face wearing a broad smile as they strolled inside.

The museum's curator, Doctor Janet Swanson, was waiting for them. Clad from head to toe in tweed, her severe features did their best to look welcoming. "Mr Bludd, so wonderful of you to accept our invitation. It's not often we have the chance to thank one of our most generous benefactors—"

Bludd waved away her sycophancy. "Any other self-respecting businessman would have done the same," he responded. "The chance to see this unique exhibit of artefacts from the late twentieth century was irresistible."

Dr Swanson nodded enthusiastically. "Let me escort you directly to the 1980s. As you may know, we have divided the building into decades, with five floors devoted to each era. To reach the 1980s we will have to take the turbolift to the forty-second level…"

RYAN WAS ALREADY in the section devoted to 1982 when Bludd arrived. The cadet did his best to look fascinated at displays about an actress called Meryl Streep and her career, but let his eyes wander towards the new arrival.

Bludd closely resembled the images previously captured by PSU cameras, despite those pictures being at least a year old. Ryan recognised the museum's curator from his briefings. The other woman must be Bludd's confidante and executioner, Kara. Her appearance was as intimidating as her reputation. The cadet could feel her mind reaching into his as she passed, expertly probing his psyche. Ryan concentrated on blocking her, letting just a hint of his recent experiences leak out as a tease.

The cadet waited until the trio were well past before hurrying after them. He did not know how long Bludd planned to stay at the museum, nor the purpose of the crime boss's visit. The dusty contents of this facility were not an obvious target for illegal activity. Bludd and his party strolled into a new exhibit entitled "EVIL EMPIRE: The Cold War and its Casualties". Perhaps this offered some clue? Ryan pushed the thought from his mind, concentrating instead on the task at hand. His job was simple; to pick the pocket of Jesus Bludd.

Getting close to the big man was surprisingly easy. In the Evil Empire display room, Kara and Dr Swanson stood to one side, deep in conversation. Ryan noticed the blonde-haired woman's hand lingering on the curator's arm, a gesture of physical familiarity. Bludd himself was standing before the main exhibit, a precise recreation of the United States of America's command and control centre for its many weapons of mass destruction. The centrepiece of the display was an android of a US president, his hand lingering above a red button on a black box. A mechanical voice explained the tableau's significance for anyone unfamiliar with the historical events being depicted.

"During the 1980s, long before atomic war ravaged North America, the country was ruled by a former actor, Ronald Reagan. He voiced hawkish rhetoric against the Soviet Union, an old ideological enemy and a forerunner of today's Sov-Blok citi-states. Reagan described the Soviets as the 'Evil Empire', a name we have adopted for this exhibition. But during Reagan's time in office it was the US President who sponsored the development of terrifying new weapons of mass destruction, many of them being sent into orbit above the Earth for deployment in case of a global calamity. Here you can see the president, his finger poised over the fateful button, ready to declare war on his enemies. Ultimately, Reagan never launched an overt worldwide conflict and the much-feared nuclear war did not eventuate until the era of Bad Bob Booth, nearly a hundred years later..."

Ryan sidled closer to Bludd as the mechanical voice continued. The cadet had seen what would happen next and knew his opportunity was fast approaching. The robotic Ronald Reagan reached forward and pressed the red button. The lights illuminating the chamber dipped suddenly and a holographic mushroom cloud appeared in front of Bludd, startling him. He staggered back in surprise, bumping into Ryan. As they collided, the juve slipped his hands into Bludd's pockets, fingers closing around the contents.

DREDD WAS WATCHING all of this on his Lawmaster motorcycle's computer screen. The video feed from the museum's security cameras was being routed via the Public Surveillance Unit so Dredd and other Judges involved could see everything as it happened.

"Ryan's gone for his dunk," Dredd announced into his helmet radio. "All units, be ready to move if Bludd reacts. Otherwise stay back."

On screen the juve stepped away from his victim, clutching a black notebook. Bludd did not shift, all his attention focused on the display. A voice crackled in Dredd's ear. "What do we do? Our boy's moving away and the target doesn't seem to have noticed. Should we move in?"

"Stand fast!" Dredd ordered. "Watch and wait. Let the scenario play out." He kept watching the scenes transmitted from inside the museum. Ryan was now leaving the Evil Empire exhibition space, his theft apparently unnoticed. "Show me Bludd's enforcer." The image on screen shifted to Kara and Dr Swanson. The two women were engrossed in a private conversation on the far side of the room, oblivious to what was happening. Bludd's voice got Kara's attention.

"If you've quite finished," the crime boss sneered. His lover blushed and moved away from the curator, returning to Bludd's side. He nodded to Dr Swanson. "Thank you for the tour. Most instructive." Bludd swept out of the room, Kara close behind him. The curator hurried after them, leaving the exhibition unattended. A moment later, a Judge emerged from the shadows and looked up at the closed circuit cameras.

"Well, Dredd, what do you want us to do now?"

"Maintain visual contact with Bludd but don't let him see you, Giant," Dredd replied before switching radio frequencies. "Control, where's Ryan?"

"Should be coming out of the Dustbuster... now."

Dredd glared across the skedway at the museum entrance. The juve was hurrying out into the sunshine, still clutching the notebook he had picked from Bludd's pocket. Ahead of him the crime boss's hoverpod was waiting for its owner to reappear. As Ryan approached a passenger door opened towards him. The juve stopped, startled. After looking around he entered the vehicle and the door closed behind him. Less than a minute later Bludd and Kara returned to the hoverpod, Dr Swanson still trailing behind them.

"Dredd to Control – give me audio on what Bludd is saying to the curator."

"Roj that. Switching to ultra-sonics."

*　　*　　*

"THANK YOU ONCE again for the generous donation," Dr Swanson simpered. "Without your support the good work of the museum would not be possible."

Bludd smiled thinly at the obsequious woman. "Yes, yes. Well, it's time I was going." He thrust his hands into his pockets, a flicker of satisfaction crossing his face. Bludd looked at Kara. "Since you seem so enamoured of Dr Swanson, perhaps you would like to stay and talk with her further."

Bludd's executioner blushed and shook her head. The crime boss stepped into his hoverpod, Kara following after him. She shot a final smile at Dr Swanson before the door snapped shut behind her. The vehicle hurtled into the sky, leaving the curator waving a feeble goodbye.

"DREDD TO CONTROL, are we getting any signal from Ryan?"

"Negative. Bludd's hoverpod must be heavily shielded. Nothing leaks out from inside and ultra-sonics can't penetrate the vehicle's exterior."

Dredd watched the hoverpod disappear into the distance. "All units, stand down. Bludd has taken the bait. If Ryan survives the day, we may have a new operative on the inside."

RYAN PERCHED NERVOUSLY inside the luxurious vehicle, its seats upholstered with real leather. Opposite him Bludd sat glowering, the big man's eyes studying the juve's face. Kara sat with her legs apart, one of Bludd's hands stroking her right thigh. She appeared amused by the juve's presence.

Ryan cleared his throat nervously. "Your robo-chauffeur said you wanted to talk with me. So... here I am."

Bludd reached an open hand towards the juve. "First things first, give back the notebook you took inside the museum."

"Notebook?"

"Don't try my patience," Bludd replied bluntly. "Kara here knows more about inflicting pain than any person I've ever met – including myself. It gives her a sexual thrill to see others suffer. Right baby?"

Kara smiled, letting her lover's hand slide up and down her legs.

Ryan shifted uncomfortably in his seat. He produced the notebook and handed it back to Bludd. "I was hoping to get your credits, maybe something I could sell at the City Bottom black market."

"You know who I am, don't you?"

"Jesus Bludd, crime boss. Your companies are collectively known as the Bludd Group."

"I prefer to think of myself as a businessman, but I'll let that pass. You did a very professional job. Most citizens would not have noticed the loss."

"But you did," Ryan said.

"Yes." Bludd pursed his lips. "Kara tells me you were recently expelled from the Academy of Law."

"How did you–"

Bludd silenced the juve with a gesture. "The Justice Department is not the only organisation that employs those with psi-abilities to achieve its goals. You know my reputation, yet you have the audacity to pick my pocket. Either you are very brave or very foolish. Which is it?"

Ryan grimaced. "A little of both, I guess."

"You have certain skills I might usefully employ. Would you be interested in joining my organisation?" Bludd shifted forward in his seat, leaning closer to the juve. A bead of sweat ran down Ryan's face but he held the big man's gaze.

"What's in it for me?"

"The rewards are considerable," Bludd said. "But I demand absolute loyalty. If I discover you are working for anyone else, you shall suffer the most painful of deaths imaginable. Do I make myself clear?"

Ryan nodded hurriedly.

"Good." Bludd smiled broadly. "Welcome to the Bludd Group."

One

"GOOD MORNING! I'M Enigma Smith and you're watching *Mega-City News*, the best and brightest place to see all the news worth knowing! Today's bulletins are brought to you by Supposi-Thrills™, the excitement you insert, and New Improved Grot Pot®, now available in Snot and Lemon flavour!"

Tri-D screens across the Big Meg flickered into life as the first light of dawn touched the city's skyscrapers. Media mogul Ruprecht Maxwell had cut a deal with Tri-D manufacturers to ensure every new set automatically switched itself on for the early morning headlines on *Mega-City News*, a show broadcast on one of Maxwell's many thousands of channels. Enraged consumer groups and citizens' action committees had protested this blatant breach of the city's communications bylaws to no avail.

As a result, Enigma Smith's face was the first thing many citizens saw in the morning, making her the most recognised and reviled person in the Big Meg. Once just a humble announcer on the audio-only version of *Mega-City News*, Smith was now a massive celebrity. But the constant stream of death threats and attempted assassinations had transformed her fame into a curse.

She maintained a grim smile and maniacally perky persona on the air in the face of such troubles, her appealing features framed by an elaborate bouffant of blonde hair. Smith's facial expression was the result of the "Non-Stop Grinning" clause in her contract rather than any wish to make bad news seem less bleak. A thousand orphans could be gunned down at a birthday party but Maxwell demanded such news be served up to citizens with a smile on the lips and a song in the heart.

"Now, here are your headlines," Smith continued. "Representatives of Justice Departments from around the globe are gathering in Mega-City One for a historic summit. Our own Chief Judge Hershey wants to negotiate a worldwide extradition treaty, so that no citi-state can be a hiding place for fugitives from the Law. Here's what the top cop had to say about the summit earlier today."

The Tri-D image switched to Hershey standing on the Grand Hall of Justice's steps, her determined face underlining the importance of her announcement. "For too long, dangerous perps and those suspected of committing crimes have been able to shelter behind arcane treaties and procedures. Some governments have been willing to look the other way, offering a safe haven to fugitives in return for a slice of the profits from illegal activities. We want to stop that and have invited delegates from key citi-states to meet here and thrash out a compromise." Hershey leaned forwards, jabbing a finger at those watching. "Let this be a warning to all who would break the Law. Soon there will be nowhere to run and nowhere to hide. Count on it, creeps!"

The familiar voice of Enigma Smith could be heard from off-screen, asking the Chief Judge a question. "Is it true the criminal underworld has threatened to stop these talks by any means necessary? And if so, how does the Justice Department intend to ward off these attacks?"

Hershey smiled for the cameras. "I have personally appointed one of our most dedicated and capable officers as head of security for the summit – Judge Dredd. He will greet the delegates as they arrive and ensure safety for the length of their stay. Spread the word; this treaty will happen. That is all!"

Smith reappeared on screen. "*Mega-City News* understands all the delegates should have settled in by noon today. Dredd has been meeting the representatives as they arrive, ushering them through the rigorous Customs and Immigration procedures."

"I SAY, THIS is most irregular!" Brit-Cit Judge Jago Warner was not impressed. He had arrived at midnight via the Black Atlantic Tunnel and spent the long hours since waiting to be allowed entry to the Big Meg. Forbidden to touch his luggage, he had been required to fill in an endless variety of forms and forced to stand in an interminable queue without access to toilet facilities, food or drink. The Brit-Cit delegate finally snapped, marched to the front of the queue and demanded to see Dredd.

"I understood he was to be here personally," Warner explained to the sour-faced Judge at the front of the line, "to ensure I would be ushered through Customs and Immigration on some sort of fast track."

"This is fast track," Giant replied.

"But I've been waiting for seven hours!" the Brit snapped, his blue hair quivering with suppressed rage. "What precisely is taking so long?"

"Safety procedures," a deep, resonant voice boomed from down the corridor. Warner turned to see another lawman approaching, the name DREDD emblazoned on his badge. "Extra precautions are necessary, due to the sensitive nature of this summit. I'm sure you understand." Dredd had reached the front of the queue and now loomed over Warner, a scowl warning the visiting Judge against pressing his complaints any further.

"Well, of course," Warner stammered. "If you believe such extreme measures are necessary then—"

"I do," Dredd growled. He pulled a small metal device from one of the pouches on his utility belt and used it to scan the Brit's body. A steady crackle flared into a high-pitched wail as it approached Warner's crotch. "I'm picking up a suspicious object in your u-fronts. You got something you want to tell me?"

The visiting Judge was affronted by the mere suggestion and said so. "Quite frankly, the contents of a man's u-fronts are his own affair!"

"Not on my watch," Dredd snarled back. "Drop 'em."

"I beg your pardon?"

"I said drop 'em, or else I'll drop you." Dredd leaned into Warner's face. "You get what I'm saying, creep?"

"I really must protest! You can't honestly expect me to disrobe in front of all these people, can you?" Warner spluttered, indicating the long queue of weary travellers still waiting to be processed. "For goodness sake, man, I am a duly appointed representative of the–"

"Spare me the pompous protests, punk. Now strip, or else!" Dredd removed his daystick from its place on his utility belt and began thwacking the shaft against the leathereen palm of his left gauntlet.

"But I–"

"I said strip!" Dredd reached out a hand and tore the tunic away from Warner's torso, exposing pale, freckled skin and a flabby stomach. Another tug and the Brit was standing in just his u-fronts and boots, shaking hands clasped across his crotch. Dredd replaced his daystick and pulled on a pair of latex gloves from another pouch. "Now touch your toes!"

"Please, just a little privacy," Warner pleaded. "I'll be perfectly happy to–"

"I said touch your toes! And keep your legs apart!"

With a whimper Warner bent forward, struggling to reach his ankles. Dredd tore down the u-fronts and began a full cavity search. After finding nothing of interest he pointed at something dangling between Warner's legs.

"What do you call that?"

"My willy, if you must know!" By now Warner was close to tears, his shame and humiliation almost complete. He straightened up and looked at Dredd, trying to maintain some shred of dignity.

"No, I mean that!" His face curled with disdain, Dredd pointed at a metal stud protruding through the visiting Judge's penis.

"Oh, that! It's a Prince Albert. Several centuries ago our ruler's consort popularised this kind of body piercing and it now bears his name. All senior Judges in Brit-Cit are required to have one if they are to gain promotion." Warner crossed his hands back over his crotch. "Are you satisfied now?"

Dredd nodded grudgingly before turning to Giant. "Alright, you can let the rest go through now." The Judge began waving the rest of the queue past his station while Warner dressed. The Brit watched in amazement as the others were ushered past within minutes.

"You mean you made us wait all that time for nothing?" he demanded.

Dredd almost smiled. "Heard you Brits were fond of forming a queue. Just thought we'd see how long it took you to demand action." He slapped a gauntlet-clad hand heartily against Warner's back. "Remember that when you go into the negotiating room. You've got to stand up for your rights, otherwise some of the other cities will try to walk all over you. Got that?"

Warner just glared at Dredd. "May I go now?"

"Be my guest."

The Brit-Cit delegate stamped away, muttering darkly to himself. Giant stood beside Dredd and the two men watched Warner depart. "Remind me never to apply for a transfer to Brit-Cit," Giant remarked. "I'm not sure their promotion prerequisites are what I'm after."

Dredd nodded his agreement. "Who's due in next?"

Giant consulted a palm unit. "Judge Ivan Smirnoff from

East-Meg Two. Fond of a drink, apparently. Too fond. Grud only knows what state he'll be in."

Dredd grimaced. "Just so long as it doesn't involve examining penis piercings."

RYAN COULD NOT help admiring the view from inside the glasseen turbolift as it ascended the outside of Emil Jannings Block. From here you could see all the way to the Big Meg's East Wall and beyond to the Black Atlantic. The ocean might be a poisonous, polluted sludge of foul water but the rising sun could still render it beautiful. A handful of early morning skysurfers were already taking advantage of the warm air drifting in over the city, gracefully riding the updrafts and zephyrs. Ryan forgot his quiet terror for a few moments and appreciated the splendour spread out before him. But the turbolift needed only ten seconds to climb a hundred levels to the city block's penthouse. The vista vanished from view as the circular tube reached its destination. The former cadet swivelled round to the turbolift doors, mentally erecting the psychic barriers that had kept him alive these past four months. He would need them more than ever to survive this meeting.

The doors slid silently open and the gentle scent of sandalwood and cinnamon welcomed the new arrival. Ryan stepped into the lobby of the penthouse, his footfalls echoing round the marble walls and floor. Overhead was a stunning glasseen ceiling, the last stars still disappearing from the sky as day replaced night. Behind Ryan the turbolift doors glided shut and he could hear it drop away. He was alone and utterly defenceless, with just his wits, training and nerve to keep him alive. Ryan prayed they would be enough.

Ahead of him walls shimmered aside to reveal the penthouse interior: a vast open plan area filled with plush furnishings and an impressive collection of artwork, a selection of doors leading off the main chamber. Sculptures nestled among potted plants while paintings hung in mid-air, suspended by anti-grav mountings. One particular canvas caught the eye, a large image that seemed to depict an antique food container. Ryan wondered who Campbell was and why anyone would wish to immortalise his soup in a painting. The juve walked towards the picture, intrigued.

"It's a Warhol." The voice was rich and deep, unmistakably that of Jesus Bludd. The powerfully built figure emerged from a doorway, closing it gently behind himself. "I acquired it from a debtor, a private collector who gambled beyond her means. She was forced to liquidate her assets to repay those debts. There is a lesson in her plight; never gamble more than you can afford to lose, lest the consequences be too ruinous to contemplate."

Ryan smiled, uncertain of how to react to this homily. "Yes, Mr Bludd."

"You were admiring the view from the turbolift on your way up?"

The juve was startled by this remark, but chided himself for not realising Bludd would monitor all those who took the turbolift to this level. Ryan's employer had not become one of the Big Meg's most successful crime bosses without learning to be careful. "Yes, I was. You have a remarkably unobstructed view to the east, out over the Black Atlantic."

Bludd smiled. "It did not come cheap. Persuading building developers to keep their high rise projects elsewhere is an expensive luxury. Come, let me show you what I mean." He moved across the room with surprising speed and grace, drawing aside plush red curtains to reveal glasseen doors leading out on to a balcony. "Open," Bludd commanded and the doors slid aside.

Ryan followed his employer on to the balcony. Underfoot was a carpet of fine white sand, curved patterns raked into its surface. Two supple young trees grew out of the sand and white stones surrounded the base of each trunk. A pathway of pale slates led to the edge of the balcony, a metallic balustrade the only apparent barrier to stop the unwary tumbling over. Bludd waited until the juve had joined him at the edge before speaking.

"This is my Zen garden. Whenever I am troubled or uncertain, I come out here and rake the sand, finding meanings in the patterns created. I find it a very calming place, away from the cut-throat nature of daily life in this city."

Ryan asked how the sand remained undisturbed, bringing a smile to Bludd's lips. "A sensible question, one that some lack the wit or imagination to ask." Bludd reached a hand out over the balustrade. Blue light sparkled about his fingers, crackling with unseen energy. "A simple force field protects my solitude here, screening out any unwanted intrusion, keeping my business private. Too many would like to know what I am saying or thinking. That is why Kara always stays so close to my side." Bludd snapped his fingers and the force field disappeared, now just the metal barrier at waist height keeping both men from the sheer drop beyond the balcony. "How long have you been in my employ now Ryan?"

"Four months," the juve replied, a knot of fear tightening in his gut.

"To the day, I believe."

"Yes, sir."

"You were expelled from the Academy of Law after failing your final Hotdog Run assessment in the Cursed Earth."

Ryan nodded, unsure where Bludd was going with all of this.

"So you completed twelve years of training to become a Judge before being cast aside. How did that make you feel?"

"Angry. Frustrated. Counsellors from Psi-Division are assigned to give each failed cadet what the Department calls 'attitude adjustment' so you can reintegrate with other citizens after expulsion."

"They brainwash the failures, rendering them less dangerous."

"Yes, sir."

"But this 'attitude adjustment' didn't work on you."

"No, sir. I am naturally resistant to direct psi-probing or persuasion. Not only is my mind difficult to read, it is almost impossible to implant unwanted suggestions into my thoughts. That turned me into a problem case when the decision was made to expel me. There was talk of corrective surgery, neutralising the aggression centres in my brain."

"And that's when you ran away from the Academy, joined the unwanted, the unloved, the untouchables of City Bottom."

"Yes, sir."

Bludd nodded, seemingly satisfied. "Would it surprise you to know Kara has been trying to infiltrate your mind these past four months?"

"No, sir. In fact I expected it. You are unlikely to trust anyone whose thoughts you cannot know."

"Exactly. But your natural resistance has proved beyond even the talents of my delightful companion. In the past one hundred and twenty days you have been an able, willing and delightfully vicious operative on my behalf. But until we overcome the issue of trust, you will never advance in the Bludd Group. To make that happen, I must ask you to do me a favour, Ryan."

"Name it, sir."

Bludd reached into a pocket and removed a small black pill. "This is an experimental drug being developed by my biochemists. It will temporarily undo your natural psychic defences, enabling Kara to read what is beyond them. Whatever secrets you may be hiding, she will reveal them." The crime boss offered the pill to Ryan. "Will you take it? Will you let yourself succumb and prove above all doubt I can trust you?"

The juve rested one hand on the balustrade, all too conscious of the three hundred metre drop to the ground below. "I'll do it." He took the pill and slid it into his mouth, dry swallowing the black tablet with some difficulty. Ryan opened his mouth to let Bludd see the tablet had gone.

"Very good. Come back inside and have a drink. The pill requires a few minutes for its active agents to pass into your bloodstream. Once that has happened, Kara will have her wicked way with you."

Bludd clapped a fleshy hand on the juve's back and led him back into the penthouse. "It will be a most pleasurable experience, of that you can be certain."

"G'DAY, MATE! HOW'S it hangin?"

Giant regarded the burly figure approaching him with suspicion. "How is what hanging?" he asked the newly arrived Judge from Oz, the Sydney-Melbourne Conurbation, fresh off the shuttle.

"Your bobby dazzler! I reckon it'll be hanging to the ground from the look of ya! Me name's Bruce, Judge Bruce, but you can just call me Brucie. In fact, most Judges are called Bruce where I come from. Makes telling us apart a bit confusing, but it saves on name badges, eh?" The Oz lawman offered his hand for Giant to shake. Bruce's scalp was covered with a rash of bleached yellow hair, his skin was tanned deep bronze and a bushy lemon moustache adorned his top lip. After a few seconds of silence, the new arrival sheepishly withdrew his hand and dropped his luggage on the Customs Hall floor.

"I heard you lot in the Big Meg could be as snotty as a pom in a pickle. Guess that was about right! What's ya name, sport?"

Giant was only catching about half of what Bruce was saying, so dense was the variety of vernacular being spouted by the visitor. But he didn't need a degree in Allspeak to interpret the last question. The Mega-City One Judge tapped his daystick against the metal badge on his chest. "It's right here."

"Giant, eh? It's a big name, fella. Hope you live up to it. Now, where do I dump my gear? I'm looking to paint the town red and I don't want to wait around while you lot rattle your dags!"

"Rattle our dags?" Giant asked, bewilderment getting the better of him.

"Fair dinkum, mate!"

Giant looked across at Dredd, who had been silently observing all of this from one side. The senior Judge jerked a thumb at the exit, so Giant sent Bruce through to the waiting hoverpod. Once the delegate had passed out of hearing, Dredd joined his colleague at the Customs desk.

"You've been to Oz, haven't you, Dredd? Do they all talk like that?"

"I suspect he was laying it on thicker than usual to leave you guessing. Keep an eye on that one. People from the Sydney-Melbourne Conurb aren't as stupid as they look."

"I doubt anyone could be as stupid as he looks," Giant muttered.

"Never trust a man with facial hair," Dredd added. "They always have something to hide."

Giant nodded his agreement. He had read that advice while studying the many volumes of *Dredd's Comportment* at the Academy. What seemed an irrational statement at first had proven to have some truth behind it in Giant's experience. He had been a Judge on the streets for a decade. Of all the set texts that crossed his path at the Academy, it was *Dredd's Comportment* he had come back to most frequently. More often than not the old man was right – that was why he was the best Judge in Mega-City One. Whenever Giant was uncertain how to react in a situation, he found a four word mantra usually provided the answer: What would Dredd do?

Giant was snapped back to attention by a woman clearing her throat. She was a slim Asiatic, clad in the yellow and red garb of a Sino-Cit law enforcer. Her helmet was held in the crook of her left arm, while her right hand offered a selection of papers.

"If you please, Representative Chang reporting." She

arched an eyebrow at Giant, as if challenging him. Her olive skin was flawless except for a small red dragon tattooed on her left cheek. Dark brown eyes twinkled beneath jet black hair that was pulled back from her features in a severe ponytail.

"I'll deal with this one," Dredd growled to his colleague, taking Chang's papers and rifling through them. "What's the purpose of your visit?"

"We are attending the gathering of delegates, as requested by your leader. Were you not informed of our arrival?"

"I'll ask the questions," Dredd snarled.

"As you wish," Chang replied and fell silent.

Dredd waited a few seconds before snapping. "Well?"

"We wish to gain entry to your city for attendance at this summit."

"Who's we?" Dredd looked past Chang but nobody was standing behind her. "I only see one person in the queue and that's you."

"Forgive me. Our translation machine is not yet attuned to the subtleties of your language. It is most regrettable."

Dredd leaned over the desk to press his face close to Chang. "You can play the inscrutable card all you like, Lotus-Flower, but it won't wash with me. I'll be watching you like a hawk, mark my words."

"You intend to observe us while flying through the sky?" Chang inclined her head towards Dredd in a slight bow. "As you wish."

Dredd pointed at the doors. "Shuttle's through there. It'll take you to the assigned quarters."

"You have been most kind. Thank you for this hospitality and I hope you have a pleasant day."

"I said move it!"

The Sino-Cit delegate smiled and moved on. Once she had passed through the doors Giant gave a low whistle. "She's a cool customer. Didn't rise to your bait once."

"Who said I was baiting her?" Dredd replied. "How many of these creeps are we still waiting on?"

Giant consulted his palm unit. "Just two left: Smirnoff and the delegate from Ciudad Barranquilla, Judge Ramirez Belgrano. Both of them were due in an hour ago." He was interrupted by a drunken chorus from the far end of the corridor. Two men were staggering towards the Customs desk, each doing their best to hold the other upright. "This could be them now."

"Terrif," Dredd muttered darkly.

RYAN OPENED HIS eyes and found himself lying on a vast bed, naked but for a black silk sheet draped over his lower body. Over the bed was a mirrored ceiling, reflecting the juve's image back down at him. He didn't remember losing consciousness but must have done so. Last thing he could recall was swallowing a pill, a pill given to him by – Jesus Bludd! Ryan tried to sit up and found he couldn't, his limbs like lead, his body too heavy to lift. Whatever was in that pill had paralysed him, at least temporarily. He was trapped, unable to move. There could be no escape.

That's right, a silky female voice said. Ryan did not hear the voice through his ears. The words were being spoken directly into his thoughts. *One of telepathy's virtues,* the voice continued. *It removes the need for talking out loud. Instead we can communicate without anything in the way – no barriers, no word games, no concealment. Just pure emotion and meaning.*

Ryan heard footsteps moving towards him and strained his head forwards, raising it off the bed high enough to look around the room. It was a symphony of black and red, stark and not a little intimidating. Mirrors lined two of the walls, reflecting each other's image to create a dizzying effect of the room expanding sideways out towards infinity. Kara was striding towards him, her proud body encased in black latex, its figure-hugging surface brightly polished and gleaming. She jumped onto the bed and knelt down across his chest before resting her weight against his crotch. *How's that? Comfortable?*

"Yes," Ryan replied, his voice slurred and unfamiliar.

Kara reached up and pulled off her blonde wig, revealing a perfectly smooth, lightly tanned scalp beneath. *That's better. I do my best work naked.*

"Really?" Ryan felt disconnected, afloat in his own body. Must be the drug. *I wonder if there are any side-effects?*

Let's just say they heighten your sexual responsiveness. Kara began shifting her weight from side to side atop the silk sheet, letting the gleaming black latex slide across the juve's crotch. *The subject becomes aroused beyond anything they have ever known, the slightest touch being magnified a thousand-fold in its effect.*

Ryan could feel his body responding hungrily to the stimulus, despite his mind screaming at it to stop.

Don't fight it, just enjoy.

"But I can't, you're–"

Whatever Bludd wants me to be. Whatever he wants me to do, I do. He's probably watching us right now, I think it gives him a dirty little thrill. That mirror over your head? It's two-way, there's a camera filming everything we do.

"Oh grud–" Ryan gasped, trying to get away from her but unable to move. Kara rested a finger gently against his lips, silencing him.

You know the best part of this heightened arousal? It never quite comes to an end, if you grasp my meaning. I can keep you on the edge of ecstasy for hours – taunting and teasing, have you begging for relief.

Kara increased the pressure against her subject, now moving herself forwards and backwards against him, her breathing coming in little gasps. *And the more aroused you get, the less resistant your mind becomes.*

"Please, no," Ryan begged.

Already I can feel your psychic barriers crumbling. Soon I'll be able to penetrate the deepest corners of your mind. Every thought, every secret, every hidden crevice will be mine. Kara licked her lips and smiled at Ryan. *Get ready. Here I come...*

JUDGE IVAN SMIRNOFF never knew Dredd had a twin. He had been briefed about the legendary lawman, described by some as the Great Satan for having nuked East-Meg One out of existence more than twenty years ago. Smirnoff couldn't care less what had happened to the Sov-Blok's capital, nor about who was responsible for blowing it off the face of the planet. Good riddance to them, that was his attitude. They had been elitist, uptight snobs, always looking down their noses at lowly East-Meg Two and sneering about inferior productivity levels. Bulgarin's bones, there was more to life than productivity!

So when the Apocalypse War led to the annihilation of East-Meg One, Smirnoff had danced a private little jig of joy. He knew it was wrong, it was bad to rejoice in the demise of so many of his countrymen. But Smirnoff shed no tears for them. Instead he had raised a toast to the man believed to be responsible – Joe Dredd. Twenty-two years later, the delegate from East-Meg Two was surprised to find himself confronted by not one but two Dredds at the Customs and Immigration desk.

Smirnoff nudged his new best friend in the ribs. "Comrade Ramirez, can you see? They were so happy to welcome us they sent twins!"

Smirnoff and Belgrano had arrived at the shuttle-port an hour earlier, their flights touching down within minutes of each other. The man from East-Meg Two was dismayed by a large sign warning that anyone caught trying to smuggle illegal stimulants, alcohol or dozens of other banned substances would face harsh punishment.

As his own silent protest, Smirnoff immediately sat down and began consuming a five-litre flagon of synthi-vodka from his hand baggage. He offered to share the contents with anyone who passed but only one man had accepted – the bellicose Belgrano. They finished off the synthi-vodka in record time and had spent the past thirty-seven minutes staggering and weaving their way along the terminal's corridors in search of an exit.

Smirnoff tried to focus on the face of his new comrade but Belgrano seemed to have grown a second head, a most disconcerting turn of events. "Are you alright, *tovarisch*? You don't look so good."

Belgrano's two heads turned towards Smirnoff. "You crazy Russian, I feel fine! You're the one with six eyes, not me."

"Oh!" The East-Meg Two delegate shrugged and smiled. "Good. They will come in handy for spying on these decadent Westerners!"

BLUDD WAS WAITING for Kara when she emerged from the bedchamber. "Well? How did Ryan respond?"

She zipped up the front of her latex bodysuit and smiled. "He thinks he's just had the best sex of his life and I never had to touch him once. Auto-erotic suggestion is a wonderfully powerful tool. Those little black pills of yours would make a fortune on the open market."

"Yes, yes, I know that. What did you discover about our newest recruit?"

Kara sighed. "It's always business before pleasure with you, Jesus."

"Don't change the subject."

She folded her arms and looked back at Ryan asleep on the bed, the juve's face beaming with contentment. "He's definitely undergone conditioning by Psi-Division, but that's to be expected in an expelled cadet. I was able to overcome their mind-blocks in minutes. To destroy the natural psi-barriers in his brain – that would take weeks and leave him a useless, hollowed out husk. But I saw enough to believe he's genuine."

Bludd smiled, one hand reaching out to caress Kara's waist. "Good. Then he can go with you on the mission tomorrow." The crime boss pulled her closer, letting his fingers slide upwards across the latex. "Now, how shall I reward you for doing such a good job?"

A BRIEF SEARCH of Smirnoff's bags revealed he was bringing nothing more dangerous into the Big Meg than a record-breaking blood alcohol level. Giant poured the Sov delegate into an H-wagon and sent him away to sober up. Dredd concentrated his efforts on Belgrano, a corpulent figure with greasy black hair and a greasier moustache. The drunken visitor was escorted to a private interview room, along with his bags.

"Ciudad Barranquilla is a hiding place for the scum of the earth," Dredd observed as he began opening Belgrano's luggage. "The Judges are lazy, corrupt and worse than most of the criminals. If Hershey does manage to negotiate this treaty, it'll be my pleasure to come down and oversee the extradition process personally."

Belgrano belched loudly at Dredd but made no other reply before Giant joined the interrogation. "He said anything useful yet?"

Dredd shook his head. "Not unless you consider breaking wind meaningful. Knowing the boys from Banana City, that'll probably be his finest contribution to the summit meeting." Dredd pointed at one of Belgrano's bags. "You check that one. Belching boy here is just stupid enough to try and bring in a few samples of illicit merchandise."

Giant cracked open the case and reeled back from the smell it released. "Sweet Jovus! Don't they have laundry facilities that far south?"

"Put your respirator on. Smugglers often defecate in their own luggage to dissuade detailed examination."

Giant pulled down the respirator unit from atop his helmet and clamped it firmly over his mouth and nostrils.

Able to breathe freely again, he began sifting through the contents of the case. "Fouled u-fronts account for the odour – a dozen pairs of them! Also got a selection of soiled shorts, socks and shirts. All of them probably violate health regs and air pollution laws."

"Bag 'em for burning, then keep looking," Dredd commanded. He had finished with the other bags and was now trying to slap some life back into the boozy Belgrano's face. "Wake up, wetback! No dozing in here!"

The South American Judge opened his eyes and winced. "Where am I?"

"Mega-City One, stomm for brains. You got anything you want to tell us before we finish searching your bags?"

Belgrano shook his head. "I have nothing to declare, except my," he paused to belch again loudly, this time accompanied by the sound of wind breaking from his trousers, "except my genius."

Dredd pulled his own respirator unit down to escape the odours being exuded. "If that's genius, the Big Smelly must be the smartest river in the world, creep."

"Yo!" Giant called to his colleague. "We got a white powder in this bottle. Care to explain that?"

Belgrano snorted derisively. "That is talcum powder, you fool!"

Giant ran his palm-unit over the disputed substance. "Then why does my scanner analysis call it sugar – eighty-nine per cent pure, to be exact?"

"I have no idea how that got into my luggage."

Dredd joined Giant at the suspect case. He ran his hands around the lining and discovered a series of cylindrical ridges down one side. "And what do we have here, I wonder?"

"That is nothing!" Belgrano shouted. "You have no right to–"

Dredd tore away the lining to reveal dozens of cigarettes sewn into the case. "Tobacco smuggling as well, are we? Quite the entrepreneur, aren't you?"

"Those are for personal use," Belgrano said belligerently.

"There's no smoking in the Big Meg – except in authorised Smokatoria – and the importation of tobacco is strictly forbidden," Giant replied sternly. He plucked open a canister labelled *aftershave* and a drizzle of brown granules tumbled out. "I suppose you'll be telling this is gravy powder next?"

The new arrival just shrugged, smiling weakly.

Dredd picked up one of the granules and slipped it on to his tongue. "Coffee." He spat the granule back out. "Columbian roast." Dredd rounded on Belgrano, jabbing a finger in the drunken man's face. "We've got enough contraband here to put you in the iso-cubes for twenty years, creep. Give me one good reason why I shouldn't lock you up and throw away the key!"

"Diplomatic immunity," Belgrano replied, his breath heavy with the odour of synthi-vodka. "Chief Judge Hershey promised all the delegates full diplomatic immunity while inside your city. I figured it was worth trying to bring in a little something extra for the trip. You can't arrest me for anything."

"Maybe. But all these illegal substances will be confiscated and destroyed. And if I catch you breaking the Law in my city, you can be certain I'll break you too, diplomatic immunity or not!" Dredd turned to Giant. "Get this scum out of my sight!"

Belgrano gave a friendly wave as he staggered out of the interview room, accompanied by Giant. Dredd removed his respirator and activated his helmet radio.

"Dredd to Control, request an urgent meeting with Hershey."

The radio crackled back. "The Chief Judge is busy meeting and greeting the foreign delegates at their private quarters. Her staff say she won't be free for at least an hour."

"Fine. Tell her staff I'll see her in sixty minutes. Dredd out!" He switched off the radio, not even waiting for an acknowledgement. Giant returned to the interview room, shaking his head with exasperation.

"I got the king of the smugglers into an H-wagon. How long are we supposed to be baby-sitting these trouble makers?"

"Until they leave. Forty-eight hours, if the talks go well tomorrow," Dredd replied, impatience evident in his voice.

"And if they don't?"

"That's Hershey's problem. Ours is keeping these punks under control."

Two

RYAN AWOKE TO find Bludd standing over him. The crime boss was smiling broadly. "Congratulations! Kara tells me you passed the test. I believe you're ready to take part in a vital mission on behalf of the Bludd Group. Get dressed and join the others in the briefing room."

The juve smiled his agreement. Once Bludd had left the bedchamber, Ryan hastily pulled on his discarded clothes before bustling into the main area of the penthouse. The door to another room stood ajar nearby, Kara just inside it. Ryan hurried to the entrance and knocked on the door. "Is this the briefing room?"

Kara nodded and motioned for him to enter. Once inside he glanced about the room. It was dark, just the green light from a three-dimensional holographic projector providing any illumination. Six hard-backed chairs were positioned around the projector, all but one occupied. Kara pointed at the newcomer while addressing those already gathered.

"Everyone, this is Blake Ryan, our newest recruit. He was expelled from the Academy of Law and will help us anticipate the judicial response to tomorrow's operation. Ryan, these are the other members of the Bludd Group's elite strike force." Kara began walking in a slow circle around the chairs, pausing behind each one to introduce the person sat there. First was a slab-faced woman riven with tattoos, every visible area of her skin adorned with a pattern or motif.

"This is Tattoo Sue, our muscle. She was thrown off the Mega-Olympics men's wrestling team for steroid abuse."

"The men's team?" Ryan asked despite himself.

Tattoo Sue grinned and made a gesture with her fingers like scissors cutting. "I've always been a woman trapped in a man's body. After the scandal I had nothing to lose, so I had the chop."

Ryan smiled back at her weakly. "Really? How... interesting."

Kara had moved on to the next team member, a male dwarf with flaming red hair. "This is Angry Sanderson. He can break into and out of anywhere, thanks to his nimble fingers and tiny body."

"Nice to meet you," Ryan offered by way of a greeting. Sanderson replied with a scowl and an obscene finger gesture. Kara patted the shoulder of the next person, a gangling black man with oversized hands.

"Skyhook is our driver and pilot, perfect for any getaway. His biggest problem is finding a vehicle with enough leg room."

"Ain't that the truth!" Skyhook said, vigorously nodding his agreement. "Just 'cause I'm tall, don't mean I ain't got feelings!"

"Quite." Kara pointed at the fourth person in the circle, a beautiful woman missing half her face. Scar tissue was all that remained of the left side. "That's Di. Used to be a bomb disposal expert for Tek-Division, until a sloppy defusing job got half her face blown off. She turned down a teaching job at the Academy of Law and went freelance. Now she sets the most delicious bombs imaginable, don't you Di?"

The disfigured woman winked at Ryan with her remaining eye. "That's right, sweetie. Just don't get on my bad side."

"Last but not least is Fincher," Kara continued. "He likes to mutilate."

Ryan realised a laser blade was being held close to his throat. He turned to find a pasty-faced man standing behind him, mirrored sockets where eyes should be. "Nice to meet you," the juve ventured. Fincher just hissed before returning to his seat. Ryan took the empty chair between Skyhook and Di. Once he was settled into place, Kara punched a code into the projector.

"This is our target. It needs little introduction," she said.

Green light began forming itself into a three-dimensional shape above the projector. Ryan watched as the image solidified in the air, his eyes widening as he recognised the familiar building. They couldn't be planning to take on that, could they? The most heavily fortified, best protected structure in all of Mega-City One – this was to be their target?

Kara looked around the circle. "Tomorrow at noon we will attack and destroy the Grand Hall of Justice." She paused briefly. "Any questions?"

DREDD HAD BEEN waiting for two hours when Hershey finally emerged from meeting and greeting the last of the foreign delegates. Each was staying in a Justice Department safe house, partly for their own protection and partly to keep them from getting together and causing any trouble before the summit began in twenty-four hours. The Chief Judge bid a less than fond farewell to Smirnoff and walked out into the Big Meg's fresh air.

"Grud on a greenie," Hershey gasped to Dredd. "Does that man breathe synthi-vodka?"

"Close enough."

The Chief Judge strolled on towards her personal hoverpod. "You requested a meeting, Dredd. I'm extremely busy, so we'll have to walk and talk. What did you want to see me about?"

The Street Judge fell into step beside Hershey. "Diplomatic immunity. I've already confiscated enough contraband to merit a life sentence in the cubes. Grud only knows what tricks the rest of these–"

"Distinguished guests," Hershey interjected.

"These distinguished guests," Dredd continued, his voice heavy with sarcasm, "will pull in the next two days. Granting them immunity has tied my hands, made it near to impossible for us to maintain any sort of discipline."

The Chief Judge stopped outside her hoverpod. "Let's cut to the chase. You think I've made a mistake allowing these delegates to enter the city, let alone open negotiations with them."

"Permission to speak candidly?"

Hershey sighed in exasperation. "Granted."

"None of these creeps can be trusted to abide by our Customs and Immigrations rules. How can you expect them to abide by the terms of any treaty you might persuade them to sign?"

"We have to make a start somewhere, Dredd."

"Maybe, but–"

"Enough!" The Chief Judge held up a hand to silence him. "Joe, you were my mentor when I went offworld for my first assignment out of the Academy, helping you find the Judge Child. I didn't always agree with your decisions but I learned to respect your reasoning. That was nearly a quarter of a century ago. Give me some credit for having learnt a little about the ways of the world in the intervening years, will you?"

Dredd pursed his lips but said nothing. Hershey softened her voice before speaking again.

"You and I both know Chief Judges rarely last longer than five years in the job. That's almost exactly how long I've had the big chair. The responsibility of trying to keep this city from descending into anarchy, well, it eats away at you, one piece at a time. When I'm gone, I want to leave something behind, something tangible to show my time at the top wasn't just about maintaining the status quo. I've spent my entire career trying to drag the Justice Department a bit further into the twenty-second century. If I can broker a deal for a global extradition treaty, that would be a significant achievement. You know what the benefits will be just as well as I do, if not better."

Dredd nodded.

"I know the diplomatic immunity is going to create more problems than it solves," Hershey continued, "but it was the only way to get some of these citi-states to send delegates here at all. You and the others will have to turn a blind eye to some law breaking. That will stick in your guts, but you'll get over it. Right now securing any sort of compromise from the likes of Sino-Cit and Ciudad Barranquilla is more important than a few petty crimes."

"As long as that's all it is," Dredd replied.

"Agreed." The Chief Judge smiled. "Can I go now?"

Dredd stepped back and let Hershey climb into her hoverpod. Once she was seated inside, the Chief Judge opened the window to add something more. "Trust me when I say I will protect this city and its people by any and all means necessary. If I have to send a thousand Judges to their deaths to achieve that, I will – even you. No single person is more important than this city. You taught me that." Hershey gave her pilot a hand signal to leave before offering a final comment, shouting to make herself heard over the hoverpod's engines. "See you on the streets, Joe!"

Dredd moved away as the vehicle took to the midday sky. Only after the hoverpod was out of earshot could Dredd hear the voice calling via his helmet radio.

"This is Giant! Dredd, can you hear me?"

"Dredd responding. What's the problem?"

"Medical emergency signal from the safe house where our Brit-Cit delegate is staying, corner of Beaker and Honeydew."

Dredd was already running towards his Lawmaster. "On my way!"

* * *

KARA OUTLINED THE plan of attack and what role each member of the strike team would take. Ryan did his best to keep all the details in his head, knowing he must find a way to communicate them to the Justice Department.

Kara deactivated the holographic projector. The briefing room light automatically brightened in response. "I will be leading this mission personally," she said. "There is no guarantee all or indeed any of us will make it back alive. Should you die, an exceedingly generous compensation payment shall be made to whomever you have chosen. But our attack must be successful. Disrupting the extradition treaty negotiations is vital to ensuring the medium and long-term health of the Bludd Group's operations around the globe. One surgical strike against the summit and Hershey's campaign will be put back years, even decades." She looked around the faces of those present, fixing them in her gaze one by one. "If anybody wants out, well, forget it. You all know too much. If one word of this plan should leak out, the consequences would be extremely prejudicial. Do I make myself clear?"

The strike team members gave a murmur of assent, Ryan joining in.

Kara smiled, apparently satisfied. "You know what you have to do. Begin preparations for tomorrow. Leave nothing to chance. We have less than twenty-four hours before starting our attack. During that time nobody is allowed to leave the building, for obvious reasons. That's it. Dismissed. We reassemble at dawn tomorrow."

She stood aside to let the team members file out. Tattoo Sue left hand in hand with Di, the two women stroking each other's faces affectionately. Fincher was next to go, followed by Angry Sanderson and Skyhook. Ryan remained behind, hoping to talk with Kara. He approached her nervously, biting one side of his bottom lip. "Look, about what happened between us earlier..."

"Put it out of your mind," she replied coldly. "I already have."

"Right. Yes, of course." The juve smiled, thrusting his hands into his pockets. "Well, I guess I'll start on my prep work. To get those passcodes you want, I'll need to access a Justice Department terminal or comms line."

Kara nodded her agreement. "There's a scrambled link in the next room, you can hook in from there. But don't stay online more than a minute. PSU traces are getting more sophisticated all the time."

"Got it," Ryan replied with a smile. "Well, I'll... get to it."

GIANT WAS FIRST through the door into Warner's private quarters. The two Judges assigned to stand guard outside the safe house, Eaglestone and Jenkins, reported that nobody had entered or left since the Brit-Cit delegate was installed several hours earlier. Warner had accepted delivery of a small metal suitcase but nothing else out of the ordinary had happened. The first they knew about the medical emergency was when Control relayed news of the alarm button being triggered from within the safe house. The pair had stormed their way inside the building but Warner refused to let them enter his private quarters.

"He claimed to have hit the medical emergency button by mistake," Jenkins explained. "We told him procedures required us to confirm this but he wouldn't come out. That's when we called for back-up."

"You did the right thing," Giant said. He approached the doorway to Warner's private quarters. Normally the closed circuit cameras inside would tell their own story but these had been switched off by the visitor when he arrived. Giant rapped on the door with his knuckles. "Delegate Warner, this is Judge Giant. We met earlier at Customs."

"I remember," Warner replied in a pained voice.

"Can you open the door so I can enter?"

"I made a mistake. There's no medical emergency here.

I'm sure I'll be ready in plenty of time for the first session tomorrow."

"Nevertheless, we are duty-bound to protect you from befalling any harm while a guest of Mega-City One. I must insist upon gaining entry."

"No! You can't come in here. I'm not… umm… not ready for you. Maybe later?" Warner suggested hopefully.

Giant took off his helmet and rested his left ear against the door. He could hear someone hobbling about the room inside and a faint whirring noise. "I'm sorry but unless you open this door, I will be forced to break it down."

"You can't do that!" Warner cried out, his voice filled with desperation. "If you do that I will leave this city immediately and never return. Without Brit-Cit's aid your Chief Judge would never have been able to instigate this summit. If I should withdraw, you can be certain the extradition negotiations will collapse!"

Giant stepped back from the door. "Delegate Warner, I'm going to send the other Judges outside so it will be just you and me. Would that be better?"

"It's a start," the Brit-Cit Judge replied after a long silence.

Giant loudly ordered Eaglestone and Jenkins from the building, waiting until they were well outside before returning to the door. "They've left the safe house. It's just the two of us now. How about you open up so I can see that you are alright? If there is no medical emergency, I'll cancel the alarm signal and you can be left in peace. How does that sound?"

"I'm not sure," Warner muttered. "Let me think about it a minute…"

Giant pulled a chair to beside the door and sat down. "There's no rush. I'll be waiting here while you decide what to do."

"Thank you. You're being most understanding."

"You're welcome, sir." Giant stopped to listen. He could hear a motorcycle rapidly approaching. It screeched to a halt outside the safe house. Raised voices exchanged a few words and then hurried footfalls grew louder. Seconds later Dredd burst in, his mouth set in grim determination.

"Stand aside, Giant! You've tried the diplomatic approach, now it's my turn!" Dredd strode to the door and kicked it down. A high-pitched squeal of terror was emitted from inside. Dredd stomped into Warner's private quarters, followed by Giant close behind. They both stopped abruptly when confronted by the scene within. The Brit-Cit Judge whimpered at them.

"I take it you're not sitting comfortably," Dredd said.

RYAN WALKED INTO the communications room of Bludd's penthouse. It was a small, dark chamber with cables climbing the walls and snaking across the floor. Like many wishing to keep their actions secure, the crime boss had obviously learned to avoid wireless technology. The Justice Department's Public Surveillance Unit had enjoyed great success intercepting signals from wireless systems, breaking down even the most complex of encryption locks.

The juve soon located the scrambled terminal and opened an interface with the judicial comms network, hacking his way in through a portal that had been deliberately weakened. When Ryan first agreed to go undercover with the Bludd Group, he suggested creating this access route as a way of proving loyalty to his new employer. Only low level security information could be reached via the portal but it would prove his value. As a last resort the former cadet could use it to call for extraction or to pass on urgent data. But Ryan had been warned against this, the risk of detection being too great.

"Make no mistake," Dredd had said, "this is for life and death circumstances only. While you are undercover you stay there: no contact with Department personnel, no secret messages, nothing. The only time you call for help is when you want out. Got that?"

Ryan took a deep breath and began typing: BLUDD GROUP PLANS ATTACK ON GRAND HALL OF JUSTICE, NOON TOMORROW. AM STAYING UNDERCOVER TO DISRUPT OPERATION – BR. He looked around the room, his index finger poised above the ENTER button. The juve was conscious of the damp patches around his armpits, trickles of sweat dribbling down his back and legs. Once he sent this message, there was no going back. Within twenty-four hours either he or the strike team would be dead. Ryan tapped the button once and then terminated the connection.

The sound of running feet approaching the comms room became audible. Oh grud, they must have been watching him! Ryan staggered back from the terminal, looking around for a weapon, any weapon. But there was nothing. He was on his own, about to die in a room full of wires and machines, nobody else aware his life was being snuffed out.

The door swung inwards to reveal Skyhook. "There you are! I've been looking everywhere for you! Are you coming or not?"

"Coming where?"

"Mr Bludd is putting on a feast for us. It's a strike team tradition. We call it the last meal of the condemned."

"Oh, right." Ryan let out a sigh of relief. "Sounds great. Lead the way." Skyhook turned away and the juve snuck a final glance at the terminal. By now his message should have reached the PSU officer assigned to the case. It was out of Ryan's hands. He left the comms room and hurried after Skyhook, spurred on by the delicious smell of cooking food. Ryan was suddenly ravenous. Nothing like flirting with death to give you a hearty appetite.

JAGO WARNER WAS naked and ashamed. His face was flushed red with embarrassment, a bold contrast to the artificial blue colouring of his hair. The delegate from Brit-Cit was half standing and half sitting on the double bed in his private quarters. Beneath him a mechanical man was squirming about on the mattress, apparently trying to prise itself free. Only a cloth draped over Warner's crotch maintained any shred of dignity.

Giant suppressed a smile. "Now I see why you weren't eager for us to come in," he said.

"This also explains the suitcase."

"Suitcase?" Dredd asked.

"Jenkins and Eaglestone reported its delivery when I arrived." Giant carefully walked around the unusual living sculpture atop the bed and picked up a discarded silver suitcase. It was empty but for a thin booklet. The Judge began reading aloud from the printed instructions. "Thank you for buying the Big Meg Self-Assembling Pleasure Mech. We trust it will offer you a lifetime of trouble-free enjoyment and stimulation. Whatever your preference, the Big Meg is the man for the job. We guarantee you'll always come back for more with the Big Meg!"

Dredd stroked his chin thoughtfully before speaking. "Did you want to ask for a refund personally? Or would you rather it went through official channels?"

"Don't be ridiculous!" Warner snapped. "Just get me off of this thing!"

"Wait, there's more!" Giant announced, still reading the booklet. "Most of this is in Japanese, but as far as I can tell, using this device in the way he's doing is against the terms of its warranty."

Dredd shrugged. "Guess that rules out your refund."

"Please, I'm begging you! Give me a hand to get free," Warner pleaded.

Dredd turned to his colleague. "Looks like a job for Med-Division if you ask me. What do you think, Giant?"

"Med-Division, definitely. Maybe some Tek-Judges too. They'll probably have to cut that thing off. Who knows how long it'll take?"

"Hours, maybe three or four."

"At least!"

"For the love of grud, just do something!" Warner screamed before breaking down in tears. "I can't keep myself up like this much longer."

Dredd and Giant exchanged a look. Finally Giant burst out laughing, no longer able to contain his mirth. "I'll call in Med-Division," he said between guffaws on his way out of the room.

Dredd waited until Giant was out of earshot before leaning closer to the delegate from Brit-Cit. "Word about what's happened here is going to spread pretty quick unless I stamp on it. You know my reputation. I can have all mention of this quashed. Your superiors in Brit-Cit need never know about your little… mishap. But you've got to do something for me."

"I'm a little stuck right now–"

"Stay where you are, pervert! I meant when you get into the negotiating room tomorrow. This treaty means a lot to my Chief Judge and you're going to help her secure an agreement. Is that clear?"

"I don't know, I…" Warner maintained his defiance briefly, until Dredd ripped away the cloth covering the visitor's crotch. "Alright, alright! I'll do it! Just leave me with some dignity. Damn you Dredd!"

"My pleasure," he replied, handing the cloth back to Warner. "I'll be waiting outside. Remember what we agreed, because I won't forget what I've seen here, unfortunately."

Med-Judges arrived as Dredd was leaving. He jerked a thumb back at the unfortunate delegate from Brit-Cit. "He's all yours. Don't feel obliged to go gently on my account."

Shortly afterwards, residents in neighbouring city blocks reported hearing a scream of agony and relief from the building surrounded by judicial vehicles.

HERSHEY REREAD THE text of Ryan's message before passing it to the next member of the Council of Five. For nearly fifty years this handful of Judges had passed the Laws by which Mega-City One was controlled. Each member represented a sub-division of the Justice Department, each offered a fresh perspective on the challenges facing the Big Meg. Together with the Chief Judge they formed a collective entity, a gestalt mind focused on preserving law and order.

Once all the councillors had seen the message, Hershey called the emergency meeting to order. "Unfortunately, that is all the intelligence we have. Noon tomorrow is when the first session of the global extradition treaty negotiations is due to start, here in the Grand Hall of Justice. It cannot be mere coincidence these two events are planned to occur simultaneously. I believe it is safe to assume the Bludd Group and its leader plan to disrupt the session, if possible, to destroy all hopes of a treaty being agreed."

The Chief Judge glanced around the rest of the council. Nobody dissented from what she had suggested, the conclusion was both logical and inescapable. "Jesus Bludd is not alone in wanting to see the treaty halted in its tracks," Hershey continued. "Most of the crime bosses in Mega-City One are against it for obvious reasons, as are underworld elements in other citi-states. But it required someone of Bludd's daring and guile to attack the negotiations directly. We must take this threat seriously."

The head of Tek-Division, Judge McTighe, cleared his throat. He had risen through the ranks thanks to a combination of genius-level intelligence and predator-like ambition. But outside his specialised area McTighe lacked the street smarts and experience most senior law enforcers felt were required to become Chief Judge. Not for the first time, McTighe revealed an ignorance of matters outside his own field. "Who is this Jesus Bludd? I've heard of him in passing, but never knew he was such a threat."

Hershey gestured to the head of PSU. "I've asked Judge Niles to give us a background briefing on the leader of the Bludd Group..."

Niles nodded to the Chief Judge before activating a Tri-D screen on one wall of the council chamber. All those present swivelled round in their seats to get a better view. A blurry image of Bludd appeared first, grim-faced and determined. "This picture was snatched a few hours ago, our most recent sighting. The crime boss was taking the morning air on the balcony of his penthouse atop Emil Jannings Block. Next picture please."

The voice-activated computer replaced the image of Bludd as a grown man with a picture of him as a child. The boy's face was smudged by dirt and dried blood, clean lines cut through the mess by the tracks of his tears. "And this is Jesus Bludd twenty-five years ago, aged seven. That was when he first came to our attention, not long after Cal was deposed." In 2101, Mega-City One was thrown into anarchy when an insane Judge called Caligula usurped control of the Justice Department. In the aftermath of his reign street gangs had claimed sovereignty in some parts of the Big Meg.

"What happened?" McTighe asked.

"Bludd was an only child in a single parent family. His father disappeared soon after the boy was born in 2094. Bludd's mother was on welfare, scraping by in Southside Sector 41. After Cal was deposed, a gang called the Cosmic Punks set themselves up as Judges in that sector and declared the surrounding streets a no-go area. Bludd's mother was raped and murdered in front of the boy as a lesson for other citizens. The perp responsible escaped justice after the boy withdrew his eye witness testimony."

Hershey leaned forward, intrigued. "He was intimidated into recanting?"

"That was how it seemed at the time. A week later, after Dredd had single-handedly restored order to Sector 41, the perp's corpse was found jammed in a public grinder. Nobody was ever convicted of the murder."

The Chief Judge formed her fingers into a steeple in front of her face. "That suggests the boy got revenge on his mother's killer. But what are the chances of a seven-year-old child forcing a grown man into a grinder?"

Niles nodded. "Bludd was brought in for questioning and evaluation. The results were most remarkable. The boy displayed close to genius-level IQ, was able to beat any lie-detector available at the time and even exhibited some latent psi-talents."

"Why wasn't he drafted into the Academy?" Hershey asked. "He was an orphan by then, a ward of the city. Results like that would have marked him out as a prime candidate for training as a Judge, even starting his training two years after the other cadets."

"Psychological testing results raised some... issues about Bludd's attitude. A rebellious streak a mile wide–"

"Such problems can be overcome with Psi-Division intervention, even surgery," McTighe interrupted.

"–and strong sociopathic tendencies. An amorality in the boy's attitude to right and wrong that would make any hardened perp proud," Niles replied. "Nevertheless, Jesus Bludd was offered a place at the Academy. He refused it and absconded from judicial custody, disappearing for the next eight years."

The PSU head called for the next picture. Again, the resolution was poor and the image blurred, but the juve at the centre of the picture was still recognisable as Bludd. He was running and looking back over his shoulder. A second juve was following him.

"By the age of fifteen Bludd was leading his own street gang, clawing his way up the criminal underworld of City Bottom. The day this image was captured by PSU cameras was also the day Bludd came closest to being caught. The gang was disturbed raiding a shoppera and fled, running right into a Judge patrol. We had been tipped off by one of the juves. Every member of the gang was killed or wounded except Bludd, who escaped unscathed. It was only after the incident that someone thought to cross-check the recorded voice of our anonymous caller with voice prints already held on file. We found a perfect match from eight years earlier. Bludd had turned in his own gang."

"Do we know why?" The question came from Judge Buell, head of the Special Judicial Squad.

Niles shook his head. "Perhaps Bludd suspected one of his gang was about to betray him. Perhaps he just decided it was time for a change. Whatever the reason, Bludd used the Judges to rid himself of the gang and start over."

"Remarkably ruthless," Hershey commented.

"As I said before, sociopathic tendencies. Bludd defines his own moral universe, divorced from whatever ideals we or his fellow perps might have about what's right and wrong. Honour amongst thieves means nothing to this man. He makes his own rules." Niles called for the next picture. It showed Bludd entering the Dustbuster, accompanied by Kara.

"This was taken four months ago, when our operative was inserted into the Bludd Group. Jesus has put on a lot of weight since his juvie days but don't be mistaken into thinking he has gone soft – that bulk is all muscle. He could crush your skull with those hands, but prefers to have others do his dirty work. Despite our best efforts to prove otherwise, Bludd appears to be a legitimate businessman. He is a leading crime boss but keeps everything twice removed from himself, always maintaining deniable culpability. He's untouchable."

McTighe rose from his chair and walked towards the Tri-D screen. He pointed at the woman climbing the Dustbuster steps beside Bludd. "Who's she? I'm sure I've seen her face before."

"That's Bludd's confidante and enforcer, a woman known only as Kara. We believe they may also be lovers, although there is no explicit data on Bludd's sexuality to back that up. She joined the Bludd Group within the last two years. According to what little our previous undercover operatives have gleaned, Bludd collected her as part of a gambling debt from a rival. We know she's a psyker, as deadly as she is beautiful. Kara is probably the person who uncovered the last three Wally Squad Judges who tried to infiltrate the Bludd Group. It seems likely she is also the person who killed them." Niles deactivated the Tri-D screen. "Much of what I have told you is speculation and educated guesswork. Penetrating the Bludd Group is well nigh impossible. Frankly, I'm surprised the cadet Ryan has survived this long on the inside."

Buell caught the hint. His department concerned itself with monitoring the actions of other Judges, so Buell was always looking for angles involving corruption or dereliction of duty. "You think he may have been turned?"

Niles shrugged. "As I said, speculation and guesswork. Up until this morning Ryan was kept on the fringes of the organisation. At dawn he entered Bludd's penthouse and hasn't come out since. Either he's been accepted into the inner circle or else he's being set up for a mighty fall."

Hershey called a halt to the discussion. "I've heard enough. Niles, do you have any recommendations to make?"

"We have to take any threat from Bludd seriously. Most crime bosses are vain, egotistical perps who undo themselves. This one is something special, always five steps ahead. Until we know differently, we have to take this warning at face value."

The Chief Judge looked round at the others. "Anybody think otherwise?" The only reply was silence. "Very well. We proceed as planned with the treaty summit tomorrow here at the Grand Hall, but step up security by a factor of five. From dawn there will be a twenty block exclusion zone around this building, nothing to get in or out without my express permission. The same applies to the sky overhead, nothing flies through the surrounding airspace. Anyone who tries to do so will be shot down. We can ask questions later."

"That will cause chaos in nearby sectors," Buell noted.

"We've had worse," Hershey replied. "This emergency council meeting is at an end. Gentlemen, thank you for your time."

* * *

RYAN SAT BACK in his chair, bloated and unable to contemplate moving. Never had he feasted on such a succulent selection of delicacies. To eat real meat from real animals instead of synthetic munce was a treat in itself, but the range of exquisite flesh on offer had beggared belief. After helping himself to thirds the juve waved away his plate, letting the house droids clear the table at last.

Bludd entered the dining room with Kara as the last of the food was removed, applauding the efforts of his strike team. "You have eaten well and that is as it should be. Never let it be said Jesus Bludd permitted anyone in his employ to face death on an empty stomach!"

The others laughed heartily at this, so Ryan did his best to join in. But the smile faded from his lips as Kara locked the double doors, the only exit from the dining room. Bludd smirked at the four men and two women sat round the table. "Unfortunately, for one of you, that death is going to come a little sooner than expected." The strike team members exchanged perplexed glances but said nothing.

Ryan felt his lower intestine clench in fear, suddenly all too aware of how much he had eaten and how badly it was sitting within him. But he kept the quiet terror from climbing into his conscious thoughts, lest they betray him.

Bludd began walking around the circular table, passing behind each of the six operatives. "One of you is disloyal. I won't say how you were discovered. It's enough to know that you were. Time and again the Justice Department has tried to insert one of its precious Wally Squad into the ranks of the Bludd Group. Time and again my beloved Kara has found out these undercover cretins and punished them for their temerity. But, for once, it was not Kara who revealed the disloyalty. It was one of you." Bludd stopped behind the tall figure sat opposite Ryan. Skyhook smiled and nodded at the others, accepting their thanks and congratulations.

Bludd held up a hand for silence, before resting it lightly on Skyhook's right shoulder. "As soon as he was able, Skyhook alerted me to the presence of an intruder amongst us. For that, Skyhook will be given a very special reward. But first I want to give the guilty party a chance to make themselves known. Do the decent thing, stand up for what you believe in and tell us why you turned traitor. You have ten seconds to do so, beginning now."

Ryan could feel fear shifting inside him, stretching and expanding, uncoiling itself like a serpent. He clenched both his fists and drove the fingernails into the flesh of his palms, forcing them to break the skin so the pain would distract his mind. This could all be a bluff, the juve told himself over and over, this could all be a bluff. But the serpent of fear was gathering itself inside him, as if snaking upwards along his spinal column towards his brain.

Bludd beckoned Kara closer to the table. "It seems nobody wishes to confess or absolve themselves in our presence. My dear, you will have to do the honours." Bludd took her place by the exit, resting his back against the double doors. "I want you all to pay attention. Disloyalty will not be tolerated. Let what happens next be a lesson to you."

Kara regarded each of the strike team members in turn as she spoke into their minds, her psychic voice low and penetrating, the words suffused with menace. *I am reaching into your minds, one by one. Do not resist me, do not defend your thoughts. You cannot escape, cannot flee what is coming. This is the end for you, traitor. This is your death.*

Ryan tried to relax. I have nothing to fear but fear itself, he thought to himself, making the sentence into a mantra. I have nothing to fear but fear itself. He looked around the table at the others. Each seemed to be wrestling with their own inner demons, bracing themselves for what was to come. The juve felt something warm and wet dribble down over his lips and chin. He wiped a hand across his face and it came away red, smeared with crimson.

I'm having a nose bleed, Ryan realised. The other five were also bleeding freely from their nostrils, some trying to staunch the flow.

Do not be alarmed, Kara announced. *The nose bleeds are a side-effect of my psi-probing. They will pass. Brace yourselves. The worst is yet to come.*

Pain lanced through Ryan's head, like a cold knife slicing into his brain. His body went into spasm, a scream crying out through clenched teeth. Moisture soaked his seat as the juve lost control of his bowels, a dark stain spreading out from his crotch. Ryan clutched at his temples, unable to cope any longer. Stop this – please!, his mind begged.

It was then one of the strike team's head exploded.

DREDD HAD SPENT the afternoon visiting each of the foreign delegates to ensure they were safe and sound. As night fell over Mega-City One, the Judge shifted his attention to supervising final safety checks at the negotiations venue. An entire floor in the Grand Hall of Justice had been set aside for the talks. All turbolift access to that level was locked off for anyone lacking the proper security clearance and passcodes. Nobody could get in or out without Dredd's personal authorisation. He had received word about the warning from Ryan. If Bludd was planning to directly attack the talks tomorrow, the strike team would have to do so over Dredd's dead body, and that wasn't going to happen.

Satisfied with security for access to the venue, Dredd strode around the rooms set aside for the negotiations. A central chamber was the main gathering point, with tables and chairs facing each other in a ring. Doors led out to a corridor that encircled the main chamber. Surrounding these in an outer ring were smaller rooms for each of the delegates to use during breaks or for one-on-one sessions. The visitors had been given secure scrambled lines of communication back to their own citi-states, to help them maintain a dialogue with their respective leaders. Hershey had personally assured the Chief Judge of each delegate that these lines could not be monitored or intercepted.

Dredd was making a final sweep of the outer chambers when his helmet radio crackled into life. "Control to Dredd, come in."

"Dredd responding. I said I didn't want to be disturbed."

"Giant requests you meet him at the corner of Cartier and Klugman."

"I'll be there in an hour. I want to–"

"Giant says this is urgent. He called it a Crazy Zhivago and Wild Wallaby situation. Says you'll know what that means."

"Stomm," Dredd snarled with disgust. He had insisted all those involved with securing the safety of the delegates use discretion during radio transmissions. It was Giant who came up with codenames. Crazy Zhivago meant the East-Meg Two delegate had disappeared from his private quarters, while Wild Wallaby indicated Judge Bruce was also involved. "Tell Giant I'm on my way!" Dredd was already running for the nearest turbolift.

RYAN OPENED HIS eyes. "I'm still alive," he whispered and smiled. His clothes and face were spattered with viscera from the headless corpse still sat opposite. Skyhook's reward for accusing another member of the strike team was to have his brain exploded by Kara's formidable psi-powers.

"Skyhook was the traitor?" Angry Sanderson asked, bewildered. "But you said he had accused one of us..."

Kara smiled, walking around the table to the chair containing Skyhook's remains. "He did. Your late team member accused Ryan of being a spy for the Judges, sent to infiltrate the Bludd Group. Skyhook even claimed to have seen Ryan sending messages to Justice Department from within the penthouse." She placed a hand on each of the dead man's shoulders, a gaping absence where

Skyhook's head should have been. "What he didn't know is Ryan was acting on my orders, passing disinformation to the Judges about tomorrow's mission." Kara fixed the juve in her gaze and licked her luscious red lips.

"We have no illusions about Ryan's loyalty. I have tested it personally."

Tattoo Sue was wiping blood and bone fragments off her ample chest with a linen napkin.

"So why kill Skyhook, if he was just mistaken?"

Bludd answered that question. "Disloyalty will not be tolerated, as I said before. You must trust each other utterly, otherwise your mission will fail." He smiled broadly. "Any more questions? No? Then I suggest you all retire to bed. Tomorrow we make history. Tomorrow we change the future. Tomorrow, we show the so-called rulers of this world just who holds the real power." Bludd threw open the double doors and beckoned Kara to him. Once she was at his side, the crime boss wrapped a proprietorial hand around her waist and they strode away together.

In the dining room, Ryan found it hard to tear his eyes from Skyhook's corpse. Fincher approached the body and examined the cadaver with professional detachment. "Remarkable," he said in a Brit-Cit accent. "Not many birds can boil a man's brain in his cranial juices until it explodes." Fincher dipped a finger into the ghastly wound where Skyhook's neck had been. "Still hot, too."

Ryan ran from the room to find the nearest bathroom, an unequal battle with the contents of his digestive system about to be comprehensively lost. Fincher looked up in mock surprise, a disingenuous smile crossing his face.

"Was it something I said?"

Three

GIANT WAS THE third helmet to reach the crash scene on the corner of Cartier and Klugman. One look inside the remains of the hoverpod confirmed what he had heard from Control. Giant shook his head in despair before turning to acknowledge the other Judges, a female veteran called Glass and her partner Daley. "You were right to have Control call me. How long have you been here?"

"Twenty minutes," Glass responded. "We saw the hoverpod weaving across Anton Diffring Overzoom before it plunged down to the skedways, nearly decapitating a jaywalker. We pursued the vehicle but the driver didn't seem aware of our presence. Eventually the hoverpod swerved to avoid a little girl and flew straight into Emporio Kneepad."

Giant glanced round the scene. This part of Sector 87 was a high-priced shoppera zone, lined with expensive outlets like Tommi Illfinger and The Gyp. A crowd of bystanders was already gathering despite the late hour, straining to get a better look at the crash and any unfortunate victims. After failing to contact Dredd directly, Giant left a message for him with Control before assigning Glass and Daley to keep the cits back. Once a cordon was established the Judge approached the crumpled hoverpod.

The Maxi Zoom Dweebie 5000 was wedged fast in the window display of Emporia Kneepad. The hoverpod's front had collapsed backwards on impact, trapping the two occupants within the vehicle. Having been stuck inside for so long, Giant would normally expect them to be dead or crying out in agony. Instead the two men were singing in slurred voices.

"What's the matter you? Hey! Why you looka so sad?" Leading the tune was a broad, nasal accent Giant recognised from earlier in the day. The other person in the hoverpod tried to join in, his broken English and East European accent making nonsense of the lyrics.

"Ahh, shut up off your vase!"

"Nah, mate, it's 'shuttupa your face'!"

"That's what I said, *tovarisch!*"

"Nah, you said vase; not face, vase!"

"That's what I said; vase!"

Giant used a small but powerful torch from his Lawmaster to illuminate the scene inside the crumpled hoverpod. Smirnoff was wedged behind the steering wheel, a half empty bottle of synthi-vodka clutched in one hand while gesticulating at his passenger with the other. Bruce was sprawled in the other seat, draining the last dregs from another bottle. The air inside the hoverpod was close to forty per cent proof.

"Good evening, gentlemen. Been out for a little excursion, have we?" Giant asked, his sarcasm wasted on the inebriated delegates.

"Gidday, Gigantor!" Bruce shouted.

"That's Judge Giant to you."

"Yeah, whatever. See, I wanted to show Ivan here all the sights."

Smirnoff nodded vigorously. Bruce smiled. "We were trying to find the Sstadue of Juddment, bud I think we took a bid of a wrong turn. Now, if you'll juss point uss in the right direction, then everything'ss apples and we'll be on our way."

"Apples?" Smirnoff asked. "Why would everything be apples, comrade?"

"She'll be right," Bruce replied. His drinking partner looked bewildered so the Oz delegate tried again. "As good as gold? Fair dinkum?"

Smirnoff just shrugged, belching loudly.

"You, gentlemen, will not be going anywhere else tonight," Giant announced, "except back to your beds to sleep this off. In the morning we can talk about the limits of your diplomatic immunity. Do I make myself clear?"

The man from East-Meg Two smiled at Giant and offered him the bottle of synthi-vodka. "Ahh, my dusky *tovarisch!* Drink with us! Here, drink!" Giant took the bottle but, to Smirnoff's dismay, emptied the contents on the ground. "You didn't have to do that, you know. But don't worry, I have more back at the hotel."

"It's not a hotel, *tovarisch*," Giant replied tersely. "It's a Justice Department safe house. You're supposed to be..." He gave up, realising Smirnoff had fallen asleep at the wheel. "Terrif." Giant stepped away from the vehicle and summoned a rescue detail to the scene, along with Med-Judges and other support teams. Less than a minute later the sound of a Lawmaster could be heard approaching. The bystanders stepped aside to let the new arrival through, Dredd barking at the crowd to move further back.

Once he had dismounted from his motorcycle, Dredd strode directly to Giant who offered a brief report. The younger Judge knew from experience that his former mentor had little patience for extraneous detail and less for bad news. Sure enough, Dredd's face grew sourer by the second as Giant outlined what had taken place. Once the report was finished, Dredd marched to the wrecked hoverpod and ripped open the passenger door. Bruce tumbled to the ground, a sloppy grin plastered across his face.

"Gidday, Dreddy! How's it going, cobber?"

"Are you injured?"

Bruce's brow furrowed. "Ssay thad again, mate?"

"Are – you – injured?" Dredd snarled through clenched teeth.

The Oz Judge smiled again. "Nah, no worries. I'm right as rain!"

Dredd nodded before gesturing for Giant to join him by the hoverpod. "You told my colleague you were planning a visit to the Statue of Judgement."

Bruce pulled himself into a sitting position. "Yeah."

Dredd crouched beside Bruce, his voice a murmur so low Giant could only just make out the words. "Then listen up, cobber. As far as you're concerned, I am the Statue of Judgement. Unless you want to see my fist up close and personal, I suggest you and the Red Menace get your stomm together and get back to your quarters, now. Otherwise I'll be more than happy to drop kick you both back to the misbegotten hellholes you call home, diplomatic immunity or no diplomatic immunity. Do I make myself understood, mate?"

The Oz delegate nodded hurriedly, scrambling to his feet. Bruce leaned inside the hoverpod and shook Smirnoff awake. "Come on! Rattle your dags, Ivan, it's time to go. Move it!"

By the time the two drunks had stumbled out of the wreckage, an H-wagon was descending from the sky to collect them. Dredd made sure the pair were loaded safely inside and gave the pilot orders about where to deliver them. He also put a Med-Judge in the H-wagon.

"Give these two something to dissolve the alcohol in their systems, but make sure they still have a hangover in the morning," he said. "The more fragile they feel during the opening session of negotiations, the quicker Hershey will get her treaty."

Giant observed all of this while supervising the clean-up crew assigned to remove all evidence of the accident. He joined Dredd as the H-wagon rose into the air.

"You know, I don't think I've ever heard you say so many words in a row as you did to Bruce just now."

"I had to get his attention."

Giant smiled. "Is it my imagination or are you trying to stack the deck in the Chief Judge's favour for the treaty talks?"

"The sooner we get this over with, the sooner these clowns get out of the city." Dredd jerked a thumb at the remains of Emporio Kneepad. "You've seen what two of them can do when they get together. Imagine what it'll be like when all five of them are in one room with Hershey."

"Control to Dredd, respond!"

"Dredd here. What now?"

"The Chief Judge wants to see you in her office. Immediately."

"On my way. Dredd out."

Giant knew what was coming next. "Go. I'll stay here and supervise."

Dredd nodded before returning to his Lawmaster. Tyres squealed in protest as the motorcycle roared away towards the nearest ramp up to Anton Diffring.

JESUS BLUDD STOOD on the balcony of his penthouse, a glass balloon of brandy cradled in one hand, a silk robe wrapped around his body. Stretched out in all directions he could see the Big Meg in its nocturnal glory, a billion lights in the night, millions of souls wondering what tomorrow would bring, if they even thought of tomorrow at all.

Bludd smiled to himself as Kara came out on to the balcony, pulling a similar robe tightly around her naked figure. A chill breeze made her gasp in surprise. "Sweet Jovus, it's cold out here!" She walked on tiptoes along the pathway of slates to join her lover by the balustrade.

"The breeze comes directly from the Arctic," Bludd replied. "This close to the Black Atlantic even Weather Control can only do so much to regulate climatic conditions. I find the wind quite bracing."

Kara slipped one of her hands inside his robe, searching for warmth. "So I can feel. Were you thinking about me, by any chance?"

"I was contemplating the next twenty-four hours. By this time tomorrow everything will be different. Reality will be revealed to those who purport to be our rulers and I will emerge from the shadows at last."

"I suppose I should be disappointed," Kara replied. "I thought only I could get you this… excited."

Bludd reached for her, his hands pushing her robe off to reveal the taut body within. "You do, my dear." He pulled Kara close, wrapping his own robe around her, fingers hungrily reaching for her. "I've never understood how the Judges can deny themselves the pleasures of the flesh."

Kara let herself be pulled off her feet, legs wrapping around Bludd's waist. "Perhaps they prefer to save their energy," she said languidly, "for enforcing the Law."

Bludd smiled, baring his teeth. "Then they are fools. Fools who will soon be parted from control of their city." He arched an eyebrow at Kara. "You do realise this balcony is under constant surveillance from the Judges, don't you?"

"But of course!" Kara replied, her face smirking wickedly. "Let's show them what they've been missing all these years…" She pushed the robe off Bludd's shoulders so both of them were naked in the moonlight. "Let's give them a show they won't forget."

MAX NORMAL STABBED his cue forward, sending the white ball careering across the lumpy undulations of the shuggy table. The wayward shot brought a snort of derisive laughter from his opponent, a four-armed, green-skinned refugee from Rexel 56 called Bonjo. But the hilarity died in the creature's throat as the ball somehow wound its way on a seemingly impossible path to the far corner of the table, politely tapping the black and white eight ball into a pocket.

"And that's the way your cookie crumbles, my emerald-hued dude!" Max announced, snapping his fingers with delight. "I think that's ten thousand credits you owe me now. Care to go double or nothing – again?"

The alien howled with rage, gibbering in some extraterrestrial tongue. Perched atop Bonjo's shoulder was a dwarf version of the Rexellian, called Mr Rogan. He had introduced himself as Bonjo's interpreter and manager when the alien challenged Max to a little competitive shuggy earlier in the evening. Normal had been reluctant to accept – creatures from Rexel were infamous for their foul temper and tight-fisted ways – but was persuaded by the other denizens of the Acme Shuggy Hall. Bonjo had hustled his way to a small fortune in recent evenings, reducing several men to abject poverty in the process. Since Max was reckoned to be the best two-armed shuggy player in the sector, it was up to him to restore the honour and reputation of the Acme.

"He says you cheated," Mr Rogan announced loudly, struggling to be heard above Bonjo's angry jabberings. "He says you a hustler."

Max rolled his eyes. "Hey, cool your jets and stay awake! Lose the rude 'tude or I'll be forced to get in a mood. You dig?"

Mr Rogan was not listening. Instead he continued to translate Bonjo's ravings. "He says you a liar and a thief. Give back his money or you suffer."

"I was afraid you cats would lose your manners. Damn, it does this pinstripe freak no good having to kick your ass!"

By now Bonjo's rantings had finally run their course, leaving Mr Rogan free to hold a conversation. "Pardon me, please. What is pinstripe freak?"

Max stepped away from the shuggy table and held out his hands, displaying the full finery of his immaculately tailored black suit with white pinstripes. If the Big Meg Dictionary ever used pictures to replace the words in its definitions, then Max Normal would appear in the space reserved for "dapper". His three-piece suit was perfectly pressed, discreet yet stylish cufflinks held his crisp white shirt in place, and his shoes were adorned with the shiniest of spats. The ensemble was topped off by a black bowler hat, perched at a jaunty angle atop Max's slicked- back hair. In a city where crumpled clothes, oversized kneepads and synthetic fabrics were all the rage, Normal was a walking anomaly. "I got style, baby!" he said.

Mr Rogan translated this for his client but Max's cultured garb only goaded Bonjo further. The Rexellian smashed his shuggy cue across one knee and began stamping towards his human opponent, brandishing both broken halves. Max just raised an eyebrow at the approaching alien.

"I see style is not in fashion on Rexel 56 this season," Normal noted. "Anybody care to back me up?" He looked over his shoulder to see the other shuggy players quietly retreating to the far side of the hall. "Don't all volunteer at once, you cowardly cats!"

Bonjo towered over Max, making a complex series of angry gestures while bellowing Rexellian invective. Mr Rogan began to translate. "He says you prepare to die. You shall suffer and die of thousand ignominies. Then there's quite a detailed explanation of where he intends to insert those–"

"I catch your drift, daddio!" Max interrupted. "Death and maiming, nothing pretty. Are they the main features on this double-bill of doom?"

Mr Rogan listened for another thirty seconds before Bonjo finally ran out of ranting. "In short, yes."

Max smiled. "I think there's something about me your uncool cat of a client ought to know. Back in the day I used to perform a valuable service for a certain stone-faced enforcer of the Law. Maybe you've heard of him, Dredd? Judge Dredd? That name ring any bells?"

Bonjo and Mr Rogan conversed in their native tongue before replying. "We know of this Dredd; a formidable warrior. But he is not here, so we do not fear you. Prepare to die screaming in an agony beyond imagination."

The pinstripe freak shrugged. "Have it your own way, my alien adversary." He dropped into a martial arts stance, ready to fight. But before Bonjo could attack, Max straightened up again. "There's just one other thing you should know before we turn the violence dial up to ultra."

Mr Rogan sighed in exasperation. "Now what?"

"Have I told you dudes my personal combat philosophy?"

"Not yet, but I'm sure you will."

"Those who run away, live to fight another day," Max said.

Mr Rogan translated this to Bonjo but had some difficulty finding suitable Rexellian words for part of the statement. Eventually the interpreter turned back to Max.

"Please explain the phrase 'run away'."

Normal smiled. "I can do better than that. Let me demonstrate it for you."

The small alien perched on Bonjo's shoulder smiled. "If you would be so kind, Bonjo would appreciate it muchly."

"My pleasure," Max said. "It goes something like this…" As he fled the shuggy hall, Max shouted an apology to the terrified manager. "I suggest you call the Judges, my man, and make it sharpish! Tell them Max Normal, the dude who dresses formal, needs their help!"

HERSHEY WAS SAT behind the vast desk in her office near the top level in the Grand Hall of Justice. Behind her, a mighty sculpture of an eagle dominated the wall, while on either side of the desk, windows reached from the ceiling to the floor, offering spectacular views across the surrounding sectors. The Chief Judge was deep in thought when Dredd arrived.

"You sent for me, ma'am."

Hershey did not reply immediately, her fingers formed into a steeple in front of her face. Eventually Dredd cleared his throat to get her attention. "Sorry, Dredd," she said. "I was contemplating my strategy for tomorrow's talks."

"Today's talks," Dredd noted. "It's gone midnight."

"Already?" Hershey rose from her chair and walked to one of the windows. "You've heard what we discussed at the Council of Five, no doubt."

"Yes, ma'am."

"What do you think?"

Dredd hesitated before replying. "It's not for me to pass judgement–"

"I'm not asking you to! I simply wanted your opinion."

"Bludd represents a significant threat," Dredd replied. "Unlike most of his rivals, he stays in the background, keeps his hands clean. To flush him out like this, it indicates the treaty must have a good chance of becoming reality."

"I meant about the security measures for the opening session," Hershey snapped. "Have we done enough to ensure safety for the delegates?"

"You've done all you can, without compromising the Law in other parts of the city." Dredd joined her by the window. "Why do you ask?"

Hershey sighed. "Since I joined the Council of Five, I dreamed of sitting in the big chair. I knew I would have to make tough choices, be willing to send men and women to their deaths. When I finally become Chief Judge, I was ready for it. But nothing prepares you for the reality of being responsible for an entire city. Every day there's a thousand decisions to be made. Every moment of every hour, somebody wants something from you. Everyone expects you to choose for them, to know what to do next, to be ready to pass judgement." Her words stumbled to a halt, the Chief Judge's head sagging forwards as she rested one hand against the glasseen window. "I just get so tired."

"Now you know why I never wanted the job," Dredd said quietly. "Being a Street Judge, it's all I know. I never had your ambition."

Hershey smiled at that. "And look where it's got me." She straightened up again and returned to her desk. "No matter. The negotiations go ahead, as planned. If Bludd thinks he can take on the might of the Justice Department by attacking this building, he's got another thing coming. I won't be dictated to or threatened by anyone, least of all a crime boss who hides behind his underlings."

Dredd nodded approvingly. "What about Ryan?"

She shrugged. "We can't pull him out now. Even if we were able, that would certainly tip our hand. Ryan will have to look after himself. If he gets caught in the crossfire… well, that's a necessary sacrifice."

"Agreed." Dredd began to leave but stopped at the door. "If it's any comfort, Hershey, you're the best Chief Judge this city has had in twenty years."

She sat down in her chair again. "Maybe. But I've been lucky so far. The Big Meg hasn't faced anything to match the likes of Necropolis or Sabbat's zombie army or the Doomsday gambit Nero Narcos launched. Anybody can look good being Chief Judge during times of peace. It's how you respond in a real crisis that separates the best from the rest."

Four

IT WAS DAWN when Giant began transporting the delegates from their respective safe houses to the Grand Hall of Justice. Originally all five were to have appeared with Hershey in a celebratory parade through the Big Meg's streets; a propaganda exercise to show the rest of the world how seriously these negotiations were being taken. But Dredd cancelled the parade within five minutes of assuming control of security for the treaty talks. "Save the celebrations until after we've got a treaty signed," had been his exact words.

It was also Dredd who ordered Giant to rouse the delegates from their beds earlier than planned. "We believe Bludd is planning to attack the Grand Hall of Justice just as the negotiations begin. However–"

Giant finished the thought off. "However, that doesn't preclude his people trying to eliminate the delegates before they even reach it."

"Right. Get them all to the venue ahead of schedule and keep 'em there. None of our 'honoured guests' leave without my say so. Is that clear?"

So as the sun rose over the Black Atlantic, Giant was trying to get the delegates to rise from their beds.

He started with Representative Chang. According to the Judges stationed outside her private quarters, the diminutive delegate from Sino-Cit had remained quietly inside all night. She had brought her own food and drink, sought no help from her guards and turned off the lights not long after dusk. Guess we should be grateful for that, Giant thought to himself, ruefully recalling the previous day's travails with the other delegates.

He knocked on the door to Chang's quarters. Within moments she was standing before him, already fully dressed in her uniform, looking at him with curiosity. "Yes? Is something wrong?"

"We're taking all the delegates in early," Giant replied. "To avoid traffic."

The Sino-Cit woman arched an eyebrow at him. "How... interesting." She looked back into her bedroom. Giant could have sworn it was tidier than before Chang had arrived. The delegate turned back to him. "Good. I am ready." She followed Giant to an H-wagon waiting outside the safe house and climbed in. "Where are the others?" Chang asked.

Giant smiled weakly. "We're collecting them en route but..."

"But?"

"They may not be ready quite so promptly as you."

Chang nodded sombrely. "I am not surprised."

Giant gave orders for the pilot to move on to the next safe house, where Judge Warner had no doubt spent an uncomfortable night recovering from his close encounter with the pleasure mech. The Med-Judges' report said the Brit-Cit delegate should suffer no lasting disability, but he would be walking bow-legged for a few days until the bruising subsided. That should make getting him into the H-wagon fun, Giant thought, rolling his eyes at what was to come.

* * *

RYAN WOKE TO find the horrifically scarred face of Di leaning over him. "What the drokk? What do you want? What are you looking at?"

"Just admiring your skin," she replied, reaching out a hand to stroke the juve's left cheek. The once beautiful woman was sat on the side of Ryan's bed, dressed in a one-piece black catsuit of reinforced leathereen. "Mr Bludd is offering us a generous bonus if we succeed in today's mission – for those who make it back alive. I'm thinking of spending mine on skin grafts, if I can find a donor."

"Why don't you just go to a face change clinic?"

"Their machines can't cope with the sort of damage my features suffered." Di grabbed one of Ryan's hands and pressed it against the ruined side of her face. "Feel that? Like someone used a cheese grater and a blowtorch on me at the same time."

Ryan pulled his hand away hurriedly, repelled by the texture of melted skin beneath his fingers. "What did you mean, find a donor?"

Di smiled. At least, the normal half of her face curved into a smile. The scarred side was caught in a permanent grimace, unable to show emotions. "To replace such a large surface area, one that's constantly on display, you need to take skin grafts from another person's face. Of course, there's not many people alive desperate enough to sacrifice their face for mine."

The juve felt his skin crawl as he realised what Di was hinting at. "So you were examining my face, in case I die during the attack, and you might want it for yourself?"

"Hmmm," Di agreed. "Lovely and soft. Of course, I'd need to get all your hair follicles removed – don't want to start sprouting a beard on one side, do I?"

"No, I suppose not," Ryan said. He sat up in bed, clutching the sheets firmly around his waist. The juve had spent most of an hour retching after witnessing the sudden and messy death of Skyhook the previous night. Afterwards, Kara had escorted him to a private bedroom just off the main area of the penthouse. A troubled night's sleep was haunted by nightmares about exploding heads and worse, leaving Ryan feeling more tired than before he had gone to bed. The juve decided to direct some of his anger at Di.

"Did you have a reason for waking me? Or was this a social call for some face touching?"

"Keep your u-fronts on!" Di stood, smoothing out the wrinkles in her catsuit.

"You're to put on the clothes supplied and report to the briefing room within ten minutes. Don't be late." She was already walking out by the time Ryan shouted a question after her.

"What clothes?"

As the bedroom door swung shut he saw a black tunic and trousers hung on the back, cut from the same toughened material as Di's catsuit. Ryan wondered how Bludd had known what size he was.

I know what size you are, Kara's voice replied inside the juve's mind. *I know everything about you. Now get dressed!*

As DAWN BROKE, Dredd was supervising the deployment of Manta-tanks and H-wagons at the perimeter of the exclusion zone. In the distance the Grand Hall of Justice shone in the morning light, sun reflecting off the mighty building. It was a symbol of order and the Law, a potent representation of the power held by the Judges. To attack the Grand Hall was to attack the Law itself, to invite anarchy and chaos into this city. If Bludd should succeed, there was no knowing where the consequences would lead the Big Meg.

By eight in the morning Dredd appeared satisfied with the arrangement of defences. He had bawled out half a dozen Manta-tank drivers for sloppy placement and sent one H-wagon to the West Wall in disgrace after the pilot arrived too late to take his place in the formidable formation. The pilot, a young female Judge called Roker, tried to explain why she had been delayed.

"There was a fire at F Martin Candor Block and Citi-Def asked for our help, so we thought–" she began.

"You thought? You thought?" Dredd snarled, leaning into Roker's face. "I doubt you've either the wit or wisdom to think! Who is responsible for ensuring the safety of these negotiations: the Citi-Def squad of F Martin Candor Block, or me?"

"You are, sir," Roker mumbled.

"And did you ask my permission for this little diversion?"

"No, sir, but we assumed–"

"Assumed? Assumed?!?" Dredd stepped back, shaking his head. When he spoke again his voice had dropped to a growl. "Get out of my sight."

"Excuse me, sir, but where do you want us to–"

Dredd sneered. "Go patrol the West Wall. Perhaps they can find a use for you. But remember this day, Roker. Remember the humiliation. If you ever disobey an order again, I'll have your badge for breakfast and you can join the precious Citi-Def, since you seem so fond of them. Do I make myself clear?"

"Yes, sir!" Roker snapped into a salute and scurried back to her H-wagon, accompanied by the rest of her crew. Word of what happened quickly spread among all those assigned to security for the extradition treaty talks. For the rest of the morning Dredd's word was treated like a proclamation from grud himself, each unit responding with verve and lightning speed. Nobody wanted to face Dredd's wrath.

"GOOD MORNING! I'M Enigma Smith and you're watching *Mega-City News*, the place to be if you want to see the news, the whole news and nothing but the news! Today's bulletins are brought to you by Sump's Pus Capsules®, the goo that's best for you, and Grot Pot Hotties™ – all the flavour of a grot pot encased in a synthetic sausage skin and shoved between two buns!"

Enigma grinned at the cameras with a smile some might consider a deadly weapon. Certainly anyone who persisted in grinning so incessantly on the pedways and skedways of the Big Meg was likely to get themselves killed. The newsreader delivered the latest headlines with her usual breathless enthusiasm. "At noon today our own Chief Judge Hershey will begin talks with delegates from five other Justice Departments as part of her initiative to develop a global extradition treaty. A parade planned for this morning that would have featured the representatives has, however, been cancelled. The Judges denied this was due to any fears of assassination attempts by criminal elements. According to the official explanation, the parade was cancelled due to road works shutting several of the main skedways approaching the Grand Hall of Justice, where the talks are to be held."

"But not all celebrations have been cancelled for today. The Mega-City Museum of the Twentieth Century – more commonly known as the Dustbuster – has announced it will be hosting a massive pyrotechnic display of fireworks tonight, to mark the end of the Evil Empire exhibition. The Dustbuster's curator, Dr Janet Swanson, says the show has been a surprise success for the cash-strapped museum. The firework display will be one of the largest ever seen in the sky above the Big Meg and should be visible across the entire city. When asked who was funding this extravaganza, Dr Swanson said it was thanks to a donation from a private individual who did not wish to be named.

"Last but not least, the staff of Emporio Kneepad are still scratching their heads over what happened to their store last night. The high fashion shoppera on the corner of Cartier and Klugman was apparently attacked by two drunks in a stolen hoverpod. Bystanders claim that Judge Dredd was responsible for removing those responsible from the scene, but the Justice Department says no charges have been issued nor arrests made over the incident. In a minute we'll have sports headlines with Shamus McGinty, including news about a hot new alien shuggy player in town. But first, a word from our sponsors..."

GIANT DELIVERED THE five delegates to the Grand Hall of Justice by 10:00 am, several hours after collecting Chang from her accommodation. It had taken that long to extract the other representatives from their various slumbers, Judges Bruce and Smirnoff proving particularly difficult to shift. Giant was eventually forced to call for medical assistance, having the man from East-Meg Two injected with enough stimulants to wake the dead. Smirnoff was still twitching and convulsing when the H-wagon approached the edge of the exclusion zone.

The flying vehicle was forced to land and everyone inside was submitted to rigorous security checks before being allowed inside the zone. Giant talked with Dredd nearby while the search was made. "I see Hershey's taking the planned attack by the Bludd Group seriously."

The senior Judge nodded towards the H-wagon. "Those creeps give you any trouble this morning?"

"Just getting them moving. Warner hasn't stopped bitching about his injuries from yesterday, while the other three men have got flaming hangovers."

"What about our inscrutable friend from Sino-Cit?"

"Chang? Sits and watches, observing everything, saying almost nothing. The Chief Judge is going to have a tough time with that one," Giant said. He got a signal from the search party to confirm the H-wagon was good to go. "Wish I could be here with you on the front line when the attack comes. Hershey wants me to keep close to the delegates."

"Better you than me," Dredd commented. "Tact and diplomacy. I'm not sure they were on the syllabus when I went to the Academy."

* * *

THE STRIKE TEAM was split between two sleek, black hoverpods: Ryan and Kara going in the first vehicle with Fincher as pilot, while Di, Angry Sanderson and Tattoo Sue followed close behind. Bludd had not been present at the final briefing. Ryan guessed the crime boss was trying to keep his distance from the attack, to maintain denial of culpability. Kara instead had outlined their strategy.

"As we suspected, the Judges have created a massive exclusion zone around the Grand Hall of Justice. They are expecting an attack and we are going to give them one, but not in the way they expect. We'll be using hoverpods with stealth technology, that should give us an edge when we approach the perimeter. The first vehicle's job will be to breach the boundary and draw any fire. Once the Judges focus their attack on the first vehicle, the second hoverpod will penetrate the exclusion zone and begin its attack run."

Ryan asked the obvious question. "Knowing the Department's love of overkill, how will the first hoverpod survive long enough to provide a diversion?"

Kara smiled. "The Justice Department is not the only agency with a research and development division. The Bludd Group has obtained a revolutionary new force shield that can withstand direct hits by almost all the weapons currently deployed by the Judges. They won't lay a gauntlet on us."

"Terrif," the juve replied. He had examined the hoverpod's exterior in detail before climbing inside but could find no evidence of a defence system. Ryan questioned Kara about it while Fincher was prepping the vehicle. "I still don't see how this tin can will withstand the Judges' firepower. It just looks like a normal hoverpod to me, no special–"

Kara rested a finger against Ryan's lips, stilling his voice. "Leave the thinking to us. Would Jesus let me fly in this if there was any danger?"

"Ready to go," Fincher reported from the hoverpod's cockpit.

"Good." Kara let her hand slide down Ryan's chest towards his crotch. "Blake, could you make sure the others are ready too? I need to go over the flight plan with Fincher before we're airborne."

"No problem," Ryan replied with some difficulty. "Back in a minute."

HERSHEY WAS WAITING in the central negotiating chamber to welcome the delegates. Giant escorted the five visitors into the circular room where pleasantries and small gifts were exchanged. Once the formalities were over, the Chief Judge signalled for Giant to come forward. "This Judge will be your personal liaison for the remainder of the day. If there's anything you need, anything at all, just ask Giant."

Smirnoff was nursing the side of his head, his face pale and perspiring. "The hair of the dog would be most welcome," he muttered.

Hershey smiled thinly. "We are only too happy to continue offering you the benefits of full diplomatic immunity. However, we must also ask you to respect our Laws, just as we are respecting your privacy. As requested, all the delegates have been assigned their own rooms on this level of the building, each with a secure, direct comms line to your superiors. I personally guarantee these lines cannot be intercepted, traced or accessed by anyone but yourselves. Judge Giant will now show you to these private rooms. The negotiations will begin here in twenty minutes' time, at precisely midday."

DREDD WAS PROWLING the exclusion zone like a caged animal, poised for action. Cordoning off twenty blocks in all directions from the Grand Hall of Justice was a massive job, causing chaos on surrounding skedways and overzooms. Creating a no-fly zone in the sky was even harder to police, with dozens of flying Manta-tanks and heavily armoured

H-wagons forming an aerial blockade. Dredd kept his helmet radio active at all times, listening to the reports flooding in from units spread around the vast perimeter.

"Dredd to PSU, any word on movement from the Bludd Group's known strongholds?"

"Nothing yet," a voice replied. The Public Surveillance Unit had an almost limitless squadron of spy-in-the-sky cameras stationed around the city, along with access to every security system and surveillance database. There were black spots, holes in the network where perps could hide or disappear temporarily, but anyone moving through the Big Meg never avoided the PSU's gaze for long.

Dredd remembered the last sighting of Ryan had been when he entered Bludd's penthouse. "What about Emil Jannings Block? Anything there?"

"Nothing as yet. Closest we've got are two hoverpods that exited a nearby parking building within the last hour."

"Where are they now?"

"Hold on–" While PSU systems gathered the necessary data, another voice broke into the transmission.

"Manta-tank Delta Two-Seven to Dredd. We've got movement up here."

"Dredd responding. What is it?"

"Something coming directly towards us, ignoring all the warning beacons to divert."

"Any ID yet?" All flying vehicles were required to carry a transponder, so the city's computerised air traffic control system could monitor what was happening in the sky. Accidents were remarkably rare, thanks to an automatic override that prevented hoverpods and other aerial transports from colliding.

"Just coming through now…"

"PSU to Dredd. Those two hoverpods, they've just split up. Both were heading towards the exclusion zone, but one has altered course to go around."

"Dredd to PSU, what about the other hoverpod?"

"Still heading straight for your position. Both have got some sort of shielding device, we can't tell if they are manned or not. Could be set to autopilot or attempting a suicide run."

"Manta-tank Delta Two-Seven to Dredd. Got that ID you wanted. The hoverpod is registered to Red Inc, a division of the Bludd Group."

"Drokk!"

"It's the same vehicle PSU just mentioned. It's headed directly towards the exclusion zone. Should be visible to you any second now…"

Dredd began searching the skyline. Twenty years ago the eyes had been ripped from his head by a vicious enemy. Fortunately, Med-Division was able to implant bionic replacements, restoring the Judge's vision and even enhancing his ocular range. In the distance he could see the approaching hoverpod, unswerving in its course, relentless in its approach.

"Dredd to all units on the exclusion zone, this is it! We've got an incoming black hoverpod with a Bludd Group ident and there's another circling round the perimeter. If either vehicle gets within three blocks of our cordon you have my permission to take them out. Use all necessary force!"

GIANT WAS MONITORING the radio chatter from Dredd's position while escorting the delegates to their private chambers. The sparsely furnished spaces had blank walls except for floor-to-ceiling windows that offered spectacular views across the Big Meg. The Judge was ushering Chang into her room when Dredd gave the shoot-to-kill order. Giant strode to the window and looked out to the east, trying to see what was happening in the distance.

"Is something the matter?" the Sino-Cit delegate asked politely.

"No, nothing." Giant moved to the desk and showed Chang how to activate the comms line to her superiors.

"We have scrambled your link to stop it being hacked from outside the building. Once you add your own encryption codes, any transmissions to or from this terminal will be secure."

"We are most grateful for your assistance," she said, bowing slightly. "If you will excuse us now."

"Of course." Giant retreated to the door. "Negotiations begin in a few minutes. If you need anything–"

"Representative Chang will be there. Now, we require privacy."

The Judge departed, closing the door after him. Chang activated the comms line and clipped a tiny encryption lock to the side of the unit. After a few moments the screen came alive with a flurry of Chinese symbols. For the first time since arriving in Mega-City One, Chang relaxed. She was about to switch off the unit when a line of English text appeared on screen: WE HAVE TO TALK.

RYAN WAS GETTING nervous, sweat soaking his armpits and the small of his back. Fincher was piloting the hoverpod straight at the exclusion zone, whistling a happy tune. Kara appeared just as unconcerned by the formidable line of Manta-tanks and judicial H-wagons waiting for them in the sky ahead. "Isn't now a good time to activate the force shield?" he asked, trying to sound casual.

Kara shrugged and looked at the pilot. "What do you think, Fincher?"

He smiled gleefully. "No need. We can make it past those drokkers!"

Ryan was not convinced. He looked out the rear window of the hoverpod. "Hey! Where did the others go?"

Kara reached into the juve's mind. *We're the diversion, remember? They'll penetrate the exclusion zone from another angle.*

Fincher kept the hoverpod heading directly at the Justice Department blockade.

"This is quite a step up for you, isn't it Sonny Jim? Mr Bludd's showing a lot of trust including you in the strike team for such an important mission."

"I won't let him down," Ryan vowed. "He took me in after I was expelled from the Academy. I owe Jesus Bludd everything."

Even your life?

Even that, Ryan thought. He could feel Kara probing at his psychic defences, each parry followed by a feint and then another thrust deeper into his mind. The juve erected the image of a brick wall in his thoughts, stretching to infinity in all directions. The bald psyker did her best to breach it but soon relented, apparently satisfied.

"Very well," Kara announced. "Fincher, you know what to do next."

The pilot began to accelerate, the hoverpod screaming towards the edge of the exclusion zone. Ryan was slammed back into his seat by the sudden burst of speed, the breath jarred from his body. He gripped the edges of the chair, his knuckles white from the strain.

"Here it comes!" Dredd shouted. "Remember what I said, once that 'pod gets within three blocks, I want it taken out. Stand by…"

In the main negotiating room, Hershey looked around the room impatiently. All the delegates were present except for Chang. The Chief Judge frowned and snapped her fingers, summoning Giant to her side. "Where is she?"

"I don't know, ma'am. I'll just go and–"

"Please begging your pardons," a quiet but firm voice interrupted. "A thousand apologies for my lateness. It shall not happen again." The Sino-Cit representative was hurrying into the circular chamber, her cheeks flushed with embarrassment. She took her place beside the other delegates.

Satisfied at last, Hershey sent Giant to close the doors and stand guard outside. As he left the room, the noise of twelve chimes was being piped around the Grand Hall of Justice's intercom system, announcing the noon hour. The negotiations had begun...

THE HOVERPOD WAS only six blocks away from the exclusion zone now. It would be upon the boundary within seconds. Kara held up a finger as a signal for Fincher. "On my command..."

DREDD GLANCED LEFT and right, checking everyone was ready, bellowing a final order at them all. "Stand by..."

"NOW!" KARA SHOUTED. Fincher twisted the steering controls sideways, sending the hoverpod into an abrupt left turn. Ryan was flung out of his chair, and slammed up against a side wall before sliding to the floor.

"HOLD YOUR FIRE!" Dredd commanded. The oncoming hoverpod had suddenly veered off, just before reaching the exclusion zone. Perhaps the occupants had realised a direct attack would be suicidal at best. But how had they known just when to turn away? Dredd felt a shadow leaving his thoughts as though someone had been hiding inside his mind, but it was a passing sensation so he soon forgot about it. "PSU! Report!"

"The hoverpod jagged away at the last moment. It's heading south, skirting round the edge of the exclusion zone. Seems to be following the same path as the other vehicle we've been watching, towards Ed Wood Underpass."

"All units on the exclusion zone, maintain readiness! The attack from the east could have been a diversion. Stand by for further orders!"

"PSU to Dredd, we've lost them. Both hoverpods went into the underpass but neither of them have come out!"

"Stomm." Dredd cursed under his breath before ordering a dozen helmets to investigate Ed Wood. "Find those hoverpods and whoever was inside them. There's more to this than meets the eye."

RYAN JUMPED OUT of the hoverpod to find the rest of the strike team waiting for him, concealed in the shadows of the underpass. "What's going on? I thought we were supposed to be–"

"Attacking the Grand Hall of Justice?" Tattoo Sue interjected, noisily cracking her knuckles. "That would be suicidal, don't you think?"

"But Kara said the force shield would protect us," the juve protested.

"You shouldn't believe everything people tell you," Angry Sanderson sneered while cleaning his nails with the point of a stiletto.

Di smiled with the beautiful side of her face. "I'm not surprised the poor boy got expelled from the Academy – far too trusting for his own good. He'd never make it as a Judge on the streets."

Ryan frowned, not understanding what was going on. "But I thought–"

I know what you thought, Kara replied telepathically. *I've known every dirty little thing that's crossed your mind since you entered the penthouse; since you picked Jesus's pocket at the Dustbuster. Did you honestly believe those psi-barriers could protect your mind from me?*

"Please, I don't know what you're–"

No more lies, Blake, no more deceptions. I know what you are, why you are here. You tried to infiltrate the Bludd

Group. *You tipped off the Judges about our attack. But all of this, it was just a diversion. You and I, we're just pawns in a much larger game, pieces to be sacrificed for a greater goal.*

"No, you don't understand," Ryan cried.

Kara smiled at him and shook her head. "Fincher?"

"Right 'ere." The last member of the strike team emerged from the shadows and clamped a powerful hand across the undercover cadet's mouth and nose, blocking Ryan's breathing. While the juve's body thrashed about, Fincher's other hand reached towards Ryan's neck with a laser blade.

"Time to remove this piece from the game," Kara commanded. "Goodbye, Ryan. At least your death will be mercifully brief. Many more will suffer far worse than you soon."

TWO HOURS LATER the Judges abandoned their search of Ed Wood Underpass. The burnt out wrecks of the hoverpods had been towed away for inspection by the forensic scientists at Tek-Division, but a preliminary sweep offered little hope of finding anything meaningful. Each vehicle was incinerated with a fast burning phosphor grenade, scorching out the interior at incredibly high temperatures, searing away any trace of evidence left behind.

Infrared sensors showed remnants from the body heat of half a dozen humans who had gathered beside the hoverpods.

But the footsteps only led a few metres away before disappearing again, no doubt into another vehicle or vehicles that had been waiting in the underpass. The only other evidence discovered at the scene was a splash of blood in a gutter. Again, laboratory analysis was needed to confirm findings made on the spot, but there had been an unconfirmed DNA match already made. The blood belonged to Blake Ryan, a former cadet expelled from the Academy of Law four months earlier.

Dredd discussed the findings with Giant during a mid-afternoon break in the negotiations. The exclusion zone remained in place but nobody else had attempted to breach its boundary. Dredd relinquished command of the perimeter and rode to the Grand Hall of Justice on his Lawmaster, meeting Giant outside the main entrance.

"So Ryan's dead?"

"Probably," Dredd admitted. "Looks like the two hoverpods met a third vehicle in the underpass. Our man was either killed or wounded there and the body transported away, along with all the other passengers."

"Do you think Bludd might keep Ryan alive as a hostage?"

The senior Judge shook his head. "All our Wally Squad operatives were killed, their bodies dumped within hours. We can expect Ryan's corpse to surface before sundown. He's been undercover for four months – all Justice Department codes and encryption systems have been routinely updated or changed twice since then. Unfortunately for Ryan, he is of little or no use to Bludd, except as a trophy." Dredd glanced at the Grand Hall's upper levels. "How are the negotiations going?"

"Hard to say. Warner is making a lot of noise but is still supporting Hershey. Belgrano is arguing over every point being raised–"

"No surprise there," Dredd said. "Ciudad Barranquilla is the most popular hiding place on the planet for fugitives from the Law. Banana City Judges gather half their annual budget from bribes and back-handers. Hell will freeze over before Belgrano agrees to sign anything freely."

Giant nodded. "Bruce looks like he'd rather be anywhere else and Smirnoff was asleep for half the first session. Hershey could call a vote now and Ivan wouldn't have a clue which way to go."

"What about Chang?"

"Watching and waiting. We know she got a call on her comms line just before the opening ceremony, but the

Sino-Cit encryption systems are resisting all efforts to break them. No telling which way Chang will lean."

"Keep your wits about you," Dredd said. "We still don't know–"

He was interrupted by a message from Control. "Dredd, there's a robot courier at the exclusion zone perimeter with a package for you. Tek-Judges have scan-alysed it, nothing mechanical or suspicious showing up. There's a voice-activated lock. Droid says the package will only open for your voice, after you say the words 'Open sesame'."

"Patch me through to the Tek-Judge nearest the package," Dredd replied.

Within seconds another voice could be heard via helmet radio. "Tek-Judge Brison to Dredd, you wanted to speak with me?"

"Take off your helmet and place it next to the package. Once you've retreated to a safe distance, I'll deactivate the locking mechanism remotely with my voice. Understand?"

"Yes, sir. Taking off my helmet now." Dredd could hear Brison placing the helmet down before hurrying away. "Ready when you are!" Brison shouted.

"This is the voice of Judge Dredd. Open sesame!"

After a long silence the lock could be heard springing open. Footsteps approached the package. After a gasp of horror, the helmet was picked up and Brison spoke into its radio mic. "Sir, I think you'd better come over here."

"What is it, Brison? What's inside the package?"

"I think you'd better see this for yourself. It's…" Brison broke off, his words replaced with a retching sound. "Oh grud, that smell! It's like… Sorry, sir, I think I'm going to be–" The Tek-Judge stopped talking, but the noise of someone vomiting repeatedly was all too audible.

Dredd gunned his motorcycle into life and nodded grimly to Giant before accelerating away towards the exclusion zone's perimeter.

*   *   *

BRISON WAS STILL recovering when Dredd arrived, the fresh-faced Tek wiping the last remnants of vomit from his chin. Med-Judges were already gathered around the package; a black plastic cube. Nearby the delivery droid was being interrogated by Street Judges, protesting its ignorance. "Hey, I just carry parcels from place to place. Somebody gives me a delivery and I deliver it!"

Dredd screeched to a halt nearby and dismounted from his Lawmaster, striding briskly towards the package. "Get out of my way!" he barked at the Med-Judges. They hastily stepped aside, clearing a path. Dredd stopped over the container and looked down, his mouth curling downwards.

Inside the cube was a decapitated head, face down. It had been severed above the larynx, the neck neatly sliced through as though it were a joint of cooked meat. The lack of blood indicated the use of a laser blade, cauterising the wound as it cut. Dredd sniffed the air, recognising a familiar odour.

"Roasted flesh," one of the Med-Judges commented. "Probably from the wounds to the forehead. They must have used the tip of the laser to cut into the skin there, leaving that message for you."

Dredd reached into the package and turned the head around to see its face. Lifeless eyes stared up at him accusingly. Two words were visible on the forehead, each letter burnt into the skin: NICE TRY. Dredd slammed the lid of the package shut again, hiding the dead face of Blake Ryan from view.

Five

HERSHEY STARED AT the image of Ryan's severed head. The Chief Judge had seen death thousands of times, witnessed the moment when life departed a body and left behind just the slowly cooling corpse. She had lost friends and colleagues and she had killed countless perps in the line of duty. None of that made it any easier to face what the Bludd Group had done to the former cadet.

"Alright, I've seen enough," Hershey said wearily. The image on her Tri-D monitor changed as the trophy was taken away, replaced by Dredd's scowling countenance. The treaty negotiations had paused for an early evening meal, giving the Chief Judge an opportunity to return to her office and deal with any urgent matters. The call from Dredd had been first on that list. "This supposed attack on the Grand Hall, it was a ruse to draw the cadet out into the open?"

"I'm not convinced," Dredd replied. "Bludd wants to see the treaty talks fail, like every other crime boss. But forcing Ryan to break his cover by contacting us, that may have been a bonus for Bludd. Or he may have already known the juve was one of our operatives and chose to use him against us."

"Plenty of unanswered questions, Dredd. I need answers."

"The hoverpods almost attacking the exclusion zone, that was a feint. Bludd has something else planned. It may have already happened. He forced us to concentrate our attention on protecting the delegates, leaving other parts of the city vulnerable. We need to identify what Bludd's real target is, or was."

A chiming noise outside her office got Hershey's attention. "The next session is about to begin, I have to go."

"Do you want the exclusion zone maintained?"

The Chief Judge sighed. Another decision, another responsibility she had to bear. "Yes, but scale back the numbers by half. Right now Bludd is five steps ahead of us. We need to catch up fast before he makes his next move. Hershey out." She deactivated the Tri-D screen and sagged back in her chair. Her desk was strewn with unanswered memos and requests, all of which would have to wait. The chimes to call delegates back to the treaty talks resumed outside. The Chief Judge sighed and got to her feet, aware she hadn't eaten all day. That would have to wait as well.

MAX NORMAL HURRIED in through the back entrance of Dennis Price Block, checking over his shoulder that nobody was following him. The pinstripe freak had been keeping a low profile since his close encounter with the enraged Bonjo. Word on the street claimed the Rexellian wanted to get his hands – all four of them – on the human hustler and administer an almighty beating. Max imagined the alien's diminutive manager Mr Rogan would probably provide a live translation of Bonjo's threats and gloating as the blows rained down. Max had suffered a few thrashings in his life and had no wish to endure another.

The pinstripe freak stepped into the turbolift and requested a floor above the level where his con-apt was located. Two decades as an informant for Dredd had taught Max plenty about how to avoid unnecessary physical pain.

Anyone who was important in the Big Meg's criminal underworld knew Max had been a star informant for the Justice Department. Normal had always feared what would happen if word of his association with Dredd leaked out. In fact, it proved to be his salvation. Max acquired an invisible halo of protection. Few would touch a hair on his head for fear of invoking Dredd's wrath.

Better still, Normal became a conduit between the underworld and the Judges. Should perps want to give themselves up, contacting Max was a simple solution. Decide you'd had enough of your law-breaking lover? A subtle tip-off to Normal and the unwanted person got a spell in the iso-cubes. The traffic was two-way as the Judges used Max to feed information to the underworld.

Sometimes, the quickest way to catch a perp was to set other perps against them. If word spread of a dunk poaching on another pickpocket's territory, retribution could be swift and painful. Most crime bosses had a dislike of perps who favoured any form of child abuse. The Judges could send a message via Max about a particularly horrific case. Within a day the culprit would appear at the nearest Sector House, usually the worse for wear.

Normal retired permanently after an assassin from outside the Big Meg used the former informant as bait to lure Dredd into a trap. Max had almost died from his injuries. After recovering he swore off doing favours for perps or the Judges. Every now and then he relented for a one-off message or urgent case, but otherwise kept himself to himself. The seedy world of shuggy halls was Max's only vice now. He hustled a few credits to keep himself in the style to which he had become accustomed. Bespoke pinstripe suits were not cheap and having your bowler reblocked was fiendishly expensive.

The turbolift arrived at floor twenty-eight. Max popped his head out and glanced in either direction, but nobody was waiting for him. Feeling slightly foolish, he stepped out and hurried to the nearby emergency stairs.

After walking down a level he emerged cautiously on the twenty-seventh floor. Still no sign of trouble. Normal strode briskly to the door of his con-apt and unlocked it. After a final glance to either side, he slipped into the unlit room and shut the door, quickly locking it behind himself. "Lights!" he called to the voice-activated environmental control system. Nothing happened. "I said hit the lights, daddio!" Still nothing.

"Illuminate," a deep, powerful voice growled from the darkness. Gradually the con-apt's living room began filling with light. For a moment Max wondered if he had wandered into the wrong apartment, but then he realised that he wouldn't have been able to unlock the door. Comprehension slowly dawned on him when he saw three men positioned around the room. To the left was a ginger dwarf, sour-faced and pointing a powerful handgun at Max. On the right stood a pasty-faced male, lightly tossing an activated laser blade back and forth between his hands. But the most imposing figure was sat in an armchair, arms folded across his chest, one hand thoughtfully stroking his chin. When he spoke, Max recognised it as the voice that had activated the lights.

"My apologies for overriding the voice-activation codes for your con-apt, Mr Normal. It was a necessary procedure to prevent any alarm systems being triggered when we gained access to your dwelling. Rest assured, the damage will be undone when we depart."

"Whatever you say, my man," Max replied as jauntily as he could. "You're the big bad, I'm just the man dressed in trad."

"Quite." The heavyset visitor stood and approached Normal, raising a fleshy hand in a gesture of friendship. "Allow me to make the introductions. The scowling individual to your left is Angry Sanderson, while the other gentleman is known only as Fincher. I don't know if you've heard of me. My name is–"

"Jesus Bludd?" Max replied.

The visitor smiled broadly. "Exactly. I've come to ask you a favour."

"WHAT DO YOU mean it's impossible? You have the most sophisticated surveillance analysis systems on the planet and you can't track six people leaving an underpass in a single vehicle?" Dredd was giving the Public Surveillance Unit the rough edge of his tongue, frustration and anger evident in his voice. "PSU gets more than its fair share of funding from the Department. I suggest you put it to better use!"

The unfortunate analyst on the receiving end of this tirade pulled out her earpiece and threw it down on the terminal. Judge Rebecca Sharp was about to let loose a torrent of abuse when she recognised the stern-faced figure walking towards her. Tall, black and forbidding, Niles ran the PSU with clinical detachment. His predecessor had turned the division into a personal arsenal against other senior Judges, using the PSU to gather information about potential rivals. But Jura Edgar had gone too far in playing puppet-master from behind the scenes and was pushed sideways to run a detention camp out in the Cursed Earth, out of sight and out of mind.

Niles stopped in front of the terminal and picked up the abandoned earpiece. "Is this Dredd?" he asked Sharp, who nodded. Niles pushed the comms device into his own ear. "Dredd, this is Niles. I understand you're less than happy with PSU's efforts to locate your suspects."

Sharp watched her superior as he listened to a stream of invective. Around the operations room of PSU, other analysts were quietly switching over to the same channel, not wanting to miss out on the confrontation. After half a minute of harsh words Niles interrupted the veteran Street Judge.

"I've heard enough, Dredd. My people are doing everything they can to help you solve the murder of Cadet Ryan. I don't need to remind you this isn't the only case being worked on here and shouting at my analysts does nothing for morale or productivity. If you've got a problem with how I run my division, you take it up with me. Don't take it out on my Judges! Do I make myself clear?"

A long silence followed. Sharp realised she was holding her breath and let the air slip out through her nostrils. Dredd mumbled a reply to Niles, who gave Sharp a wink and smiled.

"That's perfectly understandable, Dredd. Everyone in the Department wants these killers found and punished. As soon as we have something, PSU will communicate it directly to you. Niles out." He removed the earpiece and returned it to Sharp. "I don't think you'll have any more trouble from Dredd today."

"Th-thank you, sir," Sharp stammered. "Thank you very much."

Niles looked around the operations room. Everyone was watching to see what he would do next. "Nobody said you could take a break! We've got perps to catch so get to it!" The other analysts hurriedly reactivated their terminals and resumed working. Niles nodded at Sharp before returning to his office.

She pushed her earpiece back into position and began scrutinising the readouts on her terminal. "PSU to Dredd, I've got some new information for you. Only nineteen vehicles capable of carrying six people emerged from the underpass during the half hour immediately after the second hoverpod went in. None of those are registered to the Bludd Group or Red Inc, but one was reported stolen this morning. I'm uploading the details to your onboard computer now."

DREDD BEGAN FOLLOWING the route taken by the suspect vehicle after it left Ed Wood Underpass. The stolen transport was a mo-pad, hijacked soon after dawn from a family driving across Southside Sector 41. Mega-City One had a permanent housing shortage, thanks to its burgeoning population and tendency to suffer apocalyptic disasters every few years. Such incidents frequently resulted in tens of millions losing their homes as entire city blocks were wiped out by the latest calamity to befall the Big Meg. Taking up residence in a Displaced Persons Camp was never an enticing prospect, so those who could afford to would buy a mo-pad instead. PSU estimates suggested nearly twenty million people currently resided in such vehicles.

Frequently luxurious, mo-pads were required to remain permanently on the road. Any vehicle that stayed in one place for more than a day – barring catastrophic gridlock or act of grud – lost its mobile home classification and became liable to crippling property taxes. So mo-pads were always moving, driving around the thousand million miles of skedways snaking through the city. Mobile refuelling trucks avoided the need to stop while cruise control and auto-pilot facilities meant the owner did not spend their entire life behind the wheel. Nevertheless, living in a mo-pad required a peculiar kind of citizen; one who was able to cope with a life always on the move.

Dredd tracked the mo-pad's movements for more than an hour before locating the vehicle in the Sector 87 dust zone. These abandoned industrial areas were favourite haunts for fugitives and perps, the residual radioactivity and presence of bubbling chem-pits disrupting PSU camera coverage. Dredd eventually found the mo-pad in a dead end. The vehicle had been burnt out with another phosphor grenade, destroying all trace of evidence. Scorch marks on the ground nearby suggested the occupants had switched to another pair of hoverpods. Dredd muttered to himself as he crouched to examine the scorch marks. "Five steps ahead of us... Hershey was right." His thoughts were interrupted by a message from Control.

"Dredd responding, what is it?"

"There's been a raid at the Dustbuster. A display has been stolen from the Cold War section. Judges on the scene are asking for you to attend."

"Tell them I've got greater concerns than some opportunist thief stealing a collection of one hundred and fifty-year-old digital watches!"

"The helmet in charge is quite insistent, Dredd. Judge Langenkamp believes it may be related to the case you're investigating."

"Mind telling me how?"

"The robbers left something behind at the scene; a headless corpse. Initial analysis suggests it's the body of–"

"Blake Ryan," Dredd said, already running for his Lawmaster. "Tell Langenkamp I'm on my way!"

JUDGE BRUCE WAS sick and tired. He had managed just three hours of sleep after his late night drinking binge with Smirnoff from East-Meg Two – by crikey, that bloke could drink – and a long afternoon of meaningful discussions about formulating an extradition treaty was not Bruce's idea of a good time. Mega-City One's Chief Judge might be a looker but her conversation was all business, business, and more bloody business. The Oz delegate wasn't sure how much more of this he could take. Thankfully, Hershey had called a halt to the opening day's session and told all the visitors they could return to their quarters.

Bruce was pausing in his private room to collect some papers when he noticed a light blinking on his comms unit. He had spoken with the Chief Judge of Oz during an earlier break and was not due to report back in until the next morning. Who else could have accessed the secure line? Bruce considered summoning Giant from the corridor outside. The young Judge didn't seem to have a daystick up his arse like Dredd and the other Yanks, so maybe he'd be able to help. But curiosity got the better of Bruce and he activated the comms unit. A single line of text appeared on screen: INCOMING MESSAGE, AUDIO ONLY – DO YOU ACCEPT?

"Suppose so," Bruce said, shrugging his shoulders. The

unit crackled with a burst of static, then a deep voice resonated from the speakers.

"Judge Bruce, I have information that may be of interest to you – and a warning. Once you have returned to your private quarters, I strongly suggest you watch the *Mega-City News* on Tri-D. You will see something quite remarkable later this evening, something you will wish to communicate to your superiors in Oz. Now, I must give you a warning about events to come..."

DOCTOR SWANSON HAD never been the most confident of women in matters of the heart. Ask her to give a paper about the historical era in which she specialised, the 1980s, and she was utterly at ease. Her mastery of that decade was second to none, her understanding of its curiosities and quirks unrivalled among scholars around the world. On her favourite topic Swanson could converse with Chief Judges and Tri-D celebrities without nerves or fear. But ask her to articulate the romantic feelings locked within her heart, to speak aloud the private fantasies that sent a shudder of delight through her body... then she reverted to plain Janet, a shy girl hiding behind her glasses and textbooks, terrified someone could get close enough to touch her or to show her any affection. That changed the day the museum curator first met her lover.

The Swanson family had always been academics. Janet's parents were professors at Mega-U, teaching Classics and Social History. Both had been eminent figures in their respective fields. How they had ever found time to conceive a child was a mystery to Janet, such was her parents' devotion to history. Growing up surrounded by dusty books and relics in the family con-apt at Kazuo Ishiguro Block had been a lonely and demeaning experience. No affection was ever shown, no warmth, no kinship. On the rare occasions her family ate a meal together, all discussions were conducted in the arid wasteland of academic terminology and debate.

In such a loveless environment, Janet had instinctively grasped at the one area where she might form a bond with her parents. She devoted herself to studying, becoming the youngest graduate ever from Mega-U and earning her own professorial chair by the age of twenty. But this remarkable achievement went unnoticed and uncelebrated. All her life had been given over to trying to win her parents' love and affection, all in vain. Instead they had accepted her as a fellow academic, a new addition to the ranks of petrified people whose only excitement came from living in the past.

Janet had rebelled and abandoned her professorship to become curator of the Dustbuster when it opened. After that her parents refused to even acknowledge her. She had moved outside the tiny orbit of their lives and thus ceased to exist, except as another physical presence in the family con-apt.

Dr Swanson did not believe in fate, but she sometimes wondered if chance was truly random. The invitation to give a lecture series in Brit-Cit on that nation's legacy from the 1980s had come out of the blue, but it was a welcome opportunity to get away from the dry hopelessness of her life in the Big Meg. The chances of a toxic waste hovertanker crashing into Kazuo Ishiguro and only killing two people were miniscule. That those two people should be her parents... Maybe fate was real and it had smiled down on her. She had been due back home the previous night but missed her flight. Another coincidence, another piece of happenstance.

After the freakish death of her parents, Dr Swanson had blossomed. She still wore her usual tweed suits and forbidding glasses, but gradually began learning how to enjoy life. Rather than shut herself away at the end of the working day like one of the exhibits, Janet started joining her staff for an occasional meal, even sampling shampagne for the first time. A life that for so long had appeared empty and futile was starting to come alive.

Then she met her lover. It happened at a lecture Janet was giving about the rise and fall of Reaganomics, a political movement of great influence to American domestic politics in the 1980s. Most of the audience was comprised of the usual crowd of fellow academics and students, but among them one face caught Janet's attention. Sat towards the back, this person seemed to delight in what Dr Swanson had to say, hanging on her every word. The rest of the audience began to fade away, as if Janet and this lone person were having a private conversation like old friends, sharing their most intimate secrets.

When the lecture concluded. Dr Swanson found herself blushing. The applause from the audience was rapturous and her colleagues had been most complimentary. "Amazingly passionate!" said her assistant, Miles Wilberforce. "I didn't think anyone could get me excited about this topic but you managed it, Janet. Quite, quite remarkable!"

Dr Swanson could recall little else anyone said afterwards. She had been too busy searching the crowd for that figure from the back row, the person with whom she had experienced such a strong connection. But the person was nowhere to be found, having slipped away into the night. Janet felt a gnawing sense of loss, far stronger than the faint wisps of grief left by her parents' passing. Somehow Dr Swanson knew she would never be complete until she found that person again. What surprised her most about the experience was the gender of her beloved. Without realising it, Janet had fallen in love at first sight with another woman.

Dr Swanson was not a virgin. There had been a messy, fumbled incident with one of her male lecturers while studying at Mega-U and a brief encounter with a crusty Brit-Cit professor when they both attended a symposium in Hondo City. But those were fleeting, meaningless moments where she acquiesced to the desires of others, thinking it would be impolite to say no. Her own sexuality had remained unknown, an untapped well of feelings and needs. She had pushed aside fantasies as girlish and immature idylls. She had her work. That was her life. She would not let herself be ruled by base, animal desires.

Her lover had changed all that. Janet had arrived at the Dustbuster late the following morning, having spent a sleepless night thinking about what had happened. For the first time she let herself imagine what it might be like to share herself with another woman. To kiss those luscious red lips, to feel her hands caressing another woman's body and be touched too. To undress and stand naked, to be unashamed and wanting. Janet was surprised to experience no guilt, no doubt about what she felt. It seemed utterly natural and inevitable, as if a part of herself long missing had been discovered at last.

The woman was waiting for Janet outside her office at the museum. She was wearing a taut, black leathereen dress, her angular face framed by jet black hair cut into a bob. Seeing Janet approaching, the woman smiled and offered a handshake. "Hello, my name is Kay. I enjoyed your lecture last night, but had to hurry away afterwards to a prior commitment. So I decided to come here and tell you how I felt in person. I hope you don't mind."

Dr Swanson realised she was turning crimson again and hung her head in embarrassment. "No, not at all. I'm glad you did."

Kay had looked at Janet with dark, piercing eyes. "Are you blushing? I didn't think people still did that."

Janet said nothing, just shook her head.

Kay slipped off one of the black leathereen gloves she was wearing and gently tipped Janet's head up to the light. "Don't be embarrassed, it's quite charming. You shouldn't hide your face away, especially not one so beautiful."

"You'll make me blush again," Janet replied giddily.

"Nonsense!" Kay moved to stand beside Dr Swanson and slid her hand around the curator's elbow. "Tell you what, why don't you give me a tour of the museum? I've never been round the 1980s and I suspect you will make the perfect guide. That is, if you're not too busy."

Janet had looked into Kay's face and felt herself melting. She knew she would never be able to refuse this woman anything. "It'll be my pleasure. Where would you like to start?"

Kay gave her elbow a squeeze. "Let's just begin with the tour. We can save the real pleasure for later."

They got as far as the Evil Empire display before Janet felt an irresistible urge. She dragged this woman about whom she knew so little into an alcove and began kissing her passionately. But after a few moments Janet realised Kay wasn't kissing her back. The curator broke away, confused and ashamed. "I'm sorry," she stammered. "I thought…"

Kay smiled and pointed up at the security cameras. "Are you sure we should be doing this in front of all those eyes?"

Janet waved away such concerns. "They're just for show. The museum can't afford to maintain them, so only the most valuable exhibits are covered."

Kay arched an eyebrow at this news, licking her lips. "In that case…"

They made love in a dark corner, Dr Swanson experiencing a pleasure she had never previously known. At one stage a tour party wandered past the nearby exhibit, forcing the two women to pause their frantic movements. Janet tried to pull away from Kay but found herself unable to resist the other woman's urgings. "What if somebody sees us?" the curator asked helplessly, suddenly aware of how few of her clothes she was still wearing.

Kay grinned wickedly. "They should be so lucky."

Janet bit her bottom lip, suppressing the urge to cry out in ecstasy.

All that had been five months ago. Since then the two women had spent many nights in each other's arms. They slept at Janet's con-apt, Kay always taking the initiative in arranging the next meeting. Janet felt besotted when they were together, bewitched by the power of her lust for the other woman. Only when they were apart for more than a few days did Dr Swanson begin to question the relationship. Kay refused to let Janet know where she lived, or give her a way of making contact. Kay said it kept the passion alive, helped her maintain an air of mystery. To rational, sensible Dr Swanson that seemed like an excuse, something to hide behind. But when Janet was with Kay, she never entertained such thoughts. She was too busy with other endeavours.

After they had been lovers for a month, Kay revealed a little about herself. She was personal assistant to an influential businessman and philanthropist, Jesus Bludd. He planned to make a very generous donation to the museum, at Kay's urging. In return Bludd asked only for free tickets to visit the Evil Empire exhibition on the day of his choice. Janet had been more than happy to oblige, especially when the donation of half a million credits arrived at the museum.

Bludd's visit had been somewhat perturbing for Dr Swanson. He treated Kay more like his property than his employee, and seemed to sneer at the two women's obvious affection for each other. Janet had just been happy to see a little more of her lover's secret life. But after that day their assignations became less and less frequent, Kay more perfunctory in her lovemaking, as if she were just going through the motions. Janet cried herself to sleep at night, worrying about losing the only person she had ever loved. She began losing weight, rarely ate more than one meal a day and became slack about paying attention to her job. Janet was falling apart, one piece at a time.

Then came the worst day of Dr Swanson's life, the day she discovered the truth about Kay, the day she discovered the truth about herself. After that, nothing would ever be the same again.

DREDD'S LAWMASTER ROARED to a halt outside the Dustbuster. He strode inside, taking the turbolift to the forty-second floor. The grim-faced Judge emerged in the 1980s area and abruptly stopped, recognition making his expression even more sullen. He had seen this particular exhibition area before.

"Dredd? Over here!" A female Judge was standing next to a barren display space, her helmet tucked under one arm. Brown, curly hair tumbled down around her freckled features. As Dredd approached, the Judge introduced herself. "Langenkamp. I was first on the scene."

Dredd gestured towards the empty exhibition. "What's missing?"

"The Evil Empire. It depicted the old United States' command and control centre for weapons of mass destruction. Even had an animatronic President getting ready to launch nuclear war. Quite popular, apparently."

Dredd nodded. "I know. Bludd came to see it four months ago, the day Ryan was inserted into the crime boss's organisation." He paused. "Where's the body?"

Langenkamp jerked a thumb at a corner of the exhibition space where forensic specialists were examining something on the floor. Beyond them stood the doors of another turbolift marked DISPLAYS ONLY. "We think the perps took the exhibit out using the museum's goods elevator."

"What did the security cameras capture?"

"Nothing. They weren't switched on in here today," Langenkamp replied, rolling her eyes. "Seems the museum has been skimping on aspects of its budget. Nobody expected a theft from this display. It was deemed low risk."

"But the cameras were working the day Bludd came to visit."

"Only because PSU asked for access to the video feed for this area."

"Terrif," Dredd growled. "This was probably an inside job. There was a curator here when Bludd did his tour, a woman. Where is she now?"

Langenkamp sighed. "Dr Janet Swanson, she's in her office, down that corridor. But take it gently with her, Dredd. She seems to have suffered some sort of emotional breakdown. There's a Psi-Judge with her now, trying to put the pieces back together."

Dredd scowled. "We haven't got time to take it gently. Bludd has been planning this raid for months, keeping us guessing. We need to know exactly what has been taken and why!"

The forensic Judges had finished their on-sight examination of Ryan's headless corpse. They were just lifting the cadaver on to a hover-stretcher when Dredd joined them outside the turbolift doors. He pulled back the sheet covering the remains and glared at the body, the neck severed by a cauterised slice mark. "DNA match?" Dredd asked the nearest Tek-Judge.

"It's Ryan, no doubt about it. But why did they dump the body here?"

"Bludd is sending us a message," Dredd replied. "He wants us to know who was behind this theft and this murder. But I guarantee you won't find a shred of evidence here or on Ryan's body that links Bludd to either crime. He's too smart for that."

The Tek-Judge pulled the sheet back over the corpse. "He's taunting us."

Six

Psi-Judge Karyn regarded the Dustbuster's curator sadly. It had taken almost an hour of coaxing to prise the tear-stained tale out of Dr Swanson. The poor woman was almost catatonic when Karyn started, her psyche shattered by an attack so vicious it beggared belief. A lifetime of therapy would be needed for Janet to recover from what had been done to her and even then she would never be able to reclaim the life she had once enjoyed. The curator was a numb, broken woman with no fight left in her when Dredd entered the office.

Karyn hurriedly escorted him back outside and shut the door to keep Swanson from hearing her verdict. When Dredd objected, the Psi-Judge hushed him into silence.

"Somebody has done a job on that woman like nothing I've ever seen before; total character annihilation," Karyn explained in a whisper. "The last thing she needs now is you shouting at her."

"When will she be able to talk?" he hissed. Karyn didn't need to be a psychic to sense his boiling anger and frustration.

"I don't know," she admitted. "I've got the gist of what's been happening to her. The fine details will have to wait."

Dredd looked past Karyn through a window into Dr Swanson's office. The curator was crouched over in a chair, her arms locked round her knees, rocking slowly backwards and forwards. "Tell me what you can."

Karyn leaned against a wall in the corridor, pushing her copper red curls out of her face. She outlined Dr Swanson's love affair, how the arrival of the woman known only as Kay turned the curator's life upside down. "From the description it's clear this Kay was Kara, Bludd's right-hand woman. She must be a powerful psyker to ruthlessly and effectively manipulate Swanson's emotions and actions on such a scale."

"We don't know much about her," Dredd admitted. "Kara appeared at Bludd's side last year and is his most trusted confidante. She's also his enforcer, doing Bludd's dirtiest work."

"Well, she's done quite a job on Swanson. From what I can glean it was simply a ruse to gain access to information about the museum and the Evil Empire exhibition in particular." Karyn frowned, still coming to terms with the horror show inside the curator's mind. "Kay, I mean Kara turned up today with several associates, leaving the headless corpse and taking the exhibit. Just before leaving, Kara set off a mind-bomb inside the curator's head, scrambling half her memories and letting Swanson know how she had been manipulated and used from start to finish. That bitch destroyed the curator, just for fun." Karyn paused to let the Tek-Judges removing Ryan's corpse pass. "There's something else, Dredd; a gap in Swanson's mind."

"Explain."

"It's as if someone has ripped a tiny section out of the curator's memory, like tearing a page from a book. I could read everything leading up to and following on from that section, but the missing part is a void, a blank."

"Can you tell what's missing from the context?"

Karyn shrugged helplessly. "I'll have to go back inside Swanson's mind, have another look. I can't promise anything."

"Try," Dredd urged. "I'm going to interview the curator's colleagues, see what they know. Langenkamp has them in the staff room."

MINUTES LATER, MILES Wilberforce was learning the meaning of regret. He had been complaining about being locked inside the cramped staff room with nearly thirty other museum workers. "Why are we being kept here like prisoners? We've done nothing wrong! My shift finished more than an hour ago, I should be at home by now. Instead we're stuck in this shoebox of a room, with no explanations and no apologies. Well I've had enough! I want to speak with somebody in authority and I want to do so now! In fact, I demand it!"

Dr Swanson's assistant had worked himself up into a fit of self-righteous pique, trying to goad his colleagues into action. "Look at you all – sheep! None of you knows what is going on but you all sit there meekly, accepting what the Judges tell you to do, never having the nerve to stand up for yourselves. Well I'm going to show you exactly who's in charge here!"

Wilberforce strode to the door and pulled it open. Standing on the other side was the imposing figure of Dredd, gently tapping his daystick against a gauntlet-clad hand.

"You were saying?"

"I demand to be allowed to leave," Wilberforce replied, trying to keep a tremble out of his voice. "You have no right to keep us in here like cattle!"

Dredd lifted his daystick and used the rounded end to nudge Wilberforce in the chest, sending the assistant back a step into the staff room. "Don't talk to me about rights, punk." The Judge gave Wilberforce another nudge with each successive sentence. "You have no rights as far as I'm concerned. You don't have the right to remain silent. You don't have the right to an attorney. You don't have the right to a trial, fair or otherwise. All you need to know is that I am Judge, jury and – if necessary – executioner."

Dredd gave the assistant a final, hard jab in the chest, sending him sprawling to the floor. The other staff members were cowering against the walls; meek museum workers trying to keep as far from Dredd's wrath as possible. "I dispense instant justice. Unless you creeps want a taste of that, I suggest you start giving me answers. Now, which one of you punks is Dr Swanson's assistant?"

The other staff all pointed accusingly at Wilberforce.

"I might have known," Dredd snarled. He pointed at the open doorway with his daystick. "Out in the corridor. Now." Once they were both in the hallway, Dredd closed the door behind him before turning his attention to Wilberforce. "Tell me about the Evil Empire exhibition. What's so special about it?"

"I'm not sure I understand the question," Swanson's assistant replied.

"Don't try my patience," Dredd warned. "Why would someone want to steal the exhibit?"

Wilberforce paled. "It's been stolen? But that's impossible. Unless…"

"Unless what?"

"Well, only Dr Swanson has all the information necessary to remove and reactivate the system. She's still here, isn't she?" Wilberforce looked along the corridor to his boss's office. "She was being interviewed in her room."

"What are you talking about? What system?" Dredd demanded.

"The computer system for the command and control exhibit. Only Dr Swanson knows all the data to reactivate it."

"Reactivate it? How can you reactivate a replica?"

"Oh, grud," Wilberforce murmured. "You don't know…"

Dredd grabbed the assistant by the neck and lifted him bodily off the ground. "Enough with the mumbling, punk. What don't I know?"

Wilberforce choked out his reply between gasps for air. "The command and control system. It's not a replica, it's the real thing."

Dredd released Wilberforce. The assistant curator slumped to the floor, choking and coughing as he explained. "It was decommissioned and removed from the White House in the early twenty-first century and put into storage after being superseded by more advanced systems. But some of the weapons it controlled are still active."

"Who else knows about this?" Dredd demanded.

"Dr Swanson, obviously. The museum's board of directors. Our security advisors at Red Inc. That's about it."

"Red Inc provides security advice?"

"Yes. They got the contract a few months ago when Dr Swanson—"

Dredd opened the door to the staff room and threw Wilberforce back inside. After ordering another Judge to stand guard outside the door, Dredd hurried back to Swanson's office. Karyn was emerging, a worried look on her face. She saw Dredd approaching. "I'm not sure I've got this right, but if it's accurate then we've got a serious problem," she said. Dredd outlined what he had discovered from Wilberforce.

"That corroborates what I could glean from the holes in the curator's memory," Karyn said. "Kara has stolen everything anyone needs to know to make that command and control system active again."

"Sweet Jovus," Dredd said quietly. He activated his helmet radio and called Control. "I need everything you can give me about late twentieth century weapons systems controlled by the United States Government."

"That isn't going to be easy," Control replied. "All the central records were destroyed during the Atomic Wars of 2070. Anything from before that period is considered arcane knowledge these days. You could try the Museum of the Twentieth Century. The Dustbuster's staff probably know more than we do."

"I'm at the Dustbuster!" Dredd snarled back. "Contact the Chief Judge. Tell Hershey I have to speak with her immediately, if not sooner!"

"We'll pass the message on, Dredd, but she's been busy at the treaty negotiations all day. Don't know if–"

"I couldn't give a drokk what you know or don't know, Control. All I do know is that this city is in grave and imminent danger. Now do what I ask or I'll have your badge for breakfast! Dredd out."

Karyn had observed all of this at close quarters and it scared her. She had never seen Dredd so anxious nor so angry. The Psi-Judge was trying to think how she could help when a weak voice spoke behind her.

"You're right to be afraid," Dr Swanson said. She had opened the door to her office and was watching the two Judges. "In the late twentieth century, different nations launched thousands of satellites into orbit, laden with all manner of doomsday weapons. Mutually assured destruction, it was called. They believed nobody would dare risk a global conflict using these weapons of mass destruction, for fear of being destroyed themselves. They all believed that having the power to destroy their enemy made them safe. But how many different ways do you need to wipe humanity off the face of the earth?" Swanson smiled, her face briefly brought alive again by bitter irony. "Of course, we know different now, don't we? Thanks to Bad Bob Booth." The curator sagged sideways, leaning against the doorframe for support. "I'm sorry. I'm so very sorry," she whispered sadly.

Dredd moved closer to Swanson, acknowledging a look of warning from Karyn. "What sort of weapons did the US Government send into orbit, Dr Swanson?"

She shrugged. "There was a lot of talk about a laser defence system. But many suspected the satellites were used to store atomic, biological and even chemical weapons. Little time bombs from the past, gently orbiting the planet, just waiting for the chance to explode, nearly one hundred and fifty years later." The curator frowned. "I used to know a lot about such things but I can't recall any of the details now for the life of me. I don't know why..." She wandered back into her office, standing over the desk like a puppet whose strings have been cut, just waiting to fall over. Karyn watched Swanson with concern.

"She's coming apart," the Psi-Judge whispered to Dredd. "Whatever Kara did to her, it's getting worse, like a ricochet bullet, bouncing around in Dr Swanson's mind, causing more and more damage. We need to–" Karyn was interrupted by Dredd getting a call from Control.

"Putting the Chief Judge through to you now."

Karyn listened as Dredd explained the gravity of the situation. The Psi-Judge was not able to hear Hershey's side of the conversation, but it did not require much imagination. In the past Bludd had been considered a minor but growing threat to the Law. But in a single, bold stroke the crime boss had apparently acquired a means of destroying entire cities. Karyn was so intent on Dredd, she didn't notice what Dr Swanson was doing.

JANET COULD FEEL her thoughts coming apart, her mind splintering into broken shards, all shapes, edges, and pain. She tried to picture Kay's beautiful face but couldn't see it anymore, just a grinning mask of hatred where once her lover had been. Worst of all, she knew the love they had shared was a sham, a ruse, and somehow that was the cruellest trick of all.

I don't want to have these memories anymore, Janet thought. She turned away from the desk towards her office windows. Outside, the city was slowly being enshrouded by night, the sun setting beyond the West Wall in the distance. To the east, lights were beginning to appear in a few buildings. It would be dusk soon, the end of another day. I thought I was unhappy this morning, Janet realised. I didn't know what unhappiness was.

She took two steps back, then ran forwards, launching herself at the office windows.

KARYN FELT THE psi-flash of Dr Swanson's terror a moment before the curator crashed through the glasseen, but it was too late to do anything. The Psi-Judge twisted round to see the broken woman plunging out of the window, blood trailing from the wounds sliced by the shattered fragments of glasseen. Karyn braced herself for the moment of death as Dr Swanson fell forty-two storeys to the ground below, screaming with terror all the way down.

Then it was over with just a horrible, numb emptiness left behind.

No matter how many times Karyn had experienced the death of a mind, it never got any easier, any less painful. She felt drawn into the death, a tiny piece of herself dying too. The Psi-Judge did not fear her own death. It was an ending, nothing more. When you worked the streets of Mega-City One, death could come at any moment. But the horror of feeling another person die, that lingered in the mind like a cancer, eating away at you.

Karyn turned away from the window to see Dredd watching her, still talking with the Chief Judge on his helmet radio. "Sorry to interrupt you, but Dr Swanson has just committed suicide." He paused for Hershey's response. "We'll keep interviewing the other staff, but it seems the curator was the key to the theft. I doubt the others will be able to add much." Another pause. "Yes, ma'am. We'll just have to see what move Bludd makes next. Dredd out."

Karyn apologised for failing to stop Dr Swanson. "She was out the window before I realised what was in her mind. Kara left such a mess, I couldn't anticipate what the curator was going to do."

Dredd waved away the apology. "I doubt there was much more we could have gotten from her anyway." He slammed a fist against the nearest wall, leaving a dent in the surface. "Drokk it! This creep has been playing us for fools all day. He let Ryan tell us about the supposed attack on the treaty talks, knowing it would expose the security shortcomings here. If Swanson was right, Bludd now has the power to hold Mega-City One to ransom and there's nothing we can do about it!"

Karyn volunteered to interrogate the rest of the museum staff. "With my empath abilities and a handheld lie-detector, I'll soon find out if any of them was involved with all of this," she said. Dredd was about to respond when he got another call on his helmet radio. As Karyn walked away, she heard his response to the incoming message.

"Max Normal? Alright, patch him through."

"Hey, Joe! Where you going with that Lawgiver in your hand?" Max smiled at the ginger dwarf. Angry Sanderson was threatening him with a handgun. The two men were standing by a vidphone booth on a deserted skedway.

"I'm busy, Normal. State your business."

"Always to the point, Dredd. That's what I like about you Law dudes. Just the facts, Max, just the facts."

"I thought you retired. Why are you calling?"

The pinstripe freak leaned closer to the vidphone, its screen empty but for the words AUDIO ONLY SELECTED. "Well, a mutual acquaintance of ours wanted me to pass on a message."

"Who?" Dredd asked. Before Normal could reply, the Judge added another question. "Max, are you being threatened?"

"You could say that, daddio, but I couldn't possibly comment."

"That's a yes. What's the message?"

"You're to be at the Nothing Could Be Finer Diner, corner of Campion and Cribb in Southside Sector 41, within thirty minutes. Come alone: no homing devices, no weapons, no surveillance equipment and no tricks. Our mutual acquaintance says you'll be thoroughly scanned on arrival, so don't bother trying to hide anything."

"Max, can you tell me the name of this acquaintance?"

Normal turned away from the dwarf before whispering his reply. "Let's just say I've never believed in any messiahs besides myself, you dig?"

"Jesus Bludd?"

"I knew you'd be hip to my jive, Joe!" Normal glanced back over his shoulder nervously. Sanderson had disappeared. Max swivelled round but could not see the dwarf anywhere. "Dredd, he's gone!"

"Who? Max, are you there?"

Normal relaxed again, mopping his brow with a white linen handkerchief. "I'm here, daddio. The runt that had a gun on me has gone."

"Was there any more to the message?"

"No, that was all Bludd said. Listen Joe, I know I put plenty of patois in my patter but these cats are serious – deadly serious. You catch my groove?"

"Loud and clear. Dredd out."

COSMO ZIMMER'S FEET were cold, as usual. They had been cold since he started work as a security guard at the Mega-City One Spaceport three months earlier. In the past, such jobs had been entrusted only to robots but the Second Robot War launched by Nero Narcos back in 2121 resulted in sweeping changes to the city's security systems. High risk areas such as the spaceport were now required to employ one human for every five droids.

In theory, finding people to take the job should have been simple. The Big Meg's unemployment problem was endemic with fewer than one in eight citizens having paid work of any description. The rise of mechanisation had driven most of the population on to welfare support. While most coveted the prestige of having a job and the extra income it brought, that didn't mean people were rushing to do demeaning work.

Being a live mannequin at one of the sprawling shopperas, that was high visibility, Cosmo thought. Prowling around empty hangars in the cold, well, there was nothing glamorous about that. He lived in a world of private fantasy, always imagining some extravagant scenario that would change his life forever. Anything was better than dreary reality. The spaceport jutted out into the Black Atlantic, built on land reclaimed from the toxic ocean. Once the sun started setting in the west, cold air began sweeping in off the water. Cosmo felt like each breeze was cutting him to the bone, slicing through his flimsy uniform.

The worst aspect of the mandatory orange and black uniform was the boots. Thin-soled and flimsy, they leeched the warmth from Cosmo's feet, chilling the toes and numbing the bones. He had tried putting on extra socks or fitting electric foot warmer insoles in his boots, but nothing seemed to hold back the creeping cold. Everytime he stamped his feet to get some warmth into them, the insoles shorted out in protest. Cosmo had promised his wife Helga he would stay in the job for three months. The ninety days were up tonight. At the end of this shift he was quitting. Nothing was worth this; certainly not the pitiful handful of credits the spaceport authority deigned to pay its human staff.

Having reached the furthest extent of his nightly route, Cosmo began the long circle back to the main terminal. He paused to blow hot breath between his frozen fingers, rubbing the palms together briskly, when the sound of metal striking metal caught his attention. It was coming from one of the hangars he had just passed. Cosmo circled back and saw a glimmer of light beneath the main doors. Strange, this hanger had been out of use for weeks. What was someone doing inside it now?

The night watchman decided against calling in his discovery just yet. It was probably just an engineer, pulling some extra overtime. Of course, it could be perps, trying to rob the spaceport. What if I could catch them in the act, Cosmo wondered. Would there be a reward? Perhaps a promotion too? If I showed up those drokking security droids, it'd make me look even better. His mind filled with notions of glory, Cosmo crept round to a side entrance and peered through a crack in the door.

Inside, two women were shoving a heavy metal crate into the cargo hold of a private shuttle. The crate had become wedged, defying the pair's efforts to shift it. The larger woman cursed loudly, her face livid with rage. Cosmo was startled by the array of tattoos illustrating her body; he had never seen so much ink on one person. The other woman was smaller and slighter. She was standing side-on to Cosmo, but what he could see of her face was strikingly beautiful. They didn't seem like perps to him, just two women in need of a man's help. Perhaps if he stepped in and offered his assistance, they would reward him. Two handsome women, one strong man... Cosmo's face twitched into a smile as he imagined the possibilities. Adjusting his uniform, he strode into the hangar and boldly presented himself.

"Ladies, you look like you could use my help!" Cosmo announced. He was dismayed to see the more beautiful woman was hideously scarred on one side of her face. He was more dismayed to see she was pointing a small handgun at him. "Hey, what's going on here? I didn't–"

Di shot the security guard five times before returning to the crate. "Come on, Sue, we haven't got all night. The security droids will eventually notice that simp is missing and come looking for him."

Cosmo moved a weak hand round his comms unit but the fingers kept slipping off, unable to grasp it. Tilting his head to one side, he could see the reason why; his hand was covered in blood. A large pool of it was forming underneath him too. That can't be good, Cosmo thought. Still, I'm sure there's some new surgical procedure that can save my life. You never know, I might become a famous case, mentioned in medical journals...

*   *   *

DREDD STOPPED HIS motorcycle a block short of the Nothing Could Be Finer Diner. The eatery was visible in the distance, an outpost of light and warmth on the corner of Campion and Cribb. Southside Sector 41 had long been one of the Big Meg's most dangerous areas, home to vicious turf wars between street gangs. Few citizens walked the pedways after dark. It was a wonder the Nothing Could Be Finer Diner still had any windows, let alone any customers.

It had taken Dredd twenty minutes to drive across the city from the Dustbuster. He had talked with Hershey en route, discussing tactics for the meet. The Chief Judge was unhappy about one of her Judges walking into the diner unarmed and without back-up, but Dredd dismissed such concerns.

"If Bludd wanted me dead, he could easily have me killed at any time," the Judge had reasoned. "He wants to talk, so I'll hear him out. And Hershey, don't send anybody along to keep watch from a distance. Bludd will be expecting that. Don't get another Judge killed trying to protect me."

Dredd switched off his Lawmaster's engine and dismounted. He began methodically removing all his weapons: the Lawgiver handgun, the bootknife, the utility belt and its pouches laden with equipment. The Judge opened the panniers mounted over his motorcycle's rear wheel and locked the weapons inside. After glancing around to check he wasn't being followed, Dredd began striding towards the diner. He recognised the city block standing diagonally opposite the eatery. Joe Chill Block had been the scene of more murders than any other residential building in the Big Meg, its hallways and stairwells a notorious killing ground. Few residents survived more than a year inside those walls, either dying in pain and terror or opting for a Displaced Persons Camp as the safer, happier lifestyle option.

As Dredd got closer to the diner, two men of contrasting heights emerged from the shadows. The taller of the pair, pasty-faced with mirrored eyeballs, began scanning the

Judge's body with an electronic sensor wand while his dwarf colleague watched, a handgun trained on the scene. "You're Fincher," Dredd announced to the man searching him. "Wanted in three other cities for multiple murders and mutilations."

"Shame you ain't got an extradition agreement with those cities, isn't it?" Fincher replied with a smirk. The wand crackled with alarm as it passed over Dredd's name badge. Fincher examined the heavy metallic badge but could find nothing untoward about it. Satisfied Dredd was unarmed, the perp snapped the microphone off from the Judge's helmet radio. "Don't want anybody ear-wigging your conversation now, do we?"

Dredd ignored Fincher, glaring at the ginger dwarf guarding them. "And you must be Angry Sanderson. According to our files, your real name is Audley. I can see why you'd change it. Other punks don't take you seriously now. Imagine what they'd say if they knew your name was Audley?"

Sanderson's face curled with disdain. He pointed into the diner. "You're wanted inside. Get your ass in there."

"Whatever you say... Audley." Dredd began walking towards the eatery. He smirked at the dwarf and was rewarded by the sight of Fincher having to restrain the furious Sanderson from attacking the lawman.

THE NOTHING COULD BE FINER DINER was a throwback to a bygone era, a perfect replica of the roadside cafes that spread across North America nearly two hundred years earlier. Outside it was all gleaming chrome and glass, a long, rectangular masterpiece of art deco lines and curves. Inside was even more stunning, with a serving counter dividing the interior in two halves. The area beyond the counter was the kitchen, all stainless steel and polished precision.

The other half was for customers. A row of fixed stools with circular seats ran down the length of the counter. The rest of the black and white checked floor was given over to booths, each made up of two bench seats facing each other across a table. Every seat was upholstered in red with real leather, none displaying the usual graffiti or razor slashes.

As Dredd closed the diner door behind him, a small bell above it rang. A beautiful but stern-faced woman appeared from the kitchen clad in a pristine pale green uniform, a white cotton apron fastened around her waist. A towering beehive of strawberry-blonde hair was perched atop her head, while a bored expression was fixed on her face. She chewed gum and regarded the newcomer with undisguised disinterest. "Can I help you?"

Dredd approached the counter. "I'm here for a meeting."

"Really?" the waitress replied, sarcasm dripping from her nasal voice. "Well, take a seat and have a look at the menu. Once your partner in crime turns up, I'll come over and tell you both about today's specials. Alright?"

The Judge tilted his head to one side, staring at the waitress's profile. "Have we met somewhere before, Miss...?"

The waitress tapped one of her long, scarlet fingernails against a plastic name badge attached to her uniform just above the left breast. "The name's Karrie-Ann, buster. Now go sit down and look at the menu, okay?"

Dredd nodded and wandered over to a window booth a few tables away. He slid into the seat facing away from the door and picked up the menu. The choice was surprising but limited: BREAKFAST, LUNCH and SUPPER, all priced at twenty-seven credits. Grud knew what the specials were going to be.

The diner's door opened and swiftly closed again, tinkling the bell above it. Dredd could see the new arrival reflected in the glass at the far end of the eatery. It was a man, heavyset and immaculately dressed in a perfectly tailored suit. The figure looked about the diner before speaking to Karrie-Ann. "I'm here for a meeting." The waitress made a bored gesture in Dredd's direction. The newcomer approached the Judge's booth, moving with ease despite his bulk. He stopped and pointed at the seat opposite Dredd. "May I?"

"Be my guest," Dredd replied dryly.

The newcomer slipped into the booth and positioned himself opposite the Judge. Before he could say anything else, the waitress was sauntering over from the counter, already intoning a list of specials in a tired monotone. "Good evening, gentlemen. Tonight's specials are anarchy, chaos, cunning and guile. The Nothing Could Be Finer is also happy to offer its signature dish, revenge. We normally serve this cold, but it can be heated through if you prefer."

"Very droll," the newcomer replied. "We'll just have synthi-caf."

"Two synthi-cafs, coming right up." Karrie-Ann strolled away, her high heels clicking on the floor as she returned to the counter.

"I hope that's alright with you," the new arrival said to Dredd. "You look like you could use a pick-me-up. Been a long day, has it?"

The Judge did not reply.

"I'm terribly sorry, I realise I haven't introduced myself." The newcomer stretched out a hand for Dredd to shake. "My name is Bludd – Jesus Bludd."

Seven

"I KNOW WHO you are, creep," Dredd replied, folding his arms. Bludd withdrew his offer of a handshake, instead resting both arms on the table.

"You know something? You're just as I expected," Bludd said. "Just as I remembered. I saw you once, more than twenty years ago, after Cal almost brought this city to its knees. You were dispensing justice to the Cosmic Punks gang, not far from this diner. A most impressive display."

"They challenged the rule of the Law."

"And you crushed them for that, single-handedly. Quite remarkable."

"I was doing my job."

"Maybe," Bludd said. "But there was something else going on that day. It wasn't only a Judge bringing some street scum to justice. You were imposing your will on them, sending a message to everyone else in Southside 41 and the rest of the city. You were showing them the Law was back in town, the Judges were in control once more, deploying the firm spank of authority to remind everyone who was boss. You were giving a masterclass in the application of power. I remember that day well."

"What about what happened to your mother? Do you remember that too?"

Bludd smiled. "I wondered how long it would be before you'd bring that up. No doubt the Department's profilers and Psi-Division empaths pinpoint my mother's rape and murder as the key incident that turned me to a life of crime, yes?"

"I don't put much stock in psychological profiles," Dredd replied. "All I need to know is who's breaking the Law, then I break them."

"Then why mention my mother?"

"Call it a test."

"Really? So you don't just use physical force to break perps, Dredd. You're just as happy to break them mentally."

"I'll use whatever weapons I can."

"An admirable approach. One I utilise myself."

Karrie-Ann returned to the booth, carrying two cups of synthi-caf. She placed them between the two men before straightening up again, the short skirt of her uniform touching the tops of her white mesh stockings. Bludd reached out a hand and slid it under the skirt, all the while smiling at Dredd.

"Do you like my assistant Kara? She does love these little role-playing exercises, taking on a fresh persona to suit my needs."

"She destroyed the curator at the Dustbuster."

"Really? How is Dr Swanson these days? I haven't seen her in three or four months," Bludd ventured blithely.

"Dead. She committed suicide earlier today," Dredd snarled.

"How unfortunate. Still, as you say, we should always use whatever weapons we can. You can go back to being a waitress now, my dear." Kara strode back to the counter, all the while loudly cracking her gum. "Such a sweet girl. Do you know how I acquired her services?"

Dredd shook his head.

"Payment for a gambling debt, if you can believe that, along with this eatery. Do you like it? I was contemplating starting a chain of Nothing Could Be Finer Diners across the city. I have a fondness for the twentieth century: its style, its culture, its contribution to the arts. I collect the masterpieces of that era: paintings by Warhol, films by Eastwood, novels by Wyndham. They inspire me and I wish to share this inspiration with others."

"Is that why you had the Evil Empire exhibit stolen from the Dustbuster today? To share your inspiration with others?" Dredd sneered.

Bludd ignored the jibe. "This eatery is a perfect replica of a twentieth century American roadside cafe. Of course, when I chose to move the diner to this location, I made sure everyone in Southside Sector 41 knew it was under my protection."

"That explains the lack of vandalism," Dredd said.

"My reputation does have its advantages," Bludd conceded. "A business acquaintance of mine got in over his head and felt impelled to surrender this place and his beloved Kara to me as compensation. It was only when she entered my employ I discovered Kara's many other talents. She is one of the most powerful psykers I have ever encountered, utterly ruthless and completely amoral. Better yet, she is quite devoted to me, doing anything I ask with anyone or to anyone. You could taste her talents, if you like?"

"No thanks. You should be careful of her too." Dredd leaned forward in his seat. "You never know when she might turn. Someone that fond of role-playing... How do you even know Kara is her real persona?"

"Sow all the seeds of doubt you want, they will not grow within me."

"Just don't say I didn't warn you." The Judge leaned back on the bench again. "You called this meeting, Bludd. What do you want to talk about?"

"To be honest, there are some questions I've always wanted to ask you. For instance, how can you devote your entire life to fighting a losing battle?"

"I don't."

"You must know you can never eradicate crime, not in a city of four hundred million people – every one of them a potential perp. Yet you persist in trying."

"I believe in the Law," Dredd replied. "I believe in justice."

"The two are not always the same thing, but that's another debate," the crime boss said. "One day you must lose this unequal battle, Dredd. Some perp will get the drop on you and you'll die, face down in a pool of your own blood. No glory, no fanfare. Just another dead Judge, one of thousands killed every year, all losing their personal battles to win the war against crime."

"It's not about winning the war. It's about winning the battles."

"But it's a hopeless fight."

"What's the alternative, Bludd? Anarchy? The people need the Law, they need order. Without it, Mega-City One would be torn apart within weeks, even days. Millions would die and for what? The want of the Law."

"I can't decide if your life is heroic or an exercise in self-delusion."

"Delusion is what you must be suffering from if you believe you can elude the Law forever, creep."

"No need to get unpleasant. Now that I think about it, you are the ultimate existentialist. Did you ever study Kierkegaard?"

"He wasn't required reading at the Academy."

"What a pity. He neatly summed up your approach to life, Dredd. Søren Kierkegaard was a nineteenth century Danish philosopher who believed all human existence was absurd. He suggested the only way for an individual to combat this absurdity was devoting themselves to a life of their own choosing. Doesn't that sum up the singular devotion to duty required of all Judges?"

"You tell me."

"Or there's the German philosopher Johann Gottlieb Fichte. He proposed that since we can never hope to understand why we are alive, the individual should choose a goal and pursue it wholeheartedly, despite the certainty of death and the meaninglessness of action. A neat précis of your existence, don't you think? You know you can never win the war against crime, yet you continue fighting it until you die, because that is the life you have chosen. You chose the nature of your existence, Dredd, just like I chose the nature of mine. It's what we do. We are both existentialists. We are more alike than you can bring yourself to admit."

"You're wrong, Bludd. You were offered the chance of becoming a Judge, of bringing justice to those who raped and murdered your mother, but you refused that chance. Instead you chose to become a criminal like your mother's killer, making money from the suffering of others. Why?"

"I am nothing like the man who attacked my mother. Anyway, he did find justice, just not at the hands of the Law. Your kind let him escape on a technicality. It took someone else to make him pay for what he did."

"You call being shoved into a public grinder justice?"

"He got what he deserved. Nothing more."

"And you gave him that justice."

Bludd smiled. "You don't honestly expect me to admit to that, do you?"

"You still haven't answered my question: why turn to crime? Why become like the perp who hurt and killed your mother?"

"You say I did, but you haven't proven it. If I am the underworld boss the Justice Department believes me to be, why have I never spent an hour in an iso-cube? Why am I still at large, free to allegedly commit and commission more crimes? Aren't I another example of you losing the battle as well as the war?"

"Our testing showed you possessed a high IQ, great guile and cunning. Most perps act from stupidity or passion. You think first. That gives you an advantage from the beginning. You let others do your dirty work so they do the time when we catch them. You haven't been caught, yet. But that doesn't absolve you of your crimes. Why? Why choose this life?"

"I was inspired by you, Dredd." Bludd leaned back in his seat, locking his hands together behind his head. "I saw what you could do the day you beat the Cosmic Punks. You were the best Judge then and you're probably still the best there is. I decided to become the best there was at what I do. Now, after twenty years of training myself, I am ready for my greatest coup." The crime boss took a sip of his synthi-caf, thoughtfully watching Dredd. "Your friends at the Justice Department like to foster the illusion they control this city, but you and I both know that simply isn't true."

"Do we?"

"The Big Meg is never more than one step away from anarchy. You and the other Judges keep fighting to maintain order, but what happens when you lose the war? Who will be in control then?"

Dredd folded his arms. "You want to rule the city, is that it?"

Bludd laughed hollowly. "Of course not. Nero Narcos proved the stupidity of such an endeavour. He spent years developing his scheme to usurp the Judges. One of your kind stumbled across his masterplan and Narcos felt obliged to put it into action. He smashed the Justice Department's control of this city in just a few hours only to discover running the Big Meg was a curse, not a blessing. Who would want to be in charge? Even the Judges don't want the job, if they are honest. You only assumed power by public demand after the Atomic Wars. No, I won't be repeating the folly of Nero."

"Then what?" Dredd asked.

"Consider the next few hours a demonstration of where real power resides. You can talk about justice and the Law all you wish, Dredd. But when chaos hits the Big Meg, you will see the truth." Bludd rubbed a finger against his lips before speaking again. "Have you ever heard of the old expression that in the kingdom of the blind..."

"The one-eyed man is king," Dredd replied. "What about it?"

"I've been researching the history of that adage. Apparently it's a mistake; a corrupted quotation, if you will. The adage originally sprang from the pen of Erasmus, a fifteenth century humanist and satirist, a man of letters, if you will. He wrote that in the valley of the blind, the one-eyed man is king. I find it interesting how popular usage alters words to suit itself, don't you?"

"Get to the point, Bludd."

"I just wanted to plant that seed in your mind for later. You never know when such arcane knowledge might come in handy. Your singular vision, your quest for justice may be all that saves this city in the coming crisis." The crime boss swirled the last of his synthi-caf around inside the cup and then swallowed the liquid. "Well, I must say I've enjoyed this little chat of ours. It's always a pleasure to meet somebody else who excels in their field of endeavour."

"You really are bloated with your self-importance, aren't you?" Dredd spat back, disgust evident in the set of his jaw.

"On the contrary. I am perfectly aware that as of this moment, whether I live or die is of little consequence to a vast number of people. That may change, it may not. I am not the one who suffers the delusion of believing they can control this city, that they can hold back the inevitable. I just wish I could be here to see that smug authority wiped from your face, Dredd, and from the face of every other Judge on the planet. Alas, this is where our paths diverge. We will not meet again. Goodbye." Bludd stood, signalling for Kara to join him.

"Going somewhere?" Dredd asked.

"Regrettably, yes. Much as I would like to stay and continue our little philosophical debate, business calls me elsewhere. Remember what I have said, Dredd. It may be of help to you in the coming hours."

"Whatever you've got planned, Bludd, I'll find a way of stopping it. You won our first battle today, but I'll win the war. Count on it, creep!"

"Ahh, bravado. The last resort of a beaten man," Bludd replied. Kara emerged from behind the counter, still wearing the guise of a waitress. She opened the eatery's front door for Bludd. The crime boss stopped to offer one last comment to Dredd. "By the way, I ask you to remain here for a few more minutes after we have departed."

"Why?"

"Let's just say you will hear something of value and see something of interest. Besides, if I am the notorious crime boss you claim, I need time to make my getaway. How is it Judges say goodbye to each other? Oh yes, that's it. See you on the streets, Joe." Bludd sauntered out of the diner, chuckling quietly. Kara made an obscene finger gesture at the lawman before following her master. The door swung shut behind her, leaving just Dredd in the diner. He waited a full minute before pressing the letter "E" on his name badge.

"Dredd to Hershey, did you hear all of that?"

"Loud and clear," the Chief Judge replied via Dredd's helmet radio. "Tek and Psi-Divisions are analysing everything Bludd uttered for clues about what he has planned. What did you make of it?"

"If he was like most perps, I'd say he was in love with the sound of his own voice. But Bludd isn't like most perps."

"Agreed. One thing was clear, whatever he's got planned, it's happening tonight. Bludd repeatedly talked about the next few hours, the coming crisis. The reference to a 'kingdom of the blind' must be significant too."

"Creep was taunting us," Dredd said. "He's–"

Suddenly a high-pitched electronic squeal cut through the radio transmission. Dredd cried out in pain, his eardrums assaulted by the sound just on the edge of hearing. After a few moments it stopped as abruptly as it had started, replaced by a woman's soothing voice.

"Tut, tut! You were told not to bring any communications devices to your meeting, Judge. For that infringement there shall be a forfeit. However, first things first. Look under your cup of synthi-caf."

Dredd recognised the voice as belonging to Kara. She must still be watching him. He glanced round the diner and spotted a small camera set into a corner of the ceiling. "That's right, I've got my eye on you. Now look under your cup of synthi-caf, lawman."

Dredd raised the still full cup from its saucer and peered beneath it. A small, translucent plastic disc adhered to the bottom of the cup. "Remove the device and place it against the outside of your helmet, close to the area covering one of your ears," Kara commanded. Dredd followed her instructions. Once the disc was fastened to his helmet, he could hear only Kara's voice. "The disc jams all incoming signals to your radio except mine and prevents you from calling anyone else for help. It has a few more interesting properties, but we'll get to those in due course. Our conversation cannot be traced, nor can the signal between us easily be hacked by Tek-Division. From now on you speak only to me and hear only my voice. Is that clear?"

"What do you want?" Dredd asked.

"We're going to have some fun, you and I. We're going to play a little game. Normally you are the hunter and the perp is the hunted. Tonight we're going to do some role reversal. For a change you will be the hunted, while four perps try to hunt you down. You met two of them earlier – Sanderson and Fincher. The identity of the others I will keep a secret, for now. It should make for an interesting evening."

"Why should I do what you say?"

"Remember that forfeit I mentioned? Take a look out through the diner windows. Diagonally opposite you will see a building called Joe Chill Block. How many people live in that skyscraper?"

"About thirty thousand."

"Now, imagine what would happen if that city block was suddenly destroyed by a laser beam projected from a twentieth century satellite in geostationary orbit above the Big Meg."

"Oh grud," Dredd whispered. He was already running towards the door of the diner, trying to remove the jamming device from the side of his helmet. "Dredd to Control, can you hear me? Dredd to Control, respond!"

"It's no use, Joe," Kara replied. "I told you, the disc will jam any attempt you make to call for help. Besides, the energy pulse is already coming."

THE PUBLIC SURVEILLANCE Unit's headquarters were located inside the Statue of Judgement, a massive monument constructed in the shape of a Judge that dwarfed the nearby Statue of Liberty. Inside the PSU's central monitoring chamber were dozens of terminals where analysts pored over data from thousands of sources. As well as keeping tabs on a city of four hundred million people, the PSU staff were also tasked with watching out for any external threats to the Big Meg. Judge Kerri Levene had just come on station with the night shift when a red warning light began flashing beside her terminal.

"PSU to Control, Levene here. Have we been notified about anything unusual happening in the sky overhead tonight?"

"Just a fireworks display. Why?"

The PSU analyst was juxtaposing data from multiple sources. "I'm reading a massive build-up of energy several miles above the city. I think it's centred on an old satellite in orbit."

"Those things are always falling out of the sky, Levene. They burn up on re-entry, ninety-nine times out of a hundred."

"I know, but this one isn't falling out of orbit. It's perfectly stable. The–"

Suddenly all screens in PSU were overloaded simultaneously. Around the room analysts were tearing off their headsets to escape an ear-piercing squeal of static. The lighting system dimmed and then cut out completely before being replaced by emergency illumination. A babble of sound filled the air as everyone shouted to be heard, trying to discover what had happened.

A deep, booming voice cut through the noise, silencing the cacophony. "Quiet! There will be quiet!" Niles emerged from his office, scowling with fury. "I want to hear one voice and one voice only." He glared round the room, searching for answers. "Can anyone tell me what just happened?"

Wincing inwardly, Levene cleared her throat. "Excuse me, sir…"

"Yes?"

"Before the overload I was monitoring a massive build-up of energy on board an old satellite over the city. I could be wrong, but…" The analyst's words trailed off, not wanting to give voice to her suspicions.

"What is it, Levene? Spit it out!"

"I think someone fired an energy pulse weapon at us from orbit. If the beam was powerful enough to disable all our systems as a side-effect, then it could destroy a city block in seconds."

"Sweet Jovus," Niles muttered. "Can you recall the precise location above which the satellite was orbiting?"

Levene closed her eyes and recited the longitude and latitude. Niles turned to the analyst standing closest to him, Judge Sharp. "Where is that?"

"Southside Sector 41," she replied instantly. "Joe Chill Block."

DREDD HAD ONLY reached the doorway of the diner when the energy pulse hit Joe Chill. A beam of red light shot down from overhead and penetrated the roof of the city block. As it punched through floor after floor of the building, each storey exploded outwards in a shower of glasseen and rockcrete. In less than a second the pulse had reached the bottom floor, burrowing deep into the ground beneath Joe Chill before abruptly stopping.

Dredd was thrown backwards through the diner by the first shock wave, sliding along the counter and thudding into the wall beyond. Before he had collapsed to the floor, the eatery was hit by a second wave, this one made of flames and debris from the exploding city block. The Nothing Could Be Finer Diner was crushed by a blizzard of rockcrete, the roof crumpled inwards like a paper bag. Billowing clouds of smoke and dust ensued, turning the air into an acrid smog within moments. As Dredd slid to the floor of the diner he felt blackness engulfing him. He pulled the respirator unit on his helmet down to cover his nose and mouth. That saved his life, as did the long counter keeping the roof from collapsing completely. But it was almost an hour before he regained consciousness.

IN CON-APTS ACROSS the Big Meg, millions were settling down to watch their favourite Tri-D show, the Celebrity Humiliation And Nominal Career Enhancement Reality Show. Every week a fresh crop of Z-list has-beens were dropped into a hostile environment and filmed while trying to survive long enough to be rescued. Anyone who made it out of an episode alive was granted fifteen seconds of infamy.

Shot in locations around the world, CHANCERS had proved to be a runaway hit for Ruprecht Maxwell's phalanx of Tri-D stations. Coverage was split between twenty-two channels. Each of the twelve contestants was filmed twenty-four hours a day, the footage broadcast live to air on individual channels. The other ten shows were devoted to commentary, analysis and action replays. Last week's most popular choice had been Channel 27, featuring the twin talents of mega-chested, kind hearted softcore porn star Randy Mandy Candie, despite the fact she had been killed on the first day.

Round the clock coverage of her body beginning to decompose while being eaten by wild animals attracted a hardcore audience of necrophiliacs and nature enthusiasts, tapping two previously unserved segments of the marketplace. At least, that was the defence offered by Maxwell's lawyers when ordered to cease broadcasts of the footage by the Justice Department. The Judges were unable to stop CHANCERS completely, as the show's makers were careful to film only in non-extradition territories. Even if a global extradition treaty was successfully negotiated, the production crew had a replacement ready, OFFWORLD CHANCERS. It just needed the market research team to create a credible acronym from the word OFFWORLD.

The latest edition of the show was expected to be the most popular yet, with survivors from previous locations returning for a second dose of death and dismemberment. By popular demand, Randy Mandy Candie's corpse had been exhumed and added to the cast list. She wasn't a serious contender for the top prize, having already died, but the ratings from her channel were tracking a phenomenal interest in what the corpse did next.

CHANCERS' title sequence was just finishing when a news flash appeared on screen, interrupting the broadcast signal on every Maxwell-owned channel in Mega-City One. After a caption announced "Breaking News", Enigma Smith appeared, still adjusting her chair. Realising she was on the air, the seasoned presenter beamed one of her dazzling smiles.

"Good evening! I'm Enigma Smith and you're watching a *Mega-City News* Flash! Reports are coming in of a tragedy in Southside Sector 41. An entire city block has been destroyed in a massive explosion, the cause of which remains unknown. It is not known if there are any survivors or how many died in the catastrophe. No statement has yet been issued by the Judges, fuelling speculation this was a terrorist incident. Since we've been on the air, three groups have claimed responsibility: the Mutant Liberation Front, the Mutant Liberation Army and the Popular Front of the Mutant Liberation League. More on this incident as we get it. For more information, switch over to *Mega-City News* and see the story unfold. Now, we return you to your regular scheduled shows!"

AT PSI-DIVISION, ALL Judges and cadets are tutored how best to screen out the thoughts of those around them. Telepathy might be a rare talent but it could also be a great burden for the untrained mind. A constant cacophony of other people's thoughts could quickly drive anyone insane. Extreme emotions were just as bad, like daggers thrust into the mind of a psi. In times of war it was not uncommon for Psi-Division to issue mild sedatives to its Judges, to help numb the waves of feeling that leaked from the terrified psyches of ordinary people.

When the energy pulse destroyed Joe Chill Block, thirty-three thousand, seven hundred and eighty-two people were inside. At the moment of their death, each one's mind screamed out in terror. Any Psi-Judge could cope with up to a hundred people dying suddenly nearby, or ten times that number if given warning. The simultaneous, unanticipated annihilation of almost thirty-four thousand people was beyond any psyker's ability to screen out.

The effect was akin to a chisel being punched through the head of every Psi-Judge in Mega-City One. At the school where latent Psi-cadets were trained, children woke screaming in their beds, blood streaming from their eyes, ears and nostrils. Tutors staggered from dorm to dorm, trying to reassure the weeping cadets, while themselves debilitated by the incident.

In Sector Houses across the Big Meg, Psi-Judges collapsed where they stood, unable to cope with the mental overload from the attack on Joe Chill. Those unfortunate enough to have been riding their Lawmasters drove off the road, crashing into whatever stood in their way. Dozens died from the shock or resulting trauma. The rest were left with debilitating migraine headaches, unable to focus their psi-talents or even think.

The head of Psi-Division, Judge Shenker, crawled into his office and succeeded in putting a call through to Hershey. The Tri-D screen blurred before him but Shenker closed his eyes, concentrating all his energy on staving off the darkness overcoming him. "Chief Judge," he whispered, "this is Shenker..."

"Sweet Jovus! What happened to you?" she demanded.

"Massive psi overload... thousands dead... in the city... no warning..." Shenker felt himself sliding sideways but was unable to stop the decline. "Psi-Division... out of action... Sorry..." Then the blackness took him.

"Shenker? Shenker!" But Hershey got no reply.

SEVERAL MILES ABOVE Mega-City One, *Justice Seven* was limping across the sky. The orbital platform was tasked with providing a constant flow of surveillance data to the PSU, while also acting as a relay station for Control's signals to Judges across the Big Meg. When the energy pulse was fired down into the city, a massive wave of electromagnetic interference radiated outwards from the beam's source. The wave engulfed the orbiting platform, debilitating its computer-controlled propulsion and scrambling every other system on board.

Justice Seven's commander, Judge Samantha Scattergood, was first to react when the lights went out. "Damage report!" she called, shouting to be heard above the hubbub of worried voices in the control centre. A veteran of Necropolis and the Zombie War known as Judgement Day, Scattergood had seen enough to know that panic and survival never made good partners. She had lost a limb in every major conflict of the past twenty-five years, each one replaced with a robotic prosthetic. No longer able to function effectively on the streets, Scattergood had volunteered for *Justice Seven* where her lack of mobility was not a factor. She had proven an able commander since taking control of the facility seven months earlier. "I want to know what happened, why it happened and how it affects our status, now!"

"Somebody fired an energy weapon at the Big Meg," responded Judge Grissom, one of the PSU analysts on station. "The resultant surge took out our guidance, propulsion and manoeuvring, along with almost everything else."

"How long to repair them?" Scattergood demanded.

"I'm not sure we can," Grissom replied feebly.

The veteran rose from her chair, the servo-joints in her robotic arms and legs whirring noisily in the unusual silence. "What did you say?"

The PSU analyst gestured at the blank, black computer screens around the control chamber. "Auto-repair systems are gone too, along with access to all our repair guidelines. Without those, we're helpless. It's impossible."

Scattergood stopped in front of Grissom, the commander's grizzled face made even more menacing by the flickering red emergency lighting. "There is no such word as can't. Grissom, you're relieved of duty. Return to your quarters." The commander swung round, glaring at the rest of her staff. "Anyone else here think we're helpless?" Nobody replied. "Good. We've got less than an hour before *Justice Seven* drops out of orbit and burns up on re-entry, so that's your deadline. Then we have to find and destroy whatever just fired on our city. Any questions? No? Good. Now get to work!"

The crew of *Justice Seven* hurried to assess the damage and find ways of restarting the platform's systems. Scattergood realised Grissom was still standing beside her. "I thought I told you to leave."

"Please, ma'am, I want another chance. I was panicked by the situation and I didn't think before I spoke. Give me a chance and I'll prove myself to you!"

Scattergood leaned so close to Grissom the analyst could feel her breath on his face. "One chance and one chance only. Get to it!" she snarled.

Eight

Dredd, can you hear me? Dredd, wake up! It was the nagging sound of Kara's voice shouting in his mind that dragged the Judge back to consciousness. Dredd opened his eyes to find himself lying on a hover-stretcher. Overhead, he could see the night sky through gaps in billowing black smoke. "Where am I?"

"Lucky to be alive," a familiar voice responded. Dredd turned to see the Chief Judge standing beside him, her face etched with concern. "Thought we'd lost you in the explosion, Joe. They dug you out of what was left of that diner."

Dredd sat up on the hover-stretcher, wincing in pain. A succession of rapi-heal pads were wrapped around much of his body. "What happened?"

Hershey gestured at the smoking crater across the skedway where Joe Chill Block used to be. "Looks like Bludd is making good use of his latest acquisition. Energy beam from an orbiting satellite took out that building with a single burst. Death toll's thirty thousand and rising. The trauma from so many people dying at once has crippled Psi-Division and PSU is still getting back online." She placed a hand on Dredd's arm. "What can you remember? We lost radio contact with you after Bludd left the eatery. Less than a minute later the beam hit ground zero across the skedway."

Don't tell her anything, Kara warned telepathically. *No codes, no secret gestures – we're watching you, remember? Just act dumb for now.*

Dredd shook his head apologetically. "Sorry, it's still a blur. Delayed concussion from the blast, maybe…"

"Of course. I'll let the Meds take care of you. *Justice Seven* should be back online within an hour; it'll take out that rogue satellite. You just concentrate on getting better, okay?"

"Sure." Dredd watched her turn away. "Hershey–"

Careful, Joe. Remember what I said.

"Yes?"

"How did the negotiations go?" Dredd asked.

The Chief Judge shrugged. "Hard to say. Brit-Cit and East-Meg Two are on board but Chang from Sino-Cit is impossible to read. When all this happened I sent the delegates back to their private quarters. Giant is in charge of their security for tonight."

"He's a good law enforcer."

"Yes." Hershey frowned. "Was there something else you wanted to say?"

One more word and our next target is the Academy of Law!

Dredd shook his head. Hershey smiled. "I'll let you get some rest. Don't worry, Joe. The Big Meg can survive for one night without you." As the Chief Judge departed, Kara's mocking laughter echoed in Dredd's mind.

I wouldn't count on that if I were you, Joe!

"I'M ENIGMA SMITH and you're watching *Mega-City News*. Now, here are the headlines for this hour." The ever-grinning face of the newsreader was replaced by a graphic image showing a smoking crater. "Judges estimate more than thirty thousand citizens died when Joe Chill Block in Southside Sector 41 was destroyed earlier this evening.

The Justice Department dismissed earlier reports that the explosion was the result of a terrorist incident. An unnamed spokesperson said the damage was the result of shoddy workmanship tragically combining with a gas leak. Thus far thirty-four fringe groups have claimed responsibility for the carnage."

The programme switched back to Enigma's happy face. "In other news, the Mega-City Museum of the Twentieth Century says its most popular attraction of recent months, the Evil Empire exhibition, was stolen this afternoon from the Dustbuster. The museum's curator, Dr Janet Swanson, apparently committed suicide after discovering the theft. Despite the loss, the museum is going ahead with its sponsored fireworks display at midnight to celebrate the exhibit's success. The Judges have yet to make a comment on the theft, beyond saying they were pursuing several promising leads."

The newsreader's features were replaced with a graphic depicting the face of a mustachioed man straining to achieve some unseen goal. "Now on to sports, where Big Meg superstar Hank 'Pee-Wee' Potts came from behind to win the Men's Individual section in the World Sex Championships currently being staged at the Vatican City. Potts was lying third after the compulsories yesterday, but proved a master blaster in the freestyle event despite having the smallest equipment among any of the competitors. The sky's the limit when our Hank does his thing, literally! So let's all give our onanist a big hand…"

DREDD WAS BEING loaded into a med-wagon when Kara's voice switched back to his helmet radio. "Listen up, Joe, because I don't enjoy repeating myself. The time is just after nine. For the next three hours you will be my plaything, doing exactly what I want, or else… Well, you've seen the consequences when you don't follow orders. Unless you want more people to die needlessly, you will comply with everything I say. Signal your understanding by asking the Med-Judges where they are taking you."

Dredd did as ordered by the enforcer's voice. A friendly Med-Judge called Callaghan responded. "St Peter Root Hospital, it's the nearest," she said. "Right now our own facilities are overloaded with Psi-Judges bleeding out of every orifice. Not very pleasant, let me tell you. I was almost happy when we got called out to this bombsite."

"Good," Kara said via the helmet radio. "Once the med-wagon gets into the air, I want you to seize control of the vehicle. You'll need to disable the crew: kill or wound them, I don't care which. Once that's done I'll give you further instructions. If you try to warn the crew, tens of thousands will die as retribution. If you understand, clear your throat now."

Dredd signalled his compliance.

"That's good. You're doing better, Dredd. You might live long enough to see midnight. Then... well, let's burn that bridge when we get to it, yes?"

The engines of the med-wagon roared into life and the vehicle rose into the air, ascending through the clouds of acrid smoke still rising from the gnarled wreckage of Joe Chill. Dredd began undoing the restraints on his hover-stretcher while the crew were distracted by the view outside. He dealt with Callaghan first. She was folding away a dummy used to train cadets in resuscitation when Dredd tapped her on the shoulder.

"Hey, what are you doing up? Those rapi-heal pads need time to–" The Med-Judge's words were abruptly cut off by Dredd smashing her face against a bulkhead. Callaghan slumped to the floor, unconscious and bleeding. Dredd paused to check her vital signs, ensuring she was still breathing before moving on.

Still without his weapons, he was forced to improvise while dealing with the rest of the crew. Two more Med-Judges fell before Dredd's physical onslaught, allowing him access to the med-wagon's small onboard armoury. Inside the locker was a tranq gun for dealing with out of control patients, three grenades of stumm gas and a daystick. "Very resourceful," Kara offered by way of commentary for his action. "I can see why so many perps fear you."

"Why did you switch back to communicating by radio?" Dredd asked. "Telepathy is more private, less likely to be intercepted."

"The PSU is too busy chasing its own tail to even think of looking for this signal," Kara replied. "Soon I'll be too far away for psi-talents to be effective, even with my power. Now get on with your task!" Dredd pulled his respirator back down over his nose and mouth before releasing stumm gas into the vehicle's air conditioning system. He burst into the cockpit twenty seconds later to find the pilot and copilot both unconscious. The med-wagon was slowly tipping forwards, dropping into a steep dive.

"I'd get the nose up, if I were you," Kara suggested snidely. "Otherwise you'll make a hell of a mess when you crash into that building ahead."

Dredd glanced up to see St Peter Root Hospital filling the windows of the med-wagon. He dragged the pilot out of the way and pulled back on the controls. The vehicle's descent slowed as the nose began clawing its way upwards again, but the hospital was getting closer by the second. The med-wagon would never get enough height to clear the building.

"Think fast, Joe!" Kara shouted. "Ten seconds to impact!"

Dredd gritted his teeth and yanked the controls sideways, sending the med-wagon into a desperate banking manoeuvre. Still the hospital grew nearer, close enough to see through the windows. Patients inside were screaming in terror as the vehicle hurtled towards them.

Kara kept up her running commentary, teasing and taunting Dredd. "Five seconds to impact, Joe! Four! Three!"

"Shut the drokk up!" Dredd shouted over her words, his body shaking as the med-wagon tried to tear itself apart in protest at the near impossible change in direction, G-force dragging the skin across his face.

"Two seconds! One!"

The med-wagon hurtled over the front of the hospital, the base of the vehicle just scraping the outer wall in a shower of sparks. Then it was gone, flying freely through the air again. Dredd righted the controls, gasping for breath as the med-wagon levelled out again.

"Well, that was exciting!" Kara said breathlessly. "I'm feeling all a-tingle."

"I did what you asked," Dredd growled. "Now release me."

"Sorry, but the fun's just getting started. Find a quiet place to land – a dust zone or something similar. Then we shall begin the hunt."

ON *JUSTICE SEVEN*, the lighting, life support and guidance systems were back online. But propulsion and manoeuvering remained disabled, and without them the orbital platform was heading for a fiery death. Scattergood was reporting this status to the Chief Judge via a scratchy audio-only connection.

"Everyone's performing miracles up here, ma'am, but it may not be enough," the commander conceded.

"What about the escape pods? In a worst case scenario you can still get the crew off before re-entry, can't you?" Hershey asked.

"Only half the pods are still functional. We lost the rest when the energy pulse fired," Scattergood reported grimly. The Chief Judge's voice kept fading in and out, overwhelmed by white noise and interference. "For the love of grud, somebody stabilise that signal!"

Hershey's voice phased back into audible range. "–did you say, commander? Your signal is breaking up and–"

"Stomm!" Scattergood spat out in frustration. "Now we've lost her altogether!" She slammed a robotic fist through the comms unit, destroying any chance of reinstating radio control soon. The commander looked round the control room to see most of her staff watching. "Nobody said stop working!"

"Ma'am! I think I've found the problem," a voice cried out.

"Who said that?" Scattergood demanded.

A hand appeared from beneath a console unit. "Over here!"

The commander stomped across to find Grissom's face protruding from beneath a mess of wiring and circuitry. The PSU analyst was clutching two blackened connections.

"Well?" Scattergood asked tersely.

"We've tested most of the routing systems. This is just an auxiliary, but it could give us a bypass for the–"

"Speak English, Grissom – I'm a treet Judge, not a Tek!"

"Yes, ma'am." The analyst swallowed hard. "If I reconnect these two junctions it will either restart propulsion and manoeuvring or... disable everything on board. Probably for good."

Scattergood glanced round the others. "Anybody got a better idea?" Nobody answered. The commander looked back down at Grissom. "Do it!"

Grissom pushed the two connections together, closing his eyes as they made contact. For a moment nothing happened, then control panels began surging back into life. "Did it work?" the analyst asked meekly.

Scattergood smiled as she dragged Grissom to his feet. "We're back in business! Now, let's find the satellite that fired the energy beam and take it out of action – permanently."

THE CHIEF JUDGE was shouting at Control, exasperation evident in her voice. "For the love of grud, how hard can it be to re-establish contact with *Justice Seven*? Do I have to do everything myself?"

"Sorry, ma'am. All radio contact has been lost with that location."

"What does that mean? Has it already burnt up on re-entry?"

"No, ma'am. *Justice Seven* is still showing on our system. Looks like they've restored motive power. Manoeuvring thrusters are firing too. We just can't talk to them at the moment."

"Let me know when we can. Hershey out!" The Chief Judge deactivated the comms unit in her office and slumped back into her chair. Only a few seconds passed before the comms unit was calling for her attention again, the screen flashing up AUDIO ONLY. "What the drokk is it now, Control?"

But the voice that answered did not belong to Justice Department. It was male, authoritative and richly resonant. "Feeling under pressure, Chief Judge? I am sorry to hear that. Things getting out of hand, I believe."

"Who is this?" Hershey demanded. "How did you—"

"Never mind about that for now, my dear lady. You shouldn't get bogged down in the details. As leader of Mega-City One you would be better devoting your time to the bigger picture, preparing for the chaos to come."

"Bludd!"

"How gratifying it is to be recognised by a woman of such importance."

"Spare me the sarcasm, scumbag. What do you want?"

"Scumbag? I hardly think that's called for, or advisable, considering I can decimate large sections of your city and its people in seconds."

"It's your city too, Bludd," Hershey replied.

"Not anymore. I have departed the Big Meg, with no immediate intention of returning. Knowing what is still to come tonight, it seemed the safest course of action. Alas, such measures are not available to you."

"You've been dropping hints and making veiled threats all day. Why should I believe this one? Your so-called strike team didn't get within twenty blocks of the extradition treaty negotiations."

"I would have thought the destruction of Joe Chill Block clearly established my bona fides. I can organise another such demonstration if–"

"That won't be necessary," Hershey snapped.

"Very well, then. Don't suffer from any illusion I may be bluffing, Chief Judge. I am quite serious in what I am about to say – deadly serious. Unless the Justice Department transfers one hundred billion credits into an untraceable offworld account of my choosing before midnight, your city will be plunged into a crisis that makes Necropolis look like inclement weather."

"You're blackmailing us?"

"I prefer to think of it as an insurance policy."

"It's extortion, plain and simple."

Bludd chuckled to himself. "We can argue about semantics all you wish, Chief Judge, but it will get you no closer to saving your city. The time is now approaching 9:30 pm. That leaves you a little over one hundred and fifty minutes to pull together the sum I require and complete the transfer."

"Even if I wanted to do as you ask, that isn't enough time."

"Don't insult my intelligence!" Bludd snarled, all humour suddenly draining from his voice. "Your precious Justice Department spends that much on covert operations in other mega-cities every year. Divert some funding, be inventive... A little creative accounting can do wonders."

"The Justice Department does not negotiate with terrorists or criminals," the Chief Judge maintained.

"Then I hope history will forgive you for such a foolish policy. I will call in ninety minutes with the account details you require, then once more at midnight. If the transfer I have asked for is not completed before the deadline, the consequences will be more terrible than you can imagine. Goodbye."

The comms unit went dead. Hershey quickly reactivated it, calling the head of the PSU. His stern face appeared on the Tri-D screen. "Niles, I've just had a call from Bludd. He stayed on the line for several minutes. Were you able to run a trace?"

"Negative, ma'am. Systems are still recovering from the energy beam."

"Drokk it!" Hershey slammed a fist down on her desk. "Then perhaps you can tell me how that punk was able to call direct to my office?"

"Security is shot to hell across the comms network, a side-effect of that strike on Joe Chill. Bludd must have known that would happen, so he's using it to his advantage. It'll be midnight before we're secure again."

"What about the spy-in-the-sky network? Creep suggested he was shifting operations offworld. Where did he go after leaving Dredd at the diner?"

"We lost him in the confusion after..."

"What happened at Joe Chill."

"Yes, ma'am."

"He's still winning the game," Hershey said wearily. "We've only got one trick up our sleeve and no way of playing it, unless we can find Bludd."

"I'm sorry, I don't follow you, ma'am."

Hershey realised she had been thinking out loud. "Never mind. Does the PSU know Dredd's location? We may need him after all."

"He went missing twenty minutes ago, along with the med-wagon taking him for treatment. It nearly flew into St Peter Root Hospital, then disappeared. No reports of a med-wagon crashing yet. Sorry, ma'am, I thought you knew. We've got search teams looking for wreckage in surrounding sectors."

The Chief Judge shook her head despondently. "Contact the Council of Five, along with Shenker from Psi-Division. I'm calling an emergency meeting here at the Grand Hall, beginning in an hour. We need to know what Bludd has planned for midnight and we need to be ready for it. Hershey out!"

"The rules of the hunt are simple," Kara said via Dredd's helmet radio. "You have two and a half hours to reach the Grand Hall of Justice. You are not permitted to speak to another Judge, nor use any code to ask for their help. You cannot use any Justice Department vehicle to assist your journey. You cannot call Control or relay a message to Control via a third party. You cannot remove your helmet. Break any of the rules and we will detonate the explosive charge embedded within the disc attached to your helmet. You are currently..." Kara's voice trailed away for a second before returning. "You are currently twenty-one miles from your destination. Marathon runners are expected to cover greater distances in less time, so it shouldn't be a problem for you. Of course, most marathon runners don't start the race covered in rapi-heal patches."

"What's the catch?"

"Four members of the strike team that raided the Dustbuster earlier today are going to hunt you to death. Other than that, I foresee no great impediment to your journey," Kara said cheerfully. "Except one. That disc on the side of your helmet, it's also a homing beacon for the hunters to follow."

"Why are you doing this?" Dredd demanded.

"It's just a little diversion to keep my lover and I amused while we wait for the Justice Department to pay our ransom."

"What ransom?"

"Enough questions, Dredd, it's time for the hare to begin running from the hounds. Reach the steps of the Grand Hall in time and you're safe. Otherwise... let's just say it's been nice knowing you."

"This isn't over," Dredd vowed. "You can run, but you can't hide from me!"

"You're the one doing the running, remember?"

The helmet radio fell silent. Normally it transmitted a constant, low level hum of updates and information from Control. Now there was just quiet. Dredd had landed the med-wagon in an abandoned dust zone. He made a final check on the crew before emerging into the cool night air. Bullets thudded into the ground at his feet, sending him tumbling backwards into the vehicle. At least one of the hunters had already found their prey.

Dredd used the med-wagon's infrared scanners to locate his enemy. A squat heat flare appeared at the edge of the dust zone, moving towards the vehicle. Judging from the size of the image it had to be Sanderson the dwarf. "The sooner I get out of here, the safer the crew will be," Dredd said to himself. Looking round the cockpit of the med-wagon, he noticed a lever beside the pilot's chair marked EJECTOR SEAT.

It was against safety regs to operate such a device while on the ground. The seat would be flung a hundred metres into the air, not giving the parachute enough time to fill with air before impact. But Sanderson was closing in fast and another figure was approaching from the opposite side. It was now or never. Dredd sat down in the pilot's chair and began buckling himself in. He reached a hand towards the ejector seat lever.

FINCHER WAS LOOKING forward to killing Dredd. It had irked him enormously to let the Judge walk untouched into the diner earlier, but orders were orders and contradicting Bludd was only for the suicidal. When Kara had told the strike team about the hunting party contest with Dredd as their quarry, Fincher couldn't wait to get started. Bludd had offered no prize for the winner, but he didn't need to. Any bounty hunter who could produce the corpse of Mega-City One's most famous lawman would be set for life, just by collecting the many rewards offered by the underworld for Dredd's demise.

Then there were the fringe benefits. Become the man who killed Dredd and you could pick and choose bounty hunting assignments, charging any fee imaginable. Better yet, your name would become legend, forever associated with the murder of Old Stony Face. It was a sort of immortality, Fincher decided. Not to mention the added pulling power such kudos would give him with the ladies. Oh yes, he was determined to claim the prize for all those reasons.

But most of all, Fincher liked killing. The expatriate from Brit-Cit enjoyed the terror in his victims' eyes as he flayed the skin off their still-living bodies: the agony of their pain as he cut and sliced and mutilated them, the sickly sweet taste of their blood as it spattered his face and hands. Fincher's murderous ways found an outlet by killing and maiming for the Brit-Cit criminal underworld.

Having grown bored with the quality of victim on offer in his homeland, the young Brit had relocated to the Big Meg. Fincher found he had to kill at least once a week to sate his yearning for murder. Despatching the juve Ryan earlier, that was just a palate cleanser, a light apéritif before the main course.

Fincher was cursing under his breath when he reached the dust zone. That stunted simpleton Sanderson had beaten him to the killing ground, alerting the prey to their presence. Dredd was no fool, Fincher knew that. You did not acquire such a formidable reputation without learning how to defend yourself. But the bounty hunter remained confident of being equal to the task. He could hardly contain his excitement at what lay ahead. Fincher approached the med-wagon from the opposite side to Sanderson, thinking the blundering dwarf might send Dredd his way. When the Judge did not emerge from the vehicle, Fincher began to creep closer, his laser blade ready for the kill.

Suddenly the glasseen roof of the cockpit exploded outwards, startling both hunters. Moments later a heavy object shot up into the air. Fincher's gaze followed the projectile as it rose into the night sky. He realised it was the med-wagon's ejector seat when a parachute burst open above the chair as it neared apogee. A figure in the seat confirmed his deduction. Clever sod! But Sanderson was already shredding the parachute with machine gun fire and the ejector seat began plummeting to the ground at an ugly angle. It crashed into rockcrete with a sickening thud, throwing the occupant to one side.

Fincher ran towards the body, preparing to finish Dredd off and claim the kill for himself. It might not be satisfying but the rewards on offer were worth the sacrifice. "Get away from him, he's mine!" Sanderson screamed. The dwarf was still some distance away, his stubby legs not able to generate much speed. Angry was living up to his nickname, the midget's face red with rage at the prospect of having the glory of killing Dredd stolen from him.

Fincher grinned wolfishly as he reached the crumpled figure on the ground. Pulling back the laser blade ready for the killing blow, the bounty hunter rolled the body over. But, instead of Dredd, Fincher was confronted by a blank-faced dummy. There was a small speaker where its mouth should be. "Hello!" the mannequin announced. "My name's Bobby and I'll be your training partner for today's lesson in mouth-to-mouth resuscitation. Pucker up!"

"Bollocks!" Fincher shouted angrily. "It's a trick!" The Brit turned to see Sanderson approaching the med-wagon. Fincher saw a shadow lurking beside the downed vehicle, an all too familiar shadow. "Angry, look out! Dredd's right there!"

"Don't give me that stomm!" Sanderson shouted back, shoving a new clip of ammunition into his machine gun. "You just want–"

Thwack! Dredd smashed his newly acquired daystick into the dwarf's face, sending the short man into a backward somersault. As Sanderson's body hit the ground the Judge followed up with another blow, ramming his truncheon into the killer's throat. There was a hollow crack as the dwarf's windpipe broke. Dredd grabbed the discarded machine gun and began firing at Fincher, who took cover behind the ejected pilot's seat. The Brit cried out in agony as one of the bullets shattered flesh and bone.

The Judge kept shooting until he had exhausted the new clip in the machine gun. Only when the cacophony of gunfire had died away could the gurgling death rattles of Angry Sanderson be heard. Dredd crouched beside the body and gripped the head with his powerful hands. A single twist snapped the spinal column, killing the dwarf outright. "Two down – two to go," Dredd muttered. He threw the empty machine gun aside and began running.

Behind the ejector seat Fincher was binding the wound to his hand. He had listened to the brutal efficiency of Sanderson's slaying. I've underestimated this Dredd, Fincher decided, we all have. If I'm going to take him out, I'll need an advantage; the element of surprise. Rather than hunt Dredd down, I'll let him come to me.

DREDD EMERGED FROM the dust zone on to the nearest skedway, a deserted three-lane road. A sign for Harry Alan Towers Overzoom confirmed what Kara had said earlier. Dredd was at least twenty miles from his destination, with two unidentified bounty hunters between him and safety. Worse still, he was in an area of the Big Meg most citizens avoided after dark, and not far from the crime-riddled zone known as City Bottom.

Lights flashed against the overzoom sign. Dredd swivelled round to see two vehicles approaching: a hefty purple mo-pad and a scarlet speedster. He stepped into the middle lane of the skedway, motioning for the oncoming motorists to slow down. Instead, the speedster accelerated past the mo-pad towards Dredd. The red car cut across the path of the other vehicle, forcing the mo-pad to slam on its brakes. Dredd held up his badge for the speedster driver to see but the car kept accelerating towards him. The anti-dazzle filter on Dredd's helmet enabled him to see past the speedster's headlights. The driver was a heavily tattooed woman, her face a gleeful grin of anticipation.

"Drokk! One of the bounty hunters!" Dredd stood his ground until the speedster was almost upon him before diving out of its path. The vehicle shot past, its brakes squealing in protest as the driver tried to stop. Dredd ran to the mo-pad and pulled open the driver's door. A startled woman was crying behind the steering wheel. The mo-pad's interior was the same lurid purple as on the exterior, every surface upholstered with plush velveteen. The driver was wearing a catsuit of the same material, her hair dyed purple to match.

"Did you see what that roadster did? It nearly took me off the road! I only finished paying off my mo-pad this morning and that kook nearly killed me!"

Dredd glanced up the road to where the speedster had halted, just beyond the turnoff for the Harry Alan Towers Overzoom. The red car wasn't moving, but exhaust fumes from the tailpipe showed the engine was still running. "She was trying to kill me, not you," Dredd explained. "Ma'am, I need to commandeer your vehicle."

"My mo-pad? W-why?" the woman stammered.

"Justice Department business. I must reach the Grand Hall of Justice before midnight and I need your mo-pad to do that."

"Well, I'm not sure... What if something happens to it?"

"You will be fully compensated for any damage sustained by your vehicle, you have my word as a Judge," Dredd replied.

"I don't know..."

Dredd looked back up the road. The scarlet speedster had gone. He relaxed a little, the threat of another attack gone for now. Dredd rested a reassuring hand on the woman's shoulder. "Please, ma'am. I wouldn't ask if it wasn't important."

The mo-pad driver bit her bottom lip nervously before nodding. "Alright. But you have to let me come with you.

I've spent twelve years paying for this baby and I ain't letting it out of my sight for a moment."

"Very well," Dredd agreed. "I'll drive, if you don't mind ma'am. That will allow us access to Judges-only bypasses."

"Oh! Okay," she replied, clambering over to the passenger seat. "I've never been in the same vehicle as a Judge before."

Dredd settled himself in the driver's seat and restarted the engine. "It shouldn't take us long to reach our destination," he said. "Then you can continue on your journey. Where were you headed, Miss...?"

"Just driving, I guess, getting used to enjoying this baby. My name is Diana," the woman added. She turned to face Dredd, revealing the horrific scar tissue burnt into the other side of her face. "But you can call me Di."

Nine

No SOONER HAD the mo-pad driven away than two female Judges approached on Lawmasters. The pair turned off the skedway onto the access road Dredd used to escape the dust zone. Within a minute they were parked beside the downed med-wagon.

"Langenkamp to Control," one of them said as she got off her motorcycle. "Have found the missing med-wagon. Looks like there's been an incident here. I can see a corpse, the ejector seat has been fired from the vehicle and there's evidence of gunfire."

"Acknowledged. Do you require back-up?"

The lead Judge turned to her colleague. "Karyn?"

The Psi-Judge removed her helmet, shaking out her mass of copper red curls.

s"Still got a splitting headache from what happened at Joe Chill," she muttered before closing her eyes. "Can't guarantee I'll be able to sense much." Karyn pressed her hands to her temples and concentrated, her face creasing in pain. "Several people unconscious inside the med-wagon. There was violence here recently. Blood has been spilled."

"Sounds like we need Med-Judges, a meat-wagon for the corpse and some forensic help from Tek-Division too,"

Langenkamp told Control. "No sign of Dredd. I'll keep this channel open." She drew her Lawgiver and began approaching the med-wagon. "Easy does it. Let's take this one step at a time."

Karyn moved to examine the corpse. "A dwarf? What's he doing here?" She crouched by the body, passing her hands across the dead man's face. "He was angry, hunting someone. But they got the better of him. His death was swift, merciless. The killer was... Dredd?"

Langenkamp had drawn her Lawgiver and was peering in through the broken cockpit of the med-wagon. "I can see the pilot and copilot inside. They're unconscious but no other obvious injuries." She sniffed the air escaping from the vehicle. "Can you smell that?"

Karyn breathed in deeply. "Stumm gas. The med-wagon was probably hijacked in the air and brought down here. But by whom?" She saw a trail of blood leading past the med-wagon. The splashes of crimson led to the ejected pilot's seat. The Psi-Judge followed the trail to the chair. It was riddled with bullets on the side facing the med-wagon. "Someone took cover behind this when the shooting started." She touched a pool of blood on the ground. "They were wounded. Not fatally, judging by the amount of blood. The blood's still wet. This happened minutes ago, not hours."

Langenkamp nodded. "That ties into the near miss with the med-wagon at St Peter Root. The dwarf, could he be one of the hijackers?"

Karyn shrugged. "I don't know... I don't think so. What little I can glean from the corpse, there's nothing to suggest he took down the vehicle."

A moan from the med-wagon halted their speculations. Inside, Karyn and Langenkamp found a female Med-Judge crouched on all fours, nursing a bloody head wound. She looked at the new arrivals with fire in her eyes. "Did you catch him?"

"Catch who?" Langenkamp asked.

"Dredd! He's the drokker who did this to us!"

*   *   *

DREDD ACCELERATED OFF the overzoom, easing the purple mo-pad into the slow lane of Peter Welbeck Skedway. In daylight this road was habitually choked with traffic, but now the evening crush hour had passed the going was smooth and untroubled. Dredd activated the vehicle's cruise control so he could strip away the remaining rapiheal patches still attached to him.

"What happened?" Di asked innocently. "You don't seem to have all your uniform. I thought you all carried those guns, what do you call them?"

"Lawgivers," he replied. "It's still with my motorcycle, over at Southside Sector 41."

"Isn't that where the–"

"Yes."

"Oh my grud! You were there?"

Dredd winced as he tore away the final patch from his side. Blood was still seeping from the wound where a slither of shrapnel had cut through the reinforced synthi-kevlar of his bodysuit. "Yes, I was there," he replied grimly.

Di held up her hands in apology. "I'm sorry, I didn't mean to pry. It's just… well, I lead a very quiet life. Meeting a real Judge, one as famous as you… It's a little overwhelming. Sorry if I'm babbling on and on."

"You've had a shock. It affects different people in different ways." Dredd checked the cruise control was still doing its job. "What happened to your face?"

Di grimaced. "My boyfriend. Ex-boyfriend, I should say. When I said I didn't want to marry him, he threw acid in my face. Said if he couldn't have me, he'd make sure nobody else wanted me."

"Was he punished?"

"Five years in the cubes. Should have been fifty."

"Which Judge handled the case?"

"Molloy, I think his name was – Sector House 87. Why do you ask?"

"You've been very helpful. A lot of citizens would have kept on driving. I could look into your case, see if the Judge dealt with your perp too leniently."

"That's very kind of you but…" Di let her voice trail off. "I'd rather forget about it, move on. I'm making a new life for myself."

"Still, it can't hurt for me to review the file," Dredd insisted. "A Judge Molloy, you said? I've been stationed in Sector 87 several times, but I've never encountered a Molloy there."

Di shrugged. "Maybe I got the name wrong. It was a long time–" She was cut off by a sudden jolt that jerked the mo-pad forwards. "What the drokk?"

Dredd was peering at the rearview mirrors. "It's the scarlet speedster. She must have been following us, waiting for another chance to attack."

"That slitch!" Di snarled. "She'll kill both of us!"

Dredd frowned before checking his seat belt was firmly buckled. "Strap yourself in, ma'am." He slammed his foot down on the accelerator, retaking control of the mo-pad.

"It's gonna be a bumpy ride."

"YOU'RE SURE ABOUT this?" Karyn was interviewing Callaghan while Langenkamp supervised the removal of the other crew from the downed wagon. The Med-Judge nodded vehemently.

"Dredd hijacked us. He asked where we were going and I told him St Peter Root Hospital. After that he attacked me. When I came to he was leaving the med-wagon, carrying a daystick and other small weapons from our lock box armoury: some stumm gas grenades and a tranq gun." Callaghan was resting on a hover-stretcher outside the med-wagon, her eyes not moving from Sanderson's corpse on the ground nearby. "I heard him killing that man and then shots being fired. Dredd didn't give any explanation. It was like he was possessed."

"I want to look into your memories," Karyn said. "See that the concussion you suffered hasn't scrambled what you're recalling. Is that okay?"

Callaghan shrugged. "I guess. Go ahead."

Karyn removed her gauntlets and laid both hands on the Med-Judge's head, reaching into her thoughts. The events of the past hour flashed backwards through her mind's eye, confirming what Callaghan had described. Karyn slowed the flow of memories down, then moved back and forth over them, focusing on the moments when Callaghan had been watching Dredd's face.

"When you spoke with Dredd, was he paying attention to you?"

"I guess. He was..." The Med-Judge paused, reliving the same moments Karyn was reviewing. "No, he wasn't. I didn't notice at the time, but he seemed distracted, distant."

Karyn delved deeper into Callaghan's mind, freezing an image from her memories of Dredd lying on the hover-stretcher. Something small and round attached to his helmet had been catching the light at a certain angle, a translucent disc positioned close to one of Dredd's ears. The Psi-Judge could sense Callaghan's discomfiture and let go of her head. "Thank you."

"Did you find anything?" the Med-Judge asked. "I still can't believe Dredd would attack us like that, it doesn't make any sense."

"You're right, it doesn't," Karyn agreed. She signalled for Callaghan to be removed. Once the Med-Judge was out of earshot Karyn explained what she had seen with Langenkamp.

"Could it be a mind control device?" the Street Judge wondered.

"I'm not convinced. It looked more like a tiny comms relay. Somebody could be using it to jam our attempts to contact Dredd. They could be feeding him instructions, lies, anything."

Langenkamp nodded. "From now on, we have to assume Dredd is under hostile control and treat him as a rogue Judge. I'll tell Control. You see if there's anything more we can get from the rest of the crew."

TATTOO SUE WAS enjoying herself again. When Dredd had escaped her by taking refuge in Di's mo-pad, Sue feared the worst. Di might be her lover but in the bounty hunting business they were still rivals. The tattooed woman was confident she could beat Fincher and Sanderson to the prize of killing Dredd, but Di was another matter. She was devious, cunning and deadly.

The homing device attached to the Judge's helmet made it all too simple to follow him and Di safely from a distance. The signal would cease when Dredd was terminated, so Sue knew the chase was still alive. She couldn't understand why Di hadn't finished the Judge off yet. What was the stupid slitch waiting for? With every minute the mo-pad was getting closer to the Grand Hall of Justice. Perhaps Di was trying to lull Dredd into a false sense of security.

Sue lost patience and decided to up the ante. She accelerated the scarlet speedster through the four lanes of traffic on Peter Welbeck and rammed into the back wheels of the mo-pad. It careered sideways, swiping a faster vehicle and causing a five-car pile-up before returning to its lane. Sue ploughed into the rear of the mo-pad again, exploding one of the slower vehicle's tyres. Flaps of rubbereen flew up into the air as the tyre shredded itself. Within seconds the mo-pad was lurching across the four lanes, sparks shooting out behind as it began running on a metal rim.

It could only be a few seconds before whoever was driving lost all control of the mo-pad. Sue slammed on the speedster's brakes, her own tyres screaming in protest. The pile-up two miles back had cleared the skedway of other traffic, so she had an unobstructed view of what happened next. "Drokking hell," Sue gasped. "Get out of that one, Dredd!

* * *

WHEN THE SPEEDSTER hit the mo-pad for the second time, Dredd was ready for it. He kept a firm grip on the steering wheel, cushioning the impact and keeping the vehicle in its own lane. "You said 'She'll kill both of us!'," he shouted at Di. "How did you know that red vehicle is being driven by a woman?"

"What did you say?" Di was screaming to be heard above the sound of the mo-pad's tyre shredding.

"There is no Judge Molloy at Sector House 87, is there?" Dredd demanded.

"No," Di admitted, pulling a small handgun from inside her purple catsuit and pointing it at Dredd. "Now hit the brakes and–" She was cut off by the mo-pad lurching sideways as the failed tyre was lost altogether. Metal screamed in protest as the hefty vehicle slid along on its rim. "Sweet Jovus," Di whispered.

Dredd let go of the steering wheel and slapped the gun out of Di's hands. She unclipped her seat belt and dived into the foot well to retrieve the weapon. "You shouldn't have done that!" Dredd shouted.

"Why not?" Di asked, smirking as she aimed the gun at her quarry.

"Road safety: always buckle up in case of an accident," the Judge replied. He twisted the steering wheel violently to the right. The mo-pad tried and failed to make the turn before flinging itself into the air like a wounded animal. Dredd braced himself in the driver's seat as the mo-pad flipped through a somersault, the road surface ahead pinwheeling around.

The purple people carrier then slammed into Peter Welbeck, tearing up tarmac as the front windows exploded. It continued careering forward, nose buried in the road, the rest of the mo-pad still rearing up in the air. The skedway went into an abrupt curve ahead as it turned away from a spectacular vista over the shantytown known as City Bottom. The mo-pad was sliding directly towards the crash barriers and nothing could stop it.

TATTOO SUE COULD see precisely what was going to happen next. She gunned her speedster's engine into life and roared down an offramp towards City Bottom. If Dredd survived the fall, she wanted to be the one to finish him off. Di would have done all the hard work, but I'll still get the credit, Sue thought.

"CONTROL TO ALL units! We've got a multi-car pile-up on Peter Welbeck, just after the onramp from Harry Alan Towers Overzoom. PSU reports more trouble further along the same road. Proceed with extreme caution!"

THE MO-PAD THUNDERED into the crash barriers. They had been designed to withstand a direct hit from mega-trucks travelling at full speed, able to displace the impact through hollow rubber supports and struts. But the mo-pad hit the barriers while still upended on its front. The bulk of the vehicle tipped over the top of the barriers, doing a slow roll towards the ten-storey drop on the other side. It was the crumpled carnage at the front of the mo-pad that halted the vehicle's progress. The gnarled metal got entangled with the barrier and left the vehicle dangling over the precipice, just a twisted scramble of chassis keeping it from falling.

Dredd was trying to free himself when Di stirred beside him. "Road safety tip, huh?" she asked. Bruised and bloody, the bounty hunter was free to climb out through the shattered windscreen. But Dredd's seat belt buckle had been wrenched out of shape by the crash and refused to unlock. Di stood on the passenger seat and began pulling herself out. "Guess breaking the rules can have its compensations after all."

Dredd grabbed her left leg as she passed him. "Where do you think you're going, punk?"

"Let go of me!" Di protested. She kicked at Dredd's head and hands with her spare foot, trying to dislodge his iron grip. "Let go!"

Dredd grabbed the other leg and held both of them fast. "You're not leaving me here," he snarled. "If this thing falls, you're coming with me!"

The mo-pad suddenly slumped a few inches, metal screeching as the weight of the vehicle began dragging it downwards. Di looked up in alarm, watching the tangle holding them in place slowly unravelling. "Please, Dredd! We'll both die if this thing crashes to City Bottom!"

"That's what your master wanted, isn't it? Bludd sent you to hunt me down and kill me, didn't he?" Dredd demanded.

"Yes, yes!" Di cried, beginning to sob with terror.

"Why? Why do all of this? What's his real aim?"

"I don't know!" Di shouted, fear making her voice hysterical. "Now let me go, you drokker! Let me–"

Then the mo-pad fell.

TATTOO SUE WAS still driving her speedster down the long spiral offramp to City Bottom when she saw the mo-pad begin its last journey. The purple vehicle accelerated as it fell, the weight of the engine pulling the mo-pad backwards. The bounty hunter thought she could see Di clinging to the front, screaming as the ground got closer. Then the mo-pad was hidden from view, obscured by the three-storey shanty huts erected across the abandoned sector.

Sue felt the impact before she heard it, the mighty vibration rippling through her vehicle. Then came the sound: metal and mayhem, death and destruction, violent and vicious. A fireball of flame billowed into the air, followed by clouds of ominous black smoke.

"Touchdown," Sue said with a smile. Her eyes slid to the speedster's onboard computer screen. Despite the sudden impact Dredd's homing signal was still transmitting. The drokker must have survived somehow, but not for long, the bounty hunter thought. She floored the accelerator, determined to reach the crash site in time to claim her kill.

"CONTROL TO ALL units! Reports coming in of an explosion on City Bottom. Fires are spreading from the source. Expect heavy casualties. Nearest Sector Houses to send all available units. Scramble emergency service crews and Med-Judges."

TATTOO SUE REACHED the crash site first, abandoning her speedster nearby and advancing to the scene by foot, a pistol clutched in each hand. Ramshackle homes made of scavenged cardboard were ablaze, the fires leaping from building to building. The fuel tank must have exploded when the mo-pad hit the ground, Sue decided. She could hear the screams of City Bottom dwellers from inside burning hovels but chose to ignore them. Let the Judges save this scum.

Approaching sirens meant help was only a few minutes away for the locals and hindrance just as close for Sue. She began running towards the centre of the carnage, covering her mouth and nose to block out the acrid smoke and fumes. The bounty hunter burst through the surrounding ring of burning shanty homes to find what remained of the mo-pad.

The purple vehicle was just a metal carcass. The back end had plunged into the ground, the engine burying itself. The chassis had exploded when the fuel tank blew, a scorch mark burnt into the ground around the fractured remains. The only section still intact was the driver's compartment, held in place by white foam that seemed to have filled the interior.

Protruding from the compartment were some of Di's remains. Her legs were locked inside the white substance but they ended just above the knees, the rest of her torn away by the force of the impact. Sue took a step towards the mo-pad and stepped in something soft and wet. She looked down with a crawling horror of realisation, knowing before seeing what the thing beneath her feet was. Di's torso and head were smeared across the ground like paste. Grud only knew what had happened to her arms.

Sue had witnessed some horrors in her time but this was too much. She stumbled to one side and vomited up the contents of her stomach, retching over and over until there was nothing left to expel. Once the gut-wrenching spasms had subsided, she wiped the moisture from her chin and opened her eyes again, careful to avoid seeing again what was left of Di.

The homing signal for Dredd was still active. The bounty hunter checked the handheld scanner several times but it remained steadfast in its readings – Dredd was a few metres away, directly in front of her. The Judge was alive and entombed inside the mo-pad. Holstering one pistol in her left boot, Sue approached the wreckage carefully, keeping the scanner in one hand and a pistol in the other. She reached towards the white foam and was surprised to find it was rock hard on the outside. But after a few taps the white substance began to collapse inwards, bubbling away to nothing.

I've heard about this stomm, the bounty hunter thought. New safety device fitted to large vehicles. A computer-controlled system senses danger just before impact and floods the driver's compartment with riot foam. It surrounds the occupants, enabling them to breathe but protecting them from the smash. Afterwards the foam evaporates, freeing whoever is inside. Sue checked, realising too late what that meant. Freeing whoever is–

Dredd burst from the mo-pad, using Di's severed arms as a club to smash the pistol from Sue's hand. While she scurried after the weapon Dredd clambered out of the wreckage, tossing aside the unwanted limbs and pulling the tranq gun from his boot holster. He shot a drug-tipped dart into the bounty hunter's outstretched hand before

Sue could retrieve her pistol. She cried out, clutching the numbed hand to her chest. "Don't shoot me!" she said.

The Judge wiped the last of the foam from his visor. "Why not? You were ready to shoot me."

"That was business. Please, I don't want to die," she begged.

Dredd shook his head in disgust. "Your kind sickens me. You'll kill for money but plead for your own life like a whimpering child."

Sue kept up the pretence, all the while easing her good hand towards the other pistol hidden in the boot farthest from Dredd. "Please, I can help you. I know what Bludd has got planned! All of this, it's just a diversion!"

"Tell me more."

The bounty hunter looked over her shoulder fearfully, all too aware Judges would be on the scene within minutes. "Alright, but not here. I'll trade what I know for safe passage out of Mega-City One."

"Why should I cut a deal with scum like you?"

"My life is worthless once Bludd knows I've betrayed him. Trust me, when you hear what he's going to do to this city, it's worth making the deal."

Dredd kept his tranq gun trained on the tattooed woman, the sounds of sirens drawing ever closer. "Kick the pistol over to me," he commanded. Sue did as she was told, palming the weapon from her boot. As Dredd crouched to pick up the pistol the bounty hunter took aim at the Judge.

"Die you drokker!" she screamed, pulling the trigger.

Dredd threw himself sideways and fired back with his tranq gun.

Both shooters went down and stayed down.

THE CHIEF JUDGE looked round the faces of her senior staff. The Council of Five's members were assembled, each with their individual reports on recent activity. Shenker had arrived in a hoverchair, still recovering from the debilitating shock of what happened at Joe Chill. Hershey had not given them advance warning of what was to be discussed, but none of those present needed psi-powers to guess the main item on the agenda.

"Jesus Bludd," the Chief Judge began, "is trying to ransom this city for one hundred billion credits. Unless we transfer that sum to an untraceable offworld account of his choosing before midnight, he will do to the entire city what he did to Joe Chill a few hours ago. Bludd is calling at eleven with the account number. Reactions?"

Ramos was first to speak. A veteran Street Judge, he was on the council with Hollister to represent the Department's rank and file, the men and women who had to enforce the Law every day. "We can't give in to blackmail or extortion. I'd rather see the city burn than have it capitulate to the likes of Bludd."

Hollister was quick to reinforce that attitude. "Give in to one such threat, no matter how powerful, and you abdicate all responsibility for control of this city. We're worth more than that! We've got to find the drokker and stop him."

"Easier said than done," was Hershey's dry response. "Niles?"

"Like several key divisions of the Department, the PSU was badly hit by side-effects of the weapon that destroyed Joe Chill. Only now are we beginning to put together the pieces of what happened. Earlier today Bludd had an exhibit stolen from the Dustbuster. It proved to be a fully functional command and control system for firing orbital weapons left over from the twentieth century. The energy beam that crippled Psi-Division and took out our network was one such weapon. Fortunately for us, research in the archives suggests this weapon, though very powerful, requires several hours to be recharged."

"Thank grud for that," Shenker whispered.

"That explains why Bludd has not used it again, so far," Niles added. "But it's only a matter of time before he does.

We believe *Justice Seven* has located the orbital platform where the energy pulse originated. Scattergood and her crew intend to destroy the platform by midnight. That's the good news…"

"And the bad news?" Hershey asked.

Niles grimaced. "Most records from the twentieth century were destroyed by the Great Atom War of 2070. But from what my analysts have uncovered, there were dozens of weapons of mass destruction in orbit. Many of those will have fallen from the sky and burnt up during re-entry since, but not all."

The Chief Judge looked into the eyes of her senior staff as she continued what Niles had been saying. "We're talking atomic, biological and chemical weapons, the sort of stomm outlawed by global treaties after 2071. Some of it is still up there, waiting to be fired, and Bludd's got his finger on the trigger."

"Where is he?" Buell demanded.

"Offworld," Niles said. "We believe he has shifted operations to an orbital HQ outside our jurisdiction, taking the command and control system with him."

"Outside our jurisdiction or not, can't we take out Bludd's HQ?" Hollister asked. "One or two well placed missiles, or a crack team of insurgent Judges? We can deal with the consequences later."

The Chief Judge sighed heavily. "Niles?"

"Unfortunately, Bludd's HQ has stealth capabilities, making it next to impossible for us to locate it. Even if we were willing to breach international law to destroy the threat from Bludd, we have to find him first."

"I find it ominous this perp has evacuated himself from the Big Meg," McTighe from Tek-Division said. "To me that indicates he plans a strike against our city, whether or not we pay this ransom." Others around the council table nodded. Hershey waited until everyone fell silent before speaking.

"The Justice Department will not surrender its control of Mega-City One to blackmail. No money will be paid.

We must trust *Justice Seven* is able to find and destroy these orbiting weapons. Meanwhile we shall develop a response for Bludd's demands, a stalling tactic until his orbiting HQ can be located." The Chief Judge folded her arms. "We face a difficult few hours ahead. The city needs us to be at our best. It's up to you to make sure that happens within each of your divisions. Dismissed."

The Judges rose from their seats and began filing out of the chamber, but Hershey remained in her chair. Niles hung back to speak with the Chief Judge. "Permission to speak off the record?" he asked.

"Granted."

"You look tired. When was the last time you ate or slept?"

"I can't remember," Hershey admitted.

"What you said applies just as much to yourself. The city needs all its Judges at their best tonight, you more than any of us. Grab something to eat and take five minutes on a sleep machine. You've got time before Bludd calls."

The Chief Judge sighed. "You know what happens if we make it through the night? Come nine tomorrow morning I have to resume negotiations about the treaty with our five honoured guests."

"It's the right thing to do," Niles said. "Global extradition would make a significant difference to our ability to pursue perps like Bludd. Nothing good ever came easy, Hershey."

"You're right," she admitted. "I'm going to give Giant a call, make sure the delegates are behaving themselves. We don't need a repeat of last night's activities, not with everything else that's going on."

"It's all quiet," Giant said via his helmet radio when the Chief Judge called. "The delegates took meals in their private quarters about eight and most have turned in for the night. Some of them must have learned their lesson yesterday."

"Even Smirnoff?" Hershey asked, surprise in her voice.

"The last of the great synthi-vodka drinkers seems to be taking it easy for once. Guess you can only drink non-stop for so many days before it finally catches up with you."

"Alright. Let me know if anything untoward happens, Giant."

"Yes, ma'am." The Street Judge hesitated before raising something that had been bothering him. "Excuse me for asking, but will Dredd be returning to help supervise security for the delegates? He's been gone for some hours. I don't listen to gossip usually, but I've heard whispers he's disappeared and is being considered a rogue Judge."

"You're right, Giant, you shouldn't listen to gossip. Dredd is receiving treatment from Med-Judges at City Bottom. Hershey out."

Giant looked at Eaglestone and Jenkins. All three Judges were sat on their Lawmasters outside the safe house where Warner was being kept. "Hear that, Eaglestone? I told you Dredd would never go rogue. That's two graveyard shifts you owe me."

MED-JUDGE KARTER WAS wrapping a fresh rapi-heal pad around Dredd's latest wound when the Street Judge came round. "Don't move yet, I haven't finished," she warned. "You can't expect these injuries to heal if you don't give rapi-heal time to do its job, Dredd."

"What happened?"

"Where do you want me to start?" Karter assessed the battered and bloody body beside her. Every wound, every contusion told its own story. "You were shot just above the waist but luckily for you, the bullet went straight through. Took a chunk of flesh but missed the vital organs, which is why we can still have this conversation. If it had nicked the spleen you'd have bled out before we got here. Your helmet took the full force of the other round, but the impact still knocked you out. A few inches down and left, you'd be a dead hero instead of just having what I imagine is a raging headache."

"Who shot me?"

"You don't remember?" That worried Karter. The head injury might be worse than it first looked, perhaps a serious concussion. She jerked a thumb towards the corpse lying close to Dredd's feet. "Your illustrated woman friend was the culprit. I'm guessing you two fired at the same time."

Tattoo Sue was sprawled out on the blackened ground beside the mo-pad's remains. The end of a tranq dart was protruding from her left eye socket, the rest of the dart embedded inside her skull. Karter spared a glance for the dead perp. "Never seen someone killed that way before, a remarkable shot."

"Lucky," Dredd muttered. "Just lucky." He glanced around the crash site. Emergency crews had put out the fires while Tek-Judges were examining the scene for clues to what had happened. Big arc lamps lit the area, throwing bleak shadows across the night. "How long have I been unconscious?"

"Less than an hour. It's not quite eleven…"

Karter realised Dredd was no longer listening to her. He reached a hand to the side of his helmet where a translucent plastic disc was visible. "Yes, I understand," he said tersely.

The Med-Judge was confused. "You understand what?"

"I'll make it," Dredd continued.

"Make what? Dredd, what are you talking about?"

But the Street Judge ignored her, his expression changing to a grimace as he turned to look at Karter. "Very well."

"Dredd, are you getting messages on your helmet radio? I didn't hear anything from Control just then–"

Her words were cut out abruptly when Dredd grabbed her throat. Karter couldn't speak, couldn't breathe, the grip around her windpipe tightening by the moment. She flailed at Dredd with her fists, but his pressure just increased. He leaned closer to her and whispered a question.

"Which way to the Grand Hall of Justice?"

Karter's eyes slid sideways, to the north.

"I will continue squeezing until you pass out," Dredd said. "Stay down until after midnight – it will be better for both of us."

The Med-Judge nodded with the last of her strength. Already the blackness was closing in round her.

Ten

SCATTERGOOD WAS PROUD of her crew. *Justice Seven*'s operational effectiveness was back to ninety-two per cent of normal, just a few hours after being crippled. Now the orbital platform was closing in on its quarry, the ancient satellite that had launched such a devastating blow against the Big Meg. Scattergood was surprised when she got her first good look at the source of their troubles.

"Grud on a greenie! How is that still in the sky?" she wondered out loud.

The satellite was an antique by anyone's reckoning. More than a hundred years old, its metal surface was pitted and scarred from decades of impacts by space debris. Some words were visible on the side of the cylindrical device: UNITED STATES OF AMERICA SW-1701D. Grissom was already investigating this in what remained of the pre-Great Atom War archives.

"Launched covertly in the 1990s. Part of an initiative known as Star Wars," he explained. "Designed as a way of blowing intercontinental missiles out of the sky before they could deliver their payload. Proved ineffective for that but was used as an offensive weapon against ground-based targets in 2017 with some success. Officially decommissioned in 2057 as part of an orbital weapons disarmament programme by the old United States."

"Like drokk it was," Scattergood muttered darkly. "How long before it's capable of firing again?"

"The weapon is solar powered. It takes four to six hours to recharge."

"And how long since Joe Chill was summarily demolished?"

"Just under four hours," Grissom replied. "Analysis suggests energy levels are almost fully restored. It could be fired again at any time."

"Very well," Scattergood said. "Lock our weapons on that satellite and blow it out of the sky!" A long, awkward silence followed. *Justice Seven*'s commander looked round her crew. "Give me the bad news."

Everyone else turned to Grissom. "In order to restore propulsion and manoeuvring earlier, I had to scavenge a bypass circuit from elsewhere..."

"And you took it from our defence systems?"

Grissom nodded.

"Terrif!" Scattergood scowled. "Take us closer to that satellite and prep a suit for EVA. Guess I'll have to go over there and place the charges myself."

BLUDD WAS ENJOYING the show. Since arriving at his new orbiting home he had savoured a gourmet meal, enjoyed a sexual liaison with Kara and was now ensconced in his command suite. Sat in a hovering chair, he watched a wall of Tri-D screens depicting a thousand scenes from across the Big Meg. That one plastic disc attached to Dredd's helmet was proving a boon, enabling Bludd's computers to eavesdrop on all Justice Department comms and surveillance systems. The crime boss could see and hear everything the Judges did. But he had one advantage over Hershey and her underlings; Bludd knew what was coming next.

To Bludd's side Kara was busy keeping watch over Dredd's progress. The Judge had fled the crash site in City Bottom and was now making his way to the Grand Hall of Justice on foot. He was still several miles away, bleeding from multiple wounds and armed only with two stumm gas grenades and a daystick. It would be a miracle if he reached his destination in time.

"How is the hunted man?" Bludd asked.

Kara smiled at her lover. "Slowing down. He's torn open his old wounds and even the rapi-heal pads can't staunch the bleeding where Sue shot him." She could not keep the curiosity from her face. "Why are you making him do this? It doesn't advance our goals."

"No, but it keeps Dredd busy. Before beginning this endeavour I analysed every significant threat to the Big Meg from the past forty years. In almost every case it was an intervention by Dredd that preserved Justice Department's position and saved the day if you like. Remove Dredd from the equation and our chances of success improve immeasurably."

"Why not just kill the drokker?"

"My dear Kara, I do not share your love of pain and death. To me murder is another weapon in my armoury. I do not kill when it is not required. Anyway, come midnight Dredd will be far too busy to worry about us anymore." Bludd swivelled his chair round to face a screen filled with Hershey's face. "It appears the Chief Judge is about to get some rest in a sleep machine. I think it's time I gave her another call, something else to worry about."

HERSHEY WAS ADJUSTING the settings on the sleep machine nearest her office when Bludd's call came through to her via Control. "Tut, tut, Chief Judge! Going to sleep on the job, are we?" the crime boss said.

"How did you know–" Hershey stopped, realising the significance of what had been said. "You've got access to our comms network, the PSU. How?"

"Let's just say I had some help from a new friend. He and I had a chat over some synthi-caf earlier this evening."

"Dredd? He would never betray the Department!"

"Not willingly, no. But sometimes free will is just an illusion."

"Spare me the cod philosophy," Hershey snarled. "What do you want?"

"I've already told you, one hundred billion credits before midnight."

"If you're able to see and hear everything we do, then you should already know our response – no deal. Mega-City One does not give in to blackmail!" The Chief Judge was striding back to her office, spitting out her words venomously.

"It's more accurate to say the Justice Department of Mega-City One does not give in to blackmail," Bludd replied. "You haven't asked the people of Mega-City One what they think. Would they rather be proud and dead as you soon will be, or alive and a little poorer, as I am suggesting?"

"The Big Meg isn't a democracy," Hershey said. "We choose what is best for the people, so they don't have to."

"We'll see what they have to say about that after midnight. In the kingdom of the blind–"

"–the one-eyed man is king. I know the quotation, Bludd. What does it signify?"

"You'll see soon enough. Or perhaps you won't. I am transmitting the number for my offworld account to you now. Either agree to my request or all of Mega-City One shall suffer the consequences come midnight."

"We have located the orbital platform where the energy pulse originated. Within minutes my Judges will have disabled your weapon permanently."

"Perhaps," Bludd replied. "But I never said that was my only weapon, did I? Goodbye, Hershey. We shall speak once more at midnight. After that I doubt you will still be in charge of your city, unless you meet my demands."

A brief crackle of static was followed by silence. Bludd was gone again. The Chief Judge called Niles at the PSU. "Well?"

"Bludd bounced the signal through a dozen relays but he's definitely offworld. We've got an idea what quadrant, but beyond that…"

"Drokk it!" Hershey cursed, letting her frustration escape. "You heard what he had to say about intercepting our comms?"

"Yes. No doubt he can see all our surveillance feeds, as well as listening in to this conversation. We have a serious security problem."

"Agreed. Meet me at the following location in twenty minutes." Hershey sent an encrypted message to Niles. "It's the one place we know is not covered by PSU surveillance, so it'll be safe to talk there. Hershey out."

DREDD ROUNDED A corner into a dark alley and leaned against a wall. Something was moving around inside him, probably a rib. With every step the broken bone was digging into him, its edge grinding into soft tissue. Blood was seeping freely from the entry and exit wounds where Sue had shot him, while his vision was blurring badly. Dredd rested his helmeted head against the wall and squinted at the skyline.

In the distance a familiar building was glinting in the darkness, its many lights and levels a blurred smear of hope. The Grand Hall of Justice was close, perhaps a mile away or two at the most.

"You better hurry, Dredd," Kara said via the Judge's helmet radio. "You've got less than an hour to reach the front steps. Judging by the trail of blood you're leaving behind, you'll be dead if you don't make it there before midnight."

"Drokk you, creep," Dredd muttered.

"Is that any way to speak to your guardian angel?"

"You're no angel. I know you."

"So you keep saying. I'd be more worried about the street gang approaching your location if I were you," Kara replied. "They should be with you right about... now."

"What direction are they coming from?" Dredd demanded. "Answer me, damn you!"

"I'll give you an answer," a different voice said. A female juve stepped out of the shadows, her face adorned with dozens of metal piercings, rings and chains. Her clothes were a mixture of rags and rubbereen, heavy on studs and symbols. In her hands she clutched a laser truncheon, its long metal tube surrounded by crackling blue energy. "But I don't think you'll like it, old man."

"What have we got here, Myroid?" Another juve emerged from the darkness, clad in similar garb. Instead of a truncheon she was tossing a laser blade from hand to hand, careful not to slice off her fingers with its edges.

"A Judge who's seen better days," Myroid said. "Ripe for ripping, Trace!"

Three more females joined the others, forming a semi-circle around Dredd. All wore the insignia of their gang, the Slack Magic Sluts. Trace moved closer to the Judge, sneering at his weakened state. "Surprised he's still standing. Somebody been using you for target practice, old man?"

"Punks like you don't impress me," Dredd replied. "I knew a real punk once, name of Spikes Harvey Rotten. He wore a hand grenade as an earring."

Trace laughed out long, encouraging her gang members to join in. "What a joke! You're giving us jewellery tips now? What are the Judges coming to?"

Dredd produced two stumm gas grenades he had taken from the med-wagon, having already pulled out the pins while the gang leader was talking to her disciples. "Here, try 'em." Dredd tossed a grenade each to Trace and Myroid, then pulled down the respirator from atop his helmet. Within seconds the alley was filled with debilitating fumes.

"Cover your mouth and nose!" Trace commanded, but Myroid and two of the other juves had already succumbed to the gas. The Slack Magic Sluts' leader launched herself at where Dredd had been standing, flailing at the air with her laser blade while using her other hand to shield herself from the fumes. But the Judge had already stepped aside, hiding among the thick clouds of stumm.

The other gang member began backing away, having pulled a bandanna down from her forehead to cover her nose and mouth. She heard a noise and twisted round to find Dredd behind her. He pulled the cloth mask from her face. "Sweet dreams, punk!" he whispered.

"Myroid, where are you?" Trace shouted, lost in the gas. "Cosmina? Meadow? Clamidia! Answer me, you drokkers!"

"They can't," Dredd replied, moving closer to the gang leader. "They're having a nap."

"Drokk you, lawman!" Trace screamed, hurling herself at the sound of his voice, laser blade stabbing down through the stumm fumes. It plunged into Clamidia's chest and stuck there. Dredd let go of the gang member he had been holding in front of himself as a human shield.

"You just hurt one of your own, punk," he snarled, brandishing the daystick in his right hand. "Now it's my turn."

IT WAS THREE years since Scattergood had finished her training in an EVA spacesuit and she hadn't needed to use one since. *Justice Seven* took care of its own exterior, thanks to an army of nanobots crawling across the outside constantly searching for repairs to make. Spacesuits were only required in case of sudden evacuation or for manual tasks beyond the capabilities of the nanobots. Space-walking to the satellite housing the energy pulse weapon was just such a task, much to Scattergood's regret.

Justice Seven's commander suffered from claustrophobia, something Psi-Division had detected when she was a cadet at the Academy decades ago. The condition was mild and deemed unlikely to impinge on her abilities as a Street Judge. Even when she was appointed to the command of *Justice Seven*, the veteran law enforcer dismissed any suggestion her fear of enclosed spaces would be a problem. Yes, of course, she would be living inside a metal can but so would dozens of other operatives. There was plenty of room in space.

It was only when the helmet was sealed shut and the straps tightened around her body that Scattergood felt the old fear and anguish begin to creep out from deep inside. The spacesuit was not the problem, it was the heavy strapping to keep her bound against the EVA rocket chair. This device gave her manoeuvrability in the vacuum of space, but also restricted any bodily movement. She was trapped, caught, confined.

"Ma'am, we read your pulse rate and blood pressure accelerating. Everything alright in there?" Grissom asked. He had volunteered to be her EVA buddy, keeping tabs on her progress. Scattergood was already inside the airlock, waiting for the outer doors to open.

"Just let me out of this tin can," she urged.

"Acknowledged. Opening outer doors... now!"

DREDD LIMPED AWAY from the alley, the stumm gas clearing to reveal the five bodies on the ground. He only had the daystick left to defend himself now but the Grand Hall of Justice was walking distance away. All four bounty hunters had been dealt with and it was doubtful two street gangs would patrol the same turf so close to the home of the Law.

The Judge staggered towards his goal. There were only minutes left until midnight. He could not and would not let this city down.

* * *

SCATTERGOOD REACHED THE cylindrical satellite with few difficulties. Just like riding a Lawmaster, she thought to herself with pride. Once you get the knack, you never fall off again. She powered down the EVA rocket chair and locked it in place beside the satellite. Clutching a belt laden with magnetic charges, Scattergood began clambering across the surface of the satellite. *Justice Seven*'s commander could hear Grissom's instructions via her helmet radio. "You need to position those charges in specific places around the satellite, otherwise they will not be enough to destroy it. Okay, you're coming to the first vulnerable spot. Clamp that sucker down over the letter U in United."

Scattergood removed the first charge from the belt and pressed it against the required spot. Once that was in place, she twisted a dial on the outer ring of the explosive device. A faint thumping sound indicated the magnetic lock had been activated. Scattergood tugged at the charge but it would not budge. "That's the first one fixed on, five more to go. Where next?"

BLUDD WAS AMUSED to see a warning light appear on one of his Tri-D screens. "It seems *Justice Seven* has located our first weapon of choice," he told Kara cheerfully. "Start the countdown for firing, let's see how they react."

SCATTERGOOD TWISTED THE dial on the third magnetic charge. It thumped into place and resisted her attempts to dislodge it. "That's half of them done," she announced. "Where next, Grissom?"

"About three metres round to your right, ma'am," the PSU analyst replied. "And you might want to hurry it up if you can."

"Why?"

"Our systems show the weapon is being powered up for ignition again. If you're still over there when it fires…"

"Hotter than July?"

"More like trying to get a tan on the surface of the sun."

"Terrif," Scattergood muttered. "Moving to the next location."

DREDD WAS LESS than a block from the Grand Hall when he heard the voice. "Going somewhere, Judge?" a Brit-Cit accent asked. Fincher stepped into view, positioning himself between Dredd and the Grand Hall. "I knew those stupid cows Di and Tattoo Sue would never get the better of you, but I thought I'd let them take their shot. With a spot of luck, they might do you some damage. I can see I was right. Some nasty wounds you've got there, mate."

"I'm not your mate, scumbag."

"Scumbag? Is that any way to talk to the best bounty hunter in Mega-City One? I'm going be more famous than Orlok the Assassin once I've offed you."

"You've got to kill me to get the kudos, creep. Better men and women than you have tried, and failed."

Fincher pulled out an old fashioned straight-bladed razor. "See this? It's an antique. I save it for special kills, the ones that mean something. You should be honoured, Dredd, not many people get to feel my straight razor as it slices through their neck. Course, you won't feel much of anything once I've done with you. Bludd wants your badge, but I think I'll take your head as a trophy. Probably charge people for a peek under that helmet of yours, see what Old Stony Face really looks like."

Dredd leaned one hand against a wall for support. "You planning to kill me with that thing or talk me to death?"

The Brit smiled, revealing a mouthful of decaying teeth and gums. "Don't you worry, mate, you'll be dead soon enough. I just wanted you to know that this isn't personal but strictly business. I've got a lot of admiration for you, Dredd."

"It isn't mutual."

"I mean, there's probably not a bone in that body hasn't been broken at some point. How long you been on the streets now? Thirty years? Forty? And top of the game for all that time. The undisputed world heavyweight champion of law enforcement, until today."

"You know what I hate most about punks like you?"

"Today I'll be putting an end to your brilliant career. This is the end of the line, Dredd. How does it feel to meet your match at last?"

"They can talk the talk, but they can't walk the walk."

"How does it feel to meet the man who's going to end your life?"

"Like you Brits say – all mouth but no trousers."

Fincher's smile faded. "You're gonna pay for that, mate. I was gonna finish you off nice and quick, as a mark of respect. Now I think I'll take my time instead, savour the moment."

"Don't rush on my account." Dredd drew his daystick from its leathereen strap. "You bring anything besides that razor?"

"It's all I need to finish you."

"We'll see." Dredd suddenly threw the daystick at Fincher.

The bounty hunter was surprised but still had time to duck out of the way. He burst out laughing, looking over his shoulder at the fallen weapon. "Is that the best you can do, old man?" Fincher turned round again to find Dredd drawing back a fist, ready to strike.

"No," Dredd hissed. "Try this!"

"ENERGY PULSE WEAPON is almost ready to fire again," Kara reported. Bludd was watching Scattergood clamp magnetic charges to the cylindrical satellite, using the same surveillance feed as Grissom had on *Justice Seven*.

The crime boss smiled to himself as he gave fresh orders to Kara. "Reposition so the weapon is taking aim at the Department's orbital platform. Let the Judges know what it's like to be at the wrong end of a weapon for once."

* * *

SCATTERGOOD FINISHED CLAMPING the fifth charge to the exterior of the satellite. She reached for the final magnetic device. "Alright, just one left. Where should this one..."

"Grissom to Scattergood, can you hear me? What's wrong? Ma'am–"

"The satellite's manoeuvring thrusters are active!" Scattergood replied. "It's changing target! Grissom, how long before this thing can fire again?"

"The energy pulse is ready now, ma'am. Bludd just needs to lock on target and he can fire whenever he wants."

"Stomm," Scattergood hissed. She hurriedly reached for the last magnetic charge but her fingertips only brushed its edge. The device floated away from her, banging against the side of the satellite. Scattergood grabbed at its clamps and got hold of one. "Grissom, where do I put this last charge?"

"Two metres above your current position, ma'am – and make it snappy!" Fear was evident in the PSU analyst's voice.

"Why? What's wrong now?"

"The satellite – it's taking aim at *Justice Seven*!"

DREDD SMASHED HIS fist into Fincher's face, sending the Brit sprawling backwards. The straight razor tumbled from the bounty hunter's hand as Dredd followed up with a boot into the fallen man's crotch. Fincher screamed out in agony, the breath hissing between his teeth.

"Christ, me bollocks!" he whimpered, curling up into a foetal position, one hand stretched outwards in anguish.

Dredd crouched beside the stricken murderer. "Two blows, that's all it took to stop you, punk. So much for the great pretender."

Fincher closed his outstretched hand around the straight razor's handle before smiling at the Judge. "You got that last part wrong, mate." Fincher swept his arm round in an arc. The blade sliced through the sleeve of Dredd's uniform and cut deep into the forearm, right down to the bone. The Judge screamed out in anguish, blood spraying from the wound in a crimson gout as he doubled over. "I like a little pretending," Fincher smirked as he threw a punch into Dredd's throat, sending the lawman backwards into a rockcrete wall, gasping for air.

The Brit stood and brushed himself down. "Little trick I learned during a visit to Hondo City when I was a kid. Sumo wrestlers are trained from puberty to retract their meat and two veg into the cavity from where your balls drop as it protects you from low blows. I'm quite a dab hand at it myself now – very useful in a fight, I find."

Dredd was slumped against the wall, still fighting for every breath as Fincher came nearer. The bounty hunter held the straight razor in front of his face and licked blood from the blade. "There's an old saying – the first cut is the deepest. But nothing could be further from the truth."

SCATTERGOOD PRESSED THE final charge into position and twisted the dial to clamp it down, but nothing happened. She gave the dial another twist. Still nothing, no reassuring clump to prove the magnetic seal had been made. "Grissom, something's wrong! The last charge isn't magnetising!"

"Have you twisted the dial?"

"Of course I've twisted the drokking dial! It's not clamping to the satellite!"

"Magnets must have been damaged when the charge banged against the exterior. They're very sensitive, prone to breaking. That's why we use them so infrequently, except in emergencies."

"Now he tells me," Scattergood muttered under her breath. "How do I fix it?"

"You can't," Grissom replied. "You could come back for a replacement–"

"By the time I do that *Justice Seven* will be space debris!" The veteran Judge could feel the spacesuit closing in, her breath coming in ever shorter gasps as her heart rate accelerated from the stress. "I've got five charges in place – will that be enough to destroy the satellite?"

The only reply was a long silence.

"Grissom! Are five charges enough to–"

"No," the PSU analyst said quietly. "Six is the minimum. It should be double that number to be certain. With just six, all of them must be securely fixed to the exterior of the satellite when they blow to be effective."

"Terrif," Scattergood sighed. "How long until *Justice Seven* is in range of the energy pulse beam?"

"Less than a minute before it can fire."

Now it was Scattergood's turn to fall silent. She twisted round in the spacesuit to see the Earth, the sprawling conurbation of Mega-City One just visible through a gap in the clouds. Grissom's voice interrupted her reverie. "Ma'am, did you hear me? We've got less than a minute."

"I heard you," Scattergood replied. "I'll hold the final device in place while you detonate all six charges, it's the only way to stop this thing."

"But ma'am, if you stay there you'll be–"

"If I don't do this, everyone on board *Justice Seven* will die. One life versus dozens. You do the math, Grissom."

"But there must be–"

"There isn't and you know it. Detonate the charges, Grissom, while you still have time."

"But–"

"Detonate the charges! That's a direct order!"

"Yes, ma'am."

Scattergood pressed the final charge into place and closed her eyes, remembering the words of a prayer she had learned as a child. The veteran Judge whispered the opening phrase over and over to herself as she waited for the explosion. "Yea, though I walk through the valley of the shadow of death, I will fear no evil. Yea, though I walk through the valley of the shadow of–"

*   *   *

THE SATELLITE EXPLODED in the sky above Mega-City One, a fleeting fireball in the night. Fincher saw the blink of light from the corner of his eye and paused to look up. "That's funny. I didn't think the fireworks started until midnight."

"They don't," Dredd replied, "but you won't be alive to see them." He grabbed the bounty hunter's hand clasping the razor and began twisting the blade towards Fincher's neck. The Brit fought back with all his strength, but Dredd had the advantage. "Time to die, punk!" The Judge rammed his fists forward, forcing the razor deep into Fincher's throat before ripping it sideways.

The blade cut through the carotid artery, showering Dredd with the bounty hunter's blood. Fincher clasped both hands over the wound, trying to hold back the inevitable. But Dredd punched the bounty hunter in the face, knocking the Brit backwards to the ground. The Judge crawled away from the dying perp, ignoring the last spasms as death took hold of Fincher.

A familiar voice reappeared via Dredd's helmet radio. "Still alive?" Kara asked sarcastically. "Congratulations, Dredd, you've killed four of the finest bounty hunters in the business. But you only have minutes left to reach the Grand Hall, otherwise the weapon that levelled Joe Chill will be turned upon the home of justice. Hurry, Joe, hurry!"

Dredd pulled himself to his feet, fighting back the effects of blood loss and concussion. He staggered towards the Grand Hall, each step sending a shudder of pain through his battered body.

IN THE CHIEF Judge's office, Hershey sat behind her desk, waiting for Bludd's call. Niles was with her, pacing restlessly back and forth from the door. The Tri-D screen on Hershey's desk came alive. "Control to Chief Judge, message coming in from *Justice Seven* for you!"

"Patch it through," Hershey commanded.

A careworn face appeared on the monitor. "PSU analyst Grissom reporting, ma'am. We destroyed the satellite containing the energy pulse beam weapon. It's no longer a threat to the city."

The Chief Judge smiled, happy to get some good news at last. "Congratulations, Grissom. Where's your commander, Judge Scattergood? I'd have thought she would want to tell me this herself."

Sorrow passed across the analyst's face. "We lost her, ma'am. Judge Scattergood sacrificed herself to take out the satellite. She saved us all."

Hershey's happiness faded away. Another death to add to Bludd's toll, another life lost trying to stop this creep. "Thank you, Grissom. Who's the most senior officer on *Justice Seven* now?"

Grissom turned away from the screen to glance round his colleagues. "I suppose I am, ma'am."

"Very well. As Chief Judge of Mega-City One I hereby promote you to acting commander of *Justice Seven* until this crisis is averted. Do well and the job can be yours permanently."

"Yes, ma'am. But haven't we averted the crisis already? We stopped the satellite from firing its weapon again."

Hershey grimaced. "Unfortunately, we suspect that satellite may be just the first of a dozen such threats in the sky. You and your team have to stop them all. Stand ready – Bludd isn't finished with us yet. Hershey out." She deactivated the Tri-D monitor. From the antechamber to her office a clock began chiming twelve. Niles stopped his pacing to listen.

"It's midnight."

The Tri-D monitor came back to life, the face of Jesus Bludd appearing on screen. "Good evening, Chief Judge, or should I say good morning. It's deadline time. Which is it to be, the money or your lives?"

*　*　*

DREDD STAGGERED ACROSS the skedway in front of the Grand Hall, his legs collapsing as he neared the steps. "Don't give up now, Joe!" Kara's voice goaded him. "I can hear the chimes of midnight, you've got a few seconds left."

"Drokk you," Dredd snarled. He crawled towards the stone stairs, reaching one hand towards them. With one last effort he touched the first step with his fingertips.

"Congratulations, you made it," Kara said via his helmet radio. "The good news is the weapon used to destroy Joe Chill will never be fired upon Mega-City One, just as I promised. The bad news? It seems your Chief Judge is not as cooperative as you, Dredd. Now everyone in Mega-City One shall suffer the consequences!"

Eleven

BLUDD WAGGLED AN admonishing finger at the Chief Judge. "Tut, tut! You have failed to transfer the required payment to my offworld account, Hershey. Are you ready for the consequences of such disobedience?"

"I don't answer to scum like you," she spat back. "Mega-City One will not be blackmailed. Do your worst Bludd, but heed this: attack my city and its Judges will hunt you down and kill you, no matter where you go and how well you hide. You will never be safe, never know peace again. Your days will be numbered and your life forfeit."

"So be it," Bludd replied. "You might want to look out your windows in the next few minutes, the fireworks are about to start."

MED-JUDGES SWARMED AROUND Dredd's body, trying to staunch the bleeding from his many wounds. Most of the PSU surveillance cameras surrounding the Grand Hall were still offline, so Dredd's approach had gone unnoticed. It was a passing patrol that first saw the Judge's body collapsed on the stairs and reported the emergency. Med-Division was based in another sector of the city, but the Grand Hall did have its own medical bay and staff of physicians.

Now a phalanx of Med-Judges was crouched on the building's front steps around the dying lawman. Leading the efforts to save Dredd was Callaghan. Only a few hours before she had accused Dredd of going rogue, now she found herself fighting to keep him alive. Much of his body was swaddled in rapi-heal patches but the razor cuts inflicted by Fincher were too deep for such treatment so a staple gun was used, metal bands crudely fastening the gaping wounds back together.

Handheld scanners monitoring Dredd's vital signs began bleeping in distress. "We're losing him!" Callaghan shouted as she examined the readouts. "Looks like a blood clot close to the brain. Get that helmet off him – we've got to relieve the pressure now!"

Another Med-Judge questioned her command. Blum was a stickler for procedure, an attitude that won him credit at the Academy but often proved too rigid in matters of life and death on the streets. "You can't do that procedure out here, the risk of infection is too high. He should be on an operating table, not the front steps of the Grand Hall!"

"He'll be dead before we get him inside. We do this here and now, or we lose him altogether!" Callaghan snarled. "Somebody hand me a laser scalpel."

GRISSOM STOOD IN front of Scattergood's empty chair. The Chief Judge might have rewarded him with a field promotion to acting commander, but Grissom didn't feel ready to take the dead woman's place yet. She had been a towering presence on *Justice Seven*, transforming the orbital platform's status from minor outpost to a vital part of the Big Meg's defences.

"Commander," one of the other analysts called out, but got no response from the new boss of *Justice Seven*. "Grissom!"

"Sorry," he replied. "What is it?"

"One of the dormant satellites with geostationary positioning above the Big Meg is falling out of orbit, sir."

Grissom shrugged. "Not an infrequent occurrence. It's amazing those old tin cans have stayed up this long."

"Yes, but this one fired its retro rockets first. It isn't dormant any longer. Someone has deliberately triggered the descent mechanism."

"Trajectory?"

"Headed straight for the Grand Hall of Justice."

"Terrif," Grissom muttered. "How long for us to intercept that satellite?"

"Seven minutes."

"And how long before it re-enters the atmosphere?"

"Four minutes, sir."

"Stomm," the new commander hissed. "Plot an intercept course and fire all manoeuvring thrusters. We've got to find a way of stopping that satellite!"

BLUDD FINISHED TAPPING instructions into the stolen command and control system. In an era of voice-activated computers and faster-than-thought relays, using such an antiquated device was something of a shock. How did people ever cope with this puny processing power? It was remarkable to think such an arcane mechanism had controlled so many deadly weapons. The command and control system was technologically akin to a bow and arrow, he thought to himself.

Satisfied with his efforts, the crime boss strolled back to the comms centre of his orbiting headquarters. Everything was going according to plan. Now it was time to apply the squeeze. Bludd returned to his wall of Tri-D monitors, Kara vacating his hoverchair to take her own seat. "What's the latest?"

"Dredd's circling the drain," Kara replied. "They might save him but…"

Bludd was disturbed to see static on some of the Tri-D monitors. "And what's causing the interference on these screens?"

"Meds took off Dredd's helmet to treat his head wounds. The relay disc on the side of the helmet is face down. That's interfering with our signal from Control and PSU systems." Kara pointed at the live feed from a spy-in-the-sky camera observing efforts to save Dredd's life. "You can see it there."

Bludd peered at the image. A Street Judge called Elson was picking up Dredd's helmet. As he turned the helmet over, the static cleared away from the monitors, the relay signal restored. "That's better," the crime boss said.

"Not for long," Kara noted. She amplified the audio signal.

On screen Elson was staring at the translucent disc on Dredd's helmet, puzzlement evident on the Judge's face. "Anyone know what this is?" he asked. The medics were too busy attending their patient to answer. Elson began picking at the disc, trying to prise it off the helmet.

"No, don't touch that–" Bludd urged.

Suddenly most of the Tri-D monitors went black.

"We've lost our relay signal," Kara said bleakly. "My bluff about the disc containing an explosive charge was only effective while Dredd was conscious."

Bludd shrugged. "It was good while it lasted. The pieces are in place. We can glean all the information we need from other sources now."

JUSTICE SEVEN WAS moving faster than it had since being launched into orbit eight years previously. The platform was thundering across the sky, firing all its thrusters and manoeuvring rockets in a vain attempt to intercept the satellite tumbling out of orbit. Inside, Grissom was barking orders to his crew, trying to find some way of achieving the impossible.

"How long to intercept now?"

In front of Grissom sat another PSU analyst, Rayner. She scanned the readings on her computer screen before answering. "Three minutes, sir"

"And until that thing re-enters the atmosphere?"

"Eighty seconds."

On the large view screen in the command centre, the satellite was clearly visible ahead of *Justice Seven*, a black hulk given shape by the curve of Earth below it. Already the bottom of the satellite was beginning to glow red as its temperature rose, warmed by the friction of the approaching atmosphere.

"Drokk it, there must be something we can do!" Grissom protested.

Rayner looked over her shoulder at the new commander. "Even if we could reach the satellite, how would we stop it?"

"We'd find a way," Grissom replied. "Scattergood would've managed it."

"Less than a minute to re-entry."

CALLAGHAN CROUCHED ABOVE Dredd's head, the laser scalpel clenched tightly in her hand. "I'm going in," she announced. The Med-Judge began pressing the end of the cutting tool against the lawman's scalp. It sizzled through the skin, cauterising the blood vessels directly beneath before cutting into the skull.

"Getting some resistance. Gonna press harder," Callaghan said, all too aware of how dangerous this procedure was. Go too far and she would plunge the laser scalpel directly into Dredd's brain, performing a crude lobotomy. Hold back too much and he would be dead of a brain seizure within minutes.

Suddenly the scalpel was through the bone of Dredd's skull. Blood surged out the hole, boiling as it passed the intense heat of the laser, cooking in the air with a sickening smell of metal burning. Callaghan held her hands steady.

"Withdrawing the laser scalpel. We'll let the blood clot drain out, then seal the vent. Everybody ready?"

The Med-Judge pulled the scalpel away and blood spouted from the circular hole in Dredd's skull. Once the flow had subsided Callaghan took a rapi-heal patch from one of her colleagues and positioned it over the void, while another medic secured it in place. "Vital signs?"

"Stabilising," someone nearby replied.

"Once the hover-stretcher gets here we can move him inside." Callaghan sat back on her haunches and took a deep breath, her face flooded with perspiration and relief. "We did it."

THE SATELLITE WAS re-entering the atmosphere, surrounded by blazing white light as it burnt up. *Justice Seven* plunged after it, Grissom determined to keep going until the last possible moment. Already the temperature inside the orbital platform was past all recommended safety limits and still rising.

"Sir, if we don't alter course soon, we'll burn up too!" Rayner protested.

"Not yet," Grissom snapped. "I want to be certain that thing doesn't reach the Big Meg. Do we know what the satellite's payload is yet?"

"Manifest is encrypted but I've transmitted it to Tek-Division for breakdown and analysis. Not sure if the message got through. This close to re-entry all radio signals start to degrade."

On the view screen the satellite abruptly exploded into a hail of green and yellow fragments, each burning brightly as it fell to Earth. "That's done it!" Grissom shouted in triumph. "Pull us away – now!"

"I'm not sure I can," Rayner said. "We used too much fuel getting here. There's nothing left to fire the manoeuvring thrusters!"

"Retro rockets then!"

"Gone as well, sir!" Rayner screamed as her computer exploded in a shower of sparks and flame. That set off a chain reaction as other systems began succumbing to the temperature.

Grissom sank back down into the commander's chair. "Get a message through to Control. We have tried to–"

Justice Seven exploded.

THE SKY ABOVE Mega-City One offers many exciting opportunities for the amateur astronomer. Powerful telescopes like the Home Hubble 3000 enabled ordinary citizens to observe a range of heavenly bodies. Twenty-second century fireworks were dazzling and undeniably exciting. But few pyrotechnic displays over the Big Meg could hope to match the astounding light show that began dancing overhead just after midnight.

The yellow cloud was first; light bouncing from edge to edge, bringing a chorus of "oohs" and "aahs" from all who saw it. Next came green, verdant hues of emerald and jade, bathing the city in luminescence. Then the two clouds combined to create striations of colour and intensity surpassing imagination.

Those citizens still out on the streets hurried home or called friends and family to tell them about the wonders overhead. Parents and children spilled out of bed to witness this once-in-a-lifetime extravaganza. Within minutes, news stations were being flooded with calls about the pyrotechnics and images of the spectacle were being broadcast on all the major Tri-D channels.

On the *Mega-City News*, Enigma Smith was almost speechless with awe. She had won a battle to escape from the studio, persuading her producer to authorise a rare outside broadcast from the roof garden of Ruprecht Maxwell's headquarters. Smith enthused live to air while the light show was visible behind her in the sky.

"Get out of your beds, get out of your con-apts, people

of Mega-City One," she urged. "Never in her life has this reporter seen such glory, such majesty. It makes you feel lucky to be alive this night, lucky to have savoured this wonder! Don't be selfish and wake up your neighbours, your friends, even your enemies. I can only say I feel sorry for those who can't see what I am looking at now. You don't want to miss this spectacle of spectacles."

A particularly intense burst of light overhead took the words from Smith's mouth. After watching for a few seconds she looked at the camera, tears filling her eyes. "You know what? I'm not going to spoil this moment by talking all over the top of it. Let these pictures tell the story for you."

"CONTROL TO CHIEF Judge, please respond. Control to Chief Judge, can you hear this message? Please respond!" The voice speaking through the comms speaker on Hershey's desk was becoming frantic. "Control to all units close to the Chief Judge's office, please–"

"I'm here, for grud's sake!" Hershey snapped, returning to her desk. "What's so drokkin' urgent I can't take a minute away to look at the fireworks?"

"It's about what's happening in the sky, ma'am. The director of the Dustbuster called in to say the museum's board cancelled the display this afternoon when it discovered who was sponsoring the event."

"Let me guess, Jesus Bludd," the Chief Judge replied. "Then where is the light show coming from?"

"Tek-Division believes it may be fall-out from an old satellite that exploded while trying to re-enter Earth's atmosphere, ma'am."

Hershey mused on this. "Get me *Justice Seven*. We need to know more about what we're dealing with."

"That's the other problem, ma'am. *Justice Seven* was destroyed trying to intercept the satellite. Their last transmission was scrambled with static. It's taken Tek-

Division several minutes to reconstruct the message. *Justice Seven* relayed an encrypted manifest. It seems the satellite was carrying some kind of biological or chemical weapon. No further details available."

"Stomm," Hershey whispered. "Recall all Street Judges to Sector Houses, now! If that yellow and green light show is raining a bioweapon down on the city, we don't need any more helmets being exposed to it."

"Yes, ma'am!"

The Chief Judge sank into her chair, aware of her eyes starting to itch. Probably psychosomatic, but she should get it checked by the Med-Judges. It would give her a chance to see how Dredd was doing. He'd been stabilised and shifted into the Grand Hall's medical bay just before the light show had begun over the city.

Her thoughts were cut short by an incoming call from Niles at PSU. "Ma'am, have you been outside to see the pyrotechnics display?"

"Yes, I just came back in. McTighe has already warned me about possible contaminants, so I've recalled all our–"

"Sorry to interrupt but you should switch your main screen to multiview."

Hershey pushed a button on her desk. Part of the opposite wall slid away to reveal an array of Tri-D monitors. "Show me multiview," the Chief Judge commanded. Each screen came alive, displaying a different broadcast channel from among the tens of thousands serving the city. On every monitor were scenes of chaos on the streets, people staggering around clutching at their faces, blood trickling from their eyes. After a few seconds the images were replaced with feeds from different channels. "Sound on," Hershey said. She was overwhelmed by a cacophony of voices, all telling similar stories.

"Reports are coming in about a plague of blindness that appears to be sweeping across the Big Meg. So far we've had dozens of calls from–"

"Citizens everywhere are bleeding from their eyes,

unable to see anything but a blur, everything fading into darkness and–"

"It began a few minutes ago and already our switchboard has been overloaded as concerned cits are calling us to–"

"Chaos is gripping the streets of the Big Meg as people stagger–"

"The wave of blindness is spreading faster than any disease–"

"We estimate tens of thousands are already affected and many–"

"Could the affliction be linked to the light display still going on above the city? So far there has been no statement from the Judges but–"

"The end is nigh! The end is nigh! Abandon hope as God punishes the sinners and takes their vision from–"

"Don't go outside, don't look outside. That's the warning from–"

"We've had reports of roadsters crashing into buildings–"

"Stratbats and other aircraft are falling from the sky–"

"Fires are spreading rapidly, out of control and with nobody to–"

"Apparently the first symptom is itching behind the eyes, then a trickle of blood begins seeping out. Within a few minutes the victims are blind, unable to see their hands in front of their faces. So far–"

"I'm Enigma Smith and I've been struck blind like many of you. What has caused this apparently citywide catastrophe? Who can reverse this plague of sightlessness? What hope can there be for a city where none can see?"

"Sound off," Hershey commanded. Sweet Jovus, what was happening? She felt something running down one side of her face. The Chief Judge touched her cheek and felt a trickle of moisture. When she looked at her fingers, they were covered in blood. "In the kingdom of the blind, the one-eyed man is king," she whispered, remembering the quotation Bludd had been discussing over synthi-caf with Dredd just a few hours earlier. Already the room was growing dark, although she knew the lighting level had not changed.

"Hershey to Control. I am hereby instituting a total curfew over the entire city, effective from 1:00 am. All citizens are to remain indoors until further notice. Any caught outside their homes after one will be considered looters and may be shot on sight. Have that broadcast on every Tri-D channel in the city, jam their signals with ours if you have to." The Chief Judge broke off her transmission to cringe inwardly at what she had said. Shot on sight! That assumed there were still any Judges who could see to do the shooting. Hershey resumed her message. "Contact all offworld Judges within three days of Earth and tell them to return to Mega-City One immediately. Get all Council of Five members to stand by a vidphone. I'll be conducting a conference call meeting with them beginning in fifteen minutes. Is that clear?"

"Yes, ma'am. Anything else?"

"Yes. Call all Sector Houses and Department facilities in the city. Find out how many sighted Judges they still have, we need to know just how bad our situation is. And send somebody who can see up to my office. I'm going to need them to be my eyes from now on. Make it Auburn." Hershey switched off the comms unit, her fingers fumbling for the controls.

In the time it had taken to reel off her orders, she had gone blind.

GIANT WAS ONE of the lucky ones. When the yellow and green lights began dancing in the sky over Mega-City One, the Judge was stuck inside trying to prise a bottle of foul-smelling liquid from Smirnoff. The East-Meg Two delegate had somehow managed to smuggle it past all the security checks and was drinking himself into a stupor when Giant arrived to check on him just before midnight.

"It's not synthi-vodka, *tovarisch*, but it'll do in an emergency," Smirnoff slurred before holding the bottle out to Giant. "Would you like a taste?"

"Thanks." Giant accepted it but then tipped the remaining liquid out on the floor of the safe house. An acrid stench attacked his nostrils as the spillage sank into the floor covering. "What in the name of grud is that?"

"Metal polish, cut with a little lemon juice," Smirnoff replied. "Not my first choice, comrade, but you took that away too."

"Is there anything you won't drink? You'll go blind if you keep this up."

The East-Meg Two delegate shrugged. "Least I won't be alone."

"What do you mean by that?" Giant demanded.

Smirnoff hiccupped. "You'll see, my little black friend. You'll see." He tried to get up from the floor and failed miserably. "What time is it?"

"Twelve fifteen. Why?"

"Then it has already started. Soon he'll send for us."

"What's started? Who'll send for you? Ivan, you aren't making sense."

"I never do. It's part of my naïve charm."

Giant shook his head as he regarded the sprawled mess of the Russian on the floor. "How about I get you into bed so you can sleep this off? The Chief Judge will be expecting you at the next treaty session bright and early."

Smirnoff laughed hollowly. "There will be no more talk. You will see."

Before Giant could reply his helmet radio demanded attention.

"Control to all Judges. Do not, repeat, do not go outside or look at the lights in the sky overhead. If you have already seen these lights, stop whatever you are doing and report to the nearest Sector House or medical centre. All those already afflicted by blindness should remain where they are until further instructions are issued. The Chief Judge has announced a curfew for all citizens, effective from 1:00 am. Message repeats. Control to all Judges..."

Giant found the orders hard to understand. What lights overhead, what blindness? He almost went to the windows of the safe house to see what was going on before remembering the warning. Control would not have given such a directive without good reason. The Judge crouched beside Smirnoff and began slapping the semi-conscious delegate's face. "Ivan! Ivan, wake up! How did you know about this blindness?"

CALLAGHAN WAS MONITORING Dredd's condition when the first sightless Judge stumbled into the Grand Hall of Justice's medical bay. Farrow had been on patrol nearby when the lights began filling the sky. A few minutes later the young law enforcer realised he was bleeding from the eyes and immediately headed back to the Grand Hall. Farrow abandoned his Lawmaster by the front steps and stumbled into the building as his sight faded away. It had taken him another ten minutes to reach the medical bay, bumping into dozens of other stricken Judges along the way. "I don't know what the hell's happened," he said, blood dripping from both sides of his face. "One minute I could see fine, the next, nothing."

Callaghan examined Farrow's eyes. They were bloodshot and still weeping red, but there was no obvious sign of cause or contaminant. She gave him some drops to soothe the irritation and sent him to the nearby dormitories. "There's nothing else I can do for you right now. You may need an eye specialist or even bionic replacements if the condition is permanent."

"Bionic eyeballs?" Farrow asked uncertainly.

"Don't knock 'em till you've tried them," Callaghan replied. She jerked a thumb towards Dredd, then realised the pointlessness of her gesture. "Dredd over there had his eyeballs ripped out twenty years ago. After they fitted the bionics, he thought they were an improvement on the real thing – even said he should have had them fitted sooner!"

"Really?"

"Well, that's what I was told during training. Look, if your condition hasn't improved within a few hours I'll examine you again." Callaghan went out into the corridor and found an admin robot. "I need you to escort a Judge to the dormitories. He's been blinded and–"

The robot just waved her away. "Haven't you heard? Half the city's gone blind and most of the Judges with it!" The droid hurried away, muttering and shaking its head.

Callaghan realised she must have switched off her helmet radio to concentrate while treating Dredd earlier. She reactivated it and was hit by a blizzard of radio traffic, dozens of voices overlapping and shouting to be heard.

"Sweet Jovus, I can't see a–"

"Porter to Control, need medical assist. Vision went blurry and crashed my Lawmaster into shoppera window. Believe I may be bleeding–"

"It's madness out here! People screaming and crying, all the–"

"Can't face carrying on if I can't see. Have decided to–"

A gunshot punctuated the last message. It sounded to Callaghan like a Judge had committed suicide. What the drokk was happening outside?

One voice cut through the barrage, commanding the others to silence. "Control to all Judges! All unauthorised messages are to cease forthwith, in view of the current crisis. Keep this frequency open for emergencies only!"

Emergencies only? Callaghan wondered if anything wasn't an emergency in this city. She returned to the medical bay where Farrow was stumbling around, trying to find the exit. The Med-Judge led him to the door and put his hand against the left wall.

"Go straight ahead from here. You want the fourth door on the left, it will take you to the dormitories. You got that?"

Farrow nodded. "Sounds like one hell of a mess out there. I'm probably one of the lucky ones, made it back here alive. Well, see you on the..." His voice trailed away as the young

Judge realised what he was saying. He sighed and stumbled away, keeping one hand on the wall as a guide.

Callaghan went back inside the medical bay to find Dredd trying to sit up on the hover-stretcher. "Are you determined to kill yourself?" she demanded. "We only just saved your life, Dredd. Don't undo all my good work straight away! We're going to need every able-bodied Judge we can get, from what I hear."

"What do you mean? What's going on?"

"Some kind of sudden blindness seems to have afflicted large parts of the city. More than half our Street Judges have been affected," she explained.

"Where's my helmet?" Dredd demanded.

Callaghan retrieved it from a pile of possessions lying nearby. "Let me check your cranium first. We were forced to drill a hole into your skull to evacuate a blood clot on the brain." She moved to the end of the hover-stretcher and carefully peeled back one edge of the rapi-heal patch. This remarkable invention was capable of accelerating the body's natural healing ability by a factor of one hundred. Broken bones could be reset and harder than ever within a few hours instead of a few weeks.

Already the patch had knitted Dredd's skull back together across the hole left by the laser scalpel, and fresh skin was forming to cover it. Satisfied, the Med-Judge pushed the patch back into position and eased Dredd's helmet gently on to his head. "You'll be vulnerable there for days, until the skull has completely regenerated," she advised. "Tek-Judges repaired your radio mic while you were being treated."

Dredd touched a hand to the side of his helmet. "It's gone."

"The translucent disc?" Callaghan asked. "Tek-Division has that. They think it was some kind of relay device."

"Bludd's enforcer was using it to feed me instructions."

"That's why you attacked me, why you hijacked the med-wagon."

"I had no choice," Dredd replied. Wincing from the pain, he raised himself into a sitting position with Callaghan's aid and looked at the patchwork of rapi-heals covering much of his body. "I have to see the Chief Judge."

"You're lucky to be alive. At least give yourself a chance to heal properly."

"I haven't got time to heal. The city needs me."

AFTER TWENTY-SEVEN MINUTES the yellow and green lights over Mega-City One began to fade away, their dazzling display of movement and colour dissipating. But nobody still outside was disappointed to see the end of the pyrotechnics, because nobody outside could see anymore. The contents of the satellite had done their job. The Big Meg had become a kingdom of the blind.

CALLAGHAN SIGHED AS she helped Dredd zip up the upper half of his uniform. "I still say you should remain here, under observation, at least until morning."

"I need a new Lawgiver," the wounded lawman replied.

Callaghan retrieved her own weapon and deactivated the self-destruct mechanism built into its grip. "You can have mine, but now anyone can fire it. If you want a Lawgiver coded to only your heat signature, you'll have to see the quartermaster in the Armoury."

Dredd nodded as he took the weapon, slotting it into his boot holster. The Med-Judge remained in front of him, blocking the way out. "Have you listened to a word I've said?" Callaghan asked.

"I heard you. Now get out of my way."

She stepped aside so Dredd could leave. "Fine. See how far you get."

He rose to his feet, swayed for a few moments and then sank back down on to the hover-stretcher. "Grud dammit," Dredd hissed in frustration. He glared at Callaghan, who rapidly removed the amused expression from her face. "You'll have to help me."

"I can't leave the medical bay unmanned. What if there's an emergency?"

"It's already happened," Dredd replied. "Now, are you going to help me to the Chief Judge's office, or do I have to crawl there?"

Twelve

HERSHEY WAS SAT behind her desk, listening to news reports from the bank of Tri-D screens in her office. Light from dozens of different images illuminated the room with a chaos of colours, but the Chief Judge was facing away from the monitors. Like other victims of the blindness, her eyes stopped bleeding soon after the light storm above the city faded away, but her sight had not returned. A cursory examination by Med-Judges confirmed she was suffering the same symptoms as everyone else affected, but none of the medics could offer any answers about when or even if Mega-City One's Chief Judge would get her sight back.

"Auburn, are you still here?" Hershey asked, trying to keep panic from her voice. To go blind gradually was one thing, you could prepare yourself for that. But to suddenly have vision torn from you, that was a shock. Hershey had never been afraid of the dark as a child. Now she found herself surrounded by it and the sensation was chilling.

"Yes, ma'am," the auxiliary Judge replied. Balding and over fifty, Auburn had never cut it as a law enforcer on the streets. Transferred to the Justice Department's administrative section, he had discovered a talent for strategic planning and implementation that more than compensated for his other failings. Auburn's reforming zeal had streamlined the Department's systems and freed up valuable resources for upholding the Law.

"Well, make a bit more noise, for the love of grud. Then at least I'll know you're still in the room!"

"Yes, ma'am."

"Have you tabulated the numbers yet?" Hershey asked grumpily. She hated being blind, hated being so dependent upon others. The Chief Judge hadn't felt this out of her depth since that first day as a cadet. She could still recall bursting into tears as a five year-old when her mother left her with the Judge-Tutors at the Academy. Helpless and alone, that was how Hershey had felt then. Well, at least she wasn't alone this time.

"Pulling them together now. They'll be ready in time for the conference call," Auburn assured her.

"And how long until that?"

"A little over a minute, ma'am."

"Good." A knock at the office door startled Hershey. "Who's there?"

"Dredd."

The Chief Judge smiled despite herself. No, she wasn't alone anymore. Hershey swivelled her chair round to the desk and switched off the wall of Tri-D screens. "Come in and shut the door after you. I don't want to be disturbed for the next fifteen minutes." She listened intently to the sounds approaching her. There were two sets of footsteps: one heavy and shuffling, the other awkward and staggering slightly. "How do you feel?"

"I've been better," Dredd replied.

Hershey gestured to where the nearest chair should be. "Have a seat." Someone lowered into the chair, grunting in pain.

"I'll be getting back to the medical bay, ma'am," a woman's voice said.

"Can you stay, Med-Judge...?"

"Callaghan, ma'am. If you wish."

"I do. Your input may be of value."

"Yes, ma'am."

The Chief Judge smiled. Callaghan sounded nervous. Probably never been in this room before. "I understand your prompt actions outside the Grand Hall saved Dredd's life."

"Just doing my job, ma'am."

"Nevertheless, you Med-Judges will bear the brunt of our difficulties in the coming hours and days. I'm glad to have the chance of thanking you. I may be needing you–" Hershey was interrupted by Auburn clearing his throat.

"Excuse me, ma'am. The Council of Five is ready for your call."

"Put them on audio only," she responded. No need for the other council members to see their leader blind and helpless. There was a click and the five council members announced their presence online. Hershey summarised what had happened since midnight. "I've asked Auburn to join this meeting. He has compiled statistics for the status of each division that will be useful in determining the way forward. Auburn?"

"Thank you, ma'am. The blindness has afflicted different departments to varying degrees. Med-Division has about half its Judges affected. They were either out in the open on duty when the lights first appeared in the sky or else responded to medical emergency calls before the danger was realised. Tek-Division got off lightly, only one in eight affected. Psi-Division's Judges were still recovering from the sudden shock of what happened at Joe Chill, so most escaped the blindness – only one in five are blind. These ratios are all rough estimates, I must stress. We won't know exact numbers for some days."

"What about Street Judges?" Hollister asked. "I caught a dose of whatever this stomm is, but how many others are out of action?"

"Nearly eighty per cent have been blinded. Only one in five Street Judges can still see. Most of them were asleep in dormitories or on sleep machines when this began. But they are trapped indoors until the all-clear is given. As of this moment the only Judges out on patrol are those with bionic eyes as they were not hurt by the light storm. Instead of more than ten thousand Judges on the streets, we currently have only a few hundred."

"Sweet Jovus," a voice whispered. Hershey recognised it as Buell, head of the SJS. "It must be anarchy out there!"

"Of a sort," Niles agreed. "Fortunately the PSU's cameras were not affected, so we've been keeping a close watch on the skedways and pedways. There's no looting or rioting yet as potential perps have seen what happened to anyone who went out in the light storm. But there are tens of thousands of blind citizens wandering the streets, lost and panicking, not knowing what's happened to them. Fires are raging out of control in dozens of sectors where hoverpods collided with buildings. Three stratbats crashed within the city after the pilots went blind. Robotic emergency services have been sent to deal with the aftermath of those incidents, but they can't cope for long."

"We need to get back out on the streets," Hershey said. "Suggestions?"

"Bring offworld Judges back," Buell urged.

"Already set in motion," Auburn replied. "Most are days away from Earth."

"Mobilise cadets from the Academy along with all their Judge-Tutors," Hollister said. "We'll lose some but most will gain from the experience."

"Feasible but risky," Hershey conceded. "That might solve our short-term problem but putting the next generation of law enforcers in harm's way too soon could cripple the Department for decades. What else?"

"All auxiliary Judges can be put on patrol along with specialists from the various divisions. That would significantly swell our numbers." The suggestion came from Ramos, the other Street Judge representative on the council. "They're more experienced than the cadets, too."

"Blind Judges could be fitted with bionic replacements," Tek-Division head McTighe said. "We will need to institute a massive programme of surgery."

"I have a Med-Judge with me," Hershey announced. "Callaghan, what's the feasibility of that last suggestion?"

"It won't work – at least, not in the short-term," she replied.

"Why not?" McTighe demanded. Hershey could sense his umbrage at having the idea dismissed so summarily. Pompous ass, she thought.

"The operation takes six hours, with another eighteen for recovery. You need another six days for the subject to get used to their new eyes. That's a week before any of the subjects would be of any use. Plus the Department does not have an unlimited supply of bionic eyes and the replacement optical devices are expensive. Not to mention many of the surgeons skilled in fitting them have probably been blinded since midnight. To get ten thousand blind Street Judges back on patrol could take months or even years. It's a long-term solution, at best."

"Any other suggestions?" Hershey asked. "Comments?"

"Until the streets are safe, few of those suggestions do you any good," Dredd said sourly. "There's no point sending cadets, auxiliaries or anyone else outside until you know they won't be blinded too."

"Then what do you suggest?" McTighe asked huffily.

"Reactivate the Mechanismo programme," Dredd replied. "I'm no great supporter of using Robo-Judges to dispense justice, but in this situation it's the only feasible solution for the short-term."

Hershey was amused by Dredd's power of understatement. He had been utterly opposed to the plans of a previous Chief Judge to introduce mechanical lawmen to the Big Meg, even falsifying evidence to get the Mechanismo programme shut down. Dredd was sentenced to twenty years on Titan for his crime but that was commuted after flaws in the Robo-Judge technology were revealed. Hershey had revived the programme since becoming Chief Judge, but most of the units were used offworld on Department spaceships. A few hundred remained in storage on Earth, deactivated.

"Dredd's right," Hershey said. "You should have thought of that, McTighe. The Mechanismo programme falls under the jurisdiction of Tek-Division. Get those robots active and out on the streets now. That's an order!"

"Yes, ma'am!" McTighe replied, going offline to do her bidding.

"Chief Judge, I may have our first piece of good news tonight," Niles said. "My analysts report looting has just begun in Southside Sector 41."

"They're never slow to start trouble there," Hershey noted dryly. "And how is this good news?"

"The looters are going outside but not going blind, and none of them appears to have bionic eyes or any other optical protection we can see."

"So the blinding seems to have stopped with the light storm," the Chief Judge deduced. "Hollister and Ramos, mobilise the sighted Street Judges and get them out on patrol. Buell, your duties as head of the SJS will be temporarily suspended. I'm putting you in charge of drafting the auxiliaries and cadets on to the streets. We can count ourselves lucky the majority of citizens are asleep and unaware of any of this, but that won't last long come sunrise. The curfew officially starts in a few minutes and it's your job to help enforce that."

"Yes, ma'am!" Buell responded before he and the others disconnected.

"Niles, you still with us?" Hershey asked.

"Yes, ma'am," the head of PSU replied.

"You never reported how badly your division was affected."

"We escaped the worst of it. That's what comes of never going outside."

"I was sorry to hear about *Justice Seven*."

"Thank you, ma'am. *Justice Four* is returning from a visit to Hestia. Might I suggest you have it act as replacement until a new orbital platform is ready?"

"Good idea," the Chief Judge said. "It's a Rumsfeld class spaceship?"

"Yes, ma'am. Heavily armed and armoured, just itching for a fight."

"Excellent. If we ever locate Bludd's orbital headquarters then *Justice Four* can blow the drokker out of the sky. More than a thousand people died in those stratbat crashes, not forgetting the thirty-three thousand who were inside Joe Chill. Bludd must be made to pay for his crimes when this is done."

"Yes, ma'am. I'll pass on your orders to *Justice Four*. Niles out."

Hershey sank back into her chair. "Med-Judge Callaghan, you can return to your station now."

"Yes, ma'am."

"Auburn, can I ask you to leave too? I wish to speak with Dredd privately."

"Of course, ma'am."

Hershey waited until both Judges had departed before speaking again. "What do you think?"

"You've made a good first response to the problem, but this is tackling the symptoms, not the cause. We still don't know why Bludd has done all of this or why he's done it now."

"Why try to blackmail the city if he always intended to unleash a plague of blindness upon it?" Hershey said with a sigh. "Too many questions, not enough answers. Now, we've potentially a much greater threat to this city than Bludd. Unless a cure can be found for the blindness, the Big Meg is going to wake up in the morning with half its citizens permanently disabled. How are we supposed to cope with that?"

"In the kingdom of the blind..."

"The one-eyed man is king," Hershey said. "But what was Bludd driving at?"

"He was teasing us, taunting us with hints of what was to come. Bludd kept saying we were fighting a losing battle against crime, that the city was only ever one step from descending into anarchy. Now he's taken that step."

Hershey found herself nodding. "We've been reacting instead of acting. We need to take the initiative, seize control of whatever game Bludd is playing."

They were interrupted by Hershey's comms line. "Control to Chief Judge, urgent message for you."

"I told you, emergencies only Control!"

"It's from Judge Giant. It's about the extradition treaty delegates…"

"Grud," Hershey said. Amidst all of the chaos of the past few hours, she had pushed the five foreign visitors to the back of her mind. "If any of them were out in the light storm and got blinded, we'll never hear the end of it!"

"And Jesus Bludd," Control concluded.

GIANT HAD REGAINED his senses with a splitting headache, blood down the front of his uniform and broken glasseen on the floor by his face. The stench of cheap perfume hung in the air like a lynching victim, dead and repulsive. The last thing he could remember was helping Smirnoff into the bedroom of the safe house. The East-Meg Two delegate had been slurring his words, but the secrets revealed were all too clear.

"This Jesus Bludd, I have never met him, but he calls me at treaty talks, during one of the breaks between sessions. He offers the people of East-Meg a deal," Smirnoff had said, placing one foot in front of the other with all the exaggerated care of a drunken man.

"What kind of a deal?"

"He calls it protection. I call it extortion, *tovarisch*. We have seen his like before in my state; gangsters and nogoodniks, always greedy, always wanting more from you. Blackmailers, they are all the same."

Giant had eased Smirnoff on to the bed and stood over him, trying not to lose patience with the Sov's elliptical style of speaking. "What kind of a deal?"

"This Bludd, he says he will protect us, keep us safe from ancient weapons that still circle the globe. All he asks is the chance to meet with us and discuss his terms. I was sceptical, at first, until I speak with Chang and the others. They, too, have been contacted by this man. All have the same doubts and worries as I, but we put aside our differences to agree on one thing. No matter what happens, we shall – oh, dear!" Smirnoff clasped a hand to his face, blushing with embarrassment. "I was forgetting our agreement."

"You're not making sense," Giant said. "What agreement? What deal?"

The man from East-Meg Two had patted the bed beside him. "Sit, sit!"

"Ivan, what's going on?"

Smirnoff kept patting the bed. "Sit and I will tell you everything. I will – how do you say – spill my guts, yes?"

Against his better judgement, Giant had sat beside the Russian and listened to what followed. It was only when Giant tried to call Control that Smirnoff's face hardened. "I'm sorry, *tovarisch*, but I can't allow you to tell anyone else about this yet. My new found comrades would be most upset."

Then all was darkness until Giant regained his senses, surrounded by the fragments of a broken perfume bottle. Fortunately, his helmet radio was still working. Giant called Control while searching the safe house for Smirnoff. The East-Meg Two delegate was gone, along with all his possessions. "Control, put me through to the Chief Judge. Believe me, she'll want to hear this."

HERSHEY TOOK THE call from Giant. "What's all this about the visiting delegates?"

"During breaks in yesterday's negotiation sessions at the Grand Hall, Bludd individually contacted each of the representatives. I guess he must have hacked the secure comms lines in their private offices," Giant said.

"When this is over we need to seriously review our security protocols," the Chief Judge observed. "What did our friend Jesus say to the delegates?"

"That he had taken possession of a command and control system for all the US orbital weapons satellites from the late twentieth century still in the sky. He was willing to offer their cities protection from these weapons, at a price."

"The same scam he tried to pull on us," Dredd grimaced.

"What else?" Hershey asked.

"Smirnoff and the others hadn't heard of Bludd and didn't believe him," Giant replied, "until the destruction of Joe Chill Block. Bludd gave them advance warning about what would happen to the building and suggested they watch local news channels to see he wasn't bluffing. Afterwards Bludd contacted all the delegates again, just before he left the city, I guess. He warned them not to go outside at midnight or look out of any windows when the light storm began."

"So everything that Bludd has done today, it's been a demonstration of power, nothing more," Dredd said. "Mega-City One has been blinded and tens of thousands murdered so Bludd can launch a global extortion scheme."

"That's what it sounds like," Giant agreed.

"There's another possibility," Hershey said. "He could offer his newly acquired arsenal of orbiting weapons to the highest bidder, so they can unleash them against their enemies."

"Either way, Bludd just stepped up from being a significant crime boss in the Big Meg to a global terrorist," Dredd snarled. "No one can doubt he is willing or capable of carrying out his threats. He must be stopped at any cost and by any means necessary!"

"You're right," Hershey agreed. "This isn't a citywide problem anymore. It's about the future of everyone on the planet. Dredd, you have to find Bludd and stop him. I am authorising the use of lethal force. Do whatever it takes."

"Yes, ma'am," he replied.

"There was something else," Giant interjected. "All the delegates have disappeared from their respective safe houses. Before knocking me out, Smirnoff hinted Bludd wanted a face-to-face meeting with them. If they haven't already left the city, the delegates could be your lead to finding Bludd."

"Very good, Giant," Hershey said. "That will be all." She deactivated the comms line. "Can you find the delegates, Dredd?"

"That should be simple," he replied. "When they came through Customs yesterday I planted homing devices on several of the visitors so we could keep track of them in case of emergency. Most were found and destroyed within hours but one is still active – Brit-Cit representative Warner."

"Why didn't he locate the homing device like the others?"

"It was inserted during a cavity search. Warner's close encounter with that pleasure mech probably pushed it even further up inside him."

Hershey smiled. "Maybe he was hoping the pleasure mech might dislodge it?"

"I'll be on my way." Dredd stood slowly, unable to disguise the pain from his injuries.

"Are you sure you're up to this?" Hershey asked.

"I'll survive, unlike Bludd."

"Before you go, there's something you should know about a secret weapon you can use against him. We've been keeping this in reserve, to be activated as a last resort. It will only work face-to-face. Once that happens, it cannot be reused again. You only get one chance, Dredd."

"I understand," he said. "What is it?"

After Hershey told Dredd, he nodded. "I can't wait to see the look on that punk's face when it happens. He won't know what hit him."

Once Dredd was gone, the Chief Judge called Control. "Relay this message to all helmets in the city. Dredd is on a mission of vital importance. He is to be given every assistance by all Judges, without exception. Hershey out!"

DREDD'S FIRST CALL was to the PSU. "I need a current location on Judge Jago Warner from Brit-Cit," he said while waiting for a turbolift. "You should find a homing signal on frequency 212.7 kHz."

"That's a roj. Checking now," PSU replied. "He's on the move, approaching Mega-City One Spaceport. Will cross-reference it with our spy-in-the-sky cameras, see if we can get a fix on the vehicle he's in. PSU out."

Dredd stepped into the turbolift and sent it hurtling to the Grand Hall's motorpool and garage. When he emerged there was a Lawmaster already fuelled and waiting for him. A Tek-Judge was by the motorcycle, loading extra ammunition into the panniers. "Dredd, I heard your own bike was still buried under rubble near Joe Chill. Take this one. It's been turbo-charged and should give you an extra fifty an hour in speed."

Dredd nodded his thanks and climbed onto the Lawmaster. As he roared out of the garage PSU called again. "Looks like Warner's in a hoverpod with four other occupants, judging by the heat signatures. They are just arriving at the spaceport."

"The rest of the delegates," Dredd deduced. "Any scheduled flights due out in the next hour?"

"Checking for you... No. One private charter, craft registered to Red Inc. Do you want it grounded?"

"Not yet. If I can reach the spaceport in time, I want to be on the shuttle with the delegates. They can lead me straight to Jesus Bludd." Another voice broke into the conversation.

"Dredd, this is Niles. I'm coordinating with Control, clearing a corridor between you and the spaceport. Judges on patrol are being ordered to get any blind citizens still wandering the streets out of your way. If you hurry, you might still make it to the spaceport before those shuttles leave."

"That's a roj. I'm en route now. Dredd out!"

BRUCE WAS BORED and nervous, two things he disliked intensely. Yesterday's treaty negotiations had been tedious beyond belief, an arid wasteland of serious-minded talk and discussion. Strewth, it was enough to drive a bloke to drinking! But the monumental hangover from his escapade with Smirnoff had dissuaded the Oz delegate from revisiting the bottle.

Then came the mysterious call on his secure comms line urging him to watch *Mega-City News* and the warning about what was to happen at midnight. It had all sounded a mite far-fetched to Bruce. Indeed, he had only stumbled upon the news channel while searching for a little adult entertainment on the Tri-D set in his private quarters. It was only natural; he was away from home, looking to relieve a little tension. Any bloke's mind would start to wander south of the old waistline. But triple-breasted mutants munce wrestling was not Bruce's idea of erotic thrills, so he kept flipping through the channels until he saw what was left of Joe Chill Block. That got his attention.

Crikey, Bruce thought to himself, that Bludd fella hadn't been joking. A whole city block, flattened like somebody had dropped Uluru on it. No survivors, the reporters were saying. Gas explosion got the blame, but Bruce knew the truth. Bludd by name, blood by nature. That was when the Oz delegate got nervous. This trip to the big smoke had been walkabout on the wild side up until then. Suddenly it was getting a bit serious. Bruce had closed all the curtains, locked the doors and waited for midnight. He had heard the delight of those outside watching the lights in the sky turn to fear and anguish as they went blind.

Then came the knock at the door. The hoverpod was outside, waiting to take him and the other delegates to see Bludd. Bruce had clambered in, looking round at the faces of Chang, Warner, Belgrano and Smirnoff. Ivan stank of cheap perfume, so got a corner to himself. Belgrano and Warner were ashen-faced during the journey, while Chang observed everything they passed with clinical detachment. Finally, Bruce had snapped and asked her what was so bloody interesting outside.

"I am observing the effectiveness of these weapons. Should Sino-Cit agree to meet our host's terms, such information will prove most beneficial."

"Well, whatever you say, Ms Chang."

"Representative Chang. Please call me by my correct title," she said blandly without turning her head.

"Yeah, yeah."

They had reached the spaceport without incident and were now waiting in a first class lounge until their shuttlecraft was ready for boarding. Nobody was talking, everyone apparently deep in thought. After all he'd seen and heard in the past few hours, the Oz Judge was in no rush to meet this Bludd bloke. But hanging around waiting was even worse because it only amplified his boredom and fear. Finally, he stood, unable to take the silence any more. Everyone looked at him. Bruce smiled and shrugged.

"Just gonna…" He spotted the toilets across the room. "Just gonna let the weasel see the porcelain, alright?"

The others turned away or regarded him with disdain, except Chang. "Excuse me please. What does that mean?"

Bruce looked at his crotch, then at the Sino-Cit woman's inquiring face. "Tell you what, why don't you ask Ivan? I'll be right back." Bruce hurried towards the toilets, happy to have avoided explaining his vernacular vulgarity. He entered the male restroom and began relieving himself at a urinal.

"Going somewhere?" a deep, gravelly voice asked.

"Flamin' Nora!" Bruce shouted in surprise, fleetingly forgetting what he was doing. Dredd was standing inside one of the cubicles, tapping a daystick against the palm of his left hand. By the time Bruce recovered his wits there was a fine spray of urine down the legs of his uniform. "Now look what you made me do, you bloody Gallah!"

"You didn't answer my question. Where are you going?"

Bruce finished his business at the urinal and hastily zipped himself back up before moving to the sinks. "A little outing for all the delegates. Didn't your Chief Judge tell you? Something to keep us all occupied." He wiped clean the legs of his uniform before washing his hands vigorously.

"Try again," Dredd replied. "Where are you going?"

"I told you. A little outing, that's all." Bruce dried his hands before facing Dredd. "Now, if you've got a problem with that, I suggest you take it up with Hershey. In the meantime, get out of my way or else I'll have to–"

Bruce saw a blur of movement out the corner of his eye, felt an intense pain at the back of his head and then all was darkness. A few words fell after him as he plunged into unconsciousness.

"Bruce! Are you in there? It's time to leave!"

ALL THE OTHER delegates were already clambering into the shuttle when the last representative hurried from the restroom, still adjusting his uniform. "Sorry I'm late," he said gruffly after boarding the spacecraft. The latecomer took a seat at the front of the shuttle where none of the other passengers could see his face. "Got bogged down with the, err, paperwork. You know how it is, mate."

Chang was not impressed. "Please, be silent. We have all heard quite enough about your weasel and its problems. Representative Smirnoff has explained the situation."

Once they were all seated, a droid sealed the external door and the shuttle began rolling towards its launch pad. A Tri-D screen at the front of the cabin came alive, revealing two faces. Bludd was at the centre of the image, smiling at his guests. Behind him and to one side Kara could be seen concentrating on another task, jet black hair shining beneath overhead lights.

"Welcome to my private transportation, lady and gentlemen. I will be your host for the short trip to my new orbital headquarters. For security reasons the crew cannot divulge your exact destination. But the journey should take less than two hours and G-forces will not exceed four gees. So sit back and enjoy the hospitality on offer. Loyal customers of the Bludd Group are amply rewarded for their support. Once we become business partners, I will let you sample a few of those rewards too. Good morning to you all."

The screen blinked off again and the shuttle flung itself into the sky.

JUDGE BRUCE REGAINED his senses while slumped over a toilet bowl, not an unfamiliar situation. His head was pounding, he stank of urine and had lost all his uniform except for the lucky pair of u-fronts he always wore while away from Oz. Then he remembered the close encounter with Dredd. The Big Meg bully had caught him cold and stripped his clothes, but why? Bruce got to his feet and staggered out of the cubicle to find a Mega-City One Judge's uniform carefully hung from a hook by the mirrors.

"The bloody cheek – he's nicked my flamin' identity!" Bruce realised. "I'll murder the drokker when I get my hands on him!"

AT PSU HEADQUARTERS Niles watched the shuttle leave Mega-City One airspace. Soon after it reached the outer limits of the atmosphere the craft disappeared from the PSU's screens. "Switch to the frequency Dredd gave us earlier. Even if Bludd's got some sort of stealth technology masking his shuttle, we can still follow the bug inside Warner."

Judge Sharp was back on duty, having been called in from a day off to cover for those affected by the light storm. She located the homing device's signal and displayed its location on her Tri-D monitor. "Looks like the shuttle is headed over the North Pole. Plotting course projections in case we lose the signal."

"Transmit them to *Justice Four*," Niles said. "If Dredd can't stop Bludd, Taschen and her crew will have to finish the job."

ONCE THE SHUTTLE'S trajectory had levelled out, Bludd reappeared on the Tri-D screen. "I'm sorry to say one of you is not abiding by my preconditions. Onboard scanners indicate there may be an impostor among you. I did ask for the surrender of all weapons and electronic devices. Please remain in your seats, my robot crew will find and deal with the culprit."

Dredd reached towards the Lawgiver holstered in his boot, but before he could draw it a robot was already standing over him. The droid was holding a powerful laser close to Dredd's face, electricity crackling about its end. "Surrender your weapon now or there will be... trouble."

Thirteen

DREDD PULLED THE Lawgiver from his boot and aimed it at the robot. "What if I shoot? The bullet will puncture the hull of this shuttle, causing a massive decompression. Everybody on board would die within seconds."

"Humans die. We are droids; we would simply become inactive. Commit suicide if you wish but your death remains inevitable unless you surrender the weapon – now."

"No worries, mate," Dredd replied, attempting an Oz accent. "Strewth, I just wanted to check you blokes were up to the job. Don't get your tin knickers in a twist, cobber."

The robot ran a scanner over Dredd's body, but found no other weapons. "Very well. This infraction of Mr Bludd's preconditions will be noted, but you shall be permitted to continue on this journey."

"And if I wasn't?"

"This shuttle has its own airlock. All those who displease Mr Bludd are asked to step outside." The droid gestured to one of the shuttle's windows. Part of a corpse was floating past outside, the face frozen in a screaming rictus of fear. Other body parts were visible, all preserved by the vacuum of space. "This vessel had a human crew until a few weeks ago. Mr Bludd discovered they had a Justice Department informant among their number so he dispensed with their services permanently."

"Crikey, guess it doesn't do to cross Mr Bludd," Dredd said.

The droid moved on to the other passengers. "There is still one among you hiding something. Admit your guilt and death shall be quick."

The four remaining passengers looked at each other, all wondering who the impostor could be. None volunteered a confession. The robot tired of waiting and began scanning each of the delegates. Chang and Belgrano were adjudged innocent but the scanner gave an electronic squeal as it passed over the body of Jago Warner. The Brit-Cit Judge protested his innocence but two more droids were already moving towards him.

"Please, there's been a terrible mistake. I would never do anything to breach Mr Bludd's rules. The Mega-City One Judges, they tried to blackmail and coerce me into helping force through that treaty, but I resisted their threats!"

By now Warner was being dragged along the centre aisle of the shuttle to a separate compartment at the rear. Once inside, a curtain was pulled shut, blocking the others from seeing what was happening. But the noises escaping from the compartment made it all too clear.

"Please, no, you've got to believe me. I would never–" Warner's words were overwhelmed by the sound of tearing leathereen. The Brit-Cit Judge yelped in embarrassment and terror as his uniform was ripped from him for the second time since arriving in the Big Meg. "Oh grud no, not that not again!"

"Bend over!" a robotic voice commanded.

"Please, don't do this. Don't put that... Ar-rrggghhhhh!" Warner's voice was replaced by a scream of pain. After several more anguished cries there was a whirring noise and a wet plop. The scanning device was briefly reactivated, repeating its electronic squeal.

Warner could be heard pleading for his life in a pathetic whimper. "You must believe me, I don't know how that got up there. I would never... It must have been Dredd or his Med-Judges! I was given a full cavity search when I arrived in Mega-City One. They must have implanted that device then. I'm innocent, don't you see? Completely innocent! Please, grud, believe me..."

The curtain was pulled brusquely aside, allowing the lead droid to re-enter the main cabin. The other delegates got a glimpse of Warner, naked and tear-stained, before the curtain was drawn again. The lead droid was clutching a tiny metallic sphere. It marched to the front of the cabin and stood before the Tri-D screen, activating the link to Bludd. "We discovered this tracking device secreted inside the Brit-Cit delegate's body."

"Destroy it, now!" the crime boss commanded.

The robot snapped its fingers together, crushing the sphere between them. "The delegate claimed no knowledge of the device's presence. He suggested it had been implanted by the Justice Department."

"More than likely, but he should have detected it himself and had the device removed before boarding the shuttle. You know what to do."

"Of course," the droid replied. A scream of pure terror filled the cabin before being abruptly cut off. The droid punched a button beneath the Tri-D screen. "Opening airlock now." The shuttle swerved sideways momentarily before resuming its journey. "Airlock is empty. Closing doors."

Smirnoff was peering out the window by his seat, looking backwards. "Warner's out there, I can see him! He's still alive, he's still..." The East-Meg Two delegate turned away from the window hurriedly, his face filled with dismay and disgust. "Bulgarin's ghost! That's no way to die..."

The droid stepped aside to let Bludd address the four remaining passengers. "An unfortunate incident but necessary to ensure our safety and security. We don't want the Justice Department gate-crashing our meeting. For now, sit back and enjoy the rest of the flight. I will see you all soon. Bludd out."

"STOMM!" SHARP CURSED. "We've lost it!" She had been monitoring the progress of Bludd's shuttle via the tracking device hidden inside Warner. As the tiny sphere was destroyed, the last method of tracking the spacecraft was lost.

"How long had they been in the air?" Niles asked.

"More than an hour. If Bludd's HQ is in a standard orbital, the shuttle can't be more than a few minutes from its destination."

"Transmit the final trajectory extrapolations to *Justice Four*. If anybody can find Bludd, it's Shona Taschen."

THE COMMANDER OF *Justice Four* was smiling at last. The round trip to Hestia had taken months instead of weeks, thanks to a fault in the propulsion drive. The emergency recall signal had hastened their return journey until fresh orders arrived only an hour later. *Justice Four* was to replace *Justice Seven* as Mega-City One's orbital platform, becoming a conduit for Control messages and PSU surveillance systems. "A glorified relay station!" Commander Taschen fumed after reading Hershey's request. "Grud on a greenie. Why don't they ask us to organise duty rosters while we're up here!"

"It's just temporary," Judge Tyler had said, trying to placate her. He was Taschen's deputy and rightly terrified of her fiery moods. "Until they can get another orbital platform into position."

"There is nothing so permanent as a temporary position!" Taschen snarled back.

It was only after she received permission to go after Bludd that a smile appeared on her face. "Have you got the final course projections from PSU plotted in yet?" she demanded, impatiently drumming her fingers against the arms of her chair on the command deck.

Tyler nodded hurriedly. "They're coming up on the main screen... now."

Taschen leaned forward to see the results appear on the Tri-D screen that dominated the command deck's far wall. A red line marked the path followed by the tracking device that was inserted into Judge Jago Warner. From where the red line terminated three dotted yellow lines continued onwards, indicating the most likely paths taken by Bludd's shuttle. All of this was overlaid on a celestial map of known satellites and other material orbiting the Earth.

"We know Bludd's HQ and shuttle have stealth protection, so our systems can't directly detect either of them," Taschen said, thinking out loud. "The shuttle is too small to be obvious by other means, but perhaps we can find the orbital HQ from what isn't visible..."

"I'm not sure I understand, ma'am," Tyler said.

The commander pointed at the middle path from the three dotted yellow lines. "None of the projected shuttle trajectories go near a known satellite. However, the central extrapolation does pass through a patch of empty space." Her finger indicated a blank section of blackness where no stars were visible. "Our sensors can't see Bludd's HQ, but they can't see past it either. The computers think literally, not laterally. They can't escape their programming."

"So where they see nothing–"

"Should be where Bludd is hiding his HQ," Taschen concluded. "Begin a search pattern, starting from where the tracking device was destroyed. Let the drokker think he's fooled us, but keep a fix on that patch of empty space. If Dredd can't stop Bludd, we'll have to blow both of them out of the sky."

ONLY AFTER THE shuttle had docked with the crime boss's satellite did the orbital HQ become visible to Dredd and the delegates. It was shaped liked a hoop, with support struts radiating outwards from a central hub. The droid crew opened the hatch to reveal Kara standing outside in the docking bay, her body encased in revealing strips of shiny black rubbereen. "Welcome to Mr Bludd's new home. If you'd all like to follow me, I will introduce each of you to him personally." She stood aside so the four passengers could alight, then led them round the outer hoop to one of the support struts. Dredd stayed at the back of the group, keeping his face hidden from Kara's view and his thoughts a blank. A turbolift transported the quintet to the centre of the satellite.

"A most remarkable structure," Chang observed. "How was your master able to keep its construction and location a secret from the Judges?"

"Mr Bludd is most resourceful," Kara replied with a smile. "Once you have become a loyal customer of his organisation, I'm sure he will be more than happy to share such secrets with you and your city."

"But at what cost?" Belgrano asked. "Ciudad Barranquilla is not rich like other mega-cities..."

"Perhaps not in conventional terms, but your Department controls a majority of the world's sugar and coffee supplies, along with many other illegal stimulants. Mr Bludd would be more than willing to make an equitable trade," Kara replied.

She was interrupted by the turbolift arriving at the central hub. Kara emerged first and led the others into a vast circular chamber, luxuriously furnished. She waved a hand at the many sofas and chairs gathered in a ring. In the centre of the circle was a low table laden with bowls of coloured candies and bottles of clear liquid. "Please, make yourselves comfortable. Feel free to sample the Umpty Candy or vintage vodka – nothing synthetic here. If anyone is in need of a boost, the black pills are pure Adifax, guaranteed to add a month to your natural lifespan. Mr Bludd will be with you shortly." Kara smiled and withdrew from the chamber, the door sealing shut and locking behind her.

Belgrano hurried to the table and began popping pills while stuffing his pockets with Umpty Candy. Smirnoff tore the stopper from one of the bottles and sniffed the contents. "This must be fifty proof, comrades! Will anyone join me in toasting our host?"

Dredd shook his head while Chang also demurred. "We are keeping a clear head for the negotiations," she replied stiffly. "Before then we have another problem to resolve – what to do with this impostor." Chang pointed a finger accusingly at Dredd. "This is not Judge Bruce. We noticed him after boarding the shuttle. We must denounce him, otherwise all our lives may be forfeit."

"Dredd!" Belgrano hissed. "What are you doing here?"

"Bringing Bludd to justice. Get in my way and you'll die too."

Smirnoff sank back into one of the plush sofas, clutching his vodka bottle. "Snekov's beard! Is there no escape from you, Dredd?"

"Apparently not," another voice replied. Bludd was standing behind Dredd in an open doorway, clad in his usual smart garb and flanked by Kara. "It seems I will have to replace the robotic shuttle crew yet again. Droids are useful but so tiresomely literal in following orders. No imagination, you see. My beloved Kara here has no such difficulties. She can be quite inventive in the bedroom, but it's inflicting pain where her true talents lie."

"I detected your presence the moment the shuttle door opened," Kara told Dredd. "Your attempt at subterfuge was doomed to failure." She produced the confiscated Lawgiver. "As was your feeble attempt to smuggle a weapon on board."

"So shoot me," Dredd replied, "and spare me the gloating."

"Each Lawgiver will fire only for its designated Judge, as you well know," Bludd said. "Should anyone else try to use the weapon, it self-destructs. Besides, why hurry?

I want to savour your death, Dredd. It's not every day I get to kill a living legend, and a little gloating is so very satisfying." Bludd gestured for Dredd and those still standing to sit down. "First we have to conclude the negotiations. Business before pleasure, as it were."

Once all Bludd's guests were seated, he began walking around the room, slowly circling the chairs and sofas. "You have all witnessed the power I now wield. At the touch of a button I was able to reduce an entire city block to rubble within seconds. Imagine having such power at your command! Imagine what it could do to the cities of your enemies."

"The satellite from where that weapon was fired has been destroyed," Dredd interjected. "You shouldn't make promises you can't keep."

"Since Mega-City One has chosen not to partake of the Bludd Group's generous offer of protection from such incidents, I must request you remain silent," Bludd warned. "Otherwise Kara will strike you dumb for life."

Dredd folded his arms, a sour expression set on his mouth.

"That's better," the crime boss said. "As our unwanted guest has noted, that particular weapon is no longer available. But be assured that I have direct control over more than three dozen other weapons. One of those was the chemical and ultraviolet radiation weapon that blinded much of the Big Meg after midnight. Normally the effects of such weapons are permanent, if properly dispersed. Alas, Justice Department meddling limited the scope and scale of the weapon. I believe all those affected should recover within a week but the plague of temporary blindness is creating a chaos unseen since the days of Block Mania and the Apocalypse War." Bludd paused behind Smirnoff. "I imagine you must have especially appreciated that, comrade?"

The Sov delegate nodded. "Just like the good old days, *tovarisch*."

"Those two weapons were among the least powerful in my recently acquired arsenal," the crime boss said, continuing his stroll around the chamber. "I could destroy all the surviving mega-cities ten times over should I wish to, but why would I? Far better to offer you the Bludd Group's protection against such unnatural disasters."

"This is extortion backed by the threat of terrorism," Chang said. "Why should we agree to your terms?"

"You may bow out of the bidding if you wish, but the consequences for Sino-Cit could be cataclysmic. Suppose East-Meg Two decided to expand its sphere of influence and wanted some of the valuable resources your citi-state so jealously guards? Judge Smirnoff need only place one call to the Bludd Group and your people could be decimated within minutes, your land ripe for the plucking, your glorious history and culture but a memory." Bludd stopped walking. "Let me be plain. Sino-Cit, East-Meg Two and Ciudad Barranquilla are being offered a unique opportunity. Align with my organisation and you will hold the balance of power for decades to come, no longer living in the shadow of super-states like the Big Meg. If you refuse, I will make the same offer to others. I do not doubt I will find sufficient takers to satisfy my greed."

Chang said nothing in reply, her face a mask of concentration. Belgrano was nervous and sweating profusely, while Smirnoff just took another swig of vodka. Dredd glared at the trio. "Give in to Bludd now and he'll suck you dry. Blackmailers are never sated and greed can never be satisfied."

Bludd tutted to himself. "Kara, ensure Dredd does not speak again until I allow it." The psyker approached the lawman who rose from his seat, tensed for her attack. But she stopped short, holding up an open hand before her. All of a sudden Dredd felt a mental tightening that left him virtually stunned. It was like a metal vice had clamped around the area of his brain that controlled his vocal cords. He couldn't form a single sound, not even a muffled "mmmmm".

"That's better," Bludd smirked. "Disturb me again and I'll have Kara finish you."

The crime boss pointed at the door through which he had entered. "If my three invited guests would go into the next room, they will each find a secure, scrambled comms link to their respective leaders. Consult with your masters and decide how much you are willing to pay for my services. Let's say the minimum offer must be at least one hundred billion credits."

That brought a gasp of shock and dismay from the trio. "But that's impossible!" Belgrano protested.

"You go too far!" Chang shouted.

"We cannot afford such sums," Smirnoff added.

Bludd silenced them with a gesture. "You will find a way, I am sure. The lowest bidder will be made to suffer as the Big Meg now does, to prove I am a man of my word. The other two bidders shall become valued clients of the Bludd Group and reap all the benefits that entails. Now, off you go."

The three delegates stumbled from the room, muttering between themselves as the door sealed behind them. Bludd joined Kara in front of Dredd. "I think you can let the good Judge have back the use of his tongue."

Kara waved dismissively at Dredd and his vocal cords were set free. "Jesus Bludd, you're under arrest!" were the first words he spoke.

The crime boss smiled and then began to giggle, his laughter becoming louder and louder. It took him most of a minute to recover, one hand resting on Kara's shoulder for support. Bludd wiped tears of hilarity from the corner of each eye. "I never knew you were a comedian as well as a lawman."

"I'm deadly serious," Dredd maintained.

"I don't think so. This satellite is somewhat beyond your jurisdiction so you can't legally arrest me. Even my guests have full diplomatic immunity in Mega-City One, granted by your own Chief Judge I believe."

"Immunity is only proof against prosecution, not death. I don't care about jurisdiction, I only care about justice and that's what you're going to face."

Bludd raised an intrigued eyebrow. "And how will you administer this justice, I wonder? You have no weapons. You can't call for back-up. And Kara could and would have you in a comatose state long before you ever laid a hand on me. You are hardly in a position to make threats."

"Wrong. By now *Justice Four* is probably closing in on this satellite. The commander will have orders to destroy this place unless I give an all clear in the correct code."

"You're bluffing, Dredd, and you're not very good at it."

The Judge scowled. "Check your instruments if you don't believe me."

Bludd rolled his eyes but nodded to Kara. She strode to a console set into one wall and called up the satellite's security sensors. "He's right, there is a Justice Department attack ship approaching."

"Coincidence. No doubt they extrapolated the shuttle's trajectory from that tracking device. But they still can't see past our stealth tech–"

"*Justice Four* to Jesus Bludd!" a stern voice announced via the satellite's comms system. "We have weapons lock on your satellite. Surrender within two minutes or we will open fire on your position."

"Now who's bluffing?" Dredd asked.

"No reply, ma'am." Tyler was hunched over his console, listening intently for any response from the hidden satellite. *Justice Four* had closed in on the void among the stars until Taschen was convinced she knew the location of Bludd's satellite. The commander resisted the urge to bite her nails, a childhood habit that recurred in times of extreme stress.

"Either they heard us and don't believe us, or else they are trying to pretend they're not there," she muttered.

"Or we could have got it wrong and be threatening a hole in space," Tyler added, getting a glare of disapproval from his commander.

"The next time I want your opinion I'll ask for it," she snarled.

"HAVE THEY GOT weapons lock?" Bludd shouted at Kara. His enforcer was still processing streams of data hurtling across the console. Finally she smiled.

"No," she replied. "If they opened fire now, they would miss us – just."

"It seems the game is still afoot," the crime boss said, smiling once more. "Kara my dear, activate the nearest weapons satellite we control and begin targeting *Justice Four*. Two can play at this game."

"What happens if you lose?" Dredd snarled. "You got lucky, Bludd. You realised the exhibit at the Dustbuster was the real thing, not a replica. But even with all those ancient weapons under your control, you're still just one man. What was it you said to me at the diner? Some perp would get the drop on me one day and I'd die, face down in a pool of my own blood. No glory, no fanfare. Just another dead Judge. Well, much the same will be true about you, Bludd. If I get the drop on you then you'll die too, just another dead perp. You told me you wanted to be the best at what you do." Dredd laughed hollowly. "I've seen creeps like you come and go, and I've outlived them all. I'll outlive you too, punk."

"Really?" Bludd asked, a smile on his face.

"You better believe it," the lawman replied.

Bludd turned to his lover. "Kara, do you still have Dredd's Lawgiver?"

She produced the handgun from a holster tied round her waist. Bludd pointed at the Judge. "I want you to make Dredd kill himself. Plant a suicidal impulse into his head and then hand him the Lawgiver. I want to see him take his own life. I want to savour the final moments of his meaningless existence. I want to witness him losing the hopeless war against crime he has been fighting all his career."

Kara closed her eyes to concentrate. After a few seconds she smiled and then tossed the weapon to Dredd. He caught it and aimed the gun at Bludd. "Now kill yourself," Kara commanded.

"Not before I kill you both first," Dredd spat back through gritted teeth. But no matter how he fought the impulse, the barrel of the Lawgiver was slowly twisting round in his hands, moving ever closer to his head.

"You want to die," the psyker said, licking her lips in anticipation. "You want to end it all. You've had enough, you can't go on any more."

"Drokk you!" Dredd cried out, but his hands kept moving the Lawgiver closer and closer. Soon the end of the barrel was resting against the side of Dredd's helmet.

"*Justice Four* to Jesus Bludd, you now have one minute to comply!"

"Pull the trigger," Kara ordered. "End your useless, pathetic, loveless life."

Dredd's fingers opened outwards and then one slipped itself around the trigger. Sweat trickled down his face as he battled the overwhelming psychic impulse to fulfil Bludd's prophecy.

"That's quite some resistance you're displaying," Bludd said. "But even one as strong-willed as you cannot hold back my beloved for long. Kara can make almost anyone do anything she desires. Some are able to resist her fleetingly, but all crumble before the might of her mind eventually. Even you, Dredd."

"I know," the Judge replied. "That's why she was chosen for you."

"What do you mean? Chosen for me – how?"

"Kara is a sleeper, a Justice Department operative implanted into your organisation more than a year ago. She's been so deep undercover, you've never suspected her. It never occurred to you she could be a Judge."

Bludd was shaking his head in disbelief. "Nonsense! You'll have to do better than that. She's killed half a dozen undercover Judges on my orders!"

"Volunteers," Dredd said, still fighting against the impulse to blow his own brains out. "Brave Judges who willingly sacrificed their lives to prove Kara's worth to you. Ryan and the others, they knew the risk they were taking."

"You're wrong!" Kara shouted. "Now pull the trigger!"

"Your entire personality is fake, another implant," Dredd replied, "written over the top of your real persona. Psi-Division did a real job on you, wiped away almost every trace of who you used to be, the woman you were. They buried that person where you could never find her and concocted Kara in her place, a psyker capable of doing anything to anyone, all in the service of Jesus Bludd. Before today only two other people knew about you: Chief Judge Hershey and the head of Psi-Division. Everyone else involved in creating Kara had their memories erased to prevent your real persona being divulged. Hershey told me about you before I came here. She gave me the one word that will kill Kara forever and reinstate your true persona. The trigger only works if I say it to Kara in person, face-to-face."

"Lies, all lies!" Kara screamed. "You'd say anything to save yourself."

"I don't need to say anything more except one single word."

"*Justice Four* to Jesus Bludd. You now have thirty seconds!"

"Kill him, Kara!" Bludd commanded. "Finish him off, now!"

Dredd looked her in the face before speaking. "Janus."

Kara staggered backwards, twitching and flinching as if under attack from unseen insects. Her body went into spasm and she collapsed to the ground, writhing uncontrollably. The jet black wig fell to one side, revealing the bald scalp underneath.

"Her true personality is cascading back into place," Dredd said. "Kara is being wiped away and the real persona restored."

Bludd watched his lover's contortions with horror and amazement. "This isn't possible, this can't be happening," he insisted weakly.

"But it is," Dredd replied, shifting the barrel of the Lawgiver away from his head and pointing it at the crime boss.

The woman that had been Kara sat bolt upright, blinking and dazed. "Where the drokk am I? What happened?" She looked down at the wisps of rubbereen wrapped round her body. "Sweet Jovus, who's been dressing me?"

"Meet Psi-Judge Judy Janus," Dredd said.

"No, it can't be," Bludd whispered.

"*Justice Four* to Jesus Bludd, you have less than ten seconds!"

Dredd jerked his Lawgiver towards the console set into the wall. "Janus, you'd better call off Taschen and her crew before they blow us to bits." While the Psi-Judge was contacting the nearby spaceship, Dredd advanced on Bludd. The crime boss sank slowly into a chair, still shaking his head at how quickly everything had unravelled for him.

"But I still don't understand. How could you know what I was going to do? How could you have anticipated? I didn't know about the command and control system until long after I acquired Kara."

"We didn't know the details," Dredd replied, "but our pre-cogs foresaw you would become a significant threat to Mega-City One and others in years to come. It was decided to implant a sleeper beside you, someone who could gain your absolute trust. Then, when you did become a threat, we always had a weapon to use against you; your own enforcer, the only person you ever cared about besides yourself."

"You're forgetting my mother."

"So did you," Dredd said. He aimed his Lawgiver at the crime boss's head. "Jesus Bludd, I hereby find you guilty of numerous capital crimes against Mega-City One and its people, and therefore sentence you to death. Sentence to be carried out immediately."

"No, please, wait!" Bludd begged. "I demand a trial! You can't treat me like a common criminal, I deserve better than that!"

"You're just another perp with delusions of grandeur," Dredd replied before pulling the trigger. The bullet smashed through Bludd's forehead and exploded out the back of the skull, taking most of the crime boss's brains with it. The body twitched for a moment, then lay still. "Case closed."

Janus watched Dredd pass sentence on her former lover, hugging her arms across her chest. Once Bludd was dead, she spat at the corpse. "That's for everything you made me do," she whispered.

Dredd approached the Psi-Judge. "We need to disable the command and control system, take it offline. Do you still remember how to do that?"

Janus nodded. "I remember every moment of my time as Kara. I'll go and deactivate the system. Then I need to find some proper clothes."

"I'll tell the three delegates they're off the hook." Dredd and Janus departed the chamber, leaving the cooling corpse of Jesus Bludd behind them. The crime boss had died without glory, without fanfare.

Now he was just another dead perp.

Epilogue

CHIEF JUDGE HERSHEY presided over the memorial service on the site where Joe Chill Block had stood. Four months had passed since the crisis engineered by Bludd, and for most of Mega-City One, the incident was already passing into memory. Soon it would become just another disaster in the long line of tragedies that seemed to plague the Big Meg. Give it another four months and the night half the city went blind would be more legend than reality. Everyone affected had their sight back within a week. All received regular check-ups from optometrist droids to monitor on-going side-effects but the results remained positive. The crisis had passed and order was restored.

Dredd was among those attending the ceremony in Southside Sector 41. Thirty-three thousand people had died as a demonstration of power by Jesus Bludd, not to mention the thousands more who perished after the light storm. In place of Joe Chill a small park had been erected, with real trees and grass. Normally such luxuries were unfeasibly expensive and beyond contemplation, but the Justice Department's Accounts Division had seized all of the Bludd Group's assets as compensation for the crimes of its leader. Some good had emerged from the failed power play.

Hershey stepped forward to begin her speech. "This city has suffered through many traumas, many tragedies. The death of Joe Chill Block and all who were inside it at the time is one such tragedy. No doubt there will be others. Life is never simple or straightforward, the future never easy to foresee, the present always a headlong rush towards tomorrow. But hopefully we can learn from our past and honour those who have fallen so that others might live."

"How's she doing?" a female voice asked from beside Dredd. He turned sideways to see Janus, restored to her full Psi-Judge uniform, helmet in hand.

"Good," he replied quietly. "And you?"

Janus shrugged. "Still in therapy. They let me out for the morning to come here, so that's a positive sign."

Hershey's voice drifted across the crowd towards the two Judges. "Southside Sector 41 has had a long history of problems and extreme violence. Joe Chill Block was the scene of more murders than any other residential building in the entire city. Perhaps its destruction, however wrong, however traumatic, could still have some positive effects. Perhaps the people of this sector can draw a line under the past and start afresh."

"How much do you remember?" Dredd asked.

"All of it," Janus said, bitterness in her voice. "The undercover Judges I had to kill. The murders I witnessed. The sex acts Bludd made me commit with him and with others. How I used my psi-powers to persuade Dr Swanson she was in love with me and then used that to twist her inside out, ruining her life. The moment when Ryan died, pleading for his life, all of it. I remember all of it."

"I'm sorry."

"Me too," the Psi-Judge agreed.

"Finally," Hershey concluded, "I want to dedicate this garden to the lost souls who died here and elsewhere on that fateful night. May they find a way to happiness and may this oasis of green flourish in their place." Polite applause rippled through the crowd as the Chief Judge cut a ribbon, her action recorded by dozens of news channel hover-cams.

Dredd and Janus strolled back to their Lawmasters. All the motorcycles of Judges attending the event were parked in the space where the Nothing Could Be Finer Diner once stood. Janus rubbed a hand across her forehead. "It's all locked inside here, going round and round. Psi-Division offered just to wipe everything away but I couldn't cope with losing more than a year of my life, even one as bad as that. It would be denying it had ever happened. I want to remember those people I murdered, just as I'd want to be remembered if I had been one of the victims. I owe them that much." Janus looked at Dredd. "Does that make sense?"

"Your own personal memorial."

The Psi-Judge smiled. "Something like that." She found her motorcycle from among the many and began pulling on her helmet. "Were you there when Tek-Division dismantled the command and control system? The head-shrinkers had spirited me away before that happened."

Dredd shook his head. "It wasn't dismantled."

"Why not?" Janus paused. "Grud on a greenie, they didn't take it back to the Dustbuster, did they?"

"No, it's still up there. The Department claimed all those old weapons satellites for itself. The other mega-cities know we have them now and they'll think twice before taking us on."

"After everything that happened? After everything I did to help stop Bludd? What motherless drokker thought up that bright idea?" Janus asked in disgust.

"I did." Dredd mounted his Lawmaster and gunned the engine into life. "See you on the streets, Janus."

THE END

THE
FINAL
CUT

MATTHEW SMITH

Prologue:
LIFE, AND AFTER

Mega-City One, 2126

OF ALL THE wounds on Emmylou Engels's body, it was the three-inch slash across her throat that had ended her life. As the blood fountained from her severed jugular, it had taken her last breath with it, her lungs emptying into open air with a soft rasping hiss like a punctured tyre. Her mouth had been bound with tape, so she died with barely a sound. Her nostrils flared, her eyes bulged, then rolled up into their sockets, but any cries died at source. Her feet kicked a brief rhythm on the cold plascrete floor, but she was firmly held and seconds later ceased all movement. Emmylou was two weeks shy of her twenty-fourth birthday when her arteries spewed their red spray in a five-foot parabola, a distance that everyone who'd seen it later agreed was impressive.

And yet that cut was the kindest she'd received in the five hours between groggily opening her eyes and the light dimming from them forever. It had been administered by a strong hand that wielded the knife with authority and skill. In truth, she'd prayed for a death blow long before she was granted one. Her torso and arms were a patchwork of abrasions caused by a plethora of instruments, from a pair of pliers to several lit cigarettes. They had used some kind of small chainsaw to cut off her left leg just above the knee – one of the goons held the limb aloft like a trophy, only to drop it because his hands were slippery with blood – and she had blacked out for several blissful minutes. Slapped back into consciousness, she wondered if she would go insane. The prospect of being able to crawl away into a dark hole in her brain and shut out the atrocities being wrought upon her person was welcoming. Her mind, however, remained typically, screamingly rational. Emmylou's mother had always said her daughter had no imagination.

So torture piled upon torture, in all its cruel ingenuity. Sometimes her captors improvised and sometimes they followed strict orders, but they never addressed her personally, never yelled abuse in her face, or indeed seemed to be aware that she was a living human being at all. Their faces bore the expressions of professionally bored people who had done this sort of thing many times before, and would continue to do so long after she was just a faded crimson stain on the seat of the chair they had strapped her to. She was just a body, upon which pain was to be conveniently writ in big, bold and deep red marks.

And once that sharp steel had parted the flesh from her throat, that's all she'd become: a body. Her lifeless form was of no use to them anymore, and so her bloodied husk was untied and dragged away to join the five others in the back of the small, black speedster van parked outside. Emmylou was the last to be loaded, and the evening's work needed disposing of.

It was like a mobile abattoir in there: limbs entwined, vermilion streaks painting the walls, the corpses tumbling together with the motion of the vehicle as it drove through the city, headlamps from passing cars occasionally shining against the darkened windows and highlighting a glazed eye impassively staring up from the tangle of corpses. The two-man team charged with dump duty knew the route and the course of action intimately, and they worked quietly and efficiently.

They arrived at their destination, the cloud-heavy night sky adequately concealing their task from passers-by. They backed the van up to the chem-pit, opened the doors and began to empty the contents. Although the furnace of the pit would have been enough to destroy the cadavers' clothes, the men knew enough about Justice Department procedures not to take the chance, and began to remove any personal effects that would identify them too easily. If they had had the time, they would have removed all the teeth and fingertips – those that still remained – but complete dismemberment was a luxury they couldn't afford. Anyone with any experience of disarticulation knew just how long and tiring it was to take apart a human body, so they would just have to rely on the dissolving qualities of the chemicals in the pit. Similar sites had proved useful for such purposes and there was no real reason for the Judges to come sniffing around here, provided they were careful.

Except...

Perhaps it was the heat. The night was sultry and the seething surface of the chem-pit ratcheted up the temperature by a good twenty degrees. Perhaps it was because one of the men was unknowingly incubating a viral infection. Perhaps he was worrying about his kid's eye operation in a couple of days' time. A lapse of concentration can usually be traced to a specific point of origin, from which the consequences ripple outwards and all tales take flight.

Whatever the cause, the man in question paused for a moment in his work to wipe his brow, and dirt, blood and sweat smeared across his forehead. The fumes stung his eyes and made his saliva taste bitter on his tongue. His partner looked up from rolling a corpse down the bank and into the chemical soup and admonished him for his slowness. He whispered at him to pick up the pace, reminding him what the boss would do to them if they fouled up. The first man didn't need telling twice, but still the heat made him dizzy and he stumbled as he finally pulled Emmylou's body from the van in his haste to be finished. He stripped her quickly, removing two rings from her fingers, and squinted through streaming eyes to check for any other belongings. His colleague slammed the van's back doors and hissed at him again to hurry.

Head pounding and a sickness rising in his chest, the man angrily released Emmylou without a second thought and she rolled down the bank, following where the others had gone into the greenish-yellow cocktail of substances. The bubbling surface closed over her form, accepting her into its fiery embrace, and by the time the van had disappeared into the darkness, all trace of her had vanished from sight.

Already the mix of chemicals was at work on the bodies, disassembling atoms. Marrow cooked and meat sloughed off bone. It would take several weeks for the cadavers to be reduced to little more than a liquid film on the boiling surface, but the soft parts were quick to be eaten away: the skin, lips, eyes, cartilage. Emmylou's right ear was gradually separating itself from the side of her skull, now not much more than a discoloured globule. But within it, where it had been hidden by the top of the lobe, was a titanium stud. The man who'd stripped and dumped her had missed it with his cursory glance, his mind on other things. And there it remained, a hard, black rock amidst her transient flesh. While the woman she had been collapsed around it, her earring resisted any corrupting touch.

THE EARRING HAD been given to her by her boyfriend, Callum, shortly before she left the Pan-African States for the Big Meg. He'd said he wanted her to have something that she would carry around forever – necklaces could be broken, rings mislaid. But the stud would always be there, a permanent reminder. At the time, she'd found the sentiment touching, if a little overbearing. She'd never been one for overt displays of romantic sentiment and discouraged Callum from acting too much like a simp over her, but secretly she loved the attention. He could well have been the one she would end up throwing her lot in with, she'd decided, and never intended her move to Mega-City One to last more than a couple of years. The plan was that she'd make some creds, get her face known around the studios, prove herself as an actress, then decamp back to her home country with the weight of experience behind her and watch the offers come flooding in. As a rule, the money was in MC-1, but their pictures were loud and dumb. Emmylou fancied herself maturing into a dignified elder thespian of the holographic image – a Guinevere Cathcart, for instance, or a Dame Marjorie Pickering. Sedate, respectable films, where she didn't have to scream at some big rubber monster for days on end, or shed her clothes at opportune moments.

Emmylou's parents had supported her career choice from the beginning, though in truth they felt she was a rotten actress (a view held by the majority who'd seen her performances in the handful of movies she'd actually had speaking parts in). Dudley and Janice Engels knew enough about their daughter's ambition not to even try to stand in her way, despite their reservations about the limitations of her talent and the unreliability of show business. Fourteen years ago, in Brit-Cit, Emmylou's fifteen-year-old sister Roxanne had, for reasons unknown – though the Judges attributed it to Lemming Syndrome – leapt from the bedroom window of apartment 2234/B Nicholas Blake Block where the Engelses had lived all their lives. She fell to her death on the pedway thirty storeys below. Ten year-old Emmylou was watching cartoons at the time. Dudley and Janice – driven by grief and a strange, shapeless guilt – had initiated a move from the country of their births to make a new life as far away as possible in Pan-Africa, and ploughed all their energies into always making sure their surviving daughter's wishes were granted.

Emmylou never wanted anything else but to appear on the Tri-D: she wanted to attend the premieres, wanted the glamour, the illicit affairs with her dashing leading men, the column inches written about her. She wanted all this to stoke the fires of her own vanity, sure, but she also wanted to give the trappings back to her parents, in a kind of reciprocal show of love. Once she had the wealth, she would get them out of their shabby, cramped apartment and fix them up somewhere as befitting the mother and father of a superstar.

Needless to say, none of it turned out like it does in the movies. After a long period of inactivity, firing off her expensive publicity pics to every studio in New Nairobi, all she got was a succession of bit-parts in dubious, low-rent quickies that wouldn't be appearing on her CV anytime soon. She eventually had to sack two successive agents for repeatedly putting her name down for unsuitable material.

She wanted to be taken seriously as an artist, but for some reason she couldn't break out of the Z-grade ghetto. It wasn't as if she was the archetypal blonde, with an arresting cleavage and a breathy voice, the sort that seemed to drift towards trash as if driven by a hardwired homing device. But apparently she had a homeliness about her – or so she was told by embarrassingly transparent directors – that would endear her to a large proportion of their audience. She was "the girl next door" or "the childhood sweetheart", and by the way how did she feel about taking her top off for the beach party scene?

This wasn't how she had envisioned an actor's life. It was just cheap and tawdry. The films she reluctantly took roles in – *Hard Justice VIII: Caught Handling Swollen Goods*, *The Day They Took My Son Away*, *Frat Party Massacre II*, *Confessions of a Resyk Assistant*, *Blood Worms of the Meteor* – were funded by shady Euro-Cit producers and made in the full knowledge that they were rubbish by the very people putting them together. They believed that filling the shelves with crap product was better than no product at all.

It was dispiriting, but she found her fellow thespians shared the same laissez faire attitude, reasoning that they were lucky to have jobs at all. It was one step up from vidverts, and if the producers had any more money they would be using digitally generated models, and so could do away with the inconvenient human livestock altogether. When her third agent rang her to say that he'd got her a part in *Death Block: The Block That Eats*, she realised something had to be done.

To the desperate, Mega-City One can seem like a place of golden opportunity. As it was becoming apparent Emmylou wasn't going to break into the upper stream of quality Tri-D movies on her own terms, she considered maybe a change of scene was required. Film lore often spoke of unknowns being plucked from obscurity to become the toast of the Big Meg; all it took was one breakout part and some clever PR, making sure she was seen with all the right people.

She'd discussed the possibility with her new beau Callum, whom she'd met on the set of a washing powder vidvert – she was the ecstatically pleased young housewife, he the smarmy salesman – which, despite the romantic outcome, she thought represented her lowest ebb and demonstrated just how far she had fallen from her original lofty ambitions. Ironically, her parents were quietly proudest of this piece of work, beaming at the Tri-D screen every time she appeared in an ad break.

Callum had been ploughing a similar furrow to hers for the past couple of years, trading on his good looks, boyish charm and, most importantly, his willingness to take virtually any role that was offered to him.

Her boyfriend thought the idea of moving to MC-1 made sense, if that was what she really wanted. He couldn't go with her because he had a sick father to care for, but he could see that fame was something she yearned for. Where it left their relationship was left unspoken – she imagined herself returning to him full of star-struck tales, and he sensed that as soon as her first invite arrived for a glitzy premiere, he would be the next new citizen of Dumpsville.

Three months later, Emmylou said farewell to her parents and Callum at the spaceport. She would get a flight to Brit-Cit, then change onto the zoom train that would take her through the Atlantic Tunnel and on to the North American metropolis. She'd found herself a room lodging with a landlady in one of the southern sectors, and early in-roads into finding work over there had yielded promising results. Callum gave her the earring, and she felt her eyes filling up. They told each other that they would speak every day, though neither of them truly believed it at the time. In fact, it all felt weirdly like something was coming to a close, but they couldn't have possibly guessed where Emmylou's final destination lay. Callum kissed her on the lips for the last time ever and she passed through the departure gate. She turned and waved once, and was gone.

Throughout the journey, she fretted that she had made the right decision; Mega-City One was as famous for its levels of crime and violence as it was for its size and population. Horror stories filtered across through the Pan-African media: tales of supernatural ghouls murdering citizens in their thousands, of wars and disasters, of attempted coups and the harsh brutality of living under the Mega-City judicial system. Halfway beneath the ocean bed, she began to feel homesick and wondered if she had sacrificed everything meaningful in her life for a shot at something so transitory and insubstantial.

An old woman sitting across from her noticed her discomfort and tried to soothe her fears. The woman – travelling back from a vacation – told Emmylou that MC-1 was unlike any city on Earth, and that if it ever fell, mankind would never see its like again. It was noisy, overcrowded and dizzyingly vast. The rattle of gunfire was never far away, and if you looked out over the skyline of an evening, you could often see the distant flicker of block wars burning into the night. The people were by turns selfish, greedy and breathtakingly gullible. And the Judges, they were like your guilty conscience made flesh. Those faceless lawmen patrolled the city weeding out troublemakers like grud's own avenging angels, coming down hard on anyone that stepped out of line.

"But," the old woman said, raising one eyebrow, "no other city makes you feel so *alive*."

Once the zoom pulled into the Mega-City terminus, the disembarking passengers had to pass through customs. Emmylou nervously presented her luggage and papers to the Judges on duty.

"Business or pleasure?" asked one, flicking through her documents. His badge said his name was Holden. His colleague was running a scanner over her suitcases.

"Business, I guess. I've come looking for work."

"You and about four hundred million others," he replied dismissively. "Says here you came in from Pan-Africa. Sounds like a Brit accent to me."

"I'm British by birth, yes."

"Well, either way," he reached behind the counter and retrieved a clipboard, handing it to her, "read through that and tell me if you've had any of those diseases. Bear in mind, failure to do so constitutes a crime. We'll have to give you a quick medical, anyway."

Emmylou glanced at the list and blanched. To her left, a respectable-looking businessman was being frogmarched into an adjoining room. "I lived in New Nairobi," she said indignantly, "not in the middle of the Radback. Where am I supposed to have caught *this*?" She pointed to one of the names on the list.

"You'd be surprised," Holden said. "Kid came through yesterday claiming to be from Emerald Isle, and had buboes comin' out his ears." He stamped her papers and passed them back to her. "You've been granted a six-month stay. You want to stick around any longer, you'll have to apply for an extension in writing."

"That was the plan."

"Don't build up your hopes. This city ain't exactly the land of milk and honey." He motioned towards a female officer. "Judge Campbell here will conduct your physical examination."

Two humiliating hours later, Emmylou was given the

all-clear and allowed to enter the city. She recalled the old woman's words and thought that "alive" wasn't exactly how she would describe how she was feeling at the moment; more like utterly degraded. However, nothing could have prepared her for the adrenalin rush that hit her the moment she stepped onto the street. New Nairobi was bustling, but nothing compared to this; the Big Meg in full flight was disorientating to the point of nausea. Pedways criss-crossed above her like gossamer strands between looming buildings, sky vehicles honked at surfers and bat-gliders as they soared and wheeled, and behind it all the ceaseless roar of the megways as sixteen lanes of traffic thundered constantly through the city. Bodies seemed to be everywhere, every way she turned, and she gave up apologising as she was bundled through the crowd and eventually barged into the mêlée like a natural.

The robot cab drivers she found surly and unhelpful. Once she managed to master the art of flagging one down – which seemed to involve a lot of shoving and shouting – she then had to deal with their peculiar temperament. Evidently, whoever had programmed them had decided to channel into their circuitry every obstinate and teeth-grindingly frustrating trait known to mankind. After the driver had insisted on lecturing her on the full safety guidelines, she had had to repeat her destination several times while it checked the route with its internal map software, making an odd tutting noise at the back of its voicebox. Then, once they were in the air, the droid attempted conversation, though it sounded like it was building up to a monologue.

"You on holiday?"

"No. No, I'm here to find work."

"Work?" The robot emitted a barking noise, which she presumed was the equivalent of a laugh. "Not a lot of work around here, luv. They give it all to us poor sods. Now, me, I'd be happy if a few more humes had a little more responsibility, you know what I mean? Might get them directing their energies into something a bit more worthwhile, 'stead of killing one another all the time. And if foreigners such as yerself want to come over and help us out, then all power to yer. Not as if we're short of jobs to do. What skills have you got? You looking for factory work, construction, what?"

"Um, no, not really. I'm an actress."

The driver looked at her in rear-view mirror. "Actress, huh?" It paused. "Well, that's got its... merits, I suppose. Has its place in the social hierarchy. Must give people pleasure, I guess..." It trailed off, as if it couldn't think of anything to add.

Emmylou took advantage of the silence to look out the window and take in her surroundings. They were flying at mid-height, the blocks stretching below her to City Bottom and reaching up as far as she could see to scratch the sky. Their enormity was terrifying. Off in the distance, she caught sight of the Statue of Judgement, something that she'd only read about, and again the size of the Big Meg was brought home to her. She had only caught a glimpse, but even from a couple of miles away it seemed to tower over everything.

She suddenly realised the droid was talking again.

"Of course, the city would fall apart if it weren't for us. We build your homes, make your food, sew your clothes, and recycle your dead. Thousands of years of human evolution have come to a complete standstill, to the point where you're prepared to sit back and let technology take charge." It sounded like the openings of a pet theory that the robot had been rehearsing for some time. "What's going to happen to you, eh? You rely more and more on meks to do your dirty work, and what are you doing with all this extra leisure time? Sitting at home and scratching your arses? You're becoming *redundant*, you know that? Humes gave away all their responsibilities because they felt it was beneath them, only to discover that they'd just lost their reason for living. And they couldn't get it back 'cause they knew we could do a damn sight better job than they ever could. So what's left open to them? *To destroy*. Man kills so he can feel alive."

"And art," Emmylou said, believing she should speak up for the human race. "We can create art: music, literature, paintings, films. Something no mechanical can do–"

"Art?" The droid sounded genuinely disgusted. "Since when has *that* ever changed the world?"

Feeling more depressed than ever, Emmylou alighted at the slightly rundown George Bush Snr Block and found her lodgings. Her landlady, Mrs Petri, proved welcoming and not the least bit surprised by her aspirations to become an actress. She said she'd had plenty of prospective thespians come and go under her roof, though she had to admit that she'd never heard from or seen any of them again. Emmylou once more felt a twinge of panic pluck at her heart.

Her search for work proved no more rewarding than it did at home. The parts she was offered were the same level of garbage that she'd attempted to escape, just done on a bigger scale. So many creds had been poured into these films that they had to secure a wider distribution to recoup their costs. While Emmylou tried to keep a straight face as she spoke her lines in movies such as *Kazan's Legions* and *I Loved a Traitor General*, she reconciled in her mind that her profile was wider than ever before and somewhere out there, an executive was watching a test shoot and seeing her as his next leading lady. Somewhere in the back of her mind, though, she knew this was a long shot.

She never did receive an invite to a premiere – the nearest she got were the lacklustre wrap parties, which were spectacularly ramshackle affairs – but grew to find it mattered less and less to her. She spoke to her parents and Callum at least every week via vidphone, and their absence occupied her thoughts more than she'd anticipated. Once again, she considered what she'd traded, and resolved to put a finite length on her Mega-City adventure.

On the evening of Tuesday, 6 April 2126, she was alone

in the apartment, Mrs Petri having gone to visit a niece in the North-West Hab Zone. Emmylou was using a particularly lean period workwise to spruce up her CV, but found her attention was wandering from the computer screen. She gazed out of the window at the cityscape, watching a passing H-wagon swivel its arc-lights over the rooftops and walkways. Despite the press of people on every side, she felt alone.

There was knock at the door. She glanced at the clock to see that it was 9:36 pm. Emmylou wasn't expecting anyone, but she knew her landlady was friendly with several of her neighbours and they often dropped by. When she padded across to the door and peeked through the peep-hole however, she was surprised to see a familiar face. The visitor was for her.

She opened the door to the man standing there with two companions. They chatted briefly before she invited them inside. The three men crossed the threshold and quietly shut the door behind them.

Now, AS RECENT past events disperse like vapours, Emmylou dissolves too, matter changing form into liquid and gas. The earring shifts as molecules break down, and it catches in her skull. It will snag in a fracture in her cheekbone and there it will be found.

At that moment, Dudley and Janice were sitting in their small apartment talking about their daughter and wondering what to get her for her birthday. They were hoping that she'd make the trip back to see them. Callum was acting in another vidvert, this time for kneepads, and he was thinking that he wanted to get the hell out of the business.

And Mega-City One, as ever, lives on.

Part One:
DISAPPEAR HERE

One

"The advice from Justice Department is to keep all windows shut for the next couple of weeks until the swarm moves on to another nesting ground. If possible, seal doors and vents. Remember, their sting is highly toxic – symptoms include vomiting, organ malfunction and internal bleeding. Any citizens who spot one within the city walls are asked to alert their local Sector House immediately."

"Ugh! I wouldn't want to wake up with one of those in my slipper, Jerry."

"Heh, me neither, Belinda. The Judges have issued a warning saying the little critters are extremely aggressive when provoked, so viewers would do well to let trained Verminator squads deal with the situation. We don't want Grandpa Joe going after one with a rolled-up newspaper and collapsing with a subdural haemorrhage."

"Ha ha! But seriously, folks, let's be careful out there. Onto local news now, and the beautiful people have been out in force tonight for the opening of the brand-new Fred Quimby Block in Sector Thirteen. This upmarket apartment block has been under construction for the past year as part of Councillor Matheson Peat's programme to rejuvenate destitute and irradiated areas. His high-profile campaign to repopulate sections of the city with a more moneyed class of clientele has brought criticism from civil rights groups claiming that this kind of selective housing is driving a further wedge between the 'haves' and the 'have-nots', but Councillor Peat has stated that he feels he is merely rebuilding what has been shattered by conflict. Mike Johansson is on the scene now. Mike, how's the party mood?"

"Hi, Belinda. Yes, as you can see I'm in the main reception hall of Fred Quimby and behind me the party is in full swing. There's been a strong turnout of famous faces, all adding their celebrity endorsements to this new project. Harry Hartley is here, fresh from filming the second *Body Count* movie, with his lovely wife Alissa. Game-show host Barney Cannon is holding court over there, and I can see Tony Tubbs has just squeezed through the doors. The one guest that the crowds outside are all waiting for though, is reclusive model, singer and actress Vanessa Indigo."

"I should imagine the security must be pretty tight..."

"Yes, the Judges are certainly making their presence felt tonight and keeping the onlookers under control. There have been a few arrests for minor disturbances, but nothing serious. The atmosphere is mostly good-natured and relaxed."

"Mike, what can you tell us about the background to Councillor Peat's rejuvenation scheme and the significance of this block's star-studded opening?"

"Well, Jerry, I'm hoping to grab a few words with the man himself in a moment, so you'll be able to hear it from the horse's mouth. But Councillor Matheson Peat has been in the public eye for many years now, most notably with his Phoenix Campaign, in which he has pledged to clean up areas of Mega-City One left ruined by disasters such as the Apocalypse War and build upon them anew. By no means camera-shy, the media-savvy Councillor

Peat's track record so far has been very impressive, with a number of blocks dotted around the sector standing testament to his vision. His vocal patriotism and what seems an unabashed love for this city has lent him a great deal of support amongst a select cadre of very powerful friends, and it is well known that he has a cordial relationship with Chief Judge Hershey. As he's not reluctant to point out, they both share a common goal in, and I quote, 'pulling the city up by its bootstraps to face the demands of the twenty-second century and beyond.'

"For Councillor Peat, high-profile coverage of openings such as this are vital to keep his campaign on the front pages and in the minds of his electorate. He's smart enough to know the attraction of celebrity, and has no doubt hired a quality PR agency to make sure all the right people have received invites. You only have to look around to see that this is a very tasteful cross-section of high society, and that sums up Councillor Peat's perfectly judged project – everything in its place at exactly the right moment.

"And talking of perfect moments, here comes the instigator of tonight's celebrations… Councillor Peat? Mike Johansson, *MCC News*. Could you spare a few minutes?"

"Certainly, Mike. I'd be glad to. I trust you're enjoying the festivities?"

"Ha, yes, it's quite a party. You must be very pleased with so many guests arriving to witness the unveiling of another of your achievements."

"Oh, I'm over the moon that so many of the great and the good could make it. This is a very important night, not just for me, but for the whole area and indeed for Mega-City One. Fred Quimby is a symbol of how we can pull ourselves up from the brink and stand tall. The Phoenix Campaign is all about rising from the ashes, and this magnificent building sends out a message to the world that the Mega-City spirit can never be broken."

"It is indeed a truly spectacular piece of architecture. You used Barnfold and Robinson again, I believe?"

"That is correct, Mike. Architects with a unique and daring sense of design, famous for constructing buildings that are as bold as they are revolutionary."

"And quite prohibitively expensive, I would imagine. There is the criticism that whilst your clearance programmes are beneficial to the city in general, they are only creating residences for the wealthy."

"Mike, it would be very easy for me to throw up slum tenements in disused sections of the city. But does that ever solve anything? One only has to look at somewhere like Ciudad Barranquilla to see the problems that that kind of housing causes. It was always my belief when I first undertook this personal mission of mine that I wasn't just going to cement over the ruins of the past, but draw something new from them, something to be proud of. And, yes, that does cost. But quality always does. I felt if I was going to do something for this city, it was going to be done right and proper and true."

"So where now for Councillor Matheson Peat? Are you going to continue to build upon your successes?"

"Oh, of course. I feel it would almost be an insult to Mega-City One to turn my back on it with plenty of work still to do. This great metropolis is constantly evolving, growing and changing with the times, and I want to be at the forefront of its bright new future. Don't worry, Mike, your viewers haven't heard the last of me."

"I'm sure they haven't. Councillor Peat, thank you for your time."

"It's a pleasure."

"Jerry, Belinda, I'm off to get myself a glass of shampagne. This is Mike Johansson, live at the Fred Quimby Block opening, back to you in the studio."

"Thanks, Mike. Seems like it's going to be quite some night, eh, Belinda?"

"Certainly does, Jerry. Hopefully, Mike will be joining us tomorrow at six for our showbiz hour, filling us in on all the celebrity gossip that's fit to print."

"Look forward to it. Now, men, do you suffer from weak bladders? Always making those inconvenient dashes to the public facilities? Well, the boffins at Tek Twenty-one have announced that they've been working on a very unusual device that could be the answer to your prayers..."

"THAT'S HER, DREDD."

Dredd turned his gaze from scanning the crowd to watch a sleek, white limo pick its way through the excitable throng. The windows of the vehicle were mirrored, but still the various members of the press were pushing up against the barriers as far as they could, lenses thrust towards the glass. Several Tri-D crews were positioned beside Fred Quimby's main entrance, their cameras all automatically sweeping towards the newcomer, eager to frame her the moment she made her appearance.

The car came to a halt and the chauffeur nimbly jumped out and opened the rear door. A six and a half foot minder clad in a tuxedo and wraparound shades unfolded himself from the back seat, then stood to one side as a petite woman in a tiny black dress elegantly emerged behind him. A short, fat man followed and took the woman's arm in his. A second bodyguard was the last to leave the vehicle to tower over them on their left.

The crowd went nuts. The air was suddenly thick with whistles, catcalls and cheers. Flashbulbs exploded like concussion grenades and the evening lit up in staccato bursts as pressmen all yelled at the woman at once to pose for them. She looked startled at first, as if it was a reaction she wasn't expecting. But that expression held for only a split second – imperceptibly, her professionalism kicked in and a calm, bland serenity came over her face. She tightened the shawl around her slim shoulders, smiled and waved, eyes only occasionally blinking at the barrage of cameras popping off from every direction. She made a seductive effort to play the journalists' game, adopting modelling stances with an ironic degree of detachment, but all the while she was gently guided up the red carpet by her chaperone who was intent on keeping her under public scrutiny for the shortest possible time. Interviewers pointed microphones at her, shouting questions which she gracefully declined to answer. Ordinary citizens held out their hands as if they were hoping to touch something angelic. Throughout the spectacle, her smile never wavered, but her mind was clearly elsewhere.

"She knows how to make an entrance, I'll give her that," Dredd grunted.

"If you think this is insane, you should see how they go crazy for her in Euro-Cit. Almost made her birthday a national holiday."

"Control not working you hard enough, Geest, that you've started taking an interest in pop music?"

Geest shrugged. "Pays to know what makes the citizens tick," he said. "First time Vanessa Indigo visits the city, and there aren't many people that *don't* know who she is."

"There are still a few of us with more important things to do," Dredd replied. "Just keep your mind on the job. Crowd's getting a little too restless for my liking."

Geest sighed inwardly and tightened his grip on his daystick. By grud, attempting small talk with Dredd was hard work. He wondered how the man could stay uptight twenty-four-seven and not feel the need to relax once in a while. That wasn't to say he didn't respect him – how could you not admire the living legend that had led the fight against War Marshal Kazan and Nero Narcos, who had returned from exile to defeat the Dark Judges, whose very teachings on enforcement of the Law were required reading at the Academy?

When Geest was a cadet, the name Joe Dredd had been the byword for greatness. He represented everything a Judge should aspire to be: morally beyond reproach, rigidly disciplined, supremely confident and with an unshakeable faith in the judicial system. To the young boys and girls training to be the city's protectors and regulators, Geest supposed, Dredd was himself a kind of celebrity, a Justice Department pin-up, not that any of them would have admitted as much. That degree of hero worship implied you weren't fully devoted to your duties.

And, of course, no man could live up to such a reputation. As much as the stories of Dredd's deeds circulated amongst the cadet dorms, so too did rumours of a darker side: of his doubts in the very Law he espoused so fervently, of clashes with former Chief Judges and, most worryingly of all, of a possible defect in the Dredd DNA dating back to the Father of Justice himself, Fargo.

Dredd's clone-brother Rico and the ex-Judda Kraken – all from the same genestock – had exemplified a leaning towards evil and corruption that seemed to have bypassed the old man altogether. But who knew if there was something in the blood, some rogue element waiting to surface, unchecked by Tek-Division? It was a scary thought, to imagine this man, whom Mega-City One had relied upon so much over the years and would no doubt continue to do so in the future, was essentially a mystery to them. He wasn't even human, in the conventional sense, just a blueprint from a past life. He had no parents, no memories from before the Academy and could simply be described as a tool created for a job, a weapon engineered to combat crime. Nobody knew him, not really. And now Justice Department scuttlebutt had it that there were other Dredd clones being developed, the programme accelerated to meet the demands of the citizenry, and all presumably equally humourless with the same rods shoved up their backsides.

Geest sneaked a glance at Dredd standing at his side. Close-up, you could see the signs of age etched on the senior Judge's face. There was no doubt he was probably fitter than rookies that had just graduated onto the street, and that set-in-stone jaw showed scars and crags wrought by experience. Eleven, twelve years ago, following his battle with the Sisters of Death, Dredd had undergone rejuve treatment to get him back up to strength, yet the man clearly couldn't go on forever. The presence of the clones suggested that the Council of Five knew it too, and were taking pre-emptive measures to groom his replacements. Even legends had a shelf life.

"Vanessa, I love you!" a gimp in the crowd suddenly shouted, clambering up onto the barricades and waving an obviously home-made banner depicting a crude picture of the actress, assembled from magazine cuttings. Dredd strode forward without hesitation and used his daystick to sweep the fan's legs from under him, knocking him back into the crush.

"Behind the barriers, all of you," he barked, "or else I'll start making some arrests."

"How much longer are we going to have to stay nursemaiding these creeps?" Geest asked.

"Probably go on all evening," Dredd replied, constantly watching the hordes of autograph-hunters and photographers. "Some of these cits have been camped out here since yesterday. A personal appearance by a supposed megastar always brings the crazies out of the woodwork."

"Seems to me this sort of thing should be kept under wraps, not paraded in front of a bunch of infatuated halfwits."

"Two words: Matheson Peat. You can bet he'll be wanting to get as much media mileage out of this as possible."

"You reckon he's cut a deal with the Chief Judge?"

"Councillor Peat makes some very generous contributions to Justice Department funds," Dredd answered carefully, finally looking at Geest. "He gets a little leeway now and again. But Hershey's smart, she can see right through him and knows what a fame-hungry, self-obsessed creep he is. It just happens that he's also a very well-connected and extremely rich creep. Plus he seems to have the city's best interests at heart."

Geest peered up at Fred Quimby Block, stretching above them into the night sky. "I guess it is something to be proud of, giving people a new start, a new home..."

"For the few," Dredd muttered tersely. "It's the *many* we have to worry about."

DESPITE APPEARANCES, PEAT was nervous. Usually, this kind of social gathering was his bread and butter, a chance to shine amidst the upper strata of Mega-City's artistic community and allow his ego to expand that little bit further as it absorbed every insincere word of praise. He was under no illusions that his guests were particularly interested in his work, or indeed even liked him that much, but they needed the oxygen of publicity as much as he did. It was a relationship that served all of them well, allowing Peat to bask in the glow of assorted luminaries. But right now, even he was apprehensive at meeting Vanessa Indigo.

She had the bestselling album of the year, her latest movie *Baring Bloody Teeth* was wowing audiences all over the globe, and she was currently dating Evan Frick, the aeroball player who was presently on tour in Hondo City. Peat's PR agency had performed a minor miracle to get her across from Euro-Cit to open the building tonight – though he wouldn't be surprised to learn that she was in town for reasons of her own as well – and he was unsure on how to handle her. The scandal rags, which he trusted more than any studio spokesperson, said she could be difficult. He would just have to rely on the old Matheson Peat charm when he finally met her.

He glad-handed his way across the hospitality area, warmly welcoming those he plainly didn't recognise as if they were old friends. The turnout had been exceptional and if all went to plan this evening, it would be another benchmark in his remarkable career. He reached the exclusive VIP room and knocked gently on the door. A goon in a tux opened it a crack, looking him up and down, and for a moment Peat thought he would have to embarrassingly identify himself as the host of the party, but he was admitted without a word.

On first impressions, he wished he was back outside amidst the celebrations. The room was dour, with a stultifying atmosphere, the few celebrities present whispering amongst themselves and trying too hard to enjoy themselves. That old ham Harry Hartley was here with his bimbo wife, talking with a couple of ancient, besuited executives, and a vaguely infamous rock singer – whose name escaped Peat – was drinking himself towards unconsciousness. Vanessa sat on a chair against the wall, cradling a glass of water, while another of her meatheads hovered at her shoulder looking uncomfortable, his shirt collar straining to contain his six-inch neck. She seemed bored out of her mind.

It was a peculiarity of the celebrity animal, Peat knew from his many years throwing bashes like these, that the higher you moved up the ladder of fame, the more miserable you became. At any function, A-list stars would insist on having their own private corners, where they demanded to be left undisturbed, and consequently spent much of their time silently on their own, feeling too self-important to venture outside their bubble of sycophants and hangers-on. It never looked as if their fortune had bought them much happiness, but rather it had trapped them in a self-deluding circle of anxiety and vanity. Whilst Peat spent much of his life rubbing shoulders with household names, he regarded them only as a means for his own ends. Most of the time, they were no use to anyone.

The councillor cautiously walked towards Vanessa and coughed lightly, perhaps a little too theatrically. She gazed up at him and he wondered if she'd taken something; her eyes looked glassy and her movements appeared cumbersome, as if her senses were dulled. He got the immediate impression that she didn't know who on earth he was.

"Ah, Miss Indigo?" he said slowly. "I'm Matheson Peat, the organiser of tonight's event. I just wanted to let you know how much I appreciate you coming here this evening. No doubt you saw the crowd outside. The whole of Mega-City One is going crazy for you, and we're all very excited to have you here."

"Hmm?" she blankly looked up at him.

"I'm sure Miss Indigo thanks you for your kind welcome," said a voice behind him. Peat turned to see a squat, rotund man returning from the buffet balancing a plate of finger food in one hand and a flute of shampagne in the other. He had a thick moustache, complete with a sprinkling of crumbs, and his thinning hair had been pulled back into a ponytail. He performed a quick juggling act with the crockery, and extended a free hand, which Peat shook. "Maurice Lubular. I'm Miss Indigo's manager." He, like the actress, had an accent that was difficult to place; there was a lilt to it that Peat found pleasantly musical, if unrecognisable.

"I was just saying what a great honour it is to have you here." The councillor lowered his voice. "Is she OK?"

Lubular glanced to each side, as if to check no one was in earshot, and cleared his throat. "Can you be discreet?"

"Of course." Peat nodded.

"Miss Indigo has, um, a slight addiction to FX," he said quietly. "Nothing life-threatening, of course. Just a little escape route from reality."

"She needs an escape?"

"If you had her life, screaming fans throwing themselves at you day and night, you'd want to get away from it as much as possible too. As I said, it's not serious. She's probably just imagining gremlins are eating the sausage rolls. But she's developed quite a habit for the hallucinogen. I think it helps her come to terms with the real world when she's sober."

"Jovus, I had no idea..."

"Why should you? It's not something we're planning on releasing to the press. But Miss Indigo is the perfect professional. She will not let you down."

"She'll be OK to cut the ribbon?"

"Oh yes. I will be there to guide her, have no fear. What time do you want us?"

"In about fifteen minutes. I'll start rounding up the rest of the guests, then make the announcement to the baying hordes outside."

"No problem."

Peat cast a worried glance at the star, who was staring into her water enraptured, then headed back to what he hoped was normality.

DREDD THREW THE perp into the back of the catch-wagon and slammed the doors. It was his tenth public order arrest of the evening and he had a feeling that there were going to be plenty more before the night was over. The crowd was becoming more boisterous by the hour, stoked by constant announcements from the block's PA system that Vanessa Indigo would shortly be making an appearance to officially declare the building open. Right now, the cits were chanting some inane countdown.

Like Geest, Dredd was impatient for the whole farrago to be over. In fact, he was beginning to think that maybe Hershey had played this one wrong and underestimated just how easily this gathering could spiral out of control. Peat had been given too much room to celebrate himself at the expense of the Judges' rule.

Dredd was ambivalent towards the councillor. The man was charismatic and fanatically pro-Justice Department, but there was something about him that you couldn't pin down. On the couple of occasions that Dredd had been introduced to Peat, he was left with the impression that the councillor saw everyone around him as suckers to be used at his whim. Every meeting was a photo opportunity, every publicity stunt stage-managed to attain maximum exposure.

Peat's past too, was a strange mixture of genuine bravery and revisionism. During the Apocalypse War, Peat had led his local Citi-Def unit against the invading Sovs and had won some significant victories, with McGruder personally commending him for his actions once the conflict had ended. But in his early steps into politics, he made some extremely controversial, right-wing, anti-Sov speeches that upset many and he later had to apologise for offending anyone in the more enlightened, hands-across-the-ocean times. Of course, there was a section of the populace that thought he'd gone soft and felt no apology was necessary as they agreed with his statements that it was about time somebody destroyed East-Meg Two as well.

Dredd wondered what the real Matheson Peat truly believed. Did he change his opinions to fit with the political mood? Did Peat have so little faith in his policies that they were something to be picked up or dropped depending on which way the wind was blowing? The man seemed to be pure artifice.

And now there was this Phoenix Campaign of his. His intentions were laudable, but again it was a case of style over substance. Rather than genuinely solving the chronic housing problem, the campaign merely reinforced the divisions between the wealthy three or four per cent of the Big Meg's population and the struggling remainder of it. Because only those with serious cash could afford to live in these new blocks of his, it simply ghettoised the poor, driving them ever further into the margins of society. Peat never did anything that didn't benefit himself directly, and by creating these new homes for his rich peers he was ensured of their support come election day.

"Ladies and gentlemen," boomed the PA. The crowd roared in response. "Tonight is a special night for Mega-City One, for tonight we are playing host to one of the most famous women on the planet. You cried along with her in *Twilight of the Dead*, you made 'Twenty-Second Century Blues' number one for eleven consecutive weeks, you voted her the person you'd most like to be stranded in the Cursed Earth with, and now she's here in the flesh.

Put your hands together and give a huge Mega-City cheer for Vanessa Indigo!"

Dredd was sure that the technicians up in Weather Control heard the roar that erupted from the mob; it was thunderous. Flashbulbs started popping again as Peat emerged from the front doors, leading a confused-looking Indigo, the tubby guy and the two minders to a podium that had been set up with a microphone. Beside it were two small posts with a length of red ribbon tied between them. The other celebs filtered out behind the main attraction, standing in a semi-circle to the rear, trying hard not to look envious of the reaction Indigo provoked. Tri-D cameramen moved closer as Peat raised his hands pompously for quiet, which his audience roundly ignored.

"This…" He winced as he struggled to make himself heard against the chants of Indigo's name. "This is indeed a special night. This building behind me is a symbol of the indomitable Mega-City spirit, growing from the ruins of the past and refusing to be broken. I am very grateful and honoured to be involved in such a project that brings hope to the citizens of this illustrious metropolis, and it seems fitting that it should be officially declared open by someone who means so much to all of you. Ladies and gentlemen, it gives me great pleasure to hand you over to Vanessa Indigo."

Peat stood back and allowed Indigo and fatman to move towards the mic. Fatman was whispering in her ear, guiding her with his hand as if she was incapable of acting without his support. She bent forward, not looking at the crowd, and said, "Hi."

It was enough for the fans, who bellowed back their approval. Dredd watched as one of the Tri-D cameramen adjusted his position, circling around to Indigo's side, though strangely he wasn't paying much attention to what he was supposed to be recording. He kept looking behind him, as if he was checking the distance between himself and the nearest Judge. Something was up, and

Dredd was moving before his brain had even assimilated the information.

"T-thank you so much," Indigo was mumbling. "I love you all…"

The cameraman suddenly took his video camera with both hands and cracked it open, retrieving a small blaster from the hollow interior. He pointed it at the actress.

Dredd's Lawgiver was clenched in his fist within seconds as he ran forward. "You!" he shouted, his voice straining to rise above the background noise. "Drop the gun! Now!"

The man had heard him and was clearly panicked, swinging round to bear down on Dredd. Indigo's entourage immediately became aware that something was going on, and the actress's chaperone pulled her away from the podium, the woman emitting a sharp yelp of surprise. Her bodyguards both pulled hand cannons from shoulder holsters and levelled them at the perp. The crowd had gone deathly quiet.

"You two!" Dredd snapped at the bodyguards. "Lose the weapons or you'll be going down too!"

"Drokk you," one of them spat, with a thick burr of an accent. "We were gene-engineered to protect her."

The cameraman looked distressed, his eyes flickering nervously between Dredd and Indigo's minders. Other Judges were moving towards the confrontation so there was nowhere for him to go, though he probably knew that from the start. "V-Vanessa…" he whimpered. "I c-came for you."

"Last warning," Dredd growled.

"Vanessa, answer me!" the man cried, raising the gun. A fraction of a second later his head disappeared in a red drizzle as one of the bodyguards' pistols bellowed fire. Dredd reacted instantly, putting two bullets through the minder's chest. He staggered backwards, gazing down at his wound with an expression of utter disbelief. Dredd swapped targets and drilled a hole in the other bodyguard's forehead before he could aim. They both dropped heavily to the ground simultaneously, as if their nervous systems had been synchronised and somebody had just pulled the plug. The audience, who had just watched this brief firefight broadcast across giant vidscreens, took a collective breath and began to find their voice again, screaming for the superstar.

Giving the bodies only a cursory glance, Dredd headed over to Indigo, who was being helped to her feet by the fatman and Peat. She was sobbing uncontrollably.

"You want to tell me what that was about?" the senior Judge asked gruffly.

"It happens, unfortunately," fatman said and introduced himself as the singer's manager. "A person of Miss Indigo's stature tends to attract obsessive types. He was not the first."

"That doesn't explain the mini-arsenal those two meatheads were carrying," Dredd replied. "There's the small matter of smuggling illegal arms into the city."

"I cannot take this," Indigo was moaning. "I cannot... I cannot *face* them..."

"She all right?" Dredd asked.

"She's in shock, as you would expect," Peat piped up indignantly, attempting to regain his composure. "I have to say, Judge Dredd, I was disappointed with the way that situation was dealt with. Surely there was no need for further bloodshed–"

"You break the Law, you pay the price," Dredd snapped, his temper rising. "I will not stand by and see crimes committed, no matter how famous the person. My authority will *not* be undermined."

"Dredd, it's Geest," a voice crackled in his earpiece. "Crowd's losing it. Going to need some back-up."

Dredd turned and saw cits pulling at the barricades, their shouts now angry and frustrated. The celebs were fleeing into the building as bottles and debris began to be thrown at the screens and the entrance facade. Helmets were pushing the throng back, daysticks swinging to and fro, cracking heads. "OK, request riot foam," Dredd instructed. "Start making arrests. Let's stamp down on this *hard*."

He returned to Peat. "Looks like the party's over, councillor. I suggest you and your guests stay out of harm's way before anything else happens." He looked at Indigo and Lubular. "I don't want either of you to attempt to leave the city. There's still some questions I'd like answered."

Before they could reply, Dredd headed out into the heart of the disturbance, unsheathing his daystick. His radio mic sparked into life again. "Control to Dredd, senior Judge required, Elizabeth Short Block construction site. Body dump discovered."

"Kinda got my hands full," Dredd said, bringing his knee up into a rioting cit's face. "Isn't there anyone else?"

"Negative. You're the nearest unit."

Never rains but pours, Dredd thought as he waded his way through the chaos towards his Lawmaster and the first of the H-wagons roared overhead.

Two

SO I'M STICKING my gun in this geek's face and he's moaning and twitching like he's plugged straight into Power Tower. I twist the barrel between his lips and tell him to open wide. He resists at first and I'm tempted to slam the butt against his jaw, perversely interested in seeing those tiny yellow teeth shatter like crockery. Instead, I just increase the pressure slightly, my left hand gripping his shirt collar at the back of his neck, my right forcing his head back as I push harder with the gun. He relents and the barrel slides into his hot, stinking mouth like it's making a home for itself. His eyes water with fear and his breath comes in short, sharp bursts. Looking at his sweaty, grime-encrusted skin, cheap jewellery, thinning hair and stained white suit, the temptation to squeeze the trigger and empty the contents of his skull all over the warehouse wall has never been greater.

A voice calls behind me. "Yo, Pete. Take it easy, man." I look behind me and Brett Dansky, leaning against a crate of grenades, makes a casual calming motion with his hand. I stand back a pace, but don't remove my gun from the gimp's mouth, letting him suck on it like a baby pacifier. His wide, panic-stricken eyes turn beseechingly towards

Brett, as if believing *he's* all that stands between me and the drokker's brain exploding in party-popper streamers.

If it were anyone else, I would consider him even more of a fool for appealing to a Dansky. You didn't have to spend long in their company to realise they had no redeeming qualities and zero sense of compassion or sympathy for their fellow man. Business is business to them, and if that involves dropping a competitor off a flyover or gunning down a rival gang boss in front of his family, then it goes with the turf, daddio. The Danskys don't consider anything off-limits if it stands in the way of them making a whole heap of moolah.

However, this guy sucking on my blaster, this Banana City contact, he's *known* to them. They've used him before, and to all intents and purposes they probably trust him. But it doesn't hurt to make sure an associate is on the level, so while they've asked me to go through the heavy routine, this greaseball's still got his uses to Brett and Jonny. The charade is just to make sure the drokkwit is fully aware of just who he is dealing with. The brothers have put together scams with this character before, previous to my entrance into the Dansky empire, but since he's never dealt with me, I can be the wild card that keeps him on his toes, scaring him into submission.

Brett saunters over and lays a friendly hand on the geek's shoulder. "You know we've always been happy with your work in the past, Martinez. There's no reason why we can't come to an amicable arrangement again, right, bro?" Brett glances at his younger, slightly dumber brother Jonny, who is sitting at a small card table, his feet up, cleaning the serial number off an ex-army assault rifle. Jonny grunts and nods. Brett turns back to Martinez, smiling. "You see? That shipment you brought in last time contained some high-quality merchandise, something our clients can't get enough of. Right now, we could do with more of that. As you can see, our stocks are running low and there are crazies out there with wars to fight, and

Citi-Def units looking to procure untraceable weaponry. You're our *connection*, man." Brett puts his arm jovially around Martinez's shoulder, pulling him close. The gimp tries to smile around the gun barrel and only manages a nervous grimace. "But I swear if you screw with us, if you ever try to drokk us over," he continues, his mood darkening, "I'm gonna let Trager here put a bullet through your worthless, lowlife heart." Brett turns his attention to me. "You hate spics, ain't that right, Trager?"

I don't reply but simply pull back the hammer on my pistol.

"Old Petey's a real mad dog," Brett says. "Better get on his good side. So whaddya say, Martinez? Can we do business like grown-ups, or am I gonna have to dump your dago corpse in the Black Atlantic? Trager, let the man speak."

I slide the revolver out of his mouth. As soon as it's gone, he swallows several times and licks his lips, probably trying to get the taste of gun oil off his tongue. He fishes in his trouser pocket and pulls out a handkerchief, which he uses to wipe his eyes and forehead, then blow his nose.

"You have no reason to doubt me, Señor Dansky," Martinez says quickly. "I have always played straight with you. You say yourself, we have done good business together."

"As far as I'm concerned, our past means as much as a week-old hottie, and in my experience, relationships sour just as quickly. Only thing I trust is the deal before me. So, what have you got for us?"

"I receive your message, and pass it on to the relevant people. My suppliers are keen to provide you with more of the same material, for the right price, of course."

"Price remains the same," Jonny interjects, not even looking up from his task. "Otherwise we'll take our creds elsewhere."

"Well said, my brother," Brett says. "You're not dealing with a couple of hopheads looking to score cheap arms,

Martinez, and I find it personally insulting that you even *think* you can start dictating terms to us."

Martinez is flustered. "I intended no disrespect, señors. I simply meant that my contacts in Ciudad Barranquilla are willing to sell for a mutually agreed price. I'm sure they are open to negotiation."

"So are we," Jonny remarks, working the rifle's bolt release with a sharp *krr-chak* that echoes around the warehouse.

"Indeed," Brett says, grinning. "So, Martinez, this material. What exactly are we looking at?"

"Three crates of zip guns. A dozen rocket launchers, with twenty-eight boxes of ammunition. Laser parts removed from an orbiting defence battery, enough to build a military-grade weapon, or so I am told. Five crates of stub guns and a dismantled sonic cannon. There is more, but I did not bring a list, in case I was stopped by the authorities. You will be able to see for yourself, once you agree to the meet."

I can see Brett's eyes gleaming. I imagine the thought of all that shining killware makes credit signs *ping!* in his head. The Danskys have been dealing in illegal arms for several years now and have found that it is easily the most profitable of the gang's sidelines. When they started out, they had their fingers in the usual pies – extortion, robbery, prostitution, perp-running, Umpty-bagging – but nothing was more in demand in Mega-City One than readily available and unlicensed weaponry.

For the most part, their clients are the various criminal factions wasting each other in drive-bys and contract hits, but they have built up a formidable reputation for providing heavy-duty ordnance for block wars and Cursed Earth hunting parties as well. Nothing was beyond them. Somewhere in this vast building were boxes filled with satellite components, deactivated Mechanismo parts and Land Raider tracks. Mark I Lawgivers stolen from dead Judges' hands now collected dust, experimental devices that never left the prototype stage had been sold on to the Danskys by disgruntled Tek-Division employees out to make a quick sale.

Some of the Danskys' buyers were genuine collectors, obsessed with picking up assorted pieces of hardware from the Big Meg's bloody past – the gun that Chief Judge Volt used to commit suicide was a big seller on the black market – but more often than not it was the business of killing that kept the money rolling in.

"Quite a cache," Brett says, impressed. "And the source?"

"Ah, as you know, Señor Dansky," Martinez replies carefully, "my suppliers like to keep their own contacts, how you say, close to their chests. They have their own interests to protect, as much as you do."

"I just want to be sure we're not being sold ten-year-old junk, or cheaply made knock-offs from Sino-Cit. We have something of a rep to maintain amongst our regulars."

"Let us just say somebody very close to Ciudad Justice Department's main armoury is benefiting very nicely from the arrangement and leave it at that."

Brett shares a look with his brother, then glances around the room. Besides myself, there are four other members of the Dansky gang whose principal roles are muscle, intimidation and donkey work. Strodem, Mauser and Cavell are all cut from similar cloth; their lack of intelligence ensures an unquestioning and unswerving loyalty. I wonder sometimes what path led them to their current employment as gun-runners. They look almost vat-grown for the job: all over six feet, built like tanks and with creepily blank expressions, as if breaking some poor sap's neck is no different to opening a can of Popp's Cola.

The fourth, Hogg, is different. Small, dark and quiet, you can see a brain working behind her desensitised eyes, but she's probably more insane than the rest put together. Rumour has it that she used to work as a slabwalker for the Danskys until she started cutting up her johns and the brothers realised her talents could be put to better uses. The way they reason it, they're doing the city a service by channelling her energies into something more pro-active. Left on her own, she'd probably run wild on a thrill-kill rampage.

I'm sure there are plenty of tawdry tales of their pasts that I'm not privy to and they're in no great hurry to divulge – I'm sure as hell not about to start telling them *my* life story – and so an air of general mistrust hangs over us all, like a background smell you eventually become accustomed to.

For people who live their life by the moment, you never know what's coming around the corner, and whether you might have to just drop your colleagues and walk away. Sometimes you might have to make the decision to whack them, if there are no other options available. Experiencing life on a day-to-day basis like that, friendships are fleeting, and therefore unnecessary.

"Whaddya think?" Brett asks us in general, though his decision's already made. He and his brother like to make us feel we're part of a collective, as if we've got some say in the business side of things. Truth is, the Danskys would put a bullet in the back of any of our heads if it turned out to be financially rewarding.

"I don't see why we should trust this little runt," I say, still acting my role.

"Trager, your sense of suspicion is both welcome and gratifying," Brett replies, smiling, "but while Martinez may look like something you'd wipe off your boot, he's still the man with the keys to the kingdom. The gangbangers, survival nuts and warmongers out there are queuing up for some Banana City boom-boom, and we're just the guys to sell it to 'em." He looks at Martinez. "Right?"

The greaseball smiles sickly. "Absolutely, señor. Just say the word and I'll set the wheels in motion."

Jonny straightens up, putting the rifle down on the table, and moves over to stand next to his brother. "Where are they gonna want to do this?" he asks.

"The docks, I think. I will get in touch with them and arrange a place, date and time, but they will be bringing the shipment in by boat, so the pay-off will have to be done there and then."

Brett nods in agreement. "OK, let us know the details, as and when. We'll wait on your call."

Martinez turns to go, then hesitates. "There is one other thing, Señor Dansky," he says slowly. "My contacts said they have come into possession of more of the... specialised equipment."

Brett and Jonny make eye contact for the briefest of seconds and something unspoken passes between them. It goes unnoticed by the rest of the goons – you could kick any of them up the ass and it would take their brains a full minute to assimilate a reaction – but the crackle of nervous energy visible in the glance they share piques my interest. It's not something I've ever seen before. The Danskys looked, well, *frightened* for a moment. There's no doubt that the brothers knew instantly what Martinez is talking about, and it's something they've dealt with before. The immediate desire to gabble questions has to be suppressed. I'll have to pick up as much as I can between the lines without arousing any suspicions.

Brett coughs, clears his throat. "Is that right?" He's struggling to reassert his authority.

"Yes," Martinez answers. From his expression, there's no suggestion he's aware of the subtle shift in power, but you'd have to be pretty dense not to spot it. I'm beginning to think the dirtbag is as good an actor as me. "They say they are willing to sell for a special price. You still have your buyer who collects such pieces?"

Brett looks again at his brother before replying. "I... I haven't spoken to him for a while, but... yes, I can get in touch with him."

"From what I understand, I believe he would be interested in this shipment. My suppliers tell me they are antiques, recently discovered. A good find. And a good profit for yourselves, I think."

"We'll contact our buyer, tell him we may have something for him," Jonny says, a touch too quickly.

"See that you do. An opportunity like this does not often come up, eh?" Martinez heads towards the door, opens it and turns back to us. "You shall hear from me soon, señors. Adios, and here's to good business!" He grins and disappears into the city.

Silence descends on the warehouse. The inquisitive demon inside me won't be denied for any longer. "Specialised pieces?" I say as casually as I can, holstering my gun beneath my jacket. "What the hell was he talking about?"

Brett looks at me as if he is seeing me for the first time. He blinks, then attempts to wave the question away. "Just some stuff we've sold on in the past. There's a collector we've dealt with a couple of times that has a particular interest."

"What's that?"

"Weapons of torture," he replies. "Thumbscrews, blades, that kind of thing. Y'know, from South-Am death squads. Banana City has a good supply of it."

"Torture? What in grud's name does he want with those?"

Brett shrugs. "Drokked if I know, and quite frankly I don't *want* to know, but I'm sure you can guess. As long as he pays the massive mark-up we make on 'em, that's as far as my interest goes."

"So who *is* this guy?"

Brett and Jonny once more lock stares, but neither of them answer.

It's LATE AS I make my way across sector along the still-crowded pedways. The city never sleeps. As dusk falls, when the respectable cits are tucked away in their cosy apartments, a different kind of citizen emerges, with a different kind of business to attend to. Pimps and dealers unglue themselves from the shadows, quietly hawking their wares: sugar, Uncle Umps, stookie, cigarettes, coffee beans, young bodies. Gangs of Uglies loiter menacingly on street corners, preening and showing off their boils, while in the depths of dimly lit alleyways, vagrants gather around spluttering fires. Gangbangers roll past in souped-up vehicles, hanging out the windows and passing comment on the pedestrians. The clubs are heaving, pounding music cutting through the night, the freaks and weirdos crawling out of whatever hole they spent the day in to queue up outside and impatiently wait to gain entrance.

Somewhere, perhaps a couple of miles away, a siren blares before it is cut short by a burst of gunfire and the dull thud of a small explosion. No one even looks round. To live and survive in Mega-City One is to grow immune to the turbulent surroundings, to internally adopt some kind of insanity filter that acts as a blinker. Those that fail, that buckle under the pressure, can lose their minds from sheer sensory overload. Better to ignore the craziness, to let it fade out into the background, otherwise you'll end up straitjacketed in a kook cube, drinking your meals through a straw.

I hop on a zoom for a brief ten-minute journey, avoiding a hostage situation on Clancy as some spugwit tries to negotiate his way out of the dump he's burrowed himself into. The Judges call this time of night the Graveyard Shift, when every nutjob and looney-toon seems to explode into violence simultaneously. You can feel it in the air: the anger, frustration and boredom looking for an outlet, spreading like a psychic virus, infecting others with its touch of madness.

I alight at Freddie Starr Interchange and from there it's just a short walk to my destination. The building looms large over its neighbours, and even at this time of the morning it's extraordinarily busy. As I pass the off-ramp leading to the underground bike pool, two Judges come roaring out, one giving me the evil eye before they both speed off into the distance. I decide to avoid the main entrance – too many helmets, too many unnecessary questions – and instead find one of the many side doors, punching in a six-digit code on the keypad beside it that will grant me access. Once the voice-identification software confirms that I am who I say I am, the door slides open and I'm inside the Sector House. I take the empty service el to the twenty-third floor and then it's a brisk jaunt along a nondescript corridor to Hendry's office.

As usual, the anxiety hits me the moment I leave the street. Out there, it's my home, the buzz of the city is my lifeline, and amongst the cits, I pass unnoticed, a face in the crowd. Here, in this sterile environment, I'm the proverbial sore thumb. I feel strange and ungainly, like I've taken a misstep. I lock stares with whoever I pass, daring them to say something, to demand to know who I am, so I can turn this fear into something aggressive, but they seem to sense that I belong here. The shift happens before I'm aware of it; as soon as I enter this other world, my training takes hold and my posture grows more confident, my demeanour more purposeful. Something that was ground into me many, many years ago rises from the depths of my being and asserts itself. I lose the cowed, suspicious look of a Mega-City perp and transform myself back into a Judge.

I rap on Hendry's office door and enter before he can answer. He glances up irritably from the papers strewn across his desk, then does a double-take of surprised recognition. I slump into a chair opposite him, noticing that he looks considerably older since the last time I saw him. The frizzy hair at his temples is greying and his forehead seems more lined than I remember, but this is the first time I have seen him in person for over six months.

"Trager," he says evenly, trying to sound as nonchalant as possible. "To what do we owe this pleasure?"

"Oh, you know me, Hendry," I reply. "Never been one for predictability."

He smiles, a rarity for him, and offers his hand, which I shake firmly. Hendry's been my liaison since I first joined Wally Squad some twelve years ago, and in a job in which trust and deception are our stock-in-trade, there's no man whose hands I would more willingly place my life in. His knowledge and guidance has ensured that my cover has never been blown on any operation I've been involved in, and his three decades of experience on the streets before a recurrent leg injury forced him into taking a backroom role has enabled him to develop almost a sixth sense when it comes to pulling out an officer if the situation threatens to become compromised. Never a man to mince words, his seriousness is only matched by the respect he engenders in the rest of the Department.

"You haven't reported in for…" he checks his computer screen, "eight weeks, at least. We were beginning to wonder if you'd gone native."

"The Danskys have spent the past month shifting a tonne of gear," I reply, amused at the thought of Hendry sweating over one of his officers disappearing. If he had truly been worried, I would've known about it, one way or another, probably with a couple of helmets pulling me in on a bogus charge. "That small block war over in Jim Carrey the other week? Half the ordnance was Sov-made. The Danskys shipped it in via a freight carrier bound for Luna-One. We offloaded the cargo when it was meant to be refuelling. So, as you see, they've kept me busy on one or two little errands like that."

"Even so, some names and dates would've been nice," Hendry says sternly. "They're flooding the sector with firepower and it's about time we nipped their enterprise in the bud."

"Hence the reason you see me before you this very night," I say, opening my arms wide and grinning. "The brothers are making a big buy off their Banana City contacts. They're bringing it in by boat, further details to follow."

Hendry raises his eyebrows. "Big?"

"It ain't chickenfeed, that's for gruddamn sure. These are guys they've worked with before and it seems they're getting it straight from Ciudad JD. Major players. We're talking one hell of a bust here."

My superior sits back in his chair. "And you don't know the location yet?"

I shake my head. "They're using some runt called Martinez to act as a go-between. He's getting back to them with the specifics of the meet. I should imagine the Danskys would want it fairly soon. Their stocks are running low and it's drokking hunting season out there."

Hendry nods. "That would be Enrique Martinez. We got a file on him long as your arm. Worked as an informant for the Banana Cit Judges as well as fix-it man for the Conquistadores."

"I got the impression the Danskys have a history with him. There was something else too," I add. "This piece of stomm Martinez mentioned something about antique torture devices he can get for them, alongside the regular weaponry. It seems the brothers have a specific buyer who collects the stuff."

"Torture?" Hendry frowns. "You get a name?"

"Drokkers wouldn't say. Fact is, soon as the greaseball piped up about it, the Danskys looked ready to just about drop a brick there and then. Whoever this guy is, the brothers – and let's not forget who we're talking about here – are *scared* of him."

"Antique torture pieces," Hendry muses, looking thoughtful. "Not exactly a wide appeal..."

"Exactly. And I want to follow it up. Go through with the deal. Find out what this sicko is doing with 'em."

"Keep the bust under wraps, you mean?"

"Yeah, total media blackout. Far as our nameless friend is concerned, let him think the buy went ahead as planned. I'll go ahead and meet him with the merchandise after the bust to find out what this character is up to."

"You've got your teeth into this one, haven't you?"

I smile. "You know me too well, Hendry. Yeah, I got a hunger to see it through. Curiosity is driving me crazy."

"Sounds dangerous too. What you're saying makes sense and it's a lead we've got to follow, but don't push too hard. If this creep makes the Danskys have sleepless nights, then let's keep a level head."

"Wilco, skip."

Hendry studies me for a long moment. "How are you finding it out there, Trager?"

I shrug. "Same-old, same-old. Perps are becoming more inventive and ruthless by the day, while the cits grow ever more complacent. It's a warzone at times, and I don't think it's a battle we will win. Trying to stem the tide of crime in this city is like trying to put out a raging inferno with a thimble of water. But there's nowhere else I'd rather be."

Hendry taps his keyboard, glancing at the screen. "Your message drops have become increasingly erratic over the past two or three years. You're not enjoying it *too* much, are you?"

"Gotta play the game," I murmur. "You of all people know that, boss."

"Not at the expense of forgetting who you represent. What side of the *Law* you stand."

"Is this some kind of warning?"

"No, just some advice," Hendry says with an audible sigh. "You're a natural for this kind of work, Trager, and you get results. But remember you are a Judge. You have a code of honour to uphold and a duty to protect the citizens. I've never lost an undercover officer yet and I don't want to start with you."

I hold up my hands and smile. "Hey, I'm the very dictionary definition of professional."

Hendry meets my gaze and shakes his head. "Just keep your reports up to date. And get me the Banana City meet details asap. I don't want to mobilise helmets at short notice and risk blowing the op."

"You'll know as soon as I do," I say, leaping to my feet and heading out the door.

"Keep it clean," Hendry calls after me.

"Don't I always?" I reply before returning to the street, where I belong.

Three

WHEN DREDD ARRIVED at the Elizabeth Short construction site, it was teeming with life, like ants crawling over a carcass. Med- and Tek-Divisions had already established a base of operations, and there were a couple of helmets standing guard, regulating the inevitable rubberneckers who were craning to get a view of the crime scene. The Judges on duty saw him approaching and motioned him to pass with a curt nod.

Arc lights had been set up, casting the area in an eerie, hard white glow and throwing stark shadows on the ground and walls. Dredd dismounted his Lawmaster and made his way to the hub of activity which had been covered by a tent; as soon as he entered he was hit by the heat of the chem-pit which lay at its centre. Rubber sheeting had been placed on its banks upon which there was an odd collection of bones wrapped in plastic, as if somebody had attempted to piece together several human bodies and found that too many parts were missing. Dredd saw a skull with nothing attached beneath the jawline, while next to it was what looked like a ribcage and a pelvis with a couple of femurs below it.

A maintenance crew was at work draining the pit, the sludge steaming as it was sucked out by an industrial vacuum pump. They had nearly reached the bottom and it looked like the pit was giving up the last of its secrets, with a few more remains coming to light. At a rough estimate, Dredd reckoned it had held about fourteen bodies.

A female Tek-Judge was crouching by the bones and writing notes. Seeing Dredd surveying the scene, she stood and walked over to him, introducing herself as Garrison.

"What have we got?" Dredd asked.

"Construction droids were working on the foundations of the block when they realised the chem-pit they were building over was leaking into the rockcrete. They decided to clear the pit and discovered it was filled with human remains."

"Fourteen, at my count."

"Well, we haven't fully established just how many we're dealing with because we're having to match DNA samples of every piece of bone we come across. And of course, that doesn't account for those that could've been in there for years and have simply vaporised. But yes, from our preliminary calculations, we're looking at something approaching that figure."

"How long do you think they've been in there for?"

Garrison studied her notes, frowning. "The scorch marks on the bones, caused by the chemical reaction, vary from one to the next, which suggests some have been in there longer than others. It seems whoever has been using this as a dumping ground has returned on more than one occasion. They could date back over a few months."

"It'll solve some missing person cases, if nothing else," Dredd muttered. He strode over to the nearest of the remains. "Cause of death?"

Garrison joined him, bending over to pick up a skull. It rolled inside its bag and left a black, sooty stain. "That's another variable. See the contusion here, just above the eye socket? That suggests a blow caused by a blunt instrument. Ragged tearing is a sign of a limb being either broken or amputated, which a few of them seem to have suffered. In one, the chest cavity was snapped open, the likely reason being to remove internal organs. Hands and feet have been shattered, which could've been done by either a hammer or a bullet. Teeth have been forcibly removed, sometimes leaving the root. Whoever murdered these people slaughtered each in a different way with a number of different weapons. And it's likely the majority of the damage was done before the victim was dead."

"You don't think we're dealing with a serial killer then?"

Garrison shook her head, replacing the skull on the sheet. "It doesn't fit with the profile. Pattern killers tend to stick to one method, and there's usually a recognisable similarity between the victims, whether they're young women, children or people of a certain ethnicity. I can see no correlation between these carcasses; they're a mixture of men and women, young and old."

"Terrif. So we've got no through-leads and most of the evidence has gone up in smoke."

"Get ready for some more bad news," Garrison said, grimacing. "I don't think we're dealing with just one person. I think we're looking at an *organisation* here. The number of victims that have been dumped – and I'm fairly sure they've been disposed of in groups of threes and fours, if I've got my timings right – suggests at least a two-man team. There may be more involved, if not in the actual dumping then in the murders themselves. The varying causes of death calls to my mind an orgiastic killing."

"A cult?"

"Possibly, though even ritual sacrifice tends to be fairly straightforward – just a quick knifing on an altar. This seems more measured and sadistic. They took their time with the victims, and covered their tracks well, knowing exactly where to come to dispose of the bodies."

Dredd looked over the burnt and blackened remains of what had once been citizens of Mega-City One, thinking he couldn't possibly imagine the suffering they must have gone through before they ended up here. It certainly wasn't the first mass grave he'd been called to in his years as a Judge. Hell, it was a drop in the ocean compared to the landfill sites outside the West Wall containing the thousands of dead that had perished in Necropolis. But just when he thought he had the measure of this city's inhabitants, they would suddenly throw something up at him that was so despicable and callous it made him wonder if anything he did really made a difference. Justice Department did not hide the fact that it came down hard on lawbreakers, but it was debatable whether it worked as a deterrent. When perps could be so cold-bloodedly methodical as this in the act of murder, no laws could prevent it from happening. Dredd suddenly felt an overwhelming urge to bring in the guilty party more than ever.

"Have Psi-Div been through?" he asked. Telepaths could probe the final thoughts of the deceased for latent images that could sometimes show the face of the killer, or the location of the victim's death.

Garrison nodded. "He left just before you arrived. Couldn't get anything of any use as the bodies are all too far gone. Though he did say something about war..."

"War?"

"That's all he said. Just had a feeling of war. Nothing beyond that. He said he just had a 'psychic waft'."

Dredd snorted. "Psi-Div as useful as ever. This whole case feels as if it could blow away like smoke in a second. We need some ID on those remains. Start chasing up the backgrounds of the victims, see if we can make some connections."

"We'll do our best," Garrison said. "We're following up dental and hospital records and cross-referencing them with missing persons. We could get lucky."

"Let me know as soon as you find out anything." The heat inside the tent was beginning to make Dredd feel uncomfortable. "The construction droids that called it in, are they still here?"

"Outside. They've been making statements."

He left Garrison to the task of placing names to the remains and walked out into the relatively cool night. Above him the skeletal framework of Elizabeth Short was silhouetted against the sky like it had been cut out of the darkness itself, the gentle wind whistling through its exposed beams. He headed off across the muddy expanse, passing a forensic team that was examining the soft earth.

"Anything?" he enquired.

"We've got tyre tracks, but unfortunately they could be any number of construction vehicles that may have come and gone over the past couple of days," a middle-aged, bearded man told him. He, like the rest of the team, was clad in gloves, boots and a white boiler suit, so as not to contaminate any potential evidence. "We'll run 'em through the computer, see if we can single out anything that looks unusual, or shouldn't be on the site."

"Garrison thinks they were dumping the bodies three or four at a time," Dredd told him. "So we're looking for something slightly bigger than a ground car. Probably a small van, something that wouldn't draw too much attention."

The man nodded. "OK, we'll keep an eye out for anything that matches that description. We've also got footprints around the banks of the pit, but again these have been obscured to a degree by other sources, most notably the droids who made the discovery." He motioned to the three robots that were being interviewed by a Judge in a quiet corner, away from the main investigation. "They weren't very careful, I'm afraid. You know how clumsy mechanicals can be."

Dredd strode towards the droids. He could see that one had been designed for wrecking, with a large iron ball hanging from its left arm, currently lying at rest between its feet. It was a good eight feet tall, with a wide, barrel-shaped torso, and it towered over its two colleagues, whose principal duties were not immediately obvious. One was squat and boxy and had a flatscreen face, with arms that had been fashioned into guns, probably to dispense nails or rivets; the third was the most humanoid, with a thin, spindly body. The latter was gesticulating wildly to the Judge that was standing before them.

"You gotta believe us, we never did nothin'!"

"Harrick," Dredd acknowledged, cutting the droid short. "What have our witnesses got to say?"

"Plenty, though not much of it useful. At 9:45 pm they were working on the foundations of the block, securing the supporting walls. Call-Me-Kevin there," Harrick nodded to the wrecking robot, "was clearing some nearby rockcrete when he noticed a substance seeping through cracks in the bricking. He pulled out some slabs and discovered that the chem-pit had eaten away at the 'crete and was spilling through into the basement. He pointed this out to his two workmates, Geraldo and Robert here, and they decided to cement the rim of the pit to stabilise it before 'creting over it again."

"You gotta understand, we had no idea what was in it," the humanoid robot was starting to protest again, his digitised voice a reedy whine.

"Shut up," Dredd said. "You can answer questions when they're put to you. Geraldo, is it?"

"Robert," the droid murmured.

"Anyway," Harrick continued, "in the process of shoring up the chem-pit, they realised the chemicals had become too unstable and the 'crete's just going to be eaten away again. So they decide to empty it entirely and Call-Me-Kevin starts to pull apart the banks to channel the sludge away, and that's when they first saw the bones."

"We called Judges straight away," Call-Me-Kevin said with a low rumble. Dredd couldn't help but recall the first Robot War and its revolutionary leader, Call-Me-Kenneth; the two robots closely resembled each other. Dredd didn't entirely trust mechs. With the problems they'd caused the city in the past, it was a sensible suspicion, and it wasn't easy to gauge what was in their heads. A Judge shouldn't have to use a lie-detector when interrogating a droid since theoretically, it was against one of the laws of robotics for a mechanical to tell a deliberate untruth. But robots were just too damn inscrutable.

The only droid Dredd knew of that wore its emotions on its sleeve was his old servant Walter, and even *he* had managed to surprise Dredd with his deviousness and ability to cause trouble. No, droids were a double-edged sword, a potential menace everyone had to live with. It was impossible for the city not to use them. They were more efficient, they never tired, they didn't require wages and could be used for situations which were far too dangerous for a human being, and yet mankind had grown used to relying on an artificial intelligence they couldn't always understand or even control.

"Why was the pit not cleared before construction began?" Dredd demanded. "Did you know it was there already?"

"We knew the history of the land," Robert said. "We had been briefed beforehand that it had been heavily irradiated. A Sov missile came down not far from here at the start of the Apocalypse War. But that was the point of Councillor Peat's restructuring programme–"

"Wait," Dredd interrupted. "You're saying this block is another of Peat's Phoenix Campaign buildings?"

"Yes. This was started just as Fred Quimby was in the closing stages."

"Can't seem to get away from the councillor tonight," Dredd muttered under his breath. He looked at Geraldo, who had remained quiet so far. "So you knew you were building over the chem-pit?"

"As far as we were aware," Geraldo replied in a high-pitched wheedle, "the pit had been covered over. We would not have started construction if we knew the chemicals were going to eat into the rockcrete. It would have eventually destabilised the entire building, putting the residents at risk."

"I don't understand why the pit just wasn't emptied first," Dredd said, more to himself than the others. "Surely that would've been the safest option?"

"Councillor Peat wants this built quickly," Robert said quietly, as if debating with himself about whether he should spill the beans on his boss. "Why do you think we're working at this time of night? He's put the whole thing on a fast-track, making us work overtime to get it up and ready."

"So much for Peat's 'quality first' statements," Harrick said. "Looks like he's cutting corners and neglecting safety issues simply so he can get another of his buildings up as quickly as possible and his face back on the Tri-D."

Dredd didn't reply. It didn't seem like Peat to so wilfully disregard the well-being of those he'd want to live in the block once it was completed. After all, they were going to be his wealthy friends and peers, whom he relied upon to stay in office. Why risk incurring their wrath for the sake of delaying the opening of the building? From what Dredd had seen of the councillor, the man was exacting and a stickler for detail; he did nothing without reason.

Of course, it was also perfectly possible that Peat knew nothing of the pit his workforce was building on; while he may be the instigator and figurehead of the Phoenix Campaign, he wasn't necessarily in charge of clearing the land or making the day-to-day budgetary decisions with regard to materials. Dredd would have to have a word with the councillor himself and see what he had to say. He would have to be informed in any case that his latest project was now the site of a multiple-murder investigation, which would no doubt cap his day off nicely.

"Y-you don't think we had anything to do with those bodies, do you?" Robert asked. "As I told the Judge here, we just found 'em. We never knew what we was building over. We called the authorities as soon as we knew what they were. You gotta believe it, it's the truth—"

"All right," Dredd snapped, holding a hand up. Gruddamn thing sounded as if its voicebox was stuck. "No, you're not suspects. But make sure you give Judge Harrick all your serial numbers and manufacturers' details because we may need to question you again. There'll be no more work done on Liz Short until this inquiry is over, so I suggest you find other employment. Harrick, get contact numbers."

The droids looked at each other, though none of them said anything. If it was possible for a robot to feel relief, Dredd guessed, that was what was passing through their circuitry. Once again, he felt a twinge of distaste for the machines; it was as if they were privy to information that he couldn't obtain. There was too much of a divide between human and mechanical for his liking, with the latter too easily capable of concealing matters from their masters.

"Dredd!"

The senior Judge looked around and saw Garrison beckoning him to return to the tented area. Dredd marched off towards it and he could see from the excited expression on the Tek-Judge's face that they had a breakthrough.

"We've found something," she said, leading him back to the remains. "It was something on one of the last to be pulled from the pit."

"What is it?" Dredd asked impatiently.

Garrison lifted another bagged skull before him. "Look closely, under the cheekbone. It's a complete fluke that it's caught there. It could've easily disappeared amongst all that effluent."

Dredd took the cranium in his hands and tilted it into the light. The skull appeared fairly fresh compared to some of the others that had been dragged out, and even he could tell it was female. Beneath the cheekbone was a silver pellet, half the size of a pea, which had become welded to the bone.

"Is that... *metal*?" Dredd wanted to know.

"Titanium," Garrison replied, barely able to contain the pride in her voice. "I'm pretty confident that it's an earring and as the flesh surrounding it disintegrated, it came loose and caught in the skull. As I say, absolute thousand-to-one shot. We've taken scrapings from it and are running tests now, but we think it originates from outside the Big Meg."

"The titanium survived the chemicals in the pit?"

"Just about. That's why we're sure it comes from overseas. It's probably been mixed with other polymers as it was fashioned into a piece of jewellery, and that's what enabled it to stay virtually intact despite the heat."

"Could they be imported?"

"It's very likely, which means that we should be able to run a trace on any purchases that were made in, say, the past ten years. Even though I don't think this woman was killed all that long ago – we could possibly be talking only months – she may have bought the earring a while back. However, just by looking at her skull, I can tell she was in her early to mid-twenties, so we wouldn't have to go back much more than a decade."

Dredd handed the skull back to her. "Even so, a trace running across the entire city over that period is going to take time."

"There is another possibility that would narrow it down some," Garrison said. "That she came from overseas *herself* and had the earring when she entered the city. If she was a tourist or an immigrant, then they should have records of her at customs. If we can pinpoint the source of the titanium, then we can match it with anyone visiting from that country within a certain timeframe."

Dredd nodded, feeling progress was made at last. "Good. Get on it, Garrison. Any leads, any names, pass on the info immediately."

The Tek-Judge lifted the skull up again and looked at the minute earring with something approaching wonderment. "Amazing how one little detail can throw a case wide open, isn't it? And it's sheer luck that this victim happened to be wearing something that was near indestructible, as well as it sticking to the body. From tiny acorns, eh?"

"Ironically," Dredd replied, heading out of the tent, "I'm about to tell someone just how far his mighty empire could fall…"

MATHESON PEAT SAT in the dark in his luxury apartment in Michael Douglas, with a glass of water and a couple of tablets for his nerves. His nineteen-year-old girlfriend Sondra had long since gone to bed, and from his chair in the living room he could hear her rhythmic breathing. He found it soothing to listen to, but sleep for him seemed very far away. His brain was too wired, the events of the evening playing over and over again in his head like a movie stuck on a constant loop. How could something that had been arranged so meticulously, that had seemed to be going so well, fall apart so quickly? One minute he had the press hanging off his every word and any Z-list celebrity that was worth his or her salt was desperate to scrounge an invite to the biggest night of the year. The next minute, three men lay dead in a vicious gun battle, sending one of the world's most famous women – who was here at *his* invitation – round the bend.

Lubular had taken Vanessa back to their hotel, the Mega-City Excelsior, via a back route that avoided the riot going on at the front of the building. He said he would try to wean her off the narcotics until she calmed down so they could decide what their next move would be. His other guests had similarly dispersed as quickly as they could while the Judges contained the trouble, and though he made an effort to help clear up the remains of the party afterwards, his listlessness made him more of a hindrance. In the end, he too headed for home, a strange, unfamiliar feeling gnawing at him. A feeling of failure.

He'd been sitting here for over an hour, visibly trembling. Thoughts tumbled through his head: what the headlines were going to be on tomorrow's newspapers, what his friends would think of him after such a debacle, whether it was his fault for inviting a superstar like Vanessa Indigo to an inane, dumbed-down city such as this. He really should have known better.

But the image that occupied his mind most of all was of the mysterious man who had kick-started all the trouble, the would-be assassin who was gunned down by Indigo's bodyguards. Lubular had waved away the reasoning behind such an attack, saying such crazies are par for the course when you're in the public eye, and perhaps that was true. Trying to apply logic to something as random and maniacal as this was pointless. And yet, Peat couldn't help but be haunted by the man with the gun, prepared to murder someone he loved with all his heart, possibly because he couldn't have her for himself. If he had succeeded, then Peat's name would have been synonymous with a night everybody would remember for entirely the wrong reasons.

There was a knock at the door. At this time of night, he knew it could be nothing trivial, but even so he was disinclined to answer it. He just wanted to shut his eyes and forget that this evening had ever happened. The knock came again, louder, and he heard Sondra stirring in the bedroom. He struggled to his feet and padded across to the door, opening it a crack, keeping the chain in place. When he saw who it was, he sighed and opened the door fully, letting his visitor in.

"I trust I'm not disturbing you, councillor."

"No, I couldn't sleep anyway." Peat went and sat back in his armchair, reaching for his half-glass of water. "What can I do for you, Judge Dredd?"

Dredd stood, arms folded. "There have been developments of which you should be aware. Construction droids working on Elizabeth Short discovered a chem-pit beneath the foundations. This pit proved to contain the remains of at least fourteen bodies. We believe they have been murdered and dumped there."

"My grud..." Peat's jaw dropped. "D-do you know who they are?"

The Judge shook his head. "We're working on that at the moment. Just so you know, all work on Liz Short has been halted for the foreseeable future pending the outcome of this investigation."

Peat swallowed a gulp from his glass. "OK."

"I also have to ask you, councillor, did you know there was a chem-pit beneath the construction site?"

Peat leaned back in his chair, frowning. "No... not specifically. I mean, I knew the area once had a high rad-count, because that was the reason behind my campaign – to make such areas habitable again. So I suppose I must've assumed there was every chance there might be chem-pools on the land. But it was the collective responsibility of the architects and construction companies to clear the land before building was to begin."

"Did you authorise the block to be constructed over the chem-pit, without it being cleared first?"

"What? Who's said that I did?"

"Just answer the question."

"No, of course not. It would be a recipe for disaster."

Dredd paused for a moment, glanced at his lie-detector, then levelled his gaze at the man. "Our paths seem to keep crossing, Councillor Peat. I'd hope for your sake that it's just coincidence, if you believe in such a thing. Right now, you're involved – however remotely – in a multiple-murder case, so I'm instructing you not to think about leaving the city until we say otherwise. We may require you for further questioning."

"Matheson, what's going on?" Sondra emerged yawning from the bedroom in her dressing gown, her hair tousled.

"Nothing to worry about, dear," Peat replied. "Judge Dredd has just relayed some rather surprising news regarding business."

"We'll talk again later," Dredd said. "I'll bid you citizens goodnight." He headed towards the door.

Peat followed, and as he got out of earshot of his girlfriend, hissed: "I shall be contacting the Chief Judge in the morning about your heavy-handed tactics at the block opening this evening."

"That is your right, I suppose, Councillor Peat."

"Don't think you can bully us around like everybody else, Dredd. We're not *like* everybody else. I could have your drokking badge." Peat slammed the door on Dredd before making his way back to the living room.

"Matheson, you look terrible," Sondra said. "You always work so hard. I wish you'd let me help you."

Despite her protestations, Peat had refused to let her come to the opening; partly because he wasn't keen on everybody seeing his teenaged girlfriend for fear of what rumours would start circulating, but mostly because he knew she'd steal the limelight from him.

"Why don't you come to bed?"

Peat didn't argue. He let her lead him by the hand into the bedroom and beneath the sheets. But even wrapped in her arms, he found he was shaking more than ever, and he stayed awake until the first fingers of dawn pierced the sky.

Four

IT IS THREE nights later when I get the call telling me the buy is going ahead. Brett instructs me to pack as much killware as I can surreptitiously conceal about my person, and to meet them at warehouse four-two-three on the north-east docks at 2:00 am. I can glean nothing from his voice that tells me how he thinks the night's events are going to go down. He just barks brusque directions and suggests that I would be a fool to leave without adequate firepower.

The call comes through at 11:25 pm, which will give Hendry a couple of hours to mobilise the back-up units and stake the area out. I go down to a public phone and leave a coded message on an automated reply service that feeds directly into Wally Squad, and tell my superior the where and the when. Then I head back to my apartment in Nic Cage and try to think of something mindless to do to fill the hours and take my mind off the upcoming bust.

In my experience, too much thinking can be just as dangerous as a lack of preparation – with your brain wired over what to expect and how you'll deal with it, should the eventuality arise, it can blunt your instincts. I feel I work better fuelled by adrenalin, living off my intuition and natural reflexes. Certainly, in undercover work, the moment you start doing things by the book, you risk blowing your identity as your years of training start to filter through. In the end, I elect to channel-surf my Tri-D set, maybe catch a crappy movie that will require next to no concentration.

I've been living out of my apartment for virtually my entire career as a Judge. There are tens of thousands of habitats like this one, dotted around the city and owned by Justice Department for its covert operatives, and they're not so much homes as bases. I have no personal effects or photographs on the walls, my bed is a mattress, tucked into a corner of a bare room, the cupboards in the kitchen are all but empty save a few packets and some mouldering vegetables. I have no need for luxury, for it plays no part in my life. I receive no salary from Justice Department, but it supplies me with everything I require to be a Judge, and being a Judge is all that I require. When I entered the Academy of Law, I willingly relinquished the chance of marrying or having a family, of ever being wealthy or travelling, of making my own choices. I traded it all in.

Perhaps my one concession to normality is my Tri-D set, which can be vital in linking me to the rest of the city. Whilst your average Street Judge operates best when he or she's aloof from the citizenry, to be a Wally Squad officer is to be in tune with the fashions, crazes and dialogue of your regular Joe on the slab. If anything, this side of the job is just as dangerous to your health as having a blaster rammed in your face; overexposure to the insanity that this city dreams up can send your brain sideways, with every goofball quiz show and vidiot pirate channel competing for your attention. It's well known that a proportion of undercover Judges have a slender hold on reality as it is, forced to plunge into the mind-sapping maelstrom of plastic pop music and twenty-four-hour soaps.

Living in Mega-City One is a stressful business, crammed into a melting pot of bizarrity, with four hundred million borderline psychopaths jammed either side of you that can snap at any time. To submerse yourself too far into the populace brings with it the risk that you too can succumb to the intense pressure experienced by your fellows, and jeopardise your ability to think coherently. For a Wally Squad officer, the trick is to never forget what you *are*; that while on the outside, you're indistinguishable from the next cit. As long as my moron act stays just that – *an act* – then I have some hope of survival.

But nobody ever said it was easy. Stupidity in the Big Meg is everywhere, like it's one of Otto Sump's lifestyle choices that's never stopped being all the rage. Right now, as I flip channels, the vapidity steals out of the Tri-D set and tries to lower my IQ. I can feel my eyes glazing over as the stations change, but the inanity remains the same: a cookery programme presented by a microwave telling viewers in clipped female tones how to reheat leftovers; an embarrassingly cheap drama about teenaged skysurfers that was obviously filmed by a very unskilled cameraman on a powerboard; a right-wing chat show hosted by a guy claiming to be the reincarnation of Bob Booth; alien seduction techniques; celebrity bean-counting; and so on and so on, like a descent into cathode-ray hell...

Enough, I tell myself, resisting the urge to wheel through a further hundred channels, my forefinger hovering over the buttons on the remote. I stick, as expected, with a movie, a fairly old propaganda job retelling moments from the Apocalypse War, clearly made with Justice Department approval. The simplistic black-and-white moralities on display make even me wince; the Sovs are portrayed as warmongering animals, slaughtering women and children with dastardly quips while the Meg Judges ride out of a rising sun, bringing justice to the invading hordes. It typically plays fast and loose with the facts, inventing laughable romantic subplots between Sov lieutenants and cit fraternisers that sit uneasily with the carnage it unashamedly glorifies.

I was a cadet at the time the conflict kicked off, so my experiences of the realities of the war were limited to a bunker beneath the Academy, but even so, you'd have to take a full hit with a Stupid Gun not to smell the bullshit this movie is peddling. Watching the shots of Sov tanks rumbling through the occupied streets makes me think of my eight-year-old self lying on a makeshift campbed deep underground with the other greenies, listening to the shriek of missiles streaking overhead and realising at that moment just how much we had changed, how much our tutors had moulded us into proto-Judges.

Other children of our age would normally be terrified to be so close to the noise and heat of battle, but all we felt was a steely determination and a shared desire to be out there, defending our city. I suppose if we'd been asked to visualise our emotions, they would look not unlike this piece-of-crap flick, this child's-eye view of a nuclear exchange. Fiercely patriotic and breathtakingly naive, with caricatures mouthing clichés, the programme reduce the war to the level of something like the Tri-D talent show *You Stink!* – easy consumption for people who don't like to think too much.

In the end, the toe-curling acting and lines like "But War Marshal, haven't you ever truly loved someone?" are enough to make me want to kill someone, so I flip the set off before I lose my temper. I go into the bedroom and lift up a couple of floorboards, removing two Justice Department blasters with the serial numbers burnt off to make them look unlicensed. The small ammo store I have here contains probably the most valuable items in the entire apartment. It's not a significant arsenal by any means – several hand cannons, a little explosive, some bladed weapons – but enough to make me feel secure.

I slot a loaded Zirgman P28 into my shoulder holster, then work the slide on a compact Roundlock before slipping on the safety catch and jamming it beneath my belt at the small of my back. I tape a boot knife to the inside of my trouser leg, then I pull on my jacket and drop a snubnose Jameson .38 into the pocket with a few spare slugs. The weight feels reassuringly heavy, like I've got some solid protection. I look myself over in the mirror and don't see any awkward bulges that would give me away. Ideally, a bullet-proof vest would be useful for this kind of deal, but its bulkiness would be too obvious.

I replace the floorboards then take a final look in the mirror. Breathing deeply, I stare back at my reflection and silently tell myself that the Danskys are not going to know what's hit them, and they will *never* know, because everything is going to go nice and smooth. I have no reason to panic. I am smarter than them by several billion degrees.

I switch off the light and my reflection is lost in darkness as I head out into the night.

I'M DUE TO meet Cavell at a hottie house on Johnson, so I grab myself a synthi-caf while I wait. It jangles with the zizz I scored on the way and snorted in the restaurant's toilets, but it helps flatline the paranoia that was starting to creep up on me. The drug is boosting my perception, and in the building's sickly, yellow flickering light, everything is in deep focus: the group of arguing eldsters at the next table, the droids working behind the counter, the steam rising from the frying hotties, the puddles of sauce on the tiled floor. I feel hyper-alert, but it should level off shortly into a sense of pleasantly heightened awareness.

Somebody's left today's *Mega-Times* on a chair beside me and I leaf through it, conscious of the Roundlock rubbing uncomfortably against my waist. A news item on page two about a body dump discovery catches my interest. Reading between Dredd's typically terse statements to the press, it looks like the victims were all tortured before being buried beneath a block development for some time. The story sets alarm bells ringing in my head that I know are more than just the zizz talking, and Dredd's vague comment at the end about following up "significant leads" makes me ponder. I tear the article out and stuff it in my pocket.

The scarred, hulking visage that is Cavell appears at the door and nods. I finish the synthi-caf with a gulp, then join him, the meathead already striding away before I'm out the door. Conversation has never been Cavell's strong point, and the welcome silence between us as we catch the zoom over the docks gives me more time to mentally prepare. We arrive at our destination and I follow the big lunk through the maze of warehouses, his long coat flapping ahead of me. The wind brings with it the smell of the Black Atlantic: a harsh, eye-watering stink of pollutants. In the distance I can hear the cries of dog-vultures, probably wheeling above the sluggish waves, searching for carrion, but otherwise it is unnaturally quiet. The roar of the city seems a very long way away.

I try to imagine the forces of Justice Department moving in the shadows, surrounding the area, getting into position. It gives me a small amount of comfort to envisage that our movements are being tracked by infra-red binox and rifle sights, that somewhere out in the darkness my back-up is waiting to pounce. My hand slides inside my jacket pocket and brushes against the snubnose. I hope that events don't spiral so out of control that I have to blow my cover too soon.

Cavell halts at an anonymous door and raps on it four times as I check my watch: 1:45 am. The door opens and we slip inside to be met by the sight of the rest of the gang thumbing shells into shotguns. On the other side of the warehouse stands an empty truck, waiting to be loaded with the merchandise.

"Guess we're all here," Brett says by way of greeting, snapping shut the breech on one of the weapons and throwing it to Cavell, who silently hides it within his coat.

"You expecting trouble?" I ask, nodding towards the ordnance. Hogg is strapping a wicked-looking blade to her thigh.

"They ain't gonna be welcoming us with candy and flowers," Brett remarks, adjusting the holsters under each arm. "Pays to have a little insurance."

With the amount of killware on display here, I realise that if it all goes down then I'm going to be in the middle of a small war. Even with several helmets standing over me like guardian angels, they're not going to be able to pull my fat out of the fire before both factions start swapping lead. I'm walking into a highly volatile situation, and if they get any whiff of the fact that I've set them up, then I'm going to have a dozen or so gangbangers looking to tear my lungs out and eat 'em. I've gotta hope these guys mean business and don't dick the Danskys around too much. With slimeballs from Banana City, you can never be too sure.

"OK, we set?" Brett asks the room, picking up a briefcase. Most of them are wearing long coats similar to Cavell's to hide the shotguns hanging at their sides. "From here on, let me do the talking. That includes you, Jonny. No threatening gestures, no throwdowns unless necessary. Don't underestimate these dirtwads, they'll slice your drokking throat as easily as shaking hands with you. Clear?"

Mauser, Strodem and Hogg nod, and Cavell remains impassive, like a mechanoid awaiting instructions.

Brett leads the way through the darkened alleys to the docks until we're overlooking the black expanse of the sea. The smell off the water is ripe with decades of decay and I struggle not to cough as it gets into my mouth. I keep my lips tightly sealed and breathe through my nose.

"Martinez..." Brett mutters testily, looking at his watch. I check mine and see it's just after two. I can sense the Danskys' anxiety; they obviously want this over as quickly as possible.

A light flares in the shadows to our right and we turn as one and see Martinez emerging from a doorway, casually smoking a cigarillo. He looks like he's out for nothing more than a midnight stroll, wearing the same white suit that I last saw him in. He saunters towards us as if he's deliberately toying with the brothers' nerves. I can detect again that subtle shift in power. Martinez performs as if he's holding all the ace cards.

"Señors," he says with an insincere smile, blowing smoke out the side of his mouth. "Glad you could make it."

"Martinez," Brett acknowledges, visibly trying to control his temper. "So, the deal still on?"

"*Si*, my people are here," he replies, tapping ash onto the ground. "But there has been a slight change of plan."

"What?" Jonny growls.

"Nothing serious, I assure you, señors, but my contacts, they have their own protection to think of. They would prefer that the deal went ahead on the boat."

"Wait, wait," Brett says. "You mean we make the exchange out at drokking *sea*?"

Martinez nods. "It is anchored just a couple of miles outside Mega-City docks." He gestures towards the water and the darkness beyond. "They have a small craft that will take you there, and they will help you offload the merchandise once the deal is complete. But they want to keep the negotiations on the ship."

"Why?" Brett demands.

"They are reluctant to enter Mega-City One, as you would expect. But they would also prefer it if the two parties met on ground where there is little opportunity for... unforeseen circumstances."

My mind is reeling. This is bad. My back-up is going to be snafued out in the middle of the drokking Black Atlantic, and I can only hope that Hendry is picking this up and making some fast changes, otherwise I'm on my own and up to my neck in it. My zizz-induced confidence gets the better of me and before I know it I'm saying: "This is bullshit. Why the drokk should we trust these greasers?"

"Trager," Brett shoots me a look. "Keep your damn mouth shut."

"But we'll be right where they want us," I protest, playing for time.

"Trager, make another noise," Brett hisses, "and I'll put a cap in you myself."

I shut up and in the momentary silence that descends we can hear the puttering of an outboard motor approaching. A small skimmer slides out of the night, lights swinging through the mist hanging above the water's surface, and comes to a stop parallel to the sea wall by a short set of steps. Nobody disembarks from it.

"My clients are waiting, señors," Martinez says. "It is time to decide whether you want to do business or not."

The brothers exchange a glance that suggests they are seriously not happy with this, and the tension in the air crackles. I try surreptitiously to look around me, checking to see if I can catch even the smallest glimpse of the reinforcements that are waiting just around the corner, but there's no sign. I feel my heart beating harder against my ribs as a low-level, drug-infused fear begins to take hold.

"OK," Brett says at last. "Let's do it. But I wanna tell you, Martinez, this better be the one and only surprise of the evening, otherwise your dago ass is gonna be going swimming. You hear me?"

The geek grins that nauseating crescent moon of yellow teeth and nods. "But of course, Señor Dansky. Everything will go smoothly, I assure you." He gestures for us to follow him down the steps and onto the skimmer.

Brett looks at each of us in turn with a glare that says "First sign of trouble, kill 'em all," then heads after Martinez, his brother joining him. We each take our turns to board the vessel, which is about the same size as a Justice Department patrol boat. Despite the arc lights positioned above the cabin, the darkness ensures that I can't get a good look at our two Banana City hosts: one guy is standing beside the wheel, waiting until we're all aboard before cranking the engine and turning the vessel back out to sea, while the other lounges against the side, a rifle slung over his shoulder. Martinez says something in Spanish to him, sharing a joke it seems, then tells us that it will not take more than five minutes to reach the ship. The brothers are staring the rifle-guy out, trying to intimidate him, but it's not working. From what I can see of his face in the moonlight, he just smiles back, rocking with the motion of the boat.

With the flat, black expanse of water all around us, I start to feel alone and trapped. It's easy to see why the dealers chose to meet the Danskys out here, there's nowhere to run to, nowhere to make a stand. You can't even swim for it as very few have fallen into the Black Atlantic and survived. The thick soup of chemicals and pollutants is so strong that if you swallowed a mouthful you'd be in intensive care for days, your stomach pumped dry. I realise that if we don't get back on this boat after the transaction is finished, then none of us are getting out of here alive.

True to Martinez's word, the ship hovers into view in no time at all. The large, sleek yacht is anchored out in the ocean, and I can see shadowy figures moving on its deck. As the boat sidles up against the hull, a rope ladder is thrown down to meet us. The pilot kills the engine and the skimmer bobs on the waves, rifle-guy crossing to portside and beckoning us to climb. The Danskys hesitate.

"Go, señors," Martinez urges.

Cautiously, we ascend. As we clamber over the edge, we find ourselves staring down the barrels of a dozen guns. On the deck, a semi-circle of Banana City gangbangers surrounds us, automatic weapons pointed in our direction. They're armed to the max. The brothers look around hopelessly, as if trying to find a way out, but there's nowhere to go. The greaseballs say nothing, and it strikes me that if they wanted us dead, they wouldn't be taking their time about it. I get the feeling they're waiting for an order, or just keeping us under guard. Either way, it doesn't smell like a double-cross.

"Please excuse my friends," Martinez says behind us, huffing and puffing as he throws himself over the side and onto the ship. "They just like to be extra careful."

"I get nervous in the face of so much killware," Brett says, whipping a pistol from his holster and levelling it at Martinez. "And when I get nervous, I get an itchy trigger finger. You might want to tell 'em to lower their cannons before it becomes a bulletfest."

"Please, Señor Dansky," Martinez says. "Let's not make this unpleasant."

"Give me one good reason why I shouldn't unload into your treacherous drokking face, you piece of shit–"

"Because Enrique has brought an exceptional offer your way," says a voice from behind the Banana City group, and they part to allow a slim, dark woman clad in combat fatigues to walk through to the front. Her ebony hair is pulled back into a severe ponytail, revealing a birdlike, coffee-coloured face. "I trust him implicitly, and so should you."

"Talón," Brett acknowledges.

"Hello again, señor." She nods once. "Now, I believe we are here to do business and not kill each other?" The woman makes a waving gesture and says something in Spanish. The gangbangers slowly drop their guns, though from the murderous glints in their eyes, only reluctantly. "I'm sorry we are not more welcoming, but we make no exceptions. You can trust no one these days."

Brett sheathes his gun and shakes hands with her. "You got that right."

"We should not delay," Talón says, looking uncomfortable. "Evading the forces of law and order is becoming increasingly difficult. I think we should conclude our deal as soon as possible."

"Suits me."

"You have the money?"

Brett taps the briefcase. "Right here. Forty thousand in untraceable paycards, as agreed. And the merchandise?"

"But of course." Talón barks an instruction to a couple of lackeys and they disappear into the hold. Minutes later, they return struggling with a crate between them, dropping it down in front of the brothers. "There are another three like this," she says as the Danskys peer into the crate, pulling out zip guns and random weapon parts. "I trust you are satisfied?"

"All looks good to me," Jonny murmurs.

"Did I not say you would be happy?" Martinez beams, but everybody seems to ignore him.

This is it, Hendry, I'm thinking. Now, now, now. Can't take them all by myself, man...

Brett hands the briefcase to Talón. "You'll help us get this stuff ashore?" he asks.

"I have another two skimmers at your disposal," she replies, then pauses as another of her lieutenants whispers in her ear. He hands her a small package, wrapped in cloth. "Ah, yes." Talón gives Brett a dazzling smile. "We also have this for you. I understand you have a buyer who is interested in such antiquity?" She passes the bundle over to Brett, whose face has gone pale, and he takes the package gingerly as if he was holding a grenade. "It will cost you a further five thousand–"

Then the whole world turns white.

For a moment, we're frozen, transfixed in the hard light, too stunned to move. Darkness is banished in a heartbeat, as if daybreak has suddenly exploded over the ship. But when I look up, I see a looming shadow moving in the sky, followed a fraction of a second later by the amplified voice coming from it.

"Justice Department! Nobody move!"

The H-wagon swoops in low to hover above the yacht, its engine roaring in our ears, spotlights trapping us in their glare. The sea churns in the downward blast of its jets and sprays filthy water in our faces, and after a moment of utter incomprehension, it serves to break the spell and Talón and her men are moving and shouting, looking for somewhere to hide. They're like roaches, scuttling into every crack and crevice, trying to find safety.

Brett drops the bundle and grabs Martinez with both hands, bellowing into his face. "You set us up! You sold us out, drokker!"

"Señor, I did nothing!"

Jonny puts a gun to Martinez's head and blows his brains out. "We ain't got time for this, bro! We gotta *go*!"

"Talón! Find Talón!"

Lights appear on either side of the yacht, closing in through the mist; patrol boats are approaching. Mauser and Cavell stand at the stern and start firing with their shotguns at the vessels and seconds later, a cannon lets rip from the H-wagon and reduces the pair to bloody confetti. I see the skimmer that brought us here attempt to escape, but a laser arcs out of the sky and destroys it in an orange fireball.

The ship plummets into chaos. The Banana City contingent are trying in vain to hold the Judges off, but they're picked off with ease. The Justice Department boats have now swung alongside the yacht, and helmets are boarding, mercilessly putting down any opposition. Strodem – showing a rare streak of character, or perhaps just wanting to go out in a blaze of glory – leaps at the nearest uniform and the two of them are hurled into the water, disappearing into its inky depths.

Lying flat on the deck, bodies all around me, I see the bundle that Brett dropped and snag it. I stagger to my feet and try to discern where the brothers have gone, smoke now wafting in front of me as the vessel begins to burn. I see Talón and one of her right-hand men untying a skimmer from the ship while keeping the Danskys away at gunpoint.

"You were followed, you idiots!" the woman spits. "You have brought the Judges down on us!"

"It was your drokking middleman that screwed us over," Brett snarls. "Should never have trusted that spic bastard in the first place."

"*Puta!*" Talón's goon swears violently and shoots Brett repeatedly in the chest, knocking the gun-runner back in a blizzard of crimson explosions. He slides against the outside cabin wall, leaving red streaks on the panelling. Jonny yelps in genuine grief, but before he can pull his own weapon there's a blur of movement and Hogg appears out of nowhere, throwing herself at the gunman, thrusting a blade through his neck. He gargles, feebly clutching at the knife, then collapses. Hogg realises for just one moment that there is someone behind her before Talón empties half a clip into the back of her head.

Talón and Jonny stand off against each other, pistols raised. There are tears trickling down Dansky's face.

"My brother… You'll die for that, drokker," he whines.

"Come on then, Mega-City cretin," Talón sneers. "Take your best shot."

Time for me to intervene, I think. I need Dansky alive. "I'm afraid I can't let you do that," I say, levelling my snubnose at the pair of them.

"Trager?" Jonny glances at me quizzically.

"Justice Department," I reply. "You're under arrest."

For a second, they look like they don't believe me, then realisation hits. Talón screams and fires at me. I duck and roll, ears ringing as I hear the wood shattering behind me, then come up blasting, putting two slugs through her head, dead centre. My shooting range tutor would be proud.

Even before she's hit the ground, I have to deal with Jonny. He pumps the trigger frenziedly, bullets flying wild, but I still catch one in the arm, spinning me around, dropping me to my knees, making me lose the snubnose. I yank the Roundlock free from my waistband, but take too long aiming. He kicks it from my hand, then punches me full in the face. I see stars as I lay on my back, looking up at him lining his gun up with my forehead.

"Drokkin' snitch," he says.

My hand finds the boot knife strapped to my leg and I tear it free, ramming it up into his groin. He screeches in pain, and I knock him over, disarming him before he can recover. I tug the blade free and he cups the ragged mess between his legs, whimpering.

"Freeze!"

I turn and see three Judges standing before me, Lawgivers trained. "Drop the weapon!"

"Family man! Family man!" I yell, giving the recognised code word for an undercover officer. I drop the knife with a clatter, holding up my arms above my head. Behind me, I can hear Jonny moaning.

"Stay down," one of the Judges says, slowly moving forward. "Play dead until this is over."

I nod. Play dead? I can do that.

Five

HIGH UP IN the Grand Hall of Justice, Chief Judge Hershey looked out of the window of her office at the panorama of Mega-City One spread out before her. It was sometimes difficult to believe that to all intents and purposes she was in charge of this chaotic sprawl, and that from the lowliest cleaning droid, sweeping the streets of City Bottom, all points of authority ultimately cascaded up to her. It was a dizzying thought that brought home to her just how much responsibility she wielded, and theoretically how impossible her job was.

You couldn't control the Big Meg, no matter how much Justice Department told itself it did; it was merely a holding action, a juggling act. You stamped down on one section of the underworld, ten more sprang up in its place like some mythical, many-headed beast. The city would endure, the way it had always done, and the wheels of society would continue to turn, but in her low moments Hershey sometimes wondered if her position wasn't just a bit futile. She kept the cogs oiled so the whole machine was able to carry on trundling along, but did any decision she made truly change anything?

Of course, times had changed and she wasn't the

autocrat that other Chief Judges in the past had been. Mandates had to be passed by the Council of Five, and the heads of various departments all had their say in issuing directives. Ever since she'd assumed the office, she liked to think that she'd been an approachable leader – perhaps a little *too* approachable, she thought, thinking of the hours wasted listening to block committees and dignitaries haranguing her with petty complaints – and certainly her slightly liberal outlook did not go down well with some of the more hardline elements within the ranks.

There was no doubt that some of those close to her were waiting for her to fail. They were just waiting for one of her initiatives that promoted an openness between Justice Department and the citizenry to explode spectacularly back in her face and so prompt a return to the good old-fashioned "back to basics" tactic of pummelling the poor saps into submission. She did sometimes question why she bothered offering the public a platform to voice their opinions, when half the time they clearly couldn't care less. Give them a chance to vote on something and they'd whinge that all the thinking was making their heads hurt. She guessed it came down to not wanting to spend her time shuffling papers and finding things to outlaw; she wanted to see the city develop, and for people to take charge of their *own* lives, rather than her – through the judicial system – telling them how to do it.

She wondered what Fargo would make of it all, whether he'd accuse her of living a fool's dream. She could imagine he'd certainly be astonished to see a woman of her age as Chief Judge. It wasn't bad, she had to admit. She was quietly proud of being only the second female to hold the position, and she was most definitely the youngest. Ten years ago, she'd been a regular Street Judge, with no designs on rapid promotion, and now she was at the top of an incredibly complicated chain of command. The route that had taken her there was an eventful one.

She supposed she'd always been a good organiser and took well to ordering others about, and it was in the vacuum that followed the Second Robot War and Volt's suicide that the opportunity had presented itself. Few others were prepared to contest her, and given the fate of her predecessors, it was perhaps not surprising. It was not a secret that your life expectancy dramatically shortened the moment you donned the robes of office. Goodman was assassinated, Griffin shot as a traitor, McGruder went insane before checking out in the line of fire, Silver was murdered at the hands of Judge Death, and Volt went down with a self-inflicted bullet through the brain. Hershey sometimes wondered if she wasn't safer back on the streets.

Indeed, she'd be lying if she said she didn't miss being back out there on her Lawmaster, enforcing the Law. Standing at the window, watching from a distance as the tiny trucks sped along the multi-lane megways below her like lines of insects following intricate paths, she felt very marginalised from the hub of the city. It was perhaps her biggest sacrifice upon becoming Chief Judge; that she wouldn't get to experience again the rush of adrenalin as she busted a sugar deal or pursued a tap gang. While she was up here worrying about making a difference, at least down on the street you had solid evidence of the fact; a couple of dead perps at your feet spoke volumes.

There was a knock at the door. She hadn't been looking forward to this meeting. It was not that she disliked her visitor's company, far from it, but she could see it turning into a confrontation. He wasn't somebody easily assuaged, and despite her authority she couldn't help but feel intimidated in his presence. She'd served under him many times before, respecting his forthright adherence to the Law, but now the tables were turned in their relationship despite him being a good twenty years older than her, and this made her feel a touch uncomfortable, as if she could always sense his unspoken disapproval.

Still, she reasoned, it wasn't as if he hadn't been offered the position in the past. It was clear that he was only content to be at the front line in the war against crime, receiving and acting upon instructions from HQ.

"Come in," she said.

Dredd opened the door and strode into the office. "You wanted to see me, Chief Judge?"

Hershey clasped her hands behind her back and walked away from the window to stand beside her desk. "Yes, this won't take a moment, Dredd." She looked at him, unblinking, but merely saw her reflection in the mirrored visor of his helmet. "I thought you should know I've just had an irate call from Councillor Matheson Peat, complaining about your handling of the Vanessa Indigo affair."

"I expected he would. He's not usually stuck for words."

"He claimed you unnecessarily put lives at risk. He also says you later harassed him at his apartment."

"I went round there to inform him of developments in the Liz Short body dump case. I thought that he might be interested to know that over a dozen mutilated corpses had been found beneath one of his buildings. Evidently, all he's concerned about is what the papers are going say tomorrow."

Hershey snorted in agreement. "Peat's an idiot, there's no question of that. He's also extremely influential, unfortunately. He could make life difficult for us if he starts publicly badmouthing Justice Department."

"Drokk 'em. What's the worst that happens? You don't get invited to a few functions."

Hershey sighed inwardly. Diplomacy was never Dredd's strong point. He didn't understand the subtle balancing act she had to perform to keep the city ticking over: the captains of industry and media moguls she had to pacify; the foreign ambassadors she had to meet and greet with an eye for overseas trade; dealing with the offworld contingents visiting Earth for the first time. Mega-City One couldn't afford to conduct itself unilaterally these days, despite a history of going it alone. It paid not to burn bridges because you never knew when you'd require allies.

"Even so," she replied, "it might be prudent to play this one sensitively. It's attracted a lot of attention from a number of parties." She paused. "You know I've allowed Indigo and her entourage to return to Euro-Cit?"

"So I heard. You want to tell me why?"

Hershey chose her words carefully. "I've been under pressure from the Euro-Cit foreign affairs representative," she said. "You know what they think of her over there, she's a national treasure. If we didn't let her go home, they would kick up a stink."

"So what about the charges relating to her bodyguards' weaponry?" Dredd growled. "We're just going to forget about those too?"

"Indigo claims no knowledge of what her minders were carrying. She's a certified neurotic drug addict, with a history of mental illness, so she probably didn't even know what day it was. Her manager, Lubular, says the bodyguards were vat-grown and hired by a cloning agency. He also didn't know anything about the guns."

"He say that under lie-detector?"

Hershey shook her head. "It doesn't matter, Dredd. With the Euro-creeps making a fuss and threatening to turn this into a diplomatic incident, it's easier all round if we just let them go."

"Seems to me this sets a dangerous precedent. Just shows what you can get away with if you've got enough money and the right connections."

"That's showbiz," Hershey replied, immediately regretting attempting to joke in Dredd's presence. His stony-faced countenance didn't quiver.

"I thought if you committed a crime in this city, you paid the full price of the Law, no matter who you were."

"It's not always that black and white, Dredd," Hershey said wearily. "I've got to think of the big picture, especially if Mega-City One's relationship with the rest of the world is at stake."

Dredd was silent for a moment. "This complaint of Peat's, it gonna go anywhere?"

"Grud, no. Far as I can see, you acted responsibly and did what was expected of you. I just thought you should know there might be some flak coming your way over the next few days. But the councillor will calm down eventually."

"I'm not so sure."

"Trust me, I'll keep him and his cronies sweet," Hershey assured him, smiling. "Indigo's would-be assassin, did you get any ID off him?"

"Some creep called Norris Bimsley. One previous conviction for shouting in a built-up area, otherwise utterly unremarkable. Uniforms that checked out his apartment in Jack Yeovil found a shrine devoted to her. Guess he must've just flipped when he heard she was coming to town."

"Who'd be a celebrity, eh?" Hershey remarked, raising one eyebrow, aware that even Dredd himself had a dedicated fanbase, hard as that was to believe.

The senior Judge didn't respond, and the brief silence was broken by the buzz of the intercom. Hershey went behind her desk and flicked the switch.

"Yes?"

"Sorry to disturb you, ma'am. Garrison in the med-bay was asking if Dredd could stop by after he'd finished his meeting with you."

"OK, thanks." Hershey turned to Dredd. "Seems you're wanted. This is the Liz Short case, right?"

Dredd nodded. "About time we started getting some leads. Been a dead-end so far."

"Keep me informed of any developments," Hershey said, motioning that he could go. "Oh, and Joe," she added when he was halfway across the room, "appreciate you dropping by."

"No problem," he replied, already out the door.

* * *

DREDD RODE THE el down to the med-labs on the lower levels of the Grand Hall of Justice, thinking over what Hershey had said. It infuriated him that creeps with influence could evade the full weight of the Law simply by pulling in a few favours from their pals in high office, and he was surprised that the Chief Judge was prepared to get entangled in that web of self-motivation and mutual back-scratching. She was certainly a different woman to the young Judge that accompanied him on the Owen Krysler quest. It obviously hadn't taken long before the pressures of the position had started rubbing away at the strict values she'd once held, turning her into much more of a political animal. He supposed he had to see it from her point of view as well; if you didn't want the Big Meg vilified by every nation-state on the globe, you had to make some compromises.

That was probably one of the reasons why he hadn't accepted the promotion – his temperament was not best suited to entertaining the morons that circulated at that kind of level. As far as he was concerned, it didn't matter if you were a two-bit Umpty-bagger or a member of royalty. If you broke the Law, you did time.

The el reached the intended floor and he strode into a white corridor, the large windows set into the walls showing suited technicians working at computers or over corpse-strewn tables. A few droids moved from slab to slab, bone-saws whirring or pushing trolleys containing bodybags.

Here in the med-bays, the Judges performed autopsies, identified the John or Jane Does that regularly turned up after another night in the city, conducted forensic tests on murder weapons or crime scene evidence, and patched up those that had been injured in the course of duty. The area smelled chemically clinical, and Dredd's boots squeaked as he walked across the spotless floor, searching for Garrison. He spotted her sitting in front of a screen, tapping into a keyboard. Behind her, the blackened bones that had been pulled out of the Elizabeth Short chem-pit lay across several workspaces, tagged and bagged.

"Garrison."

She spun in her chair and smiled when she saw Dredd. "Got a match on that earring," she said triumphantly. "We were right, the titanium *has* been mixed with polymers outside the city. There's a substance called clarrissium present, which originates only from the Pan-African States. The Africans use it for construction purposes because it's extremely heat-resistant."

"So the victim came from Pan-Africa?"

"Almost certainly. No jewellery like this is imported, though we can't vouch for those sent as gifts, of course. I've checked with Immigration and got them to send me a list of all those that have come into Mega-City One from Africa over the last five years." She produced a printout with a stream of names copied across it. "Some of these have since returned, so they can be discounted, as can obviously the men. That leaves two hundred and fifteen women. Narrowing those down to our victim's age, we're left with thirty-two."

Dredd could feel Garrison building to something.

"I cross-referenced those names with the Missing Persons register and got three hits," she continued. "A quick DNA match with Skully here," she patted the skull the earring had come from, sitting beside her desk in its transparent plastic covering, "and we got a name at last: Emmylou Engels."

"You're sure about the match?"

"Yep. She'd been given a medical examination upon entering the city, and Immigration took a blood sample, logging her DNA onto the database. No question, that's her."

"What about the other bodies?" he asked, gesturing to the array of bones.

"Still working on it," she replied. "Computer's churning through data day and night doing citywide DNA searches. We don't have the point of reference that we did for Engels, so it's kind of a big net we're throwing out."

"When did you ID her?"

"About half an hour ago. Assumed you'd want to be the first to know."

Dredd nodded slowly. "Good work, Garrison." He looked around the room. "Is there a terminal I can use here? I need to access MAC."

"Here, use this one," she said, getting up from her chair. "I've got to go and dissect a brain anyway." She winked and disappeared into another lab.

Dredd sat and logged into Justice Department's central computer, calling up Engels's details. She'd arrived on 14 August 2125 via the Atlantic Tunnel and came looking for work as an actress. Immigration had declared her clean, she had no previous arrest record and was granted a six-month stay in the city. She'd registered her address as 2242/b George Bush Snr, living with her landlady, one Agnes Petri. The same Mrs Petri had contacted her local Sector House on 17 May 2126, saying that she was worried about her tenant, whom she hadn't heard from in over a month. Despite a note claiming to be from Engels saying that she'd found work in another sector, and a suitcase full of clothes having been taken, Mrs Petri insisted that if Engels had gone anywhere, she wouldn't have disappeared so suddenly. She'd also left a number of possessions and was owing rent.

The investigating Judge – Parris – got in touch with Engels's parents and boyfriend in New Nairobi, but they hadn't heard from her since her disappearance, and she hadn't mentioned anything about a new job the last time they had spoken to her. The Public Surveillance Unit had no record of her movements, and in the end, Parris wrote it off as a Missing Person, adding as a footnote that she'd probably done a moonlight flit with some new beau. As a result, Emmylou had joined the thousands who disappeared in the city every year, with no motive or explanation, and were very rarely seen again.

Now, four months after she was recorded missing, her remains had been discovered.

Dredd trawled through the text, assimilating the information. Reading between the lines, it seemed to him that Parris had done only the most cursory of jobs in investigating her disappearance. From the language used in his reports, he clearly thought he was wasting his time chasing after an adult who'd probably deliberately hidden their tracks and didn't want to be found. Parris was of the opinion that he could detect no criminal activity surrounding her vanishing, and believed the landlady was being overly suspicious simply because she was out of pocket. The trail had gone cold and the last entry was logged at the end of May. Other, more pressing cases had moved to the fore and Engels was forgotten; out of sight and out of mind.

And now she's resurfaced, Dredd thought, looking at the small photo of her onscreen – pretty, plump, auburn-haired – and the investigation was kicked into life once more.

Dredd made a copy of the case file, then left the med-bay. He resolved that his next port of call should be the landlady, Petri, to see if she could remember anything several months on, but first he had to deliver the bad news to the victim's family. This was one of the most unfortunate aspects of the job and Dredd was still not comfortable with it after all these years. Normally, in a situation like this, there would be a liaison Judge to soften the blow and comfort the grieving, but with the parents based over in Pan-Africa he would have to do it via vidphone. He found their contact numbers amongst the data stored on the disc and steeled himself for the anguish that was inevitably to come.

* * *

GEORGE BUSH SNR was in the rough end of Sector 20 and looked like it could do with some major structural repairs. Broken windows had been repaired with tape, and there were a few old laser scars from a years-old block war competing with lurid scrawling to make the building appear an eyesore even from a distance. From what Dredd had learned about Emmylou, talking to her mother and father, she evidently had little money and her acting career had not been exactly going great guns. She'd moved to the Big Meg to try to land bigger roles, but lacked the talent or the drop-dead looks that would've made her a star. According to Emmylou's dad, she'd made noises about returning home, her dream unfulfilled.

The couple had taken the grim news hard, and Dredd tried his best to sound sympathetic while at the same time cajoling information out of them that might be pertinent. They had nothing new to reveal since they'd last heard Emmylou had gone missing, and had been secretly hoping that she'd grabbed herself a plum part in some touring company, even though it was completely out of character for her to go off without a word to anyone. They said they were going to scrape what money they had together and come to MC-1, to bring back her remains. Her actor boyfriend – whom Parris had earmarked early on as a suspect, before checks confirmed that he hadn't left the country for the past year – was equally distraught, but did mention something of interest: in one of the last conversations Emmylou had had with him, she'd said that she'd joined an agency. When pressed, however, he couldn't recall its name and dissolved into more tears.

Dredd rapped on the door of 2242/b, and a wrinkled, rat-faced woman in her sixties answered. She peered up at him, squinting.

"Agnes Petri?"

"That's me. If it's about that goldfish licence, I told the man at City Hall I've already paid–"

"Can I come in, Mrs Petri? It's about one of your old tenants, Emmylou Engels."

She ushered him in, saying, "You after her for rent evasion? She owes me a good three months. I've had to get a new gentleman in and put the rent up so I can recoup some of my losses. People like that I've got no sympathy for–"

"Emmylou is dead," Dredd interrupted, looking around the cluttered apartment. The carpet was threadbare and the ceiling stained with something unrecognisable. Grud knew what people paid to live here, but it was probably too much. Dredd wasn't surprised that only unemployed actors were desperate enough to put up with conditions like this. "Her remains were recently discovered."

Mrs Petri shrank against the wall, her hand fluttering to her throat. "Oh. Oh, how terrible," she stammered. She walked over to a tatty armchair and slumped into it. "Oh my grud, that poor girl…"

"You originally reported her missing, Mrs Petri. When was the last time you saw her?"

"I… can't remember," she said quietly, dabbing her eyes with a tissue. "I went out one evening – it must've been April, I think – and she was in then. She was using the computer. When I came back, she'd gone. There was a note saying she'd got a job on the other side of the city, and half her wardrobe had been packed. I assumed she'd be back in a week or so, because she'd left some of her stuff here. When it got to a month, and still I hadn't heard anything, I got worried."

"There was no sign of a struggle? Nobody had broken in?"

"No, everything was how I left it. I presumed she left of her own accord."

"She was using the computer?" Dredd asked. "Show me."

Mrs Petri got to her feet and led him to a small, old terminal sitting on a table by the window. Dredd checked the files on it, noting the dates they were last revised. The latest was Emmylou's CV, on 6 April 2126. That had to be the date her landlady had last seen her. "Are the block CCTri-D cameras working, Mrs Petri?"

She shook her head. "Juves keep vandalising them. Haven't worked for years."

Terrif, he thought. He scrolled down through the CV, noting her last employers, and decided to print a copy off. "What about Emmylou's things that she left behind?" he enquired.

"I didn't know what to do with them," she said, opening a cupboard and retrieving a box filled with clothes, papers and publicity photographs. "I thought I should forward them to her family, but I never got around to it."

Dredd looked at what was left of Emmylou. On the top was the handwritten note that Emmylou had left; it was brief and vague, with no suggestion of where she'd gone, who she was with, or whether she was coming back. He compared the handwriting with her signature on other documents amongst the paraphernalia – mostly speculative letters, soliciting for work from the major film studios – and it looked convincing enough. A headed missive caught his eye: Mega-City Casting Agency. It was arranging an appointment for her to come in so they could find her work. Dredd mentally logged the address.

He handed the box back to her. "Better keep hold of it for the moment, Mrs Petri. We may need to examine some of the contents more thoroughly. I'll have someone come and collect it from you soon. Thank you for your time." He headed towards the door.

"B-but what *happened* to her, Judge?" she asked, following him to the threshold. "Where did she go? Who would want to kill her?"

"That's what I intend to find out, citizen."

FROM ONE END of the spectrum to the other, Dredd thought, as he entered the MCCA building. The carpet was a plush cream pile, and the chairs in the reception area were an artful arrangement of canvas and chrome. The walls were studded with portraits of the agency's top clients – most of whom, he had to admit, he had never heard of – and replica movie posters. For one startling moment, he found himself looking at a picture of his own visage, snarling back at him in front of a post-apocalyptic backdrop. The film was titled *Flight of the Eagle*, and the credits said that he'd been played by somebody called Janus Krinkle. The jowls were a little flabby, he thought, but otherwise it wasn't a bad likeness.

"I see you're admiring your alter ego," said a voice. Dredd turned to see a tanned, muscular man in an expensive-looking suit approaching him. "You gotta say, Janus has you down to a tee."

"You're aware that it's illegal to use a Judge's image for monetary gain?"

"These movies have all been approved by Justice Department," he replied, pointing at the little eagle symbol in the corner of the poster. "They're what we like to call our 'promotional pics'. This one retells your mission to nuke East-Meg One."

"They're propaganda, you mean?"

"Yes. A little anti-Sov entertainment goes down well in friendly territories." He stuck out his hand. "I'm Buddy Laskin, one of the partners here at MCCA. What can I do for you, Judge?"

Dredd ignored the proffered hand. "I'm investigating a case involving one of your clients. Emmylou Engels?"

Laskin frowned. "Engels? The name doesn't ring a bell. Come through into my office, I'll check my records." He led Dredd through into an ostentatious room, bedecked in black and gold. Film props adorned a huge desk, and more posters decorated the walls. Laskin rifled through some documents in a filing cabinet, then gave a little exclamation of triumph. "Ah, yes, Emmylou. Joined our ranks some eight months ago. Terrible actress, by all accounts, but she's cheap and punctual, which goes a long way."

"When was the last time you saw her?"

"Well, according to our files, when we last found her some work. That was back in February when she got a gig working for Catalyst. In fact, she hasn't been in touch since then, which is a bit odd, 'cause she came across as very keen. Is she OK?"

"She's been murdered."

"Jovus…" Laskin went pale beneath his tan. "When did this happen?"

"Possibly not that long after you saw her. She went missing in April. What's Catalyst?"

"It's a film studio – Catalyst Productions. They make the propaganda features you saw out there. Big budget, anti-Sov, war movies. We supply them with lots of actors."

"She didn't have any other work after that?"

"Not through us, but then actors work all over. She might've done some vidverts or something through another agency."

"How was she when you saw her? Did she give any indication of being troubled?"

"Not at all. As I said, she was very keen. She was happy to accept any work that came her way."

"And she didn't say anything about going away?"

"No, she made no mention of it."

"How long have you supplied actors to Catalyst?"

"Hell, years. The movies might not be works of art, but they pay fairly well and it's a regular income. That's the most important thing to our clients."

"Any other of your actors disappear?"

Laskin shrugged. "People drop off our roster all the time. They move on, have kids, join another agency, go abroad. It's not our job to keep track of their movements." He fixed Dredd with a stare. "You don't think somebody's targeting our clients, do you?"

"I'm sure Citizen Krinkle can handle himself," Dredd said as he left.

Outside, back at his Lawmaster, Dredd checked

Emmylou's CV again. The Catalyst job was the last one listed in her employment record – a subtle number called *Total Annihilation*. If she'd done any work after that, then presumably she would've added it to her résumé when she was updating it. The gigs previous to the Catalyst job were fairly evenly spaced, then there was a gap prior to her disappearance.

The fact that there was no struggle at Petri's apartment suggested that, if Emmylou *was* kidnapped, she may have known her abductors and let them in willingly. There was no mention from her parents of her making many friends in the city, so perhaps she recognised somebody from her acting work. A fellow thespian? A director? Maybe Catalyst, as Engels's last employer, could provide some answers.

Dredd swung his leg over his bike and was about to gun the engine when shots rang out. A bullet clipped his thigh, and he instantly rolled for cover. He yanked free his Lawgiver, then glanced at his leg and saw it was just a flesh wound. He peered over the Lawmaster frame, looking for the source of the gunfire, but a moment later the gunfire came looking for him. A roadster screeched around the corner, a perp riding shotgun and spraying him with the contents of a semi-automatic. Dredd dived out of their path, then came up shooting, putting three rounds through the back window of the car. Without hesitation, he leaped onto the bike and roared in pursuit, crouching down as the creep twisted round and started firing again. Dredd thumbed the bike cannons, and the powerful ammo shredded the roadster's back tyres, making it spin out of control. It hit a central reservation barrier and flipped, crashing down on its roof.

The perp with the semi-automatic crawled out of the passenger door window and got shakily to his feet, still clutching the gun. He saw Dredd bearing down on him and tried to aim, but the Judge fired one Lawgiver shot that caught him directly in the forehead. The back of his skull erupted as he flew backwards onto the ground.

Dredd slid to a halt, just as the driver was clambering out. "Freeze!" he shouted. "You're under arrest!"

The driver looked at him, dazed, then raised his hands, a strange beatific expression passing over his face. Dredd had a fraction of a second to notice before the guy exploded with an ear-splitting blast. The detonation threw him off his bike as the perp vaporised before his eyes, windows shattering behind him and red globules pattering down onto the street. Limping around his upturned Lawmaster, Dredd looked at the spot where the creep had been standing and saw only a sooty epicentre with residue radiating outwards.

Mob blitzer, he thought to himself, waving away the smoke and cordite thick in the air. Evidently, somebody didn't want him following this line of inquiry.

Six

MY SHOULDER GIVES me a twinge of pain as I enter Iso-Block 14's infirmary, probably in phantom sympathy to the poor spuggers lying in here with missing limbs, punctured organs and scarred faces. Funny how the baddest, most evil motherdrokkers look like such sorry sacks of shit once they're laid up in bed, regulation PJs on, and heads wrapped in bandages or extremities strapped to a splint. Walking between the beds is like taking a trip into a retired perps' home: a tattooed biker sits upright, coughing violently, a drip running from his arm; next to him, some sickly looking creep with waxy skin is staring at the ceiling, as motionless as a corpse; across the way, an eldster is moaning incessantly, sounding like he won't last the night. If you met any of them in a dark alley, they'd slit your throat as soon as look at you. Now, the only danger they pose is spreading an infection.

That said, the warders don't take any chances, ill inmates or not. There are two guards standing sentry at the entrance, las-rifles slung at the ready, and the med-droids that sweep from one patient to the next administering booster shots or painkillers look as if they could turn nasty if threatened. I instinctively touch my shoulder where Jonny Dansky's bullet shattered the scapula, feeling grateful that it only took a few hours in a speed-heal to knit the bone back together. Something about receiving treatment from a robot gives me the shivers: the cold, metallic fingers grasping your arm as they search for a vein; the stiff, jerky movement of their heads as they look down at you, computing a diagnosis within their circuitry; the realisation that all it takes is one crossed wire and they could be recommending you for experimental vivisection. I, like a lot of people, get queasy around droids. When something checks my pulse, I want to be able to feel a pulse back.

I find Jonny towards the far end of the ward, lying back with his eyes shut. This is the first time I've seen him since he tried to frag me on the ship, and an urge unexpectedly builds inside me to put a gun to his head and give him a permanent kiss goodnight. I haven't taken many bullets in my years with Wally Squad, and when somebody attempts to kill me, I can't help but take it personal. Part of me thinks that pulling the trigger on the drokker would be too quick, and maybe I should try something a little more agonising, like putting his pillow over his head, for example, and watching the bastard squirm as I crush the air out of him. The urge is so strong that my fingers actually brush the butt of the gun jammed in my waistband, but then reason takes over, making me realise that whacking a perp in the middle of an iso-block med-bay isn't the smartest move, surrounded as I am by several dozen witnesses, including a pair of heavily armed Judge-Wardens. Also, I still need information from him. The yearning doesn't go away, but is flattened by the odds of getting away with it. Justice Department takes a dim view of summary executions, especially when the victim is laid up in bed with a severe groin wound and is already looking at life in an iso-cube.

Even if circumstances were different, Jonny wouldn't have the honour of being the first creep I've nailed in cold blood. Occasionally, my undercover status becomes compromised to the point where my own life may be in danger, and a quick bullet to the back of the head can salvage an operation. Sometimes the choice can be hard as it's not unknown for me to grow to like the crims I infiltrate – their ingenuity, their balls-out courage, is sometimes worthy of a grudging respect – and taking out a prospective problem before it grows into a full-blown crisis is a tough decision.

Gangbangers have shared secrets with me like I'm one of their brothers moments before I've slid a blade into their guts, or they've confessed that they think they've got a rat in the house and I've had to act shocked and point the finger of suspicion elsewhere, while at the same time fitting a silencer when their backs are turned. I'm not always proud of the things I've done to protect myself, or the methods I've employed to shake down informants. There are a few pimps and stookie dealers still walking the streets (or rather, limping) nursing broken fingers or cracked kneecaps that have never properly healed.

My light chemical dependency in fact grew out of a need to not dwell on my past. A life built on betrayals is not always easy to live with. My sleep used to be haunted by the faces of those I'd pushed under a zoom train, or battered to death in a dark alley, or dropped a few hundred feet from a hovercar. My desire to keep the truth at a distance, even from myself, meant a not-insubstantial quantity of narcotics was required. The zizz helps me create a barrier between the street player and the lawman inside, struggling to stay in control.

Dansky doesn't open his eyes as I stand over him. Seems hard to imagine that this guy with his head propped on pillows, hands resting on his chest like he's sleeping the sleep of the just, had the drop on me only twelve hours ago. I was a second away from having a slug drilled into my skull by this creep, and the slenderest of margins by which I escaped still gives me heart palpitations. I'm drokking *burning* to drive my fist into his slack-jawed, slumbering face, but it's too public. I opt instead to accidentally-on-purpose bring my elbow swiftly down on his bandaged crotch, while at the same time trying to look as nonchalant as possible as I perch myself on the edge of the bed.

"Motherdrokker!" he screams, folding up, his hands clutching at his wound. "Piece of drokkin' *shit*!"

"Oops. Did that hurt?" I ask, all mock-innocence.

"I'll kill you, you drokkin' asshole," Jonny snarls, reaching for me, then notices the commotion has unsurprisingly brought the attention of the room onto his corner of it. The guards look over, shouldering their rifles, and he slowly relaxes, easing himself back onto the sheets, grimacing as he rides out the waves of pain ebbing from between his legs.

A med-droid trundles across. "What's all the fuss?"

"Sorry, doc," I say. "I think I sat on a sore bit."

"Get this drokkin' bastard out of here," Jonny spits out through gritted teeth, eyes watering. "Spugger wants to kill me."

"Remarkable powers of intuition," I reply, "but that would be against the Law." I reach into my pocket and show the robot my name badge. "Pete Trager, Wally Squad. I'm hoping Citizen Dansky here is going to help me with my current investigation."

The droid peers at my ID, seemingly surprised – if it's possible for a mechanoid to show surprise – that I'm a Judge. A brief flash of self-realisation tells me that I probably look unkempt and dishevelled, and could do with a couple of hours in a sleep machine and a fresh change of clothes. But it merely clicks its eyes up from the badge to my face and nods. "OK. But keep it quiet. I've got sick people here."

"No kidding," I say, motioning to the four hundred pound fattie wheezing and spluttering in the next bed. "Jimmy the Badyear Blimp there murdered three hundred and sixty-five citizens before they caught him." I smile graciously. "Don't worry, doc, I'll try to keep this short." The droid appears satisfied and rattles away, and I turn back to Jonny. "But when it comes to real sickos, you Danskys are in a class of your own."

"Drokk you," he breathes.

"Or should I say Dansky singular, since your beloved brother is at this moment rumbling up the Resyk megway to become the ingredients of a grot pot."

Anger flares in his eyes, but he's not dumb. He knows I'm provoking him and he can't do anything but lose in this situation. He looks at me with contempt. "What do you want, Trager? I've got nothin' to say to you."

"Well, on a purely selfish level, I'm just enjoying seeing you suffer." I tap his leg gently and he visibly flinches. "I bet that smarts, don't it? Do they reckon you can still have kids?"

He doesn't reply.

"Ah, well, probably for the best. You rid the world of one Dansky, the last thing you need is more of the shit-eating simps filling up the city. Shame somebody didn't think of doing the same to your daddy thirty years ago."

He takes this on board before saying, "Y'know something, Trager? My only regret is that I hesitated before blowin' your drokkin' head off. You're gonna have to live with the fact you're only breathin' because of that, because of a millisecond of grace. Your ass belongs to me. Your life stood on the edge and it coulda swung either way."

"Does it all the time, pal. You ain't the first," I say dismissively. "But enough with the pleasantries, I wanna know about these and the buyer you had lined up." I pull from my small knapsack the bundle that I'd snagged on Talón's yacht.

Opening it up, there's a clink of metal on metal as I spread the contents across his bed. The strange and troubling array of devices look like they've come straight out of the Spanish Inquisition. There are five pieces in total, some with more obvious applications than others. The thumbscrews are the most self-evident, a set of mini-cuffs forged from black iron. The largest instrument is some kind of skullcap, with a tightening nut at the top and clamps around the neck area. A nasty serrated blade is affixed at throat height, presumably to slice open the victim's jugular if they were to attempt to twist their head away from whatever the torturer was about to do.

Next to that is a complicated, multi-jointed affair with a tight spring at its centre and several needle-sharp barbs jutting out at different angles. So far I've been afraid to touch it, for fear of tripping a catch and having it snap shut on my hand. It reminds me of a portable man-trap. The last two items are all the more bizarre for their immediate lack of purpose: a curved, spoon-like implement that wouldn't seem out of place in someone's kitchen, and a metallic truncheon, not much more than a foot long, with a hook at one end. Despite their innocence at first glance, it isn't difficult to envision an imaginative psycho getting a fair bit of mileage out of the pair of them.

Although the pieces are clearly antiques, they've been expertly looked after by somebody who knew what they were doing. My guess is that Ciudad Barranquilla Justice Department has an entire section of its armoury devoted to shit like this, and probably doesn't have any qualms about using them on suspects.

Jonny's attempt at acting cool fails miserably as his eyes give away his fear almost instantly. He tries to look at the instruments of torture as if it's the first time he's seen them, but recognition is broadcast all over his face.

"How many times have you sold stuff like this, Jonny?"

He says nothing, turning his head away as if to refuse to acknowledge their existence.

"Talk to me, Jonny," I persist. "Who have you been selling them to?"

"Drokk you," he replies, but there's a catch in his throat and his response lacks venom. He sounds afraid. "I-I don't have to talk to you." He looks at me at last. "Why the drokk should I help you, pig?"

I let that one slide. "I ain't gonna lie to you, Jonny. Once you're out of here, you're going to an iso-cube for the rest of your natural life. There's nothing I can do about that–"

"Seeing as you're the spugger who put me in here in the first place!"

Typical perp self-pity. Always somebody else's fault. "But talk to me, give me a name, and I'll see what I can do to make it easier for you. Maybe even decrease your sentence. You could be out in, say, twenty years. You don't wanna die in jail, do you, Jonny?"

The long, hard road of the rest of his life hits him at that moment. I can see him deflating before me, all the piss and vinegar draining out of him as he realises he'll never taste freedom again. He's weighing up the choice that all criminals have to make at some point in their lives: should he rat out a colleague to save himself, or go to his grave a principled idiot? It doesn't usually take the average creep long to make the decision – no honour among thieves, yadda, yadda, yadda – but Jonny seems surprisingly tormented. Perhaps I underestimated just how much he hates us Judges.

"You... you don't understand," he begins, nervously glancing at the black pieces of metal lying only a couple of feet away. "They'll kill me. They're drokkin' dangerous..."

"Who are?" I have to admit his fear's starting to unsettle me. "They're not going to get you while you're in custody, if that's what you're afraid of. You're safe here."

He doesn't look like he believes me. "I ain't no snitch," he says loudly, as if to mostly convince himself.

"Jonny, if your brother was alive and in your place, do you think he'd be making it this hard on himself? He was always the one setting up the deals, wasn't he? He was the one with the foresight. Now, if he was presented with an offer like this, don't you think he'd jump at the chance to grab something for himself from this mess? You're on your own now, Jonny. Can't rely on your brother for back-up. You gotta make your own decision."

The mention of Brett makes his eyes leak, and he says his sibling's name in a tiny whisper. I almost feel sorry for him.

"Do the right thing. Give me a name, and then maybe one day you'll be able to raise a glass to his memory as a free man."

He screws his eyes up tight and I think he's going to continue stalling me, but after a moment's silence his head drops forward and he says quietly: "Conrad."

"Conrad? That's the buyer?"

He nods. "That's the only name I know. That's all he calls himself."

Sounds like a cover. "And how do I get in touch with him?"

Jonny runs trembling hands over his face. "The number... it's unlisted. Four-double-two-three-six-eight. I don't know where he's based. We speak to him or one of his men and just arrange a meet. Usually at Tommy's."

"The bar on Bleeker?"

He nods again.

"What does Conrad look like?"

He shrugs. "He's a businessman, he ain't a player. Smart, expensive suits, neat haircut. He's very... sure of himself."

"So why are you so scared of him, Jonny?"

He looks at me, his eyes searching mine. "He's powerful. And we've heard what he's capable of."

I stand up and gather together the torture devices into the bundle and put it back into my knapsack. "You made the right decision, Jonny."

"So you'll talk to them, right?" he says as I start to walk away, gesturing towards the guards standing sentry at the door. "You'll let them know I was willing to help? You'll cut a deal?"

"I'll do my best," I reply, giving him a short wave. Then, as I pass one of the Judge-Wardens, I mutter under my breath, "Dansky, in the far bed. He's planning on busting out and taking hostages. Bring him down hard."

I step out into the corridor, smiling, and slightly disappointed that I'm going to miss the fireworks.

TEN MINUTES LATER, I'm standing at a public phone, punching in the number. It rings a couple of times before a man's voice answers. "Yeah?"

"Speak to Conrad?"

"Who is this?"

"A friend. Is Conrad there?"

"He's busy. Gimme a message an' I'll pass it on."

"Tell him I got his antiques, from south of the border."

The phone goes dead, the sudden silence making me jolt. I replace the receiver, unsure whether I'd said something wrong, though Jonny mentioned nothing about any kind of password. Frustration gnaws at me. This number's my only lead and if I've blown it, then the investigation will grind to a halt. As I'm mulling over the possibility of running a trace on the number, seeing if I can narrow it down to a sector – though I can imagine it being rerouted through several different exchanges, leading me on a phantom search before I finally find myself chasing my own tail – the phone rings. I snatch it up.

"Yeah?"

"Who are you?" A different male voice this time. More cultured. My immediate guess is that this is the enigmatic Conrad.

There's no reason to lie. "My name's Pete Trager." I find it easier if I keep my identities to a minimum as it lessens the chance of me slipping up by getting my assumed monikers mixed up. There's also a veracity to people's voices when they speak their own name, a confidence that's notably missing whenever anybody tries to pass off an alias. "I've worked with our mutual acquaintances, the Dansky brothers."

"So perhaps you can tell me why I'm talking to you and not them?"

"Truth of the matter is, they've been the victims of a small hostile takeover. Our friends in Banana City, they saw my organisation was much more efficient at trafficking certain merchandise, and decided to take their business elsewhere."

"Where did you get this number, Mr Trager?"

"The Danskys passed over all their contacts, and I'm more than happy to carry on doing their business with you. In fact, you'll find my prices are extremely reasonable. They were going to sell what I've got for you for eight thou, but–"

"Please." The smooth voice raises a notch. "I do not wish to discuss consumables over the phone, no matter how secure this line is. Right now, the most pertinent matter is why I should trust you."

"Why should you indeed? After all, I'm just a voice in your ear, right? You need verification, somebody to vouch for me." Uh-oh, I'm gonna have to wing this one. "I'm sure Talón will speak highly of me."

A pause. "You have met Frederica Talón?"

"Sure. You could say we both hit it off. And I'm now her man in Mega-City; all her business goes through me." I cross my fingers and take a leap of faith. "You want me to fix it so she gets in touch with you, lets you know I'm on the level?"

Another beat of silence. I get the impression he wants to avoid contact with his Banana City supplier; the least amount of guilty associates the better. Plus he's probably frightened of fraternising with an honest-to-grud gangbanger. This Conrad seems to be one of those high-flyers who thinks he's above the scum that do his dirty work. "That... that will not be necessary. Senorita Talón's judgement is usually faultless over whom she chooses to deal with."

"Usual place, then?"

"Tommy's at ten. I look forward to meeting you, Mr Trager." He clicks off.

I slam down the receiver in triumph. Oh, Petey-boy, you are *sooooooo* cool!

TOMMY'S HAS A certain rep within Justice Department for being a perp-magnet. The joint's namesake was murdered over ten years ago after an extremely competitive game of shuggy, each limb discovered in a different corner pocket, the cue ball placed in his mouth. Despite undergoing several ownership changes and varying managers, it can't seem to shake off attracting all sorts of undesirables. This might be something to do with its location, nestled as it is on Bleeker Street beneath the flyover of a north-west megway, like the building itself is trying to escape detection.

Fat chance. PSU had at least one camera trained on the area almost permanently, sure to catch a few wanted felons passing through. One thing about crims, whether they're smart or dumb, ruthless young turks or seasoned old lags, they're reliable creatures of habit. No matter what they've done, no matter how many times their mugshot might've been flashed up on every Tri-D set in the sector, they can't seem to stop frequenting the same circles. Dogs returning to their own vomit and all that. I suppose by fostering this sense of community, creating an entirely separate level of society within the city, they reason it makes Judges' attempts to infiltrate it all the more difficult. Poor creeps haven't reckoned just how far the tentacles of law enforcement have already breached their extended family.

I arrive early and case the joint, feeling that organised crime could be reduced significantly just by bulldozing the drokking place. Like its patrons, the bar is squat and ugly, its walls blackened by the exhaust fumes of countless vehicles thundering overhead. The neon sign probably breathed its last back when Cal was in charge and nobody has bothered to give it a refit. The line of hoverbikes racked outside look slightly at odds with the grungy exterior; polished and gleaming, they're the status symbols of the local Harvey Keitel Wideboys.

It seems strange that somebody as evidently high-rolling as this Conrad guy should frequent a dive like this. Surely he would stand out like the proverbial mutant at the school disco? Can't see him cutting much ice with the regulars, unless, of course, they are aware of what he's up to... Jonny knew his rep and it almost scared him to silence.

The moment I enter the joint I can feel hostile eyes upon me. Years on the streets have enabled me to exude the necessary aura of menace and unpredictability that you'd expect from a Mega-City perp, but it doesn't stop my presence arousing the creeps' innate feelings of suspicion. Rather than attempting to avoid their gaze, I ride it out by striding up to the bar and ordering a drink, then turn to survey the room. The place is not that crowded, but the clientele have managed to fill it all the same. The Wideboys, sat around a corner table, live up to their name by being huge, hairy motherdrokkers that look like they could snap you in two with a flick of their wrists. Beside me, a couple of grizzled slabheads burnt out on steroids with arms like sides of beef are resting their enormous torsos against the bar.

Although the room doesn't exactly go silent, I can see glances being constantly thrown in my direction, weighing me up, and I give them the stare back, hoping I look mean enough not to tangle with. The strategy seems to work as the threat of violence drops to a low-lying ebb, and they seem satisfied that I'm not the Law. The barman brings me my beer, looking like he'd be happier wrestling Kleggs. He bangs the bottle down with his huge fist and silently takes my creds, clearly disgruntled that I've mistaken this for some kind of public house where anyone can just breeze in.

I sip at the thick, flat synthi-lager, studying a large, dog-eared photo tacked up next to the bottles on the back shelf of the remains of the original Tommy, spread out over the shuggy table. It must've been taken just before the Judges arrived, as if the killer was rather proud of his arrangement and wanted to capture it for posterity. Some wit has scrawled on it "Now That's What I Call A Break!", and I realise as I catch a glimpse in the mirror behind the bar that the table is still there next to the window, presumably stains and all.

I check my watch. Conrad is late. There's nobody here that even approaches his description and I'm a hundred per cent sure I couldn't have missed him. The thought that the guy might've got cold feet starts to play on my nerves, as I feel a little antsy surrounded by so many crims who would cheerfully rip my head off if they had any inkling of what I was. I buy another beer and nurse it for half an hour while listening distractedly to the meatheads to my left relating unlikely romantic conquests, and watching the entrance in the mirror for any new appearances. I must be looking on edge, 'cause eventually the barman notices that I'm still taking swigs from the same bottle.

"Ain't gonna hatch, if that's what you're savin' it for," he mutters, nodding at it as I roll it between my hands.

"Warm enough already," I reply.

I expect him to take offence, but he concedes the point in surprising good faith. "Ain't that the truth. Fridge got knocked out by those drokking 'bots. Whaddya call 'em, Nacker's lot? Ain't got round to fixin' it."

"You mean Narcos?" I say, wondering with an uneasy gulp just how out of date this stuff I'm drinking is.

"Whatever. Pointy headed spugger. All I know is, he owes me a fridge."

"Long dead, my friend. I think you'll have to write that one off." Some Wideboys come through the door to join the group in the corner, and I automatically look up at their reflection.

"You waitin' on someone?" the barman asks, catching my interest.

I consider my answer, unsure whether to say anything. While I don't want every crook in here knowing my intentions, my options are fast disappearing. I decide to go for it. "Was hopin' to catch a guy called Conrad, meant to drink in here. You heard of him?"

He shakes his head. "What's he look like?"

Good drokkin' question. "Smart, stylish. Snobby type. You heard him speak, you wouldn't mistake him."

"Don't get many like that in here. Ain't exactly the Megapolitan Opera House. If I see him, I can let him know you were lookin' for him. You a friend of his?"

"Just got some business to put his way."

"You got a name, just in case he shows up?"

For some reason, I pause, feeling I'm giving too much away. "Just say that Talón was asking after him." I drain the bottle, more for appearance's sake than the taste. The fear's starting to encroach on me and I need a hit. "Gotta take a whizz."

I go into the bathroom, which is as foul as I'd imagined it would be, and lock myself into a cubicle. I take a wrap of zizz from my pocket, empty a line onto the cistern lid and then snort it up, feeling it burn away the paranoia lurking at the back of my head. I close my eyes and let the drug course its way through my system, my pounding heart pumping it along every vein and artery, igniting my senses and boiling my blood. My jaw clenches and my temples throb as the anxiety is pushed back down into the dark once more, and a chemically infused strength of purpose washes through me.

I open the cubicle door and take a fist straight in the face. While I'm seeing stars I take another two body blows, knocking me to the ground. I feel my gun being wrenched from my belt, and the knapsack containing the torture instruments is ripped off my shoulder. Then I'm yanked to my feet and slammed up against the wall, and I get my first look at the two creeps assaulting me. One of the thugs keeps his arm against my throat, barely allowing me to breathe, while the other pats me down quickly, checking for any other weapons.

"He's clean."

"Going on a trip, motherdrokker," the dirtwad pinning me to the wall says, and he slams my head hard against the tiles. Darkness descends on me like a curtain dropping before my eyes.

Seven

"FOR I WILL not rest, I will not sleep, until every Sov is wiped from the face of the Earth."

"But, Judge Dredd, half the city is destroyed! Our forces are decimated! We have barely survived the aggressor's assault! How can we possibly return from this?"

"We will rebuild, because it is in our blood to stand strong against those that wish our citizens harm, because it is the Mega-City way. From the founding fathers, from Fargo himself, whose purity and belief in righteous justice flows through these very veins, it has always been our inner strength and uncompromising vision that has seen the city endure. We have stood on the brink of nuclear extinction, but fought against our enemy and threw it back at them tenfold. The whole world knows what happens to those that threaten us, who attempt to mess with the Big Meg. We will stamp on them, and we will stamp on them hard. There is no time for weakness and grief, for we must forge ahead making sure this city will rise again. Now, if you'll excuse me…"

"Dredd, where are you going?"

"I'm sorry, your honour, but I'm needed back on the streets. While this city still stands and crime is being committed, that is my duty: to protect the people and uphold the Law."

Dredd watched himself riding off into the distance on an authentic-looking Lawmaster – although he wasn't sure the bike needed the spoilers at the back – as the screen faded to black and the Catalyst logo emerged in plain white. It had just been a ten-minute short, rough footage cobbled together from recent shoots for a promotional tool, but he had seen enough to know exactly how awful it was going to be.

Dredd knew little about films and he hardly watched the Tri-D (except when an illegal broadcast demanded his attention) but for a supposedly accurate historical epic, he thought the dialogue was laughably over-the-top and the characterisation unrecognisable. He wondered what McGruder would've made of her role in it, as the actress in question had chosen to portray the former Chief Judge as some kind of simpering dunce who went around asking everybody what was going on. As for this Krinkle idiot who was playing him, Dredd had to assume the actor was either writing his own scripts or else he was being paid by the word, because he couldn't recall ever being so verbose. Speeches had never been his forte; he liked to think his actions spoke for themselves.

The lights flickered on and the studio's PR spokesman stood smiling expectantly at him, like he'd just introduced him to one of his children. "What did you think?"

Dredd struggled for a reaction. "You've taken events in an… interesting direction." In truth, he supposed he couldn't fault the sentiment. There was nothing wrong with a little city pride, and he could hardly criticise the representation of Justice Department. In an age when it seemed every cit and his uncle was distributing pro-democracy literature and taking potshots at any Judge they could find, it made a refreshing change to be painted as the good guy for once. Of course, these films were being made with the Grand Hall of Justice's approval, so they were never going to be anything less than complimentary. "You sell these all over the world?"

"To friendly territories, certainly, who share our suspicions of the Eastern Block. Most of our sales go to Texas City, but you'd be surprised how popular they are in Brit-Cit, mainland Euro-Cit and even Hondo. I think events on Sin City didn't help the Sov reputation to improve, to say the least."

"I guess not," Dredd replied, remembering the time thousands were killed when East-Meg agent Orlok released bacterium on the floating pleasure island. He imagined the televised pictures of the dying, their eyes streaming blood, their faces contorted by swollen growths, would make a horrific impression. After that, who wouldn't enjoy seeing the Sovs getting their butts kicked, time and again? "What's this one going to be called?" he nodded at the now-blank screen.

The PR gimp at least had the good grace to look embarrassed. "*Dredd's Dirty Dozen*. But that's just a working title," he added hastily. "It follows you and your fellow Mega-City Judges in your guerrilla war against the invaders. Y'know, executing collaborators, cutting off Dan Tanna Junction, that sort of thing. We've tried to make it as accurate as possible – you should see the scene where Tanna goes down, it's very impressive."

"I'm sure." Dredd couldn't help but feel distaste for the way a tragic moment in the city's history was being re-enacted for cheap entertainment. He knew this film had a certain role to play, but even so, a lot of good men and women had died in the Apocalypse War repelling the Sovs, and to see their sacrifices captured in such a tawdry fashion was a disservice to their memory. Despite being instrumental in Mega-City's eventual victory, Dredd didn't get any satisfaction from revisiting this specific point in his past, it was too much like picking at a scab, allowing the bad blood that had already been spilled to flow once more.

His overall opinions of Catalyst Productions were mixed; on the one hand, it was without doubt a professional outfit and the various soundstages were all busy in the process of making umpteen different flicks. There was no denying their commitment either, despite the general rottenness of the final product. Serious money was being thrown at these features with a substantial sum of it coming in the form of Justice Department subsidies. The productions utilised advanced special effects and real-life actors (as opposed to the digital versions), which was a cost in itself. Distributing, as it did, its wares all over the world, this was no fly-by-night company.

And yet something about the set-up irked him. Perhaps it was because that very commitment seemed *too* dedicated, going beyond a niche market into something personal and obsessive. He had no evidence of this, of course, it wasn't anything but a niggling feeling, his loony-toon antennae twitching.

Even so, there had to be a particular mindset behind a company to continuously produce something so fastidiously one-track and unrelenting in its depiction of the Sovs as the scum of the earth. It was a psychology of hatred that he found troubling. From what Dredd could see, there was little variation in the pictures. The sets and plots took occasional detours, but the end result was always the same – the East-Meggers got nuked out of existence, and more often than not it was *him* pressing the button. To see his doppelganger up on the screen, as part of this huge, big budget celebration of atomic genocide, made him feel used, as if he was complicit in this institutionalised, corporate xenophobia.

Catalyst's politics had made it friends in high office, however. Prior to his visit he'd read up on the history of the company – what little he could find on MAC, at least – and it had been McGruder, unsurprisingly, who'd seen its potential and helped fund its fledgling productions. Silver had later increased Justice Department's contribution, enabling it to significantly broaden its market share. Both former Chief Judges were hardliners, who probably took no small pleasure in seeing once again that roiling mushroom cloud rise above the remains of East-Meg One. Hershey was a different matter, but he noticed she hadn't removed the financial backing. Ever the diplomat, she was presumably keen to stay onside with the studio's CEO.

And that CEO was the enigma at the heart of his unease; the man behind the movies, Erik Rejin. Records on him were even more skimpy: born in 2066 into a wealthy family who had made their money in kneepads, he later inherited the fortune when his parents and siblings were killed by a Sov missile that was amongst the first payload, to hit the city. Eighteen months after that, he sold the kneepad firm to one of the larger conglomerates and used the money to establish Catalyst. A widower with one daughter, Ramona, reports said Rejin hadn't been seen in public for a good twenty years or so. Dredd's attempts to talk to him had so far been benignly stalled and he'd been saddled with this simpering PR drokkwit instead, who'd insisted on giving him a mini-tour of the studio and running through the company spiel. He'd so far neatly sidestepped any questions relating to his boss, and Dredd's patience was wearing thin.

"You keep personnel records of the actors that work on these films?" the lawman asked.

"We have our employees' records on file, yes."

"I need to check the details of one of your actresses that worked for you some six months back."

The gimp looked uncomfortable. "The records are kept in our head office and Mr Rejin is very, *very* sensitive about his privacy. I don't have the authority to take you over there without his say-so—"

"Listen, creep," Dredd rumbled. "I'm all the authority you need. You continue to give me the runaround, I'll book you for obstruction. Tell your Mr Rejin there's no such thing as privacy in this city, and in my experience anyone who insists upon it usually has something to hide." He took a step closer to the PR goon who visibly cowered. "I'm investigating a multiple murder, and I don't have time for the fun and games of rich boy recluses."

The gimp nodded quickly and retrieved a tiny phone from his jacket pocket, punching in a number and talking quietly and rapidly into it, turning slightly away from Dredd so the Judge couldn't discern what he was saying. Thirty seconds later, he clicked the mobile closed. "I've been instructed to take you through to Mr DuNoye's office."

"DuNoye?"

"Mr Rejin's legal advisor, and his... well, his second-in-command, you could say," he answered. "He's basically in charge of the day-to-day running of the studio."

He led Dredd through a warren of backstage corridors. They passed metres of cabling, discarded props, and the occasional actor wandering from the movie set still dressed in full costume. Dredd couldn't help but do a double-take as Sov Judges nodded at him in greeting.

"Hey, Janus, heard you scored with that chick last night, you old dog," one of them called out, slapping Dredd on the back.

The PR guy laughed nervously and hurried the lawman along before he could reply. "Sorry about that," he muttered. "Reality tends to get a bit mixed up around here." They climbed some stairs, and the surroundings gradually became less chaotic and more plush, morphing into an office environment. The gimp knocked softly on a door and ushered Dredd in. A silver-haired suit was waiting for them, standing behind a desk. Everything about him looked dry-cleaned: his clothes, demeanour, nothing was out of place.

"Thank you, Marcus. I can deal with Judge Dredd's questions," he said, dismissing his colleague, who withdrew gratefully. "I'm Vandris DuNoye, Mr Rejin's solicitor. You say you're investigating a murder case?"

"I wanted to check one of your employees' records. Emmylou Engels. She was in something called *Total Annihilation*."

He nodded. "I remember Ms Engels. A barely competent actress. Is she a suspect?"

"She's a corpse. She was murdered not long after finishing work for your company."

"My grud…" he whispered, his composure faltering for a moment. "I-I'm sorry to hear that. What did you want to know?"

"Whether her personnel file had any mention of a relationship with another employee, or if she'd talked about any problem she might've had with a colleague. I'm fairly sure she knew her killer."

"I don't think she was here long enough," he murmured, tapping at his keyboard. "She had a minor role, came in for maybe a few weeks' filming, maximum." He looked up from his flatscreen. "No, according to her details, she was paid, went away happy and we didn't call on her again. As I said, she wasn't exactly A-list."

"Any associates that you know of?"

"No, there was no one," he replied, then paused in thought. "Wait… she did say something about a mystery man. Joel somebody, lived a few blocks away from her. I presume she was dating him."

"And that's all, huh?" Dredd glanced down at his lie-detector curled in his fist, hidden from DuNoye's view.

"That's it."

The Judge looked around the office. "Your boss at home?"

"I'm sorry, Mr Rejin is not available to visitors. He's very ill."

"I wasn't requesting your permission, DuNoye," Dredd barked. "I'm getting a little tired of you people stonewalling me–"

"And I can assure you, Judge Dredd, that Mr Rejin is not well enough to answer any of your questions. As his lawyer,

I'll make sure that if you insist on disturbing him you will be facing extremely damaging legal consequences."

"Don't spout the Law at me, creep."

"Mr Rejin has some highly influential friends that would make life very difficult for Justice Department if they felt you were harassing an infirm friend of theirs. A number of distinguished Mega-City councillors are all shareholders in Catalyst, including Matheson Peat, whom I believe is already making his opinion of you widely known."

It figured that Peat was part of this rich men's inner cabal. "I couldn't care less what the good councillor thinks of me. Right now, you're hindering my investigation into a multiple-murder case—"

"I've been nothing but helpful to you, Judge Dredd. I've told you all I know. But I will not stand by and allow you to intimidate Mr Rejin. I think I've made my position perfectly clear." He pressed an intercom and said "Marcus, can you escort the Judge back to the studio floor?"

He had to admit this lawyer slimeball was calmness personified and was completely unruffled. "Don't think I've finished with you, DuNoye," Dredd growled, jabbing a gauntleted finger in the other man's face. "If I find out you've been withholding vital information, then even your connections aren't going to save you, understand me?" He stormed out, knocking aside the PR gimp as he came through the door.

DuNoye motioned with his head for Marcus to go after him, then as soon as he was alone, reached for the phone.

DREDD RACED ALONG the Steadman expressway, feeling his investigation was taking a route he hadn't anticipated. What had seemed at the beginning like the hallmarks of a nutjob cult killing now seemed to be growing into something more sinister, more sophisticated. The lead that DuNoye had thrown him – Engels's supposed "mystery man" – was a phoney, he was convinced of that. His lie-detector had told him that the lawyer was feeding him a line, and Dredd could only assume that he had been sent on a wild goose chase, to pointlessly hunt down this mythical date of the victim's. He'd briefly interviewed many of the cast and crew before he left Catalyst, and none of them could remember Emmylou talking about this "Joel" character, or that she saw any of her work colleagues out of hours. They all thought she didn't look like somebody with problems, or who was in fear for her life.

He had a call patched through from Control – it was Garrison. "Dredd, we got the next two DNA matches from the Liz Short body dump. Darryk Fellmore, white male, thirty-two. Lived in Zeta-Jones lux-apts. The other is Ricki Haigle, black female, forty-six, resident of John Malkovich. Both single, no dependants."

"Let me guess, both actors."

"How'd you know?"

"Call it thirty years of Judge's intuition. Listen Garrison, I'm not near a terminal. Can you find out their employment history, see what their jobs were in the months leading up to the point when they were reported missing? If you can't do it through MAC, get a helmet round to their last known addresses or contact the next of kin. I'm heading back to the Grand Hall of Justice, you can contact me there."

"Wilco."

Dredd deliberately failed to mention to her what information he was after. He wanted his suspicions to be confirmed independently. If he was right, then he would have to inform the Chief Judge, who no doubt would be less than happy with his suspicions.

He left the expressway, and turned onto Brassard, weaving his Lawmaster through the traffic. A large truck rumbled past him on the outside and pulled into the middle lane to a chorus of angry horns from the other motorists as they had to decrease speed sharply. Dredd looked for a way round, but discovered they were approaching the mouth of the Naomi Watts underpass and he was going to be stuck behind this thing until he could break clear on the other side. The vehicle was drifting lazily from side to side, the driver seemingly unaware of the build-up he was causing, or perhaps being wilfully obstructive. Either way, the creep was contravening half a dozen highway laws. As they swept into the tunnel, Dredd was just about to give his siren a blast and get the idiot to pull over, when – watching the truck take a wide swing to the left – he realised a split second too late what was going to happen.

The truck slid into the inside lane, as if to allow the other traffic to pass, then slammed on its brakes and slewed itself across the entire width of the road, tyres screeching. Those unfortunate enough to be right behind it had no chance, smashing into its chassis with several thunderous bangs, accompanied by the sound of shattering glass and squealing rubber, all amplified within the confines of the tunnel. The vehicles that followed tried to swerve out of the path of the wreckage, but had nowhere to go. They sideswiped the walls of the underpass or buried themselves into the tangle of metal that now completely blocked the thoroughfare.

Dredd twisted his bike in an effort to stop himself ploughing into those in front, but lost control, the Lawmaster skidding away from him. He let go and tucked himself into a roll, his shoulder pads and helmet taking the worst of the damage as the tarmac reached up to greet him like a fist. The impact winded him, but he couldn't feel any broken bones as he staggered to his feet and, to his frustration, found his bike lying immobile beneath the debris.

The air was filled with the stink of oil, gasoline and burnt rubber, and small fires began to spring up in the ruptured engines of the vehicles twisted out of shape by the collision. Some citizens were emerging from their cars, dazed and nursing injuries, others were slumped forward in the front seats unconscious, or were unable to move because of the debris trapping them in. Dredd couldn't even get to the driver of the truck to see what had caused the pile-up, the cab rendered unreachable by the sheer number of wrecks toppled over on one another. His priority was to call in reinforcements and start cutting the casualties free before the whole tunnel went up.

"Control, this is Dredd. We have a major accident in Watts underpass, med and meat-wagons required," he barked into his mic, striding back towards the entrance. "Brassard is now completely blocked. Get helmets down here to redirect the traffic, and we need cutting equipment to free the injured–"

He stopped mid-sentence, momentarily stunned by the audacity of what he was seeing. Nine or ten men in full-face masks and anonymous fatigues were swinging down on ropes lashed to the pedway above the tunnel mouth. They had spit guns and assorted hand weapons – mostly crowbars and axes – strapped to their backs, and they acted quickly and confidently. Once they touched down onto the road surface, they began to move amongst the stationary vehicles, throwing the groaning cits aside.

"Control, this was no accident. We have wreckers working Watts underpass. Repeat, back-up required, wreckers in force in Watts."

"That's a roj. Units will be with you shortly."

Dredd drew his Lawgiver, flattening himself against the wall, thinking that he should've guessed the truck had been used to intentionally block the tunnel. Whilst he'd dealt with plenty of wreckers before – perps that caused carnage by attacking motorists, breaking their way into the vehicles to steal money and valuables – he'd never actually been in the centre of a robbery itself. The creeps had certainly picked the wrong moment to launch an attack, but if they were checking the traffic entering the underpass, they must've seen him going in with it. So why choose now to commence the assault?

Unless…

The perps were splitting up, covering the full expanse of the tunnel. Some of them grabbed rings, wallets and necklaces, smashing car windows and snatching bags from the laps of the barely conscious, but others – while to all intents and purposes appearing to be on crowd control – were scanning the wreckage, looking for something. Or some*one*.

"Move in," one of them ordered. "Keep searching. We've got five minutes, tops."

This wasn't an ordinary hold-up, Dredd was certain of that now. They wanted it to look like a wrecking job, but they were using it as a cover. The robbing of cars was cursory and indiscriminate, as if that was their secondary goal. They'd staged this huge accident for one objective; to eliminate one of those trapped in the tunnel, but to make it look like the victim had not been singled out and was just in the wrong place at the wrong time. Dredd had a good idea who that intended victim was.

Well, he wasn't going to make it easy for them. He emerged from the shadows, Lawgiver raised, and shouted: "I'm giving you creeps one chance to drop your weapons and surrender. Hands in the air, *now*!"

The wrecker Dredd presumed to be the leader pointed the Judge out to the others. *"Nail him!"*

Dredd ducked down behind a car as he was met by a hail of automatic fire. Bullets ricocheted off the bodywork of the wrecks, shattering windows. Those citizens still trapped in their vehicles were ripped apart, jerking in their seats as they were caught in the onslaught, bodies riddled with ammunition. The wreckers were pouring the fire on, squeezing their spit guns dry, paying little attention to who was in the way. Dredd knew he had to finish this quickly before any more innocent lives were lost, and before a stray round ignited the huge tinderbox they were in the middle of.

The barrage halted. Through the wheel arch of the vehicle he was using for cover, Dredd saw feet approaching in his direction. Crouching, he shot two Standard Execution rounds through the meathead's lower leg. The wrecker collapsed with a yelp, his eyes meeting Dredd's for a second before the lawman put one more through his open mouth, forcing teeth and skull shards to explode back across the tarmac. The Judge crawled rapidly round to the corpse and snatched his spit gun, reasoning he could do with the extra firepower. He stood and sighted two more of the creeps sneaking in from the right, and blew them away before they had a chance to aim.

"There!" came a cry, and Dredd rolled over a car bonnet, bullets popping all around him. He felt one ping off his helmet as he came down two-footed on the road and opened fire, both barrels blazing, his Lawgiver in his right hand, the spit gun in the left. A round from the latter satisfyingly took out two of the creeps at the same time, the ammo blowing through the first one's torso to catch his partner as well, slamming them both against the underpass wall.

Dredd moved before the rest could pin him down, slaloming between vehicles, making sure he kept all of his assailants in plain sight; he didn't want any of them getting behind him. By his reckoning, he'd taken down half their number already, and there were five of the drokkers left. Ideally, he would've liked to have fired off some heatseekers, but he couldn't be sure they wouldn't catch some of the cits still left alive in the tunnel. Armour-Piercing was another matter, though. Dredd saw one of the creeps squatting on the other side of an upturned mo-pad and put several AP rounds through the engine block, catching the guy in the neck and chest. He heard sirens in the background, and so did the remaining gunmen.

"Drokkin' jays comin', man!" one of them cried and made a break for it, heading for the tunnel entrance. The lawman sighted his weapon and shot the escapee through the kneecap, sending him sprawling, his screams echoing back along the underpass.

"Heads up, Dreddy," the leader yelled and Dredd had a moment to catch a glimpse of the grenade whistling over in his direction before he was moving again. He leaped onto the roof of a car, twisting away from the rattle of gunfire that followed his movements, and gained as much distance as he could before the explosion. Seconds later, the entire structure shuddered as the grenade detonated, blowing vehicles into the air and sending an orange fireball shooting towards the tunnel mouth, incinerating everything in its path. Dredd rolled and found cover, feeling the heat blistering his face as it passed overhead. He had to get out; the fumes and leaking fuel set alight by the blast were going to turn this place into an inferno.

He got to his feet and saw the last three wreckers also charging for the opening. Looking back, most of the vehicles involved in the initial collision were ablaze, and a small chain reaction was going off, spreading to the surrounding remains. Dredd grabbed an injured perp, blackened but still breathing, and tugged him towards the light. Street and Med-Judges were arriving at the scene, leading motorists standing at the tunnel entrance out of the way. As Dredd emerged, he ordered them to get back.

"Move out! The whole tunnel's going to—"

Before he could finish, an eruption inside sent flames spiralling out, the wave of hot air pushed out with it throwing a nearby meat-wagon off its wheels and onto its side. Fire licked at the roof and sides of the underpass, the heat forcing the Judges to retreat. A droid fire-fighting crew came forward and attempted to douse the conflagration.

"Some cits still in there," Dredd said, trying not to choke on the black smoke pouring out of the underpass.

"And who's this?" a Judge called Laverne asked, motioning to the semi-conscious perp at Dredd's feet.

"One of those responsible," he answered. "Last three got away. Did you see what happened to them?"

"Nope. Must've escaped the same way they came in." Laverne nodded at the ropes dangling above the tunnel entrance. "If you've got a description, we'll put out an APB."

Dredd shook his head. "Masked. Anyway, they'll have had a change of clothes and are probably headed to another sector by now. We'll just have to hope this creep coughs up some names." He gave the wrecker a gentle kick, getting a soft groan in response.

"Quite a mess," Laverne said, looking up at the smoke and flames. "Guess they didn't figure on holding *you* up as well."

Dredd didn't reply.

"HAVE YOU ANY idea of the seriousness of what you're suggesting?"

"I'm fully aware of the implications, if my suspicions are proved correct, of course. I don't make a habit of casting wild accusations."

Hershey sat forward at her desk, hands clasped together in front of her. "But you're accusing a major film studio – one with links to Justice Department, I might add – of being instrumental in the kidnap and murder of several citizens?"

Dredd nodded. "Something's rotten at the heart of Catalyst, I'm sure of it. Engels disappears a few weeks after working for the company and Haigle vanishes two months after her first gig there. Fellmore appears in three of their productions before his disappearance a year later."

"I've read the report," Hershey said testily, indicating the papers spread out before her. "It might just be coincidence. If someone's murdering actors, then their places of work are all going to be fairly similar."

"It's the single unifying factor between the victims. They've all got different backgrounds, different ages, different sexes, but they all worked for Catalyst at some point in their lives. They also all seem to be single, with no close family ties."

"Meaning?"

"Meaning someone's profiling them, choosing them because nobody's going to notice they're missing for a while. I looked into their Missing Persons files and Haigle hadn't been registered missing until eighteen months after her probable time of death. Nobody knew anything about Fellmore. Both their apartments had been re-let, the presumption being that, as actors, they'd found work in another part of the city, or left the country altogether."

"But you have no evidence," Hershey reiterated. "Nothing concrete. This is all supposition."

"I know that DuNoye creep lied to me, giving me a false lead to further muddy the waters of the investigation. If he's protecting Rejin, I want to know why. Plus there have now been two attempts on my life. Somebody with a lot of money is behind them if they can afford a mob blitzer or hire a wrecking crew to take me out."

"But we've got no names to connect them. The drive-by shooter was identified as some lowlife called Jove Parnell, who hadalready done time for ARVs and who wasn't even gang-affiliated. And that perp you pulled out of Watts knows nothing. Psi-Div probed him and all they got was that he was hired by a voice on the phone to do a wrecking job."

"They're the soldiers. They're not going to be told anything if it means we can use that info to get at the creeps at the top. We're looking at systematic murder here. If we're gonna break the organisation open, we gotta get at the brains behind it."

Hershey sighed. "Erik Rejin is a staunch supporter of this office and he makes many welcome contributions to our funds. If you're wrong about this, Dredd, it could prove very costly."

"I'll stake my reputation on it," Dredd replied flatly.

The Chief Judge sat back in her chair, thinking. Finally, she said: "What are you proposing?"

"We put someone inside Catalyst."

Eight

"WAKE HIM UP," says a voice even my mind, floating out on the ether, tells me I recognise. My embattled memory tries to put a name to it, but it's frustratingly sluggish. Seconds later, sharp pain lances through the haze of disorientation and consciousness rushes up to drag me out of the blackness. My heavy eyes open slowly and my body takes several moments to realise the situation: I'm being held upright, two pairs of arms supporting my weight. The room is darkened, with no distinguishing features that I can make out, other than the floor feels smooth and cold beneath my feet, like it's bare stone. There is a man standing before me, his features shadowy until he steps into the circle of light I'm in. Must be a spotlight directly above me.

"Is he awake?" the speaker asks, and now I know where I've heard that cultured voice before. His words echo slightly and I get the impression we're in a fairly large, high-ceilinged room, but even as my eyes become accustomed to the darkness I can see nothing beyond my captors.

One of the figures to my side enters my field of vision – it's one of the creeps from Tommy's bathroom – and slaps me hard. I can't help but cry out, my yelp descending into a snivelling cough as I taste the blood filling my mouth.

"Looks like it," the meathead replies.

With the return to consciousness, my senses start reporting every injury demanding my attention. My face feels like tenderised munce. Blood's dribbling down my cheek from the cut bisecting the bridge of my nose where creep number two caught me with his ring when he drove his fist into it. I'm guessing it's broken, the cartilage mashed into the walls of my nostrils. I can't breathe out of it and the razor-edged gasps that emerge from my mouth sound like wretched sobs, drawn from the harsh pit of my chest. Each swallow feels like a shuggy ball is being lodged behind my tonsils.

My head lolls forward as bloody drool spills from between my lips and creep number one wrenches me back upright, smacking me forcefully a couple of times against my temples. "C'mon," he mutters. "You ain't dead yet."

The man I know must be Conrad stands there looking for all the world like this is happening on his Tri-D set. He wears a blank expression on his handsome, middle-aged, but curiously unlined face, as if this physical, ugly element of criminal activity is happening to some creature far below on the evolutionary scale; like it's feeding time at the zoo.

My aching, drug bleary mind makes a couple of snap judgements about him: firstly, he is remorseless and incapable of feeling empathy, but at the same time he's not a regular con, but rather someone put in charge of a couple of thugs. Secondly, he's not the arch-perp behind all this, but an errand boy, a gofer acting on his master's bidding. A barely functioning, cogent part of my brain realises that while he could order me dead without a moment's hesitation and wouldn't think twice about it, he's still an employee and answers to his boss. I gotta tip the advantage my way and make myself indispensable, otherwise he'll get his goons to chop me into pieces and flush me down the pan.

"Who are you, Mr Trager?" Conrad asks evenly, flattening down his thousand-cred haircut.

"Just... answered your own... question," I manage to spit out.

He continues as if he hasn't heard me. "You carry no ID, you have nothing to verify that you are indeed who you say you are. True to your word, you have brought the merchandise," he taps the bundle of torture devices that they snatched off me the moment they pounced, "for which I am grateful. But the methods by which you obtained them still vex me. All attempts by my people to contact the Dansky brothers have been fruitless."

"T-that's 'cause they're... lying at the bottom of the... Black Atlantic," I say, wincing, short of breath. "I told you... there's been a... h-hostile takeover."

"You expect me to believe that you wiped out the Dansky gang single-handed?"

"N-no, I had help. Fuh-Frederica Talón and her men... swapped allegiances."

"And what did you offer them that they found so irresistible?"

A phrase I remember Brett using pops into my head. "K-keys to the kingdom."

Conrad takes a step closer to me, peering into my face. He can't quite conceal his distaste at the dried blood caked to my skin, the bruise swelling up on my forehead, forcing my right eye partially closed, the idiot yawning of my mouth as I gulp for air, my nose a ruined mess. Something about his disgust, the animalistic repulsion of my bloodied state, creeps me out and it occurs to me that maybe the Danskys were right to be scared of this guy. There's clearly an unhinged mind behind that smooth exterior.

Conrad reaches out his fingers to my face and traces the outline of a welt on my cheek with the lightest of touches, moving his hand up past the back of my neck. Then he grabs my hair and yanks hard, tugging my head back, and moves his lips close to my ear, so close that I can hear the wet sound of his tongue as the words curl out, hissed and heavy with menace: "Who – *are* – you?"

"You... think... that I'm... l-lying to you?" I gasp, trying to keep my voice as steady as possible. It's not just the pain that's affecting me now, but a cold, hard dread that's building in my belly. "You don't... t-trust me?"

"I don't like change, Mr Trager. Change is bad. Change brings with it problems, it can upset the status quo. My colleagues, my employer, they don't like to see new faces. They like to keep the system pure and untainted, free from those that seek to enter from the outside."

"I b-brought you the... gruddamn offer of the w-week," I reply, my watery eyes looking up into his, my hair tearing away from my scalp. "I'm your... n-new contact that can g-get you... all the B-Banana City goodies that you want, and you're gonna th-throw that away 'cause you d-don't know my face?"

"The organisation I represent, Mr Trager," Conrad says, pomposity and self-importance oozing from every pore, "takes its secrecy very seriously. We had a beneficial relationship with the Danskys because they were reliable and didn't ask any questions. Now they're gone, and out of nowhere you pop up on the scene. You'll forgive me if I'm the tiniest bit suspicious."

"S'way it is on the street. Deals come and go, people come and go. The p-point is... whether y-you're prepared to g-grab the opportunity."

Conrad smiles and releases me from his grip, patting my cheek softly. "And now it is time for *you* to go, Mr Trager. You're too much of a security risk, I'm afraid." He glances at the goons holding me. "Take him down to City Bottom and dispose of him."

"Wait, wait," I weakly protest, trying to resist the creeps as they attempt to pull me away. "This... this is a trust issue, right? You don't know me from Aaron A Aardvark, so you're gonna sling me in a garbage grinder?"

"Something like that."

"What's it gotta take, man, to... convince you I'm a square bear? You think I don't have the cojones to join your group? What d'you think happened to the Danskys?"

Conrad pulls an exasperated expression. "Mr Trager, I don't know what has become of the brothers, but I remain unconvinced you were responsible. Now, I have better things to do than stand here arguing with you–"

"Lose me and you lose all your supplies from South-Am. Talón won't deal with anyone else. Take me onboard an' you'll have direct line to torture central. Won't have to bother with middlemen."

"This is bullshit," creep number two snarls.

"Trust has to be earned, I know that," I continue. "I c-cannot be automatically granted your approval... without some show of loyalty."

"Why don't we just whack him here, boss? Only way to get him to shut the drokk up..."

Conrad holds up a hand, looking amused. "Hold on, I want to hear what he's got to say." He gestures for me to go on.

I try to straighten myself, clearing my throat. "You say you don't like those that seek to enter your organisation from the outside. W-what do you do, for example... if you need to replace one of your men? Do you take on the p-person responsible for their removal... The person who has shown themselves to be the s-stronger?"

The question flummoxes him. "I don't... the situation has never arisen–"

"But you're going to need... to replace *him*," I continue, making a sideways nodding motion with my head at creep number two, standing diagonally to my left. "Who would you t-trust to take his place but his most obvious s-successor?"

"But he's not–"

I lash out, my speed and strength catching them unawares. I elbow creep number one in the midriff, loosening his grip, then spin and sweep the legs from beneath creep number two. As he lies prone, I flatten my right hand and deliver a powerful blow to his throat as if it were a blade, directly above his Adam's apple. It destroys his trachea and he gags, unable to swallow or gasp for breath. As his hands go to his neck and he struggles to his knees, his eyes bulging, a horrible spluttering noise emerging from his mouth, I bunch my fist and drive it into his face, demolishing his nose, splintering the bone. He collapses instantly, hitting the floor like a dead weight.

Conrad and creep number one have barely had time to register the attack when I turn back to them, their eyes wide, mouths agape.

"Seems like you have a vacancy," I say.

I'M SITTING AT a bar on Feltz, nursing my sixth or seventh whiskey, or whatever synthetic derivative that I've been served, and I'm allowing the alcohol to dull my senses and soften the pain. My swollen, bruised face is attracting attention from the other patrons and the barman is giving me distasteful glances every time I order another round, but by now I'm past caring. I want to drink until I can no longer feel the ache in my limbs or the throbbing in my skull or remember the sensation of the perp's windpipe disintegrating at my touch. I think I've fractured some bones in my hand, and I'm having trouble holding the glass without it shaking.

As I suspected, a display of utter ruthlessness was enough to convince Conrad that I was genuine. Although his surviving crony had to be restrained from putting a bullet through my head, Conrad himself didn't seem that upset by the violent passing of his colleague. In fact, he appeared impressed by my casual brutality and lack of mercy, as if wiping out a rival was the way to get ahead in his organisation. Despite managing to wheedle myself into his trust, I thought I had still better watch my step if I didn't want to end up the same way.

Conrad had said he had a job for me, a trial run, that if successful would open all sorts of doors for a man of my talents. I was told to be at Tommy's in three days' time when a guy called Alphonse would pick me up and show me what the job entailed. I was blindfolded and taken on a short, ten-minute journey before being left on a street corner. Clearly, his trust didn't extend far enough to reveal the base they were operating out of. I know that he has just enough faith in me to keep me alive for the time being, but beyond that I'm going to be treated with caution.

Despite my conscience telling me that I should be celebrating having penetrated Conrad's mysterious outfit, I merely feel deflated and weary. And maybe a touch scared. My head feels too heavy for my neck to support, and every time I close my eyes I see the faces of the perps I've nixed to maintain the great lie that is my life. A blood-spattered gallery of accusatory glares, existences wiped out... for what? For the greater good? Pawns that could be sacrificed because it got me closer to the Mr Bigs, the creeps who were really pulling the strings. And what did that make me? Someone who saw life as so meaningless that it could be snuffed out at the drop of a hat? Who was I to see madness in this Conrad character, when it seemed I was cut from the same cloth? Perhaps that was what frightened me – there was something about him that was very familiar to me, a kindred spirit. We're bonded by the blood we have no qualms about spilling.

The alcohol is making me maudlin, I realise. I ought to go outside, get some fresh air, shed some of the ghosts clinging to me like cigarette smoke. But maybe one more for the road... I raise my hand slightly, trying to attract the barman's attention, suddenly dimly aware that there's somebody sitting next to me.

"You look how I feel," a sultry female voice says. I turn to look to my right, eyes struggling to focus. An attractive woman – dark hair, bright red lipstick that matches her tight little dress – swims into my vision. She doesn't attempt to hide her shock at my appearance. "Jovus, somebody sure went to work on you."

"You should see the other guy." I smile weakly, even the slightest muscle twitch giving me pain. The barman ambles over and I slide my glass towards him. "Fill her up." I glance at the woman. "You want a drink?"

"Wouldn't be in here if I didn't," she replies. "I'll have the same." When the barman's gone, she asks: "So, you walk into a door?"

"More like two doors walked into me. My fault, really, my head kept getting in their way." She laughs, the first joyful sound I've heard all day. "Let me guess, hard day, right?"

"Hard *year*; one I'm trying to forget," she whispers.

I clink her glass. "Join the club. We can have mutual amnesia." I take a gulp, the fiery liquid burning its way to my stomach. "Whaddya do?"

"Professional heartbreaker."

"I can see that. Does it pay well?"

She smiles. "Not really, but there's plenty of job satisfaction. How about you?"

"Actor." It feels good to be knowingly swapping untruths with someone, both of us aware of the yarns we're spinning, like we're creating new lives just for tonight.

She looks mock impressed. "Wow. Would I have seen you in anything?"

"Well, it tends to be underground stuff, mainly."

"There's some drokking brutal critics out there," she says, nodding to my bruises. She reaches out and lightly touches the swelling above my eye, and it takes enormous willpower not to lay my hand on top of hers and keep it there.

"They don't pull any punches, that's for sure," I reply quietly.

We chat briefly, both circling the truth like dancers. For me, this kind of invention is second nature; another skin to step into, another role to play. She keeps up with me every step of the way, obviously having done this sort of thing before. Despite the lack of honesty between us, there's a warmth to her company that I find beguiling and comforting. I always did have my head turned by a pretty face and an easy smile.

An ache gnaws at the back of my skull and I groan. "Ugh. I've drunk too much."

"Come on," she says, sliding off her bar stool. "Let's go somewhere more private."

The floor seems uneven as I join her, and my legs feel like they're going to buckle any second. Fatigue and inebriation are crashing down on me. She slips an arm around my waist and steadies me. This close to her, I can smell her scent, feel the softness of her body. As she guides me out the door, I ask, slurring slightly: "What's your name?"

"Sam."

"I'm—"

"I know who you are, Pete."

Shock sobers me up fast. I resist her pull, standing stock-still and looking into her eyes. "How do you…"

"I was sent to bring you in," she replies, motioning with her head towards the street. I follow her gaze and see two Judges beside a catch-wagon, waiting for us. "Hendry wants to talk to you." She opens her handbag and I steal a glimpse of the Justice Department badge contained within. She smiles reassuringly. "You're not the only one that can put on a performance."

I'm SITTING ALONE at a small table in an interrogation room, several cups of synthi-caf now percolating through my system in a bid to stave off the effects of the alcohol. I find the blank walls, intended to be threatening and dislocating to the suspect, oddly comforting. After too much drug-induced hyper-reality and a brain-deadening comedown, it feels good to be in some nowhere-place, where I can't get over-stimulated. The spartan nature of Justice Department holding tanks evokes the cold, brutal efficiency with which the Law is administered, and is supposed to put the fear of grud into the perp, but for me, it seems like a welcome relief.

The door opens and Hendry walks in, a cane in one hand aiding his limp. He takes one look at my sorry state and shakes his head, lowering himself into the other chair across the table from me. These are the only pieces of furniture in the room.

"I feel worse than I look," I tell him.

"Helmets said you were intoxicated when they brought you in."

"Medicinal. It numbs the pain."

Hendry sighs. "Trager, do you remember our last conversation? I seem to recall giving you a friendly warning about enjoying life on the street too much–"

"Gimme a break, chief. I'd just had the shit kicked out of me. If I'm not entitled to a drink–"

"You gave up your entitlements years ago, when you became a Judge," Hendry snaps. "Exactly what does getting drunk benefit you, other than to lower your defences and leave you compromised? You're an officer of the Law, for drokk's sake, you can't afford not to be alert."

My superior's words cut through me like a las-saw; a napalm-burst ache blossoms behind my eyes. I wince, rubbing my temples. "Sending a pretty face in there was your idea, no doubt?"

"Thought we'd bring you in gently. Good job Harvey was a Judge and not an assassin, you wouldn't have made her job too difficult for her."

"Y'know, your concern is quite touching. You haven't once asked how I came to get all these." I gesture to my bruises.

Hendry pauses for a second, then says softly: "You went ahead with the torture deal? How did it go?"

"Weird with a beard. This creep the Danskys were so afraid of, guy called Conrad, he's a complete fruit-loop.

Looks like a regular cit on the surface, but he's a drokkin' nutcase underneath, man."

"Conrad? As in Conn? As in *Beast That Ate the Beast That Ate Mars?*"

"Hey, that was a good drokkin' movie."

Hendry cracks a smile. "Hell of a movie."

"But, yeah, that's all I know him by. Gotta be a cover name. They're drokkin' paranoid about outsiders."

"They didn't trust you?"

"Eventually." I flash back to the creep on his back, my hand chopping down on his throat, the awful gagging of his final breaths. An involuntary shudder travels my spine. "I convinced them I was on the level."

"What do you think he's up to?"

"I got a meet in a few days' time, guess I'll find out then. I think they're trying to test me."

The door opens again and a figure fills the frame. At first, I think it's just a uniform come to deliver a message, but then this gruff, rumbling voice emerges from it and I recognise who it is instantly. I've heard that snarling bark a hundred times on Tri-D, growling at reporters or delivering a warning to terrified viewers about staying out of trouble. "This your wonder boy then, Hendry?"

Grud*damn*. It's Dredd.

He strides in, every bit as intimidating in the flesh as his reputation suggests, a file tucked under his arm. He throws me a look that says he doesn't think much of me at first glance, and I try to give him an unimpressed stare back, but the truth of the matter is that I'm a touch star-struck. The man's a legend, responsible for saving the city half a dozen times over, and he's the benchmark by which every Judge must test themselves. There is so much weight and history flowing through his bloodline that it is difficult not to be nervous in his presence, even if you are a fellow officer. You feel your every word, your every action, is being judged and invariably will come up wanting. There are few that are his equal.

"Dredd," Hendry acknowledges. "This is Trager, one of my best Wally Squad operatives."

I raise my eyebrows at my superior, surprised by my commendation. I had always guessed that I was a little too close to the edge for Hendry's comfort. But I suppose I do get results. "What's all this about, boss?"

"Your infiltration of the torture-buyer's organisation may have links with my ongoing investigation into a number of murders," Dredd interrupts tersely, putting the file down on the table. "You've heard about the Liz Short body dump?"

I nod, thinking back to the piece in the *Mega-Times*. "Yeah, I read about that. Dead were pulled out of a chem-pit, right?"

"The victims that we've managed to identify have all been actors, and have all worked for a film studio called Catalyst at one time or another. They make anti-Sov propaganda movies. I believe that the company is a front for an outfit that is kidnapping, torturing and murdering citizens."

"Whoa." The name Catalyst rings a bell. To be told that it was killing its actors was like hearing that Dave the Orang-utan was actually a gimp in a monkey suit – a big deal to wrap your head around.

"You sold on the instruments of torture from Banana City to your contact, I understand," Dredd continues. "Where did you meet him?"

"I was told the handover usually took place at Tommy's, that bar on Bleeker. Creep never turned up but sent a couple of goons to collect me. They knocked me unconscious and I woke up in this big, dark building. Nothing I could recognise; could've been any kind of warehouse."

"Or a studio?" Hendry puts in.

"Maybe. There was a spotlight right above me. Everything else was in shadow."

"The creeps that grabbed you, would you recognise them again?" Dredd asks.

No drokkin' kidding. You don't forget the face of a man you've killed with your bare hands. "For sure."

Dredd leans in, flips open the file and retrieves several surveillance photographs showing grainy images of three men emerging from a block main entrance with a woman. She's carrying a couple of suitcases. "We pulled these off the PSU camera trained on George Bush Snr. We've narrowed down the day we think one of the victims was kidnapped, and went through the footage. I think this is her being taken away."

I squint at the pics. "They're wearing blur-masks."

"I know. But is the clothing, anything else, familiar?"

I shake my head. "These aren't the goons that went for me."

"What about the buyer?" Dredd persists. "Did you get a good look at him?"

"Sure, when he wasn't having me used as a punchbag." I point at the swelling above my eye. "I got a fractured–"

"Save it for the meds," Dredd replies dismissively. "What did he look like?"

"Grey-haired, suited motherdrokker. Not your average crim, but loonier than a barrelful of muties."

Dredd pulls out another pic. "This him?"

I don't have to hesitate. Conrad's self-important, smooth visage glares back at me. "Hell, yeah, that's him. He got form?"

Dredd shakes his head. "This is his citizen ID. He hasn't got a record. His real name's Vandris DuNoye. He's Catalyst's legal eagle and the right-hand man to the creep behind the company."

"Drokk me," I say, genuinely shocked. "He mentioned something about his employer."

"Erik Rejin. He's the meathead at the top I want to nail, but the rich creep's surrounded himself with a layer of protection I can't get close to. That's where you come in."

"Get inside the organisation," Hendry says to me. "See what you can find. We gotta blow it wide open from the inside." He pauses, glances at Dredd, then adds: "Rejin's got a daughter, Ramona. Must be in her early twenties.

Get close to her. We, uh, know you got a rep with the ladies, so see if you can use that to your advantage. Get what info you can out of her."

"Keep me updated," Dredd adds sternly. "And don't go so deep you can't get out. Remember who you're working for."

I nod slowly. "Nothing I can't handle."

Dredd pulls himself up to full height, a lawbreaker's nightmare. "Don't be too sure. If these creeps are guilty of what I suspect they are, you're gonna have to keep your wits about you. From what I've seen of them, they are dangerous and they are remorseless."

I look down at the photo of DuNoye, his cold, dark eyes betraying nothing. I can still taste blood in my mouth.

Part Two:
THE ATROCITY EXHIBITION

Nine

"You Trager?"

I glance up at the guy looming over me and it doesn't strain my brain to guess that this is the gimp I've been waiting for. Built like a Manta prowl tank, he's squeezed into a two thousand-cred suit that looks like it's about to burst. His massive arms are barely contained within a jacket stretched to the seams, and his thick-necked bullet head emerges from the shirt collar like pink sausagemeat squeezed out of a tube.

The creep's outfit makes him immediately incongruous amongst the rest of the clientele in Tommy's, and if it wasn't for the shaved head, pinched features and cold, cruel eyes set deep in his waxy skull, then no doubt one of the bad-asses here would question his right to walk amongst them. Also, the drokker's a good six and a half feet tall; he towers over the stumpy little bikers as if they're his pixie followers. Looking like a serial killer on his way to his grandmother's funeral, he exudes an attitude that would keep anyone at a safe distance, allowing him an impressive exclusion zone. Right now, his bowel-loosening stare is fixed on me, his nostrils flaring like he's itching to spill some blood.

Take a deep breath, I tell myself. Don't sound hesitant, don't let him intimidate you. "That's me. You're Alphonse, right?" The name sounds ludicrous, applied to King Krong here. His parents must've been seriously drokking optimistic – you might meet a MCU History lecturer called Alphonse, or it's what you'd christen your robo-servant if you had lots of money and pretensions but little taste, but no way does it suit a bruiser of the magnitude that is standing before me. It's like naming one of Satanus's brood Fluffy or something; just ain't gonna work. Then again, the tag could be bullshit, just another bogus ID.

He nods. "Come on. Got the speedster parked outside."

He turns, not waiting for me to join him, and surges his way through the Friday evening drinkers, the barflies parting almost as one to let him pass. I trail behind in his wake, singularly less threatening, relieved as I step out into the cool night air to be away from the crush, though apprehensive about where tonight's events are going to lead. I won't have much of a chance against this gorilla if things turn nasty, and there won't be time for back-up to mobilise. I just gotta stay on his good side, prove that I will be a worthwhile addition to the organisation.

Alphonse is standing beside his vehicle waiting for me to catch up. It's a sleek, dark, two-man hatchback job and I'm surprised he manages to fit behind the steering wheel. He's eyeing me as I approach, cocking his head to one side as if weighing up in his mind what size coffin I would take, or how much ballast he'd need to sink my body in a rad-pit. What he's actually thinking about surprises even me.

"You got any smarter clothes than that?"

I stop and look down at myself. To blend into the citizenry means a fairly understated wardrobe that isn't going to draw attention to yourself. My outfit consists of lime-green kneepads, Emphatically Yess pantaloons with the third trouserleg tucked stylishly into the waistband, a pair of hightops and a shirt/jacket combo by the Guerre family from Cal-Hab. If you don't want to attract unwelcome comments from passers-by and risk provoking trouble, it pays not to look like a simp.

I shrug at Alphonse. "S'all I got."

He sighs like an exasperated fashion consultant, then climbs into his car, indicating that I should do likewise. "We gotta get you a suit. None of mine are gonna fit a pee-wee like you."

"What's the diff?"

"Difference is," he says, starting the vehicle up and easing it into the flow of traffic, "that it creates an impression. It puts forward an image. Most people make a decision about somebody within the first few seconds of meeting. If you meet someone and they're suited and booted, chances are your impression's gonna be that they're respectable, businesslike, and take pride over their appearance. No reason to fear someone in a shirt and tie."

The casual way he says "fear" gives me goosebumps, as if everybody had a very real reason to fear him and the clothes were just a costume, a distraction, to hide the psycho concealed inside them.

"People look at you," he continues, glancing at me, "an' they're gonna think – no offence – that you're an asshole. No reason why they should give you the time of day."

"Charming."

"Nothing personal. Ninety per cent of the population looks like you and they're assholes as well. If the average Joe on the slab turns up at your door asking questions or needing help, do you let him in? Do you say, 'Hey, whatever you need, use my vidphone, anything.'? Like drokk you do. You tell him to get lost. You don't owe any drokker anything, right?"

I nod, conceding the point. Most Big Meg citizens barely saw their neighbours, let alone spoke to them. There was too much suspicion, too much nervousness about the consequences of helping – or even getting to know – a stranger. One minute you're helping out some little old lady to cross the road, the next you wake up and find yourself being sold in an alien slave market on a far away rimworld.

The Judges had fostered a society built on dread, in which they constantly reiterated the fact that crime was an ever-present disease and that each second of every day someone was a victim of it. It left cits paralysed, scared to leave their apartments; which, of course, suited Justice Department very well. It was a lot easier to control a city if the population felt besieged by an enemy within. The cits were so busy barricading themselves into their homes that they failed to notice that their supposed protectors were removing their civil rights one by one.

"Now put a man in a suit," Alphonse says, "and watch their reaction change. Automatically, they think you're someone in authority, 'cause you don't look like them. They're deferent, courteous, eager to please – a world away from how they treat others normally, even their own family." He takes one hand off the wheel and briefly adjusts his tie in the rear-view mirror. "Here, watch this."

A Judge suddenly slides up parallel to the car on his Lawmaster and glances in. Sweat prickles in the small of my back, but the helmet simply gives Alphonse the once-over then glares at me for a second before taking an off-ramp.

"Y'see?" Alphonse asks me, waggling his eyebrows. "Model citizen, me."

"Sounds to me like you've made a study of this."

He smiles unpleasantly. "I've seen plenty of meatheads' reactions close-up. I know when I've been taken into their confidence, when they sense there's nothing suspicious about me. You get enough experience at this sort of thing, it's as easy as flicking a switch. You go from Mr Nice Guy to... someone else."

"What, exactly?" I enquire, pushing him slightly.

"You'll see," he says quietly, watching me from the corner of his eye. "Mr DuNoye, he doesn't trust you, you know that, don't you? He's pretty wary of anyone he doesn't know well. Some say he's paranoid, but me, I just think he's careful."

Mr DuNoye, eh? The need for cover names seems to have gone. "You mean Conrad?" I ask innocently.

Alphonse lets out a barking laugh. "Ha! His idea of a sick joke – just one more actor playing a role. Everything I learnt about playing up to people's perceptions I got from him. You've met him, right?"

I instinctively touch my face where the bruises were slowly fading. "Yeah, we've met."

"And you're first impression of him was?"

"He looked like a businessman, like a gruddamn captain of industry. But it didn't take me long to realise that inside he was–"

"Something different," he finishes. "That's how it works, that's how we all work. The image we put forward every day ain't necessarily the same as what we're like in private. Do you know what we'd be like if we were one hundred per cent honest with ourselves? The city would be full of naked, gibbering loons, man."

"So, DuNoye may look like Mr Respectable, but he's buying antique torture equipment from South-Am. He got a taste for the rough stuff?"

Alphonse is silent for a moment, then he says: "Mr DuNoye is a respected lawyer and the public face of Catalyst Productions with many influential friends, including some within Justice Department. He also happens to have a certain... predilection, which he shares with a select client base in a profitable enterprise."

Predilection? Profitable enterprise? Suddenly, the penny drops. "Vi-zines. He's making Vi-zines."

"A rather crude term for what we're actually achieving, but needless to say you can understand Mr DuNoye's reticence to allow outsiders into his private life. You'll see soon enough how our work is so much more than some backstreet criminal organisation, and we shall see if you have the stomach to be a part of it."

I swallow, feeling I could do with a zizz hit. "He said he had an errand for me. A test. So where are we going?"

"Why, Mr Trager," Alphonse replies, that nauseating smile returning to his lips, "we're going to pick up our next star."

WE PARK IN the shadow of Dick Miller and take the el up to the one hundred and fourteenth floor, my mentor explaining to me the set-up along the way.

"See, we can't just kidnap people when they turn up to auditions. Their agencies are gonna want to know where they are, and once they start getting suspicious then the talent's going to avoid us like the plague."

"You're talking about Catalyst here?" I ask, acting stupid. I have to be careful and make sure that I don't let it slip that I have more than my fair share of information at my disposal. "I thought it made regular movies…"

"It does. Anti-Sov prejudice sells all over the world. But it's our legitimate front and what you might call our grooming method. Mr DuNoye and Mr Rejin, they monitor the actors and see who they think has potential. Those that they like the look of often get called back."

"Rejin… I've heard of that guy. Never seen in public, right?"

Alphonse doesn't reply straight away. "He's the man at the top," he mutters. "He… tends to keep himself to himself."

"But why don't you just snatch the victims off the street, if they're gonna be murdered anyway?"

"It's all about quality, that's why," he snaps. "Yeah, any two-bit Vi-zine publisher gets its meat by snatching a couple of bums out of an alley, but what do you get? You get shit, is what." He reaches into his inside jacket pocket and pulls out a small, rolled-up periodical, handing it to me. "Stuff like this is pretty much the standard that you can buy off the black market; a shoddy, cheap hack job."

I open it out and catch the title – *Drilling Miss Daisy* – before my eyes are pulled to the explicit cover pic of an eldster getting a frontal lobotomy while clearly fully conscious. The image is grainy and badly composed, the photographer having got so close to the subject that it isn't easy to make out the details. Judging by the lighting too, it had been shot in a gloomy basement with only a bare bulb providing any illumination. I steel myself to flip through the pages and do so quickly and with the minimum of attention, trying hard not to rest my gaze on any one atrocity. The reproduction values are poor, the paper rough. Hard to believe, but a mag like this sells at about fifty creds each on the underground. A sicko and their money are soon parted, that's for gruddamn sure.

"Pretty grim," I say, giving it back to him, relieved to have it out of my sight. I notice ink has rubbed off onto my fingers and I try to wipe them down the back of my trousers, keen to be rid of its taint.

"Yeah," he says distractedly, slipping it back into his pocket as if it were the morning's *Mega-News*. "It's this sort of rubbish that we're trying to avoid. We're going for the high end of the scale – classy pics, quality production and, of course, top-of-the-range screamers."

The el' pings as it reaches our floor and we step out into the block corridor. Alphonse pauses for a moment to check the address. "Three-nine-nine-eight/B, that's what we're looking for," he says to himself. "One Bartram Stump."

"What's to stop this guy having a spouse and six bawling brats?" I ask as we head off in search of the apartment. "I mean, you ain't just gonna be able to walk out with him in front of his whole drokking family."

"Research. The bosses are not only looking for photogenic bods that are gonna look good carved up for the camera, they get us to investigate their personal backgrounds: find out if they've got next of kin or many friends, see if it's gonna be noticed if they disappear. Actors have a habit of going where the work is, so it's not unknown for them to just up and leave one day, 'specially if we leave enough evidence to point the authorities in that direction. We target the ones that are living alone, preferably new to the city, that ain't gonna be missed in a hurry."

"Have any of them ever been investigated?"

"Occasionally a name crops up on the Tri-D as having vanished, but cits go missing all the time. Judges got bigger problems than chasing round after errant actors." He stops. "Wait here." He flattens himself against the corridor wall and slides along to a junction, where up on the corner of the ceiling a CCTri-D camera is operating. He reaches into his pocket and retrieves a small canister, spraying the contents in front of the camera's lens, then he looks back at me and motions for me to follow. When I join him, he murmurs, "Freezed the circuitry. It'll drokk with its time delay. Don't want PSU seeing who Stump's visitors were."

We continue down another corridor until we halt in front of a door. "Here we are," Alphonse says. "Let me do the talking at first, OK? I wanna make sure we don't spook him too early."

I nod. I can feel myself clenching and unclenching my fists, my palms damp with perspiration.

Alphonse knocks briskly. Moments later we hear movement behind the door before it slowly opens, a head peering round the frame cautiously. For a second, the citizen looks bemused, then recognition lights up in his eyes, and he pulls the door wide. All he's wearing is his dressing gown.

"Alphonse! How're you doing?" He reaches out and shakes my partner's hand vigorously. "Long time no see."

"It's been a while, Bart," Alphonse acknowledges, that slick smile spreading across his face. "We were in the neighbourhood, thought we'd drop by."

Stump's attention turns to me and he curiously gives me the once-over. The guy's got matinee idol looks written all over him: tanned complexion, square jaw, thick, dark hair that might or might not be a wig, a smooth forehead showing evidence of several rejuve jobs, pearly white teeth and bright blue eyes. He seems vaguely familiar in a way that suggests I might've seen him in a vidvert recently or staring down from some advertising hoarding; a commercial for toothpaste, maybe, or aftershave. Something in which a gimp grins at himself in the mirror a lot.

Alphonse makes the introductions. "Bart, this is Pete Trager. He's the new casting manager over at the studio. We were discussing a shortlist of names for the next feature, and yours cropped up. I reckon it's been too long since the Stumpster has been wowing the ladies in the aisles."

"Really? A new production?" he says eagerly, turning from me to Alphonse and back again, his naked ambition embarrassingly plain to see.

"No one nails that gruff Mega-City Judge charm the way you do. Ain't that right, Pete?"

I nod, trying to generate enthusiasm. "That's the truth."

"Well," Stump says conspiratorially, modesty evidently a fairly alien concept, "to be honest, I feel playing a Judge slightly beneath me. Not much personality or motivation to work on, you understand. And I always feel a bit unclean conveying fascism so convincingly. But I do so love a challenge." Before I can piledrive my fist into his arrogant face, he adds excitedly: "You better come in and tell me all about it." He ushers us across the threshold and shuts the door behind him.

His apartment gives off more than a whiff of pretty poster-boy fallen on desperate times: the furniture looks ratty, the remains of take-out food is lying on the floor, and the walls are smothered in stills from movies, faded publicity pics and yellowing cuttings. In nearly all of them, Bartram Stump is flashing those dazzling teeth, either at paparazzi as he's snapped with a succession of beautiful women attending some premiere, or in character as he's pouring on the charm to his co-star. The general effect is headache-inducing, as if I'm standing in a hall of mirrors with reflections on every side.

Stump is babbling away to Alphonse. "Grud, when was the last time you required my thespian services? Must've been *Strat-Bat Out of Hell*... That was, what, a couple of years ago? I must say, it would be very interesting working with you guys again. What made you think of me?"

"Let's just say you got the perfect face for our next leading role," Alphonse replies, reaching into his jacket. "Now can you do me a favour?"

"Anything–"

Alphonse levels a gun at the actor. "Shut the drokk up and do what you're told." He beckons me over with a gesture of his head. "Trager, grab him."

Stump is backing away, a look of shock painted on his perfect features as I move forward and put an arm round his throat. He struggles feebly, but doesn't put up much opposition; his eyes are fixed on the pistol in Alphonse's hand.

"What... what's this... all about?" he stutters, an inflexion in his voice suggesting he's hoping that this is a game, or an impromptu role-play session, where his ability to look scared is being tested. If I was a director, I'd say he was doing a pretty drokkin' good job.

"Don't speak unless I tell you to, OK?" Alphonse warns, to which Stump nods in agreement. "OK. Now, Catalyst has a new policy on hiring actors, in which we gotta see you're capable of following orders. Can't have a loose cannon, doing what he likes, can we? Thing about making movies is that everybody has to pull in the same direction. You still wanna be in the movies, don't you, Bart?"

He nods again, fervently. Watching this guy, I realise how easy it's been for the drokkers at the studio to find victims for their sick photo shoots; dangle the promise of fame and fortune, of their name up in lights, and the poor saps are queuing up at the door, happy to be exploited for a fleeting chance at stardom. Whilst they might have known they were selling something of themselves for the lure of the silver screen, few could've expected that they'd end up sacrificing everything for that one big shot at immortality.

"I guarantee, all eyes are gonna be on you. Now, I want you to pack some clothes, 'cause you're gonna be going away for a few days. Anybody likely to come checking up on you?"

"M-my ex-wife. She'll want to get in touch if she hasn't got her monthly payment–"

"OK, then you write her a note. Say something about a job that's come up across town that you couldn't pass up an' you'll get in touch when you're back. Hey, you're the creative, I'm sure you can come up with something."

"Look, what the hell is this all about?" Stump says, trying to inject some authority into his voice. "This is all very unorthodox. You can't just rough me up and drag me somewhere against my will. Is this some kind of method acting procedure, where the actor has to go through the same treatment as the character?"

"Bart." Alphonse cuts through the actor's protestations like a las-knife. "I won't give you another warning. No questions. Just do what you're told."

"Drokk you, and drokk your loathsome pet bulldog here." He struggles to look round at me, and spits, a globule of phlegm pattering against my cheek. "I'm not going to be threatened by a couple of petty thugs." He kicks against me weakly and tries to wrestle free from my grip; with my arm still wrapped around his throat, I pull back hard, cutting off his air supply.

Surrounded by this joker's rampant and misplaced egotism, his puerile handsome blandness looming in from every side like I'm trapped inside his self-obsession, something snaps in my head and I suddenly want to give this deluded drokker a taste of reality. A darkness descends as I increase the pressure until the choking rasp emerging from his mouth ceases altogether and his hands flutter up to my arm in a feeble attempt to wrest it away. I hear my name being said and the shadows at the edge of my vision begin to disperse as I glance up at Alphonse and see him mouthing at me to stop. I release Stump and he falls to his knees, coughing and spluttering. I edge away from him, a numbness replacing the rage.

Stump makes a gagging noise as he forces oxygen back into his lungs, and gradually words begin to filter through. "Please… don't hurt me… I'll do anything… Don't hurt me…" He doesn't raise his gaze from the carpet, keeping his head bowed as if in supplication.

"No more arguments, OK?" Alphonse says softly.

Stump nods, as meek as a lamb after that, his spirit broken. He silently packs a couple of holdalls, then sits at his desk and composes a short note, which he shows to Alphonse for his approval. My partner gives it the nod, then instructs me to tidy the place up.

"Hey, I ain't clearin' away his shit," I say without thinking, pointing to the dirty dishes piled up in the sink and the takeaway boxes stacked on top of one another next to the actor's armchair.

"You'll do what you're drokkin' told," Alphonse rumbles, the threat so implicit in his voice that even Stump looks up at him, fearful. He checks himself and says more quietly, "This is a disappearance job. You think the Judges are gonna think he went of his own accord if everything's left as it was? This place is gonna stink of a kidnap."

"I'd be surprised if they smell anything over the reek of that sink," I mutter.

"Rubber gloves are over there," Alphonse replies. "Get to work."

Grudgingly, I set to giving the apartment a polish. I know this is all part of the test, pushing me to my limit with menial tasks, but going elbows-deep in someone else's mess particularly yanks my chain. It's times like this that I feel like telling the drokker just who exactly I am and see him crawl through shit for a change, but I control my temper and swallow my pride, letting him feel he's still the boss. For every greasy plate I stack, I visualise the moment when I take the spugger down.

Once the chores are done, we're ready to go. Stump looks shellshocked, like he's retreated into himself, and he dumbly follows Alphonse's lead as he picks up his bags. I try to summon some kind of guilt for nearly killing the guy, but it's surprisingly hard to find, as if my reserves of empathy have run dry.

Alphonse hands me a hood. "Blur-mask," he says. "Don't want the street cameras catching our faces with him." He turns to Stump. "OK, let's move out. I'm gonna be right behind you and the gun is gonna be lodged in your spine, so no funny stuff." He gives me a wink. "Don't want to ruin your performance."

I'M STANDING ALONE in an empty studio lot – which I'm pretty sure was where I was taken to by the goons from the bathroom at Tommy's – watching over Stump, who's been tied to a battered old chair, and I feel like I'm floating above myself, watching and wondering what in the name of all that's holy I've got myself into.

In the bright, white glare of the spotlights, I can see dark stains on the floor and scrape marks where a number of heavy objects have been dragged. There's a trolley parked next to Stump and upon it are several metallic instruments that sparkle in the light. Amongst them are some of the torture devices I snagged off the Danskys and passed on to DuNoye. The stench of death is everywhere in this place. Grud only knows how many have been slaughtered here.

A groan breaks the silence; Stump has already been beaten unconscious once, when he attempted to resist being strapped down, and now his bloodied form is stirring. I study him and it reminds me of how I was in that position not long ago. As his swollen eyes open and appeal to me for help I turn away.

"Are we ready to start?" a voice from the shadows says, and DuNoye emerges from the darkness with Alphonse tagging along beside him.

"He's coming round," I reply quietly, my throat like sandpaper.

"Excellent." The lawyer looks at me. "And Mr Trager, Alphonse says you acquitted yourself well with Mr Stump's retrieval. You seem to show to a remarkable propensity for violence, which is always gratifying to see in an employee."

I don't answer but try to look flattered by the compliment nonetheless.

"All we await now is our talented photographer," DuNoye says theatrically, turning to the blackness beyond the circle of light. "Ramona, is everything set?"

"Don't wet your pants, Vandris," I hear just before a stunningly beautiful woman in her early twenties joins us out of the gloom. My heart freefalls. Despite the casualness of her clothes, she exudes an authority and confidence that's utterly magnetic. Short, blonde hair frames an exquisite face, with blue eyes magnified by delicate round glasses. Small, kissable lips are offset by a flawless complexion. She has a couple of cameras hanging around her pale neck, the straps dividing her breasts. I try hard not to stare, but I can sense her gaze upon me. "This is the new guy, huh?"

"Indeed," DuNoye answers. "This will be Mr Trager's first session."

"Well, as long as he doesn't screw up the shots," she says, removing a lens cap.

"Oh no," he says. "I think he's going to be quite a natural." DuNoye walks past me, his feet *tip-tapping* on the hard studio floor, and stops beside the trolley. He pauses in thought, glances once at Stump, then picks up what looks like a miniature wrench. Smiling, he holds it out to me and says: "Perhaps you'd like to begin, Mr Trager? Why don't we start with the teeth?"

Ten

THE GROANS SEEMED to echo from the very walls, as if the building had been passively soaking up the pain, misery and madness it had witnessed over the years. As he passed across the threshold, Dredd reasoned that this structure had probably seen more human degradation and mental agony than most, and wouldn't be surprised to discover that its history still resonated within its corridors, like a psychic illness that had permeated the rockcrete.

The psychiatric iso-block in Sector 42 was one of the oldest in the city, and it had housed a good number of the Big Meg's most dangerously insane perps. Its age meant that its technological resources were a long way behind the more recent kook cubes that had sprung up in its lifetime, but the wardens and med-staff here didn't pretend that they were attempting to cure their charges. They were simply locking them away where they couldn't cause any trouble. The prisoners were kept sedated and occasionally recommended for lobotomies if drugs proved insufficient, but as a rule, once a crim entered the iso-block it was unlikely they would see daylight again. Futsies that had possibly suffered only a temporary plunge into madness were usually sent to one of the more progressive units where they received counselling. This place was for those who had insanity deeply ingrained into their brains, and who had retreated into some dark centre at the heart of their being from which there was no return.

It was an unnerving environment, there was no question of that, Dredd thought, as he headed into the bowels of the building. The disembodied cries that drifted from beyond the locked doors of the iso-cubes were almost ethereal, and as he passed a pair of wardens struggling with an inmate, he caught the feral look on the perp's face, virtually all trace of humanity gone. The lawman wondered how long a sane man could stay in here before he too lost his mind, succumbing to the sickness that seemed to pervade the air.

Dredd found the records department and entered a small office occupied by a single elderly Judge. It was many years since he'd last seen active duty, and he had taken this administrative post rather than go on the Long Walk. But despite his balding, wrinkled features, his eyes belied a sharp mind still at work.

"Dredd," he said. "Don't often see you round these parts."

"Denton," Dredd acknowledged. "I need to pick your brains."

The old man smiled. "Well, you've come to the right place. Picking apart brains is our specialty."

"What do you know about Erik Rejin?"

"Rejin..." Denton pondered. "The name sounds familiar. He's some kind of bigshot, isn't he?"

Dredd nodded. "He's the reclusive head of a film studio called Catalyst. Hasn't been seen in public for the past two decades. I'm investigating his company for some kind of criminal activity."

"So what brings you here?"

"I've been trying to check up on this creep, but there's some troubling gaps in MAC's data. His early years seem fairly straightforward; his family made a fortune in kneepads, I don't know if you remember them? They were behind the Supafit range."

Denton nodded. "They had the Justice Department contract for a while."

"That's right. There doesn't seem to be anything suspicious in the first half of his life, he lived with his parents and brothers, Troy and Bennett, on the huge family estate. Then came the Apocalypse War and their home takes a direct hit."

"It wiped them out?"

"All of them except Erik. Now, this is where the details go hazy. He vanishes for a substantial period of time, at least a year, I think. MAC has no record of his movements during this interlude. When he reappears – or, at least, when our files make mention of him again – he's inherited the kneepad business, which he goes on to sell off eighteen months later, and then founds the film studio."

"So it's that gap that's interesting you?"

"I can't see how he could've got out of the city, not with the war on, and he couldn't have survived on his own. He might've been injured and it's very likely he was traumatised. The length of time he was missing seems consistent with possibly a period spent in incarceration. I'm wondering if he was admitted to a Justice Department facility, and this would've been the nearest psych-unit."

"But if he was in here, then the records would be on MAC."

"Exactly. That's what's worrying me. It seems too convenient that this bracket of his life has just disappeared into a hole."

"Hold on, I'll enter his name into our inmate database, just in case." Denton tapped at his keyboard and waited while the computer completed its search. "Nothing." The old man stroked his chin. "There are quite a few gaps in our data, Dredd. Wars, Necropolis, Judgement Day, they've all destroyed important records. It's not surprising that a handful of cits fall through the cracks."

"This seems more... intentional to me," Dredd replied. "Targeted. If we'd lost all the details on Rejin, then you could put it down to a glitch in the system. But just to have the details missing for one year strikes me that somebody is covering their tracks."

"You think the data's been erased off MAC?" Denton asked, incredulous. "To do that would mean someone with very high-level clearance had accessed the files. In other words, somebody within Justice Department."

"I'm aware of the seriousness of the implications," Dredd said sternly. "But until I'm proved wrong, that is my suspicion." He glanced at the elderly Judge's terminal. "Can you run an ident match? You can grab a photo of Rejin from before the war off MAC and cross-reference it with your intake from 2104."

Denton did as he was asked, pasting a citizen ID of Rejin on one half of his screen, then instructed his machine to compile any similarities from kook cube detainees that had been processed in that year. Hundreds of faces flickered past as the computer churned through its records: eyes, noses, mouths, all compared and dismissed.

"How old was he when he lost his family?" Denton enquired.

"Late thirties by my reckoning. Thirty-eight, thirty-nine. He was single – didn't marry until a while after his reappearance."

The computer flashed up a message to say it had finished its trawl and all it had was a partial match. The visage it displayed to the right of Rejin's was of a wild-eyed man of roughly the right age, but thinner around the cheeks and with a heavily lined complexion. The screen said his name was Marcellus Blisko.

"Could be him," Denton mused. "Grief and madness can change a man's appearance quite severely." He scrolled through the perp sheet. "Hmm, that's odd. The charges against Blisko, the reasons for him being sentenced here, don't seem to have been entered." He read further, then peered up at Dredd, an uneasy expression passing over his face. "And he was... released."

"When?"

"About eleven months into his stay here. Just says that his release had been approved, but not by whom. That's extraordinary. Next to no one gets freed from here. They're all lifers."

"This was over twenty years ago. Who would've handled the paperwork?"

"At that time, it was probably Judge Warnton. He died a few years back. Heart attack." Denton ran a hand over his hairless pate. "I just don't understand... He was such a stickler for detail. Can't think why there's so little info entered on this Blisko character."

"Unless it's been removed, like the data on MAC?"

The elderly Judge shot a look at Dredd. "Not on my watch. I'm the only one in this iso-block that can access these records."

"So we're looking at an outside job," Dredd said. "Some creep hacks into the Justice Department mainframe and removes anything incriminating relating to Rejin."

"Jovus, they'd have to be good to get into our system."

"I think they're getting help from on high, the same way Rejin did twenty years ago. Somebody's covering for him. A friend." Dredd turned and headed for the door. "Thanks for the help, Denton. I'll call in the Tek boys, see if they can run a source program on your terminal and follow the trail back to the hacker."

Meanwhile, Dredd thought, I'm going back to where it all started.

COUNCILLOR MATHESON PEAT sat at his desk in his office in the chambers of commerce, staring at a blank computer screen. He'd been motionless for the past hour, his expressionless face bathed in the green glow of the monitor. He was meant to be composing another of his audience-pleasing speeches – about how Mega-City One needed leaders with vision to drive it forward into the next century, about every citizen facing up to their responsibilities of being part of the most progressive society in the western world, blah, blah, blah – but the words would not come.

Normally, this kind of oratory was his bread and butter, and he'd delivered variations on the theme more times than he could remember. It was a reliable old stand-by, and it went down well with Justice Department. But recently, those phrases that would slip out of his mouth so naturally now seemed hollow and desultory, nothing more than insincere platitudes. He could not summon the enthusiasm to once more praise the city and its custodians without wishing to expose his words for the overcooked mix of hyperbole and lies that they were.

This metropolis was not some sparkling testament to mankind's indomitable spirit any more than the Judges were an even-handed force of truth and righteousness. The reality was that the people were victims, trapped in an industrialised nightmare, bullied into submission by an unelected regime that crushed democracy at every turn. It used every trick up its sleeve to hang on to its precious power, discrediting – even quietly removing, if the rumours were to be believed – those that dared to criticise its authority, and resorted to extreme levels of violence to demonstrate its belief in supremacy through strength. If he stood up now in front of a collection of fellow politicians and judicial representatives and spouted his usual media-friendly soundbites, he felt he would choke on them.

Needless to say, Councillor Matheson Peat's mind was otherwise occupied.

He couldn't concentrate, his thoughts constantly returning to the events of the past couple of weeks. He felt his carefully planned, expertly arranged life was spinning wildly out of control. First the farce at the Fred Quimby opening, then the murder investigation after the unearthing of the body dump beneath the foundations of Liz Short, and now irate phone calls from friends about

Dredd snooping around Catalyst and making menacing noises.

It was too much. It was threatening to destabilise everything he had spent his political life working towards, and even now he could sense his intricate network of colleagues and acquaintances coming apart at the seams.

It had been bad enough to allow a star of Vanessa Indigo's standing to be put in a position of danger – the attempted assassination was broadcast all over the city to a dumbstruck Tri-D audience – but questions were also being asked about his working methods following the Short case. His Phoenix Campaign had never had so much negative publicity, and where once his buildings were considered the desirable blocks to be seen in, now it was being alleged that they were constructed on unsafe land. Despite going on a charm offensive after the story broke in the press, he could not shake the feeling that those with influence who had once given him their ear were subtly distancing themselves from him, like he was a pariah. When bad news hit, you soon found out who was prepared to stand by you, and in Peat's case he discovered the answer was not that many.

Even the celebrities, once keen to align themselves with his projects, seemed cool towards him, as if they could sense when someone's spot in the limelight was fading. They were like parasites, he thought angrily, feeding on the attention he had engineered for them, sucking the last drop of exposure they could gain from his connections before abandoning him when the reporters and photographers turned their microphones and cameras elsewhere. He didn't consider any of them close.

In truth, he used their fame to promote his policies as much as they used him to get their faces on the front of the papers, and the relationship was never anything more than pure business. But it riled him to think that they couldn't even be bothered to disguise their loathing of being too near to him, as if he were a social leper, and to come into contact with his ill fortune would spread it disease-like amongst their cliques.

The damage seemed irreparable, and he felt trapped in a circle of despair that was alienating Peat from everyone around him. His girlfriend tried to reassure him that it was just a run of bad luck, and that he simply had to ride it out.

"People have bounced back from worse disasters," she had reasoned. "Aren't you always saying Mega-City One will stand tall no matter what is thrown at it? And that the city endures because the spirit of the citizens refuses to be broken? Well, if we can survive wars, invasions, despots and madmen, then you can take a few knocks and still come up smiling."

He wished he could believe her. But as sweet as her naivety was, she couldn't comprehend just how much trouble he felt he was in. He hadn't had a decent night's sleep since the problems had begun, and consequently he drifted through his waking hours like a mournful phantom, a shadow of his normal effervescent self, refusing to be comforted by Sondra, shutting her out of his dark despondency, turning her away from him.

He couldn't blame her for feeling hurt by this, and for wanting to spend as little time as possible in his company. Evenings in their apartment were silent, dour episodes. The frustrations and anxieties inside Peat grew more malignant and bitter the more he brooded on them, and he barely noticed if Sondra was there or not. Peat suspected that Sondra was seeking solace with the apprentice taxidermist down the hall, but he could not bring himself to feel jealous or aggrieved by her infidelities. And this lack of emotion made him start to question his own sanity.

Was he that hollow, to watch deadened as his life fell apart and not attempt to save it? Had he been seduced by the fame game, the need to present an image, to the point where that was all he had left? He wondered if he truly felt passionate about anything, or if it was all just spin to keep him in the public eye, empty words and gestures signifying nothing. He was alone at the centre of his world, and nobody could touch him.

Through his haze of self-pity, Peat suddenly realised that his intercom was buzzing. He sighed and flipped the switch. "Yes?"

"Judge Dredd to see you, Mr Peat," his secretary said sullenly. Keisha too had been affected by his moroseness these past few days, struggling to get him to make decisions on council matters or agree to meetings. She was increasingly having to make excuses for his non-attendance at various functions, and was clearly getting tired of mollycoddling him.

"Send him in," Peat replied, but the lawman was through the door before he'd finished speaking. He stood before the councillor as rigid and uncompromising as a granite statue. Although Peat's stomach tied itself up in knots in the presence of the Judge, he felt anger towards him too, for all the misery he had brought down on him, for almost single-handedly destroying his life and career. He shouldn't be able to get away with it. Peat wasn't some drug-dealing scumbag who offered nothing to society but a cheap hit. He was a well-respected citizen, who'd fought for his city, and he was damned if this jumped-up fascist bullyboy was going to intimidate him.

"Judge Dredd," he said through gritted teeth. "To what do I owe this pleasure?"

"I'd like to ask you some further questions, councillor. I trust you can find the time?"

"I thought I told you the last time we spoke, Dredd, that you had no right to treat me like a common criminal. I have done nothing wrong and for you to keep hounding me like this is really quite unacceptable–"

"As I told you, councillor," Dredd cut in, "you remain a suspect in an ongoing multiple-murder inquiry. Until the case is satisfactorily closed, then I will decide the course of the investigation. Now, we can either talk here or I'll pull you down to the local Sector House for a thorough interrogation."

Peat's face reddened. "Th-this is atrocious! You have no right–"

Dredd had heard enough. He strode up towards the councillor's desk and wrapped his fist in the man's shirt, yanking him over the desktop towards him. The pompous windbag popped sweat immediately, his skin draining of colour as quickly as it had flushed. "And I am drokking tired of hearing your whining, creep. Now if you don't start being a little more cooperative, I'm gonna arrest you for withholding evidence and recommend you for truth drug administration, deep-brain scan, the works. If the only way to get you to talk is to cut you open and physically extract the information, then believe me we'll do it."

Peat whimpered like a kicked dog and Dredd released him, letting him slump back into his chair. He ran a shaking hand over his face, then whispered "What do you want to know?"

"Your association with Erik Rejin."

The councillor stared. "Erik? H-he's a business colleague, that's all. What's he got to do with–"

"I'll ask the questions," Dredd interrupted. "You have an interest in Catalyst Productions, don't you?"

"I'm one of the shareholders, yes. I've helped the company secure funding, a lot of which comes from Justice Department, I might add."

"I'm aware of our contribution to the propaganda market. I'm more interested in how you came to first meet Citizen Rejin."

Peat looked uneasy. "I don't recall…"

"I'm going to keep this simple, councillor," Dredd said evenly and retrieved a small device from one of his belt pouches, placing it down on the desk between them. "That is a lie-detector; what we Judges call a birdie. As the name suggests, it tells me when a suspect is not being entirely honest. Now, you're going to tell me everything about your first meeting with Erik Rejin and every beep I hear from the birdie is a year you're going to be spending in the cubes. Do I make myself clear?"

Peat opened his mouth, then shut it again. Eventually, he nodded, cleared his throat and began to speak.

"DOWN! STAY DOWN!" Peat ordered as his squad came under heavy fire. The Sovs had them pinned. Their tanks were moving up on Barrymore, crushing any resistance before them, and ground troops were mopping up in their wake. Peat had seen four or five Judges on Lawmasters leading the charge against the invaders vaporised by just one shell, catching them dead centre. Once the smoke cleared, all that was left of Mega-City's finest was a tangle of wreckage at the base of a huge crater. He did not hold out much hope for his Citi-Def unit while they were in the open as they did not have the ammunition to enter into a stand-up fight with Sov artillery. Hit and run, that's all they could do. Guerrilla warfare.

He looked around at his men, crouching low behind the ruins they were using as cover. Not that long ago there'd been twice the number in his squad, which had originally operated out of Charlton Heston Block, and over the course of the past few days, the unit had been gradually whittled down. Run-ins with those drokkers over in neighbouring Mike Moore had caused severe casualties even before the whole city went ballistic, and now, including himself, there were just five left of the Crazy Heston Frontliners.

At first they'd directed all their energies defending their block, but when they saw the mushroom clouds blossoming on the horizon, they realised that a new enemy was taking the conflict to a whole different level. They might have had their differences with Mike Moore, but upon discovering those commie rats from East-Meg One were looking to take over not just their homes but the entire metropolis, suddenly this fresh target seemed much more worthy. His men hadn't needed convincing – they'd been fighting solidly for forty-eight hours, but their aggression was undiminished and they took to this latest adversary with renewed vigour.

Peat had led his unit proudly into battle with a foe befitting the stature of the Frontliners, but it soon dawned on him just how much he had underestimated the Sov armour. The squad's small arms were barely making a dent in the East-Meg onslaught, and all the time his unit was losing soldiers in every skirmish. They could not afford to take any more casualties.

"What do you think, sir?" his lieutenant, Mattocks, asked, squatting down next to Peat. He absent-mindedly scratched at a las-scar on his cheek.

"We can't stay here," Peat replied, watching the tanks advance through his binox. "Won't be able to get through Sov infantry, and certainly can't hold 'em off. Gonna have to retreat." The commander pointed out a route through the collapsed masonry of nearby buildings. "We'll have to hotfoot it across country, find somewhere we can lie low. Tell the men to get ready to go on my word."

Mattocks nodded and shuffled off on his belly to pass on the order. Peat continued to watch the artillery rumble down the street towards them, black smudges against the boiling sky. They needed a diversionary tactic to keep the Sovs occupied while his squad made a break for it. He spied an overhang, part of a half-demolished structure that lined the route the tanks were taking, and beckoned to Rawlinson who was carrying the RPG.

"Just before the nearest tank is under it, aim for that ledge," Peat instructed. "It's gonna be tight. We're gonna have to wait until they're fairly close before we hit 'em, but we need a smokescreen to cover our escape."

Rawlinson understood. He sighted his weapon on the overhang and waited for the mobile armour to move closer. For interminable seconds, they all crouched motionless, listening to the ever-present thunder of the tank tracks draw nearer. Peat looked at the faces of his men as they anticipated the order to move: some had their eyes screwed shut, others unconsciously fingered their rifles, heads bowed. The noise of the tanks seemed to fill the whole world, the screeching of metal getting louder moment by moment. Then, suddenly, there was a burst of flame, a rush of air, and the RPG on Rawlinson's shoulder bucked in his grip as he fired. There was a fraction of a pause before the explosion split the air, throwing chunks of the building in all directions.

"Go!" Peat yelled, and the unit stood as one, dashing for the escape route. The commander glanced at the advancing tanks and saw with some satisfaction that the rubble had put one of the vehicles out of action, rockcrete piled on top of it. Dust billowed before them, concealing their movements for a few vital seconds. The rattle of gunfire emerged from the clouds of debris and smoke, but the Sovs were aiming wild, evidently unable to see their attackers. Peat patted Rawlinson on the back and told him to get moving since they wouldn't have long before the East-Meg army was on their tail.

The Citi-Def squad moved fast, clambering as quickly as they could through the ruins, but the few minutes' grace they had bought did not get them far before they heard the Sovs shouting to each other and shots began closing in. They had been spotted. A shell arced in the air and detonated to their left, throwing out a lethal rain of shrapnel, and Peat watched helplessly as Mattocks took several hits in the face and chest, his uniform reduced to bloody rags. The lieutenant turned and unleashed a furious burst of fire at their pursuers, impotently trying to channel his rage before falling dead to the ground.

They had to find a hiding place. Peat looked around desperately for somewhere to head to, then he realised that they were running parallel to the perimeter boundary of some sort of estate. Chances were it was big enough for his squad to lose themselves in. He shouted to his men to find a gap in the iron fence. Fortunately, the area had been subjected to intense bombardment, and there were big enough rents along the border of the property for them to squeeze through. They stumbled onto crater-riddled land and fixed their sights on the remains of a large house, which lay at the summit of a shallow hill. Peat glanced back and could see no sign of the Sovs so he felt reasonably confident that they'd given the invaders the slip.

As they drew closer to the mansion, they saw that it must've taken the full brunt of an airburst. The roof had collapsed in places, the walls were blackened, the windows mostly shattered. It looked derelict.

Topley whistled appreciatively. "Must've been some pad, once."

"I think I recognise this place," Peat replied, frowning. "I'm sure I've seen it on the news..."

"Looks like a celebrity shitheap," Marriott said.

"Well, whatever it was, it's our hideout for the time being," Peat murmured, heading towards the front door which dangled off its hinges. "But we'll scope it out, make sure there's no nasty surprises waiting inside." He signalled his unit to follow. "Keep 'em peeled."

They entered slowly, flipping on the torches attached to their rifles to penetrate the gloom. All the power seemed to be out, and the destruction wrought on the inside seemed as extensive as that on the exterior. A grand sweeping staircase led up to the first floor, but it was blocked by a huge shard of the roof that had fallen in. They moved cautiously through the hallway, checking as best they could each room they came across, dust dancing in their beams, the silence enveloping them like a shroud. Whoever had lived here had had plenty of money and taste, the expensive works of art now lying shattered beneath their feet.

"You reckon the residents have fled?" Rawlinson asked.

"Seems likely, if they're not buried under a ton of rubble," Peat answered.

"This place safe, d'you think?" Marriott added, swinging his torch up at the exposed rafters. "One strong breeze and the place could come down like a house of cards."

Peat was wondering the same thing himself. "Can't say for sure. We'll only stay for as long as we have to. Any sign—"

A moan echoed through the structure as if the mansion itself was shifting on its foundations. At first, Peat thought it was the wind, but then it came again, louder, and there was no mistaking the sound's human origin. His men eyed each other nervously, shouldering their guns, and turned to their commander who put a finger to his lips and motioned for them to spread out. Peat cocked an ear and tried to follow the source of the noise, which seemed to be getting more insistent. He led his team into what had once been the kitchen and stopped, waiting for the groan to come again. When it did, he peered down at his feet.

"Trapdoor," he whispered, gesturing to the opening set in the floor that was partially covered with heavy blocks of rockcrete. "Must lead to a basement. Marriott, Rawlinson, help me clear this debris, then on three, open it. Topley, keep me covered, but don't shoot unless you have to."

The men lifted the rubble clear then stationed themselves around the trapdoor, looking at their superior expectantly. Peat counted down silently, then nodded. Marriott and Rawlinson tore open the door and a crimson blur exploded from the opening, throwing itself at Peat.

They toppled backwards, grappling at Topley's feet, who tried to sight his gun on the attacker but couldn't get a clear fix. It seemed to be a man, but he was coated almost entirely in blood and he was making a keening whine like a wounded animal. Topley reached down and got his arm around the maniac's throat, lifting him off Peat. Close up, he could smell the man's foetid stench and realised that what he thought was a mewl was actually a breathless litany.

"Kill them all… kill them all… kill them all…"

"Drokker's raving," Marriott said, helping Topley as the man struggled in his grasp. "Grud, he stinks too." He glanced at his CO. "You all right, skip?"

Peat got to his feet, rubbing his head where it had cracked against the kitchen floor. "I'll live." He got his hand under the lunatic's jaw, lifting his face into the light so he could get a better look. "Must've been trapped under there for days, poor spugger." He looked closer into the man's eyes, wild with fear and madness, then Peat spat into his hand and wiped away some of the dirt and blood caked to the guy's skin. A gasp escaped his lips. "Jovus drokk!"

Marriott looked at Peat. "Chief? What is it?"

The commander rubbed away more of the grime. "I've seen him before. This place... I thought I recognised it. It–it's the Rejin estate. You know, the billionaires?"

"The kneepad people?" Topley asked.

"Exactly. My grud, this guy must be one of the sons. Erik, is it?" The man moaned louder in response. "They've been all over the press in the past. The Rejins are one of the richest families in the city."

"So where's the rest of them?" Marriott wanted to know.

"Uh, sir?" Rawlinson piped up. He was still standing by the open trapdoor, shining his torch into the darkness below, his face pale. "You might want to take a look at this..."

"He had partially consumed them," Peat said, gazing at his hands folded before him on his desk. "Can you imagine what that did to his mind? Trapped with the bodies of his parents and brothers, crazed with grief and hunger, he'd been forced to cannibalise his own flesh and blood. When we found him, he was covered in them, head to foot, and he was raging, *raging* against the Sovs that had murdered his family."

Dredd stood before the councillor, impassive. "And so you took him to a psych unit under an assumed name. You were working an angle already, weren't you? You saw an important future ally and you helped protect him."

"I was a businessman before I was a politician, Dredd," Peat replied simply. "Here was the sole heir to one of the largest kneepad manufacturers in the city. I felt I could help both our causes if we kept this as discreet as possible."

"How did you get him out of the kook cubes?"

"The company lawyers, plus some significant leaning on certain elements within Justice Department by myself and my colleagues. We convinced them he could be kept under control."

"But he couldn't, could he? You released a dangerously insane man because it made sense to your career. What did he do? Fund your election campaign?"

Peat stood and crossed to the window, his back to Dredd. He sighed and rested his forehead against the glass. "I... I thought Erik deserved more. He was too important to be left rotting in some padded cell. I believed his energies could be directed into something more... worthwhile." He paused, then added, raising his voice, "For grud's sake, Dredd, this was twenty years ago."

"The Law is the Law. You used Rejin the same way you use everyone else, to climb the greasy pole and to increase your own publicity. And you attempted to cover your tracks by trying to erase the past. How did you hack into MAC's files?"

Peat turned and looked Dredd straight in the eye. "I'm not saying any more."

"Fair enough. We'll talk further down at the Sector House."

"No," Peat replied, reaching into his jacket and removing a small blaster, pointing it at the Judge. "I'm going nowhere with you."

Dredd stared him down, unfazed. "Don't be ridiculous, Peat. You're only making things worse."

"How can they possibly be worse?" he replied, his eyes watering. He sniffed, then shouted "Keisha!" Seconds later, his secretary entered, glanced at the two men, then spied the revolver, her jaw dropping. Before she could speak, the councillor reached over and pulled her to him, his left arm snaking around her throat. He placed the gun barrel against the side of her head. She whimpered and he shushed her quiet.

"Now, I'm walking out of here, Dredd," he declared. "Try to stop me and you'll have blood on your hands too."

Eleven

I'M SITTING IN a small room, adjacent to the studio set, my eyes closed, trying to control my breathing. In the darkness behind my lids, all I can see is blood and a face twisted soundlessly in pain, as if the images are burned onto my retina. No matter how much I shake my head or pound my temples with my fists, nothing can dispel them.

They're imprinted there, indelible, and a part of my mind not paralysed with shock at what I've just taken part in is terrified that they will never fade, like a stain on the inside of my skull. I fear that every time I shut my eyes, I'm going to see the gore-streaked features of Bartram Stump, dying in the most perverse and brutal manner imaginable. And I was the one who was responsible for his horrifying injuries because I had no way of backing out of this horrible mess this group of callous, monstrous perps have dragged me into. It's going to replay in the theatre of my mind like my very own private snuff movie on a permanent loop: star, director and audience all in one, anguish and revulsion keeping the spools turning.

I open my eyes and stare at the ceiling, wanting a hit of anything – zizz, alcohol, even a sugar rush would do – to destroy my nerve endings and render me numb. I want to crack open my head and rip out the darkness festering inside because I know it's only going to grow and grow before it consumes me entirely. What's scaring me even more than the acts I've just performed on another human being is the voice I'm starting to hear asking why I'm being such a hypocrite.

You knew what you were getting into, it's saying. Nobody forced you into anything. Don't act all mortified about what you've witnessed. The truth of the matter is that you took some gruddamn pleasure from it. The first time you met Stump, didn't you want to drive your fist into that handsome, bland face? Haven't you always longed to destroy everything that offends you with its puerility? Look me in the eye and tell me you didn't get a thrill from the power you wielded, released from the moral obligations of being a Judge. You embraced the black, cancerous heart that pulses inside you and allowed it to blossom. It's always been there, don't deny it. It's right there, right at the core of who you are.

I can feel tears trickling down my cheeks and I cover my face with my hands, trying to stem their flow. I don't want to hear what this voice has got to say, it's cutting too close to the bone, but I can't escape it. If I stuffed my ears, buried my head, it wouldn't halt its condemnatory monologue.

You don't want to hear it, it replies, because you don't want to accept the unacceptable. Take a look in the mirror, pal. Come to terms with it.

"No... no..." I murmur, unaware the words are escaping from my mouth.

In answer I hear a different, female, voice. "You all right?"

I lift my hands away from my hot, wet face, blinking back the tears. It takes a moment for her features to coalesce into focus, then I see Ramona peering round the door, her camera still dangling from her neck. She doesn't look concerned, merely moderately surprised to see such a reaction. She eyes me curiously as if I'm some sort of freakshow attraction. She glances back behind her briefly, then slips into the room, shutting the door after her.

"No need to ask how it was for you," she says with a little more warmth, a slight smile playing on her lips.

I do my best to straighten my appearance, wiping a hand over my tear-streaked cheeks. "Sorry," I say, clearing my throat. "Not very professional."

She leans against the wall opposite me. "No need to apologise. You wouldn't be the first guy to freak out after a session. Not everybody can do it. Lots of them think they can, but when it comes to it they lose their nerve. It takes guts and a certain strength of will."

"Sounds like you've done plenty of these... sessions."

"A fair few," she says, absent-mindedly removing her glasses and cleaning them with the edge of her T-shirt, affording me a tantalising glimpse of her pale belly. If she notices me looking, she doesn't make mention of the fact. She replaces the spectacles and fixes me with those piercing blue eyes. "Vandris seemed to think you were a natural for this kind of work. I have to say, you looked like you were in control of the situation. The best performers hit a kind of plateau, as if they're sculpting a work of art and are taken over by a... creative revêrie. But the comedown can be a bitch, can't it?"

I nod, thinking that sounds like the understatement of the drokkin' century. "Doesn't it ever affect you?"

She shrugs. "I stopped being troubled by my conscience years ago. My father taught me just how transient the human form was, how the flesh was a disguise, hiding our true selves." She taps her camera. "I'm capturing the unveiling of that truth, in all its multi-coloured glory."

I feign understanding, thinking that the daughter sounds as mad as everyone else around here. Gruddamn, though, she *was* beautiful. I feel like a besotted juve, but it's worth hearing her speak just to watch the shapes her mouth makes, the way her tongue flicks against her front teeth, the movement of her slender neck.

I'm suddenly aware that *she's* studying *me*. She's looking me up and down with her photographer's eyes, trying to get the measure of me. "So how did you get involved with Vandris?" she asks.

I actually struggle for a couple of seconds to think of a credible answer. Is she really entrancing me that much that I'm incapable of lying to her? Normally, the cover stories would fly from my lips without hesitation, but for some reason the dishonesty niggles me. I stamp it down quickly. "I was just a street hustler," I reply, which is hardly a lie at all. "Another bum trying to make a living underground. I came into possession of some merchandise, which Mr DuNoye was interested in–"

"The instruments from South-Am," Ramona interrupts. "They're beautiful, aren't they? It makes such a difference, working with a craftsman's tools."

I nod queasily. "They're… unique, I'll say that. Anyway, I wanted… I don't know, to prove that I could be useful to this organisation. Maybe I felt like I needed a place to belong, that I'd been on the streets on my own for too long. Maybe it was my mercenary instincts telling me this was where the money was. Or that I recognised–"

"Kindred spirits," she finishes. "I think it was more than the lure of a quick cred that brought you to us, Mr Trager. You felt the dark pull within your soul, a craving that perhaps you did not fully understand."

I say nothing, and for the first time I can't meet her gaze. I look down at my palms, still speckled with crimson.

"I could see it in you, in your performance out there," she continues. "It's impossible to fake, you either have it or you don't. And you have it very much within you, Mr Trager. It burns, doesn't it, this cold flame that can explode into violence? Directionless, without reason… But here it can be cultured, refined, into a thing of beauty." She steps closer to me and takes my hand in hers. "Let me show you."

Ramona leads me back into the darkened studio, now empty of life. All that remains of what had taken place here is the chair lying forlornly on its side, liquid patches of shadow on the floor around it. The rest of the torturers have disappeared along with their tools of the trade, presumably to dispose of Bartram Stump's corpse in yet another chem-pit somewhere in the city.

I briefly wonder, as I follow her into a backstage corridor littered with props and costumes, just how DuNoye and his men know where to dump the bodies. They seem to have intimate knowledge of every rad hotspot into which they can dissolve the evidence. It smells to me like they're getting help from outside the organisation, and that someone is priming them on the best places to go; someone with a vested interest.

We climb a set of stairs, leaving the filmmaking apparatus in our wake, and emerge into an office area. The lights are off here too, but I can feel the brush of plush carpets beneath my feet. Ramona heads towards a door, then fishes in her trouser pocket for a key.

"This all part of Catalyst too?" I whisper, glancing around me.

She nods. "This is the business section. Vandris's office is just down there," she says, pointing vaguely behind her, "and my father's quarters... are at the far end."

She looks uncomfortable, as if she doesn't want to say anything further, and turns her attention back to the lock, twisting the key and tugging down on the handle. The door swings open and she enters first, slapping on a light that casts an eerie red glow. I follow, pulling the door shut after me.

"Your father lives here? At the studio?" I ask. Once my eyes become accustomed to the lighting, I realise it's a compact but fairly high-tech darkroom: various pieces of photographic equipment and developer chemicals line the shelves.

Most immediately striking is the plethora of pictures – mostly all of them black and white shots – tacked to the walls or hanging from makeshift washing lines. It's a grotesque gallery of suffering as men and women of a wide range of ages are caught in mid-scream, their agonies frozen for the camera. Despite the horrific nature of the photos, and it's impossible for the eye not to be drawn to them, flitting from one atrocity to the next, there's evidently a talent at work that's equally hard to ignore.

Whilst the majority of Vi-zine pics are flat and unimaginative, or grainy to the point of illegibility, these are approaching art, with a style and sense of composition that far outstrips anything I've seen before. I begin to understand now what Alphonse had been talking about when he maintained that Catalyst was going for something more upmarket, and it is clear that the driving force of the talent is Ramona Rejin. She is capturing death and creating something new from it.

"My father's family home was destroyed in the Apocalypse War," she says quietly, setting her camera down on the work surface. "He was the only survivor. After that, he was uncomfortable living alone, so he made his work his life. Catalyst is everything to him; he lives and breathes what we're doing here. And this is where I feel safest," she says, gesturing around her. "Alone with my photographs."

"These pictures," I say, continuing to gaze up at the photos, genuinely impressed. "They're like nothing I've ever seen before."

"You like them?"

I pause for a moment, trying to conjure up a word that sums up my simultaneous fascination and repulsion. "They're... unforgettable. I've never seen Vi-zine shots like these before."

She pulls a face. *"Vi-zine."* She spits out the word as if it were poison. "Such a patronising and inaccurate term. It was the Judges that coined that phrase, did you know that? A catch-all expression for something they've sought to eradicate."

"Then what are you doing here?"

She shrugs. "Literally? A Pictorial Study of Human Transformation, if you want to give it a grand title. Does art need to be pigeonholed and labelled? I'm making something new here, something aficionados will not have seen before. You know the kind of rubbish that's out there on the black market."

I nod. "I've seen them."

"Pulp hackjobs like *Dismemberment Today*, *In the Flesh* and *Shreddies* – they say nothing and they offer nothing, other than a cheap voyeuristic thrill. The subjects are often vagrants, the photography is ugly, with no semblance of skill or sincerity, and they're treating their audience with a shameful disdain. However, what my father and I are doing here is creating beauty from the inbuilt flawed nature of human physicality."

"Come again?"

"Us, our bodies, are fundamentally flawed. In our minds, we're misshapen, unable to conform to the aesthetically pleasing archetype that's paraded before us on Tri-D and in the movies. We try to change ourselves, transform ourselves, but rarely to our satisfaction. The image in the mirror is never perfect. In reality, we're prone to infection and disease, constantly fighting against the defects that lead to illness and death." Her eyes glow with a preacher's zeal, sermonising what's clearly her life work. "But take apart this human jigsaw puzzle," she holds her hands to her chest, "expose the interlocking pieces and it takes on an abstract beauty. Through my photographs, I demonstrate that mankind contains an inner light so rarely seen."

The cynic in me wants to ask her to point out the artistic worth in the pic above her head showing some poor sap having the tips of his fingers sheared off, but in truth the passion in her oration is incredibly overwhelming. I feel almost dazzled by the bright flame of her self-belief. If Ramona sees her mission as unveiling our inner light, then it's shining from her right now, sparkling from her eyes and mouth.

"You're tellin' me *you're* misshapen?" I ask. "I've never seen a more perfect example of beauty." I'm laying it on a bit thick, but unusually, I'm not lying.

She looks confused for a second, then smiles to herself, lowering her gaze. In the blink of an eye, her guard is broken and she's gone from zealot to an embarrassed young woman, her cheeks flushing. Her restive fingers look for something to do and she opens the back of her camera, removing a small disk which she then plugs into a terminal.

"I promised to show you something," she says quietly.

She flicks the screen on, opens a desktop folder and scrolls through the digital photos of me participating in the torture-murder of Bartram Stump. After the fourth or fifth picture, I turn my head away, scarcely recognising the man before me, and Ramona glances sideways at me, noticing my discomfort.

"Do you see it?" she asks. "The way you wield the knife, as if it feels natural in your hand? Do you see the violence in you boiling away, looking for an outlet? You can't deny I've captured your true–"

"I'm no killer," I try to assert.

"No? Some kill because they have no choice, or do so by accident, and others do it because it's in their blood and every life they take reaffirms their identity. They kill because they can only know themselves in those final, precious moments. I would say that you're a natural born killer Mr Trager, and that you've at last found your calling."

There's still some small scrap of conscience inside me that wants to refute her theory, but maybe she's right. Maybe it's always been inside me, this ease with which I can take life, and I use the Law as an excuse to give vent to it. I could've easily gone the other way and become one more nutso mass murderer. Instead, I kill for the city; a sanctioned executioner.

"I'm capable of violence, I admit," I mutter unconvincingly, "but it's not who I *am*. It doesn't *define* me." I gesture to the photos. "Your– your audience... Who are they? What do *they* get from it?" There's a hint of desperation to the words. I feel like I'm falling apart before her, or at least, the character I've thrown up around myself is crumbling. The light blazing from her is melting it.

"We have an established client base which is growing all the time as word of mouth spreads," she replies, fixing me once again with her unwavering stare, stepping nearer. "The distribution network of Catalyst's propaganda films ensures that my pictures are shipped all over the world. All sorts of people are interested in my work. Perhaps they like to feel so close to death because it makes them closer to a higher being or something. Maybe they're drawn to taboo. The bottom line is that nobody else is doing what I'm doing. I'm breaking through boundaries."

She reaches out past me, her arm brushing my shoulder, and removes a pic from the wall of a semi-flayed face, which looks in close-up like the spread wings of a butterfly. She studies it, smiling. "Transformation, you see? We're all capable of taking on new forms." She glances up at me. "Even you, Mr Trager."

The room suddenly feels suffocating, surrounded by so much horror, and the red light is beginning to make my head ache. My hand fumbles for the door handle. "I'd better be going."

She waits until I've turned away before she speaks. "Thank you for what you said."

I pause. "Hmm?"

"The compliment. It was very sweet. You weren't just being polite?"

"No," I reply, with a short shake of my head. I still haven't actually turned back to face her for fear that she will see how much I'm trembling. My heart's pounding like crazy.

A hand alights on my arm and gently pulls me round so I'm gazing into her brilliant blue eyes once more. "My father has always taught me never to trust anyone," she says softly. "He says that everyone is steeped in lies and the truth was buried deep within. But I see in you no need for lies because the truth is so close to the surface – we've both witnessed it emerging tonight. You have demonstrated that you have nothing to hide from me."

"Ramona, I–"

"Would you like to kiss me?"

"Listen, your father…"

"He brought me up on his own when my mother died, sheltered me, instructed me as to how the world works. He taught me everything. But I'm making this decision for myself." She puts a finger to my lips briefly. "Now, answer my question."

My throat has dried up, so all I can do is nod. She smiles prettily, removes her glasses and places them on the worktop, then pulls me forward and we embrace, my hand cupping the back of her neck, my mouth locked to hers. Her skin feels wonderfully soft and smooth as my fingers trail beneath her T-shirt, caressing the small of her back and her waist. I close my eyes to shut out the frozen screams of the dead hanging above us.

I AWAKE WITH a start, disorientation flooding through me until I see the curve of Ramona's back as she slumbers beside me, her shoulders imperceptibly rising and falling. We'd talked into the early hours, lying in each other's arms on the floor of the darkroom, until we drifted off into sleep.

I sit up gingerly and struggle into my clothes, careful not to disturb her. My joints protest at having been trapped in an awkward position for too long. Gently stroking her hair, I gaze down at her. In sleep, she looks just as beautiful, her lips slightly parted as she breathes lightly, the soft exhalation the only sound in the room.

I've never met anyone quite like her, the magnetic aura she exudes is so powerful. It's her self-belief that's so compelling, her total conviction behind her "art" and the truths she's uncovering about the human condition. In a city in which dumbness and moronic gullibility are the pervading traits of the population, to come across anyone as fiercely intelligent as Ramona – no matter how *disturbed* – is a moment to be celebrated and cherished. Coupled with her extraordinary beauty, the desire she evokes in me makes me ache with a need to take her away, far away, from the corrupting influence of her father's homicidal insanity. I don't know whether she can be cured of her funereal fixation, or indeed that she *wants* to be. But however this mess is resolved, I want to keep her safe from harm. With this in mind, betraying her is going to feel like slow torture from which there's no escape.

I stand and snatch a torch from the work surface, also grabbing a small camera, then cross over to the door, easing it open slowly and checking behind me that Ramona hasn't stirred. I peek out into the corridor and, discovering it empty, slip out of the room and into the shadows. My watch says its 3:30 am and I'm hoping that Catalyst goons don't habitually patrol this area. I hug the walls, my ears attuned to the silence, listening out for any sign of life, the soft carpet absorbing my footfalls. It's almost oppressively quiet, my breathing sounding unnaturally loud.

Passing an office door, I flash the torch on and catch DuNoye's name stencilled on the glass, the room beyond in darkness. I swallow nervously and try the handle but it's locked. Crouching, I slip my hand into my shoe and retrieve my Justice Department lock override, inserting it into the mechanism. Seconds later, the door clunks open. Another quick look around me to check that I'm alone then I disappear inside.

The beam of the torch highlights an expensive office with posters for studio movies on every wall. Moving across to DuNoye's desk, I pick up a couple of folders left strewn upon it and give the contents a quick look: it's mostly a list of shipments for Catalyst products, detailing quantity and destination.

Jovus, they're going everywhere. Ramona said that the Vi-zines were shipped out through the company's distribution network. If that was true then they were being sold all over the world.

The Vi-zine racket, by its very nature, is a small-scale, covert operation that deals with a highly selective client base, and I've never seen an outfit with such huge resources behind it. Catalyst must be flooding half the major cities in the world with their brand of high-quality snuff rags: Texas City, Hondo, Brit-Cit, Emerald Isle, Pan-African States... Serious numbers were being pushed out to all of them, right under their respective authorities' noses. As the propaganda flicks were coming with Justice Department approval, Customs must be rubber-stamping them automatically. The lists don't specify customers but I have a feeling they would be held on DuNoye's computer. I'm loath to touch it, however, in case it's alarmed. This is one for the Tek-Judges to hack into once the uniforms are called in. I take a couple of quick snaps of the shipping documents as evidence. It's disturbing just how many sickos must be out there, lapping this material up.

Exiting the office, I pad further down the corridor, discovering meeting rooms or supply cupboards containing shelves groaning with glossy torture mags. *Click*, *click*, goes the shutter on my camera. I poke my head round the door of an empty edit suite, the bank of monitors gleaming in the torchlight.

The corridor ends in a large, ornate door, which I can only assume leads to Erik Rejin's quarters. I place my ear to the wood but hear nothing on the other side. I weigh up the choice: if I'm discovered breaking into Rejin's rooms, then it's game over. No amount of fast-talking is going to convince them I don't have a suspicious agenda. But this is the gruddamn dragon's lair, the point where all roads have led to. Dredd and Hendry instructed me to explode Catalyst from the top down, and finding proof that the big cheese is fully aware of what his company is up to will be enough to close the whole operation down for good. There's no argument. I unlock the door and tentatively twist the handle, wincing at the smallest creak.

Playing my torch over the surroundings, it's clear that this is some kind of viewing room. An impressive wall-mounted screen dominates the area with chairs and a sofa positioned in front of it. On the far side, there's another, smaller door, and crossing over to it quickly I can hear the rhythmic sound of snoring coming through the divide. It must be Rejin's bedroom. To be in such close proximity, and knowing that it's probably not going to take much to wake him, galvanises me into action.

Ramona had made a fleeting mention of her father watching movies here and presumably Rejin would approve anything that the studio produced, so I check the Tri-D system standing before the screen, sorting through the labelled discs lying next to it. I try to find something incriminating, but they all seem to be typical Catalyst films, with names like *Eagle Down*, *East-Meg Apocalypse*, *Perils of the Black Atlantic* (rough cut) and *Sov Strike Squad*.

I dig deeper, moving the discs aside to get a look at the others that appear less new. Some of them have no titles and I can only guess at their contents, but one catches my interest – *Anna*. I retrieve it, turning it over in my hands, casting a glance at the connecting door which separates me from the slumbering CEO behind it. My curiosity won't be denied so I insert it into the Tri-D, making doubly sure that the speakers are disconnected, then turn the machine on, light and shadow dancing on the ceiling. I listen for any disturbance in the snoring pattern coming through the wall, but there's no change, and I turn my attention to the three-dimensional images projected in front of me.

It's not a professional movie; it's been shot with a handheld camera, jittery and unfocused. The subject is a young woman, maybe in her thirties, and I immediately recognise similarities with Ramona, but the woman on-screen is too old to be her. Also, the woman's clothes and those of the occasional bystander that crosses into view date this film to be a good ten to fifteen years old. I suddenly realise that this is Ramona's mother – Erik's wife.

The opening shots are of her performing onstage, evidently an actress of some note. With the sound off, it's impossible to gauge her performance, but judging by the applause and bouquets presented to her, she's clearly popular and talented. I fast-forward through cuts to parties and holidays, sometimes catching a glimpse of a five-year-old Ramona running into shot, or being held in her mother's arms, but the focus of attention is always on the woman, Anna. There's no sign of Erik, and I guess he must be operating the camera, the adoring onlooker.

I continue to flash past more images of her, but as time goes on she appears troubled by the camera rather than welcoming its presence. At one point she seems to be shouting, pushing the intruding lens away. Then a jump-cut and the material changes entirely: Anna is tied to a chair, her mouth gagged, her eyes terrified and pleading, and as the camera moves closer to her a knife emerges from under the frame, presumably grasped in the cameraman's hand.

I watch Ramona's mother's protracted murder for several minutes before I look away, my eyes blurry with tears. My gaze rests on the threshold to Rejin's bedroom and I take an involuntary step towards it, shaking with anger and an insatiable desire to go in there and throttle the sick old drokker in his sleep. My trembling fingers reach out to turn off the Tri-D, but before I can do so the main lights flicker on. I whirl round to find DuNoye standing in the main doorway, a couple of creeps behind him.

"Enjoying Mr Rejin's home videos, I see," he says, smiling menacingly, and he takes a moment to stare up at the events displayed on the screen, the violence reflected in his face. "Not quite happy families, is it?"

I start to instinctively back away. "Look, DuNoye, t-this isn't what you think…"

He waves my protestations away. "There's no need to explain. I know everything… Judge Trager."

Twelve

"I WANT SPY-IN-THE-SKY cameras trained on him every step of the way," Dredd barked into his radio mic, swinging astride his Lawmaster. "All units to relay his movements, but not to apprehend unless expressly instructed. Fugitive has a hostage at gunpoint – we can't move in until we can secure her safety."

"Roger that," Control replied. "PSU cameras report vehicle matching your description is heading north on Massey, approaching Kevin Spacey Interchange."

"Keep me informed," he muttered, gunning his engine and speeding off in pursuit.

It was ridiculous, there was nowhere for Matheson Peat to go. Surely he would be aware that Justice Department was not just going to let him waltz out of the city, with or without his secretary as a prisoner? They had the surveillance technology to trace his route across the city, and with the Black Atlantic on one side and the Cursed Earth on the other, he couldn't make his own way beyond its walls.

The spaceports and harbour guard were put on alert and were told not to allow the councillor passage but to stall him as much as possible. Justice Department had a roster of excuses it could use to stop potential hijackers commandeering a craft to escape in: mechanical failure, weather problems, unnecessarily convoluted red tape. By the time the perp had experienced enough of these, they were ready to just about give up.

It was a risky proposition, when a citizen was being held against their will and could end up being whacked by a frustrated gunman, but Dredd felt the alert would work with Peat – the man was not a murderer. He was a coward and a weak-willed idiot who had covered for others to help advance his own career, and who had used his position of power to aid and abet a series of horrific slayings.

It gave Dredd no small sense of satisfaction to think that when he apprehended the councillor, the creep would be staring at the inside of an iso-cube for a very long time, but even so, the man was not violent or cruel or capable of taking life. Peat was panicking, that was all. His secrets had been discovered, and fleeing was the only response he had left, even if it was just making the situation worse for himself and simply delayed the inevitable.

It had been frustrating for Dredd to watch as Peat had backed away, out of his offices and onto the slab, his gun jammed under his secretary's jaw, a look of fevered desperation on his face. He had known the game was up, but was going play it out right to the bitter end. Sweaty, wide-eyed, his cheeks stained with tears, he appeared every inch a man on the brink, and it was difficult to tell who seemed more scared, the captor or hostage. In such a state, Dredd knew that the councillor's finger could squeeze the trigger at the slightest provocation and so he had to relent, reluctantly permitting him to make his way out onto the street. With the barrel jabbing into her chin, the lawman sensed too that if he tried to bring the perp down with a leg-shot or even go for a straight Standard Execution between the eyes, all it would take would be a nervous twitch and the secretary would be minus a head.

Dredd carefully shadowed Peat's movements, all the time telling him to give it up now before events got even more out of hand. He couldn't tell if the councillor was listening to him – the words certainly had little effect – and in truth he wished his negotiation skills were a tad more polished, allowing him to project a note of empathy with the criminal. However, even the most judicious of his colleagues would admit that he was not known for his sympathetic side so Dredd tended to leave that aspect of the job to those who were trained for it. All he wanted to do was get the cit out of the way so he could take a shot at the meathead.

Nobody messed with the councillor as he made his way down to ground level. The office staff had stared as their employer had passed them, stumbling backwards, one of their colleagues held close to him, her head tipped back by the gun barrel wedged under her jaw. Some of them had risen from their seats, their mouths dropping open in shock and disbelief at what they were seeing. They'd looked enquiringly at the Judge, but he'd just made a calming motion with his hand, his attention focused on Peat, and they could do nothing but silently watch as the three figures disappeared down a set of stairs and onto the street.

Outside, Peat had ploughed his way through the crowd, citizens parting in waves when they saw the blaster, and once at the kerbside had managed to force a vehicle to stop. He'd swung the gun in the driver's direction, yelling at him to get out, smashing the barrel against the side window. The man didn't argue and tumbled out onto the tarmac, arms held high in surrender, as the councillor threw his hostage into the passenger seat then jumped behind the wheel. The speedster had torn off, tyres squealing, the other traffic swerving wildly to avoid it as it careened across the lanes and powered onto a megway. Dredd had called in a full description of the vehicle and approximate location, knowing that the cameras would do the rest.

Peat couldn't escape. He was running in tighter and tighter circles, and eventually he would come to a stop.

"Suspect still heading north, now on Gulacy," Control crackled in his ear. "He's left the main thoroughfare and it looks like he's heading into a residential district. Might have a particular place in mind."

"What sector is that?" Dredd asked, thinking the name sounded familiar.

"Thirteen."

"I'll be on his position in five," Dredd said. He had an inkling about where Matheson Peat was heading.

KEISHA HAD STOPPED crying. She was curled up on the passenger seat, staring straight ahead, an expression of grim stoicism on her face. Peat glanced across at her as he drove, his left hand gripping the wheel, his right still pointing the gun in her direction; she looked mighty pissed. He'd always been slightly intimidated by her when they'd worked together – he found her no-nonsense efficiency and frankness disconcerting – and he'd often suspected she took him for a self-serving fool. Maybe she'd been proved right.

"Keisha," he started, "I'm sorry I've dragged you into this. You've got to understand... I had no choice."

She didn't answer at first, continuing to gaze blankly out of the windscreen. When she finally spoke, her voice was strained. "Are you going to hurt me?"

"No... Not if everybody does what they're told." In truth, he hadn't planned for that eventuality. He wasn't cut out for the life of crime, he decided, that was becoming abundantly clear. He wasn't nearly ruthless enough. "I don't want any... unpleasantness."

"What is this about?" she demanded, at last meeting his gaze, her temper rising as she sensed she wasn't in any immediate danger. "I knew something was wrong, but I never thought you were in trouble with the Judges. Is it some financial thing?"

"No," he snapped, then added softly: "No. I just made a mistake, many years ago. I thought what I was doing was for the best, but... these things have a habit of coming back to haunt you."

"And you think this is going to help?" She snorted derisively, her glare withering. "You're an idiot, Matheson. Where do you think you're going to go? The Judges will get you, no matter where you try to hide."

Her words stung him, but he attempted to maintain his composure, anxious to prove that he had the power here. He was the one that was meant to be calling the shots. "They won't stop me, not while I've got you. They'll have to do what I say."

"Jovus, what drokking city are you living in, man?" Keisha was shouting now. "You're going to end up arrested or dead, that's all."

"Keep your voice down," he warned.

His secretary ignored him. "You've got to give yourself up. Stop the car and maybe we both won't be going to Resyk."

"I said shut your damn mouth. I won't tell you again."

"Stop the car!" she yelled and lunged forward, grabbing hold of the wheel, wrenching it to the right. The speedster swerved across the road, oncoming traffic having to screech out of the way. Peat fought to wrest control back from her, but he only had one hand available. Desperately, he swung the gun and slammed the barrel into her face. Blood spattered the dashboard and windows as her nose shattered and she let go instantly, slumping back into her seat. He steered the vehicle back into the correct lane, casting a glance at his hostage who was holding her face and trying to stem the flow.

"Keisha... I'm sorry, but I'm not stopping, not now. I'm not going to the cubes." He was impressed by the newly defined, steely resolution in his voice. Maybe his future lay in crime after all. He'd certainly descended into violence quickly enough, even going as far as to pistol-whip a woman. Perhaps this potential had lain dormant within him all along, and he was at last discovering his true calling. Whatever the case, it seemed he was set on a path from which there was no return. "The Judges are going to fly us out of the city, and once my safety is assured I'll let you go. Just stay calm and you'll have no reason to fear."

She studied him, her bloodied hand masking the lower half of her face, her eyes burning hot with fury and contempt. "They're not going to let you step on an aircraft. They'll have every spaceport in the area under observation, there'll be snipers to take you out the moment you try to board–"

"We're not going to the spaceport," he interrupted. "We're going to be picked up in more… neutral territory."

Even her anger couldn't disguise her curiosity. "Then where?" she asked, her brow furrowing.

In answer, he swung the car off the main slab and headed towards an unpaved, fenced-off area, roped with Justice Department "Crime Scene" markers. The gate set in the fence was locked shut, but Peat made no attempt to decrease his speed.

"Hold on," he said.

"Peat, what the hell are you doing?" Keisha screamed, but any reply was lost as the vehicle smashed through the gate, wire ripping shreds from the bodywork, the air filled with the cacophony of rending metal. Once they were through, the councillor struggled to keep control of the car, the wheels sliding on the soft earth beneath, the tyres torn from the collision. He stamped on the brake and it began to skid, threatening to tip over onto its side any second. In response, he steered into the swerve and directed the vehicle towards a mound of soil, bracing himself for the crunch. It hit the bank and shuddered to a stop, the two of them banging forward then back in their seats.

For a moment, there was silence, the only sound the quiet ticking of the engine as it cooled. Then Peat recovered his senses. He wrenched the door open, staggering slightly as he climbed out, then walked round to the other side and dragged a dazed Keisha from the car.

"W-where are we?" she asked, looking round at the excavated land and construction machinery in puzzlement.

The councillor couldn't resist a little theatricality. "Welcome to Elizabeth Short," he said with a grandiose flourish, motioning to the half-built block towering above them.

DREDD ARRIVED AT the site minutes later, following the trail of destruction. Swinging himself off his bike, he drew his Lawgiver and cautiously checked the battered car, its bodywork dented and scratched, the doors left hanging open. He noted the scuffed footprints in the mud heading away from the vehicle towards the block itself, and started to follow. The diggers and trucks stood silent within the shadow of Liz Short as they had done since the bodies were discovered. The only sound was the wind whipping over the tent the Judges had established to examine the remains, the tarpaulin ruffling and flapping in the breeze.

"Control, can confirm fugitive Peat and his hostage have abandoned vehicle at Liz Short construction site," he murmured. "I suspect they are in the building itself. Continuing pursuit."

"That's a roj. Units are rolling to surround the area. Will have Short cordoned off within the next ten minutes."

Dredd made his way into the rubble-strewn entrance hall, wondering where the councillor was likely to be hiding. He couldn't get very far because there was simply nowhere to go; the upper floors had not been built yet, plus the el' would not be working. Peat would have been forced to drag his hostage up the stairs. Dredd guessed that it wouldn't take Peat long to tire of the chase. He must know by now that he was cornered.

The Judge had begun to move up to the first floor when he heard the woman scream. He gauged it had to be several levels above him and began to run, taking the steps three at a time. With the block little more than a shell, the corridors he passed through often opened into empty air, exposed beams jutting out, semi-finished floors revealing the cabling beneath. On more than one occasion he had to catch himself, as the set of stairs he attempted to climb had no supporting wall and to his right was a drop of a couple of hundred feet. The cityscape stretched around him, the growing wind whistling off the scaffolding and swirling rockcrete dust. Dredd tried to ignore the realisation of just how easy it would be to lose his footing and plunge to the ground below, and continued his ascent.

Another scream, much closer, and Dredd doubled his speed, concentrating on throwing himself up the steps. At last he caught sight of Peat and his secretary standing on one of the rafters that poked out of the building, his gun held to her temple. The rafter was little more than five feet across, and there was nothing beyond them but the vertiginous descent to the streets.

"Didn't take you long to find me," Peat said as Dredd appeared before him.

"You were never going to escape us," the lawman replied. "Plus I had an idea where you might be heading." He motioned to his surroundings with his Lawgiver. "It always comes round full circle eventually. What did you hope to achieve?"

"Don't presume too early, Dredd. You try to arrest me, I'll blow her drokking brains out."

"You're not a murderer, Peat. You haven't got it in you."

"You think so? Are you prepared to take the risk?"

Dredd could see that the secretary had taken a beating; her nostrils were caked in blood and a livid bruise had swollen across her face. She looked understandably terrified, her eyes constantly darting either side of her to the dizzying drop. Maybe he shouldn't underestimate the councillor, he thought, as he was evidently quite capable of meting out acts of violence when pushed.

"You're going to get yourselves both killed if you stay out here," Dredd said, a conciliatory note to his voice.

"That's where you're wrong," Peat answered. "You're gonna order us up a hover-cab, just a small one, enough for the two of us and the robot driver. It's going to pick us up from here and fly us out of the city. Any attempts to stop me, she dies. Once my safety is guaranteed, I'll let her go."

"Only got your word for that."

"Then that's all you'll have to go on."

"I'm not in the habit of negotiating with creeps, Peat."

"Too bad, 'cause I don't see you have much choice. Not unless you want Keisha here to go splat."

"You kill your hostage, then what are you going to do? Hand yourself in? Jump?"

"Maybe. But imagine what the papers'll say about how Judge Dredd stood by and allowed an innocent cit to die. The very people you're sworn to protect. Won't do your public profile much good." The councillor jabbed the gun harder against her head. "Now get that gruddamn cab here."

Dredd radioed in the demand, then listened to the response. "It'll be here in a couple of minutes," he said.

"It better, or I'm gonna start getting impatient."

The Judge took a small step forward. "Seems to me, councillor, that it was always *you* that was worried about the press. You were always the one courting the media. They're going to have a field day with you after this."

"Yeah. Shame I won't be around to see it."

"You had quite the career, didn't you? Quite a celebrity. And you've thrown it all away protecting a madman. Was it really worth it?"

Peat didn't reply immediately. "You take your chances when you see them. I wasn't the only one covering for Erik. He's got plenty of friends in high places."

"Fixing to get him released from the kook cubes, wiping his files, and I'm guessing more than one of your

Phoenix Campaign Blocks is built upon a body-dump. You were guiding Rejin's operation to the best rad-pits, then constructing over the evidence, weren't you? Half your rich pals are living on top of mass graveyards while you lapped up the fame and exposure."

"Where's this cab?" the councillor demanded angrily.

"And what about you, Peat?" Dredd continued, taking another step along the rafter. "You ever get your kicks from a little torture-murder too?" The secretary looked at the lawman questioningly and Dredd played on it. "Didn't you know your boss had a sick little sideline, citizen? That he's partly responsible for the disappearance of an unknown number of men and women, all of whom had been tortured to death? Kept that council business to himself, did he?"

Control crackled in the Judge's ear. "Vehicle will be with you in thirty seconds. Stand by."

"Matheson, what the drokk are you involved in?" Keisha whispered.

"Tell her," Dredd said evenly. "Tell her what your friends get up to."

"Drokk you!" Peat roared and swung the gun from his secretary to bear down on Dredd.

At that moment, an H-platform piloted by a couple of Judges rose vertically and slammed into the rafter with a sharp clang. It was enough to knock the councillor off balance, and the lawman snatched hold of the hostage and pushed her onto the safety of the platform.

Peat lost his footing and stumbled, then slipped off the beam, his gun spiralling downwards, one arm snaking around the cold metal as he fell. He dangled precariously, yelping in panic, as Dredd inched along, holding out a gloved hand for Peat to pull himself up with.

"Quickly!" the Judge shouted at his colleagues as they lowered and positioned the H-platform below the councillor, then pulled him roughly aboard. Dredd swiftly followed, leaping onto it from the rafter.

He snapped cuffs on Peat, then spun him round and lifted him up by the lapels. "Now," Dredd snarled in his face, "you and me are gonna have a chat about your best pal Erik Rejin."

Peat's numbed, sandblasted expression cracked to give way to a tiny smile. "Y-you might want to t-think about *your* l-little friend too…"

"What are you talking about?"

"Your u-undercover friend. The one you've g-got inside Catalyst. I imagine he's in very s-serious trouble right about now…"

"How did you–"

Peat giggled. "That's classified."

"Drokk!" Dredd turned to the pilot. "Get us down now! I've got to get to Catalyst studios!"

Thirteen

I'M DREAMING I'm flying over the city. I'm drifting on the breeze like a batglider, clipping the rooftops, twisting through the rockcrete canyons, my feather-light body reflected in a million windows, flashing silver in the sunshine. It looks so peaceful from up here, this heaving metropolis that I call my home, the megways snaking through the sectors like fast-flowing rivers, condos rising like immense cliffs. It stretches for as far as the eye can see in every direction, the landscape a mass of buildings and pedways knitted together; a nest of humanity.

But as I float here, buffeted by currents of hot air, diving and climbing, enjoying the freedom and beauty of my surroundings, I realise the reason that it's so peaceful is that there's no trace of life beneath me. I'm all alone, without a skysurfer or a dog-vulture to keep me company, soaring over a deserted city. The thought of my isolation casts a shadow across my mind, souring the pleasure of my flight, and there is a crinkling at the corner of my brain that tells me something isn't right.

I decide to investigate closer, tumbling down into the gloom of the towering citi-blocks, searching for a sign of occupancy. After the cool, crisp taste of the air up above the furthest spires of the metropolis, down here it smells rank, like the liquefying underbelly of roadkill. The lower I go, the worse the stink gets, a putrid, cloying odour that seems at odds with the sparkling curves of the architecture. Nothing moves down here: no citizens walk the streets, the freeways are empty of traffic, shops, factories and offices are abandoned. The silence is oppressive, the background hubbub of a busy conurbation noticeable by its absence. Even the air is still, as if thick with disease. It coats the back of my throat and makes me gag.

I feel uneasy passing through these empty avenues, wondering what has happened to everyone, what has happened to my home. The darkness seems to be encroaching as I drift ever downwards, as if the buildings are closing in and blocking out the light, stopping me escaping. I decide I don't want to be here anymore. I want to be free, wheeling across the blue sky, leaving this decaying industrial wasteland far, far below me. I want to ascend back up to the heavens, but I can't. It keeps dragging me down, the atmosphere growing heavier, more stifling, to the point where I think I'm going to suffocate.

Then I spy something below me, gleaming pale white amidst the grey surroundings, and moving closer I can see it is a skeletal arm sticking up through the rockcrete from the centre of a square, bony fingers left grasping at nothing but air. I understand at last what has become of the inhabitants. This is a city of the dead, an enormous mausoleum under which the population rests and rots, returning to the earth. Paved over their remains, the metropolis endures; a tombstone for four hundred million people, it both conceals and commemorates the deaths that it clutches to its black heart.

My feet finally touch City Bottom, the darkness looming around me, and I can hear a faint noise cutting through the silence. It seems to be coming from beneath me, so I get to my knees, my ear pressed to cold stone, trying to discern the source of the sound. I close my eyes in concentration and realise that I'm listening to the wails of the dead rising up from their burial ground, weeping and moaning and screaming, trapped perpetually within the shadow of this great sprawling cemetery. It gets louder, as if the dead masses are travelling up from their deep abode to meet me, to claim me. I try to get to my feet, but the skeletal hand suddenly grabs my hair and grips me, vice-like. I panic, struggling to be free, but I cannot pull away from its grasp. The screams rise in pitch and the ground begins to split open, light rushing up, burning my sight, my name repeated over and over again...

"Trager." The word is punctuated by a slap across the face, and I'm pulled into consciousness like a newborn, kicking and mewling. Even though I'm awake, the vestiges of my dream still cling to me for the screams continue to ring in my ears. I open my eyes, trying to gauge where they are coming from, then I see they belong to Ramona. She's being held back by the companion of that meathead whose throat I destroyed and she's looking at me, her cheeks wet with tears, and she's struggling to reach out to me but the creep won't let her come near. Something about her face tells me I probably don't want to look in a mirror right about now. There's pity there, and a horror at what has been wrought on me.

The instigator of the mess that has been made of me is the one who called my name, and he's standing over me, his suit spattered with blood, his hands dripping. Vandris DuNoye. He seems slightly out of breath, but his smooth face and expensive haircut are unruffled. I can't quite decode his expression; it falls somewhere between hatred and the pleasure he'll get from exacting his retribution.

My memories of what happened prior to being strapped to this chair in the middle of an abandoned Catalyst soundstage start to filter through. I remember being caught in Rejin's screening room, of making a feeble attempt to talk my way out of the situation and not even believing myself, let alone convincing this lawyer spugger. I remember thinking that once they had me there was going to be little to stop my inevitable execution, and I fought back desperately, trying to recall my Academy training. I landed several satisfactory punches, and put one guy on the floor with a suspected broken rib, but I was shocked at how rusty I'd become, at how slow my responses were, at how long it took me to recover from every blow landed. Too much chemical indulgence had blunted my edge.

So here I am, the man in the chair, shortly to be the recipient of the pain that not long ago I had administered with a frighteningly eager hand. I've got a fair idea what they're going to do to me. The camera's set up on a tripod – I doubt they'll get Ramona to take the photos this time, so my moment in the spotlight is going lack a certain finesse – and the trolley's standing beside me, a smorgasbord of torture weapons laid upon it. Amongst them are several of the Banana City devices obtained from Talón an eternity ago, and in a nice slice of grim irony, my way in seems also to be my undoing. I take deep breaths. I don't want them to see just how scared I am.

"Back to the land of the living, Mr Trager?" DuNoye asks me softly.

"Vandris, please, I'm begging you, don't do this," Ramona cries, still trying to pull free from her captor.

"Ramona," the lawyer snaps, turning his head in her direction. "I've asked you to be quiet. Your father is on his way down. He will deal with you."

She locks stares with me and I can see a conflict raging inside her. On the one hand, I've betrayed her and she drokking hates me for it: hates me for making a fool of her, for lying to her, for using her to get further inside the operation. That side of her would quite happily see me gutted and dismembered, the occasion captured in a series of graphic glossies. But there's a genuine stirring within her that means she can't stand by and watch me murdered. She broke free of her father's shadow for once to be with me, and that intimacy meant an enormous amount to her. For her, it was possibly one of the bravest things she had ever done. I'd got under her skin, and had been closer to her than anyone since the death of her mother.

DuNoye fixes his attention back to me. "It seems I was right to mistrust you, Mr Trager. I had my doubts right from the start, but... let's just say that your enthusiasm impressed me. Rarely do you meet someone with such a natural propensity for casual brutality. Of course, now that I know you work for Justice Department, it seems obvious."

There seems little point in continuing the charade. I cough, finding my voice. "How did you know?" My words sound slurred, unsteady, as if they have trouble leaving my lips.

"We have a little bird close to the Grand Hall of Justice," he says, taking no small delight in imparting the information. "He has access to all sorts of sensitive material." When he sees me bow my head, DuNoye adds, "No one likes to discover that their organisation has been infiltrated, do they, Mr Trager? You've compromised our operation, you've put us all at risk, including Mr Rejin's daughter. You're a danger to us and you have to be eliminated."

"Give it up now, DuNoye," I breathe, fatigue starting to take its toll. Every muscle and bone seems to be aching simultaneously. "Your sick little studio is finished. You think that by whacking me you're gonna stop them coming to take you out? Wheels are already in motion, pal. They don't hear from me, they're gonna blitz this place."

The lawyer laughs. "Oh, don't worry about us, Mr Trager. We've already made our emergency plans to get out of the city. We still have a few friends of influence that can ease our passage, and some substantial donations here and there will keep Justice Department off our backs. Still, it's nice to know that you care so much about Ramona that you're happy to see her carted off to the cubes."

I can barely summon up the courage to look at her. She's stopped struggling and is just studying me, like a laboratory specimen; some new species of human being that is worthy of investigation. I want to tell her that not everything I said was part of a performance, that my actions were motivated as much by a genuine attraction and desire as by the demands of my role as a Mega-City Judge.

I don't want to see Ramona hurt. She's been brought up by an insane father, bombarded by his mad, monstrous philosophy, and no doubt knows nothing about the truth behind her mother's death. He's made her in his own image, corrupting her view of other people to the point where her talent only emerges as she strives to reveal the secrets beneath the skin. She needs counselling, maybe a spell in a psych-unit. Encubement could only prove to damage her further. I resolve that if by some miracle I come out of this alive I will recommend she gets help. But she, along with the rest of these creeps, needs to be stopped right now.

DuNoye's watching me, sensing my discomfort. "Not pretty, is it, coming face to face with someone you've been deceitful to?"

"That's rich," I hurl back, determined not to have his gloating features be the last thing I see before I die. "She's been lied to all her life. Born into this drokking charnel house, she's known nothing but her father's warped vision. What story did you spin for when her mother disappeared?"

"Trager, what are you–" Ramona blurts out, her words tremulous.

"Ramona!" DuNoye barks again, silencing her. He glares at me, fiery eyes looking straight into mine. "I'm growing tired of the sound of your voice, Mr Trager. I'm thinking it might be best all round if we cut that devious tongue from your head."

He reaches for the trolley beside me and plucks up what looks like a pair of tinsnips. He studies them for a second, as if he were a surgeon selecting the right equipment, then moves closer to me.

"Alphonse, if you would be so kind to capture the moment?" DuNoye asks as my erstwhile partner mans the camera. "Don't want to go for the money shot too soon," the lawyer says to me quietly, grabbing my hair and pulling my head back, "but a little blood will make a nice opening splash image." He motions to another goon standing nearby. "Get his mouth open."

The meathead grasps my jaw and wrenches it apart, despite my best efforts to avoid his clutches. I'm squirming in the chair, trying to make it as difficult for them as possible, but they're both holding on tight. I attempt to retract my tongue until it's virtually choking me. DuNoye edges in closer with the implement and I feel the cold steel against my lips, taste the merest hint of oil upon them. I summon my strength and twist my head a few centimetres, enough for the snips to graze my cheek and chin. Pain lances through me, but it's enough to grant me a few seconds respite as the lawyer stops briefly, looking exasperated at his minion.

"Hold him the drokk still," he says tersely.

"Vandris, I don't want this," Ramona howls. "Not this way, please–"

"Ramona, I won't tell you again–"

"No, I agree, DuNoye," a new voice says, immediately silencing the room. "Not this way."

I'm released at once, my mouth clamping shut automatically. DuNoye drops the snips back onto the trolley and turns to meet the newcomer, who moves further into the light. "I'm sorry, Mr Rejin, I thought you wanted the traitor dispatched," the lawyer says, deferent.

"And so he will. But by *my* hand. His soul belongs to *me*."

Finally, I can see the figure: Erik Rejin, the movie-maker, the elusive creep at the heart of Catalyst. If I was expecting the Devil, a wizened creature whose physical appearance matched the evil deeds that he had presided over, then I was disappointed.

This is very much a man, and all the more terrifying that insanity could reside in someone who is normality personified. He's surprisingly sprightly for his years hidden from public view, his movements not betraying his age – he has to be somewhere in his sixties – and there's not a trace of the ravages of madness across his face. On the contrary, he has bland, almost nondescript, features: pale blue eyes behind tiny glasses, a tidy sandy-blond haircut going to grey, a small pursed mouth. His skin is unnaturally white, as if he hasn't seen sunlight for most of his adult life.

The more I look at him, however, the more I think that this person possibly doesn't belong to the same species as the rest of us, that he has in fact distanced himself from the human race. There's not a trace of emotion behind those watery eyes, no cracks appearing in that blank mask of a face. He's a cipher; a hollowed-out character who's found that the only way to feel is to see others reduced to the same basics as him. He's the nearest thing I've seen to a living, breathing robot, and when he speaks, his voice has the monotone timbre of someone who died inside long ago.

"What did you want here, lawman?"

I don't know how to answer. He's regarding me strangely, like he's looking through me, and the effect is unnerving.

"You want her, is that it?" Rejin grabs Ramona's arm without even turning and pulls her close. "You want this offspring of mine for yourself?"

"Father, please, I-I didn't know," she sobs, looking petrified of her own parent.

Rejin's head swivels mechanically towards his daughter. "You have betrayed me, child, welcoming this snake into our home. Everything I taught you about the untrustworthy nature of man, you have disregarded." He walks her forward and picks up a las-saw off the trolley. "Haven't I told you that truth lies within? That only once you go beyond the flesh can you slough off the reptile skin and reveal the light of purity? Look, I shall show you that even this being, this *man* of *law*," he spits the words at me, "contains the simple beauty of truth." He goes to raise the saw above my chest.

"No," she replies, shaking her head. "I don't want to see…"

"Then you are a fool!" he rasps and lashes out at her with the handle of the saw, smacking it against her temple. She collapses to her knees, holding the side of her head, weeping.

"Rejin!" I roar, finding my voice at last. "This has to *stop*!"

"You are not in a position to give me any kind of order, deceiver. You have infected my daughter with your lies, you have spread their taint around my domain. And damned though you may be, I shall show that redemption can be extracted from even the most foulest of creatures."

He whips the saw across my chest and the short laser beam crackles as it slices through my shirt and parts the meat beneath. I scream, straining against the ropes binding me to the chair, smoke rising from the slash-mark, the stench of burning flesh reaching my nose. He strikes again, higher, catching my bare neck and shoulder, and white-hot agony paralyses my left arm. There's little blood, as the laser cauterises each wound even as it appears, but the skin around each blow blackens and crisps.

"I want this lawman's transformation on record," Rejin demands. Alphonse hurriedly starts snapping, zooming in on my face contorted in pain. "Can you imagine what this will sell for?" the madman continues. "What the connoisseurs will say when they get to see this Mega-City Judge broken apart by my very hand? It will elevate my work up to a whole new level!" He swipes the saw downwards and slices me across the face. I feel my hair burning, then I black out.

I come to possibly only seconds later. Ramona is clutching at her father, staying his hand, repeatedly asking him to stop.

"Vandris, take her up to my room," Rejin says.

"Sir, we should really be thinking about leaving," the lawyer replies. "We don't know how much the Judges know about us, but they could have the building under surveillance–"

"Not until I have finished with our friend here," Rejin says, gesturing to me. "There is still too much work to be done." He suddenly grabs me under the chin and lifts my head up, levelling the tip of the saw just above my right eye. "I want my revenge on this offender…"

At that moment, an explosion rips through the outer part of the studio. Rejin releases me, steps back and looks around. DuNoye just has time to say, "What the hell?" before there's another burst of automatic fire and the far wall of the soundstage collapses in a cloud of dense smoke. There's a rumble of a powerful engine and Dredd comes surging through the rent in the wall on his Lawmaster, screeching towards us.

Fourteen

SMOKE. CONFUSION. THE perps scattered as if a grenade had been lobbed into the centre of the room.

"You are all under arrest!" Dredd hollered as he sped towards the group. "Drop your weapons now or face the consequences!"

"Sir! This way!" DuNoye shouted to Rejin, dragging Ramona with one hand in the direction of a back exit. The CEO followed rapidly, bodyguards shielding him and returning fire.

Dredd ducked low and powered into the melee, bike cannons blazing, cutting a swathe through those creeps that had remained to take him on, bodies jerking as they were riddled with high-power slugs. A meathead let loose with a zip gun and Dredd rolled off the Lawmaster to seek shelter, leaping behind a stack of crates. While the bike slammed into a wall with a jarring crunch, he unslung his Lawgiver and came up shooting, putting three Standard Execution rounds through the crim's skull with barely a fraction of a second's aim.

The survivors saw that this was a good time to flee and backed off, pouring on the automatic fire to cover their escape. The Judge timed the gaps in the barrage and picked his targets, taking out a further two with pinpoint accuracy before those that were left disappeared from view. When he broke cover and headed across to Trager, the soundstage was deserted, the floor littered with rubble and half a dozen bodies. As the lawman reached him, the undercover officer was slouching in the chair as far as his bonds would allow.

Dredd crouched down beside him, lifting his head up to check his wounds. There was a livid gash across his face from his hairline to his jaw, the skin puckered around it like a burn. He could hear the man breathing lightly, and his eyes flickered open, taking a few moments to adjust to Dredd's presence.

"Hold on, Trager," the senior Judge said. "Back-up is on its way." He quickly untied the straps and lifted him to his feet, noticing the scorched marks on his chest and belly. "Can you stand?"

Trager nodded. He swallowed several times and tried to push himself away, attempting to steady himself without Dredd's aid. "I... I can make it," he breathed. "How did you know I needed help?"

"Matheson Peat. He must've alerted 'em that they had a Judge in their midst. As a politician he had access to sensitive Justice Department records, so he could've discovered files relating to your infiltration."

"The councillor? He's involved in this?"

"Up to his damn eyeballs. Been covering for Rejin and the whole Catalyst operation, him and his circle of rich pals." Dredd nodded to the camera set-up. "Vi-zines?"

"And then some."

"Guessed as much." The senior Judge looked Trager up and down. "You were lucky we found out your cover had been blown when we did. It's unfortunate that you had to be put in this position. We'll have to review our security procedures."

"All part of the job," he murmured, wincing as he ran his fingers over his facial scar.

"Wait here for the med-wagon," Dredd said, noting his discomfort and already starting to head off in the direction that the perps had taken. "It won't be long."

"No," Trager replied, his voice growing stronger. "I'm coming with you."

"You're in no fit state to pursue them, Trager. You'll put both yourself and me at risk."

"I'm seeing this through to the end. Give me a gun."

"This is no time for heroics."

The Wally Squad Judge looked behind him, then uneasily walked over to one of the bodies, stooped and retrieved a couple of blasters, his face grimacing in pain. He turned back to Dredd. "I'm coming with you whether you like it or not. Don't worry about me, I'm fine."

"You're not and you know it," Dredd growled. "I don't have time to argue, but I will say this: you collapse when you're meant to be watching my back, you'll have me to answer to, understand?"

"You're all heart, Dredd," Trager said, striding past him.

The two of them reached the door that led into the backstage area. Dredd signalled for Trager to cover him as he edged his way through and appraised the corridor beyond. It was empty. He nodded and the undercover Judge followed him, a gun in each hand, head moving from side to side as he checked both left and right.

"There an escape route this way?" Dredd asked.

Trager shrugged. "No idea. This leads out to the admin offices, though DuNoye did say they had their passage out of city sorted."

"Terrif," the senior Judge rumbled. "Well, we've got units in the area, and an APB's out on them. Won't take long for them to be picked up if they get past us."

"Dredd, I gotta say something." Trager turned to him. "The daughter, Ramona, you gotta go easy on her. She's emotionally unbalanced. Rejin murdered her mother and brought her up, instilling some fruitcake philosophy into her. He's brainwashed her into thinking this whole operation is like a psycho art exercise; cutting open cits to reveal their true nature. He's off the looney-toon scale."

"No kidding. Rejin was trapped with the bodies of his family during the Apocalypse War and went full-blown nutso. Ended up eating half of them."

"Jovus drokk…"

"But the daughter's just as responsible," Dredd continued. "She'll take her chances with the rest of them."

"She didn't kill anyone," Trager replied, his voice hardening. "I'm not excusing her actions, but she just took the pics."

"She's an accessory to multiple murder, no matter what her mental state is. You were warned at the beginning not to get too close, and I can see it's already affecting your judgement. Don't make this personal. You were sent in on a job and it's now time to take these freaks down. If you haven't got the guts for that, then sit it out. But if you have, don't let feelings get in the way."

"I told you I wanted in on this," Trager said, starting to move along the corridor. "Come on, let's get it done."

Dredd watched the undercover officer make his way, wobbling slightly, through the backstage area and followed, wondering just how much of a liability he was going to be. Despite putting on an impressive front, the man was clearly in a great deal of pain, and he was allowing his effectiveness to be blunted by some personal mission of his own. Did he really think he could save this daughter of Rejin's? In Dredd's experience, such an enterprise was normally doomed to failure. When a Judge started getting too close to the perps – whether it became an obsessive vendetta to bring them down or a relationship growing between the two parties – then the Law itself became compromised. Justice should be delivered with absolute objective authority, otherwise they might as well just hand over the city to mob rule right now.

Dredd resolved he'd have to keep an eye on Trager as well as the creeps they were hunting. Both could equally cause trouble.

The Wally Squad Judge had reached a corner, and was peering round it furtively. He looked back at Dredd and motioned him over. "Thought I saw the glint of a gun barrel," he whispered when the lawman reached him. "Smells like the ideal place for a trap."

Dredd took a peek and silently agreed. The corridor ahead was littered with discarded props and several large boxes had been stacked against the walls to create a narrow channel that someone would have to squeeze through. They could conceal any number of triggermen waiting for them.

"What do you reckon?" Trager asked.

"Let's tease them out," Dredd replied, reaching down into a nearby crate and pulling out a replica stumm gas grenade. He turned it over, grudgingly impressed by its realism. Catalyst had certainly known what it was doing. "As you haven't got a respirator, we'll have to see if they can be fooled by an imitation."

The lawman crouched and threw the grenade down the length of the floor, watching as it skittered between the boxes. The result was instantaneous; two meatheads leaped from their cover, panicked by the device. They moved to kick it away, emerging into plain sight, and Dredd gunned them down where they stood.

He got to his feet and crossed to the far corridor wall, Lawgiver clutched in both hands at waist height, alert for any more resistance. He edged further up towards where the bodies lay, smoke still rising from their wounds. It was ominously quiet. He glanced back to see if Trager was following; the undercover officer was sliding along the opposite wall and met Dredd's gaze. At first, his expression advised caution, then his eyes widened and a split second later Dredd was turning, aware that someone was behind him.

"Dredd!" Trager's shout came a fraction too late.

A perp had jumped onto one of the boxes and pointed a sawn-off shotgun in the lawman's direction, letting off a deafening blast. Dredd threw himself sideways, feeling the high-calibre ammo shred the back of his uniform and pepper his skin with buckshot. He rolled, twisted and fired in one movement, pumping the trigger of his Lawgiver, but the pain igniting his back threw his aim off as he drilled a series of holes in the wall before catching the creep in the leg, shattering his kneecap. He squealed and dropped to the ground behind a stack of boxes, but Dredd sensed he wasn't out of the game just yet.

Trager scuttled alongside him, ducking low, and laid a hand on the senior Judge's shoulder. "Bad?" he asked.

"Had worse," Dredd answered, looking back and seeing a fine spray of his blood on the wall. "More pressing, spugwit ain't finished with us. I think I just winged him."

"OK, stay here. I'll deal with him."

"You're worse off than I am."

"Yeah, but I'm younger than you, old man. I carry it better."

"Shame your instincts weren't sharper. You might've spotted the punk earlier before he nearly plugged me." Dredd winced; his back felt as if it were on fire. He still had feeling below his waist and his legs were doing what he told them, which was a good sign, but he wondered how close the shot had come to his spine. That was all it took; one lucky creep with a half-decent chance and he could be put out of action permanently, spending the rest of his days teaching cadets interrogation techniques from a wheelchair. It wasn't how he had planned to spin out his twilight years. "But be careful," he added. "Creep's gonna be reloaded and waiting for you."

Trager nodded and started to inch through the channel, blasters slippery in each sweaty palm. His breathing seemed to reverberate between the walls in the eerily silent corridor. He came to the edge of the boxes and stopped for a second; the gunman was more than likely on a hair-trigger and the moment he put his head round the corner, the guy was going to blow it off. Trager knew he had to cause enough confusion to get a clear shot at him.

He looked back at Dredd, who had pulled himself to his feet, and signalled to the ceiling of the corridor and made a rebound motion. Dredd nodded, raised his Lawgiver, selected the correct bullet, aimed and fired.

The dum-dum ricocheted off the right angle where the wall met the ceiling and arrowed down behind the boxes, the creep yelling in surprise. Trager took his chance and leaped sideways, pumping both triggers before the man had a chance to recover, ammo hitting him in the chest and neck. The Wally Squad Judge curled and rolled as he crashed into the floor, coming up two-footed, feeling the wounds on his torso scream as they were torn open.

He stumbled, unconsciousness bearing down on him, the agony sending stars pinwheeling before his eyes, and leant heavily against the wall, covering the creep's death throes. The guy was feebly kicking his legs against the floor and holding his hands up against his throat to stem the flow of blood spewing forth, his shotgun lying forgotten beside him. Trager booted the gun away and crouched next to the dying man, waving a blaster barrel in his face.

"Your drokking boss," Trager breathed, swallowing down the nausea that clawed at him. "Where is he?"

The meathead gurgled. The Judge reached forward and grabbed his hand, pulling it away from his neck, the severed artery spritzing a crimson arc into the air.

"Tell me and maybe I'll get a med-wagon here in time to save you."

A glint of hope sparked in his rapidly dulling eyes. He opened his mouth to speak, a raw sound emerging from between his lips. "Th-they're b-burning it all," he gurgled, coughing up strings of bloody matter. "Whole d-drokking studio's gonna go up…"

"Where are they?" Trager demanded. "Where's Ramona?"

The creep was barely conscious enough to answer. He pointed further down the corridor, his head flopping back weakly as if the bones within him were softening.

"Where are they, you drokking piece of shit?" he snarled, but there was no reply. In a fit of anger Trager blew a hole in the guy's skull and let him drop to the floor. He got to his feet, breathing out slowly and trying to control his temper, aware that Dredd had emerged behind him and was hovering at his shoulder.

"What happened?" the lawman asked.

"Drokker wouldn't tell me anything, then tried to make a fight of it. Had to waste him."

Dredd looked at the ground and noted the shotgun lying several feet away. "That right?"

"Creeps never learn," Trager muttered dismissively, then started to continue along the corridor. "Come on, we're losing time."

Dredd looked once again at the gore-spattered remains of the gunman, then at the limping form of Trager disappearing around another corner, and followed without a word.

ON DREDD'S ORDER, Judges had sealed off all exits around Catalyst studios, plus DuNoye's description had been circulated to every unit in the area. They were instructed to apprehend him on sight in the unlikely event that he should escape their barrier. Helmets were also told to be on the lookout for an eldster and his daughter attempting to flee – Erik and Ramona Rejin were wanted in connection with numerous fatalities.

A squad had already entered the building and were mopping up the destruction that Dredd had left in his wake following the firefight. Med-Judges carried out body bags to waiting meat-wagons and Tek-Division were also starting to analyse the evidence, taking away the camera equipment and torture implements for study.

From the periphery, Judge Devenson watched the activity with interest, curious and quietly amazed at what was being discovered within the building. He remembered he'd once worked crowd control when some of the actors in a Catalyst feature had made public appearances and he'd been impressed by the company's attention to detail.

To learn that the outfit was a front for all sorts of nefarious deeds was a shock. He was certain repercussions were going to be felt in the Grand Hall of Justice itself. Catalyst had been approved by Justice Department as a producer of propoganda flicks, and questions were going to be raised about how it could have operated so secretly and autonomously within the Judges' protection. By all accounts the man in charge of the studio was madder than a sackful of spanners, but surely somebody must have pulled some strings at a very senior level to keep all this under their hat.

The media too, couldn't believe their luck. Tri-D crews were clamouring behind the Judges' line, trying to get a statement from the helmets on duty, but so far they had been told zip. It was the kind of story that reporters loved; a famous recluse is discovered to be harbouring a terrible secret, there was a substantial bodycount, and enough dirt to throw at the authorities for them to editorialise about.

The stories they were filing at the moment were filled with spurious suppositions and accusations in the absence of any hard facts. The realisation that Dredd was still in the building hunting down the lead perp led many to speculate that the lawman was using the opportunity to cover up Justice Department's involvement in the company by destroying vital records. Some rumours had Dredd actually aiding Rejin to escape so as to not publicly embarrass the Chief Judge. Devenson watched this circus with a certain degree of distaste, feeling they could do with cracking down on the freedom of the press even further.

He turned his head to survey the crime scene, making sure that nobody was attempting to cross the lines, and caught sight of a vehicle parked fairly close to the Catalyst offices. It was an expensive model, and not the sort you expected to see stationed on the slab. A couple of cits were seated inside it, seemingly waiting for something, explicitly ignoring the commotion. Eventually, the driver clambered out and wandered over to a gate set in the wall a few hundred metres away. Devenson recognised it as one of the many bolted entrances to the Undercity. The driver loitered nearby, trying to look innocuous, cocking an ear as if expecting a message to come from the other side.

"You!" Devenson shouted, striding over to the car. The creep jumped and turned, guilt written all over him. He eyed his colleague in the vehicle nervously. "What are you doing here?"

"N-nothing," the guy replied. "Just taking the air, Judge..."

"Don't mess with me, pal," Devenson snarled, pushing him against the wall. "Let's hear the truth." He signalled to the meathead sitting in the passenger seat. "You too, creep, out of the vehicle."

"We're not doing anything wrong, sir," the first gimp said.

"I'll be the judge of that," Devenson muttered as his partner slid from the car. "Come on," he called out. "Over here, now."

There was something about the way this second creep was taking his time that sent alarm bells ringing in Devenson's brain. He looked like he was building up to something, angling for the right moment. Out of the corner of his eye, he saw the driver fractionally moving his head; a slight nod indicating something to the other guy.

Devenson threw his suspect to the ground where he was out of the way and unholstered his Lawgiver, all in one movement. "Hands in the air!" he ordered, pointing his gun at the oncoming creep. "Don't move!"

The guy was either stupid or had a death wish. He must have plainly seen the game was up and yet he still went for it. His right hand delved inside his jacket and pulled out a semi-automatic, just in time to be blown backwards by three shots from Devenson, all catching him in the chest area. He spasmed onto the car bonnet, a bullet passing straight through him and shattering the windscreen. He lay there unmoving like a hood ornament.

The Judge yanked the driver up by the scruff of his neck and growled in his face. "Start talking, creep, or you'll go the same way as your friend. What are you doing here?"

TRAGER AND DREDD had reached the carpeted Catalyst admin area and smoke was drifting in the air, getting thicker the further they went. The orange flicker of flames crawled up the walls, devouring promo posters and files, melting furniture and computer terminals.

"They... They're destroying the evidence," Trager gasped between swallows of thin oxygen, his arm held across his nose and mouth.

Dredd didn't reply and barked instead into his radio mic. "Control, we need a fire-fighting team in here, priority one. Suspects have set fire to offices."

"That's a roj. Any sign of the perps?"

"Negative."

"A street helmet has just picked up a creep hanging around outside, close to an entrance to the Undercity. We're shaking him down now but we think he was going to be the fugitives' means of escape."

"Who does he work for?"

"That's what we're trying to establish, but it seems likely one of Rejin's business associates arranged it. In the meantime, the logical conclusion is that the suspects are using the Undercity to flee the building."

"The Undercity? How the drokk are they accessing the Undercity?"

"We don't know yet. But be aware that that's where they are likely to be heading."

"OK. Dredd out."

"What's happening?" Trager asked, coughing as the smoke began to billow before them in black clouds. A glass panel nearby shattered from the heat.

"Creeps are going underground somehow," Dredd replied, sliding down his respirator which gave his voice an even more menacing, mechanical timbre. "If you want to turn back, go ahead," he added. "No point getting this far and choking to death."

"I'll be all right." The Wally Squad Judge wiped his sooty brow and strode ahead, looking to Dredd like he was increasingly desperate to prove himself.

They ran down the corridor, half crouched, trying to stay low enough to escape the worst of the smoke, passing offices now fully ablaze. Trager recognised Ramona's darkroom and stopped momentarily to watch her works of art turn to ashes. The screaming faces that festooned the walls blackened and crisped, curling up and disappearing before his eyes.

"You know where they could've gone from here?" Dredd demanded.

"Rejin's living quarters are at the end of the hall. That seems the likeliest."

The two of them reached the double doors and shoulder-barged their way through, recoiling instantly at the heat that exploded in their faces as flames crawled all over the viewing room. The big screen at the far end had warped and split apart, the Tri-D set below it a molten mess of plastic and chrome.

"His bedroom!" Trager yelled, pointing to the connecting door.

They barrelled through, just having enough time to mentally note that the fire had not yet spread to this antechamber before the realisation of their surroundings hit home. The grand four-poster bed, the exotic furnishings, the expensive furniture they expected were all there, but what made them pause was what lined the shelves of every wall. Sitting there like a private art collection were hundreds of jars filled with human body parts.

For a second the two Judges were speechless as they gazed up at the sight before them. Hearts and tongues and scalps floated in liquid like pickled specimens. Some specimens were difficult to identify: pink jellyfish wafting lazily in a yellowish brine, brown stumps like wet, chewed cigars. Others stared back, dead eyes impassive.

"Son of a bitch..." Trager murmured.

"Missing Persons are gonna be busy," Dredd said.

"How did the insane drokker get away with all this for so long?"

"You'd be surprised at what we've got away with," a voice behind them said, and both Judges turned as one in time to see Alphonse swinging a massive fist and connecting with Dredd's jaw, sending him flying backwards.

Trager fired and put two bullets through Alphonse's chest, but the creep barely flinched. He walked forward and wrenched the weapons from the undercover officer's hands, then smacked him onto the ground. It felt like a block of concrete landing on his head and Trager struggled to remain conscious. Meathead must be pumped on something; blood was flowing freely from his wounds and he didn't even notice.

Alphonse picked Trager up clean off the ground. "Drokkin' rat," he growled. "We drokkin' trusted you an' you ruined everything." He casually threw Trager away from him, slamming him against a wall, the specimen jars wobbling off their shelves and raining down in a blizzard of moist flesh. Trager felt glass cutting his hands as he rolled out of their way, his own injuries screaming in protest.

There was the sound of several rapid bangs as Dredd shot Alphonse half a dozen more times with his Lawgiver, one even catching him on the side of the head, but they didn't seem to slow him down at all. The perp launched himself at the lawman and the two of them flew onto the bed, Alphonse's mammoth paws fixed around Dredd's windpipe.

The Judge couldn't throw him off, Alphonse's weight pinning him down, so he tried to improvise by flicking the ammo selector on his gun with one hand to Armour Piercing, ramming the barrel into the creep's side and pulling the trigger. Alphonse's midriff blossomed with a crimson halo as a substantial chunk of his torso was vaporised. The pressure eased off Dredd's neck for a moment, but incredibly the guy wasn't going to be stopped.

Dredd felt somebody yanking his boot knife from its sheath before Trager appeared behind the goon, pulled his head back and drew the blade savagely across his throat. Alphonse released Dredd and stood, his jugular spraying in all directions. He turned to face Trager and took a couple of steps forward, but the severity of his wounds finally caught up with him. An expression of puzzlement passed across his features before he started to stumble, then careened into the walls. One hand went to his neck in a futile attempt to stem the flow while another pounded the paintwork, a rough gasp emerging from his mouth. As he sank to his knees, he feebly punched the wall nearest to the bed and a portion of it disengaged, swinging open like a door. He shuffled towards the threshold, then collapsed and was at last still.

Trager took a peek beyond the secret doorway and saw stone steps descending into darkness. "Gruddamn."

Dredd joined him, his uniform ripped and drenched in red stains, livid welts on his neck. "Let's just get this finished."

FEAR BEGAN TO grip DuNoye, an emotion that he was unused to. Overseeing the running of Catalyst Productions, he'd always been confident of his abilities to sweet-talk the authorities, and draw on the company's resources and network of allies. But maybe it was overconfidence that had destabilised the operation. They had underestimated the Judges as well, thinking they could get away with their little operation right under Justice Department's nose. DuNoye suspected the Judges had stumbled on it by luck rather than skill, but that hardly mattered anymore. They were undone. Once the Liz Short bodies were discovered, they should've ordered a retreat there and then, escaping out of the city – even off-planet – before the heat came down on them. But DuNoye's arrogance had led him to believe he could deal with Dredd himself, trying to throw him off the investigation. That was a gross error, and all their work building up the outfit came tumbling down as a consequence.

Now, as they attempted to scramble to some kind of refuge, they found that that too was rapidly vanishing. Attempts to contact that idiot Peat had proved useless and he was no doubt at this moment in custody. The help that should have been present to aid them in their escape was nowhere to be seen, and their exit from the Undercity seemed to have been blocked. The gate was supposed to have been altered so it could be opened from the inside, but it wasn't budging, which left them trapped in this netherworld. They'd known from the beginning that it would be a risky route to take, and now they couldn't get out, and they couldn't go back to the studio either. They'd literally burnt their bridges. All DuNoye could do was keep trying to contact one of Rejin's associates in the hope that they could get to them before the Judges.

The old man was standing with his daughter, looking out at the blasted cityscape of New York. It was difficult to judge how Erik was feeling, or indeed what he was planning to do. He was completely emotionless, his face a blank mask. Ramona had tried to apologise to him for getting too close to the undercover Judge, but he hadn't answered and simply gazed at her as if seeing her for the first time. DuNoye felt uneasy, unsure how this was going to resolve itself.

But it wasn't his only worry. He could feel eyes upon him, shapes moving in the darkness, a whispered grunting echoing between the concrete canyons. DuNoye was aware of the dangers that lurked in the Undercity, and the longer they lingered here the more they became a vulnerable target for attack. He tried his vidphone again, nervousness starting to claw at him, his fingers visibly shaking as he punched in numbers for someone to get them out of this hole. He wished they'd kept back a couple of triggers for situations like this, but the drokking Judges had wasted half his men.

A rising whistle sliced through the air and the lawyer yelped in surprise as a crudely fashioned spear arced out of the gloom and knocked the phone from his grasp. He looked around for the weapon's owner, but heard only the sound of running feet.

"Sir," he said, his voice breaking with panic. "We've got to go."

Rejin turned and studied him. They were standing on steps leading away from the ruins of a twenty-first century bank, its palatial columns long since crumbled to rubble. "Go where? We are nowhere. We are abandoned amongst the dead, reduced to history like everything else."

"But if we stay around here..." DuNoye began, watching the shadows as pallid faces leered from them. They were everywhere. He backed away, head turning from side to side. "We've got to get out of here."

"Father, please, they'll kill us," Ramona pleaded.

"They are the ghosts of our pasts, come for revenge. We cannot deny them their vengeance."

DuNoye started to run, all thoughts of loyalty forgotten. His footsteps clattered in the oppressive silence as he descended towards the street, but he didn't get far. Another spear fired out of the darkness and sank into his thigh, sending him tumbling. He yelled in pain and fright, trying to crawl to shelter, but the underground dwellers now emerged, their misshapen forms like something from a nightmare. They wore only rags to cover their pale, scabrous skin, carried flint axes and daggers, and they gibbered to each other in a guttural, impenetrable language.

DuNoye tried desperately to escape them, but they descended upon him with ease, the forerunners swinging their weapons above their heads with a whooping noise and burying the blades into his back. The impact laid him out flat, and they grabbed his arms, pulling him into the shadows, DuNoye struggling weakly. The hunger got too much for one so he hacked off a hand, bringing the severed wrist to his mouth and tearing at the flesh.

When another beheaded DuNoye, Ramona screamed.

THE TWO JUDGES had entered into the slate-grey environs of the Undercity when they heard a shout rebounding off the ruins. Trager recognised it instantly.

"Ramona!"

The Wally Squad officer tore off at speed, following the scream's dying echoes, Dredd trying to catch up with him. They ran up a main street, spotting a group of troggies descending on a pair of figures ahead. Dredd fired his Lawgiver in the air several times and the subhuman creatures scattered instantly, shielding their eyes from the muzzle flash. He put a bullet through a couple of them to make sure they'd keep their distance.

Trager was the first to reach the pair. Rejin was pulling his daughter close to him, slowly retreating. The undercover Judge halted a few feet away from them, breathing heavily.

"Step away from him, Ramona," he ordered.

"She is not yours to command," the old man said.

"It's over, Rejin. Your little business is finished." He turned back to the daughter. "Please, Ramona, come with me. I can help you."

She looked at him, wary and scared. "I trusted you... and you lied to me. Everything you told me was a lie. You used me."

"I know," Trager replied, feeling his guts churn with self-loathing. "And I'm sorry. But this had to be stopped. Your father, DuNoye, they all had to be stopped. You can see that, can't you?"

"We don't have time for this," Dredd growled. "Troggies are gonna be back for more, and grud knows what else." He levelled his Lawgiver at the couple. "You creeps are under arrest. Hands in the air, now."

"Dredd, please," Trager said. "Can I just speak to her for a sec–"

"Trager, the operation is over. Your role is done. Now these two are lookin' at serious cube time."

Rejin suddenly crouched and grabbed a flint dagger from a nearby troggie corpse, jamming it against his daughter's neck. "We created such beauty, and you infected it all with your lies," he said to Trager. He studied her ashen face. "You even corrupted my flesh, to the point where I don't recognise this creature as being mine."

"F-Father," Ramona whispered, "I never wanted to hurt you..."

"Ramona, you don't owe him anything!" Trager yelled, fury boiling out of him. "Everything you've been brought up to believe in, everything you've been told, is a sham!"

"Don't listen to the deceiver," Rejin murmured.

"What did he tell you about what happened to your mother? That she left when you were a child? Was that it? That bastard murdered her! Strapped her down and filmed himself killing her!"

"No..." Ramona said quietly.

"I saw the film myself, Ramona. Anna was just another of his victims."

"You don't understand..." She started to weep.

"How can you carry on defending him?"

"Because she knows the truth," Rejin retorted. "Because you only saw what you wanted to believe."

Trager felt himself pause. "What?"

"Once she was old enough I had to teach my daughter how purity lies within the human body. That could only be done if she were to discover it by her own hand."

A terrifying realisation slammed through Trager like a ten tonne truck, stunning him to silence. The movie flashed back in his head and he remembered how he never saw the hands that wielded the blade or the camera, only the fear on the woman's face. Was it horror as she watched her own child approach her?

"Ramona," the Wally Squad Judge pleaded. "Tell me that isn't true…"

She looked at him directly, tears flowing freely, but there was a steely hardness behind her gaze. "What do you know about truth?"

"She is her father's daughter," Rejin said. "And you will never have her."

"This has gone far enough," Dredd barked, shooting a warning glance at Trager before turning his attention back to the old man. "Drop the weapon and step away from the girl, meathead."

"You think I will allow you to corrupt her further?"

"Drop it!" Dredd demanded again.

"Better that she is free, away from your touch," Rejin continued. Ramona closed her eyes as if in resignation. "Better she remain unsullied." And he plunged the dagger into her throat.

Trager didn't hear the gunshots as Dredd put half a dozen bullets through the old man's chest. His ears were filled with a roaring sound as he collapsed to his knees, cradling Ramona's head and keeping a hand pressed to her wound. He was shouting for a med-wagon, but his words seemed distant and muted like he was underwater. He was dimly aware of Dredd standing over him, saying something, but all he could do was gently rock the young woman in his arms and sob into her hair, feeling the slow beat of her heart beneath him and her shallow breath brush his skin.

When the med-droids finally arrived, it took them several minutes to extricate her from his grasp, but by then it was too late.

Epilogue:
FADE TO BLACK

THERE WAS A brilliant blue sky hanging over the Mega-City One skyline when Dredd pulled up outside Resyk. Striding inside the monolithic building, it never ceased to amaze him how quiet it was within; all he could hear were his boots echoing off the solemn corridors and gentle organ music lilting in the background. He knew that massive machines were at work beneath the surface, taking apart the corpses that were fed into its maw and reducing them to their usable components, but you wouldn't know they existed from the tasteful reception area. Here, grieving relatives could be consoled and were led to believe that their loved ones were going to a better place.

But once you entered the cavernous inner sanctum, the factory-like workings of the recycling plant became very clear. A huge conveyor belt dominated the space, upon which hundreds of cadavers travelled to the bonesaws waiting for them, and it was on a walkway above it that Dredd found Trager listening to the final words of the priest droid. There were no other mourners, and the robot was evidently on a default setting, giving a pre-recorded sermon and inserting Ramona Rejin's name where necessary. He supposed there would be nobody to give a personal touch to her passing because nobody ever knew her. Having been brought up in seclusion by her demented father, would anybody in the city actually know she was gone? Like Catalyst's victims, she became one of the metropolis's many disappeared.

Dredd hovered behind Trager until the droid had said its piece and trundled off to the next group of bereaved, then joined him at the safety rail looking out over the belt. The Wally Squad Judge didn't turn to face him, his hard, stern face simply watched the naked bodies tumbling past. Only his eyes betrayed his emotions.

"Dredd," Trager finally acknowledged.

"Trager."

"She's down there somewhere," he said, his voice cracking slightly. "I thought I might catch one last glimpse of her before she... before she went." He swallowed. "But there's so many down there, I've lost her. Lost her completely." He gripped the rail, his knuckles whitening.

"How are you feeling? Physically, I mean?" Dredd asked.

Trager glanced at the lawman for the first time and a light smile grazed his lips. "I'll be OK. A spell with the speed-heal sorted me out. I won't lose this," he gestured to the scar down the right side of his face, bisecting his cheek, "but I don't mind. It means every time I look in a mirror I won't be able to forget."

"Trager, you did what you could. You did what was asked of you as a Mega-City Judge. You can't afford to take it so personally."

The younger man shook his head, gazing below him. "It's easier for you, Dredd. You've had your feelings... severed. I just can't turn mine off like that. Every treachery, every lie I tell, is like a knife twisting in my guts. I disgust myself sometimes, the way I sell these people out."

"But justice has been served, that's the important thing. Creeps broke the Law and paid the price."

"We all pay the price," Trager said quietly.

They stood in silence for a moment, a muted sobbing coming from the far side of the walkway. Eventually, Dredd asked, "You want to know what the inquiry found?"

"Go ahead."

"First off, they commended your actions throughout the operation, which brought down a major criminal organisation. And the ripples are continuing to spread as we follow up leads from both Catalyst's records and Peat's contacts. There was a big ring of premier-league businessmen involved in the distribution of the Vi-zines, and who helped cover for Rejin in return for substantial kickbacks. So far, seven companies have had their accounts frozen pending investigation."

Trager raised his eyebrows, impressed.

"The inquiry also felt your life was put unnecessarily at risk by Peat leaking Justice Department files, following which the Grand Hall is undergoing a review of security measures. Tek Division ran a source on the MAC infiltration and we've arrested a hacker that was working for the councillor. It looks like, thanks to you, politicians are going to be cut out of the info-loop even further."

It was the first time Trager had heard Dredd sounding genuinely grateful.

"However, my report mentioned certain times where I felt you overstepped the boundaries of being a Judge, and where life was taken at a personal level. Some of these charges were serious enough to warrant a trip to Titan... but given the circumstances, the inquiry edged towards leniency, and the final ruling was that you should be stripped of your badge. Also, that you leave the city."

The undercover officer nodded slowly. "What did Hendry say?"

"He walked out halfway through. Said we were throwing away a damn fine Judge."

Trager smiled. "And what do you think?"

"I think you threw it away yourself."

Trager was silent for a moment. "Maybe. But I won't miss it. I've seen enough death, enough broken lives." He looked the lawman in the eye. "You know how many people you've killed, Dredd?"

"No."

"No, neither do I." He pushed himself off from the rail and started to walk back towards the entrance. "I'll see you around, Joe." Then, he was gone.

Dredd stood for a moment, watching the dead pass beneath him. The case still troubled him. The degree of Rejin's insanity and the scale with which Catalyst had got away with mass murder, right under the nose of Justice Department itself, made him uneasy. He couldn't help feeling that McGruder or Silver – who had been strong supporters of the propaganda material in their day – must've realised the extent of his madness, and turned a blind eye, content that his raving anti-Sov films were being distributed all over the world. How much else could they have condoned, in the spirit of a "special relationship"? It was impossible to tell now, just more secrets that had been taken to the grave.

He wandered down the walkway, wincing as his back injury flared up. Getting old, Dredd thought, as he headed out into the light.

THE END

FEATURING THE GALAXY'S GREATEST CREATORS
KELVIN GOSNELL // GERRY FINLEY-DAY // PAT MILLS // JOHN WAGNER
CARLOS EZQUERRA // MICK MCMAHON // MASSIMO BELARDINELLI
IAN GIBSON // BRIAN BOLLAND

JUDGE DREDD
THE COMPLETE CASE FILES 01
JOHN WAGNER // BRIAN BOLLAND // MIKE MCMAHON

HE IS THE LAW!

Mega-City One, 2099. This vast urban nightmare has sprung up from the post-apocalyptic ashes of North America's east coast. Each of the 400 million citizens based there is a potential criminal and only the Judges can prevent total anarchy. These future lawmen are judge, jury and executioner. Toughest of them all is Judge Dredd - he *is* the Law!

Discover the roots of this legendary character in this vast and Thrill-packed series of graphic novels collecting together all of Dredd's adventures in chronological order, written and illustrated by some of the biggest names in British comics.

ISBN 978-1-906735-87-6
US $19.99   CAN $27.00

WWW.2000ADONLINE.COM

BRIAN BOLLAND // KEVIN O'NEILL // ALAN DAVIS // CAM KENNEDY
STEVE DILLON // SIMON BISLEY // DAVE GIBBONS // TREVOR HAIRSINE
CHARLIE ADLARD

THE ART OF LAW!

it takes a special kind of judge to police the mean streets of mega-city one
and the best artists in the business to portray him. His name is Judge Dredd
and he IS the law!

Featuring stories illustrated by the most revered artists working in comics today,
including Dave Gibbons (*Watchmen*), Brian Bolland (*The Killing Joke*) and Kevin
O'Neill (*The League of Extraordinary Gentlemen*) with stories from John Wagner (*A
History of Violence*) and Alan Grant (*Batman*) amongst others, this is a collection
bursting with action, humour and breathtaking visuals!

ISBN 978-906735-92-0
US $19.99   CAN $27.00

WWW.2000ADONLINE.COM

ANDY DIGGLE // JOCK // JOHN WAGNER // HENRY FLINT // STEVE DILLON
ROBBIE MORRISON // SIMON COLEBY // ALAN GRANT

FUN-LOVING CRIMINALS!

It takes a special kind of criminal to survive on the mean streets of Mega-City One. Here are some of the best.

Meet Lenny Zero; an undercover Judge who mixes with the worst kind of scum that Mega-City One has to offer.

Slick Dickens, master criminal and style trendsetter is always ahead of the pack. He's a master assassin with an eye for fashion – but can any real person ever be this cool?

Featuring the first collaboration between Andy Diggle and Jock, the creative team behind *The Losers* and additional stories from such talents as John Wagner (*A History of Violence*), Henry Flint (*Omega Men*) and Steve Dillon (*Preacher*), this fantastic collection of sci-fi noir is not to be missed!

ISBN 978-1-907519-76-5
US $17.99   CAN $21.00

WWW.2000ADONLINE.COM

ROB WILLIAMS // HENRY FLINT // SIMON COLEBY

ROB WILLIAMS ★ HENRY FLINT ★ SIMON COLEBY

LOW LIFE
PARANOIA

IT'S A HARD KNOCK LIFE!

It takes a special kind of judge to go undercover on the mean streets of Mega-City One — especially in the crime infested Low Life; the nastiest part of the 'Big Meg.' This division of the Justice Department known as the 'Wally Squad' contains some of the bravest individuals working the streets and also some of the most unhinged!

Judge Aimee Nixon has operated the Low Life for over eleven years, infiltrating ground-level crime syndicates with fellow 'Wally Squad' Judges Thora the oldster, 'baby Judge' Eric Coil and the aptly-named Dirty Frank.

Featuring the writing of Rob Williams (*Cla$$war, Star Wars Tales*) with art from Henry Flint (*Judge Dredd/Aliens, Zombo*) and Simon Coleby (*Judge Dredd, The Authority*), this is sci-fi noir at its very best!

ISBN 978-1-907519-88-8
US $17.99   CAN $21.00

WWW.2000ADONLINE.COM

ALAN GRANT // CARLOS EZQUERRA // TREVOR HAIRSINE // BOO COOK

DON'T EVEN THINK ABOUT BREAKING THE LAW!

Mega-City One, a futuristic metropolis sprawling across the east coast of North America. This hostile urban nightmare is policed by the Judges - tough lawmen with the ability to act as judge, jury and executioner. Within the Justice department is a section known as 'Psi-Division' which specialises in Judges gifted with extraordinary psychic abilities.

Cassandra Anderson is one such Judge - a powerful telepath with a rebellious streak and a talent for getting into trouble...

With never-before collected *Judge Anderson* stories by *2000 AD* legend Alan Grant (*Batman*) and featuring stunning artwork from Carlos Ezquerra (*Judge Dredd*), Boo Cook (*Elephantmen*) and Trevor Hairsine (*Cla$$war*), you don't need to be psychic to know that you need to add this book to your collection!

ISBN 978-1-907992-54-4
US $20.99   CAN $23.99